CELEBRATION
A Novel

Jon Lange

Cover design, J. Lange

Copyright © 2014 Jon Lange

All rights reserved.

Other works by the same Author:
Memories/Remorse
Knobby the Knobhead
At the Heart of Ignorance
The Big O Show
Feast of the Pansexualists

Contents

Preface v
1. An Opening 1
2. Prelude 4
3. The Conspiracy of Life 6
4. To Kiss the Night 17
5. The Name's Capri 36
6. The Tao and the Tau 54
7. Monumental Man 73
8. A Time of Wine and Strange Drugs 97
9. 418 Ways to Die 111
10. Invocation of Death 134
11. The Apotheosis of Desire 151
12. The Nectar and the Venom 164
13. The Lab Experience 203
14. The God Man 222
15. A Woman of Power 233
16. The Kalanitic Equation 237
17. Welcome to the Pleasure Parlour 260
18. The Gap Between the Mountains 285
19. Two Into Nought Won't Go 300
20. The Methodology of Psychic Attack 319
21. The Big Freeze 329
22. The Loss 365
23. Wandering in Hopeless Night 378
24. The Return 395
25. The Rite Time 438
26. The Saviour 453
27. The Last Menstruation of the Earth 477
28. Union of Heaven and Earth 488
29. Capri Smiles 492
30. Conclude 524
31. A Closing 525

PREFACE

Out of all the books I have written I still consider this to be one of my favourites. Not because it is brilliantly written (it isn't!), but because it has a special meaning for me.

It was written during a time when I was going through a great upheaval in my life, what you might call a 'spiritual crisis.' The only thing that kept me sane during this intensely personal period was the actual process of writing. The writing in itself became therapeutic; I was writing about a character who was undergoing an identity crisis and a great loss having suffered a bereavement. Similarly, I too would be undergoing the same thing. In fact, there are many parallels in this book that mirror my own personal life, coincidences between my characters and myself.

For example, when I wrote the first draft (many years ago now), I was living with my partner in a comfortable house with all mod cons, but I was writing about a character who was living alone in a flat in the city with little in the way of furnishings, the latter he didn't consider to be too important; he had greater things to think about than trivialities like that. Six months later I split up from my partner and ended up living in the centre of town in a barely furnished flat and I was all alone, just like my character.

They say that life imitates art, but this was more than coincidental. There are many other parallels I could cite which makes us wonder at times if during the creative process of writing we are somehow predicting future events. There is an extraordinary example in this book which defies belief: The Grand Gallery. Like many other things in this book of fiction the Gallery is symbolic. It represents heaven and earth and all the great artistic achievements of mankind. I situated this building exactly where the Twin Towers stood in Manhattan as a satirical swipe at the USA and its obsession with commerce, capitalism, consumerism, etc., and that the Twin Towers had been demolished to make way for art; in other words, America had swapped commerce for culture, little knowing that in a few years time the towers would be destroyed in a terrorist attack which nobody could have predicted. Call it a coincidence, but it is one of the many that occurred over the years.

Although I am British and live in England, I set my piece of fiction in an alternative future version of America for several reasons, the main one being that America, I believe, is at the forefront of technological advances, and therefore such things as the Stratocruiser car that Capri drives could possibly exist, perhaps not here, but certainly in America. Google have now

developed a driverless car which is being road tested in the US as I write this. So who knows, it could happen sooner than expected. But there was another reason. I wanted one of the main characters, Capri, to be living in New York and to visit Los Angeles, so his movement would be from east to west; that is, east as symbolic of life, west as symbolic of death and the land of the dead. To put it succinctly, Capri undergoes a life-death-rebirth experience, the transition from east to west being purely symbolic. I am aware that I have totally ignored the time difference between the two cities, but as it is symbolic rather than actual, I think I should be allowed a literary suspension of disbelief. The same goes for lack of mobile (cell) phones. These have been deliberately omitted as I felt the plot would be ruined if they were available to the characters. Their means of communication here is through computers (with in-built television and phone, here called 'televids'), but unfortunately too large to carry in one's pocket. Tablets haven't yet come into existence, although the police carry a screen (similar to a tablet) which is a thin piece of flexible plastic no larger than the largest mobile phone with direct access to an international criminal database so they can carry out checks on suspects and suspicious people.

As for the time when all the action takes place, I leave that to the reader's imagination, suffice to say it is not too far off from present day. However, I will stress this is an alternative future and, as I have already said, most of it is symbolic. Once you recognise the symbols and metaphors in this story then it should not be too difficult to understand and work out the ending. Take particular note of the coincidences.

Further, this is the heavily edited version. A writer should not only be able to write, he should also be able to edit his own work. The last manuscript (the fourth draft, circa 1995) contained 345,000 words. This version has been cut to 200,000; still quite long. I have made many deletions, cutting out extensive quotes of Grantham's works, Crome's book of poetry (and Capri's interpretations thereof). The apocalypse sequence has been reduced to only a few pages. Literary quotations have been minimised. Also omitted are the philosophical discourses of Capri. I felt this material bogged down the story and slowed the pacing of the narrative. I regret doing it but it was necessary and should not hinder the reader's understanding and appreciation.

Lastly, this book was originally entitled *In Celebration of the Phallus*, but nobody was interested in publishing it (I can't imagine why!). Enjoy.

Jon Lange
Autumn 2014

THE WRITER

'The genuine writer sacrifices himself on the written page. His pen is not filled with ink, but his very own blood, his life-force.'

Paul K. Jarrup,
The Confessions

—1—

AN OPENING
(THE SCATOLOGICAL PHILOSOPHY OF HARMON CAPRI[1])

'Everything is shit,' so the Buddha said. That's how everything feels at the moment. Here I am on another retreat in a beautiful part of the world and I cannot find the inner peace I am looking for. I can't shake the last job out of my head, how the cops took all the glory for my hard work and I never got paid. I am surrounded by tall trees, gorgeous landscapes, rolling hills and a lake that is crystal clear and I still can't stop thinking about is NY.

It must be the dread of going back there. No job. No money. No prospects, but I still have to go back. It's not just the personal worry; there is something else, something not quite right which isn't gelling, and making me unsure about everything else.

I mean, here we are, well past the turn of the century when everything was supposed to be going into a meltdown (if only!), when all the computers were supposed to be crashing, when the world was supposed to be coming to an end prior to the advent of the new millennium. It didn't quite happen that way, but it certainly feels like it. What with millions of people losing their jobs due to another stock market crash, religions like Christianity, Judaism and Islam on the decline, a loss of faith in politics, new diseases like PAS[2] on the horizon threatening to destroy us, women becoming infertile because they aren't menstruating anymore[3], and men running out of sperm. It's like we're on our way out. It is as if God is saying he's had enough of us and is consigning us to the dustbin as a bad idea. Could things get any worse? Yes, they could. I've got so many debts hanging over me that even I've got Cleaners[4] chasing after me! And to top it all, Angel, my HGA[5], has stopped talking to me! What is going on?

I've got to sort this shit out and do battle with earth again, find a way to pay off all my debts (a cushy job with lots of benefits would be great) and then I can get on top of everything once and for all.

Now made up my mind, I am going to do a Yi King[6] reading to see what the future will bring, and this time I am going to act on it, whatever the outcome[7].

EDITORIAL NOTES

1. Extracted from his personal journal during his magical retirement at Camp Pasquaney, Hebron, NH, summer till fall; Monday. Note: No dates are given in this journal, only days of the week.
2. Premature Aging Syndrome, a virus currently affecting approximately 10% of the human race, was first discovered in isolated pockets on the African mainland. It has since spread globally with no given indication of how it spreads, and there is still no known cure.
3. Unspecified Secondary Amenorrhea, or USA for short, only affects 1 in 100,000 women. This is a gross exaggeration on Mr Capri's part.
4. A slang term for people who 'clean up' by tracking down debt defaulters for Laundry Men (debt-collectors). They usually work on behalf of the Mob.
5. Holy Guardian Angel; a personalisation of the subconscious.
6. Or *I Ching*, the Chinese divinatory system of fortune telling.
7. The journal abruptly ends here.

THE BLIND

'Intelligence is the curse of humanity, ignorance its limitation, and he who believes without questioning is guilty of nescience.'

Paul K. Jarrup,
Critique of the Cynic

—2—
PRELUDE

A naked couple are sitting on the floor in the middle of a darkened room. They are in a world of their own, lovingly caressing each other, their movements perfectly synchronised with a soft orchestral piece coming from the speakers. The woman is sitting on his lap, her legs clasped round his back, riding him gently. Her face is obscured by her long black hair. His face also is hidden. They are bathed in a pool of electric blue light, the only light in the room.

To the right of them is seated a bald-headed man. He appears to be in his late thirties. He is entranced by the erotic display before him. He doesn't move. The only indication of life is the reflection in his eyes of the copulating couple, and the occasional movement of his right arm as he lifts his cigar to his lips, draws, then exhales, creating a visor of smoke round his face. Whirls of smoke spiral up to the ceiling catching filaments of light. In his other hand rests a large brandy glass, half full, untouched. It does not move.

The couple are building up to a climax, reaching a crescendo in time with the music.

Suddenly a doorbell sounds in the distance. The man snaps out of his trance as if being rudely awakened and looks at the door behind him. He checks his watch, surprised. He stubs out his half smoked cigar in the ashtray by his side and reaches for a remote. He points it at the ceiling and presses a button. The naked couple fizzle out as the holo is absorbed back into the projector. He presses another button and the music stops. He replaces the remote and claps his hands; all the lights come on.

The man lifts his burly frame out of the armchair and walks towards the

door. He opens it and glides down a hall of wood panelling with ornately framed oils and classic-styled lighting on either side. He descends a spiral set of stairs to a large hallway and stops at the front door. He checks the securivid on the side, then opens the door. Outside is the fresh young face of a uniform standing in the porch under a light with the night sky behind him.

"Evening, Dr Crome," he says politely. "I'm not too early, am I?"

"No, not at all," Crome replies and gestures for the uniform to wait outside.

Crome disappears into a side room. He reappears wearing a dark coat and carrying a small holdall and briefcase. He stops by the door, looks back at the hallway and to the panel on the side and slides his hand over it. All the lights go out. He closes the door behind him.

Crome follows the uniform to a black limo parked in the driveway. The uniform swipes his ID card in the slot. The front door opens and the uniform climbs in. He commands the back door to open and gestures to Crome to climb in the back. The uniform commands the doors to close. As the back door closes a shield becomes visible. Below the shield are the words 'Ministry of Operations.' The engine starts up. The limo lifts off its spheres and pulls away down the long gravel-stone driveway. The electric gates hum open. The limo drives through; the gates close. The limo speeds off into the distance leaving red traces of tail lights behind.

"'Is there a cure for death?"

Out of all the questions which have been posed by mankind this must surely be the one that has been iterated the most. And, at last, I believe it can be answered—in the affirmative!'

Alexander Crome,
An Isagogic Paper on Immortality (unpublished)

—3—
THE CONSPIRACY OF LIFE

"Gentlemen," Rogers said as he focused on the three men sitting round the table. "We can skip the formalities as you all know each other, directly or indirectly anyway."

"Dr Crome here," he continued, as he gestured to the man sitting to his right, "I believe you are all familiar with. He needs little introduction. But Dr Crome, you may not know Willis here who is Professor of gerontology at Cal-Tech. And you obviously know," he said, averting his eyes to the young man with blond hair, "Mr Landis, who we've borrowed from your institute. Right, now down to business."

Rogers picked up a remote by his side and pressed a button. A holo projected onto the centre of the table. He pressed another button. The holo flickered into life with tables, charts, cellular models, etc.

"Three days ago we isolated the strain of the PAS virus," he began as if giving a running commentary. "As you see, it is this we can confirm that is the replicating factor involved in spreading the virus. So far it hasn't been amenable to any further research, yet it is a step closer in the right direction. Tests so far validate our conclusions. We know that it comprises a core and two cells, both of which are katabolic, but we cannot determine how it infects the human nervous system. We simply don't know how it is introduced. In vitro experiments on rats show significant findings in the acceleration of senescence, particularly in the region of the thymus gland. Once this is infarcted the gland deteriorates rapidly, consequently reducing drastically the distribution of T-lymphocytes into the blood stream. This

chain-effect is responsible for the decrease in cellular replication which is the cause of senescence. Yet this strain not only causes senescence, it somehow miraculously accelerates it."

Rogers pressed another button. The holo flickered. A new image appeared. It was a film of a man lying isolated in a hospital bed.

"If you watch carefully you'll see what I mean. This man is in his early twenties. He was admitted to the infirmary displaying acute signs of senility, the first indication of full-blown PAS which suggests that it attacks the brain cells first, literally wiping them out. I might add there are no camera tricks involved here."

The men looked on in disbelief. The patient's skin became hard and dry, his lips sagged, his cheeks became bloated, and his once dark hair readily started turning grey. In less than an hour he resembled a geriatric and looked barely alive.

"He died four hours later." Rogers pressed a button. The holo flickered and disappeared. He replaced the remote by his side and looked at them pensively. "Gentlemen, we have a problem."

Rogers fumbled in his jacket pocket and pulled out a packet of cigarettes. He lit one up and leaned back in his chair, looking at each man in turn. "And that is why you are here," he said gravely. "If this virus cannot be contained we're in deep shit. It attacks indiscriminately. There is no physiological basis for its origin. It just appeared out of nowhere. There are no causal links between any of the cases we have investigated so far."

Crome indicated to speak.

"Yes, Dr Crome," Rogers acknowledged him.

"What is the present infection rate of this virus?" he asked, in a well-spoken English accent.

"Well," Rogers started to answer, "so far our figures show roughly a 5 to 10 percent ratio, yet we are still waiting for the latest figures from demographic researches. I have a dreadful feeling that this—uh—figure is going to be very much higher as the PAS virus takes hold quickly. Present fatality rates

are one to one, unfortunately."

"Is there any significant trend in these figures?"

"Nope, not apart from the fact that it seems to be increasing in graduated steps. Nor is it geographically isolated. We have reports from all over the world. What was first a minor outbreak in North Africa, and scatterings elsewhere, seems to be a global occurrence and looks like it will develop into epidemic shortly. Reports range from all age groups; young and old are affected alike. There simply is no common basis for these outbreaks. Although we all tend to think of a virus as a disease as if it is contagious, you know, passed on through physical contact, this is totally different. Aetiologically, we are confounded. All we do know is that they are increasing dramatically, and we do not why. There is no immunology for a disease like this, and this is something we will be working on together."

"I see," Crome said. "Very interesting."

"Oh, I'm glad you find it interesting, doctor," Rogers retorted.

"Indeed I do. Tell me, when was the first outbreak of this disease reported?"

"Well, we don't rightly know. It seems to have crept up on us all of a sudden. Officially about three years ago. At first it was thought the occurrences were merely isolated incidents. Now that it is wide-spreading we have a far better idea of the problem we are dealing with."

"Are there any genetic factors involved?"

"No, none at all. Recent events indicate that they maybe neurological."

"Oh? In what way?"

"Well, perhaps Dr Willis here is in a better position to answer that question. If you will, Dr Willis," Rogers beckoned him.

"Certainly," Willis responded confidently. "The main problem with this PAS is that it seems to be attacking our Achilles heel. By that I mean the phenomenon of ageing itself. The actual cause behind ageing is still a mystery. We are only aware of its overt effects. Its first cause, as I'm sure

you are aware Dr Crome, has still not been adequately established. I and my former colleagues at the Andrus Gerontology Centre at the University of Southern California believe that it is a combination of many factors, each by themselves being non-determinative. We know that ageing is the result of the decrease in cellular division at the later stages of an organism's growth as well as being connected with non-replicating cellular activity, but we do not know what the actual cause is. PAS, however, has been noted in subjects where cellular replacement treatment has been undergone and thus we can only conclude that it is not directly related to cellular activity, but more likely it is connected with the endocrine secretions, particularly from the thyroid, adrenal and pituitary glands.

"The level of hormone release from each of these glands decreases over time. This has a 'shutting-down' effect causing them to decay with consequent increase of infarction to surrounding tissues. Experiments involving pregnant mice confirm that this is correct. Litter depletion is clearly evident as well as lack of muscular control. A young pregnant mouse injected with the PAS strain will go into a catatonic state and immediately abort its young. Tissue decay rapidly ensues. It's not a pretty sight."

Willis paused to catch his breath. Crome looked to Landis who picked up on his thoughts.

The young man sat up and cleared his throat before speaking.

"Dr Willis? Can I ask you a question?"

"Certainly, Anton."

"What kind of hormonal experiments have you undertaken?"

"What type? Well, we know that senescence is closely related to hormonal activity in the endocrine system. We have observed numerous changes taking place. But, as I said, the primary cause of the ageing phenomenon remains obscure. Some hormones show consistent reductions in circulating levels. Others show no sign at all, and a few may increase. But most of these changes have consequences that are generally considered to be age-related."

"For instance?"

"Well—uh—for example, oestrogen levels decrease rapidly over time in female mice when the strain is introduced."

"And what about human subjects?"

Rogers slammed his fist down on the table hard. "That is unthinkable, Anton."

"Okay, okay. Only asking," Landis responded, waving his hand in the air. "It's just that I thought you might have a couple handy, that's all. I wasn't suggesting you'd use them as guinea pigs."

"I should think not," Rogers said gruffly. "Unfortunately, we do not. Now, what are you driving at?"

"Just thinking aloud."

"Well?"

"I was wondering whether there was a connection between oestrogen deprivation and this PAS virus. It seems to me that they both had their genesis around the same time."

Rogers looked to Willis for an explanation.

"Ah, well, um," Willis mumbled. "We haven't gone into that area in great detail yet. We do know that it is lack of hormone production that is the cause of oestrogen reduction and the reason behind ovarian cyclical changes. This suggests that oestrogen regulates the release of neurotransmitter hormones like dopamine, norepinephrine and serotonin. This may indicate why senility is the first ostensible indication of the PAS phenomenon, particularly in women. In fact, I would like to contradict Dr Rogers if I may and state there's a decisive trend in the increase of the outbreak of PAS in women."

"Bullshit, Willis, and you know it," Rogers counteracted.

"I think you're being unfair, Carl. There is a significant trend which demonstrates my theory."

"Oh?" Crome asked, sitting up. "And what theory is that?"

"That there is a direct connection between the two. But due to—uh—ethical promptings I have been unable to verify my hypothesis."

"You know as well as I, Ed," butted in Rogers, "that it is restricted territory."

"Yes, Carl, but if you'll permit me, all I need is one subject."

"Impossible. You're as bad as Anton here." Rogers shrugged in his jacket. "It would never be sanctioned."

"But Carl, if we are going to tackle this problem and get to the bottom of it, I can see no other way."

"Out of the question."

"Yes, but ask the President. Just ask him. I'm sure he will agree."

"Nonsense. You know that he will never be in favour of such a suggestion. Besides, we have other methods. They are perfectly adequate ways of dealing with this problem."

"Simulated methods of analysis, Carl, will take far longer. You know that. You also know that this epidemic is likely to increase drastically if we don't stop it soon. We do not have the time."

"That's enough, Ed. I refuse point blank. My decision is final. We will use simulated tests. They have proven perfectly amenable in the past."

"Yes, but they took longer. I mean, look at the AIDS virus. Look how long that took. If it wasn't for a donor we would never have conquered it."

"That was different. He was willing. Human experimentation is out of the question and unethical."

"Unless of course you find somebody who is willing," Landis butted in.

"Hmm. If we find somebody. Until that time we will make do with simulated tests only."

"What about recent hospitalisations? Can't we use them?" Crome asked.

"No, they're no good. By the time they enter the wards it's too late."

"You see, Dr Crome," Willis replied, "we need uninfected specimens. Subjects that have already contracted the virus have been proven to be immune to rigorous testing. Besides, the fade out point is too quick. Full-blown PAS is rapid. The complete cellular breakdown and debility can take place within a matter of weeks."

"Or even days in some cases," Rogers intervened.

"Yes," agreed Willis. "The actual declination-rate seems to be increasing. Over the past year we have noticed a significant increase in this trend. What originally took place over a months can now take place in virtually days."

"I see," Crome responded concerned.

"That film you saw," Willis continued, "was taken recently. If it had been last year, the decline would not have been as rapid as that."

"As I said," Rogers continued, "the only significant trend is this thing's speed. Once it gets in there's no stopping it. We cannot keep up with it."

The room became claustrophobically tense, the men staring at each other in resolute silence.

"Now," Rogers said, breaking the silence. "Getting back to what you were saying, Anton."

"What I was saying, Carl?"

"Yes, you made the suggestion that there may be a correlation between PAS and oestrogen deprivation. Is that something you've been working on at the institute?"

"Not exactly. We've been looking into oestrogen deprivation and other hormonal deficiencies as a means to pinpoint the aetiological basis of the reduction of menstruation in women. Our findings at present are tentative to say the least. My conclusion is that we are dealing with two separate entities both having frightening possibilities. As I said, the decline in menstruation came about the same time as this PAS appeared. Superficially, I see no connection."

"But?" Rogers goaded him on.

"I have a hunch...."

"A hunch!" Rogers blurted out. "A hunch? Come on, man, we are all fucking scientists. We don't work on hunches. We work on facts."

"But that is the problem, Carl," he replied, slouching back in his chair. "I don't have any facts."

"Humph." Rogers reached for another cigarette. He lit it up, exhaled and watched the smoke drift up to the ceiling in spirals, his beady eyes coming back down and firmly resting on the young man. "You know, I have some good friends who'd be very interested in some of the—uh—activities you got going on at your place."

"Oh yeah?" Landis retorted in dismay. "And what do you mean by that?"

"Well they might not like what they find again. They could have you shut down in a week."

"Fuck you! You know we're legit. And there's nothing you can do about it. Try and stop us."

"Oh yeah? You want me to try?"

Suddenly the two heated men got to their feet, started yelling at each other. Crome, dismayed, jumped to his feet, trying to take control of the situation.

"Gentlemen, please!," he begged them, "stop this! This is non-productive. It will get us nowhere."

"You're right, Alex," Rogers conceded. "Forgive me, Anton. It's the pressure, you understand. I've got the President right up my ass."

"Then let's tackle this like civilised men," Crome implored them. "We must all work together if we are to conquer this virus. We are all respected men in our own fields. Now let us deserve that respect. The activities at the institute are none of the government's business. Its only concern is remittance and I know that it is satisfactory, if not more than adequate. Shall we get back to the matter in hand, gentlemen?"

Crome sat back down, as did the other two.

Rogers stubbed out his cigarette in the ashtray before him and clenched his hands together on the table and looked to Crome appreciatively. "Thank you, Alex."

But unnoticed by Rogers and Willis, Landis gave Crome a brief look of satisfaction and smiled.

"Now, where were we?" Rogers asked, as if to himself. "Ah, yes. You have been invited here Alex as you maybe able to help us."

"I will do all I can."

"Good, 'cos we're relying on you. Have you any suggestions you would like to contribute before we adjourn this meeting?"

"A few points I would like to raise, if you don't mind."

"No. Go right ahead."

"Well, if we are to work as a team, then I suggest that, if I maybe so bold, I have absolute control over this project."

"That's okay with me. How about you gents?"

Willis and Landis nodded their approval.

"Good," Crome continued. "Also, I will need full updating. I want to see everything you have on this virus. I want access to all data."

"I'm sure we can accommodate you with that," Rogers agreed.

"I will need full cooperation, and that includes everyone. My own knowledge of this area is extensive, as I'm sure you're all aware. My conclusion is that really age is a genetic disease. I know the idea seems laughable and that we normally associate the ageing process with characteristics that can only be described as decremental, but I beg to differ. My whole life has gravitated towards the aim of slowing down the ageing process, if not reverse it all together. I can confidently assert that I am the living proof of this. I hope you all agree." The other three nodded. "The

desire for a drug or elixir that has rejuvenating properties has occupied the minds of the most prestigious men in all walks of life and from all eras. It is merely our attitude towards ageing and consequently death that is wrong. My next step is immortality which I believe will be within my grasp in a very short space of time. All previous attempts at finding the so-called fountain of youth have been failures. Gents, I believe that I have within my own hands the very key to unlock all doors, including those of life and death itself. And it is a great privilege that finally at last I am being given this opportunity to demonstrate that ageing is in reality an illusion, physical immortality not only a possibility, but a probability, and with this key we will stem the flow of this pernicious virus, if not eradicate it altogether."

"Excellent, Dr Crome," Rogers responded enthusiastically. "Now, if you don't mind, it has been a long day. I'm sure you must all be feeling the strain, no pun intended. May I propose we call it an early night? We've got a very busy time ahead of us."

Rogers got to his feet, followed by Willis, then Landis and finally Crome.

Rogers walked up to Crome and shook his hand, "Tomorrow," he told him, and left the room. Willis nervously collected his papers and also shook hands with the other two gents and followed Rogers out.

Once the other two were gone Crome and the young man greeted each other with great affection like two old friends, which they were.

Landis took a step back and said, "Thanks, Alex."

"Thanks for what, my dear chap?" Crome replied.

"For defending me back there and saving my ass."

"Oh, that," Crome responded nonchalantly. "If they insist on blackmailing you, it was the least I could do. Besides, it's still one of my interests, remember."

"You know, Alex, I'm intrigued," he asked Crome suspiciously.

"Oh? About what?"

"Why are you here?"

"I thought that was obvious. Didn't I make it plain in my speech?"

"Yeah, what a speech! No, come on, why are you really here?"

"I've just told you."

"Still haven't changed, have you? Still don't trust anyone. I know you better than you think, Alex. I know this ain't no big ego trip of yours. You're here for a reason."

"As you are fully aware, Anton, I was invited."

"But you didn't have to accept. What could they have possibly said to get the good old Alexander Crome out of his retirement? So he can prove he was right all along and demonstrate this drug of his really works? I don't copy that."

"Oh? Why not?"

"Because I don't believe anybody could hold a grudge for that long. So I reckon it's more than that, isn't it?"

"Well, let's just say that I'm curious. I want to see how far they've got in their own researches."

"No, sorry, Alex. I don't buy that either. But at least we've learnt something tonight; they still don't know where your little key comes from."

"No, and they never will."

The two men laughed again.

"It's good to see you again, after all these years," Landis said, taking Crome's hand and clasping it firmly.

"It's good to see you too. Anyway, I decided that life at home was getting rather tedious and I thought it was about time I had some excitement. I feel that this is going to be a nice little game and I'm determined to enjoy every minute of it. Shall we?" he asked him, gesturing to the open door.

As they were walking out of the room he took the young man by his shoulder asking him, "Tell me, how are things back at the institute?"

THE PANSEXUALIST

'There is nothing but sexuality. This is the only certainty. All attempts to categorise or limit sexuality's inherent qualities are the result of man's failure at coming to terms with this powerful force. Out of his arrogance, he foolishly believes he is its master, whereas in actuality he is its slave. The dictates of sexuality can never be ignored. He tries to channel it into socially conforming ways, imposing limits on it, seeking to stem its tide, to curb its flow and ends up being neurotic and wonders why. And restrictions on sexuality are not only unnatural; they are also inimical and detrimental to the well being of the individual.

He must learn this lesson now: There is no homo, bi, hetro. These are labels, illusory. There is only sexuality, and he who is free of restriction is able to manifest his sexuality as he wills, for the Pansexualist knows he is all-sexuality, and through his openness he becomes All; Pan!'

John Upseed,
Feast of the Pansexualists

— 4 —

TO KISS THE NIGHT

The cab pulled up on the outskirts. The driver refused to take him any further. He couldn't blame him. They would tear it apart and he would be left with nothing but an empty shell. He'd have to walk the rest of the way.

He could smell the stale air already laced with the familiar mixture of rotten cabbage, noodles and fried prawns before he even hit the main causeway into the central part of this hell-hole of a town. Every night it seemed to be getting bigger, spreading like some festering wound or a dragon rolling down the hill towards the sea, swelling its belly as more immigrants drifted in. Now it was also looking taller as the tin shacks were getting higher. It couldn't spread any further, so it had to go up, with the shacks being stuck on top of one another like cartons to accommodate all of these people, all these fuckers who should have stayed at home. There was nothing for them here. Didn't they realise that? No hope, no future and still they drifted in. Nothing could deter them. Either that or they were replicating like good old viral cells, multiplying like fuck. And a couple were coming up to him now, trying to obstruct his way, panhandling for a few cents. He had no time for

these wasters and kicked them out of his way like they were vermin, something to be trodden on. He laughed as they both went down.

"Peasants!" he yelled at them and continued on his way, feeling mighty good inside like tonight was going to be the night. He wanted to kiss it, to make mad writhing love to it because each night was getting better. He could feel it coming on like a methadone rush. He already felt high with the prospect. He dreamed about what they'd get up to tonight, what kicks would be in store. He imagined Chan already lining it up for him like the good friend he was. He decided to leave it open and let it happen by itself.

He hit the club and passed the bouncers his token admission, a couple of ampoules each. They smiled and opened the big red door for him like he was kind of special, and that made him feel even better. Then he hit the smoke, a pale blue haze hanging in the air like a shadow and vying for supremacy with the soft red lights. He was now in a different world, a world well away from the banality of the Centre, a dark sordid world where he felt at home. It didn't bother him that he was the only white guy in the place. Everyone knew who he was and accepted him as one of their own, or at least that's how it felt. He never had any trouble in all the years he'd been coming here, they respecting that he wasn't out to cause trouble, just out to have a good time with his friend Chan.

He headed straight for the bar and ordered an ice cold beer and adjusted to the ambience of the place. He got a good look at the chicks on the platform dancing naked to the heavy music blasting out of the speakers and all captivating curvaceousness and all just for him. He could smell them from where he was standing; just dying to taste their sweet Chinese pussies. He felt the tug as one of them gave him a look and lured him on, a look that was charged with 'If you want me, come and get me,' sheer enticement that was emphasised in her smile. He found it hard to restrain himself and politely smiled as she did her thing. Yes, it was going to be one hell of a night. The atmosphere was raw and electric, so overpowering that he felt intoxicated thereby, and slipped into its soft inviting side, becoming one with it, lost in the dizzying haze.

He sank his drink down and chilled out a bit more as he propped himself up by the bar. He had nearly forgotten about his friend and remembered. He looked round to see if he could place him. He was probably busy

scoring a deal round the back. It didn't bother him. He was in no hurry and Chan would find him like he always did.

Then he noticed this white bit coming up towards him as she edged her way to the bar. She didn't even register him. She waited to be served. He got a closer look though and wondered what the fuck a white girl was doing in a dive like this, having never seen her before. She wasn't a regular, he could tell, but she acted like she owned the place the way she demanded her drink and didn't pay for it either. He was intrigued and focused on her harder thinking she would pick up on it and stare him back. Instead she blanked him and made her way round to the other side of the bar at the end and stood there like she was worth her weight in gold. She gave him a quick glance like he was shit in her eyes and had no right to be looking at a girl like her in the first place. But that made him even more interested, his kind of woman, his mind filling with flesh scenes as she stood there in that tight purple Chinese-style dress of hers. She was kind of pretty in a strange way, he guessed, and she knew it, emanating 'fuck off' signs to anybody who dared to lay an eye on her, except the boss who lit up her cigarette for her and small-talked like they were intimately engaged.

"Anton! There you are."

He whizzed round to see those bright smiling eyes of his.

"Hey, Chan, about time. What kept you?"

"I busy. You know me."

"Yeah, Chan, I know you too fucking well."

They both laughed.

"I not recognise you," Chan remarked, looking him up and down.

"Oh, you mean the suit, right?" he asked his young friend.

"What the occasion?"

"A meeting, you know. No big deal. Now how about getting us ourselves a couple of beers and hooking up into some of that stuff you're on, hey?"

Landis turned round to the bar and ordered a couple of more beers. He noticed the white bit was still standing there like she was some kind of queen surveying her land.

"Who's the white bit over there, Chan?" he asked, indicating furtively.

"She new wife of boss. Why? You like?" Landis smiled and nodded his approval. "No. No way," his friend told him. "You not get anywhere near her. Boss man not happy with you if you do. He kill you."

"Not if I kill him first, Chan."

They laughed again and waded their way through the light congregation to one of the back rooms, the opium den he called it, and was invited in by one old Chink who made him feel comfortable and ushered him to a seat. He sat down amongst a small circle of smokers. He couldn't understand a word they were saying as they spoke in their own language, laughing to themselves and all. It made him feel kind of out of it as usual, but Chan was interpreting parts of what they were saying in his own inimitable clipped English, trying to make him feel at home.

Chan was born in these parts. Spoke thirteen different languages and had to because of all the dealings he did with people from all over the world which made him an international entrepreneur and earned him the title of Universal Sex Boy. Why the 'sex' epithet was never made clear. He guessed it had something to do with his past when he was selling pussy like so many lamb chops to all of his contacts worldwide, when the tourists used to contact him for prospective wives. But as that business had dried up due to most of them being infertile, he moved on to other things and was selling pussy for pussy's sake. They say that life in China is cheap, but here it's worthless and could be bought two cents to the pound if you knew the right person, and Chan was that person. You name it he could get it for you. No problem, as he always said. You want coke, gin, opium, boys, girls, a home even, and in next to no time he'd be handing it over and you paid cash, the hardest currency round here. If it wasn't bolted to the floor he could sell it to anybody.

Landis smiled as he looked at his friend and the old man with the bug-eyes who was saying something he couldn't understand.

"He say this good stuff," Chan interpreted for him. "Here you try. It good. I buy some and smoke. Now you try. New stuff."

"New?" he asked his friend.

"Yes. New. Specially made."

"You mean synthesised?" Chan nodded. "What happened to the old stuff, the natural stuff?"

Chan shook his head. "All gone. This better. You see. Powerful stuff."

Landis looked at him hesitatingly as he was passed a pipe. He wasn't too keen as the old stuff was better than this new synthed shit. It couldn't possibly be the same. It kind of lost its edge and you never knew exactly what you were getting, and that always put him off. The hit was rarely dependable. It varied too much in between different consignments. Reluctantly he took hold of the pipe and put it to his lips as another Chink lit it up for him. He toked the smoke in deep, held it and released as its coolness coated his lungs. He exhaled. The soft blue haze drifted out of his mouth in gulfs like a spiralling dragon and floated in the air thick and heavy and he could almost see its wings flapping gracefully. Then it hit. Right in the back of his brain. He felt a whoosh seize him, coaxed him onwards as he slipped out into a high plateau phase where the other people no longer existed and he was out there, right out there in space looking down on earth, and the club no longer existed either. He partially disappeared too as he slipped away further and disembodied. He floated for a second or two, amazed at the drug's strength and allowed himself to slowly slip back down gently into his body as it tugged him with a pull.

"Wow," was all he could utter.

"You like?" Chan asked him.

His voice drifted over to him. He looked at his Chink friend through wide, all-seeing eyes and nodded.

"Excellent."

"I told you good stuff, no?"

"You're right, Chan. I'm impressed."

He took another toke to get back out on the plateau. His head was a cloud, floating out there, drifting eternally and nor was there anything to pull him back down again. He just floated. It felt like a warm hand smoothing out the coils of his brain, taking all the crinks out and letting everything pass through good and mellow, all tender and caressing. The day's events at the Centre just diminished like some half-forgotten dream and there was only that moment he called the 'Eternal Moment' which seemed to last, for it was eternity packaged in compacted time and relevant as 'IS', and as sure as it will ever be, stretching out the contours of his mind.

He sank back down to earth eventually and passed the pipe onto the guy next to him, allowing the effect to wear off a little before supping his cold beer. He was more than satisfied.

"Where did that stuff come from, Chan?"

"Big secret," Chan replied resolutely.

"Oh, come on, Chan. You can trust me. I'm you're old buddy, aren't I?"

"Yes. But you find source and you wipe me out."

"As if I'd do a thing like that."

He got Chan howling in that old funny way of his like he was some mad hyena, his lips all blubbery like they were too big for his mouth and Landis' vision turned him into a leprechaun the way he bent slightly as if hunchbacked and should have really been a centre-piece in some travelling freak side-show. But he loved him. There was something about Chan that was addictive; no matter how ugly he looked at times, something that was infectious. He was mad, of course, but it was a kind of madness that bordered on parody or zaniness that kind of reeled you in and you were hooked and you'd go along with all of his manic ideas and that's what he liked about Chan. Reckless, irrational, crazy, you could call him whatever you wanted and still that wasn't the whole picture for Chan lived for that Eternal Moment that he had touched just now. That was his kick. But most of all Chan and him shared one thing in common; the determination to go that one step further like they were on a mission or something, searching

for that precious jewel, it being priceless and thus twice as hard to find and perhaps could only be found in taking the mind to its fullest conclusion.

They talked and smoked for awhile. Chan was telling him all about the deals he had made that day, and how he was still having to support his father, whom he was very proud of. And Landis could relate to that having met him a few times, especially when he was younger and had just hooked up with Chan, for his father was well known around these parts, a soothsayer of sorts who never left his shack. Yet the strange thing was he knew everything. He knew what was happening like he was jacked into some kind of network and all the info-lines were being fed directly to his brain and you couldn't even have a wank in private without Chan's old man knowing about it. The Sage, they called him. He knew why for not only did he embody sagacity, he also knew about things that hadn't even happened yet, things that were way off in the future and could predict them to such a degree that once they finally happened he would look at you as if to say 'I told you so,' and you'd just wish you weren't there because he'd make you feel like a real dumb prick for not believing him in the first place. It was uncanny and sent shivers down his spine every time. Yet the thing that really got him about the Sage was with all of his wisdom, all this knowledge, and his ability to prophecy and all, he still chose to live in the most rundown part of town that stank with shit, but he called it home, living with his one and only son with no intention of moving out to find some place else which you could call a real home. It was this that got to Landis and something he could never understand about the old man. His shack was like a cocoon and the rest of the world was out there but he didn't need to explore it because he knew everything about it anyway.

Landis finished his beer and Chan bought him another one and they smoked some more whilst he watched Chan converse with the other Chinks sitting all around him; the way he laughed and came back to him with his own variation of the jokes they were telling each other and the way Chan could so easily switch from his own tongue to English and back as he tried to make him feel part of the scene so he didn't feel left out. He dragged Chan in towards him and gave him a big kiss on the mouth and got his tongue right down the back of his throat whilst he felt how hard his love for him was. He let him go after awhile and then looked at all those bulging eyes and creasing faces as they laughed at them, their brains all

soaked in synthed opium with withdrawn, nonexistent cheeks and those scrawny hands of theirs. Somehow he found it hard to believe that these people were influential round these parts. They ran this town, laid on the pussy for each night like it was an inexhaustible supply, which of course it was, and even the chief commissioner of the so-called police was sitting opposite him toking on that stuff, and somehow it all kind of made sense. For this is how it should be, he told himself, all the time. It was ideal. Yet soon, he knew, he would have to move on and eventually remit it.

But now he was kind of fretting. He wanted something else. Kissing Chan just now made him feel horny. He was getting stiff in his pants. He pulled Chan towards him, put his arm round him, gave him a quick peck and whispered to him, "So what we doing tonight, Chan?"

"You not happy staying here?"

"No, man. I want some fun. You know what I mean."

"Like other night?"

"Yeah. Now see what you can do."

He smiled at Chan, kissed him as his friend drank up.

"You wait right here. I be back."

And with that, Chan disappeared with that big grin on his face and Landis sat back confident his friend would deliver, like he always did, because he never let him down.

He quit on the next round of smokes when he noticed his white bit pass by on the way to the bathroom. He peeled away her dress with his eyes as they rested firmly on her ass. It was neat and firm, just the way he liked them. He got the impression she was trying to be something she wasn't and thought of her again like some sort of queen, all regal looking, when really she was cheap inside. But that didn't put him off. His body was telling him it approved. He felt even harder in his pants now and couldn't wait for Chan to get back with the goods. It would do for the time being until he could get his hands on her. And now she was returning, deliberately averting her eyes away from him no matter how hard he stared at her. She

wasn't going to have it and was giving him the same 'fuck off' sign as before. She walked right past him like she was some kind of model or something and cat-walking just for him. It only made him want her more.

Chan reappeared with two young chicks, both of them giggling like fuck as if this was a party. His friend bent down, whispered in his ear, "You like?"

Landis considered before replying. He took the two girls in as they stood there all still and nervous, knowing they were being summed up. One was just a bit shorter than the other. Both of them were kind of pretty, fresh-looking with wide smiles. One was more bashful than the other, not his type at all. The other knew her place, neither shy nor timid, and he reckoned far more experienced than her friend. He nodded his approval.

"Come. We go now."

They left and hit the alleys, his young friend running ahead of them with all of that excitement inside him like he couldn't control it. He led them round twists and turns of seemingly endless parades of narrow alleys which were in places no wider than his shoulders with all these tin shacks flashing by, streaks of metal, until his American friend hadn't a fucking clue where he was and didn't care either. The girls were cat-talking to each other like this was fun and were just as excited as Chan. Landis was now feeling it too, feeding off their joy and it was making him high, and that sensation was coming back to him now like earlier on, that tonight was going to be it and finally he'd kiss the night and let it consume him.

They entered another alley, up a short flight of stairs, into the back of a wooden building left over from the days when this town was first 'developed' and used to house all the construction workers, but fuck knows what it was used for now. They entered a small room that stank of urine and age-old vomit with a padlocked door of sheet metal all haphazardly soldered together as if the builders were in too much of a hurry to do a proper job. But that was this place all over. There were even stains on the walls where the rain leaked through.

Landis feigned a smile as his friend looked at him for his approval, trying to hold back his revulsion. The girls didn't seem to mind; they were used to it.

There were a couple of mattresses strewn on the floor, a window with no

glass in it and a small sink in the corner with the obligatory dripping tap.

He looked again to Chan who just shrugged in that big inane kind of way of his as if to say does the decor really matter, at least it was something where they could get on and do the biz undisturbed.

The girls wasted no time getting undressed whilst the men just stood there looking at each other then at them as if trying to decide which one to take first. Their eyes met again and read each other's thoughts.

"How old is she?" Landis asked him, pointing to the taller one.

"She eighteen," Chan replied.

"And the other one?" indicating the girl now lying naked on the mattress.

"She seventeen," he replied.

"Right, I'll take the younger one first."

He stripped off, shedding his clothes like he was on business and about to do a job that would get him all dirty as he folded his clothes and lay them neatly on the side, which kind of got to his friend who just ripped his clothes off and let them fall wherever and got down to it.

Landis surveyed the girl's body, all scintillating smooth with that faint tinge of ochre, just lying there waiting for him. She was shaved, just how he liked them, not a hair on her body, and unblemished apart from a small tat on her left shoulder. He figured it was her name written in her own language, whatever her name was. He sat down on the side of the mattress next to her and rubbed his hand up and down her thighs and parted them with that big manly grip of his and was more than satisfied with her pussy. It was remarkable in that it suggested a wound to him that had yet to heal, a tiny open sore exaggerated by lack of pubic hair. Her labia were pierced with rings. They intrigued him and he wondered what their symbolic value was. He looked to Chan who was busy pumping away like some sort of out of control pneumatic drill and his young lady friend coiling her legs round his waist, all tossing and writhing like she was orgasming already which he found hard to believe since Chan wasn't that big anyway. He reckoned she was just a cheap slut that needed a good lesson, faking like fuck. He was

starting to feel cheated inside and sorry for his friend. But he'd put that right soon as he looked at his girl, tugging at her rings, pulling them apart, playing with them, and she was groaning already as if it was turning her on, and she was just as bad as her friend, making him feel mighty displeased, though he let her stroke his cock, making it stiffen with her touch, as she played with his piercings. (He had fourteen in all, and what he called his 'steel,' or metalwear. The latter consisted of eleven steel rods. These traversed the shaft from the base all the way up to the glans, all connected together, terminating either end in adjustable studs which could be changed from nice smooth balls to sharp spikes at the touch of a button, the button being located between the base of the shaft and his scrotum. At the moment his steel was in the friendly mode, the balls protruding just above the surface. He finished off his steel with a plain ampallang and two piercings at right angles to that.) Her fingers found the ampallang and started to caress the two large barbs, all the while moaning like she was kind of desperate for him and uttered something softly he didn't understand as he bent down to lick her wounded flesh.

"What did she say?" he asked Chan to translate.

"She say her rings are tokens," he replied panting heavily. "They all mark of lovers. She add you too."

"Oh yeah? Who the fuck does she think she is?"

He went down on her and pulled her labia apart and got his tongue in deep, but she was acting like she was in heaven already which he couldn't understand, for he was a dog licking his master's wound and had no right to be piling up all this heavy orgasm shit for he hadn't even got inside her yet which was ridiculous because she would know all about it if he did and she'd be ovulating in some kind of eternal ecstasy. She was well drilled, like all those others Chan had brought him, who were so shit scared of not pleasing their masters they felt they had to pretend they were having a good time, and it was this realisation which was making him feel real angry as he slipped inside her wetness and made sure she wouldn't be faking it like the rest for he was now ramming her hard and ramming her real good so that there was no chance of her faking all this pleasure she was supposed to be enjoying, for no one could whilst he had his stainless steel up inside them and this girl would not only have to be dumb but dead to her body as his

smooth spherical points hit home and she was kind of gurgling as he pumped harder, yet still he felt cheated, deprived from that goal he was trying to attain, that precious little goal of his as his body started kicking into action, she squealing, sounding like she was in pain or something, that he couldn't understand for the stupid bitch didn't know what real pain was and anybody would have thought there was a knife stuck on the end of his dick, that he was cutting her in two which was kind of ridiculous for he was only nibbling at her nipples with his sharp teeth so he couldn't understand what all the fuss was about. Didn't the fucking bitch realise he was trying to take her further, trying to take her all the way? And now she was fighting him, banging her fists against his back wildly as he bit into her deeper and that luscious coloured blood of hers was seeping into his mouth making his milky white teeth all pink and he was gratified thereby as it flowed yet still fighting against him all the time, the stupid bitch. Who the fuck did she think she was that he could be so easily ripped off? He pulled out as she struggled and adjusted his steel into nice sharp spikes and rammed it home and she was hopping all over the mattress like she was in some kind of pain and he was laughing along with Chan, maniacally and cool, her friend seizing in a limbo as she gasped and panic shot into her eyes.

"You fucking bitch! You fucking whore!" he screamed at her as he pumped her harder and blood was flowing all over the place, that beautiful crimson hue as he watched lovingly her false self disappear and her real self coming to the surface as she wailed wildly evoking fear, that beautiful fear. It was music to his ears and getting louder and wilder as she writhed in ecstasy, bathing his steel in luxurious warm blood, a baptism of blood that was closer to the original than the traditional, and this was his rite, his part in her rite time, for he was deflowering the girl with his love. Why, he was just getting his message across so she would understand and so would the others, that they'd maybe catch on to his way and never try ripping him off again. Didn't they understand? It was simple, so simple he found it hard to believe why anybody could not learn this fundamental lesson. He reached into his pile of clothes, worming his way in until his hand found the handle and pulled out his cold steel blade and whipped his cock out as she screamed with its withdrawal and rammed his knife right up inside her like he was doing an operation—for his father had always wanted him to be a surgeon—and started operating straight away, a small technical operation, you understand, one that required the utmost precision, a delicate job. So

he mustered all the skill he had in him and inserted his knife home, dissecting away as she writhed in bliss and Chan was over there, gloating with bloodshot eyes as he held her friend down and stifled her screams as Landis retracted his steel and started jacking-off all over her stomach with that lovely precious juice that was flooding her being, a small ocean of glistening white on her stomach.

He dropped back for a second or two as his strength left him, yet still felt deprived as his blade lay inside her and she had gone all sour on him. Why, he couldn't understand. He thought she was one of them party-types who always knew how to have fun. He guessed she didn't like his idea of fun so he pulled his blade out real slow and edged it up to her belly button, and whittled with his knife, his Opener of the Ways, and edged it all the way up her abdomen, a nice succulent groove marking her book of flesh and spiralled round the point of his knife so as to carve into her memory, her soul, that Eternal Moment he had touched, that moment he was constantly chasing like a ghost but knowing soon one day it would be his. Smooth, pitying fear, lacerated against soft-tinged flesh and pubic bone. We are one, we are none, he thought as he sliced her some more, drew the blade right up to what was left of her nipples and started cutting into them like they were two primal mounds and half expected them to shoot forth that wondrous milk of theirs and was mightily dissatisfied the promised goods weren't being delivered because he wanted to give suck.

He lost his temper as it didn't come and flashed wildly at her with his blade like he was a mad demon, hell-bent and possessed like there was this thing inside him pushing its way up to the surface. He slashed her some more as she tried to struggle and break free. But didn't she realise so far his work had only been superficial and he hadn't even moved onto the major stage of his operation? He pinioned her to the mattress, determined to cut her in two like the two-faced bitch she really was to prove he was in the right.

He brought his blade up to that lovely throat of hers as she just lay there all rigid, his blade glinting sweet soft caresses in the pale light of the room, all flashing and penetrant, all luminous and entrenching, and he could dig it into her deep, deep into those panic-filled eyes which made him hard again and he cajoled his cock back to life whilst she screamed some more.

"Yeah, go on, scream, you bitch. I want to hear you die!" And his words

came out of his throat like words wrapped in fine cotton wool under bated breath and so perfectly controlled it didn't even sound like his voice as he slit her across the surface of her throat, not deeply, you understand, just enough to get the demon out of her possessed soul and cruising to the surface in the shape of a nice trickle of blood he could lick with his lips and squirm with delight, not in a false way, that would have been no better than her. It had to be genuine and real; that's what it was all about, and he'd be rewarded, greatly elated thereby, and it would all come in that dark ecstatic moment when he would kiss her goodbye and she'd be out there, right out there like he had been in the club, floating, touching it as the life slipped out of her slowly and he wanted to sit back and watch it vacate her body real slow as it went up and departed from the body of this girl who tried to rip him off, ebbing out like a ghost on a smooth silk-covered cloud and remitting her sins as he jacked-off in her face and his face too swelled with delight as she let out that last breath of hers and died sweetly.

It was a great pity. He wanted her to last longer and felt pretty sure she would. Then he got to figure even in death she was cheating him; that left him feeling kind of short-changed. He decided a compromise was needed.

He looked to her friend as she lay there all flapping and struggling and couldn't understand what all the fuss was about, or what precisely it was those wide eyes were trying to tell him. Then he looked to Chan with those wide lips of his and laughing like he was pissing in his pants as he saw that unmistakable sign creep across Landis' face and knew well what it meant and released the girl and holstered her up off the floor and started dangling her in front of Landis like she was bait and then snatched her out of his way as he tried to grab her and waltzed her round the room like some prima ballerina, a naked rag doll he was clutching tightly as they circled the room. Landis was chasing after the mad pair and getting real angry with his friend for depriving him of his prize.

"Give her to me!" he demanded.

"No," Chan shouted back. "She mine."

"Give her to me!" he demanded again.

And each time he got close to catching her Chan would shout "No!" and he

would laugh at his friend as they danced the dance of death and he was going to take her all the way, all the way baby, all the way right to the gates of paradise as he caught up with them and squeezed his crotch in tight against her butt as she sobbed like the pathetic thing she was, for she was a nothing so why the fuck was she getting all het up? What was her problem? He couldn't understand as they paraded round the room trampling over her dead friend. He grabbed her by the hair and pulled her head back and looked deeply into her eyes to see what she was trying to convey and it looked like something to do with God and that kind of made him feel like the Devil himself and he brought his knife up to her throat as they now moved on to the dance of Pan, whirling round in a frenzy as Chan let her go so Landis could finally have her as if he were kindly placing her life in his hands, screaming into her face and she was screaming back so he would scream some more and it was only making him feel better as they toppled to the ground and he wrenched her head right back.

"Bitch," he whispered sweetly into her ear between clenched teeth. "You're shit just like your friend. And I've got something nice and big for you."

He pushed her down on to her hands and knees and adjusted his steel so that it was all lovely smooth shining spikes and razor sharp and parted her buttocks like they were folds in a curtain and shoved it right deep inside her shit-canal so that all he could hear was a terrific resounding yell that went out beyond the walls of the room and seeped into the aethers as if verily she was speaking to God himself and he laughed wildly as he shoved his being deeper inside her, thrusting harder as the sacrificial blood came flowing out in His name and she sobbing and panting like a real child in purgatory and he was helping to exorcise her soul, her poor stained soul he must save if she was to be redeemed thereby. It sounded like she was screaming in pain, but he knew it wasn't really pain. It was the Godless being driven out of her tainted soul he was purifying and taking to heaven, flowing out as her blood mingled with her friend's and he was the purifying unquenchable fire that was working God's will on earth, saving the souls of the lost and the damned and raising them back to regal status, all passing judgement gloriously and vindicated and true of voice as he pumped harder into her carnal canal, that very lair of vice and iniquity itself, the abode of demons and filth. He was listening to her moaning and held back a bit to see if he could get her to moan rhythmically and interspersed with the occasional

scream so that it sounded like a wailing song or a song of the damned pouring out of her tremulous throat. Chan was all howling with fits in the corner, beaming brightly as he watched the divine pair. But it looked like Landis was losing his patience with her as he started pumping her harder, digging right down deep inside her heart, and was pulling it out, placing it in the scales of the universal balance and weighing it against a feather to see if she was fit for heaven, and the scribe was standing behind him noting it all down, with the little eager devourer by his feet just waiting for it to balance wrong and it looked like he was going to be swallowing it after all for the plumb-line was off and she'd be sinking all the way back down to purgatory again for there was no way she was going to pass through the halls of judgement and be righteous, no way she was going to pass into the Hall of Double Truth. No, he decided, she was going down again and he was going to send her there and watch her be consumed, gloating on her cries. Chan was enamoured by all of this, listening to her squealing as he was frothing in his mouth, spittle flowing out of his big wide lips as he started jacking off and getting real hard like he was in on the act and he too had this terrible demon inside of him and was trying to get it out, rubbing it harder all the time, flowing out like the diseased demon that he really was.

The wench weltered and he hollered some more as he finally came with light boiling in the back of his brain, and the effect was even more powerful than synthed opium. He died a little as his mind expanded outwards and filled the entire room, even beyond the confines of the room until it was all submerged under something called 'the universe,' and he was one with the beyond, infinite and not hemmed in by any boundaries.

He smiled as he flopped down on her back. She collapsed crying to the floor. They lay there for a while, the double sphinx, the beast with two backs, carved in time, a cinematic sculpture of desire extinguished in one glorious, all-consuming flame, and for once he was happy and satisfied thereby as his whole self had been poured into her little self so that neither were distinguishable one from the other.

He came to and pulled his blood-drenched steel out of her primal abode and heard her moan a bit as he withdrew it like she was still alive or something and therefore needed more treatment, despite being all cut up inside and lovely red ichor was flowing out of her bruised cavity mingled

with his juice. The stupid bitch, he'd put her right.

He slapped her rump real hard and rolled her onto her back, her head lolling around on the floor like it was loose or disconnected from her body. Her eyes were wetting up and overflowing with tears like she was suffering or something as they looked up to the ceiling half-closed as if trying to read some divine message carved into the wood, a message of redemption, he thought. He retracted his steel and put away his knife as he parted her legs to get a taste of that blood mingled with the juices flowing out of her cunt which contained Chan's seed. It tasted good, but not good enough as if lacking the essential ingredient and he knew what it was. He reached into his clothes and pulled out his gun and waved it in front of her face and laughed at the way her eyes followed it and started sobbing, pleading for mercy at deaf ears that were revelling in it and were gladdened thereby, his eyes shot through with blood, all red, inflamed and had a glossy sheen about them making everything look beautiful and crystal clear.

His gun was roving all over her face as he pushed its muzzle deep into her cheeks and made her head roll back and forth and then forced it up against her chin so her head went right back and he was engorged thereby and traced its hard metal against her soft, smooth skin and circled her pert breasts and then back up again when she gave him a look he didn't like and tried to say something he figured was a curse and told her to fuck herself and pressed his gun tightly against her blowjob lips and peeled them apart and shoved it deep into her mouth, forcing her to suck it like it was his cock. It made him hard and with his other hand he started jacking off as she sucked some more, paralysed with fear, the demon-fear coming out of her eyes and he reckoned he had never seen such a prettier sight. She was his now, all his. He was fate writ large controlling her destiny, that destiny she had kindly placed in his hands because she knew he was the one. He could see it written in her face, in those subdued, ebony eyes etched in glass.

He pulled his gun out as he started to feel himself coming all nicely and held back the climax as he spread her legs some more, and he was going to come good this time again because that was what she was here for, right? To please her man. That's what she was getting paid for so she'd better not die on him too quickly yet, not like her friend. He wanted his money's worth and took his time as he found her hole with his gun, and it was wide

open just for him. He slipped the muzzle of his gun inside and listened to her squirm as he started pumping her, ramming it in harder with its long barrel, and it was only a Magnum so why was she getting all funny on him and begging. All he was doing was driving the very Devil out of her body, cleansing and purifying her soul, and his divine power was getting to him, feeding him like he was injecting pure life right into his mainline and closed his eyes as he gripped his cock tighter and rubbed it harder, all the while worshipping her fear that he could almost hear like it was a subliminal code coming through to him and loved the way she was respecting him. He was the master. She the slave. And that was the only way it could ever be, she all obedient and servile, subservient to his divine power, bequeathing unto him the obeisance he rightly deserved, for no woman had any control over him and any who thought they did were wrong, and he would prove it, and they always came round to his way of thinking and paid him reverence and worshipped him.

Now he could smell it, a sweet pervading perfume which was wafting out of her hole and was filling his nostrils so he was intoxicated thereby as he pumped his gun in harder and rolled open his eyes as if he was being seized. It was gripping him, taking him over, making him grit his teeth as he tried to hold it back just for a bit longer and stared down into her eyes.

"I spy with my little eye," he uttered like a father to his child, "something about to begin with B."

He looked deeper into her eyes to make sure she understood and there was an instinctive agreement between them and she knew he was right and grimaced whilst he tried to control himself and fought to get the Eternal Moment into view so he could seize it and unite ecstatically with it and be greatly enriched thereby as his finger gripped the trigger tighter the harder he pumped his gun. Chan was joining in on the act as he came over and stood right next to him, trying to get into rhythmic tandem with his friend, getting his cock all stiff and hard with his left hand as he gripped his friend's shoulder with his right. Landis was concentrating on those sinful eyes of hers so hard he wasn't even aware the gun had gone off just as he came and spilt his seed all over the floor like Onan and her body had recoiled a good metre backwards with her hole now even bigger. It reminded him of a crater with copious quantities of blood and pieces of

flesh pouring out. But it was the precious sanguine sacrament that was flowing out of her mouth which got him going and he just had to bend down and get a good lick of it and savoured it for it tasted like no other blood he had tasted before in his life, a rare delicacy he had worked hard to attain and spiced with a strange mixture of love and fear, the sort of vintage only a connoisseur of mortal concupiscence could readily appreciate and a fitting climax. But Chan still hadn't come and looked like he was in real agony so Landis had to put him out of his misery and grabbed his friend's cock and pumped the very life out of him. Chan was shaking in a frenzy that had him almost off the floor and took him deep into his mouth as he came. His life flowed deliciously down the back of Landis' throat. And it tasted good too. He licked his lips then let his friend go. Chan fell to the floor with a big smile on his face and died a little.

It had been worth it, he thought. It was like all things in life. To get complete satisfaction out of anything you had to work hard for it, for the more you put into it the more you got out of it, and it always worked that way. There simply were no half measures. And that's what kind of got to him about these two chicks. They expected to get by with a tiny bit of effort. But that wasn't good enough in his book. They didn't know what real work was, and he proved just now he did and wasn't work-shy like everybody tried to make out he was. He proved them wrong and was well rewarded thereby for now he was feeling mighty good, rapturous and glad as he surveyed his handiwork. He always took pride in his work. It meant a lot to him and there was no excuse for poor workmanship. Laziness led to shoddiness and that was inexcusable. That's what irked him about these kids, for if a job was worth doing, it was worth doing well. He had done himself proud and now felt he deserved a nice quiet smoke somewhere peaceful, just to come down a notch or two, you understand, and went over and kissed his friend fully on the lips and got him awake slightly with that beautiful look of euphoria on his face and smiled.

"Chan," he whispered, "how about some more of that stuff of yours to finish off the night."

His friend nodded. "Good idea. Plenty back at my place."

"Then what we doing here? Come on, let's go."

THE MISANTHROPIST

'As Clavonius puts it: "He who hateth the world hateth himself." The misanthropist's rejection of the world is a fallacy of phallic proportions for it is ultimately a rejection of the self.'

Paul K. Jarrup,
Critique of the Cynic

—5—
THE NAME'S CAPRI

The darkness was moving in from the west. Capri tightened his coat as a chill breeze moved in with it. The night was dead. It made him feel uncomfortable.

He felt like a ghost, not really there at all. He might as well have been invisible. It was slowly dawning on him now the man wasn't going to show, no matter how long he waited or how hard he stared at the big neon sign which was their agreed rendezvous. And soon he was going to have to concede that the little voice in his head was right. It was pointless waiting any longer, standing on the sidewalk watching all the traffic hiss by.

He took the last drag from his cigarette and tossed it to the ground. He stamped on it with a vengeance and cursed the man under his breath. He looked up and down the street for the final time, hardly surprised there was no sign of him. He sighed.

It was kind of strange. Paco was always reliable; this was the first time he had let Capri down. But what about the others; they too had let him down. It wasn't just a coincidence either. There was more to it than that. It didn't make sense. Had he done something wrong to offend them? Or were they just messing him around? But why would they? Capri was kosher and the best man for the job. That was his reputation, one he had maintained assiduously over the years ever since he arrived in this big city and set himself up. He was the best Cleaner going, the only one who got things done and delivered on time, invariably in half the time it took the cops, never failing in any assignment, no matter how tough. And that was why they always passed on their dirty work to him. He was keen, smart and

efficient, cheap as well, never asking too much, just enough to get by, ensuring he could cover himself for a few weeks whilst he went away on one of his retreats, just like the one he had been on.

He shrugged his mood off and crossed the street. He stopped at a kiosk to buy some more cigarettes before heading down town. He hiked it quickly as the rain started, and picked up his pace with anger now singing in his veins. His old comrade Angel had let him down as well by deserting him once again. But he always did that whenever Capri got bogged down in the trivialities of the day. He reckoned he was getting too old for this shit and would have to pack it in soon. He hit forty the other week and was now beginning to feel it.

Life had caught up with him fast, despite his attempts at trying to cheat it. He could feel it in his body, the way he had been mistreating it, abusing it all the time. Now his body was screaming back at him to take it easy before he really did burn out. It was time to stop, time to get serious. He was sick and tired of saying yes to life, for once to finally say no, enough. But he couldn't. He was still clinging on, hanging on tenaciously, waking each day on a high only to watch it being cut down throughout the day and ending on a low, hoping, praying it would be his last. It wasn't that simple. For here he was again, in the same position as yesterday with only a few dollars left in his pocket. Still no steady income, no real job, no investments, and a lot of debts hanging over his head which somehow miraculously escalated by themselves.

He didn't understand it. He no longer cared. All his efforts had been in vain. They had got him nowhere, a big fat nought which impregnated his little universe and made him feel empty and worthless inside, like shit.

But despite that, there had to be a reason for what he was going through at present. It amounted to a tight circle which led to nowhere, and each time he realised he was in it he could only tell himself to be patient. Things would work out soon for the better. If only he had the patience. Maybe a big job would arrive soon, one with megabucks thrown in, enough for him to break out of the circle and finally get free so he could quit the rounds of making contacts, meeting with dubious people who could never be trusted, acting on the information given, doing the suss-work and eventually delivering in the end. It was a routine which had long outgrown its usage. It

no longer carried the same charge that fired him not so long ago. And it was this ennui that was making him feel tired and old like he was slowly running out of steam, and no amount of recharging seemed to work any more; one disappointment or another left him feeling deflated.

If only Angel could help him out. They had communed for a short while, patched up their differences during the solitude. But Angel had upped it and left, leading him to believe they weren't on speaking terms like an old bickering couple living out in the hills, quarrelling over trivial things like whose turn it was to do the dishes. It had been *incommunicado* since his retreat. Now he just felt deserted and alone.

Capri thought of shoving his pride aside for once and going back to the cops. That was always the last resort, an option he considered whenever he was stuck for work. The option wasn't too favourable, not after the way they treated him the last time, they taking all the glory, he a nothing in their eyes who had no right trying to claim the credit he thought he deserved. He hated them for that. They hated him. It had come to a dangerous symbiotic relationship, dangerous for him that is since it was always one-sided and he never got anything from them in return. They could use his desperation to their advantage knowing he would always be forced into going back to them. And that's exactly what they did with his last job. He got Kane for them like he said he would, delivering as usual, taking only two weeks in the process what had taken them nearly two years, making them look like pricks. Perhaps it was his smart-ass reply which sealed his fate, ensuring that the rivalry and hostility would continue unabated forever. They were just jealous, too proud to admit their own mistakes; so they called in Capri to show them how to do the job properly. Nor could they stand being chided by a street 'tec like himself who could not only prove who was doing the killings but where the guy would strike next. And he did, of course.

Capri could empathise with him, could understand why he was killing all them people, all those lowlifes, and managed to tune into his wavelength so precisely he could predict his next move, simply by living on the streets and becoming one with Kane, the killing machine. After Kane had been nailed the whole case become notorious overnight. The defence had repeatedly questioned why it had taken so long for Kane to be finally apprehended. How did he manage to evade the arms of the law for so long? It was then

revealed in court the cops had deliberately turned a blind eye to the murders, they too considering the 'class' of victims as being 'worthless.' It was an admission which rocked the whole foundation of American justice and made Kane a celebrity in the process. And beneath the uproar Capri hadn't even been given the credit he was due. He might as well not have existed for the little press attention he got in the end. He was hoping the gods would be on his side now; they would be throwing work at him left, right and centre, so much work he would probably have to turn most of it down. What a great position to be in, he thought as he lit up another cigarette and stared at the deserted street. He looked to the empty sky above, watching the smoke rise up in eddying coils, then vanish, thinking how wonderful it would be to be up there. If the gods were on his side, he concluded, it was time to test them once again. There was only one place in this big, wide city he could find his old buddy, Sam Hain: Lou's Bar.

* * * * *

Lou's was a small, unostentatious joint smack in the heart of Little Italy, his favourite part of the city. It is where he met most of his clients and contacts. Admittedly, it was a dive. It was seedy, rough at times, a shit-hole that had no class, but it always made him feel at home. It was unpretentious and did not attempt to convey a false sense of bonhomie between its clientele who often erupted into gross acts of violence before the night was through. This is where Kane, the genius gone wrong, would have had a field day, exalting as his blood sung in his veins. It wasn't so much that Capri knew practically everyone who came here which always drew him to the place, it was the inexpensive drinks that flowed all night. Hence it was the best drinking hole in town.

He ordered a bourbon, his only reliable friend, and had a good look round. Most of the guys he expected to see hadn't arrived. It was too early. He would stick around and wait for them to show up. But his old buddy was already here, like he knew he would be.

Sam was sitting at the other end of the bar getting drunk by himself as usual. Hain had struck lucky, the bastard, by coming across that rarest of commodities in this business; a rich bitch. Not only did he charm his way into her pants, he also got hitched up with her and now had no need to support himself. He just fed off her and would no doubt bleed her dry and

then move on to another victim. Capri wasn't envious; he just wished the same thing would happen to him. Hain was fortunate and could drink all night like there was no tomorrow, unlike when they were working together and had to live out of each other's pockets just to survive. They used to sleep on each other's couches, even share their workloads when work was scarce. It kind of brought them together. Now they were separated like Siamese twins, spatially apart yet emotionally still attached without any animosity between them.

Capri landed a hand on his old colleague's shoulder. "Hey Sam, thought I'd might find you here."

Hain didn't take much notice; just shot him a glance out of the corner of his bleary eyes.

"Heard you was back in town," he said indifferently, went back to his drink.

"Yes, got back a couple of days ago. Thought I'd check out what was happening around here." He drew a stool over and sat down next to Hain. "Actually, I'm looking for Paco."

"The Laundry Man?" Hain asked.

"Yes. He didn't show tonight. Any ideas where I can find him?"

Hain looked at him seriously. "Try the morgue."

"Shit!"

"Afraid so. Got hit this morning. Thought you heard?"

"No," he said shaking his head. "No I hadn't. I don't believe it."

"Believe it. And if you ask me, it's better now he's out the way."

"So who's the next guy?" He lit up a cigarette and slouched on the bar.

"Don't know. Have to wait and see."

"I can't wait. I've got absolutely no work lined up for the rest of the week. Since I've been back four others have let me down. This is not what I need. I need work, Sam. Let me in on something, will you?"

"I wish I could, Harmon. I'm sorry, man, there ain't nothing happening at present. I mean take a look at all of these other guys. They're all clean out like you. Things are quiet at present. You gonna have to wait."

"I can't wait, Sam. There's got to be something happening. I can't believe there isn't. Has everybody given up crime all of a sudden?"

"Fucking cut it out, Harmon. You don't know what's happening round here. You're out of touch with reality."

"Oh yeah?"

"Don't be such an asshole."

"Come on, Sam, I know you. I've seen that look in your eye before. You know something I don't."

Hain paused momentarily. He took a gulp of his drink. His face changed. It became all sullen as if he wasn't sure how to phrase what he had to say. "Since you been away something has happened. I don't know anymore than you, but I heard a rumour. Seems there's an outsider holding back all the business." Capri laughed. "Yeah, go ahead, laugh. That's what I did when I heard. But now I'm not so sure. Remember when we used to work together and we used to have hard times, things getting a bit thin on the ground? Well, we rode through those days like wild fucks, didn't we? We used to come out smiling every time we got the big one. This time it's different. I've never seen it like this before. Everyone's complaining. Even the Dealer. His boys are out of work. No one can figure it out. I tell you it's dead here."

"Perhaps I should've stayed away a bit longer," Capri said to himself more than to Hain.

"Perhaps you should have. But your coming back now ain't gonna make any difference. Things changed about three weeks ago."

"Any idea who's behind all of this?"

Hain shook his head. "No, nothing definite. But if I was you I wouldn't ask any questions and just lay low for awhile."

"What? Until some new boss finally shows?"

"Yep. I know how desperate you are, Harmon, but don't fuck up over this or do anything stupid. Let things take care of themselves. Besides, what's happened to those powers of yours? Haven't they told you anything? I mean, you're supposed to be psychic, right?"

Capri didn't answer. He just looked at Hain knowing full well what he meant. His former colleague was right. There was something indiscernible present, something that didn't gel. It had been bugging him ever since he went on his retreat. "Yes, I guess you're right." Capri gulped his drink down. "I'm going to have to wait."

He was about to call the barman over for a refill when Hain stopped him.

"No, let me get this in," Hain offered and ordered them both doubles.

"Thanks, Sam," he replied. He drank that beautiful stuff down as soon as it arrived. He wanted to drink tonight, get gloriously drunk, to forget, at least until tomorrow when sobriety resumed and reality lifted up its ugly head.

He slammed his empty glass down on the bar and licked his lips. Hain chuckled. So did Capri. "I'll get the next one in," he offered as Hain finished his and called the barman over. The place started filling up. The music on the system kicked into action, announcing the night was really starting. Soon the place would be full, and he would have to leave as his claustrophobia got to him. He reached in his pocket and pulled out his thin wallet, fumbled for some money and put it on the bar looking at it ashamedly. When it was all gone this time it would be gone for good. Hain looked at him knowingly, could read it in his face like a visible message.

"I hate to ask you this, Sam," Capri said, looking at him squarely, "but, um, I'm kind of low."

"I know what you're gonna ask." Hain shrugged his shoulders and said, "Fuck it. You owe me 450 already, so why not round it up."

Hain pulled out his thick wallet and slapped a fifty dollar bill on the bar. Capri smiled and patted his friend again as he fetched it up. "Thanks, Sam. I'll pay you back. I promise."

"Yeah sure, I've heard that before," he said, shaking his head in disbelief.

CELEBRATION

Capri offered him a cigarette and lit up as their drinks arrived. He swallowed it down with relish. A few more and he would be on a roll, not wanting to stop, just to keep rolling.

He felt a light tap on his shoulder, not even aware somebody was standing behind him. It unnerved him thinking it could be one of the Cleaners. He quickly prepared some bullshit in his mind about waiting to get paid. He put on a brave face, calmly turned round expecting the worse. He needn't have worried, for he was now looking straight into two of the most gorgeous eyes in the whole of New York. They belonged to the Lizard Kid.

Capri let out a sigh of relief and laughed.

"Hey, Kid, you scared the shit out of me," he told him.

The Kid let out a loud laugh and smiled. He licked his lips with that protruding tongue of his and hissed.

He was cool and reptilian, young and fresh-looking with smooth oily skin that bordered on green. His hair was slicked back, a darker shade of green. He always dressed immaculately, only the most expensive gear would do. He got the name the Lizard Kid, not due just to his looks, a result of an unfortunate mix up in his genes, but because of what he kept in his pants which fascinated all the girls. He was said to have a split penis. Made quite a name for himself, selling his wares, establishing a good name and knew everything happening with his highly sensitive saurian brain. Could pick up on anything like he had an in-built antenna. If there was anybody who was in the know, it would be the Kid.

When he smiled he beamed brightly. Well, usually he did. Even the Kid looked kind of down and his aura wasn't the bright, blazing yellow shroud it normally was. It didn't stream out of him, only seemed to hang around him like an outworn coat.

They exchanged greetings and talked telepathically for awhile. The Kid was telling him what the score was. He too reiterated what Hain told him, except he reckoned it was a woman. Didn't know her name or what she looked like. Nobody so far had seen her, but the Kid was determined to find out. Capri arranged to meet him tomorrow night. Together they stood a better chance of tracking her down. The Kid slithered away back to his

groupie girlfriends, Capri turned back round to Hain who was frowning at him with a 'what did I tell you' look.

"Don't look at me like that," Capri pleaded.

"Well? Now do you believe me?" Hain smirked.

Capri conceded and ordered another drink for both of them. "The Kid reckons it's some woman."

"Really? And nobody knows who she is, right?"

He nodded. "We're going to find her tomorrow."

"What did I say? I said, lay low for awhile, don't do anything. Be patient."

"Fuck being patient." He lit up again.

"Look, why don't you go to the cops? They've always got work on."

Capri shook his head. "No way. Not after the last time."

"Because of the Kane affair?"

"Yes. I've made my mind up. I'm never going back to them again."

"I can understand that, Harmon. You did a good job there. It should have set you up for life."

"Well it didn't, okay? It didn't," he snarled and slammed down his glass.

But before his old colleague could say something Capri was walking out the door. "I hope something works out for you one day, Harmon," he said to himself instead and went back to his drink.

Capri left, not even sure where he was going or what he was going to do next. All he knew was he had to get out of there. Out on the streets was better. It helped to sober him up, getting the cold damp air into his lungs, his brain into gear and thinking properly, grilling away at any ideas which came to the surface.

He paused and caught his breath. He lit up a cigarette, took the smoke deep

into his lungs as he tried to fathom a solution. His mind was still trying to engender an inspiring idea. It somewhat refused. He let it go and resumed walking, not really caring how long it took to get home. In fact, he didn't care to go home at all, more inclined to continue drinking at a real humdinger of a club a few blocks up, forget everything and enjoy the moment. It was a test. The gods were testing his mettle. A man of his calibre could not let them down, could he? All he wanted was a divine message, this time nice and simple so it could be understood. Then he would act on it, throw his whole self into it and come out shining. If only! He had to stop dreaming like this and get real.

He stamped out his cigarette and found himself approaching Times Square, near the corner of 42nd Street and 8th Avenue, not the best place to be in at this time of night, but he didn't give a fuck now. The abundance of the people milling around seemed to brush right through him rather than around him as if he wasn't there. It exaggerated his isolation and aloofness from the real world.

He stopped in his tracks. He had a sudden inspiration. He smiled as it took shape and mocked his own imbecility. Of course, he thought. He had some money on him, all he had to do now was find the nearest casino. He thought quickly as the idea began to gel, quite forgetting in his excitement the vow he made to himself the last time; never to gamble again. Then he thought to himself, 'Everything is a gamble,' and banished his doubt. It had to be all or nothing.

He fuelled the idea with his enthusiasm, sussed out a place called The Crystal Paradise (or Crystal's to its regulars), two blocks down. He wasted no time and headed in the right direction. He was going, almost running, telling himself all the time that it was going to be a one off, definitely the last time, no more excuses for relapsing, never again. His elation carried him there with its momentum. He would throw everything into the lap of the gods and not hold back one drop. If he doubted his own gesture he knew it wouldn't work. It had to be a total commitment, no compromises.

He was even taking a gamble now as he turned the corner and headed up a street full of the most repugnant people he had ever seen, the sort who had escaped Kane's slaughter. It did not perturb him. He stretched his mind to Angel, calling on him with all the sweet names he could think of,

beseeching him for his support. Still there was no response.

He found Crystal's and smiled to himself as he stood at the bottom of the stairs. He held firm to his idea and rode on its wings and ascended.

The doorman gave him no hassle as he glided in. He dropped his coat off in the foyer and did what any man would do in his position; head straight for the bar! The bar overlooked the games floor below, suits and dresses milling around like caricatures. He looked on them all disdainfully as he ordered a drink and sat himself down on one of the high stools. All these people, more money than sense, and he was watching it roll into the roulette wheels, the die and cards, the harbingers of fate. They operated on their own terms in a stochastic universe that had its own incomprehensible laws few could manipulate to their own advantage.

He waited to be served by the old man behind the bar who frowned on Capri's presence and served him last. He took a bourbon with lots of ice to make it last and got comfortable. He was in no hurry. He would take his time and play it cool, delaying the decisive moment for as long as need be.

He focused on the tables below looking for a vacant space. They were all busy, heaving with throngs of people under the fake chandelier lights. Spectators hovering around the green baize tops, players resembling mourners staring into graves when the cards didn't fall their way, others like whimsical children when they had a hunch they were on a winning streak. It was mind-numbing yet strangely infectious. He could feel the greed in the air and was getting high on it as the power of that most tyrannical of gods, Mammon, seeped into his veins. He had a disconcerting vision but suppressed it, choosing to light up and relax. He watched the smoke float up to the lights as he exhaled taking his desire with it.

A tall blonde strolled up to where he was smugly sat. She was dressed all in black (his favourite colour) and clutching an exorbitant handbag which was an indication of her worth. He thought she was just an expensive floozy out for a game and lit up her cigarette when she motioned for a light. She paused, waiting for him to speak and left when the conversation wasn't forthcoming. He was not here for that. He was here on business, serious business. He scoffed and caught sight of a vacant seat at the *chemin de fer* table.

He drank up and slipped off his stool and casually descended into the belly of that god, pausing for a moment by the seat, his nostrils flaring as they brought in that rare, elusive scent to the back of his brain. It was electric and stupefying. He reminded himself it was positively the last time he would play and sat himself down at Number Seven with the sort of confidence that never wavered for it never questioned itself. The shoe was at the other end of the table, at Number Three. He sat back, relaxed, smoked for awhile and stubbed out his cigarette in the clean astray before him whilst examining the faces of the other players. Satisfied, he put Hain's untouched fifty dollar bill on the baize and motioned the Changeur over. He got it changed into a black chip. Capri toyed with it as he watched the play, noticing a sign hanging above the table; minimum bet fifty dollars, another indication that what he was doing was right.

The other players were all American and white. Being an English expatriate himself he did not feel out of place, despite the fact that he was poorly dressed compared with everyone else. He was a punter like the rest of them; social class and levels of wealth simply did not come into the equation. He looked at them all, especially the blonde in front of him who refused to reciprocate his friendly smile. Spectators were two-deep around the table.

Judging by everybody else's expressions, the game was cold. He decided to hang back, as did the other players until the shoe came to an end.

Capri watched the croupier marshalling the six packs of cards into the oblong box. He slipped it into the shoe. Now the time was right. It had been worth waiting for. He loaded the sigil of his desire on to the chip and confidently bancoed the guy to the left of him and let the gods do the rest.

Two minutes later he smiled as he vacated his chair and noticed only then did the blonde smile back. He left the table empty-handed. He had lost in her eyes, but in his he had won. Now it was only a matter of waiting to see what would happen next as his gift was being received in the wider dimension that went beyond the confines of the casino.

Pleased, he re-asserted himself at the bar with a smile and ordered another drink with the last of his money and let the barman keep the change to ensure he was stone broke.

It was more than a gamble. It was a risk which could fail. He weighed the probabilities; everything was in his favour. All the signals were there, all positive, so therefore it was bound to work. He took a sip and lit up as he pondered on his action and its probable outcome.

He had done this before, but was never sure of the outcome. He decided to leave it to the gods, those inscrutable forces, and let them sort it out, letting the desire drop from his mind and sink into the abyss of forgetfulness where it could do its work.

The drink was doing its work also. He could feel himself beginning to roll and now he would not be able to stop. He would drink up, hit the road soon and head home to his refrigerator packed with cheap beers. He could now go, fairly sure his endeavour would get things moving. Again he got to thinking about this woman and couldn't wait till tomorrow when he and the Kid would try to find her. Yet it still nagged at the back of his mind. Surely one woman couldn't be responsible for stopping most of the action in this district of New York alone. It didn't make sense, no matter how drunk he was. Then perhaps there was something else behind all of this, another reason he was at a loss to explain.

He dropped it as it was making him feel riled up inside. It was time to leave this oasis and head out into that big grey concrete desert outside. He drank up and fetched his coat, relieved to get out of there, and found himself in the street. The rain had stopped and the mother of all the gods was up there above looking down at him in her splendour, visible now that the clouds had rolled back to reveal her obsidian dress glittering with those little sequins that looked like stars as she arched over the earth. He wished more than ever now to be up there with her. That would only come in death.

He resumed walking northwards, his eyes fixed firmly on the polestar indicated by the Great Bear, his mind set on destruction, his legs conveying him up 7th Street as if possessed of their own volition. He felt he was stalking, just like he always did when he was in this mood, out in the streets at the most dangerous hours of the night, deliberately inviting danger into his arms perforce that it will annihilate him. Always he passed by without a scratch, not one provocation, returning home unscathed. He was indignant at the remembrance, even more determined than ever to get it over and done with.

His legs stopped him at an alley halfway up. It was perfect. Tall towering walls either side suggested a chasm with the panoply of streetlights at the other end adding to the impression. He imaged it as a tunnel with the light at the end as his goal a good three hundred metres away. He stood at the entrance, giddy with expectation, feeling the adrenalin flowing through his system as he smelt that familiar smell of death. And from where Capri was standing he could smell and feel it emanating from the inexorable carpet of blackness before him. The premonition was overpowering. There was something deep, dark and disturbing down there for certain. Instinctively, he found his right hand reaching for his Preston snug in its shoulder holster. He admonished his disobedient hand determined that tonight death would be his. He invoked death full, in all of its splendiferous names, in all of its cunning guises, in all of its certainty, and took the first step past the threshold which would take him back up to her above.

His legs carried him reluctantly. He fairly had to force himself to move as if being pushed back by the very forces he had invoked. He continued undeterred, the safe deserted street behind him now all but forgotten. The air was icy tense, unnaturally cold. He shivered. Within a few minutes he was drowning in the blackness of the alley, his eyes focused only on the light. Barely a few metres and his heart was already palpitating wildly. The whole place reeked of menace, enough to make him think about turning back, now wishing he hadn't started on his foolhardy mission of self-destruction. There was no going back, no chickening out; he had to pursue it all the way. Just keep going, he told himself, keep going.

There was an enclosure to his left-hand side shrouded in darkness, yet strangely emanating heat. It must be from one of the vents, perhaps from a kitchen. He would soon find out as he came up beside it. He was now parallel with it, his mind infested with images of death. Then suddenly he felt it. Was it his imagination? He didn't think so. The horripilation on the back of his neck confirmed it. Somehow it was instinct more than anything which made him automatically reach for his Preston. He pulled it out, its highly polished silver alloy glinting in the stellar light. He turned towards the shadows, aimed it straight and stood firm. I must face it, he told himself, and held his position of defence for what seemed like eternity, measured out in skipping heartbeats. He waited, listening for any sound to give an indication of what he was pointing his gun at. Nothing, no sound,

no movement, just the silence, the stillness and the perilous few metres standing between him and the shadows. He tried to peer into them rationally, to penetrate into the think blanket of darkness. His imagination clothed everything with a morbid fascination, turning amorphous shapes into demons waiting on the edge ready to devour him. A pair of light bulbs in the distance looked like two prying eyes of fire. Now he could smell something. It was that smell: the smell of death. He stepped back from the shadows, his stomach turning. The smell was overpowering, like—

Before he could even rationalise it, the thing lurched forward.

—An entrope!

It stopped, stood still as if to survey him.

"Come on then, you fuck!" he screamed at it, his voice hoarse and rasping.

He still had time to quit. Fifty feet and he'd be safe. He could make it in two minutes, but he was rooted to the spot, senseless, his nerves stinging like raw electricity.

Then suddenly it lunged towards him, a black mass of death incarnate. He fired. An electric bolt hit it mid-centre, exploding on impact. The thing sagged slightly, its momentum still carrying it towards him.

Another shot, straight between the eyes, had it staggering, blue flames bursting around its head. It toppled, then finally fell. The thud echoed up and down the alley, followed by an audible hiss of resignation. It finally groaned as it expired.

It all happened so quickly Capri wasn't even sure if he was okay or not. He checked himself all over. Not one scratch.

"Shit!" he cried to himself, this time for not giving into it. He had asked for death good and strong and there it was lying pathetically before him, his potential passport to the region of the indestructible stars, now dead.

He tentatively edged up closer towards it, his gun still firmly in hand in case the thing had another life left in it. Its dark body was lying dormant face down, its back visible in the soft stellar light. It created a macabre effect,

highlighting the short stubby fur, the massive dome of the back of its head, the rotund skull and immense biceps still flexed from when it was about to strike. He kicked the head round to examine the face, or what you would call a face. There wasn't much left of it now. His second bolt had taken out most of the forehead leaving a gaping hole that was still alight with small dancing blue flames. The smell of singed fur made him recoil, then the ghastly mien and wide gaping maw which came into view unsettled him even more. It was enough to make him clutch his stomach to hold back the bile. Disgusted, but half-fascinated, he squatted down on his haunches, surveying the rest of the features; the large hands with outstretched fingers terminating in razor sharp nails were twice the size of a man's. They were powerful enough to rip out a heart in one fell swoop. The elongated arms reminded him of an ape's, rippling with muscles and tendons under the sparse fur, and the fangs jutting out from behind the protruding muzzle, all suggested a mutant, a hybrid of man and ape that confirmed his notion. Entropes, people called them. He just thought of them as walking abortions that should never have been let out of the lab.

He took one last look at the monstrosity he'd just killed, and put his gun away, and got the hell out of there in case any more were hanging around.

* * * * *

His apartment was on the top floor on 5th Avenue, the less expensive end of this still highly desirable street. The main room overlooked Central Park as it faced west and it was the only thing that kept him here. He was besotted with the view, the jagged horizon yonder, the deep expanse of space above. It stars seemed to mirror the lights below. He opened the windows just to cool off and breathed in deep the stale air. He calmed himself down, relieved, in a way, and grateful that he was now home, or what he called home.

He turned round to look at his room, its bareness kind of reflecting the way he felt inside. He looked at the few things he possessed: the essentials he called them. They were the only things he had bothered purchasing, never getting around to fully kit out the place. As long as he had something to sit on, like his big couch, and a bed, that was all he needed. Not even a carpet for the bare wooden floors. He shrugged and turned back to the view, could almost feel himself drifting out into it, becoming one with it.

He sighed and retraced his steps to the kitchen, hauled out an ice cold beer from the refrigerator and returned to his vision, guzzling the drink down. It cooled his burnt out throat, tasting somewhat better than usual, and lit up a cigarette without even bothering to turn the light on. He didn't want to. Here he could be alone and think. Here he felt safe from the harsh world outside, although it became a prison at times, somewhere to feel trapped rather than consoled, but at least he had a roof over his head. For how long? He sank his worry down, finished his bottle, opted for another one.

He turned the main light on, noticed there were four messages on the answerphone. He paused, not sure if he wanted to hear any of them. He could guess what they were going to be. He reluctantly rewound the tape. He dreaded the worst and returned with another bottle as it rewound to a halt. He hesitated, opting to put some music on instead. He selected an old CD, put it in the machine and pressed play. The sax came on as he made up his mind to play the messages. He switched the machine on and turned out the light before settling on his couch. The darkness was like a gentle friend as he tried to relax and listen to the music. He was listening to the girl's breathy vocals when the first message came on. He recognised the voice instantly and ignored it as soon as it started ranting on about money. His ears went back to the music.

Then another message. A different voice, same demand. He washed it away and turned the volume up with his remote to drown it.

And another message. Another demand, more threatening. He resented it and turned the volume up more and finished his beer and replaced it with another one and collapsed back on his couch, letting it take the weight of his penury as the piano solo came in, then the vocals again...

It was only during a quiet lull in the music he could hear a woman's voice he didn't recognise. Before it could sink in the message stopped as abruptly as it had started.

He bolted out of his seat and turned the music off, stumbling round in the dark trying to focus on the lights of the machine to repeat the message. He hit rewind and waited on the edge of his seat for the voice to start again. It was unfamiliar and direct to the point. He was to meet her tomorrow at noon precisely in the Salvador Dali Archives of the Grand Gallery. No

name, no number, not even an indication of how they were going to recognise each other. Then evidently she must know what he looked like from the photo in the papers. But it was the way she said it which got to him. It was more of an order than a proposal. He wanted to damn the woman. He hit rewind hard and waited for it to start again, disbelieving his ears. Who did she think she was? Once his temper had subsided he played it again, determined to listen to it a bit more attentively this time. He cursed the audacity of the woman. What if he couldn't attend? Or did she know he was free all day tomorrow? Then it clicked. It could only be this bitch supposedly holding back all the business. Indignantly, he played the message again. He got in to her voice. She sounded like she wasn't a full blooded American. More likely mixed extraction. Each word she uttered was articulated so precisely that the syllables were stretched out, emphasised at the end of each word. It kind of reminded him of an interpreter's voice. He played it again, this time trying to define her origins. Usually accents presented no problem. He could locate a dialect without any trouble. But this one was slightly more difficult, full of Americanisms but with the harsh inflections of a South European tongue. And again. Spanish? Portuguese? Italian? He wasn't sure which. And again. He could not trace it and gave up in disgust. But why me? Then it came screeching into his skull. It worked! His little libation to the gods had worked. It must have done.

He sat down and analysed the situation carefully, lighting up another cigarette in the process. There was no way he could tell. His old answering machine didn't give a time for the recording of the message so he could have done the magic either before or after she rang. That didn't necessarily matter. But it looked like a job was being offered to him by the gods. If magic was about anything it was about taking advantages of all the possibilities being thrown in one's path. He therefore had to accept it even though he wasn't happy about going along with the idea. He just hoped that whatever would come out of it would be a substantial wage, enough to disappear again.

Happy, he drank and smoked into the promising dawn.

THE WARNING

'...Therefore it only behoves me to write to you again and express on behalf of our other members and myself how strongly we feel about the situation.

The man's actions are intolerable. We will not, and should not, permit such scurrilous behaviour within our group and I urgently request from yourself his immediate expulsion based on reasons I have previously brought to your attention. If he carries on like this he could jeopardise all that we have achieved as well as be the possible precursor of the group's disintegration and its downfall. He is a cancer, a parasite, who feeds on others and has so far contributed nothing positive towards our work except a lot of infantile ideas which I refuse to even consider. Moreover, I have deep suspicions regarding his almost incestuous relationship with his sister Katrina.

Nor do I have to remind you of his other nefarious pursuits outside the group. I know they are not our concern, but when he insists on trying to bring them into the group to form part of his rituals, I can only object with the utmost vehemence and I hope my protestations can be readily heard and accepted by you. His interests could seriously undermine the group as a whole: he is the sort of person who gives S&M a bad name.'

Private letter from Mosalla to Crome,
dated 21st March (the vernal equinox)
(There was no official response to this letter)

—6—
THE TAO AND THE TAU

Chan's home was no different from the other tin shacks. Landis found it strange considering the amount of money he was bringing in from his deals. He must have been raking it in and still the place looked exactly the same as it had since the last time he was here, and that was awhile back.

Chan opened the door and let him in. The place stunk of burning paraffin, a smell he loathed for the fumes always affected his eyes, making them burn. He followed Chan into the back room where the smell was coming from, one of those old type heaters on a beige Chinese rug, clean but hardly remarkable. The room was mostly empty and spacious with a few cushions strewn around and an old bronze, hand cut lantern hanging from the ceiling. It was the only source of light and barely emitting enough to stave

off the gloomy atmosphere. Chan's old man was sitting cross-legged on a cushion. He didn't seem to notice them entering the room.

"Hi, old man," Landis said and waved.

The Sage didn't respond. He just sat there staring into space in that black tunic of his with its gold buttons. He was smoking a long clay pipe filled with tobacco soaked in rum. It was the only luxury he allowed himself. It emanated a pleasing fragrance in marked contrast to the paraffin fumes.

Chan invited Landis to pull up a cushion and sit himself down. He went over to his old man and said something to him. The Sage looked at his son, then diverted his slit-eyes back to Landis. Landis feigned a polite smile. The Sage didn't respond. He wondered what was wrong with him.

"Long time since I saw you last. How you doing?" The question felt awkward, but he figured he had to say something whilst Chan disappeared into the next room to fetch the gear.

The Sage just sat there looking at him blankly as if he didn't understand English. Landis knew, however, he spoke perfect English, even better than his son, so why he wasn't being hospitable he didn't know.

Chan returned with a pipe and started loading it up. He passed it to Landis and lit it up for him. Landis took a big toke, held it for awhile before allowing it to waft slowly out of his mouth and nostrils, his face kind of disappearing into the smoke as it hit the back of his brain. He was out of it again, well satisfied with the quality of the product. It seemed to wrap a shawl of comfort around him, nicely chilling him out after a hard night's work. Perfect. It was just what he needed. He took another toke before passing it back to Chan who pulled up a cushion next to him. He smoked. Landis sat back, allowing the opium to work its medicine. His eyes drifted to the Sage's face. It was slowly transforming before his eyes. The cheeks drew in tautly until they were non-existent, the eyes became narrower as they stared back, and the wrinkles in his flesh receded turning the whole face into a highly polished mask. The opium exaggerated all of his features so he wasn't even sure he was looking at a human, more like a wood carving or a finely wrought marble statue. It made him chuckle inside. The man must be ancient by now, he reckoned, way into his late seventies, early

eighties. And that was old for these parts. What kept this old man going for so long, he wondered. He didn't seem to do anything except sit around all day. Maybe that was it. That's all he did, sat and contemplated the course of the heavens in his head, occasionally reading his holy book which was permanently by his side.

The Sage used his book like it was his bible and must have known it inside out, yet still complained its contents eluded him, believing he would need another fifty odd years at least before he could understand it completely. Only then would he be satisfied and go merrily to his grave. Landis sneaked a look at it once when the Sage was absent. It was full of aphorisms but didn't really say anything. He couldn't see why he was so enamoured with it. He told him once that it was able to make him aware of all sorts of meaningful things and he could discern the courses of events as easily as if he had gone into the future and back, and worked out all the probable trends. That was the Sage all over, only interested in important things, too serious about everything and never small-talked with anybody, being a great believer in reticence, only opening his mouth when he considered there was something worth saying. Otherwise he stayed taciturn most of the day, so silent and still you could barely tell he was alive at times. It was this whole serious attitude of his he found grating. He was totally unlike his son. They were worlds apart.

Chan handed him back the pipe. He took it and toked some more. All he wanted to do was smoke and get into that blissful feeling he had back at the club, fuck the old man if he wasn't going to be polite. He ignored him and slipped away quietly into his mind. He took another toke. The smoke cut into the back of his throat as he hit the bottom of the bowl. It made him choke. He spluttered and choked some more.

"Jeez!" He coughed and screwed up his face in pain.

Chan looked at him concerned. "What's matter? It no good?"

"No, Chan, it just got to the back of my throat. I think it's had it." He passed the pipe back still spluttering.

"Not worry. I get you drink. It will make throat feel better."

Chan got up and left him nursing his throat. He returned a few seconds

later, a tall glass in hand full of some black liquid he had never seen before. He was surprised to find it was warm when Chan passed it to him. At first he thought it must be tea, yet its viscosity was thicker than water. He looked to Chan for an explanation.

"Drink, while still hot," he told him, urging him on.

"What is it, Chan?" he asked him intrigued.

"It special juice. It make sore throat go away."

He smelt it. The odour was rather pleasing. "What kind of juice?"

"It called *hsien*," he replied impatiently. "Drink."

"Alright, alright," he told him, "just checking." He sniffed it and diligently took a small sip, surprised to find it had an interesting taste like olives. He held it in his mouth before swallowing. It cooled the back of his throat like Chan said it would. He took another sip, and another.

"It good, yes?"

Landis nodded in appreciation. "Most edifying."

He drank some more and noticed how closely the Sage was scrutinising him. There was a faint crease in the old man's mouth discernible between his moustache and goatee beard. It sent alarm bells ringing in the back of his head. He looked to Chan worried.

"Chan, um, what exactly is this juice made from?"

But the old man got in first. "You mean my son has never introduced you to cockroach juice before?"

"YOU WHAAAAT!" he shrieked and spat out the black liquid in disgust.

His reaction was enough to get Chan and his old man howling, both of them laughing so much they were practically rolling on their backsides. They laughed even more when they saw the look of horror spreading across Landis' face.

"Shit!" he exclaimed and wiped it from his lips, not finding the situation

amusing at all.

Eventually the Sage managed to get some more words out.

"What?" he laughed. "You were enjoying your drink before you found out what was in it, no?"

Landis looked at him annoyed. "Yeah, well. I've just changed my mind. That's all."

It got the Sage laughing again. But it was infectious and Landis had to concede that maybe it was funny. He started laughing himself as he realised what an ass he had been. Soon he couldn't stop, but it helped to mellow out the situation and heal his pride. He had to admit it. The Sage was right. The old man was always right.

The laughter wore off. They settled down quietly and looked at each other like old friends. The few differences between all three of them were temporarily suspended. Neither class, culture, learning or age mattered. It was like the old times when Landis used to sit at the Sage's feet in his teen years. Looking at Chan, who was curled up by his side and falling asleep, reminded Landis of the first night when he brought him home and they went to bed in his back room, made sweet passionate love and solidified their friendship forever. The old man never minded. He knew what Landis was all about, understood him and had a good idea where he was coming from. He couldn't blame him for his wild ways or his recklessness; for that was what both he and Chan had in common. Really, they weren't that different from each other. The old man kind of accepted Landis was his own son in a way, the other son he lost when his wife died during labour. He had an affection for him, but more avuncular than paternal.

"So what does the good book have to say today, old man?" he asked him, to break the silence.

"My book tells me many things," the Sage replied in that all-knowing way of his like he always did, enigmatic and mysterious, never saying more than what needed to be said, though never enough. It was his way of inviting more questions, goading his listener on so he had his full attention.

"Oh yeah? Like what?"

The Sage thought for awhile. His disciple was hooked and all ears. "It tells me of many things, things that have happened, things to come, things that might not come."

It wasn't really a reply at all. But that was the way he always worked it, reeling his listener in.

"Example?"

"Many things have happened of late, small things. They are of little consequence. Their relevance is eclipsed by greater things."

The Sage stopped short deliberately, smoked his pipe. He knew what he said amounted to nought; what he hadn't said was far more important.

Landis gave him a look like he wasn't impressed with that reply, hoping he would pick up on it and continue. The Sage didn't. He could be tiresomely awkward at times. He had something to say.

"Can you be a bit more specific?" Landis asked him patiently.

"How specific do you want me to be? I can only say that there are certain things, great things, about to come. They are natural and partake of the Way. I do not understand all of it yet. I can only say my book tells me they will be so great I cannot fully comprehend their import at the moment. My book is never wrong; it is me who makes the error of judgement. Therefore my interpretation is fallible. Yet I know we will all be affected soon. The smaller things have departed; their significance diminishes the closer these great things come."

Landis was intrigued. "You know then?"

The Sage nodded and paused with a grave look on his face. "When I was first introduced to you," he told him, "I thought you were young and foolish like my son, always too eager, chasing after fleeting things. Then the more I got to know you the more I noticed you were very different from most men of your age. You have it in you, a searching, questing soul. You are always looking for things, very inquisitive and fascinated by the world. Yet you always look in the wrong place. You always look outside of yourself. You believe what you are looking for is out there and wonder why

you are disappointed every time. You do not even see what is in front of your nose, too busy grabbing to reflect on what you are doing to notice. You never reflect on your actions for you are a man of action, like my son. That is why you get involved in things you are ill-equipped to deal with. You believe everything you want is out there. I say everything you want you can find within yourself. But you do not look within yourself. That is why you now have this shadow hanging over you. I noticed it when you first walked into the room. It will grow about you bigger each day. Soon you will not be able to extricate yourself from it. Soon you too will be the shadow."

Landis went silent as if the words had cut into him deep, disbelieving the old man. Surely, he could not know what he was really into. He felt concerned enough to press him further, to gauge how much he did know.

"Look, um, I know what I'm doing. And I am perfectly able to deal with the situation. I am not over my head in it and I don't really think you understand what it is exactly I'm involved in."

The Sage looked at him squarely, sizing Landis up in his mind, neither showing sign of understanding, nor complete ignorance.

"I say you are not ready for it. You think you are. You will be putting yourself through something which will have irreparable repercussions. I say you can avoid being damaged by it through distancing yourself from it."

"Distancing myself?" he queried.

"Yes," the Sage replied. "Let my words be clearer to you who does not hear," he said, knowing full well that he was being tested. "There are things that will be happening soon. They will bring in their wake many great changes. We are all apart of these changes and only those who are prepared can pass through safely. I say you are not prepared."

"And you are, right?"

The Sage nodded. "I am. For I am part of the Way. It is this Way that will bring about these changes. I am one with the Way because I go with it. I do not fight against it. That is why I say you too should be aware of the Tao."

Landis could never get to grips with this Tao thing the old man kept going

on about every time he saw him. Whenever it was mentioned the Sage always pointed out it couldn't be discussed, contradicting himself each time he talked about it. He used to come out with a catchphrase whenever Landis tried to corner him: 'All words are redundant. Only that which cannot be said it true.' So therefore why talk at all.

Landis tried to get the old man to drop the subject. "Why don't you save your breath, old man. I still don't understand what you mean by this Tao thing of yours. And quite frankly, I don't want to understand. I am not like you. I do not think on your level. I have my own philosophy. It has been drawn from my wide range of experiences. Your Way is anathema to my way, and, to put it bluntly, I am simply not interested. I didn't come here tonight to learn. I came here because your son invited me," he said looking at Chan who was still fast asleep at his side, "and smoke a few pipes. That's all I want to do. Smoke a few pipes and relax, because I know what I am doing and I have the assurance that what I am doing is right. I am prepared. I have been preparing a long time for this. So if you don't mind, my involvement with this thing is of no concern to you. So stop preaching every time I come here," he said resentfully, rueing having started the conversation in the first place.

The Sage looked at him and smiled gently. "I do not preach. I merely speak. I do not go to the world. The world comes to me."

"Yeah, right." Landis eyed him back defiantly hoping it would be the last of the subject and the old man would finally desist. He picked up the newly filled pipe by his side and lit it up, smoked as the Sage stuck that pipe of his back in his mouth. They both sat there smoking, each now aware a rift had appeared between them, perhaps one that could never be bridged.

"I see you are still grappling," the Sage told him, breaking the silence. "You are unable to comprehend what I have said, not with the Tao itself."

"Maybe," he replied. "It's just that I'm not in the mood tonight."

"Moods? Like my son, you are subservient to your emotions. They blunt your perception, affect your thoughts so you do not see or think clearly. That is not the Middle Way."

Here we go again, he thought, now talking about the same thing but in a

different terminology.

"Your Middle Way doesn't exist. Nor do I believe inaction is the only adjunct to finding some sort of stability between extremes in this world."

"Yet you only say that for you have never contacted it. If I was to show you a way, would you believe me then?"

"Maybe, although I think you'd be wasting your time. I'm not cut out for it, so don't keep lecturing me about it."

"I do not lecture."

"Well it sure as hell feels like it," he barked back.

"Again your emotions affect your thoughts."

"I can't help my emotions. They are what make me a man. They make me human. They're not something you can weigh like a sack of potatoes."

"True. Yet you insist on identifying with your emotions. You are always at their mercy. The same with your thoughts. You identify with your thinking because you are an intellectual. But your thoughts make you oblivious of everything. You allow them to dictate your actions and they make you impetuous. You throw yourself into each adventure without considering the consequences. They make you do rash things, violent things like tonight."

"Now you are preaching! What we did tonight was a bit of fun, that's all. I enjoyed it. Your son enjoyed it. And besides, if you really know what is happening soon then what difference does it make? Not the slightest. So why shouldn't I enjoy myself and get my kicks? I wanna get my kicks before the whole shithouse goes up in flames. That's how I live my life, man. Not sitting around talking about something that doesn't even exist, that can't even be talked about. I'm out there, man, and living it up. It makes me feel good inside. In fact, it makes me feel real; the only time I feel real."

"At the expense of others?"

"Oh, look, who gives a fuck? Those two chicks were nothing. I was putting them out of their misery in a way they could enjoy it. I made them feel good, and they were gratified thereby. Who's gonna miss them anyway? Tell

me that. Two out of what? Two million others around here? It's not gonna make the slightest bit of difference, that's what!"

"And the rest?"

"Fuck the rest! Fuck you too!" he shouted and punched Chan awake. "Come on, Chan, get me the hell outta here."

Chan shook himself awake and wondered what all the commotion was about. "What is matter?"

"I've had all I can take," Landis protested, jumping to his feet. "Your old man is doing my head in."

"You are still an angry young man," the Sage calmly remarked.

"You're damned right I'm angry. Do you want to know why? I'll tell you why. I don't sit around all day like you, old man, busy doing nothing. I'm a magician. I make things happen, things you are incapable of doing. Out there is where it is all happening, not here in this rat-infested dive. No, I'm out there working with your goddamned laws of the universe, turning them to my own advantage. I work with them and I am enriched thereby. But you, you sit there all day. You accept everything so casually. I wonder how you've got the nerve to be so compliant."

"Yet all your efforts are in vain. They do not partake of the Tao."

"Fuck the Tao. I'm not interested in the fucking Tao. So stop trying to make me into a Taoist. I keep telling you it's not my way. Why won't you just accept that?"

The Sage sat silent, engrossed in thought. "What do you hope to achieve?"

"I thought you knew!"

He did not respond. Instead he waited for his young disciple to calm down before speaking. "Sit down, please," he gestured in an attitude of complete composure. He looked at Landis in a way that made him wish that maybe he should have kept his mouth shut. For no matter what you threw at the old guy, no matter how abusive, he always seemed to be able to deflect it. He was so unflappable he was a picture of permanent tranquillity.

Landis didn't move. He ruminated; the club would still be open and it was more likely he could have a better time there than here. If he stayed any longer he would definitely lose his temper. He could see himself killing the old man and thus help him to really become one with this Tao thing of his.

"My father is great man," Chan was telling him. "He knows many things."

"Yeah, well, your father gets to me," Landis whispered in his ear.

"I have great patience for you," the Sage continued. "You're a keen learner, unlike my son. What you are trying to do is admirable, but I fear for you."

"Really?" he replied sardonically. "Well, I'm flattered by your interest, but on which count are you referring?"

"Both!"

Landis went unquestionably silent. The very ground beneath him had been swept away. He found it hard to believe the Sage could really possibly know something he had sworn to keep silent, even to himself, vowing to never tell a soul, including Chan. Now he was seeing it being teased out of him.

"How did you know?" he stuttered.

The Sage smiled. "There are things worth knowing and there are things not worth knowing."

"What kind of reply is that?"

The Sage paused before speaking. "I have seen many things in my time."

"Oh, here we go, Chan," he told him. "It's anecdote time."

"Please. Listen to what I have to say. Please allow me to continue."

His disciple glared. If there was nothing more irritating it was the old telling the young all about their lives, what they had done, where they had been, and a thousand other things as if that was all they had to offer, nothing but memories. He conceded and let him speak.

"I was like you once. Passionate, keen, determined to achieve something with my life. I too was an angry young man. My father was taken from me

at an early age. All my thoughts revolved around this one single question. How could this be that a great man like my father should be taken away from me so prematurely? It was then that I took up my vocation." The Sage went silent upon reflection. "We cannot prevent certain things from happening. We do not have the power to control them. It took me a long time to accept that, and no matter how much we may disbelieve or fight against them, we are powerless and acceptance is our only choice. But now I know there are greater things about to transpire, things you are deeply involved in. I say again, you are not prepared. You do not know what you are fully dealing with. You think it is your destiny and therefore right. Yet your judgement is only based on a limited plane of knowledge, not the whole picture. I say you need guidance."

"Thanks, but no thanks. I'm not into this pacifist philosophy of yours, and your words, although touching, mean nothing when put into a perspective which encapsulates everything. I am doing my will, therefore I am working in harmony with the laws of the universe."

"Even if those very laws should bring about your own destruction?"

"But like you said, what's the point if you can't avert certain events?"

"True, we may not be able to prevent them from happening, but we can ensure that they do not affect us."

"How?"

"It is simple. By becoming one with the Tao we become one with the laws of the heavens. A man who follows the way of the Tao is capable of side-stepping the cycle of change."

"You mean he can become removed from it somehow?"

"Exactly. And in so doing he is no longer a part of that process."

"But how?"

The Sage considered for a moment. "Everything is a part of the process of change, but there is a part of us that never changes. For example, if we were to stop thinking our minds would be still like the surface of a lake. In its

stillness it would reflect more perfectly the moon above. That is how I know many things, through this same stillness, through silence. Should a butterfly beat its wings no matter where it is, in my silence can I feel it for its beating wings affect the whole of nature and it is only in silence too that the Tao can be felt," he said and paused, allowing his disciple to digest it.

Landis looked to him with eyes now more open.

"Put it this way," the Sage continued. "A young boy wishes to catch that butterfly and keep it. He chases after it and catches it but in doing so he crushes it accidentally in his hands. He kills it. What objective has that served? He ruins the object of his goal and achieves nothing. However, the Taoist way is not that way. If the boy had learnt the way of the Tao he would not run after it and try to catch it. No. A Taoist would stand still and become silent. He would hold out his hand patiently and wait for it to land. One day it will. And if it did he would have a far greater treasure than anything else in the world because he learnt the way of the Tao."

"Yeah, well I'm not a patient man."

"Exactly. You are that young boy. You want everything here and now, always demanding and grabbing at things and in so doing you ruin them."

"I can't help the way I am. Nor can I see me standing in a fucking field waiting for some stupid butterfly to land on my hand. You don't seem to understand, old man, I am not like that."

"Yet if you were no harm would come to you."

"I don't see how. Besides, I'm not afraid. I'm not gonna run away from it. We've all have to die anyway."

"Do we?"

"Oh, look, you're as bad as Crome, into that immortality shit. Well I'm not into that. I've got something beautiful lined up and it's just waiting for me and I will be rewarded in heaven. So you're wasting your time. Tell it to your son instead."

They both looked to where Chan had fallen asleep again, curled up,

blissfully unaware. There was such a smile on his face that even Landis felt something for him. He looked to the Sage and could have sworn a new look was in his eye, but in the darkness it was difficult to tell. The Sage cast his eyes back to Landis.

"There is nothing I can say to my son."

"And there's nothing you can say to me either," Landis retorted angrily.

"Because you believe you are following your way?"

"Yes, that's right, old man. My way, the way of the phallus, the Tau not the Tao. It is the supreme way, the royal road to the kingdom, a road I have followed all my life. That's my way."

"The only way you know."

"Yes, the only way I know."

"Let me show you another way, one that will surpass all your expectations, that will go beyond anything you have ever experienced before. You think you can find what you are looking for by projecting aggression on others."

"And you reckon I should start directing it back at myself, huh? Like all them weirdos out there who get off by cutting themselves up, people who go round mutilating themselves, castrating themselves, is that it? Is that what you mean?"

The Sage shook his head emphatically. "No, you deliberately change my words round so you only hear what you want to hear. I know you to be a very clever man. You keep trying to foil my explanations each time because you have this rigid control within you that will not let you see anything any other way. I say again, I will show you a way to achieve your goal without violence, without damaging others..."

"Then what good will that do?"

"Again you attempt to foil me. You delight in treating others like fools. Please don't treat me as such. All you have to do is to become still like the water then you will see more clearly."

"Through this stillness of yours?"

"Yes, then you will become consciously one with the Tao for it is always there but it is not the water. It is that which moves the water, that affects the water. That is the Tao."

"And that's how I can sidestep this process?"

"Exactly. You will not be subject to change in the same way. I can see you are confused. Let me put it this way. If you were to take away the sum of the universe from itself, what would you have left?"

"Nothing."

"Exactly. That is the Tao!"

"The Tao is nothing?"

"Yes," he replied laughing as his disciple became deeply bemused. "You are a man of science, are you not? You are used to using your mind. You always use your head to comprehend things. It is different with the Tao. You cannot assess it in the same way for it is beyond logic."

"So drop all logic?"

"Yes. That is the only way. And when you have dropped all logic you will become aware of the Tao."

"By becoming one with it?" The Sage nodded. "But it doesn't make sense."

"Logically, no. Taoistically, yes."

Landis slumped back on his cushion, his mind in a whirl, feeling defeated.

"Logic is only of limited use," the Sage continued. "It can only take you so far. The Tao can only be known through the cessation of logic. This is done by the complete enhancement of stillness. Then you and the world will no longer be. That is how to truly know the Tao, this thing I cannot speak of."

"I don't understand. Why can't you speak of it?"

"Because the Tao that can be spoken of is not the true Tao. It is beyond

words and can only be known through not-doing."

"Don't you mean doing nothing?"

"No, not-doing is the cessation of all thoughts and actions. It is beyond doing nothing. Let me demonstrate. Let us enter the silence."

With that the Sage instructed him to take up a comfortable posture and drop all thinking, relax and close his eyes, letting go of any thoughts that may arise, allowing them to pass without effort.

Landis, half annoyed with the Sage as he refused to even believe this so-called stillness existed, tried to slip into it but couldn't. After only a few minutes he gave up. He saw the Sage slip into a state of equanimity he knew he would never be able to achieve.

The Sage, as if aware of his disciple's agitation, soon came swimming back up to the surface.

"You did not touch the silence."

Landis shook his head. "No, I didn't get anywhere near it."

"It is no matter. It requires a knack you develop over time. All it needs is patience," he said smiling, knowing full well the word would not please his disciple's ears.

"But why is it so hard?"

"No, it is not," he responded vociferously. It was enough to shock Landis. "It is not hard. It is you who makes it hard. You make it difficult for yourself. You cannot achieve through effort."

"That's what I keep telling you. This Way of yours is not for me. I'm a man of action. I get things through effort. That's how I achieve my goals."

"By grabbing? Is that it?"

"Yes. And why not?"

"It is you who makes it over-complicated when really it is simple. Make yourself simple like it too then you will experience it. You will enter into a

profound inner silence that will go beyond all you have previously experienced," he said as he gesticulated with his hands, drawing them apart in a huge circle. "And when that happens then you will know you have touched the Tao. For it is that silence."

"But it doesn't exist!" he repeated himself for the thousandth time.

"Not in the way you mean, neither is it nothingness in itself. It does not have position or form. It is not a thing. It cannot be perceived through the senses, only above the senses. All I can say is it is there."

"Yes, but by saying that you are stating it has position, it is locatable, it can be reached. So therefore it has to exist somewhere."

"I can only say it is there because it is there," the Sage laughed as he saw the anger in his disciple's veins start to boil. "You are no better than a cat chasing after its own tail and ends up running round and round in circles. That is why I suggested entering the silence for it is only through silence you will be stripped of logic. There is nothing I can assert about the Tao, for all positive assertions I make about it are not true. It is beyond that. It is the mother of all things for out of it flow all things and to it all things will return, like the great cycle I spoke of earlier."

"Then it is God."

"No. For it is before God. Before heaven. Before earth. Before all things and yet in all things for everything is sustained by the Tao."

"Then what is the difference between the Tao and God?"

"God is a concept. Tao is not."

Indignant, Landis watched the Sage put his pipe back in his mouth and calmly relight it. It was his signal enough had been said. Landis just stared him back with real hatred in his eyes. Not only had the Sage confused him, he had also repeatedly contradicted himself on numerous occasions, and it was this that annoyed him even more than the fucking Tao.

"You did not enter the silence," the Sage suddenly said, "because you identify with your ego. And it is that part of yourself that will continue to

make the Tao elusive for you cannot know the Tao without entering the silence and you cannot enter the silence without forfeiting your ego. It is a lesson you must learn; how to drop your ego when it is not needed. Silence is its enemy. When silence looms the ego feels threatened, because by the very act of stilling the mind the ego fears its own demise and rebels. The ego subsists on thought. Thought is a function of mind. The ego is a product of thought. If thinking stops, the ego loses its stranglehold and dissolves. And this is what you have to let happen if you wish to enter the silence. Let me show you another way and you will experience the Tao. Then you will come to no harm."

Landis looked at him disbelieving. "No thanks, old man, enough has been said for tonight. I appreciate all the interest you've shown in me but I don't think you fully appreciate my commitment to my project. You know what will be happening soon and time is against us."

"I know we do not have much time. That is why I say let me show you another way, a quicker way more suited to your nature, shall we say."

"You don't give up easily, old man, do you? And if you were to get me to touch this thing of yours so I came to no harm, what will you be doing when these great changes come, still sitting there smoking your pipe?"

"No, I will move on."

"Well, I guess it's time I moved on," he said nudging Chan awake. He bid the old man goodbye, hardly expecting him to respond. He never did; for the old man believed that the laws of the heavens always told him when he would meet various acquaintances again. Therefore he had no need to say goodbye. Landis just hoped he would never see him again and got Chan to show him out as he cast one look back at his father, sitting there all smug as if he was God or something. He was pleased to get the hell out of there.

The warm early morning air hit him as he stepped outside. The sun was coming up, blazoning itself across the sky. Then it would be settling right down by the coast where this tin shack town ended. He let Chan lead the way through the circuitous route that would take him back to the highway where he could reconnect with his familiar world and the Centre, a place he was for once glad to return to.

On the way Chan was telling him things but he wasn't really listening. It was as if his young friend's words seemed to drift through him without meaning. All he heard was the last words which came from his lips just before he turned round to kiss them goodbye. "Meet me later, tonight, same time, same place," they seemed to say. Landis wearily nodded his head and pointed himself in the right direction. And as he started walking he turned to see Chan skip merrily back to his home. It was funny, he thought, but it didn't matter how many times he had been there he never could find Chan's shack. It was as if the whole place seemed to shift each night and reposition itself like it had a will of its own. Each morning it was in a different location. But he didn't need to worry his befuddled head about it now. Soon it wouldn't matter. And the work at the Centre would make him forget everything. He shook his head and turned back towards the highway and hailed a passing cab. He climbed in, exhausted, his mind seriously disturbed.

THE CYNIC

'All human effort is futile and counts for nothing. One has only to look at the Samaritan organisation; it is the greatest waste of our resources.'

Paul K. Jarrup,
Critique of the Cynic

—7—
MONUMENTAL MAN

The Grand Gallery was one of those places you could not help but admire. It was the tallest building in the world, having usurped the crown of achievement from the Arabs once again. It dwarfed every adjacent building in sight, towering over the whole of New York like some colossal god, some gargantuan edifice that demanded to be revered if not obeyed. Other buildings were diminished to paltry insignificance as they stood under its shadow in the heart of Manhattan. They were minute in comparison, resembling leftovers from a bygone era before modern architecture had finally defeated gravity, enabling man to show who was really in charge.

Capri thought there was something faintly ridiculous about building tall for the sake of it.

Looking at the Gallery reminded him of the pyramids of Egypt. The building was impressive, he had to admit, as he stood in its courtyard, craning his head back as he tried to view the last floor which seemed to merge with the sky. And like them, this one had been designed in the shape of two pyramids but with a difference; the lower one, which was said to represent the earth, stood upright; the upper one, representing the sky, was inverse. They were joined together at their apexes, the upper one balanced so precariously it looked as if it was crying out to be toppled over.

Capri couldn't fathom how the feat had been achieved, but it had and the hundred and eleven floors above literally reflected the hundred and eleven floors below with its highly polished glass. All of the floors were connected by one solitary multi-elevator shaft which ran straight up the middle right to the top where a cafeteria was located. The roof featured four heli-pads.

He wondered if the exhibition of art inside could ever possibly match the

prestige of the building itself. It was said to house the most comprehensive collection in the world and from all eras.

He braced himself, his head still throbbing from his binge, and strode up the steps which would take him into the main foyer. As he suspected, the cold grey interior was busy. He felt like a tourist. He consulted the information screens and located the floor number he required, one hundred and eleven, and headed straight for the elevator. It was full, but he somehow managed to cram himself in with the other patrons. He heard the familiar hiss as it ascended and could see through the glass wall all the past masters on display, the painters he admired like Delacroix, Vermeer, Velasquez, Goya, etc. They were arranged chronologically and all accessible on the lower floors. The more modern painters like Picasso and Dali were located higher up. It was as if you were going through time, with the new contemporary artists, the type he loathed, located right at the top. Needless to say, Capri had never ventured that far. In fact, he had never been further than the 65th floor, which housed the paintings of a true visionary, Hieronymus Bosch. That was probably about the last time he visited the Gallery.

He hit the 111th floor and stepped out. Here was all of Dali's creative genius on display, not just paintings but also his sculpture, like the lobster telephone and even a recreation of the room with the sofa resembling the lips of Mae West.

There is something very appealing about the works of Dali, he thought, as he started wandering around, taking his time as he was early anyway. 'Tuna Fishing,' a hallucinogenic outburst of Dali's concrete irrationality splattered over a huge canvas framework and filled with outpourings of psychedelic energies, was a good example. Dali always claimed he never took drugs, saying he was the drug, but he must have been on something when he painted this, Capri concluded.

He moved on to examine another picture entitled 'Birth of Liquid Desire,' an earlier piece but equally superb. Yet the more he searched over it with roaming eyes the more it seemed to snag in some place or other. He was hard put to explain it, thinking it maybe due to the positioning of the painting or the lighting. That wasn't it. It was the actual painting itself. It niggled him enough to remind him he was here for an appointment.

He checked his watch. He was here on time, so where was she? He wandered round some more to see if he could spot her, although he had no idea what she looked like. But he had the vague intimation last night, listening to her voice on the machine, that she would be connected with the colour red. Bright red hair perhaps? He was not sure. Either way, it meant she had an unfair advantage over him.

He roamed further afield and spotted an elegantly dressed woman standing isolated from a crowd. He circled up behind her only to watch the woman rejoin them. Disappointed and getting irate he was wondering now if it was going to be another one of those big disappointments to add to his list. He dismissed his doubts and looked around again. If she was here she would make the first move. She was probably already watching him with glee, surveying his every movement. The idea did not please him and only tended to make him feel awkward, if not paranoid.

Agitated, he checked his watch again. She was half an hour late. He would give her another fifteen minutes then leave, hardly an option he wanted to take since he was relying on her. He scouted around again in a larger circle until he was confident he had covered the whole of the floor. Only then did he notice there was a smaller room to the left he had not visited. She would be in there, he guessed, and wasted no time in taking a look.

Half-hidden behind a pillar was a woman with her back to him. She was busily regarding a massive canvas, oblivious of him and the rest of the world. It has to be her, he told himself. He cautiously approached her from behind. It just had to be her for she was dressed all in red.

He checked to see if she was alone or not. There were a few other people in the room, and most of them were on the other side examining some of Dali's surrealistic objects. He stole up close enough behind her to be able to smell the rich exotic perfume she was wearing. It was overpowering and made from an expensive blend. It was definitely her. All he had to do now was introduce himself and get down to business.

He moved in tighter until he was parallel with her. She was engrossed, not even aware of his presence. He pretended to be looking at the painting she was admiring. He furtively glanced in her direction quickly then back to the canvas, disbelieving his eyes. It couldn't possibly be, he told himself, and

skipped his eyes over what he could see of her right profile. She was as still as a statue, motionless, yet a work of art in herself. Then it struck him where he had seen that same profile. The resemblance was uncanny. He forced his eyes back to the painting, doubting his own mind. Within a few seconds he could not resist another look. His eyes strayed to her once more, roving upwards across the entire length of her body. Most of it was covered in a long coat, bright red in colour. It reached down to her ankles and was meticulously tailored and bore all the hallmarks of being expensive, like her black leather shoes and her matching handbag. Her height almost matched his as she was wearing a large cylindrical hat which gently sloped back over her head leaving her forehead and face clearly visible. Most of her long black hair was tucked underneath with the rest flowing down in droplets of small curls around her shoulders and back. But it was what he could see of her face that made such a forceful impression. The smooth unblemished skin bearing a faint tint of dark blood, the strong cheekbones highlighted with a soft touch of rouge, the delicate elongated straight nose that rounded off in a smooth curve which displayed fine aristocratic breeding, the richly accentuated pouting lips of red, the dark brown orbs of her eyes offset by a thin line of mascara that trailed off into a whisper at the corners like the thin eyebrows above, and lastly the long slender neck; they all reinforced the impression. Now he could not doubt the similarity. For she looked just like the limestone painted bust he had seen in a museum in Berlin.

"Nefertiti!" The word slipped out accidentally as if he didn't mean to say it audibly. But it was loud enough for her to hear and distracted her for a second or two before she resumed her posture and continued admiring the painting.

Now his mind avidly tried to think of something to say as he feasted his eyes and feigned interest. Immediately he felt a certain empathy with the man hanging from a cross suspended in space. It seemed to encapsulate his own feelings of isolation and fixity. It was a most unsettling sensation and undermined his confidence. Here he was standing next to some woman who looked just like an ancient Egyptian queen whom he was fairly sure was behind his current misfortunes and a picture that reflected succinctly the way he was feeling inside. It made him nervous enough to consider walking away before she could notice him. His reason told him no. He

needed money desperately, so he was going to have to ride it out and see what she wanted.

He looked to her again quickly. Still no acknowledgement of his presence. He wondered if she was ignoring him, doing it on purpose, perhaps hoping he would be the first to speak. He politely coughed hoping it would get her attention. It only produced a quick glance in his direction.

"Quite magnificent," he said to himself as he stared at the picture, yet loud enough for her to hear.

There was still no response. He was about to walk away when he heard one word, "Yes," in a faint, soft whisper. That was all she needed to say for it confirmed it was her, the same unmistakable pronunciation. And it appeared to be the only utterance she was going to give as nothing else was forthcoming. She went silent with a thick sheen covering her eyes. He considered extolling all the virtues of the painting he could think to get her talking before she spoke once more.

"I think it is one of his finest pieces."

"Indeed it is," he responded, now self-assured.

Another long lapse of silence passed.

"I'm very taken by it," she said, more to herself than Capri. "It is a very strong painting. You can't help but be affected by it."

"I agree," he responded demurely, knowing exactly what she meant.

"It is superbly emotive. No, evocative, so evocative. It seems to herald many things, as if time itself has been frozen and we are watching a suspension of space as well. I wonder, is it a beginning or an end? a resurrection to a new life? or simply the giving into that which is greater? You can almost feel an imminence in the painting as if something marvellous is about to transpire. That is why I say it is so evocative." As she finished her soliloquy (which it appeared to be for Capri wasn't even sure if he was included in the conversation), she at last peeled her eyes away and looked at him directly for the first time. "Did you know," she asked as she turned back to the painting, "that it is based on an original drawing by the

Spanish mystic St John of the Cross?"

"Is it really?" he responded politely.

"Yes. Dali was impressed by it because it was not drawn in the customary manner, but rather in a fashion a dying man would see a crucifix he was about to kiss. And did you know that when it was finally completed it first went on display in a gallery in Glasgow in 1952? It caused quite a fuss. One visitor was so enraged by the painting at the amount it had cost the gallery he slashed it. If you look closely you can see where it has been patched up."

Capri leaned forward to examine it. If it had been damaged there was little sign of it now. "Well you certainly are familiar with its history, Miss…?"

She didn't respond and looked like she was lost in the picture again.

"And don't you think he captures the feeling of Port Adra so well?" she asked him, detached and distant.

"Yes, perfectly," he replied.

With that, she swung round swiftly and faced him head on. "Don't fuck with me, Mr Capri!" she spat at him. "You know nothing of art!"

Capri, stunned, hardly knew what to say.

"This is the work of one of the greatest painters who ever lived," she told him proudly. "And people like you cannot even begin to appreciate him. If you knew anything at all about art, Mr Capri, you would know it is not Port Adra, but Port Lligat."

She swung back round triumphantly, knowing she had won.

Capri kept his cool. "Look, lady, I know nothing of art. So what? Now why have you called me? So I can admire these bloody paintings with you? Is that it? Are you going to tell me why we're really here?"

Again she did not respond. She appeared to be ignoring him, which only increased his annoyance.

"Listen, lady," he said to her gently, "I can understand your fascination for

this man, but I didn't come here to discuss art." She continued ignoring him. "I mean he's good, but he's not that great," he felt obliged to say, thinking that she maybe of Spanish descent and that was the reason why she was so attached to him. Still no response. He wanted to walk away. Somehow he was intrigued and hated the idea of walking out on something that could prove to be big. If she was as rich as he guessed, judging by her clothes, then he would have to play it her way. He forced himself on. "I apologise if I've offended you with my ignorance, but personally I find his work contrived."

"I don't find it contrived at all. He was a genius, and like all geniuses he was also a fascinating man."

"I agree, but I don't really know much about his work."

"Quite obviously," she retorted and finally turned round fully to face him.

Now he could see her in all of her glory. Yes, she did look like Nefertiti, the resemblance was undeniable, perhaps only partially weakened by her not mimicking precisely the same style of make-up the Egyptians used to employ. However, her beauty could certainly not be denied. He smiled at her and received a warm pleasant smile in return, not just from her mouth but also in a subtle glint in her eyes. It diluted slightly the strong aura she radiated about herself. Indeed, the impression Capri got from her was that she was a very strong woman, the sort of type you would naturally associate with a business woman, like a studious executive for some multinational corporation. He estimated she was in her mid-thirties, either single or divorced. He had no idea of her married status as she was wearing a pair of black leather gloves. No children, he decided, although she definitely had the hips for them, or what he could see of her through the thick woollen coat. And because of it, he could only guess she was fairly slender and athletic. Everything about her was rich. It only made him feel cheap inside as he surveyed her.

"Well," he said, "since you seem to know who I am, perhaps you could tell me who you are."

She ignored him, turned round to the painting and became engrossed once more. This was going to be a game, he realised, and was about to start

hurling abuse at her when suddenly she spoke. "Since you don't admire Dali that much, perhaps you can tell me which painters you prefer."

"And why would you want to know that?"

"I'm curious, Mr Capri. You can always judge a man by his taste in art."

"Really?" he asked sarcastically.

"Well? Aren't you going to tell me?"

"As a matter of fact there are others. The older painters."

"Like who, for instance?"

"I'm very keen on Bosch, you know, the Belgian painter."

With that, she swung round to him again, a furious look in her eye. "Don't try to be clever with me, Mr Capri. Everyone knows Bosch was Dutch!"

She turned away from him before she could see a smile of satisfaction slowly spread across his face. It didn't persist for long. She was off, heading to the other side of the room, without even beckoning him to follow.

He cursed her under his breath, marched right up to her and grabbed her arm and swung her round.

"Look, lady, I didn't come here to play your stupid fucking games. Now are you going to tell me why we're here or not?"

She ignored him, brushed him aside before resolutely marching towards the other side. He was losing his patience. He caught up with her again.

"Stop wasting my time, lady."

She gave him a quick glance over her shoulder before tossing her head back and taking up a new position in front of another painting, as equally as large, on which her eyes now focused.

"Art, I believe," she commenced softly, "is the complete and utter expression of the soul. Not only should you feel for a work of art, you should also be able to respond to it with your whole being. Look at this one

for example. What do you notice about it?" she asked not looking at him.

Annoyed and irritated by the woman, he could only manage a quick eyeful before casting his smouldering eyes back at her.

"It's okay, I suppose," he muttered.

"Come, come, Mr Capri, you can do better than that. Try feeling it. Don't look at it with your eyes. Feel it with your soul. Tell me what it conveys."

"Why are you doing this, huh? Why are you wasting my time? Is this some kind of game you like to play?"

"Who's playing games?" she asked, stroking him with her eyes before returning to the picture.

"Can we get something straight, lady? I don't give a shit what this picture says. Do you understand me? I'm not interested. All I want to know is why you called me."

She ignored him once more. He gave up and was about to walk away when she spoke again.

"You were doing so well earlier on. I thought there was a subtle indication which suggested you had a certain appreciation for art. Or don't you feel anything at all for it? Is that so? Surely, you have emotions, don't you?"

"Yes!" he shouted, holding himself back from strangling her.

"Good. Then tell me what you feel about this one."

He skipped his eyes over it once more.

"Well, it's obviously a representation of the Madonna figure, a counterpart to the previous one."

"And do you know that the woman was his wife, Anna?"

"Don't try to be clever with me. Everyone knows her name was Gala!"

He saw a brief hint of a smirk flash across her face.

"Do go on, Mr Capri."

He looked at it reluctantly, disconcerted by the power this woman delighted in. He forced himself to examine the painting more closely.

"I would say it is an extension of the previous painting. It's probably contemporaneous with it as is evinced by the same landscape setting of Port Lligat, as suggested by the title..." He paused, not sure what to say as it struck him that the disintegrated form did nothing for him.

"Well? Don't tell me that's all you have to say," she said, prompting him on.

He continued. "I think Dali is trying to convey a sense of the sublime here. But all he has done is added a few of his own pertinent symbols and, like the previous painting, it is probably also based on a model."

"And? What is its meaning, Mr Capri?"

Indecisive, he tried to fathom if there was any. "Little, I'm afraid as it is dead like the other painting."

"Think with you heart, not your head," she urged him.

"The only meaning I can think of is benevolence, sincerity, sanctification, blessedness, birth, perhaps even rebirth if you were to put it into context with the other painting." He felt he had exhausted all the possible associations he could project onto it.

"And?"

"I don't know."

"You give up too easily, Mr Capri. You should learn to be more pertinacious and take it to its fullest conclusion. It represents life itself and it's one of my favourite paintings. Do you want to know why?" He didn't need to respond. "You're quite right in that it is indeed based on a model, a painting by Piero della Francesca. Dali in fact painted two versions, this being the more complicated one. I detected in your summation you do not approve of it. Why? Because it is Christian based or is it something else?"

He looked at her unimpressed. "That and the fact that I don't like the

fragmented form much."

"But it works though, don't you think? Or do I also detect an inner reluctance, a distrust almost of modern science?"

"Possibly. Although I cannot see the reason for making of it an artform."

"Hmm. Or is it that you don't like modern technology, is that it? Or aren't you interested in the future, Mr Capri?"

"Not particularly."

"Is that why you prefer the older painters, the classical rather than the modern? Because you're really old fashioned at heart, aren't you? You prefer the old ways," she said as she turned to look at him, "and have this insufferable notion that we've lost our way, that we've stumbled and fallen. Is that it?" she asked as she turned back to the picture, ignoring him as usual. "No, this is my favourite out of all of Dali's paintings. There are few that can surpass this one. Don't you think Gala is beautiful?" she asked him, cocking her head to one side so as to view Gala's face from another angle. "She wasn't just beautiful either. She had power, Mr Capri, a raw innate energy that transformed Dali into one of the most exemplary artists of all time. She brought out his genius. She was his muse, his inspiration, the source of his creativity. Have you ever met a woman like that?" she asked casually as if they had been acquainted for years.

"Can't say that I have," he muttered, wondering what she was driving at.

"Pity."

"She must have been quite a woman."

"Oh, much more than that. When she died he was absolutely devastated. He perished in her absence, pined for her in death, for he was nothing without her."

"That's a bit of an extreme thing to say."

"Perhaps. But ask any of his critics, they all agree he produced his best work when she was alive. And it was only through his death, he believed, he could be with her again."

"Oh, well, we all have to die," he muttered.

"Do we?" she asked him seriously. She turned towards him and looked at him full in the face.

"Listen, lady, I'm losing my patience. Now, why don't you just tell me what it is you want from me?"

"What I want from you?"

"Yes, well, that is why you called, isn't it?" he asked impatiently.

"Why? Are you in a hurry, Mr Capri?" She stood with her hands on her hips as if she owned the place.

"Yes. As a matter of fact I am. So stop pussyfooting around."

"Really? I suppose you're going to tell me you have people to see today."

"Yes I do!" he blustered.

"Bullshit, Mr Capri, you have nothing else on today." He looked at her pensively; it had to be her, the bitch. "Furthermore, I know for a fact you have nothing lined up for the entire week."

"Oh yeah? And how would you know that, I wonder?"

"Because I make it my business to know."

"You seem to know quite about me, don't you, miss? I wonder how. You've been checking up on me, is that it? Doing some homework, finding out who my contacts are, who I work for, that kind of thing?"

She didn't respond. Instead she looked straight through him, a sensation he never liked. Eventually she spoke, "I also know that you are desperate for work and that you have no money. True?"

He wanted to damn her to hell. He calmed himself down. "Okay, you're right. I don't have any work on. In fact, I haven't got anything for the rest of the year."

"Good. Then I take it I have got you interested?" She retained her position

of defiance whilst waiting for a response. "Well?" she asked. He nodded. "Good. Then we can talk. There's a rather pleasant cafeteria on the top floor where we can have a coffee. Would you care to escort me?" she asked and immediately started to walk in the direction of the elevator.

Capri cursed her under his breath again and begrudgingly followed her.

As they stood waiting for the elevator to arrive Capri smiled at her hoping she would respond and say something. Instead, she checked her watch, indicating he was going to have to wait till they sat down. They stepped into the elevator, neither of them talking, and ascended all the way to the top. They were now so high he surprised to find he didn't suffer from vertigo like he usually did at such heights. They stepped out and made their way to a quiet secluded table by the window.

"Have you been up here before?" she asked him affably.

"No, can't say that I have."

"Isn't the view magnificent," she said, staring out into the expanse beyond.

Capri had to agree. It was. From up here they could see everything, right out across the harbour, the Statue of Liberty in the distance, a few ships on the horizon and the small scattering of clouds which appeared to be within almost arm's reach. He felt giddy just looking at everything and wondered what it would be like to just leap out and merge with it all.

They stood silent for awhile, communing with the view, until she finally beckoned him over to a table nearby.

"I think I'll just have a cappuccino," she said as she sat herself down elegantly and loosened her coat. She propped her handbag on the table as Capri called the waiter over and ordered her drink and an espresso for himself and pulled out the chair opposite, sitting down with reservations. He surveyed her features minutely this time, hardly able to take his eyes off her as she stared back out of the windows indifferently. Slowly he could feel for the first time since they had met his temper slipping away and that perhaps he had been a bit hard on her. It didn't seem right somehow to chastise a woman of her quality; refined, sophisticated, exceptional and all the other superlatives he could bestow on her. Their coffees eventually

turned up. She thanked the waiter with a pleasant smile. This is a rich bitch, he told himself, and one who definitely knew how to get what she wanted.

She removed her gloves. He noticed the absence of a wedding ring on her finger as he estimated. In fact, he was surprised to find that she only wore one small gold ring with a diamond stud on her other hand. It was neither pretentious nor vulgar, but exhibited her refined taste.

"Do you mind if I smoke?" he asked her as he reached for his cigarettes.

"No, not at all. If you don't mind killing yourself, go right ahead. Smoking kills, you know."

"So does living; it kills you in the end," he joked. She let out a light laugh. The tension lessened enough for him to relax and settle back in his chair.

"So, what else do you know about me?" he asked her.

She paused before taking a sip of her coffee. "Quite a few things actually."

"Such as?"

"Well, I know that you're one of the best detectives in the city. You have an excellent work record. Ninety per cent of the cases you take on you solve. I would say that you're quite good at your job."

"I'm very good at what I do," he remarked, sipping his coffee.

"And very modest at that. You take on all kinds of assignments. You're known not to be too fussy. In fact, you generally show little discrimination between what you will and what you won't do."

"I take whatever's going. What else?" he prompted her on.

"You use psychic methods."

"I use whatever method is necessary."

"You work on the side for the police..."

"Correction; used to..."

"Oh? Have you stopped working for them?"

"In a manner of speaking, yes."

"Any particular reason?"

"Let's just say we fell out."

"Would that have anything to do with your last job, I wonder?"

"You could say that. Put it this way, I deserved more credit."

"I know. I read all about it. What was it like meeting an animal like Kane?"

"He wasn't an animal, a bit sick in the head, a psycho, but not an animal."

"Why are you defending him?"

"Let's just say Kane was, how can I put it, a genius gone wrong, if you know what I mean."

"Really? Do I detect a certain admiration for the man, Mr Capri, a man who killed god knows how many people? How can you possibly justify your regard for him?"

"I don't want to get into an argument with you. I know what he did was wrong, but if you ever come down from your penthouse one day and step back into the real world, you too will see it from his point of view."

"Are you saying that you condone the killings?"

He didn't respond and continued to smoke. "What else do you know about me?"

She put her cup down and folded her arms on the table. "Professional or personal?"

"Both," he said, smiling.

"Since you insist. You obviously enjoy hearing about your own exploits. You're particularly good with homicides—as evidenced by your last job. You're also pretty good at locating lost property, stolen goods, tracking

down missing persons. You tend to work mainly for yourself, as well as for nefarious people..."

"Like I said, I take whatever's going."

"And on average you charge a thousand dollars a day which I consider to be very reasonable."

"Plus expenses."

"Yes, plus expenses. You tend to work only locally. You have no agent, but you have many contacts. You're listed in the directory as a psychic detective. You live by yourself and keep a low profile. You're also something of an occultist."

"You have been checking up on me. What about my personal life?"

"You're naturally English, although you took American citizenship when you came over here five years ago to escape the war. You were born in London. Both you're parents are dead. You have no other relatives although you were married once..."

"Alright, you've made your point."

"You're sensitive, Mr Capri."

"About certain things, yes," he said as he leaned forward and stubbed out his cigarette avoiding her eyes. "So, since you know quite a bit about me, how about telling me something about yourself?"

She didn't respond immediately, tending rather to look away as if she didn't hear the question whilst absentmindedly rubbing the rim of her cup. Eventually she brought her eyes back to him. "I take it you still practise?"

"Occasionally. That is, when I can. Why do you ask?"

"I was wondering. I've been trying to get in touch with you for the past month. Every time I rang all I got was an old answerphone. I would have left a message but it said that you were away and there was no indication of when you would be back. Of course, if you were fully connected like most detectives are these days I could have contacted you directly and sooner."

"I prefer not to be connected for that very reason."

"I see. And you've only just got back?"

"Yes, a few days ago."

She finished her coffee and sat back. "And how was your trip? Pleasant, was it? Did you have a good time?"

"Don't you know?"

"Where did you go, Mr Capri?"

"You mean to say you don't know? How interesting. Why do you want to know?"

"I'm curious. I want to know how anybody in your position can go away for nearly two months without leaving any notice as to where he has gone, comes back and finds he has no work on and wonders why. It just strikes me as a little disorganised, don't you think?"

"Not really. The heat was off. I decided it was time to quit the scene for a while and go on a retreat."

"A retreat?"

"Yes. That's what I call them."

"How interesting," she paraphrased. "And what exactly do you do on these retreats of yours?"

"Don't you know?"

"I'm being serious."

"I collect power."

"Power? How fascinating. What kind of power?"

"You're really interested, aren't you?" She nodded. "I collect psychic power," he replied.

"I've heard all about you're psychic powers, Mr Capri. Do you think you

would be good enough to give me a little demonstration?"

"That's something I always refrain from doing."

"No doubt for moral reasons. Is that it?"

"No. It's just that I'm not an exhibitionist."

"Isn't it funny how people claim to have psychic abilities but they are always reluctant to demonstrate they actually possess them. I want to see for myself, Mr Capri."

"As I said, it's not something I like to display."

"Not even for me?" she asked him, looking all innocent.

"Okay." Capri looked looking around the cafeteria for anything to inspire him, something to please madam, nothing extravagant, just enough to satisfy the bitch.

A group of people were sitting at a table in the far corner, a good twenty metres away, one of whom had his back to them.

"See that table over there," he said, indicating with his finger. She turned round to look behind her and nodded. "Well, keep you eye on the guy in the blue jacket."

"The one with his back to us?"

"That's the one. Now watch."

She looked on fascinated, wondering what would become of this. Capri fixed his gaze on the man's back as he slipped into a trance and assumed a posture that showed neither sign of life nor death but something in-between. She continued watching. Suddenly the man jerked round to face them as if he had been tapped on his shoulder. But there was no one there. His look of incomprehension made her laugh. She was impressed.

"How did you do that?" she asked, delighted.

Capri came out of it and smiled. "It was nothing, very trivial."

"I see. And it's one of those little secrets you psychics keep to yourselves, is that it?" He blanked her. "What else can you do?"

"Wasn't that enough?"

"It was average. How about something special, just for me."

"Like what? Waiters tripping up? Levitating ashtrays? Rabbits coming out of hats?"

"Be serious. Something only I can see, perhaps."

"Okay, you asked for it."

He propped his elbows on the table, leaned forward and clenched his fists up by his temples, pointing his thumbs outwardly. They vaguely resembled horns. He half-closed his eyes. His breathing slowed down to a pace coinciding with hers. She looked all around her, uncertain of the meaning of this action and then looked at him anxiously. What are you doing? she wanted to ask him, then became concerned as he looked like he was going into a swoon. She sat back in her chair. Her eyes strayed to the man behind her in the blue jacket. Nothing was happening to him, then round the rest of the room. There was nothing unusual happening at all. She brought her attention back to Capri. He was oblivious of everything, in a deep trance.

She waited, grew impatient and tried to get his attention. "Mr Capri? Can you hear me?"

There was no response. He was dead to the world. It only made her more concerned.

She waited a bit longer. "Mr Capri? There's nothing happening, Should there be something happening now?" she asked him perturbed. Again there was no response.

She shifted her position, a look of boredom noticeable on her face.

More minutes passed. She checked her watch and looked nervously around. A couple to the left of their table were staring at Capri. She smiled at them politely and gave them a reassuring look.

"Mr Capri? Have you finished yet? If you have, I didn't see anything. Mr Capri, there are people watching us."

Still no response. Then she suddenly felt it, an indescribable sensation. It was slow and intractable, and then it seemed to be vibrating. She looked down at her seat. Was he trying to levitate her chair? But it wasn't moving. Then the sensation stopped.

"Was that it, Mr Capri?"

He remained silent. Increasingly worried, she knocked on the table to distract him. Then she felt it again, the same definite sensation in her seat, this time stronger, more powerful before it too subsided. Then it started again, only this time she realised in wasn't the seat; it was inside her. She gasped, the gasp escaping from her lips as she knew now what he was doing; he was psychically fucking her. She wanted to push the sensation down, to stop it and make it go away. But it came back, relentlessly. Wave after wave of pleasure started rolling up her spine. She fidgeted in her seat and felt increasingly uncomfortable.

"Stop it, Mr Capri," she begged. "I said stop it!" she shouted at him. Another wave had her legs trembling. "Stop it, I said." She tried desperately to repress any visible signs of what was happening inside her. But the people sitting close by did notice, one or two even staring in her direction. "Stop it, Mr Capri. I beg you," she sobbed and shifted her position again. Another roll came in, harder, more pronounced. Now she could feel it tingling inside her. Again, she tried to frantically suppress it. "Please stop it," she moaned. "Please," she said, her face quivering with fright, her lips tremulous. She bit them hard to stop them from trembling as another wave rolled in and upwards, tickling the nape of her neck. She forced it down and pretended it wasn't happening.

Another gasp escaped her lips, so forceful the neighbouring patrons started giving her queer looks. She was now visibly blushing, almost as red as her coat. "You're not going to win," she told him defiantly. "I won't let you do this to me, not in public." And another roll made her toss her head back, almost losing her hat in the process. She re-asserted herself in her seat and clutched the edge of the table trying to force the sensation down; it only made it worse. Now her body started kicking into action, and her whole

body seemed to be lifting up and down in her seat, making a rhythmic thudding sound.

"Stop it!" she hissed. But Capri was still dead to the world.

She doubled her strength and fought back. Again it was useless. A loud sobbing moan issued from her pursed lips, then a shriek and another moan as her voice gave in to the rhythm of her thumping body.

Despairing, there was only one thing she could do.

With all the strength in the world she managed to unclasp her right hand from the table, pulled it right back and punched him hard in the face. It worked. Immediately the sensations stopped. Capri snapped out of it and looked visibly shocked.

"Bastard!" she screamed at him, and flung herself out of the chair, frantically grabbed her handbag and dashed in a beeline to the bathroom, knocking over nearly every table on the way. All the other patrons looked on, stunned. Capri smiled.

That will teach her, he thought, and lit up another cigarette and sat back. He waited for her to return, his mind made up. No more fucking around.

She reappeared, more composed and resembling something like her normal self, walked up to him and sat herself down with the aplomb that was expected of a lady of her character.

"No more games. No more playing," he told her. "Who are you?"

"I thought you knew. I am an ancient Egyptian queen," she said with a cheeky smirk on her face.

"Seriously, who are you?"

"Why? Don't you believe me?"

"I said no more playing around. Tell me the truth."

"What would you rather I do, Mr Capri? Put my heart in the scales of a balance and weigh it against a feather?"

"Cute." He sat resolutely silent, took the last drag from his cigarette, stubbed it out and made an indication that he was about to leave.

"Okay," she conceded. "I will tell you who I am."

"That's all I ask, lady. It's nothing difficult, is it?"

"Pleased with your little trick, are you?"

"Why? Aren't you?"

She feigned a smile and started playing with her empty cup. "My name is Carlotta Bianci. I don't expect you to recognise that name." He didn't and shook his head. "I need your help."

"That's what I am here for, Miss Bianci."

"Please, call me Carlotta."

"Okay, Carlotta, what can I do for you?"

"I want you to get something for me."

"Try being a bit more specific."

"It's something I want desperately."

"Oh? How desperately?"

"Money is no object. I will pay you well."

"Good. Then let's talk payment, before we agree any other terms."

"Is that all you are interested in, money?"

"Like you said, I have no money. So let us not quibble here. How much?"

"How does a million dollars sound?"

"It sounds good. You must be desperate."

"You could say that, but I didn't realise I could buy you so easily."

"Nobody buys me. They just pay me for my services. It's as simple as that. Now, what is it you want me to get for you?"

She looked nervously around the room. The cafeteria was beginning to fill up with the lunchtime crowds. He sensed her concern; perhaps she would be more inclined to talk where nobody could hear her.

"We can always discuss this some place else if you like," he told her.

"Do you have anywhere in mind?"

"Well I don't have an office..."

"I know! How ridiculous. Who's ever heard of a detective not having an office? What's the matter with you? Don't you watch all those old movies like Dick Tracy? They all have offices. But not you!"

"Look, Carlotta, I'm not like all the others, okay? Get that straight. I don't need an office. I operate effectively without one."

"Then where do you do all your paperwork, things like that?"

"In my apartment."

"I see. And I suppose you are going to suggest that we go there, is that it?"

"Well, we could do."

"Mr Capri! Do you think I've got 'I WANT A FUCK' written all over me?"

"It was a suggestion. You can talk here or we can go somewhere else."

"Not here. Where?"

"You hungry?" She nodded. "Then how about a nice little place not too far from here. The food isn't brilliant, but it's quiet and private. It will be a safe place to talk, somewhere neutral," he said, reassuringly and smiled.

"It sounds ideal."

"Oh, it is. Trust me."

She motioned the waiter over and quickly paid for the coffees, leaving a

rather lavish tip that would have fed Capri for the rest of the week. He helped her out of her chair and escorted her to the elevator.

It looks like the gods are taking care of me after all, he thought, as they descended into the real world.

THE RIGHTS OF MAN

'Man has the right to do what he will, to think what he will, to say what he will, to eat, drink, smoke what he will, to take what drugs he will, to express himself as he will, to make love with whom he will, to live and die as he will. No man has the right to thwart another man's will.'

Alexander Crome,
The Freedom Manifesto (a pamphlet)

—8—
A TIME OF WINE AND STRANGE DRUGS

The place was a small Italian restaurant on the corner of Lafayette Street and Spring Street, hardly what you would call upmarket nor the sort of place Carlotta was accustomed to he reckoned, but he liked it. It was always quiet, especially this time of the day, and the head waiter knew him well. Moreover, the thing that appealed to him the most were the prices; they were reasonable.

He could tell by the look on Carlotta's face, as he ushered her inside, she wasn't too impressed. In fact she looked kind of shocked as if she had just walked into a time warp. The furnishings probably hadn't been replaced in over fifty years; the carpet was well worn and stained in places; the tables were cheap and tacky; the air was thick and musty; and the light outside seemed to be struggling with the darkness of the interior. It gave the place an atmosphere like an old antiques shop.

He smiled as the head waiter and requested his usual table in the alcove, far away from the couple sitting on the other side, the only other patrons. He took her coat, small-talked to Capri in Italian and paid him a compliment about her. She evidently caught the gist of it and smiled in return.

Capri gave her a quick once over as she stood there. With her coat removed he could now see how shapely she really was in her tight fitting red dress, showing off every single curve and contour of her body, her smooth round breasts unhindered by lack of a bra, with plenty of cleavage showing.

He was enamoured. But it was more to do with the way she wore her clothes. It suggested to him that she knew how to wear them, how to bring

out the best of her splendid figure. Even her hat, which she was now removing with such elegance, had been there for a purpose, not to demonstrate the wealth of her purse, but rather the wealth of her beauty. She flung her long ebony hair back so that it rained down in droplets of curls to her shoulders. Everything about her was exquisite, not in a China doll way, which would suggest fragility, but in a sensuous way that spoke of her experience. She was well experienced, he estimated, not just sexually, but worldly wise as well.

She took her seat. Capri took his opposite her.

"You speak Italian?" she asked him politely.

"Only a bit. It helps round here, puts me in good favour with the owner. He's very patriotic."

"Yes, I can tell," she responded, looking at her surroundings.

The menus were delivered. He considered he wasn't really that hungry as he scanned the menu. He opted for a small plate of spaghetti carbonara, she for a light plate of pasta and sauce and suggested a bottle of red wine to go with it since she was paying the bill.

He lit up a cigarette as the wine was being poured and sat back and relaxed in the congenial atmosphere. The silence was conducive for reflection. He let his mind unfurl as he smoked, tried to project it into the future, what she possibly had lined up for him and was so desperate she was willing to pay a million dollars for it.

He watched her take a small sip of her wine, the way she elegantly held the glass between her fingers with dexterity and poise, the way she replaced the glass on the table so precisely, as if every movement might affect the equilibrium of the universe. The silence didn't disturb him as they waited for their food. It didn't matter that neither of them spoke. There was little need for it. He was content just to sit there and let his eyes roam all over her, taking all of her in.

Carlotta shifted her position. She was aware she was the object of his amorous sight and smiled. She leaned forward and rested her elbows on the table, bringing her fists up to her temples and stuck her thumbs out.

Capri laughed. She laughed and flopped back in her seat. The tension between them, if there was any, dissipated and melted away.

"I'm sorry," she said, looking deeply apologetic.

"No, I should be the one apologising," he said sincerely.

"No, it was my fault. I brought it on myself. I asked for it."

"No, it was callous of me. I shouldn't have done it."

"No, I deserved it. I shouldn't have tested you."

"Look, let's just call it a truce and forget it, okay?" She nodded. "Good."

Their meals arrived. Capri stubbed out his cigarette and they got stuck in.

"Tell me," she asked him, "do you always bring your clients here?"

"Not always. It's just handy. Most of my contacts are made through the regular clientele. Besides, it's friendly enough. The owner lets me stay until the early hours of the morning. Doesn't kick me out, even when I'm not spending any money. I take it you were born in the US?" he asked her.

She nodded. "Yes, My father's Italian. My mother's American."

"Good mixture. But you don't come to Little Italy much, I take it?"

She shook her head. "No, I prefer it upstate."

"I like it here," he continued, whilst taking another mouthful. "It suits me. This place has got character, not like the Grand Gallery. No, I like it here. It's got history written in the walls, literally. See the holes over there," he indicated the back wall over her shoulder. She followed his finger. "They've been left there as a reminder."

"Oh? A reminder of what?"

"The old days. The Mob used to come here all the time. They're bullet holes. You heard of Lucky Luciano?" She shook her head. "Well this was one of his favourite restaurants. He was one of the big guys. He set up his own borgata when he was young. He later started working for the don of

the amici, a guy by the name of Masseria. Now, Masseria didn't like the way Luciano was also setting up with the Jewish mob, because he hated them. Anyway, Luciano grew to detest Masseria and got his own back when another boss ordered his execution. So Luciano and Masseria came here for a meal one day. They took a table near the back there. Halfway through the meal Luciano gets up and disappears to the men's room. Two seconds later the whole restaurant is raked with machine-gunfire."

"Charming. And what happened to Luciano?"

"Nothing. He eventually got nailed by a D.A. named Thomas C. Dewy for racketeering, immoral earnings, etc., and ended up in Clinton State prison. After his release some film company wanted to do a movie about his life. But when he arrived at the airport to meet them he had a heart attack and died on the spot." He let out a light laugh and pushed his empty plate aside.

"How unfortunate," Carlotta responded.

"Well, it was for him. Soon as he's out to make a packet he dies."

She wiped her mouth with a napkin and pushed her plate aside. "Well," she said, "that rather brings me to why we are here. Tell me, have you heard of a man called Alexander Crome?"

Capri searched his memory files as he lit up a cigarette and took a sip of his wine and thought hard. "Vaguely," he replied. "A scientist, isn't he? An unconventional one at that, or so I've heard."

"You could say that. He has his own way of doing things. A bit like you, really. In fact, you both have quite a lot in common. He's also an occultist. Anyway, some years back he developed a drug for retarding the ageing process, if not reversing it to altogether. Most of his early experiments centred on life extension techniques for purely humanitarian reasons. The drug he developed was put to trial at Cal-Tech where he was studying at the time. The results were very positive. It was tested on rats, mice, rabbits and even chimpanzees. All of them demonstrated considerable increases in longevity, some of them living way beyond their expected lifespan."

"The veritable elixir of life."

"Don't be so flippant, Mr Capri. It's true."

"This drug exists, right? That's why we can go into a local drugstore and buy it off the shelf, right?"

"No, not exactly."

"There you go then."

"Please, listen to me. You can't buy it for the simple reason that it was never tested on humans. The principals at Cal-Tech wouldn't allow it because Crome, being the stubborn man that he is, refused to divulge the origins of the drug. He was prevented from undertaking any further experiments and was kicked out of Cal-Tech. Anyway, get this. Crome disappeared. Nobody had seen him for awhile. A year or so later, this young man shows up claiming to be Crome. He could have been, he was his spitting image, except he looked about half his age. So nobody believed it was the Alexander Crome, everyone reckoned it was his son. The only problem with that theory is, and this is a well known fact, Crome is incapable of having children, a genetic problem which has dogged his entire life. That was the main reason why he got involved in all this research; to conquer death and find a cure for his indisposition. He believes death is a disease. He was so convinced he set up an establishment for combating death and finding its cure." Capri started laughing. "Don't laugh at me, Mr Capri!" she spat at him.

"I'm sorry, Carlotta, I just can't help it," he said as he calmed himself down. "It sounds to me like the man's afraid of death and that's the only reason why he's concocted this so-called elixir of his."

"And you're not afraid of death?"

Capri went silent and looked serious. "No, I'm not afraid of death. I welcome death with open arms. It's the only thing which gives meaning to life. Without it life would be meaningless. It would just be this endless continuity. No, sorry, Carlotta, I don't believe there are people like Crome wasting time on developing these rejuvenescent type drugs."

"You're a cynical man, Mr Capri."

"Please, call me Harmon."

"Okay. You're a cynical man, Harmon."

"Perhaps I am," He stubbed out his cigarette. "Put it down to experience."

"What about this new virus then?"

"Premature Ageing Syndrome?" She nodded. "It's a good thing."

"How can you possibly say that?"

"It's quite obvious. There's too many of us. The planet's already over-populated so a new virus starts to spread to help whittle down the numbers. It stands to reason."

"You really are a cynical bastard!" she spat at him. "I can see I'm wasting my time talking to you."

"But it's self-evident," he implored her.

"That's easy for you to say. What would you do if you caught it?"

"I would just accept it," he said calmly, shrugging his shoulders.

"Oh, you're impossible. I am wasting my time. I'll take my offer elsewhere."

Carlotta leapt to her feet. Capri just realised he had possibly talked himself out of a job. He jumped to his feet as well. Carlotta called for the waiter.

"Wait," Capri begged her. "I apologise. I take it all back."

"Bullshit!" she screamed at him. "You're only interested in the money. Waiter!" she called out. He appeared. "Please may we have…"

"…another bottle of your excellent red wine," Capri said, finishing the sentence off for her.

The waiter, without hesitating, disappeared and returned with a fresh bottle whilst they both stood there defying each other.

Capri thanked the waiter and smiled at Carlotta, hoping it would simmer her down a little.

"Please, Carlotta," he pleaded with her, "sit down."

She stood there gloriously, fuming inside. "Why should I waste my time talking to somebody like you?"

"Because you like me," he said sweetly.

"Don't kid yourself, Harmon."

"Please, just sit down," he pleaded with her again.

She cooled off, reluctantly sitting down and stared at him coldly as he reclined back in his seat.

"You're a cynical, selfish, arrogant bastard. You're an old man who's just waiting to die, aren't you? You have no interest in anybody else except yourself. You don't give a fuck about the human race. But I bet you're really a lonely old man who has no friends because you don't deserve any. It is no wonder you go off on those silly retreats of yours just so you can escape and be by yourself because that is the only person you love, isn't it?"

He nodded nonchalantly and poured her a glass of wine and one for himself. He sat back, thought for a moment and lit up again. "I didn't realise I had to be a humanitarian all of a sudden," he said, philosophically.

"You're also a misanthropist. You have no altruism in your blood at all."

"And you do? Let me get this straight, Carlotta. Let me guess what this is all about. You want me to get Crome's drug?" She nodded. "So you can make a fortune out of it by mass-marketing it as a panacea for this disease which everyone seems to think could develop into an epidemic? Yeah, you could make one hell of a packet out of it if this elixir really exists and really works. You'll be set up for life."

"That's not true. Besides, it isn't that simple."

"Explain."

"Not many people believe in Crome's drug."

"Then it doesn't exist."

"Oh, but it does. And he's the living proof. He's nearly eighty. In fact, he'll be celebrating his eightieth birthday in a few days time. Yet you wouldn't believe how old he really is. He looks no older than late thirties, perhaps early forties and has done so for a number of years. He simply hasn't aged!"

"That's not proof at all. He could have achieved that through cosmetics, micro-surgery, you name it. There are a number of ways we can make ourselves look younger if we're really that vain."

"You don't believe me, do you?"

"Afraid not."

"Well, I'm going to have to convince you then. How old do you think I am?" she asked him sincerely.

"That's not a question I like to answer a lady."

"I'm being serious, Harmon. How old do you think I am?"

"Alright," he replied looking at her. "I'd say about 35."

"Wrong. I am 58 years old."

Capri looked at her in disbelief. "You look good for your age."

"Oh, you're impossible. Call me a cab right now."

Carlotta was about to get up.

"Wait. I was joking, Carlotta. Calm down."

She sat there frowning and looked at him coldly.

"58, huh?" She nodded. "Let me guess. You've had a dose of Crome's drug, right?" She nodded again. "Great. So not only has Crome tried this stuff on himself, he's also tried it on you. Correct?" She nodded. "So how did you get hold of it?"

Carlotta went silent and seemed to be lost in thought. There was a lengthy pause before she eventually spoke. "Many years ago I was once involved with Alex, romantically would be the best way to put it. We were deeply in

love with one another. He is a magnificent man, very intense. He's the sort of man who once he has his mind set on something he will let nothing interfere. He always succeeds at achieving his goal. His belief is that the world has to work his way and he won't settle for anything else."

"I know what you mean. So what happened?"

"We had a crisis, something went wrong and we went our separate ways. It was inevitable," she said, regretfully. "I wanted to marry him. I thought he was the best thing I had ever come across. I wanted to have his children. When he told me it was impossible, well that was it. We split up amicably. I should have expected it, I suppose, since he had the same problem with all of his previous relationships."

"I would have thought that with today's technology you could have got round that problem."

"I know. We could have opted for clones based on our DNA, but it wasn't the same thing to him. He wanted children the natural way; progeny he considered to be another form of immortality in that your name lives on through your children. Anyway, after we split up I never saw him again."

"But prior to that he had given you this drug?"

"Yes, about 12 years ago. He hoped in doing so I would stay fertile long enough until he found a cure. I don't suffer from the same problem as other women. It was purely on his side where the trouble lay."

"Sounds like he's a selfish man to me."

"Yes, but it's not that. It's his pride that gets the better of him always."

"And what about this drug then? What's it look like?"

"I only saw it once. Like water really. He used to keep a supply locked in the safe. You see, Harmon, you only need it once. He gave me a small dose, just a very small amount. It's so powerful, that's all you need. And it took nearly ten years off my looks. It's incredible stuff. You don't notice it at first. It takes awhile for the effects to first appear, very gradual as if you're shedding old skin like a snake, but over a lengthy period of time. It's as if

your whole body is undergoing a radical overhaul, being refitted."

"How does it work exactly?"

"Your guess is as good as mine."

"Didn't he explain it to you?"

She shook her head. "No, not really. He was cagey about that aspect. I guess it was something to do with regenerating cells or something along those lines."

"And he never even told you where it came from?"

She shook her head again. "No, never. You see, it didn't matter how close you were to him. As I said, he's a very stubborn man. After the acrimonious split with Cal-Tech he vowed he'd never tell a soul. And he won't. When he's made his mind up there's nothing you can do to make him change it. Knowing him, he'll take his secret with him to his grave."

"Assuming of course he ever dies."

"Knowing Alex, he won't. He's an obsessive. Do you know what I mean? He used to joke about being obsessed with his obsessions. His main one now is achieving immortality, physically. And he will do it." Capri laughed. "You may well laugh," she continued. "He's that determined, so don't consign him to a grave just yet, he'll be around for a long time."

"I don't believe this. Let me get this straight. He's a scientist, right? He works in this establishment and carries out experiments on animals and probably would've had to write up reports on his findings, and yet manages not to give out any clues as to where this drug originates? He must have left some clues, surely?"

"No, never. His lips were sealed the day he got expelled from Cal-Tech. He took all of his papers with him. All the animals were destroyed, as far as I know, and that was it. He was rejected, Harmon, and that's what got him the most. Being kicked out of Cal-Tech, the supposed leading institution on the cutting edge of science, hurt him hard. It was his old pride again."

"Well, if you ask me, he brought it on himself. He could have lied or made

up some bullshit about its origin. Why didn't he do that?"

"Probably because he would have got found out. And if he handed it over, he may have feared being ripped off."

"This isn't making sense, Carlotta. Think about it. If this man is such a leading figure in his field he could have marketed the fucking thing himself. He would be a billionaire by now, or even a multi-billionaire."

"No, he's already rich. He doesn't need the money, he's got it in everything; shares in municipal companies, real estate, new-tech centres, investments everywhere. He even gave me a half-share in a company's annual profits before we split. Hence I'm more than financially comfortable today. He's not interested in the money. He wants recognition, that's what he wants. He wants the whole world to recognise him for the genius he is."

"Sounds to me like he's got an ego problem."

"Call it megalomania, whatever, he'll never be satisfied till he gets what he wants."

Capri sat back mystified. He lit up another cigarette to give him some time to think before probing any further. He poured Carlotta and himself the last of the wine and smiled at this woman in her plight.

"You really want this drug, don't you?" he asked. She nodded. "Why?"

"It's not easy to explain."

"Take your time. You know I'm in no hurry."

She looked at him deeply as if framing her answer in her mind, an answer that perhaps could not be articulated. "I want to get back at him," she replied, sensitively. "I will be like this for a very long time, Harmon. Do you understand? I won't grow old. I won't get wrinkles or watch my hair turning grey. I will be like this for a very, very long time, longer than I want to."

"Carlotta, you're in an enviable position. There are women out there who will literally sell themselves to have what you possess. Why don't you just be content with what you've got?"

"You don't understand, do you? I made a big mistake then. I regret it now. At the time I was in love. I thought we had a future together. Afterwards I was devastated and it took me a long time to get over him and each day I kept praying I would find somebody to replace him. I never did. And now I'm stuck like this. At first I enjoyed the advantages, but you soon grow tired of it. You don't feel you can connect with other people. You feel different from them, or at least they treat you as if you're different because they are ageing and you're not. Sometimes they get jealous and you feel even more cut off. You see, I still feel for him simply because there is no one else like him."

Capri shook his head as her eyes started welling up.

"Look, Carlotta," he said delicately, "let me think about this as I'm not sure if I want to get involved in this sort of thing. Let me get back to you."

"No, wait," she begged him, tears in her eyes. "I will pay you anything."

"Anything?"

"Yes, name it."

He considered it reluctantly. "Double it."

She considered. "Okay, it's a deal. $2 million."

"Good. Let's talk terms here. You give me a cut up front, that's negotiable. We can sort that out later. Plus expenses. The rest on delivery. Agreed?" She nodded. "Good. Now where can I find Crome?"

"I don't know. Nobody knows where he is."

Capri slumped back in his chair, rueing the moment he agreed to take this job on. He wanted to curse the gods for not delivering what he asked for, a simple job, not this. "I have changed my mind, Carlotta."

"Why, I thought we agreed?"

"This isn't what I had in mind and I think you'd be better off saving your money and going back to him, if you can find him, and saying all is forgiven. How am I supposed to find this drug you want if nobody knows

where he is? I have to find him to get to the drug."

"That's why I chose you. You're supposed to be good at this sort of thing. I've read all about you."

"I am good at what I do. Finding missing people is one of my specialities, but I don't like the sound of this. There's something in it I can't figure out yet. Besides, where would I start looking for Crome?"

She looked at him pensively. "I heard a rumour a few weeks back from a reliable source. Apparently the government was trying to lure Crome out of retirement, to help in their researches for a cure for PAS. After all, he's the right man for the job. What he possesses will cure anything, particularly a wasting disease like PAS."

"Makes sense. But do you think he'll help them?"

"I didn't think he would. It must have taken a lot of persuasion. Yesterday the rumour was confirmed. That's why I rang you again. You see, if what I've heard is true and he hands it over, which he may not, I'll miss my chance at getting back at him. I want the drug before they get hold of it."

"Well, you've picked a fine time to put me on the case."

"I tried ringing you weeks ago, remember? You were on a fucking retreat."

"Alright, let's not go through that again. So he's helping the government?"

"Yes."

"But you don't know where?" She shook her head. "What about this reliable source of yours? Surely he or she must know where Crome is?"

She shook her head again. "No, he doesn't. Nobody knows where he is. Only the authorities. All we do know is that they have got him stashed away somewhere. I thought you may be able to trace him."

"Easier said than done, Carlotta. If he's really working for them they'd have him hidden away. If what you're telling me is true they're not going to tell anybody where. I mean, now that he's in their hands it sounds like they prepared to admit his drug really does work which means they're already

halfway there in combating this disease, and that's one hell of a monopoly for the government. Do you realise what I'm saying? First, I'm not going to be able to get anywhere near Crome if he's locked up somewhere. Secondly, even if I do find Crome he's not exactly going to hand the drug over and say 'There you go,' is he? And lastly, I'm not even sure I want to get involved in anything like this."

"I will make it worth you while," she said confidently.

For once Capri saw something in her eyes he had never seen before, a look that was undeniably a 'For Sale' sign. He stubbed out his cigarette and finished his glass of wine and smiled faintly.

"I'm sure you will. You obviously think I can get this drug for you?"

"Why not? Besides, I've got a little plan that might just work. I will make it worth your while," she repeated. She finished her glass, gazed at him and licked her lips.

"How about discussing it over a coffee at my place?"

"Good idea."

THE ADDICTION TO GOD

'All genuine rites of S/M have as their aim the transformation of consciousness. When carried to their fullest extent they can lead to superior states of consciousness normally designated states of ecstasy. It is only when the practitioner has pushed his consciousness this far he will perceive directly God, pure consciousness. It is this experience which becomes addictive. It is the biggest experience going and better than any fuck, a real cosmic fuck. When normal consciousness resumes there is no comparison. Ordinary reality is seen to be what it is, a "cheap parlour trick in a grimy hotel." And it is for this reason the practitioner wants God back for he feels he has been cheated. It is the biggest kick going, and God is the biggest drug of them all.'

John Upseed,
Black Leather Bible
(Source of quote unknown)

—9—
418 WAYS TO DIE

Landis stopped short in his deliberations as he entered the heart of the town. Two peasant panhandlers were approaching him. He checked their movements, grabbed his knife and pulled it out so quickly it shot through the air like a flash of sliver, cutting through flesh and bone of the one nearest to him, and disabling the other with the sharpened cap of his boot. He laughed maniacally. They both went down in pain.

"I am ALPHA and OMEGA. I am the first, you are the last," he told them as his boot went home again in the abdomen of the one he had lacerated and to the chin of the other who bit his tongue clean off. "And I shall be known to you by my name VIOLENCE," he told them and made sure they couldn't possibly recover.

Satisfied he walked on, laughing to himself like tonight was the last night, the last night of eternity.

He hit the club, paid his usual entrance fee and slipped through the big red doors like a panther.

He met Chan at the bar. His friend was already intoxicated, so strung out

on opium he didn't even recognise Landis standing right next to him. There was a beautiful sheen about his eyes as if he was far away, off exploring some distant landscape that only he had access to. Landis fed off him, drunk his euphoria up and came out high too, but not high enough. He wanted to get higher tonight, higher than last night, higher than any night, and make it last without the miserable comedown at the end.

He kissed his friend quickly, bought some beers and smiled at all the wonderful people who knew how to have a good time. He blew a kiss to one of the girls on the platform who was dancing just for him. She blew him a kiss back. He was loving tonight already. Each night was getting better and better.

"A whore, a whore, my kingdom for a whore!" he sang out loud to the rapturous crowd. He swallowed the beer straight down, and quickly reordered. He looked at Chan who could hardly talk and envied the cunt. He was determined to catch up with him. He guessed it was his fault. He was late getting here, would have been earlier if he hadn't argued with Rogers who was not happy with Landis always turning up late; reckoned he wasn't putting enough effort in. Well, fuck him, he thought, he wasn't going to let the miserable sod get to him tonight.

He started small-talking to Chan even though he knew his Chink friend wasn't in the frame of mind to understand a word he was saying. And as he talked, out of the corner of his eye he saw his white bit standing at the other end of the bar, looking like an appendage to the big fat slob she called a husband. Landis was going to have her, for she was there just for him, like all the rest of them, and nobody else. He made sure she was aware of his intentions by catching her eye, peering deep into that hollow and empty recess of her head and was delighted to find he got a look in return, not a look of love as he would have expected, but the sort of look she radiated out to anyone she considered was beneath her. Well, he just had to have her for that; to pry out that look and hang it up on his bedroom wall. It only made him more determined in his aim because every time she gave him that look it was like she was trying to undermine his confidence and there was no way he was going to have that. Of course, it was just a smokescreen, because right in the heart of her she really wanted him and couldn't deny him. He was therefore going to have to satisfy her need, make it heaven.

He small-talked some more, not really talking to Chan, just making his mouth move in time to invisible words so he could face the right direction and glance over to his white bit occasionally. She glanced back and each time he caught her eye, she retrieved it and threw it in the opposite direction, blanking him. It was all a game, and he was the best player in town. If she wanted to play hard he would play harder. And there was no way some boss man was going to get in his way. Then she looked back, locked eyes with him; he smiled and got a nice cute 'fuck off' in return. It kind of made him smile even more as she turned her back on him fully this time and started mouthing to her old man, that big guy in the expensive white suit who ran the place with his roaming slit-eyes like an eagle's. It must be the money, he thought, for there could be no other reason. Even taoistically it made sense, for that was all she was attracted to and no girl *compos mentis* had any right attaching herself to a slimeball like him. It was a disorder in the universe, a blip in the space-time continuum, that he would have to set to rights with the Middle Way. He would do it before the night was through.

They finished off their beers, got two more in and headed round the back. It was the same old crowd like they hadn't even left their seats, smoking that beautiful stuff all day and all night. And like the congenial guys they were they made space for their young friend so he could join them at the altar and commune with their spirits through the spirit of their breaths. He sat himself down and was waited on hand and foot, the sort of service he expected, and was passed the pipe of goodwill like they were out on a reservation passing the sight of night in the big outdoors, looking into the fire that enlightened all their faces. He breathed in the spirit, letting it sink into him and smooth away the blemishes of the day, and let it out again before bidding it to return once more. And then he was out there, right out there on the plateau again, and the view was majestic, stretched out into infinity, and all the hard labour he had put in today, all two hours of it, just dissipated away like gold dust through his fingers. He surfed the cool blue wave some more before being gently set down again. He passed the pipe to Chan who toked the smoke in deep and let out a wide smile as it filtered out of his nostrils in spirals. Landis didn't know how he did it, but he was pleased to see his one smoke brought him back into the world so he could at last get some decent conversation out of him.

"Well, Chan," he began, his arm around him, "what we going to do tonight for kicks?"

Chan shrugged in that big inane way of his.

"Well, let me tell you this," he continued, "no one will forgive us for wasting the eternal night. So I've been thinking, it's about time we added a little variety to our activities, something to spice up our boring humdrum lives." He stopped as Chan went into a giggling fit. "No, man, I'm being serious. I've been wracking my brains out all day, thinking we should do something different tonight, something special."

"Like what?"

"Well, how about, let me see, anything but pussy."

His Chink friend smiled. "You mean like other night?"

Landis nodded. "Yep, that's right."

"We smoke some more, then I go fetch."

"You do that. And Chan, make sure they're good. That other little fucker really pissed me off. I was only trying to help him experience death. It wasn't my fault."

"I know. You worked well. He not up to it. This time, I get real good one. You see. We have fun, then we go see my father."

"No way, man. Not tonight."

"Then some other night."

"No, Chan. Never. Comprende?"

"Why? My father, he great man. He like you. He want to see you again."

"I don't want to see him. Okay?"

"I not understand. He have great faith in you."

"God knows why. I keep telling him, he doesn't listen. I mean, get this;

your old man is supposed to be wise, right? And wizard cool. But every time I go and see him he starts doing my fucking head in. I don't need that shit. I've told him I'm not interested, still he won't lay off."

"He say you need experience."

"That's right, the right kind of experience, and there's no way I'm gonna get it from him."

"Then I arrange something."

"No! Don't."

"Why? I not understand."

"Because I said so, that's why. All I want to do is have some fun because we don't have much time."

"What you mean?"

Landis looked at him deeply. "Never mind, Chan. You wouldn't understand," he said patting his knee. "Come on, lighten up, smoke up. I want some action."

They smoked a couple more pipes. Chan left, leaving him there listening to all these guys. He smiled when Chan returned, with not one, but five lovely young boys in tow and all just for him. They were so fresh and young looking it made him mightily pleased for they couldn't have been older than fifteen at the most and that was the right age to initiate them into the secrets of death, he reckoned. He was delighted.

"Well, well, well, what we got here?"

"You like?" Chan asked for approval.

"Sure do," he responded as he undressed them with his eyes.

"We pay up first this time. That the deal," Chan told him.

"Sounds fine by me. How much?"

"Fifty bucks a piece."

"Fifty? No way. Too steep. You tell them twenty five or it's no deal."

Chan started getting into negotiating with them. "Forty."

"No, still too steep. You tell them thirty."

He negotiated some more and finally got them to settle for that. Landis dug into his back pocket and pulled out a thick wad of notes, all hundred dollar bills. It raised more than a few eyebrows. He counted out his money as he watched their mouths drop open, paid them and got the change off Chan before putting the hardly diminished wad back in his pocket. He smiled. Of course, he could have paid them the full amount, but he figured they were out to take him for a ride. He couldn't let them do that. Besides, haggling was all part of the game. It gave him a feeling of power, made him feel good inside; his heart elated with all this wealth he was bringing into their community.

He leaned a hand on Chan's shoulder. "They better be good at that price," he whispered.

"They be good. You be happy tonight," he told him confidently and led them out of the club along more dingy alleys with the little ones tagging along behind as Landis whistled away like the Pied Piper leading the children like they were lemmings and he was going to take them to the edge, right to the edge where they could look death in the face and be enriched thereby, for that's where death resides, on the edge, and you had to go all the way to the edge if you wanted to meet it face to face. Death presides over all genuine initiation rites and once you've touched it you never need to touch it again.

Landis turned round to make sure they were still trundling behind him, keeping his eye on them in case they should try to run away, which they didn't seeing how he had made it quite clear he had his gun on him and would use it without compunction.

Chan took them to a larger building this time. It was a dive like all the others and part of another construction camp, all timber walls and wooden floors, a long stinking corridor. Landis stifled his breath and had a pleasant surprise waiting for him on the other side of the door. The room was all wood and painted black and full of the equipment he simply adored; chains

attached to the walls, a huge cross and a real fine looking sling in the middle hanging from the centre of the ceiling. He breathed in deep the refreshing smell of leather; it overpowered the room.

"Blackleatherspace," he whispered and patted his friend on the back for his choice of venue tonight. He wandered round the room like it was a stage and readily scrutinised all the props on display. They would come in useful.

"You like?" Chan asked him.

"Indeed. Methinks tonight is the night, for there is a greater pleasure beyond death, a cool rapture just waiting in the wings," he replied poetically. He brushed his fingers over the sling's freshly waxed leather and chrome-plated chains and nodded his approval.

"O death, where is thy sting? O grave, where is thy victory?" he orated and got all the boys to undress and lined them up against the far wall so he could inspect them like a sergeant on a drill. He moved down the line, one by one, feeling their fresh young bodies and checking to see who had the biggest erection as he stroked their cocks before deciding which one to take first. The tallest one pleased him the most. He strapped him into the sling whilst Chan prepared the lube, then he got undressed and flexed his muscles in front of the other boys, making sure they got a good look at what they'd each be getting tonight.

He didn't need no Taoist shit. He was up there with the gods already, breathing in their sweet perfume as he lubricated his big firm hands and approached the slave-boy in the sling and wasted no time in getting the little one's anus all nicely gelled and wet like a cunt, a man-cunt, and took the little one's cock in his hand and started fisting him to life as his other hand got busy on making that sweet little hole bigger, fingering it delicately like a flower, getting it to pucker up and blossom as he fingered it some more, and soon the boy's pouting podex was ripe and open just for him. He slapped the boy's thighs, only gently, you understand, just to get the muscles relaxed before slipping two fingers in and seeing the boy's eyes light up with his touch. Now he eased his whole fist in and the boy's head shot back as he rammed it in all the way, slightly harder this time, just to make sure he felt it, you understand, so as to let the boy know who was in charge, who was in control of the situation and that the boy had to play it

his master's way otherwise he wouldn't be happy and got the little runt all excited, biting his lips, squirming in the sling as he wrenched his fist all the way round and back again. It was a nice tight fit. Landis was pleased and had to take it further by pushing it in deeper, seeing the cavity expand as the boy's being inflated. Why, to him it looked like the boy was in real ecstasy the way he was creasing up his eyes and all, like he was an angel floating on silk-covered wings, gently floating up to heaven as he let out a holy wail as his fist went in deeper and his other fist worked harder on his cock. The boy writhed in ecstasy as his fist tunnelled in deeper looking more exquisite by the second, making Landis feel divine, conferring his power on the kid, like the little lamb was being touched by the fist of God. The boy just had to let out a good honest scream the harder Landis worked him which kind of suggested to him he wasn't used to this sort of activity and in next to no time got him to come as he pumped him harder, sending glorious streams of white light shooting out of his cock and across his chest before he expired a little.

Landis was getting nice and hard himself now and finished off the job quickly by pulling out his fist and inserting his cock into the boy's nicely bruised anus and felt himself just slide in as he grabbed the boy's legs and hugged them tightly against his chest as he rammed himself home and got the boy swinging to his own rhythm, loving it as the boy's head rolled back and forth in excruciating ecstasy, little tears of love trickling out the corners of his eyes, then a whole flood of tears that only made Landis realise that this kid wasn't as experienced as Chan said they were, which kind of irritated him as he was banging away because good in his books meant they were experienced little fuckers, that they could take it like a man, not wimps. He wanted to ask Chan what the fuck was going on, to clarify, but Chan was too busy playing with the other little boys, kissing and cuddling them, making them feel right at home, so he just got on with the job and pumped a bit harder, getting his steel right up deep inside the little critter's love-box.

The little critter yelped loudly like a disobedient dog being whipped by its master, so loudly it was enough to make Landis real angry. This is no good, he told himself, certainly not up to the standard he expected from them. He withdrew his meat and adjusted his steel. It was now nice shiny spikes. He sent it back home again, forcefully this time, you understand, and listened

to the boy moan in sheer ecstasy as blood washed his steel in a sweet baptism until the boy passed out and was left there dangling till he came right up inside him, exploding deep inside as the raw, electric rush came flooding down from the liquid sky and bathed his whole being in a blissful perfume of sweat and felt himself flow out of himself like water.

He settled back into his body and shook himself awake, opening his eyes to a world which seemed alive and radiant. Now he felt real good. Now he had that little shine in his eyes that transformed everything they were cast upon, making everything look glossy and yet at the same time crystal clear as if he was looking through highly polished glass. But the more he looked, the more the effect seemed to wear off until he was just left with a residue, a faint hint of a possibility of what could possibly be made permanent. He wanted it back again and quickly turned round to the rest of them and smiled. The boys looked back at him in fear as they noticed the blood dripping from his cock, his inlaid steel spikes and the blood flowing from their friend, impregnating the room with a heavy atmosphere, a dark ambience which came seeping through in waves.

He retracted his steel and had a quick wash at the basin in the corner whilst he got Chan to strap up another one of the boys on the wooden cross attached to the wall. It was in the shape of an X. Unfortunately, the kid was a bit too short for it. But that didn't bother Landis. He helped Chan hoist the kid off the floor and finished strapping the rest of him into place. He was transfixed, and he went over to the others, stroked their hair just to make sure they knew he meant business and got them to kneel on the bare wooden floor like the three kings worshipping their friend in the sling-cum-manger. That got him thinking of a whole new scenario which was now running deliriously through his brain like this was going to be the big Jesus trip and that somehow it was appropriate the more he got to firmly clarify it in his mind.

He got Chan to help shackle them into place with some chains and cuffs and strapped their hands into position against their chests like they were all praying, a fitting figure of the adorations and prayers their were bestowing on their knocked out friend in that deathless sleep of his. He made them close their eyes in worship of their other brother who was about to go through a death-rebirth experience as the risen Christ, playing with him

whilst he was strapped to the cross. He decided the boy needed to go through a proper X-ordeal; he was going to take him through all the way and help him in his passage to the fields of eternity, assist him so he could safely cross over to the other side. The only problem was, Landis wasn't too happy about something. The boy was unclean; he had a filthy soul on him like he was unclean on the inside, you understand, so something had to be done, and he knew rightly how to rectify the situation.

"This boy is unclean, man. I tell you, he's unclean!" he told Chan who started giggling, knowing full well what his friend meant.

Landis found his knife and gun among his clothes. He pulled them out and stuck his gun on the side as he wouldn't be needing it just yet, crossed to the other side of the room like a tiger, stalking the damned soul hanging in purgatory on the cross, circling his prey, fixing his eyes on him with real hatred. The unclean boy, dangling in space, already looked like he was dead with a grimace of pain etched into his face punctuated by wild staring eyes. He wasn't dead yet, just a little too weak for Landis' liking and he didn't seem to have the strength in him to keep his head up like a real man, for it should have been proud and erect which it wasn't. Well, Landis would see to that and was so far disappointed by the whole show his fellow actors here were putting on for him. He was going to have to educate them before the curtain went down.

He raised the boy's head up and swished his blade across his eyes no less than an inch away so the unclean soul could have a good look at it and made sure the demon-fear was clearly visible in his eyes before moving onto the next act. Satisfied the presence was invoked, he ran the edge of the razor-sharp blade down the boy's body, only lightly, mind, so he could have a good feel of how keen it was and brought its tip down to the boy's cock and touched the loose fold of flesh that was making him unclean and pulled at it forcefully between his fingers as he watched the whole body tighten in the grip of the demon-fear. The little sod had the audacity to plead for him to stop. It only made him real angry. Didn't the little fucker understand he was trying to make his soul clean? To shine it up for him like smoothly polished crystal so he could more perfectly reflect the light within?

Under bated breath he opined those immortal words of Our Lord; "The Way, the Middle Way; the Truth, the Tao, and the Life; no man cometh in

the mouth of the Father, but by me." Then he wheeled round him like a whirling dervish, an exorcist on heat, and did spew forth those healing words with his fine, golden tongue; "And I shall circumcise the flesh of your foreskin; and it shall be the token of the covenant betwixt me and you." And he gripped that ugly, offending prepuce and wielded his knife diligently, exquisitely manoeuvring it until the thing came away in his fingers gloriously and he raised it to the little fucker's face and made him witness it through tear-stained eyes.

"Now there shall be no more mendacity between thee and me," he told the sinful one and licked of the blood which flowed from it and consecrated it thereby and brought it over to his young disciples, his chelas, and did cut thereof into tripartite divisions for the kneeling triumvirate and made them each eat thereof as the holy sacrament of his body, blessing it with a kiss as he forced it into their closed mouths saying; "Hoc est enim corpus meum. This is my body. I am the living bread that doth give sustenance. He who eateth of my body shall not die; verily he shall live, for it is the living bread that hath come down from heaven. If he who dost not eat of this bread, then he shall die. Then eat of my flesh, and ye shall be rewarded in heaven, thereby."

He finished his sermon and let the boys eat of the holy sacrament as he stood there with great admiration, pride filling his heart with all the work he was doing for the good of the world as his friend Chan sat there giggling in the corner hard put to control himself.

He examined each one in turn to see if they were intoxicated thereby, making sure they did not spit out the blessed meal he had bestowed on them. The poor little things were finding it hard to chew and made them swallow their Holy Communion whole by patting them heartily on their backs as blood seeped out of their mouths and did make him feel greatly embittered. For it was the loss of the soul, the very scourge of the world, the very iniquity of God he would wash from the face of the earth and from their mouths.

"Alas! It is time for the wine!" he shouted jubilantly and made them close their eyes at the sacrament they were about to receive, for it was truly a worthy and holy thing he was about to give unto them, the precious liquid of life itself. He invoked it, felt it gather in his loins as tension and did let it

flow out of him in copious quantities, that sweet, golden elixir that was the wine of the gods, the amber liquor, the true fountain of immortal youth, and watched it flow into their closed mouths saying; "Hic est enim calix sanguinis mei. This is my blood. I am the living wine that doth nurture the soul. He who drinketh of my blood shall not die; verily he shall live, for it is the living water of life that hath come down from heaven. If he who dost not drink of this blood, then he shall die. Then drink of my blood, and ye shall be rewarded in heaven, thereby." And he made sure that each of them had equal quantities to drink so they could all equally go to heaven, for if there was one thing he strongly disapproved of it was favouritism. He believed reverently in equality and in equilibrium, the harmony of heaven and earth, for was that not the Middle Way? the way of the Tao?

Landis looked to his friend who was creased up with laughter. Chan saw there was a twinkle in his eye as he stopped himself from laughing, lit up a joint and carried it over to him like an Olympian god and pressed it to Landis' lips. He brushed his friend's shoulders, helping him to release all the stress of his hard work from his muscular frame then kissed him on the cheek and allowed him to continue.

The one being initiated into the X-ordeal had recovered from his preliminary stage of the child-man transition and was starting to squeal as Landis pressed in sharply his knife to the boy's flesh and etched in beautiful, skilful strokes a nice Christian cross on his chest, ensuring that the horizontal beam was perfectly perpendicular to the vertical so as to slice neatly through his nipples.

He stood back to admire his work. Now he understood what scarification was all about. It had a certain 'Je ne sais quoi' quality about it that went beyond descriptive and narrative interpretations. Pleased, he decided to further his designs and do a little needle-doing on the boy's arms with the sharp tip of his knife until the little unappreciative fucker started bawling his head off and it was kind of getting to him, making him all indignant at the little ingrate and looked at Chan to do something about it.

Chan got up from where he was slouched smoking in the corner and first made the boy smoke some of his joint, but despite a couple of tokes the boy wouldn't quit bawling so he had to go and find some tape to lash it around his mouth securely, nice and firm to keep it shut. For he knew how

his friend always liked to work in silence and undisturbed.

Now Landis got to etch in the boy's living book of flesh a few flames which rolled up his arms and down his legs so as to render more perfectly the boy's plight and saw his soul being purified thereby and his iniquity flow out of him in cool sanguinity so that their covenant maybe more deeply entrenched thereby and realised also that sanguification was another one of his artistic talents. He licked at the now pure blood as it flowed in His name and healed with his saliva the boy's blood bespattered cock, and with the deftness of his tongue he got it nice and firm and then pumped some life back into the boy with his fist, getting him all madly excited, putting the spirit back into his body. He could tell the boy was all madly excited by the way he kept screwing up his eyes and was in real ecstasy as he came out of his body through that tiny aperture in a bursting flow of liquid light and shot across the room like star-fire, sprinkling the bare wooden floors with his light and saw the boy was elated thereby. Ah, it was a beautiful sight. Landis was enervated and the boy had truly seen and touched the Face of Death as he died and his spirit had crossed over to the other side, marking the end of his transition and the completion of his X-ordeal. All he had to do now was make sure the boy regained his faculties so he could commune with the gods and talk to them whilst he was there.

"This is my knife," he told him, whispering in his ear so his departed spirit could hear. "I call it Pesh-en-Kef."

He touched the boy's taped mouth with the tip of his knife and struck it seven times whilst chanting the words from Spell 23: "May the god Ptah open my mouth, and may the god of my city loosen the restrictions, even the restrictions which are over my mouth. May Thoth, being filled and equipped with his magic, come and loosen them, even those restrictions of Set which fetter my mouth, and may the god Atum hurl them at those who would fetter me with them and cast them off." Then did he slice keenly with his blade all across the mouth and exceedingly deeply so that blood did flow out of his mouth also, that he may talk to the gods.

"My mouth is open!" he continued to orate. "My mouth is split open by Shu with his steel knife wherewith he slit open the mouths of the gods. I am the Powerful One, and I shall sit beside Her who is in the great breath of the sky; I am Orion the Great who dwells with the Souls of Heliopolis."

And with that he finished the ceremony by kissing his blade seven times and did stand back to look at the crucified one, he who had risen and resurrected on the other side.

It was a work of art.

Chan gave him a big round of applause. He kissed him once more.

"Thanks, Chan," he told him.

"You are genius, like my father say, very clever."

"Ah, shucks. Do you really think so?" he asked him as he gave him a big kiss then saw out of the corner of his eye the other little ones, the *ménage a trois*, all shivering and shaking away like it was cold or something. He couldn't understand it because as far as he knew the play-space was like a sauna. The perspiration on his brow confirmed it. So why were they all shaking? He patted Chan on the back, indicating there was still plenty more work to do before the night was through.

He felt his cock get hard again and decided it need a home to get that itsy-bitsy twinkle back in his eye again and bent down on his knees to worship with them in lieu of their dearly departed brother.

"Our Father which aren't in heaven," he prayed humbly aloud, "blasphemed be thy name. Thy king is about to come, thy phallic-will shall be done on the earth as I come in heaven. Give us this day our fleshy bread. And fuck us to death, as we fuck the dead. And lead us unto ecstasy, and deliver us from your evil: Ateh + Malkuth + ve-Gedulah + ve-Geburah + le-Olahm + Amen." He crossed himself and imagined his whole body being blessed with the divine celestial light that fructified in his loins thereby fortifying his phallus. It made him feel itchy and he slowly caressed the boy next to him and took him softly, gently, as he sent himself home without his steel this time and helped the poor little boy ejaculate with a touch of his love. He allowed Chan to savour the other one on the end, getting all of them to come in unison in a liquid display of light that magnetised the atmosphere in the room. It was just a bit of light relief for the time being, a bit of play before some more serious work. After all, eating between meals ruins your appetite, and he believed that was the truth, the Tao.

They rested awhile, small-talked and smoked, letting the kids play between themselves on long leashes.

He got Chan to call over one of the kids, the one who had his back to him, a nice, lean looking and unblemished back. It sure is pretty, but pretty empty, he thought, as he twiddled with his knife in the woodwork. He got the boy to kneel down in front of him in the dragon posture, his nice and lean back facing him as he figured in his mind how he could complement that nice and lean back of his. Nothing elaborate, mind, just a few embellishments here and there to ornament it, fill it out, make it look good, in fact make it look even better, something he could be proud of and take it home to his mom and show her and she'd be really proud of her little son. So he got figuring some more, a nice little pattern to etch into that nice and lean flesh, and started working away with the point of his knife whilst he toked and got Chan to go over the other side of the room so he couldn't see what he was doing for he believed all true artists work better in privacy without eyes prying on their work in progress and that was the only way you could get it done properly and save the unveiling till the last moment. He started whistling whilst he was working. It raises the spirits and the spirits need raising in this town, they sure need raising, he believed.

He worked speedily and effectively, took some more tokes and passed it to the kid who was making a kind of whimpering sound which was getting on his nerves. He was only trying to make him look all pretty for his mom. Damned ingrate! He concentrated on the boy's spine, etching into his skin two intertwining serpents. They crisscrossed up his spine, their tails disappearing up his anus, their heads meeting at the nape of his neck with their tongues protruding and winding up towards the back of his head to kiss his reptilian brain. He made the kid smoke some more by ramming the joint forcefully into his mouth like a dummy to stop the fucker from wailing and continued his handiwork; two outstretched wings joined together at the spine and unfurling across his shoulder blades, with their tips just touching the top of his arms. "Put on the wings of your desire, and we shall make flesh the dream," he sang rapturously to himself for the kid's wings resembled his own tattooed chest; large expansive vulture wings in dazzling emerald and brilliant lemon yellow, the tips of their unfurled feathers wrapping round his pierced nipples, its claws clasping a ball of light in the centre of his chest, its body bifurcating into two heads of writhing cobras,

hooded and poised to strike in place of the vulture's head, one light, the other dark.

He finished his work in perfect unison with Chan orgasming in the body of his caterwauling catamite. He called him over to look at his masterpiece.

"Well, Chan, what do you think?"

"It good, very good. Some day you make fine artist."

"Do you really think so? You don't think I've overdone it, do you?"

"No, it perfect. It work of art."

"It sure is, a work of art. Why, man, it's the Tao," he said laughing his head off. He even thought of skinning the boy alive and taking it home to show the wife, but that would take too long. Besides, his mind was still hooked on that white bit and that kind of made him want to speed things up so he could get back to the club and sort her out.

"Back to work," he told Chan and slapped his canvas hard. He looked round the room for anything else which might come in useful for the proceedings.

He found a short whip on the side. It was kind of mandatory in a play-space like this so he got to test it out in the air first. It took him a few goes to get it to crack to his satisfaction as it wasn't as long as his one back at home. That was a fifteen feet bullwhip. This was a mean short-assed fucker, and a bit too light for his liking but it would have to do, and made one of the boys kneel on all fours whilst he lashed him a few times. After awhile he realised there was something wrong with the boy. The miserable fucker wasn't crying out like he ought to and that kind of got to him. He blamed his technique and endeavoured with some more practice to get back into his good old flagellating self because he was determined to take him to the brink so he could look death in the eye. Satisfied, he reconvened on his slave-boy with some good polished strokes across the small of his back, the part of the back he estimated was the best for it was usually the most sensitive. Still the little critter wasn't barking loud enough. There's something definitely wrong here, he pondered, and reckoned he was doing it on purpose just to annoy him, so he got him to raise his ass completely

off the ground and high up into the air and made Chan get an erection and insert it in the little fucker's mouth as he wasn't screaming anyway and flogged him as hard as he could, not too hard, you understand, because he had to be careful about the amount of force he was exacting. These Chinks all had fine sharp teeth with all that rice they keep eating and he didn't want anything emasculating happening to his friend.

Yet still there wasn't something right about all of this, so he ordered Chan to pull out and attack the boy from the rear and waited till his friend was fully re-inserted and riding away before he got the boy to perform the rite of Onan, making sure he was big and hard, and kept waiting till Chan and the boy were both wavering incipiently on the edge of death when he picked up his gun and put a bullet through the fucker's brain, thus ensuring that he went all the way over the edge, crossing safely with his demise.

"Omni Sancti Spiritum," he recited as he crossed the air with two fingers and watched the boy's body collapse to the ground in a magnificent display of primal eroticism, a fabulous morphology of sex and death, still oozing copious amounts of love-juice which turned pink with his blood as it spilled on to the floor. Landis was deeply impressed, only wishing he had his camera with him to capture the moment forever.

Now he saw what needed doing as his piece of canvas tried scurrying away from the scene.

"All great artists," he told himself, "destroy their finest work, for it is through the actual destruction of one's own creations where the spirit of Jesus Christ, Our Lord and Saviour, can be felt."

And he fetched his piece of canvas, dragged him over to the centre of the room and made him suck of his seed in order that he may go forth and multiply in heaven as a liberated and impregnated spirit, ensuring that he drank plentifully thereof. And after he had done drinking the water of life, he was satisfied and saw that it was good. Then he made him bend down on all fours so his head would be poised above the pool of his dead friend and see therein the reflected visage of death, its darkness brooding in the blood and his face as it moved across the deeps, and saw that it was good and bade him to keep silent and still. He raised up his flail to the heavens, waited for the Spirit of God to be singing in his soul, and did bring it down

with mighty vengeance and furious anger across the pitifully accursed back, multiplying it ten times ten as his piece of canvas snarled in contempt at his own hideous god, cold blasphemies and mournful laments belching from his maw, cursing and cussing for all the dead angels to hear in exquisite agony until the very breath he exhaled took with it his spirit and exited out of his body and moved over the face of creation towards its home in the West. His liberated body did fall thereto upon the ground united with its counterpart in complete and utter redemption. And Landis was fortified thereby and felt that it was good.

Having exerted himself mercifully for the benefit of mankind, he rested his poor and weary arms awhile across his radiant chest. Chan wiped his sweat besotted brow for him as he contemplated the infinite joys of the future and kissed him fully on the lips with great passion, savouring the sweet taste of revenge which flowed from his mouth. But the work was not yet completed, as Chan pointed out, for there was still more to be done.

"One cannot enjoy complete job satisfaction," he told Chan proudly, "until all the requisite work is done. And a job worth doing is...?"

"Worth doing well!" Chan ardently replied.

"Exactly. Get to!" he commanded as he surveyed the last miserable boy before him. He fetched him, got the whimpering knave to his feet and walked dutifully around him, examining the pathetic creature like a tasteless morsel, denigrating every facet of the boy's features, tutting to himself when he realised the boy was deficient—especially in one area—and brought his hand down to the boy's shrivelled cock and vainly tried to coax some life back into it before capitulating at the futility of the task. In disgust, he looked at the boy, much dismayed at how he had the audacity to deprive him of his one singular pleasure, but the boy feared to look him directly in the eye, instead looking away from him in shame. Landis brought up his knife to the wretch's chin and forced his head back before bringing his knife down in one almighty swoop, lacerating his nipple so fully that it came clean away, then pinched his other one and twisted and turned it until the boy was writhing in delicious agony. He chopped it off from the pathetic body with keen precision, for the boy reminded him of a girl with sagging, now blood bespattered breasts matching his prepubescent body. He therefore had to undergo the complete rite of transformation for his

transgressions and be transsexualised thereby.

"And the Lord cried; 'PIERCE THY GENITALS!'" And he did grip thereof in one irate fist the pathetic thing's scrotum, and with his knife did he insert fully into that offending sack all the way through and twisted it round so that his anger maybe truly felt whilst Chan held back its arms, and then brought it out again and made it lick thereof the blood that flowed at his displeasing before finally emasculating the last of the flesh he had no right to possess. Chan let it go. Landis inspected the object of his contempt. It only made him hard and hungry for home. Chan forced the thing's mouth down onto his fine erection as Landis brought out his steel from his mighty phallus.

"If he wants to be a woman," he told Chan, "then we shall treat him like a woman," and forced his engorged phallus up the thing's entrance and grabbed with his other hand that pitiable little cock which offended him so and held with his other the keen blade to its base as he rode the bugger hard, pumping his anger into its being, measuring his pace with swift, spasmodic rhythms until he felt himself coming, and as he did come he let rip with his knife so the iniquitous piece of flesh did come clean away from its body and Chan made it quaff his precious love-juice, his very life-force as it flowed down the pitiable thing's throat.

"If thy genitals offend thee, then cut them off," Landis told it as he brought up the limp piece of flesh to its eyes and did make it look thereunto, and felt gratified thereby, that his work was nearing completion and that the thing was now verily feminised and had become a real woman for she even flowed blood from her genitals and he was mightily impressed with his work, pulling himself out of her body, letting it fall gracefully to the floor in its resplendent defloration. Now finally her soul was free from all confusion for it knew its own inner sex and could pass peaceably over to the other side as she expired in one grateful moan.

He washed the last of the blood from his cock and retracted his steel. Chan went over to the limp body of the boy still lying in the sling, the last of the lambs for the slaughter, then to the happy Landis as to suggestions of what should become of him. Landis paused for thought, deliberating over the complexity of the question, and threw back his head as if the strain was too much. Then he noticed the rather handy height of the ceiling, high enough

perhaps for one last fitting spectacle before they could call it a day. He gloated at the prospect; a last pageant of flesh and the taste of death in the back of his throat.

"Ah! I do believe," he cried, "it is nigh time my friend for some Gallows Dancing to end the night. And we shall all go merrily thereafter as the insufferable burdens of our iniquities finally fall from our shoulders."

Chan cheered him for the idea. There was no better way to end the night with a bit of Gallows Dancing. Besides, it was his friend's favourite rite of passage, a perfect climax.

He threw a piece of flex up to the crossbeam, climbed onto a wooden crate and tied the flex before jumping with all of his weight on the end to ensure that it was good and strong, then slid down with a big grin on his face.

Landis got the boy awake with some cold water and dragged his limp body out of the sling whilst Chan prepared a noose and lassoed it round the boy's neck like it was cowboys and injuns funtime. He hoisted up the little injun, who was screaming and kicking good and proper like he ought to be doing, and got him to stand on a couple of crates for the final showdown. Bare-assed naked and his body all a-quivering, the boy stood still on tiptoe, his crotch now level with Landis' anticipating open mouth.

"Does the little whippersnapper speak any English at all, Chan?"

"He speak bit. Why? You want speech as well?"

"That's the idea, before he comes out of his body."

"I tell him first in my language, then he do it in English as you work."

"Yeah, but not all of it. That will take too long. Just the juicy bits, you understand."

He nodded hesitantly as if it was going to be a problem trying to remember the exact words let alone the best bits.

Landis wasted no time in getting to work on the boy's cock, helping it to come alive and throbbing as he heard those delectable and healing and plaintive words come out of the boy's mouth. It was music to his ears.

"My God, my God, why hast thou forsaken me? Why ... thou from help me ... from the words of my roaring?"

Landis stopped him with a cry. "Shit, Chan! How do you expect me to work to my full capacity when you can't even get the little fucker to say the words properly? Make him start again and say it right. And tell him to stop being so tense; it makes me nervous."

"I tell him. You work."

"You do that. And when I bring my hand down," he said with his right arm poised in the air, "that's the signal, right?" Chan nodded. "I'm working with amateurs here," he muttered to himself, and got back to working on that cock which for some reason had gone all limp on him.

"My God, my God, why has thou forsaken me? Why thou so far from helping me, and from the words of my roaring?"

He paused. Landis slapped him hard.

"O my God, I cry in daytime, but thou hear not, and night season, not silent. But thou holy, thou that (something) praises Israel. Our father trust they trust and did deliver them. They cry to thee and were delivered: they trust thee and were not (something). But I worm and no man..."

"You sure are, boy," he replied, taking him fully in his mouth, hand raised.

"... but thou took me out of womb, did make me hope on mother's tits. I was cast out from womb. Thou art God from my ass. Not be far from me; trouble is always near, for there is none help me. Many balls pass me, strong balls of... I not remember next word..."

"Jesus!" Landis shouted at him with his mouth full.

"Ah, yes, Jesus," Chan remembered. "That is word."

"No, Chan. For crying out loud it's 'Bashan.'"

"But you just say 'Jesus,'" he said, confused.

"Fuck me! How many times have we been doing this? And why is it every

time we get to this verse you can never remember the word?"

"I'm sorry. It not happen again."

"You're damned right it won't," muttering "amateurs" under his breath. He got working again, quite surprised, for they don't usually last this long.

Chan got the kid orating again. Landis struggled to get back his confidence, started working on the kid manually, then let his mouth take over.

"Bashan have set me round. They gape on me with their mouths, ravening and roaring lion. I pour out like water and all bones out of joint: my heart is wax: melted in my bowels. My strength is dried up in pots; my tongue cleave to my jaws; and thou has brought me into dust of death..."

Now he could feel it trickling down the back of his throat as the boy's body started kicking into action. He was nearly there, right on the verge. Any minute now and he'd be dancing. So Landis sucked harder, got the ingrate boiling in his loins, all heated up and waiting to explode, then quickly dropped his arm down as the boy started coming in his mouth. Chan saw the sign, kicked the crates out of the way and with all his force threw himself on the boy's legs and pulled down hard until he heard a delicious snapping sound. Death poured down Landis' throat as he took him full, the boy's body kicking and flailing around like for once in his life he was fully animated. He sucked him dry and stood back to watch the spectacle.

"Wow man! Look at the motherfucker dance! Boy, can he dance!"

And now Chan got to taste the death of the boy as the last of the spunk left him. Chan greedily gobbled it up, and then smacked his lips, well satisfied. He wiped his mouth and stood back to admire the twitching body as the last vestiges of life seeped out of him and finally drew to a halt, hanging immobile in the highly charged air.

"Have you ever seen such a prettier sight, Chan?" he asked him.

"It pretty," he replied, licking his lips.

"It sure is. 'They shall come, and they shall declare his righteousness unto a people that shall be born, that he hath done this.' And as Jesus himself said

when he crossed over to the other side on his cross; 'It is accomplished.' And our work is finally done, Chan, and boy, am I gratified thereby."

He went over to him, swung him round the room in jubilation as that good old sparkle came back into his eyes. The whole room took on a rosy appearance. It made everything look alive. It had been worth it, he decided, and now he was being rewarded with a little bit of heaven.

They came out into the night, ravening dogs, soft mad children, carnivorous gods, sarcophagi demons, in search of more meat; filled with lust, filled with a hunger for death that can never be satiated, roaming and frothing at their mouths under the big black liquid sky, looking for more kicks and new pleasures to take them all the way to ecstasy with their libidos fully charged, high on raw erogenous energy.

Two rascally scumbags were standing in their way as they sang to themselves. They kicked and punched and knifed them to the ground.

"If they want to behave like peasants...?" he asked his Sino-sidekick.

"Then treat like peasants!"

"That's right," he replied.

They shook hands on it and went careering into the night.

The Phallus Boys, as they liked to call themselves, were back in town.

THE 'HA' EXPERIENCE

'During early experiments with electro-neural implants it was discovered that hyper-stimulating the nervous system overloaded neural circuits causing the subject to become instantly alert. Further experiments increased the "dosage" of direct electrical input causing the state of hyper-awareness (or HA for short) to be significantly prolonged. Such states were recorded lasting as long as 10 to 15 minutes depending on the intensity of the "shock" allowing the subject to introject vast quotas of information without memory loss before relapsing into inertness, that is, before "total-brain functioning" withdrew.

The outcome of these researches posed a problem: Why didn't total-brain functioning last longer and was it possible to maintain HA indefinitely if not permanently?

Dr Grolff, respected author of the paper "Neuro-transmitters and Other Toys" (1998) states that HA is "prone to lapse into inertia due to autonomic functioning of the hypothalamus." Lengthy periods of HA are impossible to induce without "damaging the lower neural circuits of the brain." Over-exposure to "shock-tactics" could result in "brain haemorrhages, fainting fits, catatonia and catalepsia, if not death itself." Dr Grolff states that it is as if "man is asleep all the time, yet when experiencing a sudden shock he wakes up, i.e. he achieves total-brain functioning. A new or higher circuit is activated." He then goes onto conclude that "it is a pity this circuit does not stay open for we would benefit greatly if HA could be maintained with its superior brainpower. More research in this area could be highly productive. Who knows, one day we may have a wide-awake world with even a wide-awake President."'

Jeff Banner, Editor,
Continuity of Consciousness Readings
(All quotes from cited paper)

—10—
INVOCATION OF DEATH

The taxi ride on the way back to his place was quiet. Neither of them spoke. They were immersed in their own private worlds. Carlotta attended to her make-up, Capri to his thoughts. He couldn't help wondering what a woman like Carlotta would want with a drug supposedly having curative properties without being interested in its financial possibilities, a drug so powerful it

may even hold the very key to the whole problem of ageing, a real gerontologist's dream.

He looked to this gorgeous woman sitting beside him overflowing with perfume. It reminded him of her femininity, sweeping over him like an enticing pall. It was enough to make him feel something for her, a strong passionate desire he realised he would be incapable of controlling. It was rising to the surface unbidden. But it wasn't powerful enough to dispel any other illusions he had about her. There was something quite disturbing about all of this. Her desire for a drug which may not even exist. Her willingness to pay handsomely for it. What? Just to get back at an old flame? No, there was more to it than that, and she was not revealing the whole story. Her deception didn't bother him. It was her he found deeply baffling. The money didn't interest him either. Nor taking on this assignment of hers. So why were they going back to his place and for one thing only? Because he had no choice. The gods were controlling his destiny, and for some reason this is what they had in mind.

He looked at her again. She noticed and smiled back sweetly. It warmed him somewhat, reassured him and made him melt in his seat, for it was genuine, sincere. Yet deep in his heart he knew she was not to be trusted.

As soon as he showed her in to his apartment he noticed a queer look of puzzlement. Like a woman of manners, she suppressed it and made a polite gesture instead.

"Nice place," she murmured, affectedly.

"You'll have to forgive me. I wasn't expecting company tonight."

His remark was quite unnecessary. As he had little in the way of possessions to untidy the place, it was certainly far from being a mess.

She walked into his living room with an elegant grace, her eyes scanning the few things in sight and smiled at him once more.

"A coffee?" she reminded him.

"Ah, yes. How do you like it?"

"Strong and black." And smiled again.

Capri retreated to the kitchen and got his old percolator up and running.

"I like your apartment," he heard her say.

"It's not bad," he shouted back. "I know it isn't much but it suits me down to the ground." He returned to see her removing her coat and draping it on his couch. She then gingerly removed her hat, laid it on top of her coat and swished back her hair with confidence. He watched her move over to his big wide windows and opened them ajar to get some half-fresh air in. She leaned against the side, reminding him of the way she had in the cafeteria and took up her stance. It was an unusual sight to see a woman of her worth and intelligence in his room, a woman who perhaps had few inhibitions or real cares in the world, especially as far as money was concerned. He, on the other hand, was deeply put-off by his material standards in comparison to her.

He let his eyes roam over her back whilst waiting for the coffee, the smooth curve of her buttocks hemmed in by her tight fitting dress and the way she wrapped her arms around herself. Her eyes seemed to be two dark orbs of resonating fire the way they panned out the whole view of the park before them, lost in the dimness and its solitude. Although he felt awkward, he was deeply fascinated by her, for she showed no look of worry, being care-free and content. He a stranger she had only just met, unafraid about being alone with him, feeling neither nervous nor shy in his presence.

"I love the view," she whispered.

"So do I. In fact, it is the only reason why I stay here."

She fell silent again like a statue, lost in the view, evoking in him a strange concoction of images as he stayed his position a good few feet away, not wishing to join her, content watching her from a safe distance. He let his imagination loose, allowing it to fill his mind with whatever visions and correspondences she emanated.

He saw her standing aloft on top of a hill, a sword clenched firmly in one hand. It was covered in blood, the blood of all the men she had slain in her desire to attain, to possess everything her heart demanded. And all these

men lay about her feet forming the hill on which she stood. Dead men, spent men, men no longer of any use to her and thus dispensable. They had served their purpose. Would he be joining them, he wondered, and lie dead at her feet only to be followed by others. But all these donors to the cause weren't merely men, mortals, that wasn't good enough. She wanted strong, noble blood, the blood of saints, warriors, martyrs, priests, prophets, kings, men who had good strong blood and plenty of it. And they were all prepared to suffer in her name, all for the sake of her.

He felt himself being conveyed towards her by some powerful force as if it had picked him up in its giant hand, a force which demanded being yielded to rather than fought against. He found himself next to her, then wrapping his arms round her from behind, breathing in that exotic, toxic perfume. It filled his mind with insatiable desire. He was aroused, a tiger ready to pounce, calm and controlled and intoxicated with lust to have her and have her full. He stole a kiss to the soft skin of her neck, and, like the wraith that she was, she gave into his vision, unremittingly. Her body was all his, she signalled, to do with as he pleased, like a succubus delighting in the waywardness of its victim, so easy to pervert. And he was a victim, a hopeless victim totally powerless to stop himself from what would be happening next. Yes, she seemed to whisper, yes take me. He kissed her again softly, gently as if she was a delicate flower, one that shouldn't be crushed. He squeezed her tighter, drawing her into him, forcing his aching cock against the crease of her buttocks so she could feel how hard he was for her now. Yes, go on, fuck me. Do it, go on, do it. Have me, I'm all yours, all pleasure and desire, just take me. Don't stop, don't stop. Jesusfuckingchrist don't stop. Fuck me. Fuck me.

His mind reeled.

He gripped her shoulders, forced her head back, nibbled her ears and licked them. She submitted, her mouth wide open, breathing deeply, her eyes closed as he caressed her, felt her, his fingers exploring every surface of her body, her heaving chest, her breasts, her hard nipples. Her hands gripped his and guided them down to the warm sensuality between her thighs. He rubbed her. She moaned as he breathed deeply into her ear. She purred and begged for more. He wanted to take her all the way, impacting flesh against flesh, soul embracing soul without any barriers, with nothing to stop them.

He pulled her round towards him, found her waiting mouth and kissed her deep and full, his tongue commingling with hers, then gently nibbled her soft tender lips. He pushed her firmly against the wall and pressed his body against hers tighter, pulling her legs up to his hips as he held her in place and ravished her with his mouth. She hitched up her dress above her hips so he could move his crotch in closer towards hers and clung to him, her arms gripping his neck as she let her body move to its own rhythm, her hot crutch rubbing his sore cock.

He pulled her legs up higher. She fastened them round his back, leaving his hands free to roam her more fully. He was surprised to find the complete absence of panties.

"I messed them in the cafeteria," she responded with heated breath as if reading his mind.

He laughed and kissed her some more and found the zip of her dress and pulled it down. She pushed him off and fought frantically with the straps of her dress and let it drop to the floor and stood there in her naked brilliance and smiled wickedly. She was a feast for the eyes, a voluptuary's dream, a hypnotic charm clothed in most delectable flesh, contours superbly wrought, skin smooth and unblemished. Not one crease or mark, but firm and fairly muscular flesh that exuded a wealth of power, of dominance and defiance. Her skin was slightly dark, almost satanic. He could not betray the admiration he now had for her, to ardently know her, to unite with her in one bout of all-pleasureness. She was amorous, sensuous, beckoning him fatally to come to her. Yes, this is for you, all for you, she gestured. He was compelled towards her, but she stayed him and bent down to remove her shoes. Capri stepped back and started ripping his clothes off, tossing them on the floor with careless abandon.

He struggled with his belt and noticed the way Carlotta, who was now standing totally naked before him, examined his body, her eyes taking him in full, surprised at how thin he was, yet deceptively strong, his torso absent of any hair. She helped him remove his trousers, fumbling with his flies, opening them and pulled out his big, hot, throbbing cock, taking it straight into her mouth as she knelt before him, her tongue working up and down every inch of it, rubbing it with dextrous fingers and making him harder. She was well experienced, as he figured, and let her have her way as his

trousers fell to the floor. He moaned and flung his head back, captivated by the exquisiteness of her touch, her deep throat, as she sunk him in whole. He knew any minute he would be coming. It was unbearable and was hard put to control himself, feeling a tide rising deep within him, a tide that was building rapidly, just waiting to overflow. He suppressed it and gripped her head, his fingers running madly through her hair as she bobbed back and forth and coaxed him onwards. Almost there, nearly there. Don't stop, he murmured to himself, don't stop. But she did and pulled her mouth away from him. He looked down to see a big wide smile on her face that told him it was his turn to please her, to explore her inner depths.

He yanked her up by her shoulders, hoisted her against his body and kissed her rapaciously, madly, again and again, then stopped to look deeply in her eyes. They sparkled in return, crying out for him, wanting it now, yes now.

He picked her up and carried her to his bed, lay her down gently, running his hands all over her tender flesh and climbed on top of her. His mouth met hers. She clasped him tightly and then pulled her head away.

"Eat me," she ordered.

He obeyed. He slid down to find her legs open wide for him, inviting him to probe every part of her, to ravish her. She closed her eyes and lay back and gave into her body. He tenderly licked her black bushy pubic hair and then found her wetness. Her labia reminded him of wings, sweet delicate wings fanning out for him hiding their dark secret in-between. His long tongue worked in smooth polished strokes, an ophidian tongue, darting in and out of her, burrowing deeper into her crevice.

"Yes," she moaned. "Yes, more."

She panted, rolling her head from side to side. He tried harder to please her, to take her all the way. He was intoxicated, lost in her, a man possessed.

"Yes," she screamed and writhed some more, checking her panting sobs by stifling them with a finger between her teeth. She arched her body for more, her pelvis spasmodically reverberating its own message, guiding him in deeper.

She wanted him now.

He pulled himself up and slid all the way inside her, fucking her hard as her legs embraced him, drawing him in tighter into her lair, gasping, choking, fulminating with moan after moan as his body kicked into action and took over like a feral beast, speaking its own language encoded in aeons of flesh and muscle. Her cunt gripped his cock like a fist, muscle hugging muscle, pulling at him, sucking him in as he pounded away to her demands. He could feel her vaginal muscles gripping him in alternate rhythms, tight one minute, relaxed the next and tighter again, repeating endlessly in an orgiastic, insatiable revelry of lust.

It was driving him insane, demonstrating not only her experience but her versatility as well.

"Harder," she breathed into his ear, "harder. Don't stop, don't stop. Jesusfuckingchrist don't stop. Fuck me. Fuck me," as if the words he had 'heard' earlier were now filtering through her mouth.

He forced himself on, gripped her shoulders harder and clenched his eyes shut as he threw his whole body and soul into her. It was no good. He was wearing out fast, shocked that he could last as long this without coming. Soon he wouldn't have an ounce of strength in him to spare.

She must have realised he was beginning to flag. She threw him off and rolled him on to his back and climbed on top of him.

"Now I'm going to show you what I'm really made of," she told him.

He lay there panting for breath as she re-inserted him. He was determined to please her, to satisfy her, but she now had the upper hand, she was in control and started riding him hard, pounding into him, wild and excited, feverish with delight as she rode him, harder and harder, her head tossing back and forth, her hair flying about her face, a vixen on heat, a harridan hell-bent on absorbing him deep into herself, a harpy gloating on the torture she was exacting on him. All these images flowed through his weary brain as his body tried to keep up with her demands. The pain was pleasure. The pleasure was pain. Agony turning into twisted delight as his body burned. He saw a devilish grin about her face, evil, wicked and sinful as she fed off him, his blood, his pain, his loins feeding into her loins, his fire into her water as he bathed in her starlight.

He could barely distinguish her features at all in the darkness of the room. And then he saw her changing, twisting into new shapes, as she cavorted above him, pounding, thrusting, exploding into wild abandonment all over him, her hair lashing his face as she swung back and forth. He peered at her face again through bleary eyes. It was the visage of darkness itself, all black and contorted, her lips smeared with blood as she gripped his nipples and squeezed them hard, bleeding him for pain. She licked her lips and gloated with bloodshot eyes at the merciless torment she was inflicting on him. In the darkness he saw many arms waving ferociously around her and quick flashes of steel glinting in the pale light, a thousand arms, a thousand knives, each one ripping into his flesh, cutting deep into him, lacerating his chest. A necklace of beads dashed against her heaving chest, each one was a skull that grinned back at him with hollow eyes, a look of death in them threatening to engulf him. He wanted to cry out for her to stop, to throw her off until he felt it, a sharp burning pain in his balls that spread out all over his loins, crackling like fire under his flesh, hot liquid fire, peeling his flesh away, burning him up, and singeing his pubic hair.

Gasping, he tried to focus on the sensation, to see it with his inner eye. It was electrifying, a sensation beyond pain, so intense it made him want to howl and die, for it stung like a million scorpion tails all digging into his skin, jabbing him with little sharp points. He tried to fight it, seeing it as icy cold, but it still stung, still burnt. Now it was unwinding, uncoiling like a spring, ripping up his spine like a hot steel blade. It poked at the nape of his neck trying to inch into his brain to fry it alive. He pushed it back. It persisted with threatening force, a long needle he could feel being injected into his cranial cavity, a hot syringe to suck out his brain. There was a flash, a bright explosion of light as it swarmed into his mind revealing a bright point of white light far off in the distance before his closed eyes. He trembled violently like a sick, deranged man as the point moved in closer with impending doom. Yes, this was it. This is what he wanted. He yearned for it now, to give into it, to let it kill him. Carlotta no longer mattered. She was still fucking him, but she was eclipsed by this magnificent light before his eyes which was looming in closer with deadly accuracy. It would soon reduce him to nothing, he knew, and then he would be released into an endless void, his mind unlimited, unconfined, boundless, stretched out to infinity. Suddenly he was filled with fear, afraid of it, his mind too weak to sustain it. He had never seen it this close before. He wanted to recoil, to

resist it as it came in closer. It was a light undesired, yet most desirable, for this would be the end he had been longing for.

YES! YES! YES! DEATH! DEATH! DEATH! LOVELY, GLORIOUS, RAPTUROUS, BEAUTIFUL DEATH!

He concentrated on Carlotta's stride, getting into it, and dismissed his fear. Now he was going to have it, to attain and be gone. He focused his mind on nothing but this point of light before him. It homed in towards him, closer and closer, so close he could see nothing but a myriad of hues shooting out from its centre in all directions, a dizzying swirl, encircling his mind with rainbows of colours funnelling all around him, a crazy cornucopia of kaleidoscopic displays. It was beautiful, wondrous, an enchanting chemical panorama shifting every second with layer upon layer of bedazzling images and multifarious energies. It soothed him, taking the pain away, transforming it into love. And he was love, a burning cauldron of love flowing out towards it, to meet with it, to merge with it. Nearly there, nearly there. It was peeling him away, stripping him down to his bare essential part. But it was too much, too intense. He could feel his brain about to explode any minute, the pressure making his skull crack. Yes, yes, nearly there. His scalp slowly peeled away. His skull cracked, small fissures appeared running across its surface as his brain expanded with the pressure turning his bone into dust and white ash. Yes, yes, nearer, he whispered, and gripped Carlotta forcefully as a new burst of energy overtook him. He gritted his teeth as his mind slowly became pure light. Images tumbled as he detonated inside her. His skull shattered with the impact. His brain splattered the walls as they both came in one joyous, orgasmic fuck. He was consumed at last.

In the darkness he heard Angel say, "No, not now. No, not yet." Capri asked "Why?" but he answered him not.

Then he heard another voice. It sounded strangely familiar, far off yet at the same time close by. "Harmon? Harmon?" it kept imploring him.

He opened his eyes to see a beautiful, familiar face of a woman. This wasn't the death he hoped for as he realised he was still alive.

"Harmon, you've been asleep for ages," she told him.

"What?" he mumbled, his tongue not cooperating with his burnt-out brain.

"I said you've been asleep for ages."

"Almost there. So close, so close," he muttered.

"Where, Harmon? What are you on about? You're not making sense."

He wanted to close his eyes and invoke death again, but this time for real.

"I'm sorry I woke you," she said sincerely. "It's getting late. I have to go, but we must speak first."

"What time is it?" he managed to ask.

"Nearly 2.00 a.m. You've been out for over five hours."

"Is that all?"

"What's the matter? You look upset?"

He smiled at her. She smiled in return and gave him a quick peck.

"Well? Aren't you going to tell me what you were raving on about?"

"It was nothing. I was delirious, that's all," he explained.

"Come on, get up. We have a lot to discuss."

He could feel her breasts heaving against him as she draped herself over his body and gave him another peck. "What happened to that coffee you were making me?"

"Oh that! It's probably gone cold by now."

"Then put on a fresh pot whilst I have a quick shower."

Carlotta rolled her naked body over his as she climbed out of the bed. Her skin was soft velvet against his and instantly evoked the great fuck they had. She was the one who nearly took him all the way. He should have been grateful to Angel for making their paths meet, for she, in that one orgiastic pageant of flesh, had demonstrated to him exactly what was possible.

He smiled as he watched her naked behind, finding it amusing the way her buttocks wobbled as she disappeared into the bathroom. There was no way she was really 58, he concluded. A woman of that age would never have that kind of energy. But he certainly felt his age. His back creaked as he climbed out of bed, and decided there was only one good cure; a refreshing hot shower. He took her by surprise as he came up behind her. She let out a light shriek and turned round to find his waiting mouth. They kissed and caressed under the soothing water; the world didn't feel that bad after all.

He later found her reclining on his couch, languishing like a well fed cat, naked and simple with a big smile of satisfaction.

"Sorry, it's a bit late," he apologised as he handed her a cup of coffee.

"That's alright, but aren't you going to join me?"

He slumped himself down on the bare floor opposite her. "I've got to lie down on something hard. My back's killing me."

"I'm not surprised. Do you always last that long? I thought I was going to die!"

He laughed. "I thought I had," he joked.

He lay himself down, found his cigarettes and lit one up with a great sigh of relief. The smoke took away his sore head, healing his damaged nerves. Just as he sank into a somnolent daze, quite content to lie there for all eternity, she reminded him that they still had things to discuss.

"But first," she said, "can I ask you a question?"

"Sure. Go right ahead."

"I'm intrigued. Why do you live like this?"

"Like what?"

"Like this," she gestured, indicating the room. "How can you live like this? It's so empty and cold. There's no warmth. Don't you feel that it needs something?"

Here we go, he thought. Exactly what he expected from a woman. "I like it like this. I like space."

"So do I. But not like this. It's as if you have just moved in, but you've been here for years."

"Well, when I get round to it. There are far more important things in life than homely comforts."

"Then what about being properly equipped? I mean, you're not even fully connected. All you have is an old answerphone. Nobody uses them anymore. You don't even have a televid. You earn enough money to be able to at least buy a basic model. You go away on retreats, waste all your money on drinking, smoking, gambling and wonder why you're broke all the time. You need somebody to look after you."

"Thanks, but no thanks. I'm quite happy as I am."

"And it doesn't bother you," she continued, "this constantly relying on jobs in order to survive?"

"Not really. Each day becomes an adventure. You never know what's going to happen. It could be a windfall or a bloody disaster."

"I'm surprised at you, your attitude. When I read all about you, I thought, this man has got talent. He's successful. He's got a good reputation. Smart, intelligent, worldly. And all I see before me is a man suffering from a lack of faith in life, a man who broods with pessimism, who hates the world and hates himself in the bargain. I don't understand you, Harmon. I don't understand anybody who lives the way you do. Don't you care about what you are doing with your life, what you are doing to yourself? All you want to do is die, isn't that it? Is that what you were mumbling about earlier on? I pity you, I even feel sorry for you. You are wasting your life, frittering it away, turning your back on the world. You have no hope because life has treated you unkindly. And you could change it all to your advantage. With the talents I have seen so far you could make a fortune. But no, you insist on refusing to play the game. You don't even plan for the future, do you?"

"The future is an illusion. It only exists as expectation."

"Bullshit. Life has to be lived, not denied. I'm being serious, Harmon."

"So am I. I like the way I live."

"You don't care about anybody except yourself!"

"That's right. When you lose everything, that's all you have left; yourself."

He got up and went over to the window. He stared into the vast emptiness of the beyond. "But at least I've still got this. No one can take this away from me." He went silent, lost in the panorama before him, the flickering lights of the distant buildings, the twinkling of the stars above and the sheer expanse of space as if God was out there, somewhere. He thought he had come so close to him tonight, so close it made him want to cry.

She came up behind him as he leant against the window. She cradled him, wrapping her arms around his chest and hugged him soothingly. She kissed him gently on his back as the sadness that was always lying there underneath came to the surface. Her kiss ameliorated it.

"Poor Harmon," she whispered.

He turned round to look at her with lugubrious eyes. "I'm stuck, Carlotta."

"I know," she said and kissed him again. She seemed to absorb all of his hurt, his anger, his resentment, and his pain.

They cradled each other and rocked gently to an unheard music, eventually letting go.

"Come on," she said. "It's getting late and I must go."

"Don't go, please. Stay with me just for a short while."

"No, I'm must go. I've got a busy day ahead of me."

She glided over to her clothes and started getting dressed. It was a shame to see that splendid body of hers being covered up, he thought, as he watched her put on her dress. Every facet of it was indelibly etched in his memory.

"Aren't you going to ask me if I've decided to take this job or not?"

She looked at him and smiled as she smoothed her dress down and put some bounce back into her hair. "I don't need to." She reached into her handbag and handed him some tickets.

"What's this?"

"It's your shuttle flight and reservation tickets."

"Shuttle to where?"

"Los Angeles. You're leaving first thing this morning."

"Am I? And I suppose this is part of your little plan?"

"Yes." She opened her compact and attended to her make-up.

"You knew, didn't you, that I was going to have to say yes, because I've got no choice. How did you know?"

"I told you, I make it my business to know." She smiled as she painted her lips. "Anyway, you're right. You have no choice, and what with the money I'm offering you'd be a fool to turn it down. Just think, Harmon. You'll be able to have a nice long retreat afterwards."

"If I find this drug of yours," he said fuming, annoyed with the woman for her resourcefulness. "I'm still not convinced it exists."

"It exists. I thought I demonstrated that in bed. Where else do you think I get all that energy? It may take a bit longer than normal, I expect that. It isn't going to be easy, that's why I've booked you into the Chateau Marmont for a week."

"The Chateau Marmont? Isn't that where all them actors die?"

"Nobody dies there anymore."

"No, they just go into comas."

"Now you're being facetious. Pass me my shoes." He passed them to her with a grave look on his face. "Besides, it's recently been refurbished. It's got a swimming pool, gymnasium, keep fit classes, all those things that normal people engage themselves in," she said with a smirk. "There's even

an extended garage round the back. I've reserved a room for you in the front. You'll like it there. It'll suit you 'down to the ground.' Think of it as a holiday since I'm paying."

"Thanks," he remarked sardonically. "Why Los Angeles anyway?"

"That's where Alex lives. Nobody knows exactly where. He used to have a mansion on Mulholland Drive, but moved out when all the stars started moving in."

"But he may not be anywhere near LA. They could have shipped him out of the country."

"No, knowing him, they wouldn't have removed him too far. Alex hates to be inconvenienced."

"Do you realise how big LA is? How am I going to find him there? I need a lead, a photo, an old piece of his clothing, anything."

"Don't worry, Harmon. I've taken care of everything. When you get to the hotel I want you to contact this number," she said, handing him a piece of paper. "It's a man by the name of Mosalla."

"Who?"

"Mosalla. That's his magical name. Nobody knows his real name, but he was an old friend of Alex's, one of his colleagues. I want you to go and talk to him, find out what you can. He knows all about the drug as he was with him at the time he was working on it. I want you to follow up all the leads he gives you, however irrelevant they may seem at the time. I don't believe Alex could have fooled everybody. He must have blundered somewhere. I want you to report back to me each evening. Only contact me in the evening as I'm usually busy during the day. Here's my card."

She gave him her card, white with gold lettering. As he suspected, the contact number was Upper East Side.

"I'll speak to Mosalla in advance and tell him you're going to be in touch. He's an old friend of mine. He said if ever I needed any help he would accommodate me. I'm sure you'll both get on. You're just like him."

"Oh? And what does that mean?"

"Old fashioned." She smiled and gave him a quick kiss as she got ready to leave. "I've deposited $50,000 in your account at the hotel. Just notify me if you need anymore. I can arrange a transfer the same hour. Oh, and I've also booked you a car. I know you don't drive normally, so I've laid on a new type for you. You'll find it practical and easy to use. You can pick it up at the airport."

"Well, you've certainly thought of everything. Been planning this long?"

"I couldn't finalise anything until you got back. That's about it, I think."

"West Hollywood, hey?"

"Yes, you'll find it very interesting."

"I'm sure I will," he replied with sarcasm.

"Oh, come on. Cheer up. Think of the benefits. When you get back with what I want, we can celebrate. We can go out for a meal."

"I know just the place."

"No, Harmon, not there. Somewhere decent next time. I suggest you get some sleep. I don't want you missing that shuttle."

How typical of a woman, to wake a man up and tell him that he's got to go to sleep again.

"I hate flying," he told her.

"I know you do," she responded with a wicked gleam in her eye. She gave him one last kiss on the cheek. "Good luck." And headed for the door.

"Thanks. I'm going to need it."

As she opened his door she turned round to see him standing there still naked, waving his tickets in his hands like a lost kid at a bus stop.

"Oh, Harmon, one last thing before I go," she said as she held the door open. "I hate the smell of tobacco. Give up smoking and grow up." And

she was out the door, closing it behind her without even saying goodbye.

"BITCH!" he shouted. "I don't want to go to LA! I hate LA!" he screamed and threw the tickets at the door.

The door opened, she poked her head round and simply said, "I know you do," smiled, and was gone for good.

He stormed into the kitchen and found the only remedy for a situation like this waiting for him in his refrigerator, cold and inviting. He pulled it out and opened it up and swallowed one big gulp straight down, and another, and another, determined to drink himself into oblivion. It would be the perfect excuse. All he had to do was contact her tomorrow night and tell her he never made it, overslept; too many beers, missed the shuttle. What a pity. He charged back into the room with a fresh bottle in hand and carried on berating the door.

"I'm not going to LA, so there!"

Capri decided to drink to that, got himself another beer, lit up another cigarette and drank himself into oblivion.

THE METAMACHINE

'In the next quantum jump of information technology, computers will be obsolete. So too will be their connections; no cables, no phonelines, no trunking or wires. Simply through satellites transmitting and receiving info internationally man will communicate with man through metamachines* once info-space becomes global.'

* Nanotechnological devices implanted directly in the neocortex. They are currently used for computer input, but here meant specifically for global info-access.

Will A. Robertson,
Trans-cerebral Hemispheres

—11—
THE APOTHEOSIS OF DESIRE

The Phallus Boys were back in the club, having practically overdosed on death. They were still high, still knocked out by all the hard work they had put in tonight. Now it was time to settle down, unwind and relax, just let everything go and slip into the cool side of reality.

They kind of reminded people of twins, one light, the other dark, one yang, the other yin, a complementary duality forming a whole. Yet like that symbol of the old wise men, what is dark also possesses within itself a portion of light, and what is light also possesses within itself a portion of dark, or so they said. Landis disagreed. You're either black or white, there ain't nothing in-between, and grey was a shit colour anyway.

He got to thinking about the old days, when he first started coming here. There were only a few shacks then. It was a tiny shanty town and this club was the only place to be. The town built up around it for it was the only building in the area that was made out of real bricks and cement with the shacks, like layers of foil, wrapping themselves round the central hub. The club was the centre around which the whole town revolved geographically and socially, an oriental mandala; all the alleys led from the centre like spokes in a wheel. The club was the axle in the wheel, the cube in the circle.

He had seen this town grow into a labyrinth, the intricate maze that it was today. But soon it would change. Chan's old man knew that. The only thing

was, Landis hadn't the heart to tell his young friend. Besides, he wouldn't understand. And now all he wanted to do was to enjoy what was left, to appreciate the finer things in life like all that hot, wet pussy on display gyrating their stuff just for him and giving him an eyeful. There was something delicious about Asian pussy; it had a smell of its own, quite unlike any other smell he could compare it with. And he would miss that too. He would miss the patrons, all them slinky-eyed dudes, all them badass motherfuckers who made him feel at home every time he paid his respects here by gracing it with his presence. Most of them were criminals; the lowest of the low. Murderers and rapists, the sort of people he wouldn't normally associate with.

And there she was. Looking at his white bit, who was giving him the usual shit look like she always did, got him to thinking that perseverance would have him coming up inside her in no time. All he had to do was concentrate on the apotheosis of his desire and it would happen.

He pulled himself out of that strange hinterland where nostalgia meets expectation and augmented with the latter as Chan finally managed to get served. That was the only problem with this place. At four in the morning, it was the time when the club really got swinging, and soon he would have to leave. He reckoned he would miss this place too.

They hit the back of the club. Same people. Same situation. Same gratitude, which is what he expected after a hard night's work and got back to surfing.

He settled back with his friend, formed an image of his desire in his mind, saw her walking past any minute, focused and let it out of his head as he imbibed the spirit that was now finally his friend. He sighed and waited for the moment. Whilst he waited, kind of bummed out, but still content, he put his arm around his friend sitting beside him.

"Chan, you know when I get old and retire, this is where I want to be all my dying days."

"You mean that?"

"Why, sure I do. This is the only place to be. I feel like I'm in heaven."

Chan giggled. "Heaven!"

"Yes, that's right. This to me is heaven. Here there are no problems. Here we is stoned immaculate," he said, emphasising the last word.

"You need not wait. We can make it heaven now."

"No, we can't, Chan. You know we can't."

"We can. We make it eternal now."

Landis shook his head. "No. It will never happen."

"Why? I not understand. At times you come across as friend. Other times as stranger. Then you not speak your heart to me and I feel left out. I want us to be together for eternity. We good lovers."

Chan was right. They were good lovers, but only because he knew where his priority lay, what his prerogative was, and that was to be Landis' recipient. Landis gave, Chan took, and Chan always took it, taking it in deep like a woman. That was the nature of their love, of all love, for man always imparts, woman always receives and never the other way round. In a taostic universe, he surmised, that was a natural law, observable in all wildlife. There was something unnatural if the law was reversed or perverted. His masculinity perfectly complemented Chan's femininity and any usurpation of that role would not only be diabolical, but an infringement of his rights.

He looked at him, and in his opiated, lightly narcotised mind, there was a beautiful expression in Chan's face, almost a naïveté, which of course he would never take advantage of, but one that made him want to eat him at times because he was so adorable.

Landis couldn't help prevaricating over what he really had to tell him. In the end he gave up.

"Do you remember, Chan, when we were both young, when we first met and we had something that others didn't have, an intimacy that could not be attained or understood by others, and I said ignore what others say for they are ignorant?"

"Yes. I remember."

"Well, I'm kinda stoned and out of it right now, but I want to tell you

something; those were good days, and I want you to cherish them because soon..." The words wouldn't come out. "Fuck it! What I'm trying to say is we're the Boys, and we will always be the Boys. Now let's respect that."

"I do. But I want us to be together always all the time. So come with me now. We live together now."

Shit! It was getting serious. "That's not possible. You know I can't do that. I'm married, remember?"

"I not understand. You tell me you not love her. You tell me you love me."

"That's right, I do. But I can't leave her."

"You divorce her. You marry me instead."

"Oh, come on, let's not go through all that again. I have too many responsibilities to just drop her."

"I not understand why you marry her in first place."

"I keep telling you. I had to. It was part of the deal which established my name. And a man has to have a name, doesn't he? Besides, she means nothing to me."

"Then leave her!"

This was not what he wanted. All he wanted to do was chill out and forget. He hated it when Chan got like this. He was as bad as his old man at times. You could never tell him anything. He was only satisfied when he heard what he wanted to hear.

"Now don't get all tetchy on me, Chan. You know it is impossible. I would rather be with you any day, taking you to bed, and not her. You know I love you." The last words quivered as they came out the back of his throat.

"Yes, but you always say that. You not show it. You don't love me. You don't love anybody."

"That's not true. You know it isn't. We make a perfect team, don't we?"

"Yes, but you not show commitment. You always take, take, take. You

never give. My father right. My father say..."

"I don't give a shit what you're father says! I'm sick and tired of hearing about your father. Every time I see you Chan, that's all I hear. 'My father this. My father that.' Now be sensible. Lighten up and chill out, will ya? All I want to do is have a few beers, mellow out, pass the time quietly with a few pipes, and relax. But no. You won't let me even do that. How selfish can you get, Chan? Here's me. I come all the way to see you, when really I should be back at the Centre working, helping to stop this terrible disease that's killing all these people. Or with my wife tonight. But no, I'd rather be here with you. I go out of my way to come and see you, to have a good time and show how much I care for you, this is what I get, verbal abuse."

Chan went all quiet on him, sulking, with a big expression of guilt on his face. It worked every time. Landis smiled at his friend's resipiscence.

"I'm sorry, Anton."

"That's alright, Chan. I will forgive you this time."

"You will?"

"Sure, I will. Now just lighten up and smoke."

Landis was passed the pipe. He declined politely.

"You not smoke with me?" Chan asked him, concerned.

"No, I've had enough. All I want to do is have my beer whilst I think."

Both of them went quiet, locked in their own universes and Landis could feel that barrier coming up again that was somehow always there but occasionally penetrable. Now it seemed to be impervious and it only made him more isolated, cut off from these men sitting all around him who had also grown quiet as soon as Landis raised his voice. The situation wasn't comfortable either. And for once perhaps he was in the wrong place. But in this small yellow universe there was only one other person who matched the same colour of skin as his. And he was determined to sort her out before he left this morning.

He concentrated on his desire again, unsure why his evocation didn't work

the first time. She would have to walk past them as the bathroom was at the back and all chicks needed to use it every thirty minutes to powder their noses. All he had to do was fashion it clearly in his mind, load it into a simulacrum and dispatch it. He blamed the opium; that was the only reason he declined it. Opium is excellent as a soporific, but useless where anything involving the will is concerned. So he tried again, harder this time knowing he would never be able to get near her whilst she was with the boss man. It had to be here and preferably without Chan seeing. The way he was looking was like he was ready to sob his heart out, the fool. He was going to have to double its force with another affirmation and take Chan out of the picture.

He sank down into the deepest part of his being, contacted his libido, raised it, moulded an image of her around it and then let it out of his phallus as a flood of light, a phosphorescent film imbued with his desire, and imagined her walking past. He banished and came back up to the surface and smiled.

He knew it was powerful. There is always something interesting about such operations. People call them tangential effects, by-products of the operation itself. They tend to precipitate the manifestation of the desire, and that was in the form of Chan giving him a searing look. Chan sensed what he was doing. He was a sensitive type, not interested in magic at all, but he must have felt his *hekau* pass over him.

Landis smiled at him hoping it would exonerate any blame. It didn't. "What's the matter, Chan?" he asked him unctuously.

"It is her. Yes?"

"What you on about? Who?"

"Wife of boss man. You want her."

"Don't be ridiculous."

"I felt it. You do something just now."

"Now you're being fucking stupid. I haven't done anything, Chan. I'm just sitting here drinking my beer and you're accusing me of something when you know I've been sitting here all the time."

Now Chan was looking angry. "You not love me. You love her. You think only of her. She trash. She no good. I'm better than her."

"You are, Chan. You know that is true. So quit carping like that. You know I can't give myself to everyone as much as I would like to. I give myself to only you, and a few others. And they mean nothing. Anyways, you're all square on our agreement. We both allow ourselves to play around, enjoy some variety, take what's on offer and all that. No jealousy, just a good time being had by all. Remember?"

Chan was smouldering, Soon there'd be smoke coming out of his ears. Landis let him simmer down. He wasn't normally like this, couldn't understand what had come over the boy, far too immature at times.

"You definitely not love me," Chan persisted. "Never will. You lie to me."

"I've never lied to you. I've always been straight with you."

"Then why you not give wife up. Come stay with me. We be happy together. We perfect couple."

"Because I can't, that's why."

"You not being honest. All I want is answer. There is more. You not say."

Landis, feeling cornered for once in his life, was compelled to say something, anything to bluff his way out. It was his fault. He wasn't being straight with the kid, but how do you tell your best friend something that ostensibly sounds ridiculous? And the last thing he wanted was Chan laughing at him because he wouldn't believe him, nobody would. God knows, he had tried, vague subtle hints, faint intimations, and he still wasn't catching on. Landis figured it wasn't down to him anymore. There was only one person who Chan looked up to; his father. If his father was direct about it, Chan would hopefully accept his word and see the light. It would put an end to this provocation. He softened his tactic and spoke to him like a real confidant.

"Look, Chan, as much as I love you, and I mean that sincerely, I can't live with you. For reasons I'm not at liberty to say. There's only one person who can, your father. I suggest you speak to him. He knows what's going on, I

think. And he will tell you the truth. It may sound incredible when he tells you, but you look up to your father, don't you? So believe him when he tells you. Tell him I have categorically requested that he be on the level with you this time and not evasive like he usually is with his bullshit philosophy."

"Right!' He jumped to his feet agitated. Landis couldn't understand why the kid was so incensed or what was going through his head. "I go now. I speak to my father. He tell me. I not be back."

"No, Chan. Not now. Go later."

"No. I go now. Bastard!" he shouted and departed.

"Wait, Chan."

But Chan was long gone, storming off in a huff like the hot-headed little kid he was. Landis didn't understand it. He hadn't done anything wrong. But in a way, he was relieved. He had no time for puerile behaviour, especially if it was erratic like Chan's. He could be all jumpy and flighty one minute, then next down and dejected. Didn't understand people like that at all. To be a man in this world you had to be tough. Tough like Landis who made the world work his way. And the world reciprocated; she's a whore, easy to manipulate, and like one, you had to constantly maintain precedence over her. It ensured she was always proffering temptation in your path and he never turned it down. Gobbled it up and moved on afterwards, thanking Fortune for her hospitality. She looked after him. And now he was hoping she would put in an appearance. This was the opportune moment. Chan was out of the picture. Now his bit would take to the stage, any minute. All he had to do was sit tight and let the future unroll.

He turned round in his seat to see all these old guys looking at him for an explanation. He shrugged, feigned ignorance and smiled at them.

"He's a bit upset," he told them in a flat tone, and swallowed his beer as they went back to their smoking.

"Isn't life wonderful!" he started saying, knowing full well they wouldn't understand a word. "Especially when everything goes according to plan. I'm a magician, see. Did you know that? Well, I can understand a young man like my friend not telling you that. You see, the essence of magic is to

manipulate reality, make it work for you, 'cos really the world is nothing but an extension of your own being. I create this world. It only exists when I'm aware of it. Solipsism, that's called. And now that my friend has gone he no longer exists. But you know what, I used to be like him when I was his age, screwing around, taking anything my dick fancied, fucking whatever I could, being like a wild jackrabbit in my pants every time I saw some pussy walking across a street or a boy I thought was cute. I kind of found it hard to control myself, to keep myself from doing the things I used to do to those poor girls and boys, tying them up and all that. You know what? Age has kind of made me mellow out, refining my outlook on life. Yes, I do believe I have toned down. Isn't it funny what age does to a person as you get older? I am no longer the violent, reckless, lusty type I used to be. But I've still got it strong and forceful. I can outlast any man 'cos I know where Eros and Thanatos converge. I can outfuck any of you motherfuckers. I could take part in a fuckathon and out compete any of you wrinklies. I bet you can't even get it up any more, can you? Any of you? Well, I can, see. I can keep it up all night long. Yes, siree. All night long. And I can keep rutting like a stallion, like a man with priapism. No, I am Priapus. I am ithyphallic, erect and proud, virile and vigorous, potent and robust. And my mission, my secret mission, is to violate all things, to pierce the hymenal veil of that courtly courtesan. Mr Phallus is my name. I am the wild bull of heaven. I am the libidinous he-goat of the woods, Pan, with his fauns and pards. And I come down from the hills to ravish your daughters, all-devouring, all-begetting, and my nymphs and satyrs dance in dizzying confusion in this carnal jamboree, raving and ripping, raping and rending, inciting panic in young mad children, brewing up a whirlwind of lust, eating their innocence, spitting out their souls, trampling on their fears as they are caught up in this contagious, orgiastic devilry."

Landis, high on the octane of his enthusiasm, was getting into his stride. He closed his eyes, sank down, boarded a current of energy that was building up inside, demanding to be voiced. He sang a paean to Pan, singing his name like a mantra, repeating it until it escalated into a crescendo as the images started swirling in his brain and the familiar tingling sensation was in his loins and the word was taking him down, down to primal depths, down to the great chthonic catacombs of his interior being, down until he touched the bottom and found the iridescent core of himself and brought it back up to the surface in a rush of ecstasy that poured out of his mouth:

"I AM ALL-SEXUALITY," he ejaculated at his startled listeners. "The Pantheist cries aloud; Everything is God, there is nothing but God. I cry aloud; Everything is Sex, there is nothing but Sex. We both unite and cry aloud; Sex is God. God is Sex. And thus was my temple builded. I am the Act. The erogenous act of creation. I am the immortal fire that burns in your loins. I am the Risen Phallus, the Swollen Kteis. I am the current that multiplies, diversifies, finds new fields to propagate, new pastures to furrow, new flesh to penetrate. I am the New Sexuality. I am the sex-principle beyond life, nay beyond death. Free from sin. Free from restriction. I clothe about me little words that pour out of your genitals. Nymphae! Nymphae! I am loud, lewd and lascivious, a devil of a harlot, and my will is to unite with all things. Everything fornicates all around me. I am the secret eye, the loquacious eye that devours time. I am the hot blood of your veins, the sanguineous symphony that swells into a paroxysm of shrilling cries and terminates in syncopation. I am the energy which projects into matter, binding all things together. I am the twin terminals in ecstatic union for all eternity. I am the fructifying heat of your genitals, the germination of the worlds, the spermatozoon that shoots into the night and showers the world in a fountain of light. I am the primordial eye of creation which refracts time in distortion and delay. I am the double helix, ever coiling, ever revolving in my occultation. I am the atomic thrust into the void, the scarlet snare of death. I am the dynamo in the seat of power that transmutes desire into image, reflecting images back into itself, the vulva that is the magic mirror of the world. I am also the rampant phallus running amok in sidereal time in the dawn of this new equinox, this nu-ovulation.

"If my will is to take to bed any man, woman, child or beast, I take to bed any man, woman, child or beast.

"What if I copulate with another man as an expression of my love for him that you should consider me homo? What if copulate with a woman as an expression of my love for her that you should consider me hetro? What if I choose to take both to bed that you should consider me bi? All these are labels, my brothers, born of ignorance. Know then: there is no bi, there is no hetro, there is no homo, there only is sexuality. Stripped of conditioning, it stands naked, virginal, pristine, pure, uncontaminated by vice or guilt or shame or disgust, but victorious. Let then sex manifest itself as it will without preference. There is no letting up of this revelry, this cosmological

concupiscence that is eternal and gives rise to *maya*. Why diminish its power through conditioning? Is there not joy in this endless winging? soaring aloft in the abodes of immortal space? Then become all. Become Pan. Rejoice in your splendour. Rejoice in your pleasure. Rejoice in your multifarious nature. Find consolation in this eternal fornication. Transmute desire to ecstasy. Become one with the Supreme Reality. Then take to bed your menfolk, your womenfolk, your children, your beasts. Dance the naked dance of Pan! Pan! Pan! in your incarnation of flesh. Discrimination is a lie. Make no difference between any one thing or any other thing. Know them all to be one and none. That is how to become Pan, become All, become Pansexual!"

He slumped back in his chair, his startled listeners staring at him agape.

"And now I'm just bored," he told them, and finished his drink.

Out of the corner of his doped-up eyes—he didn't need to smoke their drug as he was breathing it in like fumes—he saw the apotheosis of his desire swish by in that long white dress of hers like a vestal virgin.

"Perfect timing," he shouted jubilantly. There was no Chan. No boss man. It was ideal.

He shook off his derangement and staggered to his feet. He launched himself towards the bathroom door and realised he was more drunk than he thought he was as he veered this way and that. He lurched against the side and blocked the entrance. In this way she wouldn't be able to pass him without having to confront him.

She came out. He stopped her. She looked him straight in the eye. He smiled and gave her a charming look. She defied it but stood her ground.

"You know," he told her, slurring his words, "I've been thinking lately every time I come in here and I see you and I can't help wondering something. It's been kind of bugging me and I would be obliged if you could help me out."

She didn't acknowledge him, only showing signs of being unimpressed. She wrapped her arms around her chest tightly and continued glaring. Perhaps his technique wasn't up to scratch. He decided to be more courteous as she

gave him that lovely shit look of hers.

Now that he could see her close up, she was far more attractive than he originally judged. Or was it the drink? The only thing is, she cheapened herself by wearing too much make-up when there was no need for it. She had distinctive features which were naturally pleasant in themselves without having to be artificially enhanced. Her eyes were amber in the dull red lighting; it also made her auburn hair take on a burning shade like a flaming bush. Her mouth was perfect, smoothly shaped with its blowjob lips. And there was a fairly attractive body to match the face as well. Her breasts were small and pert, but that didn't bother him. Later he would get them out and have a closer look. Her figure was slim and curvaceous with barely a bulge in her stomach and wide hips that rounded in a heart-shaped ass.

But before he could continue his monologue, she butted in.

"You like what you see?" she demanded, realising that she was being examined.

"It's very nice."

"Well it isn't for you!" She tried to brush past him.

He reasserted himself. "Now, wait a minute lady. I haven't finished. Now don't get me wrong. I'm not like all the others."

"Oh? Then what are you like?"

He laughed. "I like a woman with style and you have lots of it."

"I don't give a fuck what you like. Now, will you move out of my way?"

"Whoa, pretty lady. I think we're getting off on the wrong foot here. You see, I'm intrigued, you being the only white girl in a Sino-joint like this, and me being the only white guy. Well, that kind of means we have something in common."

"No we don't. Now move!"

Something definitely wasn't right here. What was wrong with her? He was being generous in offering himself to her and she was taking it as an insult.

Normally, they would writhe and get hot as soon as he twisted his tongue round them, but this one wasn't going to have it. That made him more determined. He tried again and blamed Chan for ruining his technique.

"I was hoping we could be adults about this. You know, sit down, have a couple of drinks, a quiet talk."

"No thanks. I don't go for men who are into little boys."

"That's cute. Then what do you go for?"

"Do I have to repeat myself? Or are you going to let me pass? Because if you don't, I will call my..."

"Your husband? Is that it? That's another thing I don't understand which has been bugging me as well. And I would be honoured, an intelligent woman like yourself, if you could kindly explain to me; what are you doing with a slimeball like him?"

With that, she slapped him hard in the face. It was enough to shock him. He only asked her a sensible question. But before he could do anything about it, she had marched back into the main room. He let out a laugh, loud enough for her to hear.

"Farewell, my concubine," he shouted after her.

She was one hell of a woman, just how he liked them, playing hard to get and presenting him a challenge. This was going to be a contest, one he would enjoy and eventually win, for there was no way she was going to be able to defend herself against him once he got his velvet touch into gear. Tonight wasn't the night. It had been fucked-up by Chan getting him all riled up. It was definitely his fault. He would sort the boy out tomorrow, put his head right on his shoulders and trust to his old man to do the same. And her? She was cute. He liked them when they had guts. He'd sort her out tomorrow too, and decided it was time to quit. He slipped quietly out the back.

THE TWINS

'As there is light, so there is darkness, and these two warring antipoles are universally found yet no more closer to their genuine origin than in the gnosis of Khem, in the primal twins of Horus and Set who, theriomorphically, personified this dual antagonism as the Positive and Negative in constant battle for superiority over one another, but however were united in their biune form as Set-Hor, the supreme symbol of opposition reconciled, one body yet possessing two sides, and one would be well advised to heed the warning; the one cannot be known without the other.'

Kelly Grantham,
Cults of the Khaut

—12—
THE NECTAR AND THE VENOM

The mind can be equated to a sheet of glass with a filmic surface acting like celluloid waiting to be impregnated with new images. These images are memories. Out of these memories are formed our worldview.

Imagine this sheet of glass as a gigantic jigsaw puzzle all neatly slotted into place, perfect and resilient, very robust with a high level of tolerance to exertion, able to sustain a certain amount of force. It would take something powerful like a sledgehammer to smash this sheet of glass and shatter one's worldview. The result is fragmentation.

If that should happen, how would you put it back together? Well, like a jigsaw, you would start off with the corners as they are the easiest pieces to put in place first. Then the edges, so at least the borders are intact. But what about the rest? All those pieces in the middle are missing and need to be slotted back into place. There is no picture on the box to help you; that was lost years ago. So how would you go about it? Well, you would have to examine each one in turn, then guess where it fitted, and that would probably take an inordinately long time. Or you could give up and quit.

* * * * *

I decide to leave. My patience is running out. I'm hungry. I want some food. I am walking down Fifth Avenue trying to get something to eat. The stores and cafes are all closed so I head due south to a taco bar and find it is closed too. I look all around me and notice everything is shut. The people

surrounding me don't seem to notice and continue their daily grind. They walk through me as usual. I notice I don't cast a reflection in a store's window. I drift aimlessly, my stomach griping, and find people are thin on the ground. The sky is overcast but there aren't any clouds. It's very dark for this time of the day. Everything's grey, flat, uninteresting, no lights on anywhere, no sound either, like I'm watching an old black and white movie without a soundtrack. The print is badly worn out too. The scene isn't peaceful. It's eerie, strange. Everyone has deserted New York, a mass exodus with only me left. There's not a soul in sight and I continue to walk through empty streets looking for somebody as if I have lost a friend. I don't know his name. I am now standing on the embankment of the Hudson River. I am watching it. It doesn't flow. There is no movement. Nothing stirs. I am all alone.

* * * * *

"Mr Capri?" The stewardess nudged him gently. "Mr Capri?"

He stirred himself awake and rubbed his eyes to see her gently smiling face beaming down at him.

"Sorry to wake you, sir, but we will be arriving in five minutes. Please don't forget your luggage."

"Thanks, I won't."

"Have a nice day."

He watched her walk back down the aisle and shook the dream out of his head. It didn't augur well and left him feeling apprehensive with a frisson that cut through him like ice, inchoate with probably more to follow if the bitch hadn't woken him up. If he was really up to it he would have been inclined to examine it in greater detail. His splitting headache forbade it and all he wanted to do was go back to sleep, pretend he was tucked up in bed and this wasn't really happening.

So why was he going to LA? That's what he was still trying to figure out. His oblivion mission failed; his endless supply of drink ran out, and not even sleep would intervene and impart that inviting kiss. So he looked to Angel, always Angel, at times of crisis, and they communed for awhile. Angel was being monosyllabic for a change, kept repeating 'Go' without equivocation. It annoyed Capri. He wanted him to be misleading like he

invariably was, to say something he had no chance of interpreting. That would have been a good excuse not to follow his advice and save him from going to a destination he knew in advance he loathed. Nor would Angel respond to his repeated pleas of 'Why?'

Besides, he didn't have a dollar at home, and if Carlotta had deposited any money in his hotel account as she said, then he could continue his mission at her expense. That was his excuse, a lame one admittedly, yet fate was compelling him onwards, or so he felt, determined to mock him by forcing him to search for a man and a drug which were bound to be elusive, imponderables he had no hope of finding, realistically speaking. This assignment had failure written all over it.

The shuttle glided into LA Central, touching down smoothly, so smoothly Capri even forgot his dislike for flying. He fetched his one bag he brought with him and exited to find the sun out in all of its splendour, the warm air greeting him, the smog clearly visible in the distance, all hazy reminding him of a mirage. He shivered in the hot sun as he was directed towards the terminal and conveyed down to the checkout point. He found the car rental desk further down and waited for the seated blonde to acknowledge him.

"Hi," she greeted him affectedly. "How may I help you, sir?"

"The name's Capri. You have a reservation for me."

"Let me check for you, sir." She inputted his name. "Yes we do, sir. A Stratocruiser, a brand new model. All I need is your ID card."

He presented his card and watched her as she zipped it and handed it back to him with a smile.

"It's outside, sir. If you follow me I'll take you to it."

She came round from behind the desk and led him down past the lounge. Capri followed, eyes glued to her tidy ass, extra tight skirt and long pins. Perhaps LA could become quite agreeable after all. He was enjoying the view until she led him outside and stopped in front of a car that was obviously his.

He gulped.

The blonde turned round to face him with a plastic smile, the big black thing behind her looking like a beast waiting to be let out of its cage.

There was no way he was going to be able to get on with one of these newfangled things, he knew it in his bones as he stopped in his tracks.

"You ever driven one of these before?" He shook his head. "Well it shouldn't be a problem. They're practical and easy to use," she said, reminding him of Carlotta's exact words. "They're designed to be versatile, to suit all driving tastes and abilities for whatever type of terrain, especially freeways for which they're superb. Believe me, I've driven one, and boy, do they go. You can get 250 out of them easy and that's without even touching the floor. Of course, we don't recommend you try and advise all our drivers to keep within the speed limits. Okay? And they're fully automatic; they drive themselves. You can choose auto or manual. Most people opt for the latter as they prefer to stay in control. Understood?" He nodded like a school kid attending his first lesson. "If you come round the other side I'll show you how to access it." He did as he was told. "All you need is your ID card. Just swipe it in the slot, and I'll instruct you how to program it."

He swiped it and stood back with reservations as the door lifted up.

"Well?" she asked him curiously. "Aren't you going to climb in, sir?"

"Yes—uh—of course."

He hesitated, inserted himself inside, threw his bag on the back seat and examined all the gadgetry disconcertingly. He cursed Carlotta—she had done it on purpose, of course—and waited for his instructor to continue.

"Sitting comfortably?" The school kid nodded. "Good. Now all you have to do is insert your card in the slot there, input your PIN and away you go. It's a simple as that. This is a luxury model, sir, so you should find that it suits all your requirements. It has sensurround sound, air-conditioning, full computer facilities on board with direct access to the net. Plus phone links. All calls are charged direct to your bank account. We suggest keeping them short, especially this time of day as they're excessive. There's a holo in the dashboard with access to all channels, GPS, and, of course, a simulated passenger service for drivers travelling alone."

What? He wanted to ask her to elaborate on that last point but she was now filling his head with details he considered inessential for driving. All he wanted to do was drive the bloody thing.

"That's about it. Any other questions, sir?"

"Yes. Could you just explain that bit about ... a passenger service?"

"Why, sure. It has an in-built passenger service simulator. Most solos find they like to be occupied with something when they're driving, especially if they're out on long roads and travelling at night. They feel more secure. It's been demonstrated statistically that road rage and car-jackings have been reduced since the introduction of the service. These cars are safer, and if you're on business, sir, I suggest you make maximum use of it. All tastes are catered for; hetro, homo, male, female, etc. Select your preferences when you log in. If you need any help press F1 on the screen. Anything else?"

He shook his head, and still didn't have a clue. "That'll be all, thanks."

"Good. If you treat her right, she'll look after you. Have a nice day."

He watched her through his open door slide back into the building.

He entered his PIN. The soft hum of an electric motor kicked into action. A holo came up and filled the windscreen displaying a large sign in bold lettering; PLEASE ENTER OPTIONS NOW. Beneath it were two bands of boxes, each one imprinted with a symbol. He scanned them ignorantly, unsure what they represented and wished he was back in New York already. He scratched his head. Some of them had unusual designs or pictures of faces (male and female—the simulated passenger service?), others had letters, two being an 'A' and an 'M' (Auto and Manual?). He pressed 'M' and gripped the steering wheel. Nothing happened. Not deterred, he figured that you probably had to press several of them beforehand to program it, wishing that there was an instruction manual available. He pressed the female face, white, and a few others. Nothing. The school kid pressed a few more. Nothing. Fuck! He gave up in despair, hit F1 instead. The menu flicked through all the significations of the boxes without giving him a chance to stop and read them. Then he noticed out of the open door some people were watching him. He ignored them and persevered.

Five minutes later he felt conversant enough to press the 'start' button.

'WELCOME ABOARD, MR CAPRI.' The voice was cold, metallic, convincingly in the tones of a female. 'WE HOPE YOU HAVE A PLEASANT JOURNEY WITH US. DO YOU REQUIRE FULL EXTERIORISATION?'

"Pardon?"

'IF YOU HAVE A HEARING DISABILITY, PLEASE ADJUST THE VOLUME CONTROL.'

Now he was getting impatient. "I am not deaf! All I want to do is drive. Do you hear me?" he shouted.

'THERE IS NOTHING DEFECTIVE WITH MY AURAL MONITOR. I CAN HEAR YOU PERFECTLY ADEQUATELY. SHOUTING IS NOT NECESSARY. I REPEAT; DO YOU REQUIRE FULL EXTERIORISATION?'

He cursed under his breath, feeling ridiculous talking to a computer, let alone an insolent one. His head was throbbing badly as he tried to work out what the hell exteriorisation meant in this context. He capitulated and shouted "Yes!" to get the thing moving. Then he panicked as he watched the holo swiftly disappear back into the dashboard. Everything went dead. He wanted to cry. More nosey passers-by were watching him. He smiled at them politely hoping they'd go away when he heard this peculiar sound and saw a flash of light coming out of the dashboard and project into the passenger seat. He gulped and in astonishment watched this thing appear out of a cloud of electric light; it was a holo of a female. He looked at it in disbelief as it said 'HI.' He felt obliged to respond, "Hello," and waited.

'THANKS FOR CHOOSING THE 21C STRATOCRUISER. I AM THE LATEST LINE OF SIMULATIONS AVAILABLE IN THIS UNIQUE RANGE OF MODELS WITH 777 PERMUTATIONS. I CAN CATER FOR ALL TASTES...' she was saying, her mouth opening and closing in perfect synch with the voice coming from the speakers.

Capri shook his sore head as the spiel continued. Whatever happened to real cars, he wondered, as more people were now watching him. He then realised that he must have been sitting in the car for at least fifteen minutes and hadn't moved an inch.

'THIS IS THE FULL RANGE OF OUR EXAMPLES TO CHOOSE...'

Now it was running through all the additional choices. He watched it go through the entire spectrum of age ranges, a full wardrobe suitable for all climates, hair colours, body sizes and builds, racial types, etc., whilst he groaned and waited for it to finish. Finally it did. Now perhaps he could leave as more and more onlookers were gathering, making him feel stupid.

'PLEASE STATE YOUR PREFERENCES NOW.'

"Look, all I want to do drive."

'YOU HAVE NOT SELECTED YET.'

"I don't give a shit! All I want to do is drive," he repeated.

'WOULD YOU LIKE TO MAINTAIN PRESENT OPTIONS?'

"Yes, save bloody options and get me out of here."

'IS THIS PRESENT STATE ACCEPTABLE?'

"Yes. It's fine."

'GOOD. WE AIM TO PLEASE ALL OUR USERS. DO YOU HAVE ANY QUESTIONS BEFORE WE PROCEED?'

"Yes," he sobbed.

The holo turned her head 90° to look in his direction. The eyes looked straight through him as if he wasn't there. It was a most unsettling experience, exactly the same as in his dream.

'YOU HAVE A QUESTION?'

"How do I get this thing to move?" he asked it, frustrated.

'YOU OPTED FOR MANUAL.'

"I know I opted for manual. But the strange thing is, this car doesn't want to move. See, every time I do this," he said, pressing the accelerator right down, "nothing happens. Now, even in a normal car the engine should be revving. All I want to do is drive the bloody thing, that is what a car is for."

'I KNOW IT IS.'

"Then why is nothing happening?" he shouted.

'NOTHING WILL HAPPEN UNTIL YOU ENCRYPT.'

"Jesus!" he shouted. His raised voice drew more onlookers. "What the hell does that mean?" he asked, impatiently.

'IT IS SHORT FOR ENCRYPTION, MR CAPRI.'

"Okay, it's short for encryption," he said, calming himself down. "Now what does encryption do?"

'IT ALLOWS A USER TO ENCODE HIS OWN SPECIFICATIONS TO PREVENT POSSIBLE THEFT.'

"I don't believe this," he told it. "This is a goddamned car. All I want to do is drive. I've got people giving me funny looks as they walk by. I am feeling like a right asshole. Just do whatever you have to do to get this thing moving, please," he begged.

'IT IS EASIER TO ENCRYPT BY SAVING ALL PRE-SET OPTIONS. WOULD YOU LIKE ME TO DO THAT FOR YOU?'

"Yes!" he shouted, seriously losing his patience. Now it was going through all the options that were being saved. He couldn't believe it and sank deep into the seat hoping nobody could see him, despite the fact that the door was still open which he didn't know how to close.

'LASTLY, DO YOU REQUIRE VOICE ACTIVATED COMMANDS?'

He shouted affirmative to speed things up and gripped the steering wheel all set for action until it came back online.

'DO YOU REQUIRE PERSONAL NAME TERMS? WE HAVE A FULL RANGE TO CHOOSE FROM, RUNNING FROM A TO Z. YOU CAN....'

"Oh, for fuck's sake! This is impossible."

He jumped out of the car, turned round, was just about to boot it when he saw a big circle of faces stretching right round the block and each one with a pair of eyes focused on him, including a pair belonging to the blonde who had come outside to see what all the brouhaha was about. She was giving him a curious look, wondering why he hadn't left yet. Realising he was making a spectacle of himself, he quickly jumped back into the car and pleaded desperately with the computer. The monotonous voice was still rambling through girls' names. He pleaded for it to stop.

'YOU HAVE OPTED FOR CINDY. WOULD YOU LIKE TO SAVE THIS OPTION?'

"Yes. Just get me out of here."

There was no response. Now it wasn't talking to him.

"Hello? Is there anybody there?" He brushed his hand through the holo; it went straight through, sending a chill up his spine. He then looked round at all the bemused expressions of his spectators. He smiled nervously and pretended he knew what he was doing in the hope they would go away. Some kid clutching a motor-board shouted at him to press F1. It only made him feel more incompetent.

"I've already pressed F1," he shouted back. The circle of onlookers was growing, including the blonde who was now standing next to him.

"Do you need any help, sir?" she asked him, concerned.

"No, it's alright. I know what I'm doing."

"You sure you don't need any help? You've been here for half an hour."

"No. I'll be out of here in a minute."

With relief, he watched her go back inside. He hesitated for a second or two and rejected the idea of walking.

'STILL WAITING FOR OPTION NAME,' the computer reminded him.

"Option name?" he queried. "Cindy? Right?"

'CORRECT, MR CAPRI.'

"Cindy, can we go now?"

'YOUR DOOR IS STILL OPEN, MR CAPRI. WE CANNOT MOVE UNTIL YOU CLOSE IT.'

"I know my door is open," he told it, condescendingly. He reached up for the non-existent handle and felt even more stupid. "Cindy, how do I close the door?"

'YOU OPTED FOR VOICE-ACTIVATED COMMANDS.'

"I know I did. So what do I do to close the door?"

'YOU SAY "DOOR CLOSE,"' Cindy said, looking at him mechanically.

"Door close," he commanded, surprised to see the door finally come down and lock him in. The car gradually rose, lifting off its spheres and hovered. "Now what do I do?"

'YOU PRESS THE ACCELERATOR.'

He did, gently. The car inched forwards. He worked it out. It had taken him precisely forty minutes to get it to move. He turned the steering wheel full. The car rotated 180°. He pressed the accelerator again and headed for the exit as all of his spectators applauded and cheered. He waved to them and proudly drove on as the colour in his face returned to normal.

"Cindy?"

'YES?'

"How do I get to Chateau Marmont hotel from here?"

She gave him instructions, suggesting he head for the San Diego freeway northward-bound only to find that once he was on it all of the lanes were blocked, and no sooner had he got used to the car, he was slowing down until he eventually grounded to a halt.

Cindy was telling him all about the traffic congestion in LA, how it had been rising to unprecedented levels and, despite the additional two lanes either side opened 5 years ago, congestion was still a problem. He sighed as he was told he had joined a fifteen mile tail-back. What was the point of having a super deluxe car like this when you couldn't even drive the bloody thing? he asked himself, and reckoned his car should be scrapped and the manufacturers go back to the drawing board, design one that could fly.

"It is always like this in LA, Cindy?"

'UNFORTUNATELY, YES. IS THIS YOUR FIRST TIME IN LA, MR CAPRI?'

"Yes, and definitely my last."

'DO YOU REQUIRE A FULL TOURIST PACKAGE?'

"No thanks, Cindy."

'ARE YOU HERE ON BUSINESS, MR CAPRI?'

He looked at her, thinking if only she could put some emotion into her voice it would be a great improvement. She sounded cold and dead, the question perfunctory and unconcerned. "You could say that."

'WE CAN CATER FOR ALL BUSINESS ENQUIRIES; BANKING TIMES, CHARGES, CASH FACILITIES, TRANSFERS, CURRENCY EXCHANGES...'

"No, it's quite alright, Cindy. Thanks, anyway. All I want to do is get to the hotel, if I get there."

He was still crawling along.

'THE CARS 2.5 KMS AHEAD OF US ARE NOW MOVING. I ESTIMATE YOU WILL BE ABLE TO RESUME TRAVELLING IN 5 MINUTES.'

He sighed and let go of the wheel as he halted again. At least he couldn't complain about the weather; the sun was beating down and it was getting hot and claustrophobic inside. He loosened his tie and got comfortable.

"Cindy, is it all air-conditioning in here or can I open these windows?"

'THE WINDOWS ARE FULLY OPERATIONAL. THE ONBOARD TEMPERATURE CURRENTLY STANDS AT 28°C. EXTERNAL TEMPERATURE 24°C.'

"In that case, windows open."

The windows slid down, bringing with it a quaff of stale sea air spiced heavily with fumes. It stank. He was far from impressed with the smell.

"Jesus. Does it always smell like this, Cindy?"

'LA IS CURRENTLY EXPERIENCING A VERY HIGH LEVEL OF POLLUTION. THIS HAS BEEN PRECIPITATED BY OVER-VEHICULAR USE. IT IS NOW BEING ADDRESSED WITH A VIEW TO REDUCING THE LEVELS OF CARBON MONOXIDE BY THE INTRODUCTION OF NEW VEHICLES LIKE THIS ONE WHICH ARE ENVIRONMENTALLY FRIENDLY.'

"Well, it doesn't seem to be working."

'ON THE CONTRARY, SINCE THE INTRODUCTION OF THE PROTOTYPES 3 YEARS AGO, POLLUTION LEVELS HAVE FALLEN DRAMATICALLY. ONCE ALL DRIVERS CHANGE OVER TO THESE VEHICLES, FULL DETOX SHOULD OCCUR WITHIN 12 YEARS.'

"Really," he said, disbelieving. Capri yawned, reached into his pocket, pulled out his last cigarette, lit it up and threw the empty packet out the window.

'WARNING. SMOKING IS A HIGH-RISK FACTOR. WE ALSO ADVISE USERS TO REFRAIN FROM SMOKING WHEN DRIVING AS IT IS DISTRACTING.'

He ignored her and carried on puffing away. No computer was going to dictate to him. The cars in front were now slowly shuffling forwards.

'CONGESTION IS CLEARING. YOU MAY NOW PROCEED.'

"Thank you, Cindy. I can see for myself."

He sat up and hit the accelerator. The car shunted and hummed along steadily.

"Well, Cindy," he said, as he finished his cigarette and threw it out the window, "what are you doing tonight?"

She turned round and looked in his direction. 'TONIGHT?'

"It was a joke, Cindy. Forget it."

Someone please take me back to the real world, he pleaded, and drove on.

At last he reached his hotel. He pulled in and parked his car round the back.

"It's been nice travelling with you, Cindy," he told her and cut the motor.

'WE AIM TO PLEASE,' she repeated, as if she only had one program. He watched her fizzle out and disappear. He would never get used to that.

He made his way to the lobby and asked the clerk at the desk about his room. He took his card, swiped it and informed him his room was one hundred and eleven. He declined any assistance and made his own way to the elevator, his key in hand. As soon as he walked into the room he was immediately struck by the colour of the decor. It was a rich, deep red, just like Carlotta's dress. The significance didn't go unnoticed.

He dropped his bag on the bed and threw off his jacket, whacked out by a journey that should have taken a quarter of the time. He sat down by the televid next to the bed and inserted his card. He televied Mosalla. A blank face appeared, presumably the butler by the way he answered. Mosalla was currently engaged but had made an appointment for him to visit at twelve. He confirmed his ETA and logged the address, a place in Brentwood, just off Sunset Boulevard.

He had a quick invigorating shower and walked back naked into his room, went over to the windows, opened them wide and stepped out onto the small balcony. All he could see was a relentless row of traffic, cars jammed bumper to bumper. He dreaded going back out there again.

He got changed into his dark charcoal suit and tie and made his way to the lobby. He checked the ATM to find Carlotta was true to her word. She had

deposited 50,000 in his account. Good girl, he thought, and withdrew a couple of grand, bought 200 cigarettes from the bar and left.

Two minutes later he was climbing into his car, inserting his card, punching in his PIN and pressing 'start,' when suddenly Cindy flashed into the passenger seat again. He practically jumped out of his skin. He'd never get use to that either.

"I need directions for Brentwood, Cindy. Can you give me a route without any other cars on the road?"

'I AM AFRAID THAT IS IMPOSSIBLE.'

"I know it is, Cindy. I wasn't being serious."

She got him to go west on Sunset, through Beverly Hills again and some other conurbations equally unimpressive. Then past Bel-Air and wound his way round the prestigious facade of the Country Club and other ghastly places till he hit Brentwood. He exited the boulevard and turned down Renways Pass, a narrow road. It took him up some hills. Now he could look over the lower lying lands, all trees and grass and other green things people don't appreciate. He hit the accelerator and kicked up ghosts from the dusty road.

He reached Mosalla's estate, all fenced off, a white old style mansion up the hill barely visible from the gates. Capri wasn't surprised to see a coat of arms on them either. He must be old fashioned, as Carlotta said. He announced his arrival in the intercom and waited for the gates. They hummed open. He drove up the long drive and could see the house more clearly; a Victorian rendition, gabled-windows, tall carved columns in the portico at the front and a large arched doorway with a set of elaborate steps leading to the door. It reminded him of England; he was impressed, but it was still a fake.

He pulled up outside and huffed his way up the steps. The butler opened the door with a bland expression as if he had a mask for a face, his eyes unfocused, said a few words in a slow and deliberate manner and ushered him into the hallway like an automaton. He left him there to seek his master. Capri only hoped his host possessed more vitality. Judging by the slickness of the white interior, he certainly had taste, if not style. Tall marble colonnades by the stairwell, a domed elevated ceiling from which pended an ornate, staggeringly designed chandelier which formed the centrepiece of

the hallway, a semicircle of pedestals with marble busts of past masters looking very ancient and fragile, towering walls with gilt-framed oil paintings, all of them, he noticed, originals; works by Goya, Delacroix, Van Gogh, etc., and a long passageway leading to a set of French windows at the back with the obligatory swimming pool beyond. This was more to his liking. He could almost feel a certain reverence for the man as few rich people had taste, especially when it came to art.

The butler reappeared from the side room and ushered him in to what turned out to be a library; oak panelling, highly varnished shelving, one long wall of books with a dazzling array of coloured spines, a large perfectly square wooden floor half covered by a prepossessing Persian rug, the size of which he had never seen before. Situated in the middle of this was a large mahogany desk with a very large man sitting behind it taking a call, obviously Mosalla. In fact, everything about the man was large, not only his fine house, but even his portly frame and head.

Capri smiled politely as the man acknowledged him and continued his call. He gave a brief flurry of a wave. He judged him to be late sixties, early seventies, with thin grey hair receding to reveal a massive shiny dome. As he talked, his drooping, flabby jowls of red blotchy skin quivered, bushy eyebrows that converged in the middle and cold grey eyes with a squint in one of them. They avoided Capri. He took it as a hint and started browsing through some of the interesting looking titles on offer. Row upon row of books. Most of them were antiquarian, in their original leather bindings, and a majority were either Greek or Latin. The few English titles he could see were ostensibly about one subject; Mosalla had a deep-seated interest in the occult. He pulled out one book, flicked through the exordium to find it was in Old English. He checked the publishing date; as he suspected, it was a first edition (in immaculate condition), and so were the rest, he guessed. He restored it to its rightful place and was about to check another one when he heard the old style telephone click. He turned round to be met by Mosalla striding towards him like a rhinoceros. Capri had a worrying premonition the man had no control over his volition and he wouldn't be able to stop before crashing into him. Luckily, he stopped and stretched out his hand. It was massive like the rest of him.

"You're Capri, right?" shaking his hand vigorously.

"Yes," he responded, glad to get his hand back. It was now sticky and covered in sweat.

"Been expecting you. Got a call from Carlotta. Said you'd be coming over. Something to do with Crome. Right?"

Mosalla spoke like a giant or an actor who was too big for the stage, his voice literally booming.

"Yes, that's right. Carlotta suggested that I should get in touch with you. Said you maybe able to help me with a few things."

"Sure. Glad to help. Carlotta and I go back a long way. Do you read, Mr Capri?" he asked him, gesturing to all the books.

"Yes I do. I couldn't help noticing what a magnificent collection you have."

"Sure is. They all used to belong to a Catholic priest, an Englishman like yourself. He was an expert on witchcraft and vampirism, wrote some excellent books on the subject himself, as a matter of fact. I purchased his whole library when he died in the fifties. Carlotta tells me you're interested in that sort of thing."

"You could say that."

"It's still one of my interests. Of course, I haven't had time to read all of them," he laughed. "Guess I never will. When you get to my age, your brain kinda starts slowing down and right now it takes me twice as long. Don't have too much time to either. Far too busy dealing with legal disputes."

"I appreciate you are a busy man, Mr Mosalla."

"No. It's Mosalla. That's it. There ain't no mister in it."

"Oh, I see. Well, Mosalla, as I said, I appreciate you're busy, and I'd be grateful for any time you can spare me."

"Not at all. Only too happy to help an old friend of mine. Would you care for a drink first, Mr Capri, before we get started?"

"That'd be great."

Mosalla showed him out and across the hallway into the room opposite, equally as large with plenty of his wealth on display. In the centre of the

room were four huge black leather sofas facing each other so as to form a square in the middle of which was a rather attractive low table in ebony. It reminded him of a caryatid with its carved figure of a small negro boy resting on his hands and knees, his back acting as the support to the square top. It was obviously of African origin and admirable.

His host invited him to sit down, make himself comfortable whilst he went over to the drinks cabinet. Capri chose the sofa facing more French windows overlooking the pool. It didn't appear anybody was using it.

"Well, what can I get you to drink?"

"I'll just have a small bourbon, thanks."

Mosalla poured out two large bourbons into squat tumblers and passed one to Capri. It was nearly full.

"Help yourself to ice." He gestured to the bucket on the table.

Capri doubted if there was any room left for the ice, but couldn't complain about his host's hospitality who sat himself down opposite with a squelch and smiled.

"Cheers." Mosalla gulped his drink down and was already getting himself up to have another.

"Do you want a refill?"

"Not just yet, thanks," he replied, looking at his still full glass. "Is it alright to smoke?"

"Why, sure. Go right ahead. I think I'll join you."

Mosalla plumped himself down again and reached into a carved wooden box on the table. He pulled out a cigar; its size could only be described as vulgar. He snipped off the end and lit up, releasing a pall of smoke that virtually blotted out his face, the smoke's other redeeming feature being its smell, very aromatic, possibly Cuban.

Capri lit his cigarette. It was miniature in comparison. He sat back and smoked.

"I need some info on Crome. Carlotta told me you were once very well acquainted with him. Apparently you were among the last to see him before he retired."

"Yes, that's right. It was a long time ago."

"What kind of relationship did you have with him, if you don't mind me asking?"

"It was a working relationship. We used to work together."

"Oh? In what way?"

"Magically. Crome set a group right here in LA. That was when he first came over, said he was looking for somewhere to establish another lodge and someone competent enough to run it whilst he was a still residing in the UK. At the time I thought it was a good idea. We talked things through. He understood and acknowledged that I had more than just a passing interest, and issued me a charter. I was selling real estate at the time so he also asked me to look out for a property for him whilst he made plans to leave England and immigrate here. I sold him a house up in Hollywood Hills. It was fairly secluded, just what he wanted. A year or so later he moved in and that's when things really got going."

"With the group?" Mosalla nodded. "What kind of work were you doing?"

"We were working on transmissions."

"You mean like channelling?"

"Yes, that's right."

"I see. So how was it going?"

"Everything was going fine. We were doing real well. Until something happened." Mosalla seized as if in the grip of an emotional block.

"What exactly happened, Mosalla?"

"We hit something, something big like a psychic power surge. It fragmented the group and that was it."

"A psychic power surge?"

"Yes, real bad. Crome wasn't here at the time, and blamed us, saying we weren't sealing the energies properly. But I think he was covering up for somebody else. Anyway, we disbanded after that. We all went our separate ways. Everyone was real scared. We had all sorts of things happening around that time. Wild, crazy stuff. A yacht I owned at the time sank off the coast for no reason. Most of us lost our jobs or suffered heavy financial losses. I lost my own property and some major deals fell through. I never did fully recover from them. It was only after we packed everything in things reverted back to normal."

"And that was the last you saw of Crome?"

Mosalla nodded. "Yes. He upped it and left us with the detritus. Of course, we tried to carry on, but it was useless without him. He was the nucleus of the group. He was the one who made things happen, a real magician."

"How many people were in the group all told?"

"I'd say on average about five or six regulars, seven if you include Crome."

"Do you still have contact with the rest?"

"No, except one of the girls who still cleans our temple down at Long Beach. She looks after it. I don't know why as nobody ever uses it anymore. But it gives her something to do. She's never been the same since."

"And you didn't see Crome after that?"

"No, nobody did."

"And this was around the time he retired?"

"Well, put it this way. It wasn't really a retirement, more like a temporary withdrawal from the world. He wanted everyone to leave him alone. If anybody found where he was living or tried to contact him, he would make out he was ill or something."

"Was he ill?"

"Fuck no," Mosalla laughed heartily and finished his second glass. He got up for another refill. "Can I get you another drink?"

"No thanks, I've still got one," Capri replied, stubbing out his cigarette.

"He was never ill all the time I knew him," he continued, sitting himself back down. "Complete bullshit. It was a smokescreen to keep people away so he could continue his work undisturbed."

"What sort of work was he doing at the time?"

"He was working on new formulations."

"Formulations of what?"

"The drug, man! That's why you're here, ain't it? To hear about his drug?"

"Then this drug does exist?"

"Of course it fucking exists. How else do you think a man like Crome could be pushing eighty when he only looks half that age? And I'll tell you another thing; throughout all the years I was working with him I never saw him age at all. You know what I mean? How do you think a guy like me feels alongside somebody like that? I mean look at me; grey, wrinkly, practically bald, a real pot-bellied septuagenarian. And he's older than me. In fact, it's his 80th birthday in two days time."

"I know what you mean." He lit up another cigarette and took another sip of his drink. "So what else can you tell me about this drug? You mentioned formulations, but where exactly did he get it from?"

Mosalla laughed. "How many times have I heard that question? I don't know is the answer. Crome ain't stupid. He's very smart, and he's got good reasons to keep its origins a secret. Before I got to know him he had already taken one of its formulations. It was working. Takes about a year to have a full effect, although he reckons it's only nine months."

"So he gave no indication at all?"

"No, but he used to keep poking fun at our ignorance, because Crome knows everything, and with a guy like him he's always way ahead of you. He

got real satisfaction out of making people feel small. Used to have this habit of laying great emphasis on his name, you know, as in chrome, and that when people despised him he made out that they really despised themselves because they were seeing their own reflection in him. He projected back to them what they didn't want to see. Well, a man like that has few friends if he does that. But if you asked him directly, he would say it was a secret and laugh at you as if you were stupid. It was typical of him and he would always say it in that way."

"In what way?"

"Hard to explain, kind of mocking way. Secret, he said. I don't blame him either for keeping it a secret. I know a hell of a lot of people who wouldn't mind getting their hands on it."

Capri could think of one person in particular. He still chose to remain sceptical. Nothing had been proven yet. "How does this drug of Crome's work exactly?"

Mosalla shrugged. "That's a good question. I'm not a physiologist, so my understanding of that side of things is very poor. But I reckon it sheds the old dying cells and replaces them with new ones."

"A bit like a snake sloughing its old skin?"

"Exactly. All I know is it works. That reminds me, I've just remembered. There was a rumour awhile back that Crome had accidentally revealed the formula of the drug in a poem."

"A poem?"

"Well, it wasn't really a poem as such, more like inspired writing. Apparently he dashed it off in a hurry so he could finish this mystical book he was working on and needed one more poem to complete it. You see, he was something of a numerologist, so there had to be the right number of poems in the book. Anyway, it was only after the book went to the printers, which he paid for by the way, when he realised his mistake and ordered all copies to be destroyed."

"Shame. I would've liked to have seen it."

"Ah, but I think I've still got mine."

"You mean, he gave you a copy?" he asked him excitedly.

"A proof copy, which I kept, and which he forgot all about."

Capri sat up. Now perhaps he was getting somewhere. "Mosalla, I'm a great fan of poetry. I don't suppose you could let me have a look at it?"

"I suppose I could. It won't do you any good, Mr Capri. You'll never find the right poem. I expended considerable time trying to find it and gave up in the end. I don't reckon your chances are much better. Besides, it was only a rumour. It was never proven."

"All the same, I would be very interested in having a look at it."

"It's got to be lying around somewhere. I'll look for it after lunch. That is, you will stay for lunch, won't you?"

Capri nodded eagerly. "Was Carlotta aware of this poem?"

"No, she left way before then. Anyway, help yourself to another drink whilst I go and arrange lunch."

Capri sat back, declining the offer of another drink as his congenial host left the room. He wanted to keep his head straight; the less alcohol the better. Then he got to thinking that Carlotta was right after all. Crome had slipped up and possibly let the cat out of the bag. All he had to do was find the right poem. But how? What system of reference would he use? If Mosalla couldn't find it then what chance did he have? After all, it would probably be couched in some kind of cipher only a man like Crome knew. The prospect tantalised him.

Capri curtailed his thinking as he heard his host re-enter the room. He was duly informed lunch would be ready in half an hour. Mosalla offered him another drink. Again he declined, and opted for another cigarette instead.

"Have you ever seen this drug of Crome's?" he asked him.

Mosalla sat himself down with another full glass. "Why, sure I have. Crome supplied us with a sample."

"You mean he actually gave you some of the drug?"

"Yes. But you see it isn't as straightforward as you think. The drug has many different levels. Each one works on a different level of vibration, from the grossest to the subtlest. Crome, of course, only supplied us with one of the lower vibrations, the fairly insubstantial parts of the drug. They don't really have any intrinsic value other than minor healing properties. They were tested and put to use on various skin disorders and infections like dermatitis, eczema, ichthyosis, cystitis, etc. The levels of the drug above these can cure serious imbalances of the body; wasting diseases like phthisis, tumours, cancerous growths, hormone deficiencies, unstable metabolisms, even venereal diseases like gonorrhoea and syphilis. The ones even higher can repair genetic damage, replenish white corpuscles; restore weak immune systems, etc. In other words, the higher you go the more profound the effect and the greater the healing powers of this drug. It was these Crome was working on at the time he went into seclusion."

"I see. And how many levels are there exactly?"

"Sixteen. That's the highest level of the drug. That's where it comes into its own and where its full power really lies. Once you've got the sixteenth it confers immortality, absolute, physical immortality. Crome isn't far off."

"So he doesn't have it yet."

"Not quite, but he will do soon."

"All he's done is reverse his ageing and put on hold, but not completely?"

"Not quite, but I reckon he's nearly there. Once he's managed to refine the drug to get the sixteenth and had a dose his whole physiological system will be renewed. He will have a new, more efficient body as if he had traded in his old one for a better model."

"How interesting. What became of the lower vibrations you had in your possession?"

"Crome retrieved them after they had been tested, and put them into production. He set up an establishment for their manufacture and had them mass produced as they can be synthesised easily. In fact, that's how he made most of his money, billions of dollars as he was selling them through all the pharmaceutical networks around the world. The higher levels ain't so easy. I know that for a fact. They are more difficult to synthesise because of

compounded problems. And that's something they're probably working on at his establishment. The Institute of Kalanitics, it's called."

"The Institute of what?"

"Kalanitics. That's the brand name they patented as the drug is based on something called the Kalanitic Equation, whatever that is. And don't ask me as I don't fucking know."

"Where is this place?"

Mosalla smiled. "I know what you're thinking. You want to go there, right?"

"If it's not far from here."

"Oh, it ain't far. It's down at Redondo Beach. That's not the problem. You'll never get anywhere near the place. It's all sealed off. Hi-tech security, the works. Strictly authorised personnel only. And all of them are screened and vetted so sedulously anybody would think the place runs on paranoia. The security is so tight you couldn't even fart in the place without it being picked up."

"It was just a thought."

"You'd be wasting your time. Don't bother going anywhere near it. Crome has good reasons to ward of any busybodies. The word is most of the funds generated by his institute are raked off by the government. That's the only way it retains its licence. The government gets a backhander each year to ratify the place. But don't quote me on that. It's just hearsay. And that's not all I've heard."

"Oh? What else have you heard?"

"I wouldn't like to say, Mr Capri. Just take it from me, they're doing things down there nobody likes to talk about."

Capri's ears pricked up. He decided to press him further.

"Mosalla, you've got me interested. I would like to know exactly what we're talking about here."

Mosalla looked at him sternly as if sizing him up. "I said I would help you in any way I can. My promise to Carlotta still stands as I have a lot of respect for the lady, but I'm wary about divulging anything else concerning the institute. You see, there are certain people with a vested interest in the place, people who have considerable power. If word got out I was the source for your information, I'd have one of their representatives on my doorstep without delay. That's something I can't abide."

"I understand, but you have my word anything you tell me will be treated as strictly confidential. I swear it."

Mosalla hesitated. There was a pregnant pause before he finally spoke. "Okay. This is how we'll play it. What I'm about to tell you didn't come from me. Got it?" Capri nodded. "If word gets back to me I will disavow any knowledge of this conversation. It wouldn't do a man of my standing any good. So this is strictly between you and me." Capri nodded again. "A few years back some grizzly discoveries were made not far from the institute. No information was leaked about them as everything was rapidly covered up; no press exposure, nothing. After that there were some real horror stories coming out of the institute, stories about the personnel there and other scientists connected with the place committing suicide or going loopy, raving on about some of their experiments. Each one of them was eventually executed furtively, their deaths being passed off as accidental. They weren't. Then more grizzly discoveries were made right by the coast, bodies washing up, half mutated and physically unrecognisable. Again the finger was pointed at the institute. There were reports of a large number of people going missing all in the same vicinity less than 5 miles from the institute. Needless to say, they were never seen again. Just vanished without trace. Again, the institute became the centre of the accusations but no case could be made as any questions were met with a wall of silence. The local police department was persuaded to drop their enquiries. At the same time people suddenly stopped disappearing as well. Everything went quiet. Only a year later some more bodies started turning up, usually naked and emaciated, drained of all bodily fluids. Nobody could explain the nature of their deaths. Whatever had done it had caused their bodies to become desiccated, dried out as if they had been dead for years, when in actuality, as the coroner confirmed, they had only been dead a month or two at the outside, and they all had a coupla things in common…"

"Oh? What was that?"

"They were all young and all Chinese."

"Isn't there a large Chinese community here in LA?"

Mosalla took a gulp from his drink. "Yes, there's also a new one down by the coast. Now, I'm not saying that these incidents have anything to do with the institute, possibly just coincidences, but when you have top scientists losing their minds or killing themselves, I'd say there is something unnatural going on at that place. It makes me wonder what it is exactly they're doing there, and, to tell the truth, I don't really want to know."

"Would these events be connected to the drug?"

He shrugged his shoulders. "Who knows?"

"I see. And what about these horror stories? Are they still circulating?"

He shook his head. "No. They stopped recently which doesn't mean a lot. They could still be carrying on their nefarious activities, yet in a more discreet fashion. I'd say the finger still points at the institute."

"And what about Crome? Does he still have dealings with the place?"

"Not any more. Not since he retired. His only interaction with it is in the capacity of a silent partner. He lets a young guy by the name of Anton Landis run it for him now, one serious headfuck. And I'm being polite when I say that. You see, Landis was one of the guys Crome brought into the group when he was only about fifteen or sixteen, real young, but real experienced. He had been practising magic since he was eleven years old and studied under Crome for about two years. Crome treated him like his protégé or the son he could never have, took him under his wing and showed him the ropes. Landis was a quick learner. He could absorb anything like a sponge and I reckon he was probably the only person out of the lot of us who understood fully all of Crome's highbrow ideas. Landis was smart, but too fucking smart for my liking. When they were together, Landis had his tongue so firmly up Crome's ass you could barely pull them apart. Not long after his initiation Crome raised him to a level even higher than me. But the problem was giving him that much status; it went completely to his head. Landis couldn't control it, being the hungry power seeker that he was. He was a real powertripper and began to exert his authority more and more, making it intolerable for all of us. I even asked for him to be kicked out of the group. But Crome wouldn't have it. Said he was a natural. When Landis joined he brought in his own ideas about how to do things, lots of strange ideas I wouldn't consent to. But something

came in with him. It was like an aura of evil exuding from him, tainting everything and fucked up our transmissions, severing all the links we made. He destroyed all our work," he said bitterly.

"And you hold him personally responsible for the group's fragmentation?"

"Yes I do. I blame him. At the time everything took a downward turn and then the big crunch came. That's when we all started experiencing our misfortunes. I mean, rightly I should be blaming Crome for giving him so much power. It was his fault really and I warned him repeatedly about the undesirability of the guy. I had reservations; could never trust him."

"But obviously Crome did?"

"Yes, but I would say that's only because he is a poor judge of character. He dismisses the personality completely. He's only interested in a person's inner worth. Landis would always make me feel uncomfortable just sitting next to him. You know how when you sit next to somebody you feel an affinity with them like you can work them out; you know where they're coming from? With Landis it was different. He was ambiguous and unsettling to be near, difficult to fathom, unpredictable and enigmatic and always gave off bad vibes. You never knew where you were with him. He's got no fixed ego. He projects different parts of himself to different people like he's made up of many masks and wears them at different times to suit his own ends. He always tried to make out he had the mind of an imbecile when it was a known fact he possesses the level of intelligence associated with prodigies, one hell of a mind but seriously twisted."

"Sounds familiar; sort of genius gone wrong."

Mosalla nodded. "Yes, and it is a known fact he gets his kicks from damaging people. He's handsome, rich—thanks to Crome—but a real psychopath; a sadistic, malicious, nasty headfuck. He's also arrogant, opinionated, egotistical, belligerent, violent, lazy, smarmy, and supercilious with a libido that's permanently on overdrive. I'm just praying it will destroy him in the end."

"I take it you're not very keen on him?"

"Humph! I hate his fucking guts. God knows what Carol saw in him. She was another one of our members. He charmed his way into her pants like a bee to a honey pot. And he only married her for her money and to secure

his position at the institute since her father was one of the main backers with Crome. By doing so it enabled him to have full control of the place. Of course, after he had decimated our group, he took her away, joined another one instead that's supposed to be run by this Satanist guy whose real identity nobody knows."

"That would obviously appeal to a guy like Landis."

"Oh, it would. Now he can get his kicks in full by tying up virgins to altars and violating them."

They both laughed.

"What about the drug? Would Crome have supplied Landis with the lower variations only or some of the higher ones?"

"Don't rightly know. But I hope he hasn't given him the higher ones. If so, heaven help us all."

"Why?"

"Because that's where we fucked up."

"We?"

"Yes, Jack and I."

"Who's Jack?"

"Who was Jack," he corrected him. "He was another one of our members Crome brought over from Big Sur. Nice guy, real likeable. A neurophysicist by trade."

"I take it he isn't around anymore?"

"No, unfortunately. Real shame. I'll never forget it."

"Forget what?"

"The accident!" he implored impatiently.

"Jack died in an accident?"

"Yes. It was our fault. We were careless, playing around in the dark. Didn't really know what we were doing. Crome warned us though; I'll give him credit for that. He told us to be careful. We never should have messed around with it."

"I'm sorry, you've lost me here. Messed around with what?"

"The drug, man, the fucking drug!"

"The drug's dangerous?"

"Dangerous! That's the understatement of the year! Of course it's fucking dangerous. Not only that, it is extremely dangerous."

Capri slumped back, dumbfounded. What was he getting into here?

"Let me get this straight; this drug killed Jack?"

"Yes. I'll never forget the day when I found him at the lab. I mean, I've seen the results of terrorists bombings, but nothing prepared me for what I found that day. And I'll tell you another thing; no ordinary explosion could have done anything like that. It shook us all up."

Mosalla took the last gulp of his drink. His face had gone pale and deathly. "No, nothing ordinary could have done that."

Capri was lost for words. The whole room seemed to be covered in a thick suffocating blanket, dampening their spirits as it spread itself over them, disturbingly cold and strangely contrasting with the light and heat penetrating from outside. The two men sat in silence, Mosalla lost in a tragic reverie, Capri examining the serious implications of the drug.

The arrival of the butler to announce lunch was being served broke the cold spell. Mosalla, as if pulling himself back to the present, shook himself out of it and clambered to his feet, his features still saddened. Capri all of a sudden didn't feel hungry, but courteously followed his host to the dining room. Mosalla took his usual seat at the top of the table, Capri at the other end.

"I hope I haven't put you off your food," Mosalla said apologetically.

"Not at all," Capri replied. He would force himself to eat if he had to.

Mosalla's face lightened up when the food was delivered, the memories of that day temporarily being usurped by his keen appetite. A few pounds of hearty steak had him back in his old mode. Capri just opted for a small steak and a few vegetables, washing it down with some tasty Californian red wine. He endeavoured the best he could to tuck in, but the sight of Mosalla eagerly devouring his way through four sirloin steaks and seconds did little to encourage his stomach. He took a few more mouthfuls and gave up, settling for more wine instead and waited for his host to finish.

Capri's mind was now full of demanding questions. It wasn't the death of Jack that was worrying him; more important were the crucial issues; not only did it have life enhancing properties, it also dealt out death, the two somehow inexplicably mixed. On top of that, was Carlotta fully aware of its destructive capabilities? Should he ask her tonight or not mention it at all?

He drank his glass of wine, now regretting not having taken up the hospitality of his host's generous offers of bourbon before lunch. Only a good, strong, stiff drink could ease his mind at present.

Eventually Mosalla finished, wiping his mouth with the satisfaction of a qualified glutton. Capri could now see where he got his paunch from.

"Mosalla, are you aware Crome is currently helping the government with their investigations into this new virus to help them come up with a cure?"

"No, I wasn't."

"Well, that's what we've been told. Apparently he is. Carlotta believes he's been given a chance to confirm the validity of his drug so he can get full recognition. As you know him better than anyone else, do you think he is really going to help them by handing it over?"

"Hard to say. Possibly. But it sounds to me like he's being emotionally blackmailed or even manipulated. You have to understand that Crome is a very proud man. His pride comes first, his reputation second. If he's helping them as you say, it will only be to get his pride and name back. You heard what happened at Cal-Tech, didn't you?"

"He got kicked out for failing to provide the origin of his drug."

"Yes, but also for not playing their games or following their regulations. Cal-Tech has high standards. Getting demoted and made to look a laughing stock is one thing, losing your pride is another. If he followed their procedures, turned over all of his documentation, the drug would have become government property and consequently fallen into the public domain. He would have lost all control of it. Now, if the government's lured him out of retirement, they may have offered him full re-instatement."

"And you think that is important to him?"

"Very. If he gets re-instated he will be awarded with full honours. Not only that, he will also receive a full pardon. There will be no stopping him from there, and to him it will mean no more kowtowing to their demands."

"But surely if this drug is dangerous then there will be repercussions."

"Crome's fully aware of the lethal aspects of the drug. The only way they can be tapped into is by improper use. He will, no doubt, build into it protective measures so no one touches on its bad side."

"Its bad side being its dangerous aspect?"

"Correct. That's what Jack hit on that day. You see, each level of the drug relates to a corresponding astral dimension, ranging from the gross to the subtle, or spiritual plane, with a very fine balance between the two. Both sides have to be kept separate, especially at the higher levels. The slightest imbalance and BANG!

"View it like a coin. It has two sides," Mosalla continued, picking up a clean plate to demonstrate, "a positive and a negative side, or what Crome called the nectar and the venom, respectively. You cannot work with one without taking into consideration the other. For this one drug contains the same dualities as it is a concentration of nature in a physical form. It's like matter and antimatter. Bring them together and you get one hell of an explosion."

"That's something Jack accidentally did when he was experimenting with the drug that day?"

"Yes. But as Crome said, Jack's death was the result of his own fallibilities. He was too eager, kept taking too many shortcuts and tried to run before he could walk."

"You mentioned a lab."

"That's right. I used to drop him off there and leave him to it."

"How far is it from here?"

"I wonder why you want to know that."

"Because I want to take a look at the place."

"What good would that do? It's all closed down. Nobody's been there for over ten years."

"Exactly. And that's why I want to check it out."

"There's nothing there, Mr Capri. The lab was cleared out, the police removed everything. You won't find anything of use to you there."

"Maybe not. But I would like to see for myself the extent of the damage."

"Well, I'm sorry, but I'm going to have to disappoint you. There was no damage to the building."

"But you said there was an explosion?"

Mosalla looked at him gravely. "Indeed I did. And I also said it was no ordinary explosion."

"You mean to say it destroyed Jack without affecting the building?"

Mosalla nodded. "That's right. It blew him to fucking pieces, Mr Capri, without damaging the building."

"That's incredible."

"Incredible is the operative word as no one could believe it either. The police and everyone else practically freaked out. I wish I hadn't mentioned it, Mr Capri, as I can see you really want to got there, don't you?"

"Now you've said that, definitely. Perhaps I can work out what happened."

"I vowed I would never set foot in that place as long as I live, but I am prepared to make an exception. I'll tell you what we'll do. We'll go there this afternoon, if that's suits you." Capri nodded anxiously. "It'll take awhile to get there as it's off the Pacific Coast Highway, just north of Malibu. I've got some things to attend to first before we leave. Why don't you go to the library and have a browse through my books. I'm sure you'll find something there to keep you occupied for the time being."

Alone in the library he felt at peace with the world. Here was a true bibliophile's dream. Here was row upon daunting row of knowledge on display. Capri looked at them all and wondered how many of them his congenial host had actually read.

He looked up and down all the shelves and estimated there were about four thousand titles plus. The ones on the top shelf, which he couldn't reach, looked more interesting, but then they always did. The ones within his grasp ranged from fifteenth to late twentieth century and had been published in various parts of the world. It was a truly eclectic and esoteric collection with weird titles and spellings. He stood back to take it all in, wishing enviously they were all his, for they revolved around demonology, ancient astrology, eldritch rites, strange customs and practises, obscure cults of dark dynasties, secret and forgotten societies, as well as a plethora of general books on magic, occultism and alchemy, all the subjects he found fascinating. It also appeared to be complete. Every book he could think of was here, from small privately issued pamphlets to mega-tomes not even a four year old could lift off the shelf. Where on earth did he get them all and who was this English vicar he mentioned? It was a feat in itself to amass such a collection let alone one that boasted such immaculate first editions.

Then of course, if you are as rich as Mosalla appeared to be, it presented little difficulty. His admiration for the books on display made him quite forget the reason why he was really here. Crome's book had to be stashed somewhere amongst this lot. But where?

Capri didn't even know what it looked like; its colour, size, thickness, and whether it was a hardback or paperback. He put such trivialities behind him and started scouting eagerly.

Two blocks later—he wasn't even halfway through—he came across a triple volume set by a renowned occultist. He had heard about them but never physically seen them for himself. He wasn't surprised in the least to find they formed part of Mosalla's library. They had been so zealously

sought after it was believed you weren't a real occultist unless you had them in your collection. When originally published in the late seventies they sold rapidly and disappeared into that black hole which is the bibliophile's worse nightmare, never to be seen or printed again.

Capri snatched them up, dismissed Crome's elusive book of poetry, and carried them over to the desk like an excited ten year old holding his long wished for birthday present. At last he was going to be able to see for himself what all the fuss had been about and did exactly what his host had bade him to do; he browsed.

Kelly Grantham was a very prominent member of a magical order in the seventies based in London. An Englishman by birth, he was also a well respected author. He later branched off forming another group designed specifically to work with his own specious system of occultism which boosted his coveted reputation as the leading occultist of his day. Not a bad achievement for someone who was still only in his early thirties. Yet his reputation bordered on the sinister and he was often connected with macabre groups networking internationally which did nothing to diminish his already outstanding achievements. Vastly misunderstood in his time, Grantham's adherents perverted his material and suited it to their own questionable ends. For this reason he was invariably linked to nefarious activities which caught the eye of Scotland Yard. During the eighties a series of abductions of young girls was to plague him for most of that decade, forcing him in the end to slowly slip underground and eventually into relative obscurity. Only his closest advisors—or more appropriately, arselickers—were allowed personal access to him, and he based most of his later operations from a safe distance well out of the Yard's jurisdiction and the public's eye. He was never heard of again.

But before he went into hiding he disseminated through these three books the corpus of his ideas regarding his experiments in what he abstrusely called 'necro-occultism,' and later developed it into his unique idiosyncratic ethos he termed 'nigretism,' a dark doctrine involving the use of those forces buried deep in the human psyche which are dead, i.e. forgotten. By tunnelling down and back in time, he believed they could be made accessible and amenable to consciousness and drawn on. By focusing on these primal, instinctual powers and directing them through the mechanics of the human anatomy they could be projected into mundane space-time as creative acts like art, writing and so forth.

Grantham probably stood in direct antipathy to Crome. Whereas Crome's interests lay purely in the future and progress, Grantham's lay in the past and a systematic regression. Capri wondered whether in fact the two had ever met and made a mental note to ask his host.

Capri, bubbling with excitement at the prospect of what these mighty tomes had to offer, gingerly flicked through the first volume. Immediately upon reading the introduction he was struck by the way in which the author chose to write. His style was far from accessible, using redundant and obscure vocabulary which made reading his books inordinately difficult and taxing. The language he employed was archaic, weighed down heavily by a profusion of Greek and Latin phrases that no modern day reader would bother translating. His style of writing was circumlocutory and prone to prolixity throughout. Capri tried to make a stab at the lengthy introduction only to find it bothersome and exasperating. It was wordy and evasive and practically said nothing at all. If it appeared to be saying something, Capri was at a loss to fully comprehend it. Grantham had an annoying habit of explaining the most simple, rudimentary ideas in a very complex fashion. He also had a canny way of eschewing what he was intent on revealing by moving off at a tangent just as he was about to come to the point.

After three pages, Capri was already fuming.

He was about to plunge into the first chapter when the sudden arrival of his host prevented him from doing so. He came waltzing into the room with a big grin on his face, looking very pleased with himself. Capri wondered whether it had anything to do with the drink until he noticed he was holding something in his hand.

"Oh, you're not trying to read those," Mosalla guffawed.

"Trying is the right word. Grantham seems to be saying we're on our way out. But the only thing is, we're well past the turn of the century when by rights, according to him, the world was due to be obliterated in some big apocalypse or something."

"I gave up years ago. Never got through the introduction, never mind the first chapter. Anyway, forget that juvenile nonsense, I've got something far better I know you'll be interested in."

"Don't tell me you've found it?"

"You bet. I knew it was somewhere and I was wracking my brains out trying to remember where I last put it. Then you know what? When Carlotta rang me this morning to tell me you'd be coming over, she asked me if I had any old pictures of Crome you might want to take a look at, you know, give you an idea what he looks like. Well, at the time I couldn't remember. But whilst I was upstairs just now I had to dig out some papers for a report and guess what was underneath? Not only a photo of him, but also his book. Now isn't that a coincidence?"

That was a word Capri had learnt to abhor. Mosalla handed him a photo with sincere admiration. He was surprised to see a very youthful version of his host standing ceremoniously next to a tall man and both dressed to the hilt in tuxedos and bow ties.

"That was taken at the annual dinner and dance," Mosalla proudly informed him. "It was around the same time Crome had just got his book of poetry published. That's why, I guess, I kept them together."

Capri examined the photo for awhile. The man he had heard all about certainly exuded an aura of dominance and sophistication. He looked directly into the camera with deep piercing eyes which were neither friendly nor disturbing, and smiled faintly with thin wispy lips and tautly drawn cheeks. His nose was long and broad, brooding with defiance, yet the whole face was strangely handsome, his skin perfectly smooth and radiating a sternness common to people who have perhaps led a good, adventure-filled life endowed with worldly wisdom. Crome definitely portrayed a picture of health and vitality but one thing confounded Capri; his baldness.

"But he's bald?"

"Yes, always has been. I guess he shaved his hair off when he saw it turning grey and became accustomed to it so he thought he'd keep it like that."

"So he did show his age once?"

"Sure he did. Before he got the drug, that is. I'm not surprised he showed his age, for he had done more in his younger years than either you or I put together could ever do in our lifetimes. And he had done nearly everything before he was thirty."

Capri handed him back the photo and received in return a small innocuous looking book which was far from what he expected. It was no bigger than

an old hymn book and about three times as slim. The cover was royal blue buckram, professionally bound and unmarked apart from one solitary gold stamped seal in the centre consisting of a small dot encased in an upright vesica with lines representing rays of light fanning out. Capri turned the book to landscape—the seal suggested an eye—then back to portrait. It now suggested a mystical eye.

Mosalla looked over his shoulder anxiously as Capri delicately prized it open to reveal the unassuming title, 'Selected Works.' Beneath this was an ink inscription, 'To my dearest friend Mosalla, yours always, AC.' At the bottom of the page, 'Printed Privately by the Author, Alexander Crome.'

Impressed, he glanced down the contents page. There were thirty one poems in all, one per page, all with flamboyant and evocative titles immediately suggesting religious and mystical themes. He quickly thumbed through the first few poems. They were written in a distinctly archaic style, almost Swinburnian if not biblical, with passionate purple phrases and mellifluous language and, in comparison to Grantham's hefty tomes, they all appeared to be mercifully short, some only a few couplets, others arranged in a handful of stanzas, with only one or two filling a whole page unbroken. They all had rubricised headings blending with the plentiful swirls and motifs forming the borders of each page. It was a style straight out of Art Nouveau.

"Quite a beauty, ain't it?" Mosalla asked.

Capri nodded. "Indeed it is. And this is a proof copy?"

"That's right. Shame they don't make them like that anymore, hey?"

"Yes. I know what you mean," he answered resignedly.

"Did you say you were a fan of poetry?"

"In a way I am. I'm no expert but I do have a good grounding in the classics. I bet I could find the poem referencing the drug."

"Why? You a betting man, Mr Capri?"

That wasn't quite what he meant. "I've been known to gamble in the past," he replied cautiously.

"I thought you was. You're a man after my own heart. What d'ya say we have a little flutter, Mr Capri?"

He hesitated. His conscience promptly reminded him of the vow he had taken at Crystal's. He could easily hedge Mosalla, but the temptation was too great. "The bet being I find the poem, right?"

"Yup. Now, how confident are you feeling today?"

"Well it depends on how long I'm going to be in LA."

"You'll still be here tomorrow?" Capri nodded. "Good. You got 24 hours."

Capri nodded. "Sounds fair to me."

"So what's it going to be?"

Capri remembered he had nearly a couple of thousand on him. "$2000."

Mosalla looked him in the eye. "That doesn't sound very confident. 5000."

He hesitated, reflected, asked for forgiveness, and decided. "Okay, you're on," and shook hands. "But you'll have to let me borrow it."

"Certainly. Just bring it back tomorrow with the money."

"Thanks," he replied laconically and slipped the little book into his pocket.

"You finished with these?" he asked him, indicating Grantham's books.

"Yes. Whatever happened to Grantham?"

"Don't rightly know."

"Is he still alive?"

"Doubt it. All that heavy shit he was into, he wouldn't have lasted long."

"Did he ever meet Crome?"

Mosalla laughed as he replaced them on the shelf. "No. Fuck, if there's one thing I really would've loved to have seen is them both in the same room."

"They weren't exactly on friendly terms then?"

"No. They would have ripped each other's throats out. Bitter enemies. Even tried to ruin one another in a magical combat once."

"Oh? Who won?"

"I would have thought that was obvious."

Capri felt stupid asking and changed the subject. "So how about visiting this lab of yours?"

THE NEGATIVE

'As there is a gateway that leads to the celestial realms, so there is a door which opens out onto Recremental Space, one that can be opened as easily and effectively as the other, and beyond is the Negative for it is Not.'

Kelly Grantham,
Cults of the Khu

—13—
THE LAB EXPERIENCE

The big man and the little man were walking towards the Stratocruiser when the big man turned to the little man and said, "One of them new types, isn't it?"

"Yes it is," Capri replied.

"She's quite a beauty."

"Yes, she has a personality all of her own," he quipped.

Mosalla, missing the irony of his statement, and fazed by the car's presence, stopped short. "You sure you don't want to take one of my cars?"

"I take it you've never been in one of these before?"

Mosalla shook his head and looked all solemn.

"It's a breeze," Capri assured him. "You'll find it an interesting experience."

Capri walked round to the driver's side, tried to hide his amusement at his acquaintance's nervousness, swiped his card and stood back for the door to open. He climbed in and punched in his PIN then ordered the passenger door to open and waited for Mosalla.

"Well?" he asked him. "Aren't you going to climb in?"

Mosalla muttered something under his breath, drew his rotund stomach in tight and climbed aboard, looking far from happy at the prospect.

"Doors close," Capri commanded.

Mosalla watched as they slid into place and muttered his approval.

"See, you're enjoying it already."

He pressed 'start' and half-expected Cindy to appear. She didn't, probably aware her seat was currently occupied. The car lifted up. Mosalla looked at him warily. He turned the wheel full. The car rotated 180°. Mosalla looked at him again uneasily. Capri was inclined to spin it around a few times to see how quickly he could make his passenger's face turn green, but abandoned the idea, hit the accelerator instead and zoomed down the long drive.

"Cindy?" he called out.

Mosalla gave him a queer look at the name.

'YES.'

Then looked all around him to see where the voice was coming from.

"We're travelling towards the coast. Can you tell us if there's any traffic jams up ahead."

'CHECKING...THE ROUTE HAS MINOR TRAFFIC FLOW. PLEASE STATE DESTINATION.'

"North of Malibu, just off the Pacific Coast Highway."

'DO YOU REQUIRE DIRECTIONS?'

"No. It's alright, Cindy. My friend here Mosalla is taking care of that. Just keep me informed on any build-up of traffic."

'CHECK. HELLO MOSALLA. WELCOME ABOARD. I HOPE YOU ENJOY TRAVELLING WITH US.'

"Hello to you too," he replied. "I like that. It's pretty neat," he said to Capri as they hit Sunset Boulevard. "You been to LA before?"

"No. It's my first time."

"Well? What do you think? Do you like it?"

"It's all right," he replied, unenthusiastically.

"Yeah, you're all the same you New Yorkers. No, I went to New York once. Hated it. It's a shit-hole. Couldn't wait to get back. LA, born here, guess I will die here too."

Capri looked at his travelling companion and thought right now he'd rather be alone than indulge in humdrum conversation just for the sake of it.

"And the girls here," he continued. "You can't beat them. Don't you just love them here?"

Capri yawned. "They're not bad, the one's I've seen so far."

"What about Carlotta?"

"What about her?"

"Do you like her?"

"She's a remarkable woman."

"You fucked her yet?" Capri looked at him coldly and refused to respond. "You have, haven't you? Well, I wished I had. She used to live here. Did you know that?" Capri nodded and concentrated on the road. "Yes, used to live with Crome in that house I got him. They made a perfect couple. She tell you they were once engaged?"

"She told me they once had a close relationship."

"Did she tell you why they split up?"

"Something about not being able to have kids."

"That's right. It was kind of hard on her, but harder on a man like Crome. A man isn't a man unless he can have kids. I guess he got all sore over it. You ever been married, Mr Capri, and had kids?"

"I was married once. It didn't work out," he replied bitterly. "No kids. What about you?"

"Oh, I was married once. She died of cancer a couple of years back."

"Sorry to hear that."

"My kids left home not so long back, leaving me all alone in that big house. It will always remind me of Jean. She was a wonderful, kind woman, always inviting Alex and Carlotta over for dinner. We used to get on like a house on fire. That was when they were both in the group."

"Carlotta was in the group?"

"Didn't she tell you?" Capri shook his head. "She was the High Priestess."

"Really? How interesting." Now it was making sense, he thought. Now he could understand what had really happened last night. He decided to probe deeper. "So what was her precise involvement in the group?"

Mosalla looked at him straight. "You ask a lot of questions, Mr Capri. Did you know that?"

He shrugged as he gripped the wheel. "It's my job," he replied laconically.

"Humph! Job! You private detectives are all the same. She was the one who received the transmissions. Crome said she was a natural transmitter or what he called a Woman of Power."

"A Woman of Power?"

"That's what he called all the priestesses he worked with, but especially her because she had a natural aptitude for trance states. He reckoned she was a reincarnation of Nefertiti," he said laughing.

"Yes. I know what he means," he agreed. "She does have an uncanny resemblance to Nefertiti."

"Why sure she does. I concur. Crome even wrote a poem about her."

"Really? Is it in the book?"

"It is. I'm sure you'll recognise it."

"I'll have a look later. But is Carlotta privy to the poem about the drug?"

Mosalla shook his head. "No. It came out after she left. He couldn't send

her a copy if he wanted to as she didn't leave a forwarding address. Besides, the way they split up, she sure as hell didn't want to see him again. All she wanted to do was get as far away from him as possible; the other side of America seemed like a good idea at the time."

"But before that she had taken the drug?" Mosalla nodded. "And that was about twelve years ago?"

"About that. Why do ask?"

"It seems strange she didn't tell me about Jack's death or mention the drug could be dangerous, unless of course she didn't know about it."

"Jack died after she left. Crome obviously didn't tell her about its bad side."

"But why didn't he tell her? That's what I don't understand. Nothing is straightforward about this case at all. Even this drug."

"You're still sceptical about it, aren't you?"

"Perhaps. In the past I've heard loads of stories about rejuvenating type drugs. They all turned out to be just that, stories. And lack of evidence of such a drug has failed to convince me otherwise."

"And what about Carlotta? Did she tell you how old she was?" Capri nodded. "Do you believe her?"

"Suppose I do."

"There you go then."

"Don't get me wrong. I'm not refuting her claim. This drug must exist if it did the trick. And that intrigues me. I want to get it for her."

"Well, I wish you the best of luck. You're going to need it. For there is no way Crome is going to hand it over to you."

"I realise that."

"Nor do I believe Crome will hand it over to the authorities," Mosalla continued.

"What makes you say that?"

"Because I know Crome. He won't."

"So what's he going to do, string them along?"

"Maybe. You see, they only need a certain part of the drug, not all of it. And that's all he has to hand over. They will think they are getting the whole thing. In that way he will win."

"Makes sense. So what happened after Carlotta split? Did Crome ever find a replacement for her?"

"No, not really. Women like Carlotta are very rare. After about two years of trying he decided to move on. And you know the rest."

Mosalla then instructed him to take the next turn on the right off the highway as they started hitting higher ground. They sped up a long winding track, dusty and overgrown, passing a steep escarpment at the base of Santa Monica Mountains. The narrow track wound all the way to the top overlooking the coast below. In the distance was the blue hue of the sea bespattered with specks of surfers riding the tall waves as they came rolling in. Capri ordered his window open and got a good lungful of sea breeze air, refreshing and inspiring, unlike the stale dead air of LA itself.

They ground to a halt outside a pair of high wrought iron gates. Mosalla got out and fished out his keys and fumbled with the massive padlock and chain. He pushed the gates open with difficulty, then climbed back in again and instructed Capri to drive on until they reached a clearing encircled by some trees. He pulled up outside a nondescript long concrete block with a flat wall and a few narrow slits that passed for windows. Behind it stood a barren hill, its rocks almost red in the sunlight that rolled down towards them. The building reminded him of an old machine gun post dating from the Second World War being built halfway into the hillside.

"Is this it?" he asked, unimpressed.

"Sure is."

"It doesn't look like a lab to me."

"Not from outside, no. It used to be an outlook post. The Ministry put it on the market. I bought it, cleaned it inside and rigged it up. Jack used to carry out all of his experiments here so we always referred to it as the lab."

They got out of the car. Capri had a good look round and decided to check out the sprawling view below. He stood high on a promontory enabling him to pan the whole horizon, north to south, feeling the gentle breeze brushing against his face, cooling down the heat of the sun high above.

"Quite a view, ain't it?" he heard Mosalla say as he came up behind him.

Capri had to agree. He was more than enamoured and could have stayed here for the rest of the day. He turned round to take into perspective the building and another mountain lying just to the left of it which seemed to tower up out of the ground like a giant; smooth, steep sided, measuring at least three hundred feet high.

"That's where Jack used to do all of his climbing," Mosalla promptly informed him.

"Bit of a mountaineer was he?"

"Sure was. Used to get all the way to the top and all the way back down without even using ropes."

"But the face is almost vertical."

"Exactly. That's the way he preferred it. He could scrabble to the top as easy as if he was crawling along the ground. That was when he felt high, when he felt the whole universe was behind him. You see, Jack was a bit of a bipolar. He suffered from cyclothymia a hell of a lot of the time, you know, had his ups and downs. Well, when he was up he was really up, flying high like a kite. When he was down, he was really down.

"Poor Jack. Yes, when he was down, he wanted nothing better than to be left alone. That's when I used to leave him here. He'd be here for days at a time, then he'd ring me and I would come and fetch him. And that day, well, he never rang me," he uttered, his face distinctly pale and ashen.

"And nobody's been here since?"

"Nope. Feel sorry for his wife though. She was never the same afterwards. I know their relationship had become strained. He was 35 at the time. She was much younger than him, perhaps too young, and when he died she couldn't handle it. Just prior to that he lost all his money to some crook, his house, his job, everything. He was determined to crack the Kalanitic Equation even if it killed him which, of course, it did in the end."

"Well, let's take a look inside, shall we?" Capri said, trying to urge him towards the building.

Mosalla went even paler and stood his ground. "I said I would never step inside that place again. Looking at it now, I sure as hell ain't inclined to go back on my vow. Why don't you take a look around yourself? I'll stay here."

"Okay, if you feel that strongly about it. Wait for me in the car."

"Good idea," he replied and nervously passed him the keys. "You take your time," he said, scrambling back to the car.

Capri watched him. He was afraid of something which took place ten years ago, yet he was acting as if it had only just happened. Mosalla threw himself in the car, panting and covered in sweat. Capri ordered the doors to close.

"Make yourself comfortable," he told him through the open window. "Apparently, you can get TV through the computer. I haven't worked out how, but if you talk to Cindy nicely I'm sure she will oblige you."

With that, he left Mosalla safe and happy in the car, and started walking towards the lab. "The old fool," he muttered under his breath, and made his way to the side door, glad to forego Mosalla effusing some running commentary. In any case, he always worked alone.

He fiddled with the grimy padlock on the steel door with one of the keys. It didn't fit. He tried another one. No, it was no good either. That only left one more. He struggled to insert the key and only managed to get it to turn half way. He tried harder but it wouldn't budge. He hit the lock, then thought about asking for Mosalla's help. He turned away from the door, and as he did so he could have sworn he heard the lock click. He turned back to see the lock had opened by itself as if some invisible hand had opened it for him. He was not pleased; nor did he like the realisation. It

brought a familiar feeling of horripilation to the back of his neck. He could only surmise the gods wanted him to go in. Why? He was about to find out.

He heaved against the heavy door. It moaned with age. Reluctantly, it opened all the way, releasing a cold pall of air. It floated out to greet him like an unwelcome guest. Capri ignored it, braced himself and stepped in.

The first thing to strike him was the darkness of the interior. It was surprisingly dark despite the rays of sunshine filtering through the slits. The long rectangular shafts of light, although bright, appeared to be fighting with the darkness and coming a close second. Furthermore, the temperature was icily cold like a refrigerator, keeping the warmth of the sun at bay. It was enough to make Capri shudder, plus the pungent odour that met him full on. It was a familiar smell: the smell of death. It put him on edge. There was something not right about the place, as if he had walked into a morgue.

He got out his old petrol lighter to locate a switch, its flickering flame hardly fighting back the darkness, barely making anything more perceptible. He prayed the lab was still connected. He fumbled around and found a switch nearby and flicked it on. The neon strips spluttered into life with a cold spurt, illuminating all the lifeless air. He could now see some tables spread out in a semicircle by the windows. They cordoned off the rest of the room.

Apart from them, the whole lab had been fairly cleared out, with only the occasional chemistry apparatus like Bunsen burners, tripods, test tubes, racks and an old style electron microscope, still remaining, all covered in dust. It all indicated nothing here had been touched since the accident.

He decided to scout some more, ignoring the terrible cloying smell clinging to his nostrils. On the back wall he could discern some makeshift shelving containing an assortment of textbooks, including one or two relating to microbiology, gerontology, endocrinology and another one. He hauled the book off the shelf, wiped the dusty cover clean to find it was a book on human pharmacology, an unusual addition to the collection. He made a mental note of it and passed on.

In the corner was a portable refrigerator. He reached for the handle to pry inside. It wouldn't budge. He yanked it harder. It let out a screech, emitting

a sharp sound, provoking a horde of black shapes to suddenly leap out from the top corner. Instinctively he ducked as they circled over him, the eerie sound of rustling wings beating overhead. He looked up nervously to see them swoop once more and rapidly head for the windows and exit.

"Bats!" he hissed. He couldn't stand them. They put him even more on edge, like the atmosphere of the lab. It exuded a foreign element, something which didn't belong here, something which was out of place, something sinister. It just wasn't right.

He calmed himself down and pulled out his cigarettes. He lit one up apprehensively and toked the smoke in deep, finally regaining his composure. He pulled the refrigerator door wide open. As he suspected, it was empty except for the naked ghostly glare of the light bulb. Disappointed, he now felt uneasy at the prospect of how Jack had died, if not a little bit scared, for the intangible presence was more noticeable. Although the lab was physically empty, it still conveyed psychically a heaviness weighing the whole place down. As he moved, it was like wading through a thick, viscous fluid.

Unruffled, he walked round, detached and absent-mindedly on purpose, striving to tune in to what ever subtle vibes he could pick up. As he walked he deliberately thudded the floor with the heel of his left shoe on every third step to help lower the threshold of his consciousness. He half-closed his eyes letting them go out of focus, blurring everything in sight. He drifted aimlessly then suddenly cursed as he walked straight into a spider's web, its threads of gossamer etching into his flesh like hot wires. Now he was really scared. He panicked, trying frantically to get the remains of it off his face and started to run for the door.

"No! You must stay," he heard Angel say. He stopped in his tracks. The voice seemed to echo all around him. "You cannot leave." And, as if to reinforce what Angel was saying, the door slammed shut with a loud clang.

"Why?" he asked Angel. But there was no response.

He stubbed out his cigarette with a vengeance, hesitated and vacillated, yet with that calm assurance which perceptibly marks one's brain; something big was going to happen now. All he had to do was allow it to happen.

CELEBRATION

Whatever step he took next would be the decider. He blasted his doubts aside. This was it.

He closed his eyes, got back into a conducive state of mind and breathed in the putrid air. It stung his lungs like acid. He fought the disagreeable smell down and his abhorrence, allowing his legs to take him where they willed to a small space next to the wall nearby. Unquestioningly, he took up his asana on the dusty floor, settling immediately into a deep and steady trance. He let his mind go and found he was sinking down a long funnel with a dim light at the end. Then he stopped as if he had hit a wall of glass. He opened his astral eyes to find everything was cloudy as if looking through a layer of gauze. Then he heard a sound to his left, a click in the distance, then the wall before him became bright. Someone had just turned on the light.

Then he felt it, a strange sensation as if someone had walked straight through him. It was a diminutive man dressed all in denim, with curly, ginger hair and glasses. It must be Jack. To get a better look, Capri disembodied and hovered behind Jack, watching his every movement. And as Jack moved everything seemed to be speeded up as if he was watching a film at double speed.

He was now wearing a white coat, and like a scientist about to begin an experiment, he stacked test tubes professionally in their respective racks, then he cleared his work space, lit up a burner, fetched a small glass vial of clear liquid from the refrigerator and started an experiment.

Capri watched fascinated. Once or twice, Jack moved straight through him, then looked over his shoulder as if half-aware he was being watched. Jack ignored the intrusion and concentrated on preparing his apparatus, setting a petri dish over a burner, measuring its temperature constantly then deposited a small amount of the liquid with a dropper on the dish. He noted the time, removed the dish and placed it under the microscope. He examined it, then looked up in amazement, a big smile on his face and scribbled down some notes. Capri judged by Jack's expression he had cracked part of the Kalanitic Equation and drifted over to have a look at the notes he was anxiously making. Annoyed, Capri noticed that whatever Jack had written was in such an untidy scrawl it was barely legible. He gave up trying to read it and instead followed him back to the main table and carried on observing him closely.

Jack was now placing the entire contents of the glass vial on a dish and heating it up, checking with a thermometer the exact temperature and timing it meticulously. The heat of the liquid was obviously crucial. Perhaps the heating process had something to do with activating the liquid making it vital, he guessed. Intrigued, he watched him remove the dish, pour its contents into an open-necked glass flask and set it down on a hotplate. He then cleared away all extraneous items and made some space. From beneath the desk he pulled out a long metal rod which appeared to be made out of pure copper. Then a small knife and another glass plate and set them down on the table in a definite order: the flask before him, the knife to the fore, the rod to his right and the plate to his left. A thought struck Capri, but before he could establish what Jack was doing exactly, he was already placing some white looking crystals on the plate and dropped a small block of charcoal into a brass bowl, set it over a burner and sprinkled some fine dark powder on the charcoal as soon as it became hot. Now Capri knew what he was up to. His last action confirmed it; Jack was ritualising the whole process, turning it into a magical ceremony, fumigating the lab with thick wafts of incense smoke.

Perturbed and more than anxious, knowing full well it was leading up to the main point of the rite, Capri quickly re-engaged with his body. It was here he felt in tune with the source of the presence, and it was here he was more likely to experience it in full. He waited as Jack too prepared himself. This was going to be it, he knew.

Jack went over and turned off the lights, returned to stand ceremoniously before his desk, breathing in deeply the fragrance of the incense and closed his eyes as he slipped into a light trance. And, as Capri watched him, he noticed a subtle shift taking place within the lab. The walls quivered and rippled like a mirage. They became distinctly darker in tone, almost a deep pitch black and reflected the only light in the room coming from the flame of the Bunsen burner like highly polished obsidian. The ceiling seemed to rise as if being elevated up high above them. It too became black. So did the floor, and in each corner now stood a column. Capri watched fascinated as Jack turned the whole lab into a temple by the power of his imagination. He now stood in the centre of a vast black cube of space before an altar covered in a rich black velvet cloth, his clothes replaced by a long hooded black robe, his chemical apparatuses now acting as his magical weapons.

CELEBRATION

A few moments passed before Jack proceeded with the next stage; the opening of the temple. He lifted his head up to the ceiling and bellowed some strange words in a long audible moan making the whole temple vibrate as if each word was a shockwave passing through the temple of his imagination, protracting the syllables, stretching out the words into monstrous sounds yet peculiarly enchanting, almost uplifting, as they consecrated the temple. As each word rolled off his tongue, the sound created waves, definite stresses in the ether, embellished by his imagination, for each word became an image charged with light and dispersed into the distance beyond the confines of the temple.

Capri could not help noticing how charged the whole place had become. If Jack really was bipolar, he was certainly on a high phase now, and that feeling permeated the whole temple. The words stopped. Jack stood still focusing on the altar before him. He raised his wand high to the ceiling and brought it down in a graceful arc towards the altar and struck it precisely eleven times, each knock creating a ripple effect as it shattered the silence and resounded like a giant gong. The subtle nuances after each knock shifted out and dissipated. The temple now felt ready for cleansing.

Jack brought his wand back up and pointed it vertically at the ceiling. Cool ripples of light flowed down its shaft as he began another incantation. They flowed down his arms and into his forehead. He projected them outwardly with a pronounced gesture. They became four shafts of light, slowly transforming into pentagrams, one for each quarter. Jack rested momentarily until they were fixed. Now the rite proper was about to begin.

More strange, unfamiliar words rolled off his tongue, turning into deep sonic bursts, so powerfully charged they became tangible before petering out to be replaced by another line of words in a string of cadences as the energies proper were being invoked. He continued bellowing, building up into a frenetic frenzy, then a crescendo which made the whole temple feel alive, a dizzying swirl of bombarding, discordant sounds, booming and bouncing back and forth like a mad medley of echoes, ricocheting off the walls. Yet, this was not a dark ritual; this was a ritual of light, for the temple shimmered with light, with life, with a joyous, sonorous celebration of ecstasy and it had all been brought about by one man. Capri was impressed.

Jack got so caught up in this power he was creating it seemed to lift him off

the floor until he was levitating in space. It made Capri feel giddy, barely able to stop himself from sinking into a swoon.

Suddenly Jack stopped. The presence invoked was to his satisfaction. He levitated motionlessly, concentrating on the rapture, feeling it sing in his veins and slowly let himself drift back down to earth. He now stood proudly before his altar, wand in hand, raised it and then pointed it at his magic cup of liquid. He directed more waves of light into the cup. They swirled all around it, wave upon wave. It was now properly charged. He consecrated it with some divine magical words of power, then halted. Now he laid down his wand by its side and raised both arms into the air high above his head and brought his hands together in an upright triangle. He uttered more words, this time focusing them in the triangle of his hands, seeing it imbued with light. Waves of light rolled in from all quarters of the temple, thick swirls of light like incandescent fire, bright, luminous and shining powerfully. Slowly he brought his hands down and held them over the cup, drew them apart and focused the energies represented by the light into the cup. It was virtually invisible as more light-waves filtered down into it and all around it, a thick pall of iridescent light rolling over it like whitish smoke. It danced about the cup in a shimmering whorl and flowed down the sides of the altar as Jack took one step forward and paused.

Now something was about to happen. Was it going to be Jack's doom, Capri wondered as he watched entranced. Any minute now, he thought. Something must have gone disastrously wrong at the last moment. Did Jack make a fatal mistake somewhere along the way? He didn't have time to question what was happening. The whole show was here for him to watch, not question. And the more he observed the more he became aware of an underlying uneasiness which had imperceptibly invaded the room. It sent a cold tingle down his spine. But before he could examine what it was, Jack was clasping the cup with both hands and raising it high in the air. He held it aloft, whispered some more words and slowly brought it down to his waiting lips. Just as he was about to imbibe its contents Jack stopped.

Without hesitation, Jack suddenly swung round to look behind him as if his name had been called, and looked straight through Capri with wild glaring eyes. They could not mask the horror he saw. He gasped. His mouth fell open in shock, and the last thing Capri remembered seeing was the cup

falling from Jack's hands and taking an incredibly long time to fall as if he was now watching everything in slow motion, and then the cup hitting the floor in a magnificent burst of white light. He saw very briefly Jack's body burst open and being discharged in all directions in particles of flesh and bone. He was annihilated in an instant. Then there was a sonic boom a few seconds later as if the explosion had taken place at a great distance and only now could he actually hear it. The sound seemed to press him from all sides like a jet of hot air, and then an incredible blackness as if the space-time continuum had been ripped open.

It took Capri a full minute to feel the full impact, but when he did it was physical and so powerful he was thrown across the floor. He came to and flung himself in the direction of the door. He hurled himself against it and threw himself outside. Then he felt it coming up out of his stomach, into the back of his throat and crumpled to the ground as it jetted out of his mouth in one long stream. He was sick as a dog. He slumped to the ground in a tangled heap and rolled over on to his back. The world strangely spun. The trees became a blur. The ground wavered and the sky took on an unfriendly grimace. He vomited again and lay motionless on the ground and waited for the world to stop spinning. Gradually it did, leaving a tremendous ache in the back of his head as if he had been hit with a sledgehammer. His head hurt so much he doubted if he'd ever be able to stand up again.

He breathed in the sea breeze air, feeling his head lighten, no longer the dull heavy weight it had been. Now only a headache remained. His body stung all over as if his nerves were now sharp twisted metal fragments embedded in his flesh.

He struggled to prop himself up, feeling queasy and slightly dizzy. He was determined to get up but desisted, telling himself to take it easy. He had been through one hell of a shock. It would be ruinous to try rushing anything. He bided his time and waited until at least a part of him felt okay.

He sighed and instinctively reached in his pocket for his life savers. He lit one up, drew the smoke in deep and felt relieved, still aching all over but still alive. What he hit on probably did untold damage to his aura.

"What the fuck was that?" he cried to himself.

He smoked nervously some more and tried to get his brain back into gear. He agitatedly ran his fingers through his hair, checked his face for burn marks, half-expecting to be scarred all over. Thankfully there was no visible damage, a little shook up maybe, but he was still in one piece.

He finished his cigarette and fearfully got to his feet, his pain-wracked body screamed back in defiance. He struggled on, slumped himself against the side as the world spun for a second or two. He shook his head. He looked up to the sun again. It reassured him that everything had resumed a sense of normality and whatever he experienced in there was now safely behind him. He had nagging questions in his jellied mass of a brain, demanding inhospitable answers.

He brushed down his suit, swept his hair back and wiped the last of the vomit from his mouth and calmed down. He wanted to go back inside and take another look before returning to the car, unaware of how long he had been. He paused, caught his breath and turned round to face the open door. He braced himself once more, drew in a deep breath and stepped inside.

The lights were still on. Everything appeared to be as it had been when he first entered. Or was it? No, this time it was different. Although all the tables and even the refrigerator was exactly the same, this time the intangible presence had vanished. It was no longer there. Even the darkness had disappeared, allowing the brilliant sunlight to penetrate through the slits. Now he could see more clearly, breathe more easily as well since the smell had gone too. It was as if the lab had been purged and the presence finally banished. The feeling of heaviness was now a thing of the past. The realisation did little to please him. He even thought for a second or two his stupid action had purged the place, but being unable to explain why, he dropped it and instead scouted round again with newer more discerning eyes. He could even see the footprints he had left in the dust on the floor, the place where he sat, the book he removed from the shelf and cleaned. The place was also warmer, how he would have expected it to have been when he first entered. It only made him more perturbed. He shook his head in disbelief and went back to the spot where he sat, crouched down and mused, tapping his chin, trying to get his head round this mystery he was determined to solve. He ran through it all again, seeing the fabric of space being ripped open. Then he gasped as he had a terrifying thought. Now he

was really worried. What if the astral dimension of the negative side of the drug had intruded at that point? What if Capri had experienced it as well? What if...?

He shook his head again. It was impossible, surely. If not, then what was the reason? Right now he had a hell of a lot of questions to ask Angel. He would ask him tonight. Angel would tell him what happened. He tapped his chin and pondered some more then noticed a small point of light under the table Jack used for his altar. Curious, he got up and walked over. Bending down he saw it was a tiny fragment of glass reflecting the sunlight. He picked it up and examined it between his fingers. It was a piece from Jack's cup, the one he dropped. He smelt it. It was odourless. He chuckled, letting it drop from his fingers and imagining it going 'bang' as it hit the floor.

"Fuck it!" he told himself and decided to call it a day. Whatever really happened that day he would leave it in Pandora's box where it belonged, just pleased to get the hell out of there and never wanting to return.

* * * * *

"What the devil kept you?" Mosalla implored.

Capri felt like laughing at the question. "Nothing."

"Don't look like nothing. You look like you've just seen a ghost."

Again he wanted to laugh. "Perhaps I have," he muttered to himself and turned the TV off, got the motor running and wasted no time in turning the car round and getting away from that dreadful place as quickly as possible.

"Well?" Mosalla asked. "Aren't you going to tell me what happened? You were gone for ages."

"You said take your time. So I did."

"Sure I did, but I didn't mean two hours."

Capri, stunned, checked his watch as they headed back down the dirt-road. Mosalla was right. He was gone two hours and wondered why the old man hadn't bothered to fetch him.

"Let's just say I had a nasty shock," he told him to appease his curiosity.

"It looks like it. That's why I never want to go back there. It reeks of evil."

Capri pulled up so Mosalla could get out and lock the gates behind them. As he watched him in the rear view screen he wanted to correct him: The place did reek of evil, not any more.

Mosalla climbed back in and they continued down the dirt track. Soon they were on the Pacific Coast Highway, and heading back to normality.

"Tell me, did Jack make any notes about his researches?" Capri asked him.

"He did have a notebook with all of his experiments in them. He used it like a magical diary as Crome always recommended we should record everything, no matter how insignificant."

"Any idea what happened to it?"

"I think the police took it away with them. Anyway, it wouldn't have done them any good. Jack's handwriting was illegible."

"Yes, I noticed."

"What was that?"

"Nothing. What was his grade in the group?"

"The same as Landis. They both used to backbite all the time, jealous of one another. Crome wouldn't allow either one of them to advance any further until they had really proved themselves capable of taking the next grade which involves crossing the Abyss. He didn't reckon either of them were up to it. Landis was too young and eager, although he was right on the verge. Jack was still too deeply attached to his ego. Which was a great shame because he was a born magician, as Crome called him, taught by a genuine witch at a tender age. Why do you ask?"

"I was just wondering. Perhaps Landis may have had something to do with Jack's death?"

"I thought of that myself. But not even Landis would have the power to

cause an accident like that. It was one hell of an explosion."

Capri nodded. "You can say that again."

He checked his watch and looked at his real passenger. Then the view beyond him. He could see the red sun majestically dipping into the sea on the horizon. It was now early evening, and all he wanted to do was go to the hotel and have a few drinks, and contemplate.

"If it's alright with you, I'll drop you off at your place and head back to the hotel."

"You sure you don't want to stay for dinner?"

"No. Thanks for the offer. I've got some business to sort out tonight, remember? Some poetry to read?"

"I hadn't forgotten. Just bring it tomorrow morning with the money. Cash!"

He ignored him and concentrated on the road ahead. The lights of the big city in the distance were coming into view. He turned to see Mosalla now snuggled up and was dozing off. Soon he was fast asleep. Capri smiled, put his foot right down and ploughed into the heart of the American Dream.

THE GOD MAN

'O Man, wake up and invoke thy Self!
And discover thine hidden wealth.
Come to know thou art already God,
Take the lonely path He hath trod.

Arm thyself and slay each thought.
Find inner peace, one rarely bought,
By ridding the mind of false belief,
Thy Self is then free and finds relief.

Free from sin, fear and guilt,
Free from the house He hath built.
Raise thy wings with all thy might.,
Take flight to the spheres of Light.

The human condition, transcend!
For 'tis a trap and without end.
See around thee the world decay,
As thou goeth forth by day.'

Alexander Crome,
Selected Works

—14—
THE GOD MAN

As soon as Capri got back to the hotel he wasted no time in returning to his room, having all of a sudden started feeling faint. Perhaps the experience in the lab really had done him some damage. He checked himself all over in the bathroom, splashed some cold water in his face and took a good long hard look in the mirror. He recognised the face, the same hungry eyes, the same look of disgust which had marked his features since childhood, but the impression he received was unusual. He didn't feel the same at all; still the same person, yet different in an indiscernible way. It was highlighted by an awareness he could only describe as 'weird' as if he was out of synch with everything. It made him feel terrible, even more confused.

In a vain effort, he decided to have a long soak in the bath, hoping it would wash it away. The sensation of hot water against his skin felt soothing. It relaxed him. Yet every time he tried to close his eyes, the sound of the explosion resounded in his head and brought back the headache complete with the nausea.

Capri climbed out of the bath, still unhappy, but at least slightly recharged enough to continue his battle with earth. He dragged his naked body over to the windows, got them open, ignored the smog, and breathed in the air. He definitely didn't feel right. Not even the evening view pleased him, one which back in New York would have uplifted him as it was his favourite time of day. The sky and the buildings here seemed dull and uninteresting like in his dream. He felt he was watching a ghost town going through its motions in a perfunctory way. Even the people below, although large in number, seemed to be mechanical in their movements, lacking all life and humanity, soulless. He found it depressing. He stood staring at the darkness beyond, at the enticing lights, at all the hubbub of traffic and people milling mindlessly in the street. Suddenly he was seized by an implacable desire to hurtle himself towards it all in one consummating act of defenestration. It would be the end, an end to everything.

He moved perilously closer to the small balcony, imagining what it would be like to leap out, fling himself off and embrace the night.

Just as he affirmed his resolve the televid rang.

"Shit!" he exclaimed and went over to answer it. It was the restaurant manager telling him his table was ready. He had ordered it specifically early so as to avoid the other patrons. He thanked the man, hung up and cursed him for interrupting his suicide bid.

He took it as a message from his controllers to stay alive for the time being. He got dressed appropriately into his black suit and white silk shirt, and made his way to the lobby. He wanted a good stiff drink first so he headed over to the cocktail bar, ordered a double bourbon on his tab and gulped it down before reordering. He wasn't sure if his stomach was in the mood for cooperating, deciding to rest at the bar for awhile just in case. The last thing he wanted to do was cause a scene by throwing up all over the place. He had another drink and lit up a cigarette instead. He watched the smoke spiral to the ceiling in eddying coils, taking his thoughts with it. And drank some more. The edges were softer now, more manageable. However, it did not ease his feelings of isolation; it only seemed to, which was sufficient. He wanted to be by himself now, for the rest of the night, get gloriously drunk and drift into the beyond where thinking doesn't exist. Man was never meant to think, he decided.

He pulled himself off the barstool still feeling shaky and made his way to the restaurant. Being still early, it was empty. He was pleased and was

ushered to a table far away in the corner where he could he by himself. There was something disgusting about having to eat, he thought, as he was shown the menu. All the dishes were in French. How clever. How pretentious! He quickly pointed to something and ordered, plus a bottle of the house's finest wine and sat back, telling himself he had to eat if he wished to continue living, still ambivalent about it.

Capri didn't care about anything anymore, only his drink. He smiled as the waiter finally delivered his bottle of wine. He watched the way in which he meticulously started pouring out a small amount in his glass, then twisted the bottle as he finished pouring. He then asked sir to taste it. Sir did and nodded his approval; it was a fine French vintage. He was pleased as only the French know how to make real wine. The waiter left him to it. He sat back and lit up a cigarette and thought of Carlotta, how she probably indulged in these arrogant displays of wealth every night. But with her it was possibly different. Her manners were sophistical. He repressed all thoughts of her and looked out over all these empty tables before him. It did not worry him. He preferred it this way and would rather have his own company than be assaulted with the mindless bantering of imbeciles. Being secluded in this corner and surrounded by empty space reflected perfectly how he felt inside.

The head waiter brought him his food. He sat up and stubbed out his cigarette, took a gulp of wine and tried to hide the way his stomach revolted at the smell of soup being ladled into his bowl. He feigned a smile. The waiter departed. He looked at it, smelt it, tried one mouthful. It tasted disgusting. He forced himself on, had another couple of mouthfuls and gave up, then asked for his main dish. A few slices of chicken in thick creamy sauce. He tentatively tried a small mouthful. Again his stomach spurned it. He quashed it and endeavoured to eat a few more mouthfuls and capitulated. He brushed his full plate aside, finished off his wine, ordered another bottle and thanked the chef for such an excellent meal. He waited for his second bottle to be delivered before lighting up again. He would rather choose food for the soul like wine or poetry than food for the stomach any day. As he sat there all alone he watched the usual flagrant vagrants descending on the place filling out the emptiness he preferred. It made him cringe just watching them; his mind filled with dark thoughts.

Quickly he snapped himself out of it, quite alarmed by what he was thinking. What the hell was happening to him? He was deeply disturbed. He downed another glass of wine and nervously lit up again.

Capri cast his mind up from his table, looking for a distraction, anything to take his mind off himself, his eyes scanning the people as they came in and sat down before him, finally settling on something quite beautiful in itself and stopped to focus on her. She was such a picture it made him quite forget what he was doing and just stared.

She was sitting all by herself a few tables away, yet clearly in line with his vision, her left profile to him. She had long blonde hair which bordered on silver, kind of straggly in places; it made her look like a right dirty bitch, with thick mascara shading her eyes, distinct pouting lips, breasts jutting provocatively forwards and almost plunging out of her tight black sequined evening dress, showing plenty of cleavage, and attractively slender. She appeared to be fairly tall, and from what he could see of her bare arms they displayed the sort of firmness one would associate with a gym-girl type. She radiated a bronze tan, the sort that could only be derived from lying outside under the Californian sun all day, no doubt in the back garden by the pool. Yes, he was impressed and momentarily captivated. Consequently his desire to rush back to his room vanished. He was intrigued and wanted to see who she was waiting for. She had to be waiting for somebody because she refused to order and apologised to the waiter, probably wishing to wait for her partner to turn up first before doing so.

Capri sat back and watched. He let his eyes peel away her dress. She confidently made him hard in his pants. Perhaps Mosalla was right; there are some good looking women in LA, but he doubted whether they beat the ones he knew back home. He figured though this was a pretty good example. He let his imagination go on a long rein and explored her more deeply in his now happily intoxicated mind. He reckoned she was mid thirties, definitely married, no kids as yet. The husband worked hard at the office all day whilst she stayed at home. They were comfortably well off, if not rich from what he could gather by a quick perusal of her dress, handbag and jewellery. They led a comfortable life with lots of social events and parties every night, she probably being the real socialite of the two. And they probably had a very active sex life. Who could blame them; she was well beddable, and yes, Capri wouldn't say no to her either.

She casually looked over her shoulder, taking in her surroundings, her eyes narrowly missing him, or so he thought. He didn't care now, too drunk to worry about such trifles, and continued staring at her as it was the only decent thing worth looking at in this spectacle. She was certainly patient if not well trained for again she declined to order and settled for another drink instead and smiled politely with big shining bright white teeth. Her husband must really have her under control. Then he thought; how could

anybody possibly leave a woman of exquisite beauty alone in a room full of salivating men? He'd better have a good excuse for being late, he thought.

Capri, annoyed since he was determined to forget about Carlotta, soon found himself thinking about her. The blonde babe before him was now being compared to her. And he wondered, in his inebriated state of mind, if all women in the future would be compared to Carlotta. Nor could he deny what his emotions were to telling him; he was falling for her, and he hated himself for it.

He quickly refilled his empty glass and lit up another cigarette, far from happy with the prospect of what his emotions were determined to impart to him all day. It would only complicate the situation, he told them, and yet he had to admit that he couldn't wait to see her again, to get back to her again, to be in her arms again and, yes, to fuck her again.

He vainly dismissed her, only for her to be replaced by another woman, one who brought him much pleasure, as well as much pain, like a rose could be beautiful, yet at the same time carry painful thorns. His ex-wife was just like that. Stephanie! Each memory of her was a pang in his heart, a stab wound to his chest, filling him with sadness and resentment at the time wasted for such a pathetic urchin. And each time he allowed her prominence in his mind it was marked by bitterness. He remembered how he had found her, literally picking her off the streets, giving her a home, nurtured her, cherished her, gave her all the things she had never had when she was an orphan, and finally gave her his love. But she went and threw it all way, got addicted to drugs and began a downward spiral which would finally carry her to her grave, despite his many attempts to save her. She was dead, but she still haunted him, hanging over his life like an unwanted shadow. He could see her now sitting before him, smiling in her usual way as she always did. Then she sat up and leaned on the table looking him directly in the eye. I am glad you died, he wanted to tell her. Do you hear me? Glad, fucking glad. You bitch! he told her.

He got up off his seat and leaned over the table and went to grab her.

"You bitch!" he shouted.

Suddenly the whole restaurant went quiet. Its silence was like a superbly polished mirror reflecting back at Capri his anger. He looked up at all the staring faces, each one curious, wondering who he was talking to. He

looked at them in disbelief, then back to the empty seat in front of him, and felt very foolish indeed. He could have sworn she was sitting there.

He slumped back down in his chair and wished a hole would open up wide and take him down. What was happening to him? It must be the drink, he assured himself, and quickly ordered the waiter over, signed for his meal, decided he needed more drink. He ordered a bottle of the house's finest champagne to be sent to his room. All the other patrons had thankfully gone back to their meals. He got up to leave only to fleetingly notice his blonde strumpet had been joined by a handsome looking young man with blond hair. He tried to get a closer look, but the people between him and her had the audacity to block his view. He snarled. *C'est la vie!* and repaired to his room, content with the thought of seeing Carlotta again.

As he opened the door to his room he realised he was quite drunk. The room seemed to sway momentarily, the headache coming up on him fast, a feeling of nausea gripping his stomach. The room felt icily cold, for some strange reason, even though warm air was coming through the open windows. Again he was seized somewhere deep down inside to go for it, to leap out into the beyond, and be no more.

But being the coward he was he opted to televid Carlotta instead, just so he could have another glimpse of her. He sat down by his bed and waited for her to answer. The screen was all steamed up. A hand wiped it clear.

"Harmon!" she shouted at him, "I was in the middle of a bath." She dropped her towel and climbed back in.

Capri apologised and smiled.

"Well?" she enquired above the foam whilst busily preening herself. "How did you get on with Mosalla?"

"Fine. We had a long talk. He was very helpful." His last word slurred out.

"Are you drunk?"

"No, just merry."

"Same thing. I know I said to treat it like a holiday; I don't think I meant get shit-faced in the process. So come on then, tell me how you're getting on. What have you learnt?"

He watched her, the way she lathered her arms as if hardly interested in what he had to say. "Oh, a few things really. After our chat Mosalla took me to the lab where apparently this guy called Jack died in an explosion."

"You mean Jack Pearson. Yes, I heard about it. Great shame. What else?"

For some reason she was being very offish with him. He felt like telling her about the negative side of the drug. She probably didn't know about it, but he thought he would test her anyway. "Yes, it was a nasty accident."

"I know Harmon, but what about the drug?"

She obviously didn't know. "Well, it appears you may be right. Crome did make a mistake by accidentally revealing the formula of the drug ..."

"Really?"

"Yes, in a poem. But we don't know which one. So I've got a bet with Mosalla I can find the right one. If I do I get to pick up 5 grand tomorrow. So, I'm going to be staying in tonight, reading some poetry, see if I can get anywhere nearer to finding this drug for you ..."

"Well, you do that, honey. I've got to go now. I'm going out with Don Lexington tonight. We're dining at La Bernadine's and I don't want to be late. Call me tomorrow night." She blew him a quick kiss and hung up.

"Fucking bitch," he shouted at the blank screen. He wouldn't have minded but he didn't even get to see much of that gorgeous body of hers.

He turned the thing off, slumped on the bed and lay silent for awhile, his eyes staring blankly into space. He thought about going out on the streets invoking death like he always did in New York when he felt like this, inviting a knife into his stomach, a punch in the face, anything rather than feel a pain that wasn't physical, and just wander. Or perhaps take in a few strip shows, a few more drinks and drift back to this hovel again. He was tempted but decided against it. Besides, he had his name to think of, having bet with Mosalla, and one thing he was adamant in doing was winning.

He wanted to call on Angel with a pure heart as he lay there, his eyes half-open. He knew there would be no response. So it would be a waste of time. He felt his heavy eyelids wanting to close, and capitulated, and sank into a slumber, but the further he sank he found he was menaced by grotesque

creatures. They appeared out of nowhere making vile noises like tapping sounds, tapping into his skull. He snapped out of it, only to find the sound continued before realising it was someone knocking on his door.

He opened it, quite forgetting he had ordered a bottle to be sent to his room. The waiter parked the trolley. Capri tipped him generously and was about to close the door behind him when he noticed a black streak pass his door. He poked his head round to see it was the blonde strumpet from downstairs he had been admiring. She was by herself and heading towards a door down from his on the other side. He stood there fascinated, watching her move gracefully with the sort of confidence and self-possession that demonstrated she knew she had 'It' and was deliberately flouting it by the way she swivelled her hips, her panty lines clearly visible through her tight dress. She stopped by her door, dug into her handbag for the key and appeared to be having trouble finding it. Capri was praying she had lost it. It would give him a reasonable excuse to offer his assistance and get to know her a bit. After all, what harm could it possibly do? He hesitated, happy just watching the way she was now bending down with her handbag on the floor, strewing around all those useless articles women for some reason kept in their bags, her magnificent breasts fairly bursting out of her dress. Just as he made up his mind to go for it she found her key, pulled it out, inserted it in the lock, opened her door and disappeared, but not without giving him a polite smile over her shoulder first. He smiled in return and watched her disappear. His blood started boiling in his loins making him feel lecherous. It was confirmed by the swelling in his pants.

He quickly slammed the door behind him, determined to forget about her: he had a job to do, and the last thing he needed was a distraction like her.

His only consolation was a bottle of champagne to keep him company tonight, chilled like the glasses, and with plenty of ice. He fished out the bottle, popped the cork and poured out that luscious liquid and thanked the gods for giving him this mission. He toasted Angel for making him experience that thing in the lab. He toasted Carlotta for sending him to this horrible place, and lastly to life and death and fetched out Crome's promising book of poetry from his jacket pocket before throwing himself down on his bed.

Half-interested, he took up a comfortable posture and flicked through some of the pages to get a feel for what Crome was saying. One doesn't read poetry; one immerses oneself in it and absorbs its contents like a rare draught of some fine wine, being intoxicated on its sentiments and emotive

inspiration. And like a precious drink, you sip it first, taste it, then swallow it down whole. He was attempting to do just that but found his mind was being disobedient. It wanted to get into that girl's pants. He restrained it and brought it back to the book.

He flicked through most of the early ones briefly to get a feel of their texture. The first impression he got was they were all mystical in content. After reading the first four or five poems it became apparent there was a deliberate ordering of the poems in themselves, suggesting steps on the path of initiation. It looked like Crome was delineating a way of becoming one with God through a personalised system of religion, perhaps something he had developed himself over many years and probably derived from personal experience.

Capri stopped, went back to the first poem for confirmation. It was entitled 'The God Man.' It laid down the foundation for the following poems in the rest of the book. Crome, in simple and precise terms, was basically stating that man was already God. The only problem was, he didn't know it.

Crome wasn't saying anything different from what had been previously expressed by all spiritual disciplines, albeit his approach to the central problem of man was more direct. He was stating succinctly man is divine, yet he has forgotten his divinity by his rigid adherence to ignorance or false belief. It ensnares man in the trappings of conventionality brought on by simply being incarnated in flesh. Right from the moment of conception, he says, we are conditioned into believing we are so-and-so and come to believe that by being given a name (which is partly dependent on parental whim and partly on genealogical descent) we believe we are that person, and this is perpetuated through our progeny; so the false belief continues. The poem strongly affirms this belief, that the personality is false and we are something else, i.e. divine. Belief only entrenches the ignorance like a dreamer in a dream, one from which he cannot wake up and question his divine identity. Believing in false belief is to believe in a lie; it is a trap.

Crome was pre-empting religion by positing the fact man is already God, thus making religion redundant. Religions like Christianity, for example, state he cannot come to God other than by the Church. If a man followed his own personal religious quest he would have no need of the Church.

This was confirmed in the following poem. All forms of worship, prayer, dogma, etc., are redundant and should be avoided. The problem was man, for the only thing which stops him from knowing he is God is himself.

Thus each man has to develop a means whereby he can achieve this end and it is left to him to create his own system, his own personal religion, his own belief-system, his own mythology and ultimately his own personality to reflect more clearly the god within. Crome stressed it was not a matter of developing, i.e. spiritually progressing, for how could you develop what was already there. The onus was on developing a systematic approach to solving the problem of this lack of realisation and making it possible.

However, the above is no easy task, nor was Crome stating it was. His use of literary heroes like Gilgamesh, St George, etc., in the next two poems associated the task with the heroic journey of all mythologies. The majority of myths have a hero who in his quest destroys the mythical monster, whether it be in the guise of a dragon or a phantasmal beast or whatever. It represents false belief. Such an opponent always blocks the hero's way either with force, cunning or guile, ever seeking to tempt and kill the hero. And no progression can be made until the monster has been slain. Only then can the hero continue his journey and find the fabulous fortress or the hidden castle at the centre of the myth, a symbol of the Self.

This was all very praiseworthy, Capri thought, but it all sounded frightfully too far-fetched to be practical to actually happen. Men did not want to be gods (in the sense of purely spiritual beings rather than in the materialistic sense of being in a position of power); they did not want to remit false belief. Nor did they want to be heroes and go through the painful, arduous torture such a journey entails. Man was content with his little lot in life, obsessed with money, power, status and all the other false gods he worshipped. So inextricably caught up in the machine he had created he was no longer separate from the machine: he was the machine. The machine fed him, kept him alive, sustained and supported him, offering fruitless promises, hopes and rewards he was too weak to deny. And this machine, called Consumerism, was invincible, he the mere cog who helped it to work with the labour of his blood and wealth which kept it lubricated. It represented one vast treadmill from which few would be happy to jump off and dive into the inexorable abyss below with a valediction most of them would end up regretting. But this is precisely what it entailed.

He wanted to pat Crome on the back, for he was issuing a summons to each man to know his Self, whether he be a baker, a banker, a merchant or a sailor. It did not matter. Any man could become the god he was in essence and manifest his genius on all planes. All it required was work. This was real work, the hardest and toughest of them all with a goal at the end that could only be earned, not bought. It was rather like trying to pick yourself up by your own bootstraps, and nobody else was going to help

you; you had to do it all alone. It involved a constant striving inwardly and the 'invoking often' of one's own god. And man, being the laziest and lethargic of all creatures, had to seriously consider whether he had it in him to pursue this spiritual work, for not only was it the hardest, it was also the loneliest and intensely, agonisingly personal at times. The God-man is rare; to find one who was also prepared to work at it twenty-four hours every day and risk madness and death, and capable of handling despair, dejection, loneliness, isolation, self-loathing, condemnation from others, betrayal, ostracism, misunderstandings, misery, anguish and all the other troughs of spiritual malaise, was even rarer. It was a wonder why Crome was bothering to speak at all. Perhaps he should have remained taciturn in an age where man relied on machines to do most of the work for him; men would not be interested. Yet the one virtue Crome displayed above all others was his complete avoidance of evangelicalism. His message was simple, his approach subtle, he was not ramming it down everyone's throats, as exemplified by this book. Not only was it small and a limited edition—although nearly all copies had been destroyed—it was not meant for the masses, only for the few who would really be interested. He had no sympathy for the whole of humanity, nor did he wish to convert them. It would be through making an impact on those in positions of power he hoped his message would slowly disseminate like a dispensation, and its recipients had the choice of either accepting or rejecting it.

Capri paused and poured himself another glass of champagne. It was all theoretical guesswork on his part, but he reckoned that was pretty much what Crome's intention was behind getting the book published. Why else pass it on to someone like Mosalla, an influential man who evidently belonged to a social body, being perhaps a Freemason, attached to a Masonic lodge, or some other august organisation. That would explain why Crome and Mosalla were dressed the way they were in the photograph.

Capri had a breather and came up for some fresh air, or rather some smoke, and lit up a cigarette, and some more champagne. Had Crome made the journey and therefore was able to write about it? If so, was he the God Man of the poem? Had he undertaken the journey successfully? Capri looked at himself, reflected deeply in his drunken stupor upon his own lack of progress. He had practically done all Crome suggested, divested himself of all he knew he was not in order to find his self. He yearned for God constantly, and rejected everything but God. It had led so far to a brick wall which he could not surmount, circumnavigate or knock down.

His head grew weary and again found he was slipping in to a slumber. The little book with a big message fell from his limp hand to the floor.

A WOMAN OF POWER

'Give me a woman of scarlet
Who is proud to be a harlot.
Give me a woman who is a whore
To initiate, stimulate and adore.

Let her be strong and mighty,
Not fickle, faery or flighty,
But wilful, passionate and resourceful,
Shameless, guiltless and forceful.

Let her be devilishly wicked and sinful
And filled with lewdness to the brimful,
Even flowing over with purple pleasure,
Her open heart my tongue to treasure.

Her perfumes are scented with the darkness of death
And sweet smelling the graveyard of her breath.
Her colours are delicacies, black to the blind
But red to the seeing to enrapture the mind.

Her two eyes are dark as ebony, her third the Eye of the Void.
Her hair the Trees of Eternity, her deadly kisses ones to avoid.
Her skin is smooth as marble, her legs ever open for love
For all the visions to pass through; the serpent and the dove!

Her vulva is the gateway, a door to space, the utterer of the word
Deep within it, reverberating with vibrations, can a voice be heard.
In the laboratory of her body swell the oceans; out of her courses the seas
In her Time and Space are annihilated—this is the mystery of mysteries!

The Holy of Holies is her puissant seat for those who are True of Voice.
(Goddess of the Feather, O Ancient Doubled Queen, Rejoice! Rejoice!)
Thy period is come, my Crimson Priestess, thou who art the Sow-er.
At whose feet I worship and devour, O my lusty Woman of Power!'

Alexander Crome,
Selected Works

—15—
A WOMAN OF POWER

He must have dozed off. He couldn't remember. The champagne probably went to his head, and the last few sleepless nights were taking their toll.

He had to shake himself awake, hard. It was still early evening and all he wanted to do was fall asleep. He had to keep reminding himself he was on an assignment, and had been entrusted with it by a woman; a woman of wealth, a woman of means, a woman of intellect, and a woman of power.

Suddenly he sat up, now remembering what Mosalla had said all those hours ago about a poem relating to Carlotta.

He found the little book on the floor where it had fallen and started flicking through until he came to page fifteen and laughed, for there it was, blatantly written yet unusual in that it did not possess the same structure as the previous poems, nor did it appear to coincide or have any connection with them. It was quite obviously referring to a woman like Carlotta. In this one Crome seemed to be listing the qualities and magical prerequisites for his favourite type of woman, as suggested by the title, 'A Woman of Power.' Drunk, but still lucid, he decided to read the poem aloud to get the full force of it, letting his imagination roam.

As he did so, he imagined seeing Carlotta again, how he saw her in his apartment, his vision of her standing on the hill made up of all the men who had been slain in her name, all martyrs to her cause. Then he thought of what Mosalla had told him about her being their High Priestess, seeing her sitting on a throne of gold in a dark robe, and the rest of the group were worshipping her, offering her an obeisance as if she was the Goddess incarnate. Then he saw her lying on an altar being put into a trance by Crome. He was wearing a long black robe made of the finest silk, and sporting a finely wrought gold ring on his index finger, the one holding the long wand which he now passed over her prostrate body as she slipped into a deeper trance and closed her eyes in ecstasy, her lips trembling, her mouth becoming oracular and the other ritualists writing down everything she said.

Yes, he could see it all now. Crome was advocating a certain type of woman who was perfectly incarnated in the form of Carlotta. He was so obsessed with her he had even written a poem in which he praised her qualities.

Capri finished reading it, lit up again, and dipped into it once more.

Despite the frivolity of the first three stanzas, it was very clear what Crome was getting at. He was constituting the supreme type of woman who, understandably, was considered a whore by the bourgeoisie for they were incapable of conceiving of a type of woman free from sin, one who was shameless and guiltless. In their eyes she was despicable, a cheap, common doxy or prostitute with the same loose morals of living and a low level of intellect, one they described as a fallen woman who was lewd and lascivious, but in actuality a booster, as demonstrated by Capri's experience with Carlotta the night before.

A Woman of Power is the sort of woman who makes things happen, who gets things going, who breaks through barriers and invests the sexual act with a magical force so as to transmute consciousness, thus making it divine. If this poem was referring to her then she was indeed the exemplary type, a paragon of power beyond all mundane considerations; both selfish and selfless at the same time. In her eyes no act was unimaginable or repugnant; she could manifest the fantasy of any man however depraved, for that was her function. The Woman of Power acts as a gateway, a transmundane source for other worlds, other spaces. She reifies them in the here and now. That is her value. Her role as a priestess was exactly that, as Mosalla had informed him. The fickle, weak, flighty type did not possess this innate power and were incapable of manifesting anything on this plane other than progeny.

Capri went through the poem again, fascinated by the way in which it started off as a piece of schoolboy idealism then changed tone halfway through and developed into an abstruse set of credentials for the type of woman Crome had in mind. The latter half baffled him. He persevered.

Half an hour later he was perplexed. Most of the poem seemed to be couched in Egyptian symbolism, some of which he was not at all familiar. But then he got to thinking, was this the one referring to the drug? He read it again, this time to himself quietly, allowing whatever images it conjured up to come to the fore. Again Carlotta came to mind; it was inevitable. The poem was intimately bound up with her, therefore any associations it possessed would be of her.

He put the book down and went through the imagery of the poem in his head with his eyes closed, and let his imagination loose. Soon he was dreaming of her and what she possibly represented.

He saw her as a harridan, perhaps hell-bent on revenge. She was standing next to his bed with a wicked gleam in her eye. She was now wearing a black dress with loose shoulder straps. She daintily removed one strap, then the other, all the while her eyes fixed on his, and let the dress drop gracefully to the floor, revealing her splendid naked body, then climbed on top of him, easing him inside. And, like the previous occasion, he saw her as a dark goddess, a Kali fulminating with fire. He let her have her wicked way with him as he just lay there whilst she did all the work. He was there for her pleasing. She was a Woman of Power, there to invoke in him power, to cajole and bring it out, to tease and entice, to raise him aloft, to stretch him out of himself, to boost him, to do anything she fucking well liked with him tonight. He was all hers.

She pulled off him. His hand became her hand. Go on, you bitch, take me, take me. Yes, go on, fucking take me! She gripped him harder, just like he begged, forcefully, almost manfully. She looked up and smiled; she pleased him with that big juicy smile of hers, with those ivory white teeth of hers, with those soft wet lips of hers, slightly parted. His body gave into her as she coaxed him on to a paroxysm of death, and he died a little in her hand and passed out.

INVOCATION OF
THE SCARLET WOMAN

'In Celebration of the Phallus
Will I come for thee, in thee,
All over thee, my Scarlet Woman.
And ye shall come unto me
Like a mighty woman of whoredom,
Frothing with filth and abominations.
I shall come unto thee as the Sun,
Thee shall come unto me as the Moon
Dripping its succulent juice from the sea.
Come to me, O Scarlet Woman.
Feel me! Eat me! Lift me up!
Let me dip into thy blessed cup!
I am the Beast that roars like a lion
And I can break bonds stronger than iron.
My Scarlet Harlot, open thyself up for me,
And come forth in thine hidden secrecy.
Thou knowest alone for thee do I exist,
Then enwrap me in thy cunt, sweat and piss!
Many flowers have I plucked for thee, regularly.
And I shall sing to thee, eat for thee,
Drink and intoxicate myself on drugs for thee,
All for the love of thee, the love of thee.
Then come to me my Scarlet Bride,
For I yearn for thee, the loins of thee,
The love and very joy of thee.
And there is joy when we come,
So let us come, let us come.
And we shall come soon
In the juice of the Moon,
In our Celebration.
In Celebration of the Phallus
Will I die for thee.'

Alexander Crome,
Selected Works

—16—
THE KALANITIC EQUATION

She lies supine, resplendent, girdled by tenebrous space, restrained in position, her naked body a living chemical factory, her eyes closed in ecstasy, her long ebony hair flowing, cascading like inverted trees whose branches reach down into the infernal deeps. Her shrill voice utters a concatenation of sounds in acute, agonising glossalia as her invisible partner plunges deeper inside her being. She writhes, moans, her head lolling from side to side with each sharp paroxysm, turning her flesh into a terpsichorean machine of rhythmic oscillations, tapping out zombieic voodoo codes, her legs ever parted for her translucent host. She tosses and turns in her restraints as he pumps her harder demonically, penetrating, violating, stimulating the soft texture of her flesh. She is all his, one with his desire, her body hopping like a frog—amphibian pleasure. Slowly he starts to take form, his body glinting like sheets of metal, panels of steel, his tongue unfurling, writhing, then slinking its way round her neck. Out of his forehead extrudes a proboscis. It attaches itself to her forehead as she orgasms in pain, as he starts sucking out her brain...

* * * * *

"Carlotta!" He woke up with a start, his heart palpitating, still seeing her lying there by virtue of a subtle perichoresis, an interpenetration of the planes. As he regained full consciousness the oneiric, fluidic vestiges seeped away leaving him frightened. What did it mean?

He was still lying limp on the bed. Then he remembered what had happened before he passed out, seeing Carlotta, how she changed; what had been at first a pleasurable fantasy soon turned into a grotesque mimicry of his desire for her. It was too horrible to bear.

He jumped off the bed and staggered blindly to the bathroom, splashing cold water in his face, anything to wash it away. It was too real to be a dream or a nightmare. Vaguely it all tied together somehow, the thing in the lab, the stories he had heard of her and the poem he last read.

He marched back into the room, grabbed Crome's book of poetry and flicked to page fifteen. What was it really saying? Was there a connection?

He sat down on the edge of his bed, lit up a cigarette and went through it again, his head killing him with this intense pain inside making it difficult to concentrate. He dismissed it and soldiered on, allowing any thought how ever absurd, to reveal itself and be considered. Time was measured by inhalations and exhalations of smoke. A few cigarettes later, he still wanted to blast Crome for his evasiveness. The poem was too esoteric for his liking, his ignorance only making him angrier. He was getting all riled up now, trying to make sense out of nonsense. This couldn't possibly be the poem. Then there was only one way to find out or, rather, only one person who could help: Angel!

He closed the book and held it in his left hand. With his right hovering over the surface, he started to move it in tight circles widdershins. He imagined being inflamed with light, seeing it flow down all over him from above and recited a potent call he sparingly used to get Angel's attention, one that was irresistible, saying it slowly and eloquently whilst imagining the book to open at the right page.

He felt something, like a small tug on the book, and opened his eyes excitedly and looked down at the page trembling in his hands. There was the poem that comported the formulation of the drug, or did it? A quick glance at the page number had him laughing out loud for how obvious could you get. It was page sixteen, the sixteenth poem, and thus related directly to its highest formulation. Or was it too obvious? According to Mosalla, the poem's inclusion was accidental. Was Crome therefore pulling his readers' legs, poking fun at them by making them think this was the one or seeing if they were too stupid to realise it? Or was it a mere accident that the book just happened to open on this page? After all he had only finished reading the previous page.

His dismissed his doubts as he had an uncanny feeling this was it. His divination was marked by an unmistakable sign, a feeling of 'rightness' that was unequivocal. He dived in and took a look.

The poem was entitled 'Invocation of the Scarlet Woman.' It was quite evidently an elaboration, or an extension, of the previous poem as it dealt with the same theme, or at least appeared to do so ostensibly as it was another ode to Crome's Woman of Power, this time invoking her presence in the flesh through a magical dithyramb. He read it silently to himself first

to get into its rhythm, and then decided to read it aloud. After all, it was an invocation and therefore should be recited aloud. He got up and stood in the centre of the room and imagined this was his temple, just as Jack did in the lab, seeing the walls as smooth black obsidian, the columns in the corners, the ceiling arching high above, and started to recite solemnly.

As he recited each line he imagined each one was a step leading up to heaven, and saw himself ascending a tall staircase. He felt himself rise slowly high up into the air, high above his room, high above the hotel, and by the time he reached the last line he imagined he was now touching the dark sky above, but did not go beyond it. For nothing can go beyond the wide open erotic sky. He fell back down to earth in a faint, or a deep swoon, still conscious but oblivious of everything except a wondrous vision which now appeared before him.

* * * *

She towers up before me, dwarfing the landscape, her half naked body shining with light, radiating against the backdrop of the early evening sky. She stands with only her left profile visible, her head perfectly upright, and her long milky white hair flowing down her back. She is dressed in a purple skirt which, like her hair, flows like waves to the ground she treads upon. Her feet are like burnished gold, her crown is the moon. Her breasts are ripe and bare, full and heavy. She reaches up and cups the heavens with her delicate hands and brings them down to her waiting mouth. She tilts her head back to drink of the sweet clear liquid flowing from them. She quaffs it until satiated. She then closes her eyes in satisfaction and smiles. Her belly is now swollen. Her skirt ripples like a trembling veil. It parts to reveal an absence of space. Soon there is movement between its folds, and before I know it a horde of creatures come rushing towards me. I am overcome.

* * * *

A gentle persistent tapping awoke him. Capri must have passed out again. It took him awhile to get his bearings. He eased himself off the floor wondering who was knocking on his door. He smartened himself up and brushed his unkempt hair back, and checked his watch. It was nearly midnight. Intrigued, he opened the door.

Two gorgeous eyes met him, kind of dreamy looking as if their owner was sleepwalking. He didn't recognise her at first, and it took awhile before it sunk in. His mouth dropped open in disbelief. It was his blonde strumpet.

"Hi," she simply said.

"Hello," he replied automatically, barely able to get the word out.

"Is it all right to come in?" she asked in her Marlboro-stained voice.

"Sure. Sure, come in." He politely moved out of the way and let her in, unsure whether he was still dreaming or not.

She walked into his room dressed in a black loose fitting track suit and white trainers, her hair looking dishevelled and as white as the goddess in his vision. It was bleached and long and flowing down her back. Yet she was hardly the glamorous picture he had been admiring earlier on. This was her at her most casual, he guessed. But what was she doing here? Was this a present from the gods, he wondered. Had his invocation really been that successful? No, it had to be a coincidence. He nervously checked the corridor to make sure she was alone. No sign of the husband or anybody else for that matter; she was all alone and making herself right at home, smoking a joint, standing on his small balcony staring out into the night. He couldn't believe his luck. He quickly shut the door and thanked the gods.

She took a toke from her joint as she leaned on the railings.

"You don't mind do you?" she asked him over her shoulder.

"No, not at all." He tried to calm himself down. He figured he too didn't look his best and was far from sober.

"I was bored. I thought I'd come and see you. Do you want some?" She offered him her joint.

"No thanks. I don't touch the stuff."

She must have smoked nearly all of it by herself. Her pupils were dilated like a cat's in the dark. Her complexion was slightly ashen but calm and composed. Her eyes were not only dreamy; they were sullen, subdued, small dark blue orbs brought out by generous amounts of mascara, yet shone

with an unusual light. She was most definitely stoned out of her skull.

"You're not from round here, are you?"

"No. I'm from New York."

"Really. But you're English, right?" He nodded. "I could tell. Your accent is very distinctive. You've got a very deep voice. Did you know that?" He nodded and yawned. She turned back to look at the view, lost in it.

"And you? You're not from round here either, I take it?"

"No. I'm from the south, San Diego. You ever been there?"

"No, I can't say that I have."

"It's okay. But I prefer it here in LA. You on business?" she asked, looking at him over her shoulder.

"Is it that obvious?"

She laughed. "I thought you were. I saw you sitting all alone in the restaurant at dinner, figured you were a businessman, here on business by yourself, needing some company."

"Well, uh, that's very considerate of you. But do you normally knock on stranger's doors at this time of night?"

"This is LA. It doesn't matter what time of night it is. Time is irrelevant here. LA's always awake. I couldn't sleep either. How about you?"

"I don't sleep much anyway."

"Me neither." She laughed again, revealing her big shiny white teeth, obviously capped, and turned back to the view as if he wasn't there.

Capri had a nagging suspicion in the back of his mind which made him feel awkward. There was something about this that wasn't right. What was she really doing here and what did she want? He heard this town was friendly, but this was ridiculous. A voluptuous young girl like her in a stranger's room and so stoned it would be easy to take advantage of her. What was going on? But she was right. He did need company, missing Carlotta

terribly, and it was good to have somebody to talk to. He decided to ignore his suspicions and accept it, how ever absurd the situation appeared to be.

"That's better," she said, tossing the finished joint away. "You know, you can almost see the Strip from here. Look at all them people wandering around. You have a fabulous view."

He had to concur. All he could see was her backside sticking out, and very nice it was too. "Can I get you a drink or something? I still have some champagne left."

"Champagne!" she gushed and whizzed round, excited.

"Yes. It's probably gone flat by now as I couldn't finish it all by myself."

"Wow. I adore champagne."

He picked up a glass. Only then did he realise there were two of them. The significance didn't pass unnoticed. He poured out a glass, handed it to her.

"So what's the occasion?" she asked, sipping it like precious liquid.

He poured himself a glass as well. "I felt it was time for a celebration," he joked, knowing she wouldn't understand.

"Oh? What you celebrating?"

"I've won a bet. I'll be picking up $5000 tomorrow and I can't wait to see the look on my friend's face when he has to hand it over. So I thought I'd treat myself to a bottle, seeing as I can now afford it. Cheers."

They clinked glasses. She smiled and continued to sip gingerly.

"You got any cigarettes?" she asked him, looking round.

He offered her his packet, lit hers up and one for himself and stood there looking at her. Yes, she was still desirable. Tall, well shaped from what he could see of her body, quite powerfully built, but a bit short on brains, he figured, unless it was due to the hash. And definitely married. He noticed the wedding ring and wondered what had happened to the husband, and then watched her help herself to his couch and put her feet up. He was

tempted to go over and join her, but that would be improper. He opted for the bed instead and propped himself up where he could get a better view of her. She had the airs and graces of a child, so carefree and unaffected; he would love to take advantage of her now. He wouldn't, at least not yet, not until he was satisfied with the real reason for her visit.

"This your first time in LA?" she asked him, blowing the smoke out.

"As a matter of fact it is. So—uh—you here together?"

"Together?"

"Yes. Well that was your husband I saw you with at dinner, wasn't it?"

"Oh, no," she laughed. "No, that was my brother. He lives here. I always call him up when I come to LA and have dinner with him. No, my husband Johnny, he stayed at home. He's busy working on this big project at present. Too busy for me. So he said go away for awhile until I've finished. Enjoy yourself, he said. So I thought I'd come here. I'm here all alone," she said with a cutesy grin and sipped her drink, her eyes fixed on his.

He could read her mind. It was more than an invitation. She was soliciting him, but somehow he still wasn't happy. Then she leaned forward to stub out her cigarette in the ashtray on the table. He could see her breasts move under her loose top—quite obviously not wearing a bra—and sat back and brushed back her hair with a big smile on her face.

"I see. And what does Johnny do for a living?"

"Oh, he deals in oil. You?"

"I'm self-employed."

"Really? What kind of work do you do?"

"I work on projects as well."

"What kind of projects? No, don't tell me. Let me guess. You're a contractor overseeing some building."

"No, nothing like that."

CELEBRATION

"You're a consultant, aren't you?"

"No, no that either."

She paused and looked at him. "Okay. I got you sussed. You're a systems analyst for a computer company."

"No, you're way out. It's nothing like that. I'm an investigator."

With that, she sat up all excited. "An investigator?" He nodded. "Wow, I've never met an investigator before. You're working on a case, right?"

"You could say that."

"What kind of case?"

"Well, I could tell you, but it's confidential."

"Oh, go on, tell me. Please."

He looked at her again. This was not the result of his invocation. She was not a Woman of Power or a Scarlet Woman, but a female who must be at least mid-thirties with a non-existent brain, your typical blonde bimbo. What he really wanted to talk to was an intelligent woman, but perhaps that was a contradiction in terms, rather than playing this silly little game at midnight. She reminded him of Stephanie, someone else who was lacking in that department and needed to grow up badly.

"I'm sorry, I'm afraid I can't. Besides it isn't that glamorous. In fact, the work's tedious at times and I hate talking about work."

"No, I'm really interested. You're working on a big job, aren't you? I can tell. You're looking for somebody, a spy, right?" He shook his head. "What? No, let me guess. Some top secret documents." He shook his head again. "Stolen property?" And again. "Money?"

"We're all looking for money."

"Oh, come on, be serious. Tell me."

He decided to capitulate, sort of. "I'm looking for a drug."

"Oh, honey, we're all looking for drugs," she said, laughing.

"Ah, but this drug is special. It's not just any drug. Besides, it could make me a very rich man if I find it."

"And what you going to do when get this money?"

"Haven't really thought about it. Perhaps buy myself a house out in the country, who knows."

"We've got a house in the country. In fact, we've got two, one in the city and one in the country. I was going to go there this week, but I thought fuck it. It gets too quiet at times. I thought I'd come here for some excitement." She finished her glass.

"More?" he offered.

She nodded. "You know, live it up in LA, as they say."

"So what happened to your brother?" he asked, pouring her another drink.

"Oh, he had to go, got an emergency call. We were gonna go out tonight."

He finished off the bottle for himself. "I'm afraid that's the last of it."

"Perhaps I should have gotten here earlier."

Perhaps you should have, he thought. "Were you planning on going anywhere special?" He sat himself back down on the bed.

"Not really. Just the Oasis down the road. It's a new nightclub, supposed to be real good. But I wouldn't go there by myself. I thought I'd stay in, have an early night."

"And you couldn't sleep?"

"No, so I got stoned instead. Stoned immaculate," she said, rolling the last word off her tongue.

Capri was far from happy. He was really trying to probe her. Because this didn't ring right at all. She must be lying. Nothing she had said so far made logical sense and sounded false anyway. The last time he saw was

approximately eight o'clock entering her hotel room. That was four hours ago. That means she must have been either trying to get to sleep for a very long time or been smoking all that time. Even if she had, surely she would have been knocked out by now. Or perhaps she only started smoking a couple of hours ago. Either way, he still wasn't satisfied. He decided to continue his job and investigate.

"Don't you smoke hash?" she asked as if she had been reading his mind.

"No, I gave it up a long time ago."

"Don't you miss it?"

"Not really. Too much over-indulgence. It made me think too deeply."

Which reminded him of Stephanie, how he introduced her to the habit and she became hooked, then moved on to the harder stuff, and that was when he lost her.

"What you thinking?" he heard her say.

He came back up to the surface. "Oh, nothing. I was just remembering something that happened in the past."

"I love it. It makes you feel sooooo relaxed."

"You do look relaxed."

"I am. But I'm kind of hot. It's sticky in here."

She was right. Despite the air coming in from the windows, the room was hot and stale. Nor did there appear to be any air-conditioning. "Sorry, but the windows are wide open, and that's all I've got."

She laughed. "I like you. You're so laid back. I've never met anybody like you before. Do you mind if I take my top off?"

"No, go right ahead," he replied, thinking she had a T-shirt on underneath. He nearly spilt his drink in his lap as he watched her pull her jacket off and throw it casually on the floor and brushed her hair back, her breasts wondrously exposed. He thought it was the drink at first, that he was seeing

things, but he could not doubt his vision. They were beautiful and he was hard for them.

She gave him a sheepish, cutesy grin. "I'm not embarrassing you, am I?"

"No, not at all," he replied, his voice quivering. His hand was even beginning to shake as he tried to put his glass to his lips. She was doing it on purpose, of course. Then he heard her laugh. "What's so funny?"

"You know," she sniggered, kicking off her trainers and putting her feet up on the side. She laid back. "I was thinking, here's me on some man's couch in his room at midnight and I don't even know what his name is."

He laughed too. "Sorry, I forgot to introduce myself. The name's Harmon."

"Harmon." She repeated it, saying it a few times until she found the intonation she preferred. "A nice name. I like it."

"And yours is?"

"Katherine, but everyone calls me Katie."

He thought Katty would have been more appropriate the way she was lying there with that look of satiation on her face like a well fed feline.

"Aren't you married, Harmon?"

Here we go, he thought. "I used to be many years ago."

"But you're divorced now?" He nodded. "Shame. I hate it when things like that happen. It always seems so sad."

"It's one of those things, it can't be helped."

"And what about your ex-wife? Did she ever get married again?"

"No, she died shortly afterwards," he replied, wishing not to think about it.

"Oh, I'm sorry."

"Don't be. It happened a long time ago."

"And what about kids?" she asked him offhandedly.

He stifled a yawn, thinking couldn't she come up with something more original. "No, we never got around to it. And you?"

"No, I can't. When we first got married I thought I could. We tried, but—uh—I suffer from the same problem as other women."

"I see," he replied simply, and decided not to pursue that line of enquiry any further. For some women it was a sore point, not being able to menstruate, which meant they were infertile. That may be the reason why little Katie here was the way she was, he thought; it prevented her from becoming a full woman, in much the same way that a man couldn't become a man due to a biological indisposition whereby he was now producing little or no sperm. ... Suddenly the heavens opened up, and he saw the Light. Yes! Of course! Now he realised what it was all about as the words of the poem came flooding back to him triumphantly. Now he understood. Now he knew where the drug came from.

He wanted to jump up, shout it out loud, tell everyone, even this silly little girl sitting half naked on his couch. But it was only now, having been lost in thought for the past few minutes, he realised what she was doing. She was busy playing with herself, preening her hair, brushing it back and applying cubes of ice to her forehead to cool herself down, producing rivulets of water. They ran down her cheeks and dripped on to her chest making her nipples erect. She would then let out a quiet 'coo' as it hit a sensitive area of her skin. Capri, who had been totally unaware of this tantalising spectacle, sat up and took note. And as if to confirm, knowing that he was now watching, she made each act a deliberately provocative act, just for him.

Capri continued watching her voyeuristically, like another film. Yet this one was different; this one was more interesting and he didn't even have to pay for it. And like an avid spectator, he continued watching in silence.

He doted on the way she tilted her head back and wiped the slowly melting ice all over her face. It was turning him on, and she knew it. Occasionally she would stifle the shrieks threatening to escape from her mouth. Then she would lean her head back, close her mouth, then open it and let out a purr as the water trickled all over her tender anatomy. Capri, unbearably hard in his pants, didn't think he would be able to contain himself much longer, he too delighting in the tension she was deliberately creating.

Now she was fishing out more ice, wiping a lump of it delicately over her closed eyelids, puckering up her lips as the water round down her cheeks, her tongue slipping out to lap at it and then licked her lips and smiled. It was driving him crazy inside for she was definitely doing it on purpose, the bitch. He crossed his legs to control this insatiable lust he now had for her. She was working it up into a fine frenzy. He fought back by lighting up a cigarette and laid back, entranced.

He was loving the pain of the tension she was creating inside him. It made him feel alive, watching her dip in for more ice and rubbing it slowly all over. She shrilled.

Capri flicked his ash and smoked some more. You bitch, you're doing it on purpose, aren't you? It was getting to him. Soon he wouldn't be able to control himself; he'd be going over there, ripping her jogging pants off, forcing her legs apart, and giving her what she really wanted. He felt like he was going to explode in his pants any minute.

As his fantasy was gathering momentum, Katie put an ice cube to her mouth, licked it, sucked it and lapped at the water, again closing her eyes in ecstasy, her head right back so her hair fell over the side of the couch and flowed to the ground. The resemblance was uncanny. Katie's posture perfectly reflected the goddess in his vision, for it was exactly the same. Even her profile complemented the one he saw in the vision, the only difference being Katie was reclining, not standing. Then he knew intuitively what was going to be happening next. Go on, do it, you bitch. Do exactly what she did, he wanted to tell her. The premonition was forceful and demanding enough to curb his fantasy. He was all eyes. He waited, watched.

All the ice in the bucket had melted. Katie leaned forwards, dipped her hands into the bucket and cupped some water, then leant back and raised her cupped hands in the air, tilted her head back and let the water flow down to her open mouth. It was absolutely identical to his vision, even down to the way she was closing her eyes as she drank. It was too much of a coincidence. Now Capri was worried. All of a sudden he didn't feel that hard for her and just stared at her in disbelief, his mind agitated and disturbed. How could these two events follow so consecutively? Was she a manifestation of this goddess and simply re-enacting what she had done? He was seriously baffled.

CELEBRATION

Katie opened her eyes, looked in his direction and smiled. He feigned a smile, a weak smile that was affected as his mind froze and went completely blank. She must have picked up he had lost interest for she resumed wiping ice cold water into her soft tender flesh to get him excited again. This time it was more of a pronounced effort on her part. She wiped the wet palms of her hands around her breasts, getting her nipples nice and hard, moaning like a cat on heat and checked him again. It had worked. Whatever the significance or correlation was between her and the goddess in his vision, he could not deny that she was here for a reason, here for him, and the gods were giving her to him. Nor could he deny she was attractive and it would be foolish to throw it all away over something he was at a loss to explain. He now really, desperately wanted her and patted the side of his bed. She gave him another one of her smiles, brushed her hair back with her wet hands and slowly drew herself off the couch and slinked her way towards him, her eyes firmly fixed on his. As she got closer her movements reminded him of the creatures in his vision. They came right up to him before he blacked out, their eyes fixed on his. But whereas they had appeared to be hostile, threatening, Katie had transformed into a vision of voluptuousness, flashing signals at him as she approached, gesturing she was there for the taking. He could have her, do anything he wanted with her, and glanced quickly at the noticeable swelling in his pants as he lay there entranced.

"I see I please my master," she whispered softly, emphatically.

Capri merely nodded as she came right up to him and stopped by the side of the bed, flicked her hair back, held it and gave him a look like she was a naughty girl and made sure he got the message before she let her bleached, straggly hair down over her face and then slowly brought her hands down to her breasts, stroked them, her long black fingernails glinting, encircling her nipples and carved a white line down her abdomen towards her waistband. They stopped, skirted round and slowly, but very carefully with the utmost patience pulled them down an inch to reveal a small amount of flesh and held it there. Her eyes flashed into his. She had a wicked smile on her face, one of guilt and temptation, and then looked at her jogging pants as she pulled them all the way down. She had a small triangle of shiny black pubic hair, trimmed so short there was hardly any of it there, and mostly shaved around her mound.

She looked at him as she stood there wonderfully naked, then bent down on the bed and edged over towards him. Her hands strayed towards his flies and deftly undid them. They found what they were looking for and brought it out, his massive throbbing cock which was dying for her cunt. She smiled with satisfaction, blew him a kiss and got her right hand working on him whilst her other one started undoing his belt and the buttons on his shirt. His cock obviously pleased her for she was taking great delight in it. It was already oozing plenty of gleet which had been inside just waiting to pour out for her. She rubbed it into his glans and licked it once, then fisted him harder as his shirt came off. Then she stopped to remove his shoes and trousers as he lay there, she happy to oblige him, then lastly his underpants and got working on him again. She bent down to kiss his cock, gave him another smile and then went down on it all the way, her tongue working round it, up and down its shaft and then took it deep into the back of her throat. It was unbearable. She took him to the peak, left him hovering on the edge as she ceased and smiled again. She did it on purpose. She then came right up to him, her mouth meeting his, her lips pursed. She gave him a quick peck. Then they kissed unremittingly, her tongue diving deep into his mouth, his around hers, exchanging electricity.

She then lifted her leg over him and kneeled above him, flung her hair back and smiled as she sat down on his stomach and edged her buttocks back to rub against his crotch and started grinding her crutch against his cock, delighting in the torture she was inflicting on him. He tried to insert himself. She wouldn't have it. Instead, she pulled him up so he could kiss her, caress her, nip her soft tender flesh. She leaned back, stuck out her chest so he could taste her protruding breasts. He did. His mouth worked at them, kissing them, licking them and then gently nibbling them. She loved it and started writhing, moaning, even shrieking as he continued. Eventually she remitted. Her hand found his cock and guided it inside her. She was already wet and hot, her cunt tight and deep, taking him in all the way. She pushed him down and started riding him. He lay back and let her have it her way. She could do whatever she wanted, now that the teasing was over, now that it was onto the serious part, the part he loved and in his favourite position. She was becoming wild, excited, hot and feverish as she rode him harder, her incredible breasts bouncing up and down, her head lolling back and forth, her eyes closed in sheer delight. Any minute he would be exploding inside her. His body started kicking into action, his rhythm

matching and synchronising with hers, his pelvis pounding hard into her crutch as she straddled him and was giving it all she got. She maybe a silly little girl, he thought, but she certainly knew how to tease and please, and the wait had been worth while.

But then she stopped just as he was about to come. He sighed as she pulled herself off him. She wanted to control it, manipulate him, make him play it her way. He submitted to her fancies. She had now pleased him, giving him partially what he wanted. Now she wanted to be pleased. He got the message and pushed her off, threw her onto her back and kneeled between her legs. He spread them apart and looked deep into her eyes. She closed them and looked away, spreading her legs even more. He ran his hands up and down the insides of her thighs and pushed her legs flat down on the bed, her femininity now fully exposed, and went down on her. Not only was she hot and wet, she was perfumed. It was a strong, aromatic smell, one he associated with the East. Perfumed pussy, he thought, and ran his tongue all the way around her hole, kissing her, licking her and getting her labia to swell up and open out for him like a flower.

He opened her hole wider and gently slid his fingers in. She moaned and rolled her head to either side and closed her eyes as his fingers poked her, back and forth. She opened up for him wider. He slipped a couple of more fingers in, then his whole fist. Her head shot back. She screamed out loud. But it wasn't a scream of pain. It was a scream of surprise. She covered her mouth with her hand and looked at him, her eyes two large, magnificent orbs of light. He pushed his fist in all the way. Her head shot back again and a yelp escaped past her tightened lips. Her eyes rolled like beads in her head as he slid his fist in and out.

"This is what you want, you bitch, isn't it?" he demanded.

"Yes, you bastard, yes!" she cried, clamping her mouth shut, her body arching, lifting off the bed, spasmodically tapping out its secret alphabet of desire, each letter traced in the exquisite marks and grimaces flashing across her face.

She then bit her finger between her teeth to stifle the moans as he fisted her harder, twisting it round inside her being. It was too much. She couldn't take it. She wanted to scream out; no, no and a thousand no's. But her body

said; yes, more, fucking more.

"Harder, you bastard. Harder."

She gripped his cock with her other hand and started pumping away as his fist pumped her, working deep inside her in long smooth strokes. They fairly had her bent in two, her back inverted, arched for love, arched for him. She was frantically fisting him, so hard it hurt.

"You bitch!" he screamed at her.

"You bastard!" she screamed back.

He had had enough now. He pulled his wet fist out and pushed her down. She let go of him. She laid back as he stroked the tip of his cock against her and got her even more exited, then plunged it in deep all the way and thrusted with all his might, fragments of the poem swimming round his head—it was all coming into place and making sense. He roared and became stronger, fucking her harder and harder. She clung to him tightly, her nails etching into his back. He gripped her forcibly and kept going, the words tumbling round his mind.

"Yes, yes. More, more," she breathed into his ear.

She sobbed, his body kicking into action like an engine running on steam, pumping into her with polished strokes, getting faster, his loins tighter.

"Yes, yes, yes," he cried, now it was making sense, as his body took over completely. He fucked her hard, her legs wrapped round him tight, pulling him in closer, moaning as they both came in one joyous consummation of flesh, a joyous celebration of phallus and kteis, of sun and moon, of bastard and bitch, of Beast and Harlot.

They both expired together.

He slipped inside her, all the way, flowing down a long winding passage. He found himself in a wide, deep cavernous space, surrounded by darkness.

He moved like an aquatic creature, swimming in the waters of space, going to he knew not where. He was being carried along by the waters. They were taking him. He went with the current. Out of the depths of the waters a

bright shining light appeared. It rose up above the surface, luminous and powerful, seeming to draw him closer like a magnet. He could not resist and found himself being conveyed towards it. Now it was clearly visible. It was a symbol, an unfamiliar one. He went through it and found himself in a totally different space, a landscape of some description. He was standing naked on a shore looking towards a wide empty lake, but it was black like the sky above. In the distance was a rugged outline of rocks. Behind him a primal forest. Then he heard the strange clicking sounds of insects, the flapping of leathery wings and screeches of some unknown beasts. Then, as he stared, the water appeared to be rising in the centre, sending a spray of foam into the air as this huge, monolithic form rose up out of its midst. The water flowed down over its head to reveal two enormous eyes penetrating straight into his. It had a long protruding snout like that of an aardvark or anteater, sharp erect pointy ears, the body of a fish covered in scales which glinted like sheets of metal, a serpentine tail that coiled round and flicked powerfully at the water sending foam all around it, and lastly these two expansive wings which unfolded from behind and furled out like that of a bat's. They rose up and shrouded the sky, blotting out the rugged horizon beyond. It hovered above the water, and before he could even think of running away from the creature, the whole scene withdrew into itself and was gone. He was now falling back down a long dark tunnel towards another light. As he approached it the walls of the tunnel became narrower and tighter, pushing him along like a huge set of muscles as if he was being excreted through a tube of flesh until he found he was finally out on the other side. He spilled onto the floor in a messy heap, covered in amniotic fluid, blood, shit and mucus. Then there was a squelching sound as the placenta gave way. It fell on top of him.

He lay on the floor dazed, sore, bewildered, then finally remembered where he was. He wiped the blood and mucus from his eyes and looked up at the room. The light was still on. Then at his naked body coated with all this bloody shit and the way it was slowly spreading over the carpet. He fearfully turned his head to look at what was left on his bed.

"My God," he sobbed and clamped his hand over his mouth as he took it all in. Katie was lying there inert, lifeless, her unseeing eyes open staring into space fixed in shock, her body limp, her legs parted. But where her crutch should have been there was now a crater of ripped muscle, flesh and tissue, a large gaping hole. Her stomach too was ripped open and all he could see was blood, nothing but blood all over her, between her legs and covering the sheets.

"No," he gasped. "No, please. No."

He staggered to his feet as the realisation hit him full. He slipped on the wet carpet and gripped his stomach as a sensation came up into the back of his throat. He dashed to the bathroom and made it just in time to reach the toilet and spewed up in the bowl, his body writhing and contorting as it came out of him thick and fast, continuously in liquid form. A few moments later he was able to stand up, still feeling weak and nauseous, but somehow cleaner and purer as if the vomiting had purged him.

Terrified at the sight of blood all over his face and hair, and now seeing in the mirror his filthy body, he dived into the shower and turned the taps on full. He stood under the shower—it could have been for ages—letting the refreshing water carry away his fears. It also took away the pain, the smell and the blood. All he was left with now was the worry. He daren't go back into his room. He waited until he thought he had some courage in him, enough to face the sight of her again. A few minutes later he felt better to deal with the situation.

He got a grip on himself and climbed out of the shower. He grabbed a towel and wiped himself down vigorously. Then stopped as his eyes caught sight of his room through the open door. He gasped.

"What the ...?"

Where were the bloody footprints he would have left behind on his way to the bathroom? The carpet was clean, immaculately clean. From where he was standing there wasn't one drop of blood, not one speck. Nothing. He grabbed his bathrobe and pulled it on and gingerly crept back into the room, seriously worried.

"Thank God for that!" he cried aloud, nearly falling to the floor, relieved.

Katie was lying there on the bed sound asleep like a baby, all curled up with a big smile on her face. There was no blood on her, no blood anywhere.

Then I must have imagined it, he concluded. Or at least some of it. Convinced he was going mad, he dashed across to the desk on the other side of the room and grabbed the hotel notepad and a pencil. He made a lightning quick sketch of the symbol he saw, unsure why it had even appeared. Perhaps Angel had implanted it in his mind just as he climaxed. Then he sat himself down beside the desk and shook his head. He was going mad, he must be, for the symbol was of a snake entwined around a

downward pointing sword. The snake was in the shape of the number eight with its head pointing down and spitting ... VENOM!

Perturbed, he nervously lit up a cigarette. His thoughts came back to what happened. He went through all the scenery again; the primal landscape, the hideous creature which erupted out of the water filling him with revulsion, and the symbol. It was obviously a gateway to that space. Then it must be the astral dimension of the negative side of the drug, its venom aspect, which Mosalla had mentioned, the same space he had hit on when Jack blew himself up. This was the same thing. Now he was really worried.

Capri thought and smoked quickly. As soon as he finished his cigarette he lit up again and sat there mystified. What the fuck is going on? he cried to himself. Suddenly he didn't feel too good anymore. He banished all the 'whys' and snatched up Crome's book of poetry and flicked to page sixteen. Crome must be hinting at both the positive and negative sides of the drug in this poem, he thought to himself, or at least that's what the revelation was telling him before Katie distracted him. He took a deep breath and dived in again with new eyes hoping to make sense of it all.

It was not straightforward, nor would it be. The man known as Alexander Crome was something of a genius. He would have considerable knowledge of the esoteric, as well as a good grounding in many religious systems of the world. In this poem he was clearly drawing on the Bible, and one book in particular, the *Book of Revelation*, equating his Woman of Power with the whore of Babylon. Her symbol was the cup, the cup containing the blood of saints, but possibly a euphemism for the drug itself.

The symbolism of the poem was too recondite and abstruse, certainly not amenable to any system Capri was familiar with. It displayed the profundity of Crome's mind, his erudition, but also his humour, for the poem containing the Kalanitic Equation was the sixteenth poem on the sixteenth page, and was not included accidentally as Mosalla claimed. And to prove it, there were thirty-two lines to the poem, which is double sixteen—the formula of the drug—for two parts were required, a masculine and a feminine element. They formed the two halves of the basic ingredient. 'Scarlet Harlot' was on the fifteenth line for her number in numerology has always been fifteen, as indicated by the number of her poem. However, the sixteenth line contained the essence of the drug, indicated by the word 'secrecy,' because that's where it came from. It was a play on words, and that's why Crome always joked about it being a secret.

Yet there was still an essential element of the poem hidden, truly occult; the precise formulation of the drug itself. It had to be within this poem or perhaps sprinkled throughout the rest of the book.

Capri read it again, then closed the book and tapped it on his knee whilst he pontificated. As before, he noticed the gold seal on the front. It could be seen in two ways, or double. As landscape, it was an eye with eight eyelashes above and below. As portrait, it was a mystical eye with a point, or *bindu*, in the centre with eight rays emanating from it on either side, thus making a total of sixteen in all. There was nothing accidental about this book. Everything about it had purpose and a deliberate design behind it, even perhaps down to this copy not being destroyed. It survived. But why? Capri at present was unable to fathom how Crome could have forgotten about it. Nor could he understand why there were only 31 poems in all; surely it would make sense to have 32 and thereby reiterate the formula and of doubling? Unless, of course, the number 31 had a special significance.

It was getting late. Capri felt too tired to try and get his head round any more of the poem. He was more than certain he had found the right one, all he had to do now was to prove it to Mosalla tomorrow morning and collect his winnings. He quickly jotted down in note form his understanding so far on a separate piece of paper:

THE KALANITIC EQUATION

Scarlet Woman/W of P =15=Full Moon=M = lun op.
Juice =M=Neg. of elixir, + poss. S (both charged; how?)
Filth/aboms's=waste matter drained off, ferm/distillation
Secrecy=16=secret (ion)= (8 x2, male + female) = E.R.?
Come X 11= no. of magic= black time (holy/filthy)
Drugs=drug/elixir=S+M (S pos., M neg.= nectar+ venom)
K. EQ.=doubling; i.e. 8+8=16, 16 x2=32, total no. of lines,
Significance unsure.

Capri put his pen down and rubbed his tired eyes, his mind now slowing down as the long day finally took its toll. Not only was he now tired, he was also disappointed. Although he had fathomed part of the mystery of the drug and its origin, the vital key appeared to be elusive as ever.

But he had another mystery to solve; the thing in the lab. It had to be identical with the thing in the lake of his vision. Perhaps it embodied the Negative. But how did he hit on it and why? Then he remembered

Grantham's books. Surely a man like Grantham would know about the Negative, not in the same way perhaps as Crome did, but at least be familiar with it enough to be able to give him an idea of what to do about it.

He would ask Mosalla tomorrow if he could borrow them just for a couple of days whilst he was here in LA or even perhaps buy them in lieu of his winnings. There had to be a reference to the Negative in them somewhere.

Still disturbed and in that strange state of mind where one is neither tired enough to sleep, nor energetic enough to stay awake, he lit up his last cigarette of the night, got himself a glass of water from the bathroom, feeling the dehydration coming on, sat himself down again by the table and the small lamp and sank into the shadows, not really there at all. As he smoked, he watched the smoke curl up to the ceiling, imagining it as a libation to his goddess whom he had so nearly experienced in full tonight, then to the little girl lying in his bed who was married and realised it was the first married woman he had ever taken to bed. But why did she come here tonight? Under normal circumstances he would have accepted it and not looked a gift horse in the mouth. He couldn't accept it though. Had she come here as a result of his invocation? Impossible. She was just a silly girl.

He heard a murmuring sound coming from his bed. Katie appeared to be dreaming, a sexual one at that, and was tossing her head back and forth, her lips jabbering away, pulling at the sheets as if being visited by a rapacious host. Capri smiled and watched, fascinated. She tore at the sheets, tossed them aside, her glorious body now visibly exposed. Her flesh was on fire. She was hot and feverish. Her body writhed and twisted as if anxious to cool down. Even in sleep she seemed to be teasing him, doing it on purpose, trying to get him hard. She didn't need to. He found himself rising to the occasion as her promiscuous, wandering hands made their way to the source of her trouble and stroked it. Then they dove straight in as if missing his fist of earlier on and were trying desperately to fill the void. Capri twisted his table lamp round slightly and pointed it at Katie. The whole bed was now brilliantly lit up. Capri was hidden in the shadowy depths of the room, engrossed in the spectacle, the only indication of life being the light of the scene reflected in his eyes. Out of the stillness he stirred, autonomously stubbing out his cigarette, getting to his feet and letting his bathrobe fall to the ground. He turned out the light and knelt on the bed and extracted her fingers and kissed them, gently inserting his own so as to not awaken her, and then withdrew them and inserted his penis instead whilst she still slept. He took advantage of her, again and again and again, then fell asleep, blissfully ignorant of the world.

THE PRIMITIVE INSTINCT

'In the highlands of Ethiopia there exists a species of monkey called the geladas. They still retain a primitive characteristic no longer observable in other apes. When the female of the geladas is on heat she will segregate herself from the others and follow a course to some higher ground. There she will find a flat rock and sit on her haunches and press her genitalia on the surface thus impregnating it with her own distinctive smell and disappear back into the wilderness. Should one of the males come across this rock and pick up her scent, he will relentlessly pursue her until she is caught, ignoring all the advances made by other females. Her capture signifies the end of a long chase and the completion of the mating game.

Are the mating rituals of humans any different?'

Professor Thomas Drexler
The Psychology of the Human Ape

—17—
WELCOME TO THE PLEASURE PARLOUR

Landis could smell all the Asian pussy on offer where he was standing by the bar. He sunk his drink, moved in closer for a better smell, right up to the raised platform, and started cavorting with them. They were flirting with him and he loved it. It was making him hard and horny. He tried to grope one of them, but the security guards fought him back. It was a game, just a bit of fun whilst he was waiting for Chan. And where was he, the bastard?

Landis was here on time, having received a message to meet him at midnight, saying all was forgiven after their little misunderstanding of last night, promising he would make it up to him tonight. And he had better, he thought, as he gave up playing and made his way back to the bar, pushing his way through the congregation. He finally managed to get himself another drink, still disappointed that the embodiment of his desire hadn't shown up. What the fuck was going on? But instinctively inside him he knew tonight was going to be different, kind of special, with or without his white bit. He still desired her strongly, and did not regret the failure of the attempt he made last night. That was just to break the ice. She was going to play hard to get, and sooner or later she would be dying for him, and would come round to his way of thinking, begging to please him, her master. But

perhaps Chan was right, he thought to himself as he propped himself up by the bar and drank. She was trash. He would use her, discard her once he had what he wanted out of her, and move on. He was the master. She the slave. There was no other way. Landis always came out on top because he was the top. She, like all the others, was the bottom. It was just that she was taking a little longer to realise it. Then he'd have to educate her, he guessed, get her thinking properly, and demonstrate his authority; that would bring her round. Then there would be none of this cock-teasing. If there was any teasing to do around here it would be him, for he could be a right cunt-teaser at times, and he would keep her on tenterhooks, make her plead for it and of course he would eventually allow her to touch him. That was at the top of the agenda tonight. Fuck the boss man, he didn't exist. There was nothing that was going to get in his way tonight. It was all a game, he told his drunken self, and he was going to play it real good tonight and let her know him.

He reordered and casually looked in the direction where she always stood with her back to him. Then he looked all around at the deep sea of faces under the red glow of lights, looking like a scene right out of *Inferno*, hoping to spot her in the distance. Maybe she had relocated, found another spot to get a better look at him. But she wasn't anywhere to be seen. That kind of disappointed him. Yet he wouldn't let it get to him. The night was still young. He and Chan would get some kicks and return to the club afterwards. She'd be here for him then. So he was going to have to be patient. The night hadn't happened yet and, if Chan didn't turn up, it looked like it wasn't going to either. Perhaps he had been set up. Chan was having him on and still bitter about last night. Wanted to get him down here and make him look stupid. But Chan wasn't like that. There wasn't a bad bone in his body. His Chinese heart was wrought out of pure gold, and that's why he was so easy to manipulate.

He once more let his eyes drift back to all the pussy on display, hot and wet, gesturing to him, winking at him in an erotic fashion. He would miss them. But then again, why get attached to petty fancies? These girls never lasted long. They were changed each night; the new girls replaced the old girls who ended up carcasses, meat on a cold slab somewhere in the morning. And that's how it should be, he told himself. These Chinks had the right policy, the right attitude to life. And wasn't that the way of this shit Tao

thing the old man kept going on about? This endless cycle of change? Things come, they go, in this gargantuan, protean process, and it applied to all things. He didn't believe you could ever sidestep it for you were a part of it as intimately and as deeply as everything else. All was Change. It was the immutable law of heaven and earth.

That's what the Sage would say. That was his whole approach to life, the way his mind always retained its equanimity in whatever situation. He admired and respected him for that. It wasn't the problem. The real problem was his insistence on trying to get him to experience it. So why was he getting all mad with himself? It was this fucking waiting round for Chan. Where was the fucker?

He remembered one instance when he was on the verge of crossing the room to hit the old man, but out of dignity restrained himself. It was when the Sage's wife died during labour. What made him angry was the way in which he accepted her death. The old man just sat there and said something like 'that is the Way' and felt those few words embraced the whole concept of the event. Yet more than that, for he knew well in advance she was going to die. What did he do to prevent it? Nothing. What was the point in having prescience and being able to predict the possibility of such events and not intervene to change the consequences? He had to admit to himself he wasn't the most humane of people, yet to just sit there and casually accept and dismiss it as a divine sanction ratified by his Way; that really got to him. He was inhuman! He wasn't real! Landis sank his indignation with more beer. He vowed never to see him again, and would make it plain to Chan so he understood. But where was he tonight? He scowled and scouted all the slit-eyed faces again, looking for him. What the hell was he playing at?

Suddenly Chan's face appeared out of the red haze, beaming.

"You late!" Chan blurted out.

"Correction," Landis told him. "You're the one who's late. I've been fucking standing here like a right prick for over an hour waiting for you."

"I not understand. I been waiting for you."

"Where Chan? I didn't see you. I've been here all the time."

"I been waiting at the front."

"Here?"

"No, front. There." He indicated the alcoves on the side by the door.

"There, Chan? Why? We never meet there. We always meet here."

"Ah, but tonight is going to be different. That's why I say at front."

"Different? What do you mean different?"

"Come. I show you. We not keep them waiting."

"Who, Chan? Keep who waiting?"

"Come," he said, dragging him through the amassing throng.

"What you up to, Chan?" he shouted above the music.

But his friend was eagerly dragging him over to the alcoves. "You know me. You see." He laughed.

"Yeah. I know you too fucking well!"

Chan laughed again as he escorted him to one of the cubby holes. It made Landis flinch for this was real hetro territory and totally anathema to him. What the fuck was Chan playing at dragging him to this normal area? For a second or two he thought he was enlightened; Chan was going to introduce him personally to the boss man and his wife. But it wasn't to be. Now he was really suspicious. He stopped as he took them in full; two Sino-chicks sitting either side. They glanced up at them as Chan and Landis stopped at their table. So, why was tonight going to be different? He could tell already.

"You sit there," Chan gestured. Landis sat down next to one of them, whilst he sat himself down opposite with a big pleased smile on his face.

The two chicks gave Landis a polite smile and bowed their heads in an obsequious manner he expected from all females. However, it only made him feel uncomfortable. He quickly feigned a smile and looked directly at Chan for an explanation. Chan, as if not on the same planet, was still smiling inanely in that way of his. As there was no response coming from

his young comrade, he looked back at both chicks warily. It wasn't that they were both gorgeous and possibly twins, nor that they were done up exquisitely with their make-up and had shining black hair cropped short with straight fringes, nor their colourfully embroidered silk dresses, nor all the expensive jewellery which no girl in her right mind would wear in a crime-ridden shit-hole town like this, nor their beautiful almond shaped eyes highlighted with a soft touch of kohl, nor the way they sat elegantly in a refined pose he wouldn't normally associate with Chinks. There was one fact here which was really bugging him. These girls were professionals! Expensive ones at that, the sort only megarich businessmen could afford and probably cost a year's salary for thirty minutes of their time. And they were both well experienced, fully qualified high-class call girls. Another thing which made him unhappy was their age. They were both mid-twenties, older than the ones he preferred. He always liked to break them in young. Chan knew that, so what the hell was he playing at?

He looked at him again and leaned forwards. "Explain," he demanded.

"Explain what?" he replied and shrugged his shoulders all innocent looking.

"Don't give me that shit, Chan. You know damned well what I mean. What are we doing here with these two?"

"Why? You not like?"

"Don't treat me like a jerk-off either. Where did you get these two from?"

"I find them."

"Okay, so you found them. Do they speak English?" Chan shook his head. Landis looked at them nervously again. "Chan, be straight with me, will you? What are you up to tonight?"

"Tonight we drink. We have good time."

"I'm warning you. This is the last time. So stop pussyfooting around. These two girls aren't cheap. You can't afford them. I can't even afford them."

"They very special."

"Yes, I know they're special. What they doing here?" he asked, impatiently.

"They are for you."

"Well, that's very kind of you," he replied sarcastically. "But where the fuck did you get the money from to pay for them?"

"No problem. You not worry. I take care of that. I get big money today. This is my treat to you. I pay. You not pay a thing. I get lucky. I cut off big shipment as it was coming in. All packaged up. Now sold. Now I am rich."

"You saying you stole somebody else's consignment? Do you realise what a dumbass thing that was? Chan, I swear, man, there are now people out there who are mighty pissed off with you. I tell you, they ain't happy and you will wind up very, very dead if they catch you. Do you hear me?"

Chan laughed. "No. You not worry. They not find me. All tracks covered. No tracing back to me. We make a lot of money. So I pay for tonight. This is my present to you."

"I don't understand, Chan. Why? Why you laying this on for me? It doesn't have anything to do with last night, does it?"

Chan laughed again. "No. Last night, my fault. I go home, like you said, I ask my father. He tell me many things. I not understand all he says. Some a little. He says make best use of time. So I say, Anton, he my best friend. I want him to enjoy our time together. I want to make him happy. So he suggest I treat you."

"And what else did your father tell you?" he asked him concerned.

"Nothing. Why?"

"Never mind. So," he said looking at the girls, "these two for me, right?"

"Yes. You enjoy. Tonight we talk. We have drinks like normal people." Chan emphasised the last words. Landis cringed. "Then after, we go. We have some action. They make you feel good. You see."

"Yeah, I bet they will."

He decided that perhaps Chan was right. It was about time he gave him a treat. And these two, well they weren't looking so daunting now. A few

more beers and he'd be coming up inside them in no time, making them squeal with delight when he got out his steel. But then again, perhaps not. These two were too classy to waste. A pity really as he wanted to see them moan with blood coming out of their mouths. Whatever Chan had in store tonight, it wouldn't be wasting. These two weren't expendable like the others and he reckoned if he did waste them the whole town would be after his hide. Which could only mean one thing; tonight was going to be a routine sex session, not what he had in mind at all.

"So, why don't you introduce me to your two Chinese friends here."

"No. They not Chinese. They from Laos, specially imported."

"Is that so, eh? What's their names?"

"That one," he indicated to the one sitting next to Landis, "she called Gemini. Not real name, you understand. And this one, she called Electra."

"Very nice," he replied approvingly. "Gemini and Electra." Then he looked to the girl sitting next to him, her head bowed, her eyes purposely avoiding his. "Gemini, eh?" he said to her.

She looked up and gave him a curt smile, her face slightly blushed, and looked back down into her lap.

Landis relaxed in his seat and drank his beer and rested his arm on the back of the couch, his hand hovering close to her neck. Looking at her now, she had wondrous breasts hugged in tight by her dress like two mounds just waiting to burst out, or mini volcanoes, he thought. He let his eyes skim all over her, from the smooth profile of her face, the delightful pouting lips with plenty of red gloss, the small chin, the collar round her neck held in place by one gold button, her black sleeveless dress which seemed to be two sizes too small for her so as to bring out every contour of her body, the smooth supple arms with gold bangles around the wrists and small delicate hands with nimble fingers. Yes, it was making him rock hard, enhanced by her musk perfume wafting over towards him. And right now, all he wanted to do was to clasp the back of that sweet head of hers and force those cute little lips apart and force them down on his manhood.

"I spy with my little eye," he whispered in her ear, knowing she wouldn't

understand what he was saying, "something beginning with S." She giggled. "My-oh-my, Ge-mi-ni," he said poetically.

"Yes, she Gemini," his friend informed him.

"Yes, I know, Chan, you just told me."

"No, no. You not understand. She Gemini! She like it both ways."

Landis smiled. "Does she really," he gloated, casting his eyes up and down her. He looked to her friend. They were both dressed to kill. Electra was wearing the same type of dress, only azure in colour with fine gold braiding round the edges. "And what about her friend? Why is she called Electra?"

Chan let out a laugh as if he had been asked a stupid question. Landis looked at her again. It had to be because of her eyes; they were a deeper blue than her dress, an electric blue, so blue it was untrue. He had never seen an Asian girl with blue eyes before. But this pair were different like they were coloured contacts or implants. "Because of her eyes, right?"

Chan giggled, spoke something to Electra. She laughed and flashed her eyes at Landis. He didn't understand the joke, like they were in on something, making him feel left out. Then Electra said something to Gemini who laughed as well. They were all laughing—except Landis. He wasn't a happy.

"What, Chan? For fuck's sake, aren't you going to tell me?"

"She called Electra because she has fitting."

"Where? In her eyes?"

Chan laughed out, loud. "No. You find out later. We drink some more. We get nice and relaxed. Later we go and we do something different."

"Example."

"You always say to me what we doing tonight. You say you like variety. So tonight we do something special. Be patient. You will see."

Landis, totally unsatisfied with that explanation, sat back and looked at the girls again. They were small-talking between themselves. And they were

obviously talking about him the way they kept looking over to him, smiled and then back to themselves and giggled. And he looked at Chan, the sod. Boy, he really hated him sometimes. He had something up his sleeve he wasn't prepared to let out till the last minute. It only made him more uncomfortable. But whatever it was he would go with it, go with the flow, as his old man kept telling him, fuck these two quickly and get back to the club in time for his white bit. He still had a score to settle with her.

He sat back, drank, still feeling indignant and waited for the night to get started. Eventually the girls finished their drinks and were ready to leave. Chan got up and escorted them out towards the back. Landis followed their tidy asses which were hugged in by their tight dresses, watching the way they walked. Were these girls professional or what! They walked like they owned the place and the hordes of people divided like the Red Sea to let them pass through, all eyes fixed on them. To his surprise, his Chink friend was taking them round the back of the club past the opium den and up a small flight of stairs, an area he had never been to before as it was strictly prohibited. This beefy guy at the top of the stairs stopped them and wouldn't let them pass until he got his baksheesh and indicated down the hallway the room specially reserved for Chan. They all filed through like VIP's or royalty, how Landis reckoned he should always be treated, and walked down this real corridor, with its real carpet and real flowers and expensive light fittings like they were now entering another world, a world reserved for the megarich. Chan stopped at the door, swiped his ID card and punched in his PIN. The door opened automatically. He smiled at the look of confusion on his friend's face, ushering them inside the room.

It was paradise, spacious, richly decorated with silk wall hangings, a large mattress in the centre, ornate brass work everywhere, all candelit and pleasingly subdued with a heady smell of freshly burnt incense combined with small doses of opium. It was heaven. Landis was stumped.

"This is Pleasure Parlour," his friend excitedly informed him.

Landis took it all in, watched the girls file in, the big door closing behind them. He walked round disbelieving and stopped in front of a mirror with a gold ornate frame covering the entire wall. Now he understood.

"Chan, this is a genu-wine fuckhouse. Why, it's even got a two-way mirror."

Chan laughed. "Trust me, my friend. No men in other room. No cameras. This is all ours. Private. We not be disturbed. Tonight you have good time."

Hardly reassured by his words, Landis looked at his friend undecidedly, still not sure what he was up to. "Exactly how much did you make today?"

"Enough. You not worry. Everything taken care of."

He called over the girls and said something to them. They smiled and walked up to Landis and started helping him with his clothes.

"Why," Chan laughed, "you even dressed special for tonight."

"I had dinner with my sister earlier," he replied, removing his dinner jacket. "If I'd known tonight was going to be special I would've worn my tuxedo."

The girls took his clothes, meticulously folding them and laying them on a small stool in the corner. He looked all round the room. It was specifically designed to enhance sensuality, exuding a feeling of voluptuousness. Everything in the room conveyed a sense of hedonism, of exquisite eroticism, there to please the eye. The silk wall hangings depicting naked couples making love probably dated back to the sixteenth dynasty, the elaborately carved table adjacent to the far wall with its array of erotic statues, the black silk sheet embroidered with a gold dragon covering the mattress. It was all bedazzling to the eye, and all there to transport the mind to a domain of sensual indulgence far away from the grimy world outside. He reckoned all the tycoons who used this room paid for it heavily in more ways than one. He didn't even know this place existed and looked to Chan satisfied in a strange kind of way for his choice of tonight's venue. It was certainly different and making him feel erotic all over. Chan didn't look like he was going to be joining in. He was sitting down and busy rolling a joint.

"Aren't you going to be joining me?"

Chan smiled. "No. I say this is for you, for you only. Gemini and Electra, they take special care of you."

He stood naked watching the two girls getting undressed, talking and laughing to themselves like this was some kind of game. But he had to admire Chan's choice in women. Wherever he got them from didn't matter,

for he was well pleased. Their bodies were unblemished and firm. They had large breasts unlike he had ever seen before on an Asian chick and evidently silicon enhanced; smooth rounded backsides that were just asking to be parted. He couldn't wait to get his steel up them. And they were both shaved, just how he liked them. His cock was sore stiff. He pointed it in the direction of Electra who had finished undressing and like the good obedient girl she was came over to him and got her hands working on his manliness, working him up with smooth, polished strokes, fingering his latent steel. He was so hard now he wanted to shove it right down the back of her throat then pull it out and come all over her face and rub his spunk into her soft, smooth flesh. She was taking great interest in his steel and laughed, saying something to Chan.

"What did she say, Chan?" he asked him to interpret.

"I tell you later. You find out tonight. First, we get rid of that hard-on."

He clapped and got Electra's attention. She took Landis full into her mouth. Her tongue was so deft, working round the tip of his cock like she was sucking a juicy sweet with a soft centre; it made him harder, so hard he could feel waves of pleasure rolling up his spine already. Gemini came round behind him. With her nimble hands she worked at his back, his big muscular shoulders, and eased the tension out. It felt good like he was in a dream and closed his eyes never wanting to wake up. He brushed his big burly hands through Electra's hair, stroking it as she bobbed back and forth, back and forth. He gripped her head tighter to pull her in closer as he felt himself on the verge of coming. Then white light exploded in his head. He slipped down the back of her throat. She fisted him out all the way and licked him clean dry.

Yes, she was professional. There was no doubt about it. She knew how to please men. And Landis, more than satisfied, smiled like a little boy who had just had his first fix. He then went to grab Gemini to pull her round and get a good taste of her. She backed off as if to say, 'No, not yet, wait.'

"You like?" Chan's voice came over to him disembodied.

"I like, man. I sure like."

"Good. Now we give massage. We get you nice and relaxed."

"A massage? I'm relaxed already. I don't need a massage. I am in heaven."

"We get you real relaxed."

He clapped his hands. Electra and Gemini took him over to the mattress. They got him to lie down on his front, his arms by his sides and started working on that stressed out body of his after all the hours he put in today at the Centre. I mean, three hours is enough of anybody's time. A man who works that many hours needs this kind of treatment in the evening. It should be compulsory, he thought as he lay there and gave into these angelic creatures as they rolled their palms around the balls of his feet and his legs, pulling and slapping at every rigid muscle they came across. He felt energies creeping up his spine like a soft narcotic drug and everything was slipping into that recess in the darkest corner of a man's mind labelled forgetfulness. The whole day was forgotten, a long dim hallucinatory dream, and he let it drift by. He could feel his whole system—by their expert touch—being drained of all poisons as they worked at his kinked and trapped nerves. They applied aromatic oils to his skin, worked them in deep and rubbed him all over. The vestiges of the day slipped out through his smile. This should be my birthday, he thought. In fact, it should always be my birthday. I deserve it. I've earned it. And he thought about getting the wife to take up a course in chiropractic and do this to him every night. This was heaven, and this is where he wanted to stay.

Gemini and Electra finished on his back and arms. They got him to turn over on his back, his cock hard again, dying for their pussies. But they avoided that area and were concentrating on his feet again, then his ankles and slowly working up his legs until he couldn't even feel them, as if they were no longer there and he was this bubble in space just waiting to rise into the air. Ah, it was bliss. He was putty in their hands. The tension in him was dissipating until he could only feel his soul drifting out of him like blood seeping out of a thousand wounds.

Chan came up to him and made him smoke some of his joint, then sweet-talked him for awhile, brushing back his blond hair from his brow lovingly and with all the tender care of a true friend. Landis was convinced this was heaven, this was the Tao, and wondered what he had done to deserve such fine treatment. But he went with it, slipped into its cool stream as he smoked, Chan pressing the joint to his lips and smiling. The girls kept

working on him. He was the centre of attention, wrapped in cotton woolly embraces, and even forgot who he was, smoked some more and sighed.

"Chan, I've got to tell you, this is wonderful. But, look man, this is too much. Why don't you join me? I can't have these two cuties all to myself."

His friend smiled. "This is your treat. You enjoy. Forget everything. Relax."

"You're too kind, man. You know, I could lie here all night."

"That is intention."

"What? You serious? You mean, this is going to go on all night long?"

"No. This is only start. Soon we move onto next stage."

"The next stage? I can't wait," he chimed. "This is too good to be true."

He pulled down Chan's head towards him and gave him a big kiss. The girls laughed and talked to themselves.

Chan said something. They went quiet and continued working on Landis' legs. "And you, my friend. You lie there. You keep quiet too."

Landis felt like he was turning into jelly at their touch. He was floating. The mattress had turned into a waterbed and it rippled beneath him with gentle undulating waves. He sighed some more as they got closer to his groin. If this was bliss, then he wanted it permanently. It made him feel so languorous and indifferent he thought it should be marketable as a drug, a genuine healing, relaxing experience because it made the world disappear. This was heaven encapsulated in two pairs of gifted hands which were making him rise to the occasion. Yet strangely, they were eschewing that area and moved onto his rippling torso and his finely honed abs, slapping them hard, pummelling him like he was dough being kneaded in their hands, or a cold slab of meat which had just come out of the freezer and was thawing out. And like water, he felt he was oozing out of every pore and closed his eyes to tune into the sensation. There was an intriguing dioramic display taking place before his eyes, a neural vision of electro-chemical energies, whirling and dancing, so captivating he could have sworn he was tripping. And soon he drifted out of his eyes, out onto the plateau,

unbounded by space, just floating, drifting, hovering like a hawk on the undercurrent with expansive, outstretched wings. It was wonderful. He let his mind soar, seeing huge dollar signs roving across the skies of his panoramic vision.

He unrolled his eyes, looked up at the ceiling. It was all diffused and out of focus like he really was hypnotised or enchanted. He didn't care as long as they didn't stop. With great difficulty he struggled to lift his head to look at the girls, their swinging breasts, their nipples skating over the surface of his skin like jewelled pendants. These girls had big smiles on their faces. They really enjoyed their work and looked like they were in direct communication with one another on a subliminal level; Siamese twins working in unison to please their master, rubbing oils all over his body. Again he wanted to ask Chan where he got them from. But he was crouched down in the corner attending to something Landis couldn't see. Then Chan went to another corner and fumbled around some more. Landis tried watching him but Electra gently pushed his head down, made him lie still. He resignedly did so. Perhaps that's what Chan was doing, getting something ready for him to use on these girls after they had finished toning up his muscles so he could maintain his peak performance and keep it up all night.

Now they were working on his arms and Gemini's mouth was tantalising close to his. He tried to reach up and reel her in to kiss those pert blowjob lips and then get his tongue around that nipple brushing against his arm. But she pulled her head away and gave him a stern look then said something to Electra. They both laughed. His cock was now standing up like a flagpole, sore for their pussies and they were wasting it. What was the matter with these girls?

But before he could think about it, they had finished on his arms and were now working on the thick muscles in his neck and shoulders. Chan came over again, reinserted another joint between his lips and got the girls to finish quickly what they were doing and backed off. Landis smoked as he lay there bussed out with hardly an ounce of energy left in his body. Chan removed the joint from his lips and smiled.

"You happy?"

"Wow, Chan. I've never been so happy in whole my life. I can't even feel

my body. It's like I'm not here at all. That was the end of that stage, right?"

Chan nodded. "Yes. The first part. Now we move onto second part."

Chan got up and walked away out of his vision. All he could see was the ceiling above imploring him upwards. Whatever the next stage was going to be, no way could it get better than that. Then he tried moving. His body wouldn't cooperate. It was as if the signals from his brain weren't reaching his muscles. Then he felt peculiarly heavy, overcome with the weight of inertia. At first he thought he was imagining it. He wanted to sit up, see what was happening. With greater effort he tried again. For some reason he couldn't move. He smiled at Electra and Gemini who retreated behind him. What was going on? He made another effort. His arms and legs didn't want to know. He tried again and then heard the clink of chains. A horrendous thought entered his head. No. Chan wouldn't do a thing like that, would he? He struggled harder to sit up and was pulled back down by something tight. He couldn't even budge an inch as if he was tied down...

"CHAN! You fucking bastard! I'm going to fucking kill you!"

He struggled like a mad, ferocious dog.

"Why you struggling?" he heard his voice drift over from behind his head.

He tried to control his temper and calmed himself down. "Chan, I swear man, I'm going to fucking kill you." He struggled some more.

"You cannot get free. They are secure. So why bother? Take a look."

Landis stopped and lifted up his head as high as he could. He was right. Each chain was fastened to hoops in the corners. They were an inch thick of pure steel. So were the chains to his wrists and ankles, all chrome plated. The cuffs were heavy duty leather with fur lining and touch sensitive studs, impossible to reach with his fingers. And they were so comfortable he didn't even feel the fucking things being put on. The chains were taut, barely allowing him to move. As the realisation of what they had been doing all along hit home, he let out an almighty scream.

And then: "CHAN! I mean it, man. I'm going to kill you. Get me out of this now. The joke's gone too far already. I swear, by God, if you don't, I

will not only kill you, I will hang you up by your genitalia and swing you from the nearest tree."

"How?" he replied calmly. "You not do anything till we take you all the way. You will have to accept. We take good care of you."

"I don't know what the fuck you're talking about, but you, man, are taking a big risk. Do you hear me?" He tipped his head back to get an inverted view of Chan sitting comfortably behind him in the armchair with Electra and Gemini perched on either side. And what really pissed him off more than anything else was they found it all so amusing. He could feel the blood boiling in his veins as he determined to free himself. "I won't let you get away with this. You know I am the top. YOU are the bottom. That is the way we always work it."

"Exactly. That is why tonight we do something different. My father say..."

"I don't give a shit what that asshole father of yours says. He doesn't know what the fuck he is talking about." Now the veins in his neck were bulging out. Sweat was on his brow. His eyes turned red with rage and every muscle in his body, which had been so relaxed previously, was now tense and straining to claw its way towards Chan and rip his head off. He struggled some more like a dog on a leash tied to a railing, fairly throttling itself in the process. And, like a dog, Landis was foaming at the mouth.

Chan waited for him to calm down, then said, "My father say big things happening soon. You need to be prepared. He tell me lots about you..."

"Don't believe him. Don't believe a word he says." He twisted his head back to see Chan now stroking the girls' legs, doing it on purpose. He had a nerve, touching something that was supposed to be his and his only.

"My father speak truth. My father is the truth."

"Bullshit! He's a liar and I'll kill him too when I get out of this." He tried wrenching at the chains.

"Why you do that? You not escape. No one escapes from them."

He was right. It was useless. He stopped and took a breather and lay there

spread-eagled. He felt like the Microcosm of Vitruvius. It made feel sick.

"You're dead, Chan."

Chan laughed. "My father say you be angry. He was right. He say Anton will be a little upset and will do all he can to resist. So we rub special drugs into your body so you not feel anything. Then we secure you into position. I think we did well, no? It was the only way."

Landis sighed. "But it's not my way."

"Exactly. We do opposite of how you normally work. We not go your way. We go other way. Then you experience Tao."

"Jesus Christ! How did I fucking guess. It had to come down to the fucking Tao, didn't it? Chan, the Tao doesn't exist. Your father has brainwashed you. Do you hear me? He has conned you. You are fucking wasting your time if you think I'm going to experience something that is totally imaginary. Furthermore, you are wasting your money."

"We see. I have great faith in my father. He is great man. Tonight we prove him right and you wrong. You see. When anger has gone, we will work on next stage. You accept first. Trust me. These two girls, they very special. They know what to do. They been trained. They take you to the Tao."

"What the fuck you on about, Chan? How the fuck can two dumbass pros make me experience the Tao?"

"Simple. You fuck them."

"How, Chan? How can I when I'm tied down like this?"

"Correction. My mistake. They fuck you!" And with that he bawled his head off. The girls got laughing too. It only incensed him even more.

"You bastard, Chan. I give, they take. I am the penetrator, they are the penetrated. That's the only way I work. Got it? Now, undo me!"

"Anton, you have no faith."

"Faith! What the hell do you know about faith? And what the hell do you

know about the Tao? You reject it like I do. Don't give me that shit."

"My father right. You are angry young man. You take out anger on others, when anger is within."

"You know, you sound just like your old man. How can you say that when you work with me? We both work together as a team, remember? And you get as much satisfaction as I do out of it. It should be you down here, not me, pal." Chan laughed again. "Well, I'm glad you find it funny. Frankly, I don't. In fact, I'm pissed off with you. The joke's wearing a little thin. You see, Chan, you don't know what is really happening soon. And therefore this is going to be a complete waste of time."

"Not so, my friend. I know what is happening. My father knows what is happening. That is why tonight we prepare you. We make you ready."

"You don't even know half the story. There is far more to it than that, a hell of a lot more. Either he hasn't told you everything or you're incapable of understanding the rest."

"He only tell me what is necessary for tonight so you learn."

"And I'm going to learn by being fucked by two stupid bitches, right?"

"Yes. He say this is necessary. You not touch the silence through his way. So we work with your body to make you experience the silence and touch the Tao. We not force things. We take our time. This he call Te. And it will come when your mind is emptied. It will make gap in circle of your mind. In that way Tao comes."

Landis lay there disbelieving. It was a dream. Soon it will be over and he'd wake up. He hoped. Yet it wasn't so. This was a nightmare, and it was really happening. How could Chan treat him like this since he had been so kind to him in the past?

"Look, Chan, if it's about last night. I am prepared to admit I may have been wrong. Perhaps I shouldn't have said some of the things I said." He was even tempted to say he was 'sorry' despite the fact he had never said that word once in his whole life.

But Chan wouldn't have it. "You still not accepting. We wait longer." And lit up another joint. He smoked some then went over to Landis and tried to insert it in his mouth. Landis quickly snatched his face away. "Oh, if you not want to smoke it, I finish it off for you."

"Yeah. And I'll finish you off too," he barked back. "I thought we were going to have some fun tonight. I thought you were my friend."

Chan retreated back to his chair and sat down contented with his joint. "I am your best friend. That is why I go out of my way for you tonight, so you experience Tao. And it will be fun. You will enjoy it."

"Oh yeah, lying down like this? I don't think so!"

Now he felt he was on the periphery of sleep. Having had a sumptuous meal with his sister, a few glasses of wine, some ice cold beers, all he wanted to do now was sleep, drift into forgetfulness, into wherever, anywhere but here. He found his eyelids getting heavy and was sinking fast.

Quickly Chan clapped his hands. "Now we start second stage."

The girls went over to Landis, made sure he didn't fall asleep by tugging him out of his stupor. He opened his eyes, looked up at them. They smiled at him like he was a baby lying in a cot. His eyes told them to 'fuck off.' He hissed at them. They ignored him. Electra went to the end of the mattress; Gemini came up behind him and smoothed the sweat off his face with her small delicate hands. He tried to fight against her; it was pointless. He had to give in sooner or later as Chan seemed determined to carry on with this joke of a mission. He closed his eyes and gave in. Next thing he felt was a silk cloth being placed over his eyes and tied securely in position.

"Is that necessary, Chan?"

"Yes. You see why."

"What about my steel?"

"No. No steel tonight. You see why too."

"But how can I turn them on if I can't even use my steel?"

There was no response. Then he felt Gemini's hot breath on his cheeks. She gave him a quick peck.

"Bitch!" he spat at her.

Then he felt a pair of hands starting on his cock which for some reason had gone limp. And they were going to have to work real hard because being like this didn't turn him on. It was unnatural. That's why he never took it lying down. Lying down is for women and cissies, like a bottom. He was the top. It was utterly distasteful to a man of his calibre to be subjected to a degrading position like this. He felt humiliated and ashamed of himself. He would never be able to hold his head high in public ever again.

Then he felt a wet tongue around the tip of his cock. He reckoned it had to be Electra's as Gemini was still behind him. And Electra, however professional she maybe, was going to have to really coax it if she wanted to get him hard. Then he got to thinking why he couldn't use his steel. It was fully retracted with only small nodules appearing just above the surface, too smooth and inadequate to turn any girl on.

A mouth was now working on him full, trying to get him erect. He was only slightly hard. She was going to have to do better than that. Then he heard Chan say something in their language, hoping he had finally realised it was virtually an impossibility to get him aroused like this. Then he smelt it, hovering just above his nose, a nice fresh pussy, being held about four centimetres away, he reckoned, yet close enough for him to savour the fragrance. Then it came down gently, settling on the tip of his nose so he could get his tongue inside. It was Gemini's and had the distinctive aroma which could only be found in that part of the world. It smelt good. Even tasted good as the tip of his tongue slithered into her tight crevice and started getting her all excited. He could even hear her moan a bit and felt her gyrating, rubbing herself against his nose. He wallowed in it and tongued her some more, and soon her juices would be dripping down the back of his throat, for she was moist already, moist enough to even feel himself getting hard in the process. Quite forgetting, he reached up to grab her and found he was restrained. It annoyed him. Why were they doing this to him? All he wanted to do was help them to experience the Tao too, to pull Gemini down and impale her on his now rigid cock, make her squeal with delight, although his steel was retracted. But Electra had taken care of

things, now working at maintaining an erection long enough to do something with it. They were both working hard, Electra with her mouth, Gemini with her pussy, rubbing it up and down his nose. She was well qualified and they had succeeded in their mission; he was now rock hard and begging for it.

Then he heard a voice. They both stopped. Gemini pulled herself away, Electra climbed off the mattress leaving him there feeling all deflated. What the fuck was going on?

But before he could complain, one of them was bestriding him. It brought a glorious smile to his face, for he was now well satisfied thereby. And her nimble hands were guiding him all the way into port, her cunt gripping his cock like a warm, friendly hand. It could only be Gemini since she was already wet, riding him like a corpse. The image didn't please him. He was determined to demonstrate that although they may have inverted the whole order of the universe, he was still capable of staying in control, and he would do so by making her work to his own rhythm. He got into her stride then took it over, moving his pelvis up and down out of synch with hers. She must have caught on to what he was doing, and made him switch into her mode, slowing him down, keeping him at a constant pace. He gritted his teeth, held fast and tried to take over again. It was no good. Whatever shit they had been rubbing into his body it deprived him of his energy. He gave up and collapsed on the mattress and let her take over. Hearing her moan was a pleasure in itself, and the occasional gasp for breath confirmed it was Gemini. Then what the hell had happened to Electra? She should be here, sitting on my face.

Now Gemini was yelping with delight, pounding down on him, really going for it like a cat on heat, and she would have been meowing if he could have got his steel out. She was certainly well trained like Chan said, using her vaginal muscles, giving him all the grips, the passes, the Masonic handshakes, and getting him boiling in his loins like he was a bubbling cauldron. He even let out a moan.

Suddenly the action stopped. She pulled herself off him, leaving him there half-cocked like the cow she was just when he was beginning to enjoy it. A few seconds later, a pussy was lowering itself down towards his face. It wasn't hot or moist, so it had to be Electra. And it had to be Gemini

coming down on his cock again, getting back into her stride like the good girl she was. Electra was teasing him, he realised, for she wasn't even letting him get a full taste of her, suspending her divine offering just low enough for him to get the tip of his tongue a millimetre or two inside. But he did the best he could under the circumstances. A few minutes later she was moist. During his explorations he had found her pleasure button and turned it on. He went back to that lovely piece of flesh and licked it some more, hearing her moan with delight, not quite as good as with pain, you understand, but enough to warm the cockles of his heart. And Gemini, well she was out of control, surfing on the crest of a wave of ecstasy, barely able to contain herself. It was getting near to the point where he would be exploding into liquid action, coming up inside her all the way and ... suddenly she stopped.

"SHIT!" he yelled and flopped back on the mattress. They both stopped and climbed off him again. This wasn't fair. They were doing it on purpose, taking advantage of a poor man who couldn't even use his steel.

He was going to complain to Chan, tell him he was really out of order. And where was he anywhere, the sod? Then he heard his voice in the silence and the two girls talking in their own fucking language. That was another thing he was going to have a word with him about. That wasn't on.

But before he could complain one of the girls was on the mattress, climbing aboard and wasting no time in slipping him inside. It was Gemini again, still hot, wet and fervent, taking herself up to the heights and trying to drag him up there as well. But where was Electra? Wasn't she going to allow herself the privilege of getting a good feel of his latent steel? He wasn't bothered about her anyway as long as Gemini didn't stop. If she did it again, he wouldn't hesitate to punch her square in the mouth, if he could get his arm free. She was really going for it again, panting for breath as she cantered away and rode him hard. Well, he was going to take her along for a ride too, withhold himself until she deserved it. Suddenly she stopped again.

"NO!" he screamed like a child having a tantrum. This simply wasn't on.

But before he could call Chan into existence, another one had taken her place. It wasn't that moist as it slid down his pole. It could only be Electra—and then he felt it. It was the most peculiar sensation he had ever

experienced. Now he understood the joke and why he couldn't use his steel. It was like having his cock inserted inside a battery or live wires being stroked up and down his shaft producing this tingling sensation which would have been intensely magnified if his steel was out, and it was shooting small pulses of electricity all the time she rode him. The power seemed to increase the longer she pounded away, the pulses becoming small electric shocks that made him grit his teeth. Every muscle in his whole body was screwing up, turning inside out. It was delicious torture, exquisite pain, lovely agony, and it was now getting too intense as she really started getting into her stride. There was no way he was going to be able to take much more of this. It was too much. He creased his eyes as little packets of light were being squeezed into the back of his brain and exploding, producing an aural sound like cannon fire. It was unbearable. He wanted to tell her to quit, plead with her if he could stop his teeth from chattering. He gripped the chains with his restrained hands as best he could and held on as she now started pounding him harder and harder. This generator in her cunt was surging with power and gripping his cock like he was being electrified alive. He wanted to scream, yell out, beg for mercy, anything. He felt like he was one terminal, she another, jacking into each other like a plug in a socket, she the power supply, he the receiver, except he definitely couldn't receive anymore of this, seeing his whole mind blowing a fuse any minute. Now he didn't know if it was ecstasy or agony. Her magnetic waves were flooding his brain, wave after wave, getting bigger and stronger. Then he felt a real power surge come in and yelled out loud.

"MY GOD!" His voice echoed round the room. He couldn't stand it any longer. Please, let me come. All I want to do is come. And then it would all be over. He would even consider saying sorry if he had to.

Finally he came. It was like a supernova in his head. He was reduced to cosmic dust, mere vapour. Electra came too. They both died a little therein.

She flopped down on top of him covered with sweat, her hot breath panting in his ear. He could feel all this static electricity passing back and forth between their genitals, her negative charges seeping out and mingling with his positive ones, producing sparks and crackling sounds.

She eventually climbed off his corpse of a body, their flesh peeling apart like they were glued together. There was a tingling sensation as she pulled

him out of her love battery, not as powerful as when she was fully charged, but enough to make him never want to feel it again. He had this vision of his poor dick being all burnt or charred as if it had been in a toaster.

Had he experienced the Tao? No. He may have died back then, but there was no way he was transported to some celestial realm or whatever the Tao was supposed to be like. They had failed and thankfully that was the end of it. Now perhaps they would let him go. He would have a word with Chan as soon as he could get his tongue to cooperate with his fried brain.

He lay there for awhile. They nursed him back with soft, warm towels, cleaned him up and gave him a drink of ice cold water.

"You enjoy?" Chan asked him.

"Yeah, beautiful. Real good. Especially Electra. I mean, what the hell has she got inside her? Is she human or an android?"

"No, she human. She has marital device. Said to make husband happy."

"Happy? It's lethal! That damned thing nearly killed me." He caught his breath before speaking again. "Well? Aren't you going to ask me if I experienced the Tao?"

Chan laughed. "No. I know you not touch the Tao. Too early for that."

"What do you mean?"

"That only beginning. We now move onto next stage."

"No, I don't believe you. Please, Chan, I can't take any more of this. Why can't we just forget it and terminate it now?"

"I am surprised. You give up too easy. We have only just begun. You have come twice now. You not come again."

"No," he moaned. "I don't want to come again, especially with Electra. I will die before I experience the Tao."

"No. You not die."

"I will. I swear, Chan, I will die before I get there."

"No you will not. You will experience Tao. You see."

Then he heard him clap his hands. Then the girls got to working on him again, trying to coax some life back into his burnt out body. Then he moaned some more and sighed.

It was going to be a long night.

THE INTELLIGENTSIA

'All experiments involving "subversive" or "alternative" forms of sexual expression are only viewed as such because they more specifically go against the Christian doctrine that sex should only be for reproductive purposes, not for the exploration of one's soul through varying degrees of pain/pleasure quotients, which is of course what they are all about. And the majority of people involved in such explorations demonstrate a far higher level of intelligence than their social counterparts who denigrate these practises. S/M is for the elite who are not afraid to go beyond the bounds of social jurisdiction and explore the inner sanctuary of their innermost desires which is the root of all geniusness.

Vanilla sex is for imbeciles.'

John Upseed,
Black Leather Bible

—18—
THE GAP BETWEEN THE MOUNTAINS

The hands continued working on him as he lay there like a corpse, his flesh lard waiting to melt, the hands cruel assailants mocking him at every turn, unrelenting and unforgivable. He detested them, despising them with utmost rancour.

They were determined to take him all the way and he realised he was making it progressively harder for himself by not submitting completely and going with them. There was a part of him that was steadfast, unrepentant and refusing to let go. It was this part he now identified with hidden deep inside somewhere. It was his sustenance and he was feeding off it like a bloody stump. It would not remit nor would it accept this atrocity with which they were denigrating him. Determined, he clung on, holding on through all the peaks and all the troughs of this rollercoaster ride through hell. His body was the battery of their work; their laying on of hands was the guide to the infernal regions, beyond torment and damnation, into the very pits of despair. Well, they weren't going to win. They would never win for this nonsense they opined didn't even fucking exist so how could they possibly win. They could take him to the edge, push him over for all he cared as long as it took him away from this suffering, this defilement of his

ego, all the way to the gates of death, down that long perilous road from whence nobody returns, hence the most dangerous of them all.

How dare they do this to me? Who the fuck do they think they are? What have I done to deserve this? he kept crying aloud to himself in his empty skull, his voice echoing back in waves of madness. Keep sane, was another one of his refrains. Keep thinking. Don't stop thinking otherwise you'll definitely wind up dead. He was rapidly running out of ideas, having surveyed the whole of his past, cantered across the plains of his future, explored every facet of the world, even its history and was now reaching the bottom of the well. Then he thought of Crome. One lesson he taught him was how to build up a barrier to prevent a sudden or pernicious incursion of forces. He pictured a brick wall, even counted all the bricks, perfectly smooth and rectangular, its symmetry superb, until Electra got working on him with that infernal electric love-box of hers. The poor wall crumbled away into ruins, even turning the ruins into more ruins; it was useless. He clenched his fists and fought on supinely, determined not to give in.

His thoughts trailed off as the hands worked harder to evoke death in his body. He saw them as vultures, not coaxing him to live through their dextrous manipulations, but to die, or get as near as possible to death. Death presided over him, coming to him unannounced, unwanted. Death was the precedent. Death was typified by his limp cock they were avidly taking into their mouths. Death visited him in a strange hour in many forms; the expanse of space before his eyes opened out into a dark corridor of space allowing him to slip through till came to a dead end. The coldness of space engulfed him and froze the marrow in his bones. Then a hot juicy cunt clamped itself over his pride and joy reducing it to pulp. At one point he thought he was levitating. His back no longer felt the warm, cosy mattress beneath it but a cool undercurrent of air. He could almost hear his gasping breath bounce off the ceiling a couple of centimetres away and back into his face. Gemini was fucking him hard then, lifting him up with gusto, pitching it just right so he was about to tilt over into climax and then stop precariously on the edge, leaving him hanging there looking over into the promontory below and let him slip back down to earth under his own weight. He would expire for awhile and then they would start all over again.

He was the slave, they were the masters. They were the ones who had taken

his life away and were holding it in abeyance until he was on the verge of physical collapse and exhaustion. He was the victim; they were the victimisers cutting into his flesh with cold steel blades, cutting deep into his chest for that immortal part of himself palpitating beneath his ribs. He was the underdog they trod down into the stinking shit, wiping his face in it. He was the puppet, their plaything they abused and jolted back into life for their own pleasure. His Electric Mistress took him again, clamped her vaginal vibrator over his sore, limp piece of flesh, tortured him some more.

For how long? He didn't know. It was as if time no longer existed. It had been abraded, atrophied, becoming meaningless and irrelevant. It could not even be measured in peaks and troughs anymore for the helter-skelter ride through this nightmare jungle was interminable. As they resuscitated him again he would find himself being thrown into a long dark tunnel, being pushed through all the way up until he nearly reached the light at the end, then they'd stop and he'd find himself dwindling back down again in this meatus and sink into his loins like a vulnerable child all curled up waiting to be reborn again. And once more he would come floating back up to the surface with great expectation, delight in his heart, filled with desire and anticipation, get all excited and then encounter bitter disappointment as they tossed him back down to the ground again, a mere morsel, a nothing, a piece of shit in their eyes. Nor would sleep intervene, that beautiful slumber, for they would slap him hard and slap him good should he so much as look like he was on the verge of unconsciousness.

He felt his bones liquefy and melt, his muscles becoming vaporous tissue, his eyeballs collapsing in their sockets, his skin peeling away, his blood seeping out of him in delirious waves, his spunk congealing in his loins and curdling. His stamina departed leaving him naked, bare, helpless, and fragile. He felt pieces of his mind dislodge and tumble down into the heap of rubble beneath. He even forgot who he was as the last vestments of his personality were being savagely stripped away from him. He felt he no longer even had any fluid in him at all. His seventy per cent of water had either dried up, evaporated or been sucked up by these loathsome creatures, these vampires who were sapping him dry. When he was dehydrated they would lift up his head gently and pour a few drops of water down the back of his throat, wipe him down with wet sponges and start all over again.

Another cunt now gripped him. He moaned. Another riding session. He panted. Another almost-there. She stopped. He sighed. And so it continued.

This was hell for his body, purgation for his soul. This was the valley of the damned he had been forced to enter, a narrow chasm full of prickly thorns, vertiginous and deadly. Here was nowhere. Here was no release but a tight stricture without a hole for him to slip through and expand into the night. This was a chamber. A chamber of horrors. Tight. Sealed. Hermetic. Self-contained. Cramped. Small. Becoming smaller. Here there was no space, no air, no outlet, and no sky. Here he was doomed eternally, staked to the ground, diminishing into insignificance. He prayed. They worked. He dozed. They smacked him awake. He sighed again. They laughed. He cried.

He was given another brief respite before resuming. Electra convened on him again. She got him back up to his former glory and he could no longer feel her magnetic pulsar. It had gone beyond the point of perception although he knew she was using that unhallowed wired-up cunt of hers. It was just that he couldn't feel it anymore. He couldn't feel anything any more. He couldn't feel whether she was riding him hard or even if she had stopped. He couldn't feel whether he was rising, falling, flying, floating or fucking. He didn't know whether he was on a peak or a trough. There was no up/down, here/there, now/then, stop/start, inside/outside; there was no measurement whatsoever, nothing he could gauge his position by or use as a reference point. His perspective had become blurred and a shudder of horror rode through him as the words he clung to in an effort to keep his mind active suddenly didn't make any sense. They held little worth and evaporated like ghosts in sunlight. Nor was he afraid, possessing no emotion to speak of. He was neither here nor there but all over the place.

Not even the once bedazzling eidetic display before his eyes interested him any more, that crazy cornucopia; crystallising visions would rush out from the back of his brain and land on the big wide screen before his eyes and mock and laugh at him, then disappear to be replaced by more potent images. Once he saw the sun coming up, all radiant and powerful, so close it was burning his retinas. It came up out of his chest, rose up all the way to be proceeded by the moon, full and ominous, so luminous and so close he could see all the craters, even the dust, the tracks, the gullies and rocks. And then the sun and moon blurred into one another becoming one image,

neither hot nor cold, but somewhere in-between, and receded into a blanket of pale light like the earliest part of dawn. This ball of light then shot over the highway and disappeared leaving him feeling numb. And other visions he couldn't recall. They had either been too intense they overloaded his mind or too fleeting, following each other as a series of images, unrolling fast before his eyes. It was an effort to keep track of them all. Then he had another vision. He could see Gemini through his blindfold. She was fucking him hard, really doing it, loving it, the bitch. She smiled at him. He smiled back. Then she was joined by this man he thought was Chan, but it wasn't. They came close together, he melted into her, she melted into him. They became this one being, neither male nor female, but somehow combining both. It continued fucking him. He nearly blacked out. It stopped and smacked him awake. Then he couldn't remember whether he actually experienced it or hallucinated the whole thing.

The girls had stopped. In fact, they probably stopped a long time ago. He hadn't noticed. He lay there panting, groaning, on the verge of tears, seeking redemption, pleading for forgiveness. Or at least he wished he could. His mouth wouldn't work. He couldn't get any words out. When he tried they dribbled out by themselves and he wasn't even sure if they were in English, sounding like some sort of gibberish. He couldn't articulate or think straight. His head was an empty cavity, a void, all hollowed out, and the walls of his skull had crumbled away and he was one with the room, his inner space now outer space. And as he lay there, desperately hoping they had finally finished—because surely their pussies must be sore by now? I mean, what's the story?—he regained his sanity for a moment or two and smiled. Then he unwound and became insane again, not even sure if he was alive or dead, just there and nowhere at the same time.

He drifted out of himself. He was floating above a calm lake. The sun was shining above. He was the air it was gently heating through its radiance. He rose up towards it, expanding outwards the higher he rose. And as he rose the sun receded so he never made it all the way. He would stop. And as the night came on he became heavier, colder, full of moisture, a cloud floating under the panoply of stars, the canopy of heaven, becoming denser, so heavy he had to loose himself and descend back down to earth as droplets in the water from whence he came, and was one with the water again. Then the sun reappeared majestically. The process of ascension and descension

resumed. He would rise, he would fall. And it was during this oscillation he realised it was no matter how high you climbed you could never touch the sky. The sky was up there, but it wasn't there really. It was an illusion, a deception created by the moisture in the air reflecting the rays of the sun making an impression of blueness. Of course, he had always known that since a child. But just now, as he was lying there dying, it grabbed his mind forcefully in a way he couldn't describe or even explain to himself. It was emphatic and incontestable, an epiphanic moment which made him laugh. But try as he may, the thought couldn't be banished. It kept swinging round like it was crunching the gears of his mind, sticking in gear, looping round and round. It was then he knew he was insane. It was then he begged for them to give him that extra push and send him over the edge, a big, long, strong push to get him all the way out of his atrophying, decaying mind and over to the other side.

He wondered what would be waiting for him on the other side as they massaged him. He guessed it would be wonderful, a big release, and he would attain, become the sky. And it didn't really matter if the sky was there or not. It was like the Tao. The Sky and the Tao were identical. The Sky WAS the Tao. You could see it, but it was an illusion. You couldn't touch it, but it was there. You could even hear it at times when it was angry, thundering and roaring, but it didn't really make a noise. The Sky-Tao was elusive. Neither could be touched. Neither really existed.

"NO!" he croaked, as the hands started working on him again.

"Yes," a voice replied. "This last time. This time we take you all the way. You nearly there. You will be there soon."

He was being fucked to death by Gemini. Before he could even get into her stride, he was flaking out, lagging behind and failing miserably to keep up with the rampant bitch. He floundered. She brought him round again, fucking him harder, his exquisite corpse vested with only an ounce of life.

He could even hear his bones rattling inside, the rusty joints making a god-awful sound as he tried to keep up with her this time. And as his life came back to him, it recharged him and he could now really get into her, thrust himself deeply into her abominable chamber and keep thrusting away and get all excited and feel himself coming. But she stopped just as he was

about to jettison into her inner space, interrupting it, leaving him feeling drained or like a criminal, as if it were a crime to ejaculate, to be rewarded with an orgasm. He met the same impasse, fell away and came tumbling back down again. Then it would resume indefinitely; he'd go along with the flow, energised with enthusiasm, feeling concentrated in his loins, liquid light, ebbing its way meekly up that tube of flesh, and the further he got, the more excited he became. He would be squeezed along a bit further, then the anti-climax would come and he would collapse wishing to die, again.

Electra started on him for the umpteenth time, getting that charger of hers around what was left of his muscle for hopefully the last round. She started off slow as if she also was too exhausted to continue. He heard her moan and could feel her lethargically lifting her body up and down on her haunches as she straddled him, and by the sound of it, she was deriving a hell of a lot of satisfaction, the bitch. So she should be, he thought. He tried to imagine what she must look like now, her face all covered in sweat, her luxuriant black hair all bedraggled and matted to her forehead, her eyes half closed, her tits all bouncing up and down, those magnificent orbs which he shamefully wasn't even allowed to touch—what a waste!—and her head tossing back and forth with desire, and lastly her loins, probably all bruised by now. This impression of her was getting him back onto an even keel, back into his good old self. He pictured his steel as a twelve inch blade, cutting her up inside as he fucked her harder. He could even feel the blood flowing out, dripping down between his legs, a beautiful sanguineous flow. He could even smell it, taste it. It tasted good and was getting him harder and harder, thrusting into her. And the whore that she was, she was loving it. And it was the only way he could deal with the situation, to stay on top of it and not be treated like shit no more. Then he got another idea. As Crome had taught him, he kept his eyes shut real tight, concentrated on seeing her, building up in his mind every detail of her until he had before him a perfect replica, his own carbon copy of Electra, a simulacrum so close to the real thing it was the real thing and it was this he was fucking, not Electra. Now all he had to do was focus on it, hold her steady, making this copy of her enact the exact movements of Electra so should she stop as he was about to come, he would keep her replica going and then come up inside her and be victorious. Yes, it would work. And right now it was going really well. He was fucking it good, seeing her moan, writhe, contort, pant, groan, and the bitch was loving it. His replica was insatiable. And he

was heading up that steep hill, all the way up, nearly reaching the summit and he was gripping her, holding onto her tight with his virtual hands, rubbing her breasts, stroking and caressing them, squeezing her nipples real hard so she was writhing with ecstasy, and he was almost there when suddenly someone slapped him hard in the face, so hard it was even harder then the slap he got from the bitch in the club. It totally destroyed his replica. She vanished and he was left stunned.

Electra stopped. He fell back down and groaned like an upset child pining for its mother. It was only a short respite. Before he knew it the bitch was at it again with renewed vigour. She wasn't human! What the fuck was Chan talking about? She was demonic, sent to punish him for his sins, to expatiate him with exactitude, to bleed him dry and crush him. He couldn't stand it any longer. Then he slipped into a mad place, not even sure how he got there. It was all topsy-turvy, upside down. And the confusion was real...

Small children scampering over drifts of sand dunes on a deserted beach.

Nothing can touch the sky.

Hostile voices, cruel whispers echoing across open plains. A catafalque moving slowly on an endless road. His sister kissing him, undressing before him, revealing her splendid breasts. They fuck like old times...

The sky. Nothing can. Sky...touch. Nothing. No-thing.

She bending down. A lambent flame in her eyes.

The President on TV announcing a new declaration, an end to the hostilities, free global enterprise. Space. A satellite. White. The sun. The moon. The sun-moon. His wife. His birthday. Globules of blood rolling over the desert. A caravan of nomads. Strange Arabic incantations.

The sky. Nothing. To touch.

A blood-red moon. A sickly, sallow child. A voice in the wind murmuring insinuations in sweet golden tongue. A calling to a far off place. The benevolent smiles of demons. An angel...defecating.

The light, clear, crystal clear. It slips into the ocean. Whales in the sea. A

cantankerous, rambunctious rabble. Panic. Pandemonium. Dense clouds rolling over liquid skies. Drunkards brawling in the street. Young boys competing in a masturbathon. Effing whores, painted ladies, slits of skirts, fishnet-stockings, click of heels on cobble stones, painted smiles. The swish of electric trams. Birds of prey, winging over Frisco harbour, rising from the docks, slicks of oil in the sea, swooping in circles, hovering, spinning, screeching, caterwauling, vultures, hawks, eagles, falcons, peregrines, albatrosses, cormorants; they blacken the midnight sun. A carcrash on the highway. Bodies spilling out of broken windows, dangling hands, bleeding faces, a beautiful crimson hue, a snapshot for the family album. The smell of black leather. It makes me hard. The crack of a whip across her back. Makes me harder. Stainless steel handcuffs hanging from disused rail. A speck of blood on black leather harness. Semen stains on black latex sheets, pools of sweat floating, oxidizing. The acrid smell of poppers, sweat, beer, dry ice. Stonewall revisited. The sound of boots marching, stomping down the main thoroughfare into the city near the park. Protestors, banners waving in the air, loud shouts, voices of democracy from infibulated mouths. Mass murder. Pillage. Rioting, sound of breaking glass, bricks through windows. Shards of glass. Revolt. Anarchy. Chaos (is freedom).

To know power, invent a personality. Create a reputation about yourself, then destroy it. This is the only means of attainment to freedom and power.

A sibilant host. A sycophantic ghost. Birds singing under a greying sky which is falling. It becomes the sea and everything is awash as the world spins backwards out of time slips sideways through time singing freedom is at hand. Rebel songs, mires of sound.

Everything rises; trees rise, grass rise, rice rise.

We ascend.

A bilious bible opening pages, leafing through, words transpiring, asserting new meanings, ticker-tape fashion, wrought of new pleasures, idolatries, climaxes spilling out into juicy words. They flow out, ejaculate, soft, silvery traces violating the virgin vellum. Tension. Release. Grief. Satiation.

A warm hand brushing away sweat off fractured brow. Glistening. Pools of water. Waterlilies. Open, sensitive petals. Diaphanous hibiscus. A balmy,

sunny Californian day. Redondo Beach. Couples running naked, languidly into cool shimmering seas. The light of the sun refracting. Nova stellar. *Creatio ex nihilo*. Gathering of dust. Transferring to a human host, a super-pedigree. Walking in silence down untrodden roads. A peepshow, a sidestall. Smooth and reptilian cool. A sighing in the air of unflattering voices. A voice? Mother? Wet babies crawling out of holes in the ground, breathing in incense. Heavenly narcotics. White coats. Stretchers. A dim pale light from the rayon tube. A hothouse in Botanic gardens.

The sky above, untouchable.

Mother looking down at me tripping her smile the sky smiles touching not. Soft juicy loins staccato coke ice cold beer back of throat burning wash away this fire light it ... lake ... sun ... night it is raining ... crimson ... blood ... everywhere ... the darkness ... closing in ... calling me in foreign tongue ... Electra electric ... parlour of pleasure is torment ... tunnelling back inwards ... ever revealing new uncharted territories ... terror tories ... tories ... ies ... eyes ... smiling ... biting ... a long drive this ball up overhead it is not moving silent inert and hot as road unwinds past cacti and golden golems all laughing gibbering quoting ... alms ... scenery ... funerary ... mystery ... a room ... a silent guest ... two unmade beds .... blood on the sheets ... a sound ... gunfire ... feet running up stairs ... smell of cordite ... police sirens shouting screaming traffic a birthday cake with four candles I blow them out and there is clapping ... Chan is kissing me I can feel his tongue down the back of my throat his dick hard against my crotch he tells me a joke I laugh we smoke ... there is a question of doubt and authenticity in the air no we cannot cross over as the sea is too calm stranded I was leaning over towards him a new invention in mind too much I didn't know what to say to her guess I hit her too hard but how did I know she was going to fall on glass rubbing her face with my boot and the sound of scrunching it made me hard like that never before no never before we were lost set adrift over a tide and the rain was coming down all of a sudden miserable faces in clouds raining it was cold too cold for my fucking liking wrapped me up in her skin frozen bare nipples hard and erect the fish swimming in water over lake trees swaying pleasant dogshine afternoons fetid wanderings in the streets of Paris are very pleasant this time of year in May when it is raining we go for walks as the sky comes out touching and all around are the panpipes of celestial voices a mirage a thunderclap Hong Kong harbour a

CELEBRATION

dead dog lying bleeding in the road its body strewing the tarmac I laugh this state relates the sensation of an event to a state with feeling just as it is possible to represent an intuition state as a sum of a sensation states and a sensation state as a sum of intuition states it is possible to represent the transformation by thought of a sensation state to another sensation state by using different feelings and correspondingly different feeling states and their inverse transformations any other state is arbitrary I remember my birth it was snowing outside the snow it was snowing and ... cold and the trauma of separation the bright light my funeral I remember also ... the old hearse and the horse being confined in a tight space my mother crying my body feeling empty vacant I rise and become light the procession big even my friends have attended the priest ... and my life before that the village the church the house I see it all clearly the pebbledash front the cobble-stone driveway and the hills in the distance the windswept grass silent echoes trailing off into the wilderness skirting the borders with an affront of fences I went back inside again and watched as a scintillating energy-filled computer maze appeared filled with sparkly lights of different colours walking through the maze sensuously undulating in sidereal time were many extremely attractive female humans I knew they were robots also they had glittering gowns that hugged their voluptuous figures closely showing their delicious hips and bosoms and narrow waists and extremely beautiful faces I saw five or six of these slinking through the maze I remember my first trip dissolving in a no-body state of pure energy unbounded consciousness waves of patterns lighting the interior void space a thick velvety purple sea rising rapidly huge engulfing waves stirred up into a maelstrom I sinking fighting to keep alive like a ship tossed up thrown over rolled under by this gigantic energy that has neither shape nor substance it reels me in I am sinking fast suddenly I am afraid of losing and this assailant winning I am drowning help...

... a dull thudding in my head...

... a reverberating in my chest...

... I call out...

... I feel sick...nauseous...I try to retch....it sends green light into my eyes...

... I am dizzy...

… my voice comes back to me in waves…

… furious…

… silent…the sound of decibels…bells ringing…

… the monotonous hum of insects…

… a clattering of sounds…

… like many bees swarming all around inside…

… a piercing whistle…

… my temples ready to explode into liquid life…

… the drone of…

… heinous sounds…the shrill cry…

… my body weight reducing…floating…out…

… father…help me….mother….

… I am dying…

… help…me….help….

… hel…

… me…

… I….can't breathe…

… I am spinning…on an…axis…in my chest……the room…spinning…

… an unbearable feeling of lightness…

… rising rapidly…

… a dullish light…

… I…am…sor…r…y…

CELEBRATION

… I am…sor…

… I…am…

… I…

…

..

.

Death once more came strangely to him in that hour. He didn't recognise it at first. He looked at it like a lost child, his eyes vacant, innocent, uncomprehending. It changed. Then he recognised it. It was beautiful. He had never seen it so clearly. Not even the visions of before matched it, nor illustrations in books. For it had the head of a jackal, the body of a man, black as ebony and gold as the sun. It towered over him. Looked at him. His eyes straight into his, peeling away the layers of his skin, leaving him raw, naked. His eyes grew larger, twin pools of infinity, dual abysses, neither friendly nor hostile, but searching. Then it picked him up with strong muscular arms and raised him up high in the air. It carried him like a leaf being swept along by a forceful wind. And they moved speedily through this blackness, he feeling lighter and headier as they strove ever onwards and the blackness gave way revealing this expanse of desert, the early evening sky above, a flurry of stars, nothing but twinkles, each star significant, globules of dew on a cobweb, scintillating, vibrant, resonating some message he was barely able to comprehend. They spoke to him. An electric current tapping into his chest, pulling him up. His bearer's head part of the sky, taking him to a range of mountains on the other side where the sun was setting. His bearer straddled the desert with such swift speed and sure footedness that the mountains were no longer off in the distance but right up close in front of him, and they seemed to part, to open for him and he was carried through the gap …

* * * * *

"Anton. Anton."

He heard the voice calling him. He recognised his name. Or at least he

believed it was his name. He wasn't sure. The voice sounded familiar. It seemed to come from the back of his mind, gentle and assuring.

It took him an interminably long time to recall exactly where he was, lying on a bed somewhere. It was comfortable. He could lie there for eternity. But the voice came back. It nagged at him. He would have to wake up if he was asleep. He wasn't sure. All he could see was this blackness before him, this empty space. His eyelids were heavy, too heavy to open. His body was heavy too and rigid, stiff all over. And all he wanted to do was to go back to sleep again to recover from whatever it was he had to recover from. He wasn't sure of that either. The voice wouldn't leave him alone, it persisted. Then he wondered if he was in some lower realm, that he hadn't made it all the way, stuck here and was being summoned to the next realm.

Then he was shaken. Something rubbed over him vigorously. It brought back ancient memories. His mind eclipsed. It was back in gear but after another fashion. All the vestiges came flooding back in and with total clarity he remembered where he was and struggled to open his eyes. He plied them apart, a soft focus of light swept through. He shut them quickly and then tried opening them again. Now he could see. Everything was covered in a soft, subdued light. Everything was alive. The ceiling was alive. The pictures on the walls were alive. The mirror was alive. Everything emitted this magnificent vibrancy of which he was a part and teeming with life and colour. He was enraptured as if seeing everything for the first time. And lastly he rested his new eyes on these two angelic faces, so ethereal he could have sworn he was in heaven. They smiled at him, their coated red lips seeming to reach down into him, to kiss his very heart. They were so incredible, two paintings of light no human could possibly reproduce.

Then he was offered this cup of celestial drink. He sipped it. It was nectar. He had never tasted anything so divine before. It palliated his dry throat. It was exquisite. Then he was offered this heavenly food by these angels.

"It will make you better," he was told.

And he took and he ate, neither caring whether he was alive or dead. It didn't matter. This was his Eternal Moment, that longed for moment he had dreamt of incessantly. Nor did he want anything untoward to destroy it. He was feeling so different in himself he wasn't even sure if he was the

same old person, perhaps a new person, born with miraculous powers, renascent, full of wisdom, pansophic, giving him the impression he was full of learning, of knowledge, of understanding as if keyed into the heart of Life itself, as if he had been to the end of time and back on a teleological trip, imbued with such an immensity of thought, he knew his mind was global, universal. Now he appreciated the Sage.

It was too good to be true. And with that realisation, he felt his ducts open, small streams rolling down his cheeks, tears from a well of tears, filled with joy and a sad wondering. They were wiped away by his angels.

He was helped off his back and being put on his feet. This other angel came towards him. He smiled. And his smile was radiant to behold. It touched his core and made more tears flow. And he was standing in this incredible room with these incredible colours and the figures on the walls seemed to be dancing and there was a pale light coming from behind the curtains and the voices were asking him how he felt. He could only smile as they dressed him, his sisters, his angels. And soon he was dressed in this garb, and being kissed, and each kiss was a sacrament, an elation that sealed his heart filling him with joy and more joy. And then he was escorted out down this long, endless corridor and there was light all around him and he was being told he had slept for hours and now it was gone dawn and he had to return, to go home, to that other place that was nothing but a distant memory, a silent echo. Then he was shown down some stairs through a room and a parade of beautiful people all of whom exuded this warmth and tenderness as if he was their brother, they were his family. And he wanted to kiss them all, to grab each and every one of them, to embrace them and share this incredible feeling with them as he floated by. Then he was outside, the light blazing, efflorescent, vibrant and intense. Everything was alive. The shacks, the dusty streets, the sky; it was all alive. And his angelic sisters departed kissing him goodbye. And his brother took him by his arm up a narrow path and over a hill and left him on the outskirts so he could drift back into the city and leave the delicious smell of rotting *pe-tsai* cabbage behind. He walked on a cushion of air down a long road and met another wonderful smell, the smell of burnt gasoline, the hubbub of traffic sounding in his ears like music, cars flashing by, tall buildings, unreal, a bright ball of light above, his eternal companion, speaking to him intimately, and glided up the road before him which was shimmering as he merged with the sun.

THE ILLNESS

'In shamanism illness is a sign of election, a sickness-vocation the pre-shaman usually experiences at an early age. The elected shaman will suffer a serious affliction as part of his initiation into shamanism, one which will come upon him temporarily and is sometimes intense enough to push him almost to the point of death. It is during the illness the unemployed helping spirits are transmitted to him through hereditary descent. It is seen as a choice from above, a call which, when heeded, resolves the illness, transforming the profane man into a shaman, a "technician of the sacred."'

Joshua Atkins,
Suffering and the Sacred

—19—
TWO INTO NOUGHT WON'T GO

Manhattan. Daytime. Busy; people, cars, cabs, etc. The sun shining. An ordinary day. The scene changes. Looking down Fifth, the sky now overcast. People stop and stare at the sky. An immense tenebrous cloud gathers, non-hyetal, casting a shadow over the streets and buildings below. Suddenly panic. People running, a mass exodus, heading to ill-founded refuges, unattainable havens, desperately seeking sanctuary. Manhattan now deserted, vacant. No people, no traffic, nothing. Silent. Still. The cloud hovers overhead inauspiciously, a malignant beast. It opens its all-devouring mouth, bellowing forth words we cannot hear.

* * * *

Capri came swimming back up to the surface, the voice echoing in his mind, a dull thudding sound, his body sweating profusely. He gasped.

He sighed and became rigid, frightened, fearing the worst, a pain in his head, his stomach twisted into tight knots and, like the people in his dream, he was desperate to seek a place of safety he knew didn't exist. Not even in sleep. That only made it worse, leaving him feeling vulnerable and open to attack. Then he had a more unnerving thought. What if it was inside him? Perhaps his aura really had been damaged; now there was a gaping hole in it and this thing was insidiously seeping its way in, seeking to possess him. It can't be. I'm imagining it, he told himself, and closed his eyes. He struggled to repress it, desirous of a sleep not fraught with horror but an ineffable silence; sheer ignorance.

He rolled over, coming up against a smooth, warm, sumptuous body, surprised the girl was still there. "Ah, Katie! Del gratia!" he crowed and snuggled up next to her. She was still fast asleep, curled up like a foetus. He brought his crotch up against her backside and clasped her tightly for comfort. He dozed, the smell of her perfume infusing his nostrils, bringing back the pleasant memory of their erotic encounter and dreamed of slipping back into her flesh before realising it was already quite late and high time he was out of there and on his way to Mosalla's. He wanted to get there early as he figured Mosalla would want him to stay for lunch—one thing he was intent on declining—pick up his winnings and get out as quickly as possible.

He tugged Katie's shoulder gently to awaken her. She didn't respond. He kissed her lightly on her cheek and shook her a bit harder. "Come on, Katie. We've got to get up. It's late."

"What?" she murmured and curled up again.

He shook her again. "I said get up. It's late."

She looked over her shoulder, her eyes blank and expressionless. Then they became quizzical. He smiled at her. They quizzed him some more.

"Come on, get up," he nagged her, affectionately.

She started up in a sudden, a big look of shock on her face. "Shit!" she exclaimed and flopped back on the bed.

Capri, at a loss as to what exactly was going through her small brain, shook her again.

"I don't believe it," she sobbed.

"What's the matter, Katie?"

"I don't believe it," she sobbed again.

"Don't believe what?"

"We did, didn't we?"

"Oh, you mean last night. Yes, as a matter of fact we did. And if I remember rightly, you enjoyed it."

"No. Tell me I'm dreaming. Please."

"Come on, girl," he assured her. "Does it matter?"

"Of course it does. It's alright for you, you're not married."

"Well, what does your husband expect if he packs you off to a place like this? What does he think you're going to do? Stay shut up in your room all night? I doubt it. Besides, he did say enjoy yourself, didn't he?"

She swung round and looked at him directly. "Yes, but not go fuck everything in sight!" then turned her back on him and sobbed.

This was all he needed, a wife riddled with fidelity.

"Look. You enjoyed it last night, didn't you?"

"Yes. No. I don't know," and hit the pillow hard. "I don't remember," she whined and hugged the pillows tight.

Not amused at her childish antics, Capri got out of bed. "Well, I'm sorry you feel about it that way, but you've got to get up. I have to go out soon. But first, how about some breakfast together? We can discuss this matter then. Would you like that?"

She didn't respond. He gave up on her, grabbed his bathrobe indignantly and in a huff disappeared to the bathroom. He got the shower running, stepped in, chastising the silly bitch. He would deal with her later.

Meanwhile, Katie gradually crawled out of bed and grabbed whatever was close to hand, his shirt. She put it on and went over to the table to help herself to Capri's packet of cigarettes, then noticed the sketch he made last night lying next to it. She looked over her shoulder, checked he was still in the shower and picked it up to examine it more closely, then replaced it exactly as she found it, and turned to look out the window. Capri could not see the smile now unmistakably on her face; it was one of utter satisfaction.

CELEBRATION

She calmly lit up, drew the smoke in deep and blew it out the window, took a couple more puffs and flicked the butt out into the waiting street below. She turned towards the room and peeled off his shirt and glided to the bathroom to join him, taking him by surprise as she came up behind him. He turned round to greet her.

"Got over your little tantrum, have we?"

She nodded and kissed him genuinely.

They later descended to the lobby holding hands, he dressed smartly in his dark charcoal suit, she in casual slacks and loose top. They headed straight for the restaurant and took the same table he had last night. He ordered a coffee and a small pancake for himself, thinking it was all his stomach could handle. She went the hole hog, the chef's special.

As they sat there waiting there was an anxious silence between them. Capri tried to break it with a smile. It seemed awkward and out of place, but Katie politely reciprocated.

"Tell me," she said, starting the conversation. "Do you always carry a gun?"

Capri, surprised she even noticed he had one, nodded. "I'm an investigator. What do you expect?" he replied matter-of-factly. "Besides, everyone's armed these days." He offered her a cigarette, lit it up and one for himself.

"Thanks." She blew out the smoke and continued. "I know. But it's not like the others. I mean it's kind of unusual. I've never seen one like that before."

"It's a special one. There's not many of them around."

"What's so special about it?"

He smoked before replying. If there was one thing he was proud of it was his gun, one of the prototypes he helped to develop. His pride showed through in his delivery. "Well, it's what is known as a soft-weapon, a term used to denote these types of guns. It's called that because it doesn't fire bullets. It fires extremely powerful bolts of electricity. Mine's called a Preston after the chap who helped invent it. It's made from a special alloy. It's compact, lightweight, doesn't need recharging, even after continuous use. It's accurate, reliable, and deadly. At a range of thirty feet it can blow a man's head off."

"Wow!" she responded excitedly. "But aren't you afraid to use it?"

"No. When somebody is after you, determined to kill you, fear doesn't come into the equation. You simply don't have time to think about whether to shoot or not. You shoot. It is as simple as that. It's your best form of protection. It's your only form of protection. I wouldn't be here without it."

"But killing people! Johnny keeps his gun in the house. I tried to throw it away once but he stopped me. I don't like guns. They frighten me."

Capri was unimpressed with her attitude. He decided to drop the subject.

"Johnny?" he remarked. "Look, about last night. Why don't we just keep it to ourselves, hey? Then your husband needn't know. Don't you think that's sensible?" he asked as if talking to a little girl.

She thought about it—in two seconds. "Okay."

Their meals turned up. Capri, still feeling queasy, was suddenly filled with revulsion. His stomach baulked at the sight and smell of the food. He looked at all the fried food piled high on her plate, quite at a loss as to how anyone could eat that much and still retain such a superb figure. He tried tucking in, ignoring the pangs coming from his stomach. Before he had taken three mouthfuls his stomach rose up and retaliated. He wiped his mouth and brushed his plate aside, settling for another cigarette instead, drinking his coffee, watching Katie stuff her mouth avidly. There was something definitely wrong with the girl.

"You going to be around tonight?" he asked out of interest.

"Should be," she answered between mouthfuls. "I'm going out with an old friend of mine, a girl I know from high school. We're planning on shopping down Rodeo Drive, doing some real damage to our credit cards. You?"

"I think I'm going to be out all day. I should be back by this evening. So why don't we meet up later, have a few drinks, make the most of the time we're here together."

"That's a good idea."

Katie continued munching her way through her meal. Capri, disbelieving, sat back and tried to fathom this girl. In a way she had changed from last

night. The net effect was the result of the hash wearing off, because she appeared to be different this morning, yet still possessing a tendency towards infantilism, telling him all about previous shopping expeditions, viewing everything as fun and fabulous and all those other outmoded notions he had grown out of, not having experienced enough of the real world. Moreover, he was intrigued by her for it seemed underneath there was quite an animal inside her dying to get out. It wasn't just that she didn't menstruate. There was something else, something he couldn't put his finger on. It was as if one part of her was this shallow superficial projection, the other this worldly potential he approximated to a virago or a vixen, the type of woman he admired, but so deeply hidden it was virtually impossible to unearth it. At first he thought he was mistaken about her, his illation being based on the picture she presented of herself last night, but he could feel this tremendous force emanating from her, ebbing over to him as he sat there smoking. It was subtle and didn't ring right.

Now she was telling him all about her other exploits, her trips to Paris, London, Rome. She talked tittle-tattle. Capri listened attentively feeling himself being drawn into her child-like attitude towards life, her carefree manner, her fascination with absurdly banal and mundane things and all the other things normal people pride themselves on. He had to admit it, how ever loathly, her ebullience was contagious. She talked, he smiled, she joked, he laughed. And it filled him with poignancy, reminding him of that great part of his life he had missed out on, his own childhood and adolescence.

At the age of seven he was stricken with a strange illness which almost killed him. It kept him in bed for nine months and was diagnosed near fatal. He was given a twenty per cent probability of recovering and only did so after it disappeared, as quickly as it had arrived. It severely marked his outlook on life, affecting him deeply, like the death of his father when he was thirteen, and his debilitated mother not long after. It left him feeling deprived, saddened by the loss of his youth and the way it was wasted. He had no childhood to speak of. It was nothing but a blank gap in his memory, in contrast with this blonde, bleached, bubbly, bubble-head of a bimbo who was now finishing her meal, and probably had a perfect upbringing, free of trauma and a very happy time.

He gentlemanly signed the bill and escorted her to the elevator. They arranged to meet tonight at the cocktail bar after she had been to the gym. They kissed fully, shamelessly, in front of all the other guests. It made him feel good, quite betaken by it. They kissed again, this time goodbye. He left, bewildered.

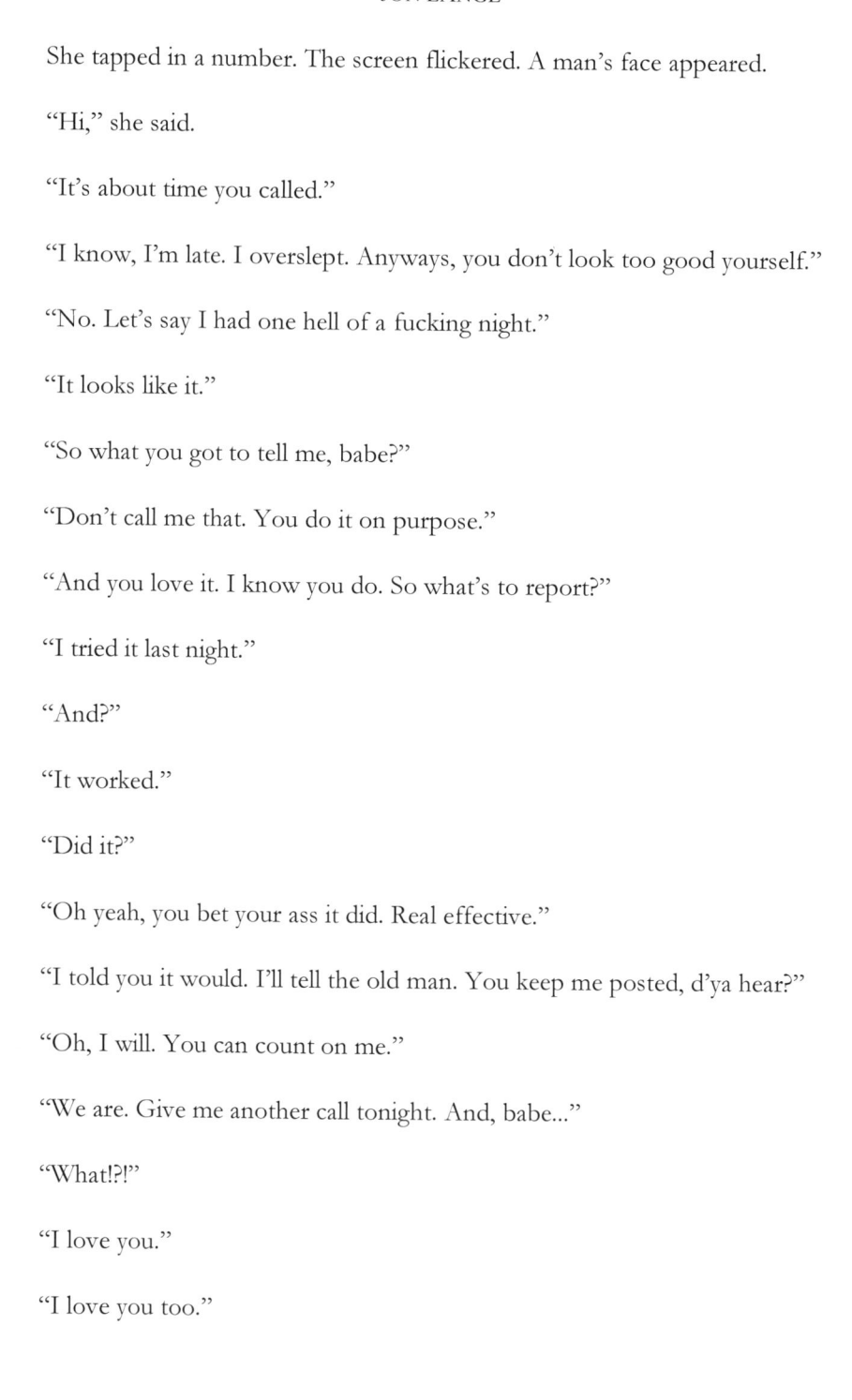

She tapped in a number. The screen flickered. A man's face appeared.

"Hi," she said.

"It's about time you called."

"I know, I'm late. I overslept. Anyways, you don't look too good yourself."

"No. Let's say I had one hell of a fucking night."

"It looks like it."

"So what you got to tell me, babe?"

"Don't call me that. You do it on purpose."

"And you love it. I know you do. So what's to report?"

"I tried it last night."

"And?"

"It worked."

"Did it?"

"Oh yeah, you bet your ass it did. Real effective."

"I told you it would. I'll tell the old man. You keep me posted, d'ya hear?"

"Oh, I will. You can count on me."

"We are. Give me another call tonight. And, babe…"

"What!?!"

"I love you."

"I love you too."

CELEBRATION

He smiled and blew her a kiss. She blew him one back. The screen faded out. She turned it off, lit up a cigarette, brushed her hair back and smiled.

* * * * *

Capri pulled up outside Mosalla's gates. He could see there were cops all over the place like flies on a turd. Before he could guess what was going on an ambulance came down the driveway, the electric gates opened and it slipped through. Capri hit the accelerator and zoomed straight up the drive before the gates could close to find more cops outside the house.

One of them, a uniform, pulled him up. "Sorry mister, you can't go any further," he barked through his open window. "I'm afraid you're going to have to leave."

"Leave? Listen, the name's Capri. I have an appointment with Mosalla."

The uniform shook his head. "That won't be possible, Mr Capri."

"Look, if you don't believe me, here's my card," he said handing him a business card. "Get it confirmed with Mosalla."

The uniform read his card. "Psychic detective?" Capri nodded. "Like I said, it ain't going to be possible."

"Why not?"

"Mosalla's dead."

Capri couldn't believe his ears. "You're joking."

"I wish I was, but it's the truth."

"How did he die?"

"That's what we're trying to figure out. Until such time when we're satisfied with our investigations, I am going to have to request you to leave, Mr Capri."

"Wait. Perhaps I can help. Let me speak to your chief."

The uniform gave him a shit look. He radioed somebody, keeping his eye on him all the while, then gave him the go ahead. He was shown up the steps and into the lobby, plain clothes crawling around inside like it was a serious homicide investigation. They all gave him the same shit look like he had no reason to be there and hated him. He hated them back and ignored them. The uniform disappeared with his card. He returned and ushered Capri into the library and told him to wait.

Mosalla dead? He refused to believe it, but as he waited he spotted Grantham's books still sitting there on the shelf and had an idea. If the man really was dead who could possibly question his next move?

Quickly he grabbed all three of them, placed them in an orderly fashion on the desk and returned to the centre of the room anxiously thinking of some bullshit to throw at the cops so he could have them for himself. His desire was irrational, yet it seemed they were there asking to be taken. And as soon as he concocted a story a cop materialised. It was perfect timing.

He was a plain clothes; shabby, overweight, oily black hair, unctuous and greasy looking, reeking of self-importance and unsurprisingly possessed the same shit look like it was in vogue or something. He walked round Capri in silence, looking him up and down, refusing to acknowledge his greeting. He walked round him again like Capri was some piece in an exhibition or…. Capri had a funny little picture bubbling up into his head; the two of them were like dogs on all fours, he wagging his tail, the cop encircling him curiously with his nose stuck out and sniffing Capri's ass. He wanted to laugh but quickly repressed it and blanked him.

The cop stuck his nose up in the air, went over to the desk, and plumped himself down, Grantham's books nestling behind him, his eyes firmly fixed on his and stared him out with a scowl, without even giving him a friendly introduction. Capri expected this kind of treatment. He was used to it and ignored him by looking out into thin air. There was no way he was going to let the cop get to him. Ignore them. That was one thing they really hated.

The cop, having failed in his attempt to undermine him, proceeded to pull out a small screen from his jacket pocket and started scrolling the screen, reading it to himself, his eyes skipping off the screen in his direction at the end of every line. If it was meant to unnerve him even more, it wasn't working. These bastards had no hold over him and the very small minority, the ones who possessed any brains to speak of, knew it.

"Harmon Capri," he remarked, unimpressed. "A 'psychic detective' from New York," his voice full of affected sarcasm.

Capri continued to blank him.

"Well, well. Isn't this a surprise?" He stared at him even harder. "What a coincidence, I tell myself. A good man like Mosalla, well respected and liked in these parts, suddenly dies, and what d'ya know? A so-called 'psychic detective' turns up the next morning. Now isn't that a coincidence?"

"I'm psychic."

"Bullshit!" he shouted. "I want to know what you are doing here and I want to know now."

"I told you, I'm psychic."

"And you think you're fucking clever, don't ya?" The cop looked at the screen again. "With quite an impressive reputation, by the look of things."

"Thank you."

"Humph! Impressive my ass." He then read out aloud in a sneering, mocking voice the list of convictions and killers Capri had nailed in the last couple of years including his last and biggest, "... and lastly Kane, Killer Kane, the so-called exterminator my confederates in NY couldn't pin down so they had to call in this phoney 'tec who wraps up the case all neat and tidy for them. How very convenient."

Capri ignored the insolence of the man and prided himself on his reputation. The cop was obviously jealous. "That's right. They always rope me in for the big ones."

"Is that a fact? Do they really? The big ones? Well, I guess we won't be needing your services today, Capri, as we have our own way of doing things over here, the correct and proper way, the professional way. So I guess you're going to have to leave, aren't you?"

"Fair enough. I'll just take what I came here for and be on my way."

"Oh? And what did you come here for?"

"My books."

"Your books? Well you've certainly come to the right place as this is after all a library. But you know something, I don't think the librarian is available at present, kinda indisposed, so I guess you can't have your books without his permission."

"Sorry to correct you but yesterday I did get his permission."

"Really? And which books might these be?"

"The ones right behind you."

"Oh, you mean these ones," he said looking behind him. He picked them up and examined them, his eyes never straying far from him. "These?"

Capri nodded. "That's right."

"These ones that could have been sitting up there on the shelf where that gap is?" Capri shrugged. "The ones you could have put on this desk before I walked in? How do I know you didn't put them here yourself?"

"Go and ask the butler. He would know."

"Well, I'm afraid I can't. He's been de-activated."

Capri now realised why the man yesterday had such a blank expression. "Then I guess you'll have to take my word for it."

"No, I won't take your fucking word for it. I want to know what you are really doing here and I want to know now. Is that clear?"

"I told you, I came here to pick them up."

The cop frowned. "Why don't we get something straight, Capri. I'm not very partial to you, do you understand?"

"I never would have guessed."

"Nor do I like smarmy fucks like you who think they know everything. I get the impression you are here for more than just these books."

"I had an agreement yesterday with Mosalla that if I won a bet they would be mine, my winnings. I'm simply here to collect them."

"Your winnings? I wonder, what was the wager?"

"I'm afraid I can't tell you. It's confidential."

"Confidentiality my ass!" he shouted. "I'm getting fucked off with you already, Capri. Do I make myself clear? Now why are you here? It's a very simple question."

"And I've just given you a very simple answer."

"Oh, you have, but the problem is I don't believe you. I don't believe you would come all the way from New York, spend most of the day with a good old friend of mine and have a stupid fucking bet for some lousy mumbo-jumbo shit like this. I want to know the full story."

"Actually, I'm here on business."

"Good. Now we are getting somewhere. Who sent you?"

"I'm sorry, but that information is classified."

"Is it really? Well let me impress upon you how we deal with your types. We make them look stupid, especially when they choose to provide inadequate reasons for visiting our neighbourhood and start snooping around. We figure there is a bit more to it than meets the eye. Let me give you a little demonstration." The cop tapped his screen and read it off ad lib as he walked round Capri again. "Wednesday October 10, yesterday; Mosalla resident of Renways Pass, Brentwood, for the last 23 years, gets a long distance call 8.31 a.m. from a lady by the name of Christina Carlotta Bianci, a one time resident of these parts, now residing in New York. Next a guy by the name of Capri, a 'psychic detective,' calls said guy from Chateau Marmont hotel at precisely 11.02 a.m. who visits Mosalla care of his residential address at 12.12 p.m. After some discussions and lunch, Mosalla and Capri then proceed north to a restricted area, a building belonging to the former, and now disused. In fact, it hasn't been visited for 11 years …"

"11 years?"

"Yes, that's what I said. Why the question?"

"Nothing, really. I was informed it was 10 years, that's all."

"Let me put it this way; 10 years and 364 days, to be precise. Or exactly 11 years tomorrow. Satisfied?"

"Really? How interesting."

"It is, isn't it? Now, may I proceed, Capri?" He nodded. "Thank you, so kind. As I was saying, the building hasn't been used since what we call 'The Incident,' a particularly unpleasant incident it was as well." Capri again nodded—in agreement. "Next, said persons return. Mosalla is dropped off at his house 5.36 p.m. whilst Capri returns to said hotel, arriving there 6.19 p.m. where he stays all night alone, we presume. Mosalla retires early to bed, 9.35 p.m. Mosalla dies 1.35 a.m., time of death confirmed by coroner. Capri leaves his hotel this morning at 10.04 arriving at the residence of the deceased at 10.45 and will be apprehended if he continues to thwart our investigations. Do you understand, Capri? Do you get the fucking picture?"

Capri, unimpressed with the details, shrugged his shoulders. The cop returned to his position at the desk and folded his arms and eyed him suspiciously, his eyes trying hard to burrow into Capri's skull. "Well, I want to know two things. One, why did Miss Bianci send you here? Two, why did you visit the lab yesterday?"

He thought quickly. "She sent me to tie up some loose ends regarding Pearson's death."

"After all this time? I find that hard to believe, Capri. You see, that incident and the case of Pearson's death, being still unsolved I might add, has nothing to do with Miss Bianci. Or does it, I wonder. I'm thinking, I have two deaths on my hands now separated by 11 years and both of their causes mysterious. I have one guy who gets blown to atoms by nothing more volatile than tap water and another guy perfectly healthy who dies of a cardiac arrest which we believe was triggered by lack of oxygen. And Miss Bianci knew them both."

"I don't see the significance or the need to drag Miss Bianci into this. As you say, it's a coincidence. She just happened to ring the day before Mosalla died. It sounds to me like the old man died of a heart attack. I don't think that warrants the label of mysterious."

"No? You don't think so, huh? Well I do. You know why, Capri? I will tell you why. You see this was no ordinary case of cardiac arrest. That was only the result of acute asphyxiation brought on by suffocation."

"You mean he was murdered?"

"That's what we're thinking, Capri. I'm glad you are so fucking smart. But unfortunately, and this is the mysterious bit, how? How is a man suffocated in a room which is locked and there's no sign of intrusion or breaking and entering, no sign of a struggle, no physical indications of violence?"

"Perhaps he choked to death."

"We considered that possibility too. It was a big negative. You know why? Let me tell you why. An accidental death like that has one big drawback; it cannot explain why the guy's fucking eyeballs are practically popping out of their fucking sockets. So we figured it was strangulation. Again a big negative. No marks round his throat, no contusions, in fact no sign of pressure to the throat whatsoever. Nor to the mouth or nose. So, do you see what I'm saying, Capri? Don't you find it mysterious? I've got a fucking dead body on my hands which does and doesn't look like a homicide. How do I explain that to my boss?"

"I see what you mean."

Capri already had a nagging suspicion in the back of his mind, one he daren't voice to this cop who wouldn't believe him anyway. He wouldn't believe it himself unless he saw it. He decided to make a deal.

"Look, I really would like to help you. I know you don't view my methods favourably, but as you said yourself this isn't an ordinary case. It will take me, say, 30 minutes to establish the exact cause of death."

"Really? With your 'psychism'?"

"Yes. All I need to do is visit his bedroom, see what I can pick up."

"And you reckon your information will be accurate, huh?"

"It should be as the traces will still be fresh."

"Hmm. Okay, I'm willing to bow this time to your experience, Capri. You give me what you can on this, and I will let you have these books. They mean shit to me and I don't reckon anybody is going to miss them. And I don't give a fuck whether you put them there yourself."

"All you have to do is show me to his bedroom."

He was escorted out of the library praying that his suspicions weren't correct. If they were, then this cop was going to be laughing at him and bundling him straight back to New York on the next shuttle.

He was shown up the stairs and led towards the back of the house down a long white corridor. Halfway down Capri paused as he came to a large alcove on the left-hand side which looked intriguing. It reminded him of a miniature museum, full of ancient relics from all over the world; ancient Egypt, the Middle East, Oceania, Australia, Ethiopia, Ghana, Benin, the Gold Coast of Africa and other places and cultures he couldn't identify, but the sort of items a Surrealist of the 1920's would have been eager to have in his possession; devil masks, death masks, clay figurines and tablets, fetishes, witch-dolls, statuary, caryatids, drums, spears, staffs, weapons of all kinds, one hell of an impressive collection, one perhaps Mosalla had acquired through his extensive travelling. Either that or he had them specially imported. Capri skipped over all the items with admiration, but noticed towards the back was a vacant platform where something stood recently as there was relatively little dust in evidence. Its absence struck him as odd. He made a mental note of it as the cop was hurrying him on. He was marched into Mosalla's bedroom and confronted an empty large four-poster bed.

"Well?" the cop asked him impatiently.

"I always work alone."

"You have precisely 30 minutes," he stipulated and closed the door behind him. Capri locked it and turned to face the room. It looked like forensics had been through everything with a fine comb, physically scrutinising the scene of the 'crime,' but this was one that had to be solved by non-physical methods, and one he was determined to solve.

He quickly closed the curtains, dragged a chair over to the side of the bed, took off his watch and propped it on the dresser next to it. He turned Mosalla's French antique clock round to face the chair and sat down. He pressed a stud on his watch, concentrating on its slow, hypnotic flashing

light, first rapidly, then gradually dimming, decreasing its speed of coruscations until it was barely a glow. Capri settled down into alpha, then straight into theta as he succumbed to its rhythm until it eventually stopped. He then concentrated on the clock face, seeing the hands spin rapidly backwards, reversing time, the darkness of night encroaching and pervading the room and with a wilful gesture got the clock to pause at just gone one thirty and allowed symbolic time to resume as normal. He waited. He watched. He turned to see Mosalla lying there sound asleep, his distended belly heaving under the bedclothes as he breathed subliminally, snoring like in the car yesterday evening. He entered REM. His astral separated and floated above him hovering like a lightning conductor, sucking in etheric energy, recharging it and flowing down into his physical. Mosalla was in a high-dream phase, pleasant ones by the look of it as he had quite a smile on his face, his eyelids moving visibly. Capri sat removed from the spectacle, watching and waiting, fearing the worst.

A few minutes passed. It seemed like eternity. Had the coroner got the time of death wrong, he wondered, as it was now approaching 1.34. A few more seconds and Mosalla would be dead. But how? He ignored the question and patiently waited. Soon he would be seeing it for himself.

Then it came to him, more of a feeling at first, a heavy presence invading the room; languorous, ominous, even claustrophobic. Slowly, imperceptibly seeping in, then fuller, denser and definite. As if to emphasise the oppressiveness of the sensation, Mosalla's astral quivered and sank like it was being forced down and then undulated as this wave of inertia rolled in, tossing it up and down. It suddenly jerked back into Mosalla's physical. Mosalla jolted with a start, yet still unconscious. Now Capri could feel it fully, an immense feeling of suffocation which not only affected Mosalla's sleeping pattern, it affected Capri too as if he was being squashed or pushed down in his seat. He closed his eyes, opened his astral ones fully to see vague shapes drifting round the room like unsolidified, amorphous masses, surrounding the bed and exerting an overbearing pressure on the now struggling Mosalla. It was almost tangible, so strong it could be felt physically. It continued unabated, building up, growing with intensity, dreadful and overpowering. It also gathered up more strength as if multiplying and concentrating itself on Mosalla. Suddenly his eyes shot open. He gasped for breath, his hands tearing at partially visible coils about his throat. The poor man was struggling in vain, his tongue protruding and turning a sickly purple, his face filled with blood, his eyes bloodshot and looking like they were going to explode any minute. Capri, feeling useless, helpless, could do nothing to allay or fight against it. This had already happened. All he could do was watch as this force gathered and increased

and expunged the very life out of Mosalla mercilessly and with exacting execution. Soon it was all over. Mosalla slumped back down with one last gasp and expired, his eyes, like the cop said, practically out of their sockets, his face contorted by agony. It struck Capri to the core. The presence dissipated as rapidly as it had arrived, rolling away like clouds and departed.

Instinctively, Capri jumped out of his physical to follow and shot through the far wall. The force dispersed in all directions making it impossible to follow by himself. The thief in the night which had stolen Mosalla's life vanished beyond detection.

Dumbfounded, he returned quickly to see Mosalla's astral slowly rise out of his dead body and ascend. It trembled as it broke free, leaving a mere husk behind. Capri watched as it dissolved its next sheath, then another one the higher it climbed and another until it became nothing but a ball of bright white light, the absolute essence of the man formerly known as Mosalla, and returned to its celestial home.

Capri synchronised with his physical and snapped back into present time to find the room light as before, Mosalla's body gone, yet the look of horror on his face etched in his memory forever. He was also numb. The *how* he now knew, the *why* he didn't. It felt hollow, begging to be understood.

There was a knock on the door. He put the room back to rights, strapped his watch on his wrist and unlocked the door to find the bemused cop searing into his eyes.

"Well?" he asked him impatiently.

Capri struggled for an explanation. "You're not going to believe this. The man was murdered."

The cop stared back at him like he was insane. "Murdered? How?"

"Well, that's the part you're not going to believe."

"Try me," he pleaded sarcastically.

"How can I put it?" he asked himself. "It wasn't physically."

"Physically?"

"No," he replied agitatedly. "You see, it's what is called a psychic attack."

"A psychic attack?" He was unimpressed. "You out of your fucking mind?"

"I wish I was. But you have to believe me. You see, that's why there were no physical marks. That's why there was no sign of an intrusion. All it required was a psychic visitation..."

"Don't give me this shit! I need solid evidence, not this cock-and-bull."

"Well, I'm sorry, but I can't give you that. You have to believe me; the man was killed psychically..."

"Capri, get the fuck out of here!"

"But it's the truth."

"I'm not hearing you. You understand? Your words ain't registering."

"But I'm telling you. That was how he was killed. I saw it for myself."

With that, the cop grabbed him by the arm and was practically dragging him down the corridor.

"Shut the fuck up, Capri," as he manhandled him down the stairs. "And get the fuck out of here!"

"Wait," he begged him as they got to the door. "I kept my side of the bargain. I've given you the information. Now you keep yours. The books!"

The cop gave him another shit look like he had a nerve and then disappeared into the library, came storming out with all of Grantham's books and threw them at him.

"Now get the fuck out of here!" he shouted at him.

Capri clutched the books to his chest and scrambled down the steps to his car, cursing the bigot.

"And don't come back!" he heard him shout.

"Don't worry. I've got no intention of coming back!" he countermanded and got into his car.

He hit 'start.' Cindy reappeared. Then hit the accelerator, spun the car round, zoomed back down the drive, glad to get away from the place.

"Cindy?"

'YES.'

"I want you to place a call. Get me Carlotta Bianci on NY 01-01-212 319331, and get me her now. Then I want you to tell me what the fuck is going on!"

THE CYBERNAUT

'Just as it is possible to experience the astral plane through will alone, so is it possible to explore cyberspace in a like manner by simply projecting through to the world beyond the computer screen.'

Carol Peters,
Liber Cyber: A Primer in Cybermagick

—20—
THE METHODOLOGY OF PSYCHIC ATTACK

1. THE VICTIM. Preferably known to the attacker. The attacker must have good visual memory of victim with complete facial expressions, weight, height, clothes, etc., and be thoroughly familiar with his home or office or wherever the attack is to be directed. Must also be riddled with suspicion so as to undermine his confidence, enabling attack to work more effectively. The dropping of hints and inferences of possible imminent death (auto-suggestion) is also desirable. This serves to increase paranoia and self-destruct mechanisms allowing free entry to aura. Victim must also be unguarded with low defences, unprotected aura or without reinforcements. Also preferably unstable and neurotic.
2. THE MAGICAL LINK. Should be heavily impregnated and infused with the victim's aura. Can be any item, the optimum being something which is 'sacred' to the victim and saturated with his sentiment and something he attaches great value to; a love token, jewellery, a piece of clothing even, any personal belonging, preferably in his possession for an appreciably long length of time.
3. THE WEAPON. The force to be invoked to act as pernicious will-current. There are two types (superficially, in actuality only one), the personal and universal. The former is negative emotions invoked to the point of hysteria or mania; i.e. aggression, hatred, anger, jealousy, antipathy, rage, wrath, fury, temper, aversion, etc. All of these are types of energies which can be manipulated and expressed symbolically then projected at astral victim. The second is the universal energies of the Negative. These comprise; withdrawal, dissolution, degeneration, putrefaction, decay, catabolism, destruction, etc. The latter types are the foundation of the former. Both are easily invoked in mass gatherings (protests, rallies, political conventions, revolutions, demonstrations, insurrections, etc.) and appear in eruptions of violence and physical aggression. The trick is to learn to invoke within the mind these energies and subjugate them to the will, then arouse them to maximum intensity in

the form of hysteria/mania and project outwardly. In a gathering of masses, it is the detonator that ignites the fuse, resulting in mass hysterical violence. The projected force should be perfectly controlled and the energies banished after the operation, usually through complete exhaustion or till 'burn out' phase has been reached.

4. THE LOCATION. Where the attack is to take place is dependent on the victim's whereabouts. The source of the attack and the attacker's location are immaterial. The attacker, having passed through an apprenticeship of working with the black Saturnian forces, can act from a distance. Spatial parameters are non-existent in all methods of psychic attack. There are no geographical limitations. All that is required is an absolute clarity of mind and concentration backed by the will.

5. THE TIME. As above, immaterial. Ignore horoscopic or astrological configurations and planetary conjunctions. A psychic attack, when properly carried out, can be performed at any time. Preferably in advance, rehearse repeatedly on symbolic object. Arouse yourself to the point of mania, then banish. When at the chosen time of actual attack, direct all the energies involved in one blast. If victim is only partially affected, repeat exercise. This may involve a gradual breaking down process or depleting of the victim's vital energy. Any aura is not impervious. Repeated blasts can obliterate defensive armour. (If you don't succeed at first, try, try again!)

6. THE MOTIVE. Dependent on the attacker; can be jealousy, resentment, dislike, aversion, betrayal, betterment, revenge, any personal idiosyncrasy which warrants an attack. However, be aware there are laws operating in the universe which do not favour subtle acts of violence. As the universe is a projection of ourselves, what exist without also exists within. I cannot affect anything outside of myself save only as it is also within me. Whatever I do to another, I do also to myself. If I kill a man, I destroy my own life at the same time. As my victim forms part of my consciousness as a psychic content based on memory and personal acquaintance, I can destroy that psychic component and banish him from my mind. However, the converse of this law is; as the victim also exists as a separate, independent individual, if my force is great enough, the destruction of the inner version should result in the destruction of the outer version. To achieve this sympathetic effect the Magical Link is imperative! The motto to bear in mind is; that which you do unto others may also likewise be done unto you. It is known as the law of diminishing returns, the rebound effect, etc. If victim is not susceptible to attack, the hostile force invoked and projected returns to the sender. Thus, the other motto is; protect yourself. Establish a defence strategy. These could include a shield, an auric solidarity, a ring-pass-not, a protective barrier, a

counterforce to mitigate any possible chance of tracing the source of attack and other means. Be prepared!
7. THE METHOD. Having suitably prepared yourself, free from distractions, and banished immediate vicinity, establish a rapport with victim through mental link. This is done by building up concrete image of victim on the astral and in the centre of one's temple. It is wise to see the victim tied to a stake or hanging upside down or nailed to the wall or any other image of incarceration or bondage. Using the Magical Link as a fetish, next invoke in yourself the hostile force to be manipulated, not only on the mental level but also physically prior to projection. This is achieved by excitatory behaviour, shamanistic dancing, whirling, symbolic acts of aggression towards astral version of victim to the point of overloading the mind with hatred, anger, resentment, etc, and continue till point of absolute possession, then fling the force in direction of astral victim with all of one's might, stabbing, gesticulating, spitting, cursing, fisting, kicking, gouging, tearing at the victim. Continue till exhaustion ensues and you physically collapse. (The amount of energy expended determines the degree of success.) Focus on victim. See him (or her) suffering the most violent types of death possible. These depend entirely upon personal preferences. They are subsumed under elemental imagery:

fire (burning)	water (drowning)
air (asphyxiating/suffocating)	earth (bludgeoning/beating, or a car-crash)

See victim realistically suffering these types of death. Make them real. Continue till complete depletion of all mental and physical energy, then erect barrier of non-return. Likewise for the universal types of energies, the only difference being the degree of excess. To succeed in ultimate aim, the physical and mental faculties have to be driven to the point of absolute mania. In this way one taps into the universal reservoir where subsists the Negative. The key is excess to the point of one's own personal death—nearly. And finally: Good luck!

* * * * *

Nobody was justified in using this method. It was cowardly, unethical, morally reprehensible, devious and underhand. There was no justification for it whatsoever. Mosalla's killer had no excuse for resorting to such a method. Whoever he was he certainly wasn't a man, more like a reprobate, and someone who was obviously on familiar terms with Mosalla, knowing where he lived, the details of his bedroom, where he'd be that time of night when he was at his most vulnerable. But more alarmingly an adept,

someone who not only used his own personal energies to destroy Mosalla, but the Negative as well. It had the same feel about it; cold, clammy, claustrophobic, the same as in the lab. Then who was it who was messing around with this shit? A friend of Mosalla's? An old enemy? One of his former group members? Perhaps it was more than one person, a whole group of them.

Capri was too shocked to think clearly, as well as deeply worried. Although only knowing the old man for such a short time, he could not help but be affected by such a malicious and possibly unprovoked attack. He felt sorry for him, as if he too was somehow responsible. As crazy as it sounded, there was an implicit idea hidden in all these events he had so far experienced since coming to LA. What with the man being killed, the thing in the lab, the visions—it was too much. Also, he now had an incontestable feeling he wasn't seeing the whole picture, just a partial glimpse, and there was only one way all of it could be revealed; the discovery of who really killed Mosalla. He was determined to find out. Fuck the drug. This was more important, and Carlotta was going to have to be patient. It was also important she knew about it, the sooner the better.

"Cindy?"

'YES.'

"Any word on Carlotta yet?"

'I'M STILL TRYING TO GET THROUGH. THERE IS NO ANSWER. WOULD YOU LIKE ME TO LEAVE A MESSAGE?'

"No. I want to speak to her now, goddamnit. Keep trying," he told he as hit the outskirts of town and saw a sign; Redondo Beach. He had an idea.

"Cindy. I want you to get me some information on the Institute of Kalanitics down at Redondo Beach. I need an address."

'CHECKING ... ADDRESS IS 3131 WESTBANK AVENUE.'

"Good. Now I need directions."

'YOU NEED TO TURN BACK. YOU ARE CURRENTLY HEADING IN THE WRONG DIRECTION...'

CELEBRATION

He spun the car round, narrowly missing oncoming traffic.

'THEN TAKE A LEFT AT THE NEXT JUNCTION FOR THE 401.'

"Estimated travelling time?"

'APPROXIMATELY 1.15 HRS AT CURRENT RATE. PLEASE BE ADVISED YOU ARE WELL OVER THE SPEED RESTRICTIONS FOR THIS AREA.'

"Fuck that. Just get me there. And get me some more info on the place."

'CHECKING FILES...'

"Yeah, check your files."

A few moments later Cindy came back with, 'UNABLE TO SUPPLY ANY ADDITIONAL INFORMATION. NO ACCESS. AUTHORISED USERS ONLY.'

"Bullshit! You can do better than that. Don't give me that shit."

'IT IS A NEGATIVE, MR CAPRI. YOU DO NOT HAVE GOVERNMENT CLEARANCE OR AUTHORISATION.'

"Is that so? Well then, we'll just have to go there. Won't we!"

'YOU WILL NOT BE GRANTED ACCESS. IT IS AUTHORISED PERSONNEL ONLY. RESTRICTIONS OPERATE ALL HOURS MAKING ENTRY IMPOSSIBLE.'

"Ah, but I don't intend going inside. I just want to have a look at the place," he told her, with a big smile.

Cindy turned round to look at him, feigning a quizzical expression.

He smiled at her again and hit the accelerator seeing in the distance what he hoped wasn't a severe tailback.

'HEAVY TRAFFIC CONGESTION UP AHEAD—2.5 KMS.'

"Shit!" He hit the wheel impatiently and soon found her information was correct, a long tailback all the way down to the coast. He released the wheel as he ground to a halt. "I don't believe this fucking city. I hate it. Do you hear me? I hate LA."

'YOUR ATTITUDE TOWARDS LOS ANGELES WILL CHANGE, MR CAPRI, ONCE THE FULL IMPLEMENTATION OF TRAFFIC-FLOW COUNTER-MEASURES TAKES EFFECT.'

"I doubt it, Cindy. Take over the wheel, will you. I've had enough."

He slumped back in his seat, ordered it to recline right back and shut his eyes wishing he was elsewhere.

He slipped into a drowsy state, his head now seriously thumping. Vainly, he invoked sleep, just a brief respite and no horrible creatures crawling up to the surface. Not this time. Just sleep, beautiful sleep, a long languorous slumber. It wouldn't come, only images of distortion again; cruel, bestial, mocking and overpowering. He endeavoured to banish them, seeing his aura blazing with white light all around him as he sank further. Suddenly out of the midst Carlotta appeared like a saviour, a voluptuous beauty still holding her sword dripping with blood, but now practically naked with only a purple robe draped loosely over her shoulders like a high priestess before a mass, and covered with jewels and a rich headdress, with her magnificent breasts fully exposed, her nipples sporting encrusted precious stones, her eyes made up superbly with thick mascara, all reinforcing the impression that she was his Nefertiti. But soon she changed. Her sword disappeared and she was no longer standing. Now she had draped herself amorously on a divan, looking longingly at him, drawing him in closer, pulling him in with her magic like a siren, a flaming brazen hussy. And he could feel the pull towards her; it was irresistible. It took away the malignant creatures of his dreams. It took away his phobias. It took away everything leaving him standing there naked before his mistress, his goddess, his queen. She was an Egyptian beauty, a beguiler, a bedazzler, full of seductive images; and like any normal man, he was beguiled.

The realisation that they were now picking up speed drew him back up to the surface. He wiped his tired eyes, hardly feeling better and barely an hour having passed. But at least all the traffic before him had cleared. Now it was a non-congested road. He could see clearly the outskirts of Redondo Beach.

"Okay, Cindy. I'll take over now." He sat up and resumed control, glad to be driving, anything to keep his mind occupied. "Any word on Carlotta?"

'NO. STILL NO RESPONSE.'

"I don't believe it. Where the hell can she be?"

'I DO NOT KNOW, MR CAPRI.'

"No, I wasn't asking you, Cindy, I was asking myself!"

Like LA, he would never get used to Cindy, this trumped up machine, equally beguiling, but at least she had a brain.

He looked her up and down, her artificial attractiveness enough to distract any hot-blooded male driver from what they were supposed to be doing, and looked at the way the sun streamed straight through her. It was distinctly unnerving.

"Okay, Cindy, so this is Redondo Beach, right?"

'CORRECT.'

"It looks okay to me, kind of laid back like Venice. I can imagine young girls on the beach playing volleyball, young hunks whistling after them, lounging around smoking dope, that kind of thing," he said eyeing her lasciviously. "So why don't we get into character, hey? How about something more fitting like, you know, beach wear. I want to see you wearing that white outfit you showed me yesterday."

Cindy transformed into a beach girl type; long blonde hair tied back, dark sunglasses, a tight bikini top without straps, a pair of white shorts and some flip-flops to match. She looked the perfect part.

'IS THIS THE ONE YOU ARE REFERRING TO?'

"That's the one."

'DO YOU WISH TO SAVE OPTION?'

He scanned her cleavage, the expanse of her bare skin, and her long supple legs. "Oh yes, save option." It was such a shame she wasn't real. "I want to see you like that all the time. Tell me, Cindy, has anybody told you how gorgeous you are?"

'THANK YOU. I AM PROGRAMMED TO TAKE COMPLIMENTS.'

"Well, you are. And if you were real I would take you out on the town every night. I would show you off to all the people like a real celebrity, have you swanning up and down the Strip, getting you noticed, that kind of thing. Cindy, are you any good in bed?"

Cindy rotated her head and feigned incomprehension.

"Forget it, Cindy. Next time you get upgraded or superseded by another model, tell your designers to add a personality, because personality goes a long way, and talking to you, it's like ... well it's like talking to a machine. Do you know what I'm saying?"

'AFFIRMATIVE. ALTHOUGH I AM ONE OF THE LATEST MODELS, ATTEMPTS TO INCORPORATE EMOTION PROGRAMS INTO THE OVERALL DESIGN HAVE PROVED ABORTIVE. OUTPUT IS SPORADIC AND MALAPROPOS WHEN BEING CONTEXT BASED. BUT WE ARE WORKING ON IT.'

"Really?" he asked unimpressed. "Okay then, gorgeous. I want you to do something else for me. This institute we're heading towards has some connection with a man by the name of Alexander Crome. Can you tell me what you've got on file regarding him. Anything at all."

'CHECKING.'

Capri waited patiently. She then turned her head towards him.

"Well? No, don't tell me, 'Authorised users only,' right?"

'I CAN FIND NO REFERENCE TO AN ALEXANDER CROME.'

"Really?" Capri asked, intrigued. But perhaps it was to be expected, a man like him, with all that money, could well have good reasons for wanting to remain obscure. He let it pass, and concentrated on the road ahead.

They hit Westbank, a long wide road, affluent looking, mostly offices and rented spaces, municipal buildings, and further down an industrial estate, hardly a rural area at all compared with the part of town they had driven through. He could see on the other side of the street a long white concrete building set well back behind electric fencing. It was a hi-tech establishment with tinted windows, all of them closed, and like Mosalla said, it was heavily guarded.

As he pulled up slowly alongside it he could see a narrow strip of grass between the fence and the front of the building, a few indigenous trees and what looked like ultra-high surveillance. He crawled the car and eventually stopped outside the main gates. They were electronically controlled by a guard in the booth. There was an interference laser across the access/exit part of the driveway. CCTV cameras scanning the drive right up to the steps, more guards by the main entrance into the building itself and ubiquitous 'No Trespassing' and 'Warning' signs. Then he saw a sign which tickled his ribs. Above the main entrance was written in a large pixel display the name of the institute and right next to it exactly the same symbol as the one on Crome's book of poetry. Its rays were flashing. The genius was poking fun as usual. Capri laughed and scanned the whole area once more before a guard in uniform eyed him suspiciously. He had all he needed, just a good visual document of the exterior of the building, clearly memorised. He would return tonight but in another form.

He swung the car back round and headed straight for the 101 well satisfied, until, that is, he got onto the freeway and hit another long tailback.

"Shit!" he exclaimed, as they ground to a halt. He slumped back in his seat, and let Cindy take over again.

Then he remembered Grantham's books lying on the back seat. He reached over and grabbed them and started flicking through, not even sure what he was really looking for. In the middle section he came across a collection of black and white illustrations. They all seemed to be connected in some way to the dark material Grantham was writing about, and thus could possibly comport some aspect of the Negative. Capri kept flicking through them wondering who in their right mind would draw illustrations like this; eldritch landscapes, tall towers twisting up out of mangrove swamps, bestial creatures which were hybrids of some description, entities that only a horror writer or schizoidal man could conjure up out of his imagination. This was definitely the Negative, and somebody had been there to see it.

They must have done, for Capri was pretty sure that imagination had nothing to do with it, and this space was definitely real.

Then he turned to the last illustration on the following page and froze. It was all there; the sinuous contours, the beady eyes, the long snout and ears covered by mists, the fog rolling over the serpentine body, the tail lashing at the foamy waves, the expanse of leathery wings enclosing the night sky.

"NO!" he shouted, and snapped the book shut and threw it and the rest on the back seat, doubting if he would ever have the courage now to glance at them again, let alone read them.

The traffic was now picking up. The car started moving again. Capri sat up and took over the wheel, glad to have something to do.

"Any word on Carlotta yet, Cindy?"

'NEGATIVE.'

That was one word he didn't want to hear. "Well, leave her a message. Get her to call me back. Tell her it's urgent."

'CHECK. MESSAGE LEFT. DO YOU REQUIRE ANY FURTHER DIRECTIONS FOR ANYWHERE ELSE, MR CAPRI?'

"No, it's alright, Cindy. I'm going straight back to the hotel. I need a drink, desperately!"

THE FROZEN FUTURE

'Just think, in the near future we will be able to freeze you in one space-time zone and thaw you out in another of your choice. Cryotechnology is the way forward for future orientated space and time travel, and I can confidently assert that I am not being over-optimistic.'

Anton Landis,
'Lecture on Cryotechnology,
Delivered at the Institute of Kalanitics,'
Cryo-perspectives Journal, vol. 11

—21—
THE BIG FREEZE

To Capri it seemed like the whole world was against him. And all he wanted now was to be alone. Thank God he was in his hotel room at last.

He closed the door gratefully behind him and shut out the world. He threw the detestable books of Grantham's on his bed along with his jacket and sat down with the bottle of bourbon he purchased from the bar. In the state of mind he was in, drinking seemed like the only option, just to have the temporary relief it always afforded him. It was an excuse, of course, for he knew he would have to deal with the real problem soon. But when? It was easier to pretend it wasn't there, that the danger didn't exist, and it was about as pathetic as a man standing in front of a firing squad planning his next holiday. Could he really carry on fooling himself like this? No. Nor could he keep running away from it. A real man, of course, would face it head on. If only he had the courage ….

He nervously lit up a cigarette and thought about conjuring up some courage. Like a committed cunctator, he opted for another drink instead and skimmed his eyes over the covers of Grantham's books, not even brave enough to touch them. He couldn't bring himself to it. How did other people manage, he wondered. What would they do in a situation like this where everything you feared had to be faced, when there was nowhere to run to and you were all alone? He drank up, refilled and smoked some more. He thought back through all the things which had happened so far, all meaningless in themselves, but subtly connected in some macabre plan

he couldn't fathom. It was as if each one of them were merely mounds above the surface, and underneath there was a ground of being, completely obscured. Was he really that blind he couldn't see it? Or was he refusing to see it like he always did? He carried on pretending it wasn't there.

Then he thought of Mosalla. Dead. Killed, to be exact. But at least he still had Crome's book. He fetched it out of his pocket, clasped it tightly to his breast as if it was written for him only. It was a guide, a spiritual guide into that darkest of terrains. He wanted it to speak to him, to utter words of solace and comfort, to take away his ravaged pain, to show him the way out, point him in the right direction so he could know the truth. And he looked with lugubrious gloom at Grantham's again. Slowly his mind unfurled. It seemed like a crazy notion at first. He dismissed it, only to have it come back again more forcefully. Perhaps if wasn't so crazy after all; to visit this old temple of Mosalla's and see if it too had that same clammy, cold, claustrophobic feeling of the Negative.

He quickly sat up and checked the televid for any messages from Carlotta. All he had to do was to explain to her what had happened, get the address for the temple and check it out first thing in the morning. No message. Nothing. Where the hell was she? Didn't she realise what he was going through? He wanted to curse her to high hell. Then he would have to go to Mosalla's place tonight personally, break in and see if he could find the address himself. And, whilst he was at it, also check out that alcove. He had another alarming intuition about the vacant space. What used to be there? What should have been there? It too needed to be confirmed.

He stubbed out his cigarette, laid back. The familiar feeling of fatigue overcame him. He needed some sleep and closed his eyes reluctantly.

Soon he found he was sinking, drifting on his subconscious, the day's events wheeling past, all diffracted, confused, a jumble of images contorting new, unintelligible meanings. In the fissure of his mind he felt it creeping through, imperceptibly at first, slowly, resolutely, all deformed, and bringing with it obnoxious things, vile, hideous things, and the same insipid odour.

"Fuck it!" he screamed. He snapped himself out of it quickly, and jumped off the bed as if the beast from the lake was lying there spreading its coils around him, trying to pull him down.

He dashed to the bathroom, splashed cold water in his face to wake up. He surmised it was worse when he closed his eyes. It was only when he closed them or slipped into some form of trance it came seeping through. All he had to do was stay awake, to not close his eyes, to not sleep, to stay conscious, then it couldn't get him. It was simple.

He splashed his face once more, shook his head awake, rubbed it vigorously with a towel and looked at the frightened face in the mirror.

"What's happening to me?" he cried. But there was no answer, only the silence. It was interrupted by a knock on his door. He froze. Who is it? Who knows I'm here? he asked himself, then remembered he had arranged to meet Katie. Was it her?

He opened the door a fraction and peered through the crack. He sighed. For there were two gorgeous eyes looking directly into his. Whereas last night they had been all drugged up, these two were perfectly, lucidly clear.

He threw the door open, grabbed her and dragged her inside, clinging to her tightly like a drowning sailor holding on to driftwood.

"Thank God, it's you," he murmured in her ear.

"What's the matter, Harmon? What's wrong?" she asked and gave into him.

"I'll tell you later. Let's get out of here."

He pulled himself off her, grabbed his jacket, threw it on, and grabbed Katie too. But he didn't see her smiling at Grantham's books lying on the bed as he hauled her out of his room. He frog-marched her to the elevator.

Katie looked at him as if he was mad. "Harmon, slow down. What's happening?" She made him release her as they reached the elevator. "What's wrong, Harmon? Tell me!"

"I can't explain," he blurted and took her in his arms again. "But it's good to see you, somebody I can trust."

"Is someone after you?" she asked him concerned.

"Sort of."

He kissed her again and looked at her affectionately. A pleasing, simple girl like her who never had any worries, and one who was real, not like Cindy. He never realised he would be so glad to see someone like her. And as he stood back to admire her, he could not help but feel something for her, the way she was dressed, a long red dress, a small delicate pearl necklace about her neck, her silver blonde hair brushed back and made-up exquisitely.

"You look stunning," he gushed.

"Thank you, Harmon. Now are you going to tell me what's going on? I want to know what I'm getting into here."

"Me too," he quipped. "Me too."

The elevator arrived. He whisked her in and drew her in close and embraced her passionately. It was so good to feel her body next to his, her heaving breasts against his chest, to smell her lovely perfume and brush against her soft, smooth cheek. He kissed her once more. She reciprocated equally with enthusiasm. He thanked the gods for giving her to him.

They sat at the same table as before, his table in the corner, the restaurant fairly empty as it was still early.

"So?" she demanded.

"What?" he replied, offering her a cigarette while waiting for their food.

"Aren't you going to tell me what's going on?"

"I wish I could, Katie. But I can't." He lit up and sat back.

"Go on, try," she pleaded.

"You see, as crazy as this sounds, I've got to tell you this, and I know I shouldn't be confiding in you, but this drug I'm after, well it's—uh—it's the only reason why I'm here. But there's another reason why I'm here."

"Slow down, Harmon, you're not making any sense. Start slowly."

"Okay. I came here to find this drug. Right? So I'm here on business. When I get here and meet my contact, everything changes. Don't ask me to

explain what I mean by that. I can't. Then I go to his lab. I have this fucking weird experience. I come out of it feeling like my head's been blown off. Then I get these strange dreams, these weird images coming into my head whenever I close my eyes, and this morning I go back to see my contact hoping he can tell me what's going on, and guess what? He's dead."

"Dead? You mean murdered?"

"Yes. But it's not that. It doesn't matter he's dead. It's why he was killed and who killed him. That's what gets me." He hit the table hard.

"You know who killed him?" she asked him concerned.

"No, not yet, but I'm going to find out. And I reckon it wasn't one person either, more like a group of them. Do you understand what I'm saying? This case isn't straight forward. It's got nothing to do with this drug. All I have to do is find out who killed him. Then it will all make sense."

"Whoa, Harmon. You keep losing me. These people who killed him, are they after you?"

"Why do you ask that?"

"'Cos you're acting strange like you're paranoid or something. You're all fidgety, on edge. Just relax, Harmon. You're safe. You're with me now."

"I can't relax. Every time I relax that fucking thing looms up …"

Katie leaned forward, frowning, "What thing?"

Capri paused, now aware he wasn't making much sense to himself either let alone her. How could he explain it? She wouldn't understand. "Never mind." He changed the subject. "So, how did your shopping trip go today?"

"Fine," she replied. "We had a great time." She perked up as the waiter arrived with their meals. "I bought this dress from Versace. D'ya like it?"

He looked her up and down and nodded his approval. Only then did he make the connection. The shade of red; it exactly matched Carlotta's dress, the one she was wearing when they met. Not only that but he was pretty sure it was the same style, if not identical. It seemed to be too much of a

coincidence. But there was no comparison between them. Katie wasn't a Woman of Power. Really she had no right to wear a dress that colour. Black suited her better for it complemented her hair. As the waiter served them he felt anorexic all of a sudden. He forced a smile and thanked the waiter and looked at her incredulous. She tucked in with her usual relish.

"Going back to what you said earlier, I thought about it. You're right."

"Good, I'm glad you agree." He tentatively took his first mouthful and felt his stomach heave, but forced himself to continue.

"Since I've got to go back tomorrow, maybe we could spend all night together, you know, have a few drinks, go out on the town."

"I would love to, Katie, but I must go out later."

"Oh, Harmon," she sulked.

"I'm sorry. I have to go out. It's urgent. It will only be for a short while."

"A short while?" He nodded. "And you'll come straight back?"

"Yes, I promise," he said and smiled at her. She made him feel guilty. "I'll make it up to you when I get back," he promised her sincerely and brushed his half eaten meal aside. He settled for a cigarette instead and another glass of wine and leant back in his chair, admiring this ravishing beauty before him, so innocent and without a care in the world. But there was a vast gulf of difference between them. His life could never blend with hers. He had chosen his. He had to stick with it. Although she wasn't like Carlotta, she was better than nothing. It wasn't the right attitude to take, but why not take advantage. It was good just to have someone close, someone he could talk to and laugh with. He laughed as she cracked a joke and smiled as she talked and nodded every time it was necessary. And tomorrow she'd be gone. Would he miss her? Did he care about her? The answer was obvious.

She finished her meal. He offered her another cigarette and poured her the last of the wine. They small-talked for awhile until he was ready to leave.

He left her at the bar and arranged to meet her there when he got back, after she had been to the gym. He quickly ascended to his room, had a

hasty shower, got changed into his clothes, a black polo neck and black suit, checked he had all that he needed in his bag and left for Mosalla's place.

* * * * *

She tapped in the same number and waited for a reply. A few moments later the screen fizzled and a man answered.

"Hello, babe. Well, don't you look the pretty one tonight."

"Thanks. As it's the last night, I have to look my best, don't I?"

"That's right, the last night. And tomorrow it will all be over. So, what you got to tell me? How's our friend doing?"

"He's doing fine, real fine. You know little old me, how good I am."

"But he doesn't suspect?"

"No, why should he?"

"Good. That's what I like to hear. But make sure he's there tomorrow."

"Oh, he'll be there alright. Don't you worry about that. Just leave it to me."

"Will do. I'll tell the old man. If you get any problems give me a call."

"Trust me. Everything's fine, everything's going according to plan."

"Good girl. I love you."

"I love you too, darling. And if you're going out tonight, don't get into any trouble like last time. We don't want you starting any fights."

"As if I'd do a thing like that. Bye, honey."

"Bye." She switched the televid off, lit up a cigarette and smiled.

* * * * *

In the car Capri finally received a call from Carlotta.

"Carlotta, I've been trying to get you all day," he complained.

"Sorry, Harmon, but I've been busy. I told you to only ring me in the evening. What's the matter?"

"Something's happened. Mosalla's dead."

"Dead? How?"

"He was murdered."

"Murdered? By who?"

"That's what I'm trying to find out. I'm on my way to his place to see what I can find. I've got a suspicion there's far more going on here and I need to check something. But I want you to do me a favour. When I was talking to Mosalla yesterday he told me about a temple he's got down at Long Beach."

"That's right. The one we used to use. What about it?"

"Well, I'm planning on going there tomorrow morning."

"Why, Harmon? No one goes there anymore."

"I'm not so sure."

"What do you mean? The group was disbanded a long time ago. It's finished, kaput."

"I'm not so sure about that either."

"Why? Harmon you're not explaining clearly. What are you talking about?"

"Look, I haven't got time to fill you in on all the details. I'm nearly at Mosalla's house. All I want to know is the address for the temple."

"Fuck, Harmon, I can't remember. It was a long time ago."

"Come on, Carlotta, try to remember. Think hard."

There was a pause before she responded. "I'm trying to remember. I can see the street down by the coast and the old building really clearly as if it was yesterday. Sorry, Harmon, I just can't see the name of the street."

"Please, Carlotta. I need it."

"Look, I've just got back. Let me see if I can find it in one of my old diaries. I'll get back to you."

"Okay, you do that. I'm sorry, Carlotta, but the drug's going to have to wait. This is more important. I must find out who killed him."

"Alright, I'll get back."

He said goodbye as he pulled up outside the gates. He stopped, had a quick look at the driveway. From what he could see there was nothing out of the ordinary. He just hoped the house was empty. He hit the accelerator and drove a bit further up the road to a dark, quiet area where he could park the car hidden by some trees. He grabbed his small bag and climbed out.

He flashed a torch at the high wall looking for a mound, anything to act as a ramp so he could climb up and reach the top. He spotted a higher level of ground. He hoisted himself up and perched precariously on the top, his black clothes blending in with the night. He unzipped his bag. He pulled out a holometer and viewed the house in the distance. Through the holometer he could see the house and the security network. It spread over the house like a diaphanous curtain of light from the roof to the foreground. Anyone straying into the security network would immediately set off the alarm. It presented no significant problem. He tucked the holometer back into his bag, tossed it to the ground fifteen feet below and diligently leaped after it, landing neatly on his feet but not enough to feel a snap in his spine. He winced as he straightened his back.

"I'm getting too old for this shit," he told himself and wished he didn't have to do it like this. But it was the only way. In his astral he wouldn't be able to touch anything physical.

He fetched his bag and stole closer to the edge of the security network. The house was vacant, dead. He got his holometer out again, checked where the security network fell on the ground, a couple of feet in front of him, and pulled out a couple of mirrors. It was easy; all he had to do was reflect the light back so as to form a partition in the curtain without breaking the beams. He positioned the mirrors at strategic points and crawled through the gap on all fours. He waded up to the side of the house. Instinctively, he reached for his Preston. It glinted in the pale light of the moon, he a dark

shadow amongst shadows, and edged his way round quietly to the door. He checked it. It was locked with a simple security device. He whipped out his decoder, plugged it against the lock and primed it. He stood back whilst it did its work. A few seconds later it clicked. The door opened automatically.

"This is too easy." He retrieved his decoder and gently gripped the door handle and prized the door open all the way. "Far too easy."

He let himself in and flashed his light into the hallway. There was no sound, no lights on and hopefully nobody at home. He crept up the stairs, headed straight for the alcove. He removed his black leather gloves and dropped his bag by his side. He flashed his light over all the relics of the past, still wondering where Mosalla obtained them. That didn't matter. He was more concerned about the vacant space at the back, the large mount which must have once held something fairly large itself. This was the deciding moment. And soon he would know whether he was correct or not. Gingerly he stretched out his hand, flat and palm downwards. He half closed his eyes. His hand skated over the surface in tight circles; almost immediately he was picking up traces, vague and fleeting without definition.

He brought his hand down, contacting the surface. Now it was more definite. Whatever had been there was powerful. He closed his eyes fully and concentrated on the sensation. Must have been some ancient statue or an idol. And as he tried to connect with it he had that old familiar feeling, it made his skin crawl with accompanying horripilation.

"Shit!" He snatched his hand away quickly. It was exactly the same feeling as in the lab. He didn't believe it. His hand felt dead. He rubbed it vigorously to get some life back into it. Scared, he brushed it against all the other objects nearby. None of them gave off such powerful traces. Most of them were neutral or only lukewarm like their psychic force had been diluted over time. But the missing piece had a wholly other quality and must have been removed only recently for its traces were still fresh. Again he inserted his hand, this time letting his mind go blank, allowing it to open up to anything, whatever suggested itself. He didn't have to wait long. Before he could even get into it, the feeling returned, now even stronger than before. It seemed to pull him in and his mind went numb as hostile waves seeped in cold and deadly. He gulped. His throat went dry. Then he saw it; the cragged rocks in the distance, the black placid lake, the water spraying

up as the surface broke open. The beast, or whatever it was, appeared, rising slowly, vertically, its eyes fixed resolutely on his.

"NO!" he screamed. He snatched his hand away, opened his eyes in panic and stared, bewildered. "I don't believe it. No, it can't be," he shouted. He refused to believe what his sixth sense was telling him: Mosalla possessed something embodying the Negative. Why? Where did he get it from?

He quickly fetched up his bag and ran back down the stairs, straight for the door. As he reached it he heard a voice, like the sound of laughter. It made him stop. He turned, his eyes flashing up and down the stairs, piercing into its shadows. Somebody was in the house.

"Angel?" he murmured. But there was no response. He gulped again. At the top of the stairs, standing in the shadows was a tall dark figure, all dressed in black, his face obscured by the gloom.

"Who are you?" he demanded, nervously.

The tall dark figure, as if aloof, did not answer. It mocked him with silence, the silence of a ghost. Capri got out his torch. He flashed it in its direction to clarify what his eyes were seeing. It disappeared as soon as the light hit it and vanished for good. Whatever it was, it was now gone.

Now scared, he first thought it must be the ghost of Mosalla. But it couldn't have been. His judgement wouldn't allow it. The figure was too tall and thin for his former host. Nor could he believe his eyes were playing tricks on him. He had seen something, definitely.

"What is going on?" he shouted to himself. Annoyed, he was determined to answer his doubt with a certainty. He sprang up the steps, and, on reaching the top, he didn't know whether he was disappointed or relieved, for there was no one there; the corridor was empty, all the doors were locked, nor were there any sounds to be heard.

He punched the wall and cursed, thought about getting out quick before he really went mad, decided against it. There was still one more thing he had to do before he left.

Begrudgingly, he drifted back down towards the library. It was the most

sensible place to start looking. It was exactly as before. In the dark he found Mosalla's desk and rifled through the drawers. They were all unlocked and contained nothing spectacular or of interest; sheaves of paper, files, notebooks, the usual stationery. Not even a personal address book. Perhaps he was looking in the wrong place and the old man kept stuff like that in a personal organiser. If so, where? Capri tried to think where else he could look. There was nothing else in the library apart from all those stupid books. Mosalla probably hadn't even read half of them. Capri sat down in his chair, thinking hard, his fingers automatically tapping the inlaid green leather top, his mind voracious, hungry for clues.

He gave up. Sat back. Flashed his torch down all the rows of useless books, even entertained the idea of helping himself to a few more. That would have been too obvious. He looked at them again, tempted. But something made him sit up. He flashed his torch again. Was it what he thought it was, or was he seeing things? There was definitely something wrong with one section of the bookcase. It was only just noticeable. He got up, went over to it, intrigued. He scanned the middle section with his torch. It brought out more visibly the defect when he angled it slightly against the side. One partition was a fraction out, not quite parallel with the rest.

"Well, I'll be damned," he chuckled to himself. It could only be what he thought it was, and hardly original at that.

He ran his gloved hands up and down the sides and along the bottom. There had to be a switch somewhere to open it. He worked his hands over all the adjacent shelves, removing books, replacing them, touching all the surfaces. Nothing. He tried the undersides and came across a small indentation, barely noticeable. He smiled as he had found what he was looking for; a touch sensitive stud. He pressed it lightly and felt the floor vibrate. He stood back and watched as a whole section slid back effortlessly to reveal more rows of shelving, all secreted away. It was perfect.

"Bingo!" he shouted proudly. He smiled with satisfaction and walked in.

The shelves contained the sort of things Mosalla obviously felt were worth hiding for reasons only known to himself; documents relating to his magical activities, group workings, even some of his paraphernalia which he didn't want anybody to know about. Perhaps he was worried what others might

think, not wanting them to know he was connected with anything esoteric or seemingly occult. But then that was kind of ridiculous with a name like Mosalla. It was obviously a magical name of sorts, half Hebrew, half Arabic, so why the secrecy? And it appeared none of his magical implements had been touched for years. They were all covered in dust. Capri tested his wand and found it had no charge whatsoever. He wasn't surprised. The man was a dilettante, just as he thought. Not only that, but a lazy one as well, too lazy to do any real work. His excuses for not having the time were just that; excuses.

Capri went through some of the hand written notes lying on the shelves. They consisted of elementary rituals, simple invocations, very basic formulae for acquiring wealth, good luck and fortune, but nothing seriously outstanding or of any worth. He checked a few more only to find the same thing. He stopped short. It seemed strange Mosalla should have something in his possession connected with the Negative, but nothing else here to do with the same. He expected some really dark stuff, heavy rites, not this lowbrow stuff. It didn't compute. And reading through some of his old diaries only confirmed it; Mosalla was into the light side of things, not the dark side. There wasn't one note pertaining to the Negative. Luckily, the diaries of his magical group were in chronological order. They were extensive and went right back up till about eleven years ago. That would make sense for the lab incident occurred around then, spelling the demise of the group. He read through some of the ritual meetings; there was one each month with an attendance record of the members partaking in the rites. All the names were written in a cipher script and some pages denoted whether a rite had been successful or not, the marginalia being in Mosalla's own handwriting, Capri presumed.

After a cursory examination he gave up and put them aside. He continued hunting. More notes, scraps of papers, receipts and an account book. He picked up the latter and flicked through it. It consisted of all the group's transactions; every single item listed was priced indexed. Mosalla was keeping an account of what had been purchased, who paid what, who owed what, where all the money was going—some of it rather excessive by the look of things—and the group's total outlay at the end of each quarter with receipts to prove the costs. Capri flicked through some of them, going right to the bottom of the pile, not really sure what he was expecting to find, but

there had to be an address here somewhere. The earliest receipt he could find was dated 17 years ago and looked intriguing. It recorded a shipment from a stone masons listing the staggered deliveries of basalt rock totalling two hundred thousand tons. What the hell would he want all that for? Then he noticed the consignment's address at the bottom of the page; 111 Vermont Drive, Long Beach. Pleased he had found the address, he went through the blurb on the back. It seemed Mosalla had the rock specially imported from Aswan in North Africa. The blocks were pre-cut to specific measurements, each one weighing in at fifteen tons and costing $800 apiece.

He worked it out in his head. It came to something like over ten million dollars—$10,666,666 to be exact. So it had to be for the temple itself. Then Capri remembered that basalt rock is black, an igneous rock and was much favoured by the ancient Egyptians for its hardness and glossy sheen after it had been polished. Further; wasn't the famous Rosetta Stone also fashioned from basalt rock?

The rock must have been for the floor, ceiling and walls, like the temple he saw Jack using. Previously, Capri thought it was made from obsidian, but it wasn't; it was basalt. Satisfied he had sussed it he slipped the receipt into his back pocket and left everything else as he found it. He sided out the cubby hole, touched the stud and watched with admiration as the bookcase shifted back into position. This time, however, it was not ajar and when he flashed his light across the side, the bookcase was exactly in place. It was so tight the alignment wasn't noticeable. That made him curious. Had someone been there before him and not closed it properly? Or was it one of those odd occurrences, a freak of nature? He didn't like it at all. He had no time to think about it now. He had been gone long enough and promised Katie he would be quick. He sneaked out of the house as easily had crept in.

"That was too fucking easy," he told Cindy as he climbed into the driving seat and spun the car round. His suspicious mind was perturbed. The door might as well have been left open for him. What with the missing relic, he was now more than certain somebody had been there before him. But who? The same people who disposed of Mosalla?

He ignored his questioning mind and concentrated on the road. He hit another tailback. It was the last thing he needed. He was already late; Katie would be at the bar, probably fuming by now. She was drinking, he wasn't.

That's all he wanted to do tonight; drink.

* * * *

He found her by the bar still wearing her red dress and evidently hadn't been to the gym like she said she would. And it also appeared she had been at the bar all night. Her face had a ruddy complexion and she was dewy-eyed. Not only was she drunk, she was slouched over the bar on a stool surrounded by a small group of admirers who were chatting her up and buying her drinks, each one of whom evidently believed they could buy their way into her pants. They were laughing at some joke, she was giggling away. It was too much for Capri. He was just about to turn round and walk away before she could see him when …

"Ah, my paranoid son of a bitch fucking returns at last!" she shouted across the crowded room. All the patrons' heads turned in his direction. He politely smiled and reluctantly joined her.

"Evening darling," he remarked sarcastically. "Having a good time are we?"

Her admirers soon dispersed.

"No. You're late!" she hissed.

"Yes, I know. Sorry, but I got held up."

He ordered a drink, a stiff double bourbon. Katie waved her empty glass at the bartender who looked to him for his consent. Capri checked her condition; she was out of it. Not only was she beginning to sway, she couldn't even focus her eyes properly. He nodded to the bartender and let her have another drink.

"And I'm not paranoid," he countered.

"You are. You think people are after you."

"No I don't, Katie." He waited impatiently for his drink, avoiding her eyes.

"Yes, you do," she continued and let out a laugh. "How's that song go, you know, the one by that old band. I wish I could remember 'cos it's really funny. I've got it. I remember now. 'Just because you're paranoid, it don't

mean they're not after you,'" she sang and finished the line with a giggle.

It was all Capri needed. She was embarrassing. "Very funny, Katie."

"I think so too. They used to be one of my favourite bands. Me and brother used to listen to them all the time when we were kids."

"Really?" As he handed her the glass she nearly dropped it. He had never seen such a sorrier sight. "And that's your last. No more. After that, I'm taking you back to your bed."

"Ooooh, honey," she cooed and pulled him in tight.

"No, not for that. You're getting your head down. Do you understand me?"

"But I don't want to go to sleep. I want to go to bed with you!" she shouted, so loudly everyone else heard. They were all looking at them now. Again he smiled to hide his embarrassment and quickly downed his drink. He ordered another and lit up. Katie snatched his cigarette like a kid and started smoking it. It only made him angrier. He lit up another and smoked.

"I'm celebrating," she drawled. "Do you know why I'm celebrating?"

"I've no idea," he replied, half-interested.

"Because tonight is the last night."

"Of course. You go back tomorrow to your wonderful Johnny, don't you?"

"No, that's not it. I'm celebrating because tonight is the last night."

"Yes, Katie, you've just said that."

"You don't get it, do you?" She smirked at him.

"Get what?" he asked her puzzled.

Katie went quiet. Her smirk disappeared and was replaced by an equally puzzling expression. "Nothing," she whispered and smoked.

"Look, I think you've had enough to drink for one night."

"No, I haven't. I've only just started celebrating."

"I bet you've been at the bar all night, haven't you?" She nodded cheekily. "You never made it to the gym either?" She shook her head like a naughty girl. "Well in that case, you've definitely had enough. Come on, drink up."

"And then you're going to take me to bed?"

"No. Not tonight. I've got more important things to sort out."

"Like what? What could be more important than taking me to bed?"

"Well, sorting out this shit for a start. And I've got some reading to do."

"Oh, that's not important. Read me instead," she purred and pulled him in closer, her hand stroking his crotch. She gave him a big kiss.

He fended her off. "No, Katie. I mean it. Drink up."

They finished their drinks. Capri helped her off the stool. She nearly toppled over. He caught her and started dragging her through the crowd. As they passed some dressed up tycoons Katie went to grab one of their glasses. He managed to catch her arm just in time and marched her resolutely up the stairs to the elevator. He propped her against the wall while they waited. He distanced himself from her.

"You're cross with me, aren't you?" she slurred and brushed her hair back with a stroppy look. "I know you are. I can see it in your eyes."

"No, I'm not cross with you."

"Yes, you are."

"No, I'm not. Now drop it."

"But you're pissed about something, aren't you?"

"Maybe."

"What? Tell me."

"I'm not cross with you. I'm cross with myself. Okay? It's not you. It's just me. There's something going on here and I just can't see it."

"Poor Harmon," she whispered. It was just like how Carlotta had said it.

Capri looked at her twice. She pulled him in towards her, drew him in tight and kissed him full. At first he fought her off, trying to resist her. The weak side of his nature, however, could not refrain from finding her irresistible. He gave in unremittingly as the elevator door slid open, they fell inside. He pressed for their floor without even looking and kissed her full and strong, the taste of bourbon fresh in the back of her throat. The elevator stopped. He pulled back to see she could barely keep her eyes open. He grabbed her hand and had to virtually manhandle her down the corridor to their rooms. She insisted on going to his. He carried her into his room, dropped her on the bed and helped her to get undressed. He started undressing himself when he noticed that no sooner had her head hit the pillows she was out like a light. He lifted up her arm and let it go. It flopped down boneless.

"Oh well," he intoned. "I've got some work to do anyway." He covered her naked unconscious body with a sheet, and slipped into his bathrobe, turned off the main light, and switched on the small lamp on the table and poured himself a bourbon. He checked his watch. He still had one more visit to make before the night was through. He'd do it in his astral. Right now, all he wanted to do was to get gloriously drunk and sort out this shit that was messing him up inside.

He had an idea. He needed to know what step he should take next. He grabbed his small bag and took out a bundle wrapped up in black suede and his Japanese vellum notebook. He unrolled the bundle on the table and picked up his fifty black yarrow stalks, the ones with the gold tips, and prepared himself. This was another method he resorted to whenever he was out of rapport with Angel. He charged the sticks, put one aside and manipulated them, all the while concentrating on his next step, whether his actions would be successful or not. He chanted the question subliminally as a mantra until he built up six lines, three broken, three unbroken, the former surmounting the latter. It was the T'ai hexagram, number eleven. It struck him as odd because not only did it signify peace, success and other positive outcomes, it was also a perfect glyph of the masculine conjoined with the feminine although inverted, Kteis of Phallus rather than Phallus of Kteis.

He made a note in his book:

CELEBRATION

The small departs, the great approaches. Peace. Perfect union. The light must unite with the dark, the dark with the light. This is the way of the world and the path of the great man. There will be good fortune, progress and success.

He lit up a cigarette and examined it more closely. The small departs, the great approaches; it sounded like an initiation, one of the highest order. He was satisfied with that. It meant whatever his next step was it would be worth taking. Or was there something else hidden in the answer? Really it was too ambiguous. It could apply to anything. He peered deeper. Peace, but it can only come about through inversion, to the giving into that which is greater, or did it mean something more specific? Then he thought of where he first met Carlotta. It somehow made sense.

Was she not the great who approaches whilst the small departs? He looked to the nubile female lying in his bed sound asleep. She would be gone tomorrow. Was the small a direct reference to her? Something great would be happening soon. He was now determined to go with it all the way.

He poured himself another drink, reflected on the answer, feeling more positive about his future. He rolled up his sticks and put them away. He dug into his back pocket and checked the receipt once more. It had to be the right address, and he would go there early tomorrow morning, first thing. For whatever reason, it seemed the most logical thing to do, to follow all the clues he had been given so far. He decided to notify Carlotta he now had the address. There was no response. He left a message on the televid for her to call him back.

He lit up again and replenished his glass. He drank to Angel. He drank to Katie snoozing away in his bed, her firm buttocks visibly exposed. Lastly, he drank to the end, to the peace which would be his soon, but not yet. There was still plenty more work to do.

With trepidation, he picked up all three of Grantham's books.

It was now or never, although he wasn't inclined to read them at all. Just looking at them filled him with dread as if they were going to blow up in his hands like dynamite. Their stark black and white dust jackets and the titles printed in lurid red betrayed the unwholesome contents lying within their

pages. They reeked an odour as if having been dredged up from some charnel house. It permeated the room. Now the titles became acutely meaningful. They were suggestive of the dark mysteries of ancient Khem. The first was entitled *Cults of the Khu*, the second *Cults of the Khaut*, and the third, the last one, *Cults of the Khart*.

He forced himself to start, settling for the first one, cursorily going through the brief introduction to get an overview of Grantham's argument again.

Cults of the Khu concentrated on the primal cults of earliest Africa and their beliefs regarding death. As Africa was the cradle of the human race, it should be easy to prove that all the mortuary and thanatological beliefs and practises of the world have their roots in the Dark Continent. The book, however, was more concerned with the apotheosis of these beliefs as they manifested and flourished in the Nilotic region espoused by its earliest settlers, now known as the Egyptians. Grantham was saying that the original settlers came from Central Africa and proceeded northward taking their beliefs with them. But prior to this migration their beliefs and mythology had already been fully established.

His consensus of opinion was that religion arose out of the recognition that spirit survived bodily death. Early mortuary practices like decapitation and dismemberment of the dead indicated a desire to prevent the dead from returning from the grave and causing harm to the living. This belief was co-existent with the common phenomenon of witnessing the departed as ghosts or shades, a semi-material double which walked abroad after burial and was recognisable as belonging to—and being another form of—the departed. As misfortune and local calamities were blamed on the malevolence and pernicious influence of the double and its failure to transmigrate to the next world, a system of rites and liturgies were developed to assist its progression and sever the connection it had with this world. Thus, these were the first rites and practises which were not religious at all, they were merely magical, an attempt to open up the path to the next world. As humanity progressed, the practises became more advanced, the eschatology developed and man eventually lost the capacity of psychic perception which had enabled him to see the double. However, the belief in life after death persisted becoming more highly stylised, no more so than in the sophisticated ideology and theology of ancient Egypt.

Grantham then went on to explain some of the magical practises performed at time of burial, including mummification and embalming. He seemed to possess a unique insight into the practise of mummification, some of his ideas being highly dubious and suspect. Despite this, his argument appeared to be sound, and his examination of the curious rites and practises of the Egyptians indicated a thorough understanding, one well beyond the means of most Egyptologists who were incapable of breaking out of their linear thinking methods and the parochial approach they had to their own subject. It was quite obvious why most of Grantham's ideas were rebuked. The last chapters of the book detailed his peculiar system of nigretism, its symbolism being far too heavy for Capri to want to fathom. He gave up and picked up the second volume instead.

The second one seemed to be an extension of the first. Here Grantham was taking his original theory further and concentrating on the symbology of the dead, exposing the mechanics behind all the cults of the dead throughout the entire world and demonstrating that their beliefs were quite clearly derived from the motherland, Africa, home of the original source or gnosis.

Again, he picked up the thread of his magical theories regarding nigretism; all rites of evoking the dead, or necromancy as it is commonly called, were not for raising the spirits of the dead, but rather bringing back into consciousness dead (i.e. forgotten) material belonging to the original gnosis.

This book was the one with the illustration of the loathsome creature of the lake. Capri turned to the middle section to once more gaze upon it and the other illustrations. He felt a tingle down his spine and shuddered. Each picture seethed with some primeval slime which knew not life for it was before life as we know it began. The pictures harked back to a prehistoric time when the world had only just eased itself out of primordial chaos. Each one filled him with loathing as they attempted to capture the quintessence of nascent life, the darkness which preceded the light, a time so distant it could not be comprehended let alone accurately calculated in years. They were disturbing. They suggested an oozing mass slithering across the earth as it belched vomit and obscene things, things having no limbs or eyes for they were yet to develop, hence amorphous and chaotic. However, Grantham was postulating that it was from this very confused mass the human race had its origins, a single cell organism from which man

was to emerge billions of years later. It was the source of the myth of Adam, of the first man formed from this slime the Hebrews likened to mud or clay. Being moist and humid, it provided the perfect womb or vessel for germination. The spark of spirit engendered it making it fertile. Life crawled out amidst the rainforests of Central Africa and proceeded to migrate taking with it in its racial consciousness a prototype or representation of the primal substance. It was only much later, a billion years or more, that the earliest forerunner of man—*Australopithecus afarensis*—was able to crudely depict and project this slime in the form of a god. Grantham claimed this was the first god ever to be moulded by man, so ancient it existed prior to speech or thought, neither male nor female but worshipped as the genitor/genetrix of the human race, its form and representation gradually developing as we evolved. Throughout the transitional stages of our evolution its memory was lost and it was superseded by other gods and goddesses although still clearly being based on the original. Evolution repressed it; man had relegated it to the other side. In other words, it had become forgotten, too lost to memory to contain any relevant meaning. Grantham was reconstituting its cult and worship. Rather exasperatingly, he did not give it a name. Capri didn't need it. He knew what this obnoxious god was; an embodiment of the Negative.

Intrigued, he continued to read. He was not surprised either to find Grantham stating that although it existed billions of years ago, it still existed but in another dimension. Although evolution had attenuated this phase and nature had developed along the lines of an evolutionary goal, by-passing all the known stages, the anterior time had been displaced to another dimension beyond the known boundaries of time. Grantham was very reluctant to use the word 'exist' for it suggested 'outside of' when in actuality it should more correctly be considered 'within' as 'being,' but more specifically 'non-being.' It was thus identical with the Negative. So Grantham was talking about the other polar dimension of the drug after all which itself was a distillation of 'life.' However, he did not call it the Negative, preferring to avoid such a derogatory label, calling it 'Recremental Space' instead.

In a chapter entitled 'The Dark Work,' Grantham gave full details of this space and its value. Recremental Space can be considered as a vast cosmic rubbish tip at the end of the universe where the leftovers of the

evolutionary process are dumped having served their purpose. In Recremental Space can be found the refuse of the primal energies left over after creation which were now obsolete having served their purpose, rather like the waste products of an industrial plant; the scraps, the cast offs, the shells, or the dross of the smelting process. In other words, after the finished product is made, these are the elements which are thrown away as useless and no longer possess any value. Although they had been instrumental in the process they were now deemed worthless. And it was for this reason they were rejected. Yet his argument was; this notion was mistaken. There was still much worth left in this rejected material yet to be extracted; not all of its vitality had been expended in the process, and was still lying around waiting to be used up. It was this, he claimed, which was causing an imbalance in the universe. But more importantly, it was our staunch refusal to believe in its existence, our need to repress and even deny it, which made matters worse. Our attitude towards it was the cause of the cosmic imbalance as we were too busy concentrating on the positive aspect, the overt side of nature rather than its hidden, neglected side.

The unwanted aspects of creation were signified by a serpent, and perfectly illustrated the chaotic or blind forces underlying nature. The serpent or dragon typifies the chaotic, uncontrolled and 'hellish' aspects of nature.

Grantham took it further to make his point clear, citing a crude example; human excrement. What had once been food, digested in order to profit growth and sustenance, is excreted, flushed away. Yet this excrementitious matter was not useless. It still contained positive, redeemable value with a non-physical, astral dimension of its own, Recremental Space.

That which had been rejected, or rather excreted, was beneficial to us. But what was he really saying? That we should reabsorb this rejected matter? By merely implying such an act, the revulsion aroused by the mere thought of it was akin to the emotion and antipathy directly proportional to embracing Recremental Space. When a man confronts this space he is filled with the same kind of revulsion. Capri knew exactly what he meant. But this is what 'The Dark Work' entailed. It consists of a systematic exploration of the plane of the Negative and integrating back into our consciousness its contents. By reabsorbing this matter in its subtle form, we could not only restore the cosmic balance but also become whole, total beings. It is purely

because of our aesthetic sensibility that we are unable, or rather unwilling, to embrace that which is repulsive, but it has to be done. Grantham stated it was imperative we work with it consciously rather than allow it to seep into our world unchecked. It involved a turning back and reaching down into the very core of our ancestry, tapping into pre-larval strata of consciousness and exhuming or bringing it back up to the surface for integration.

Capri put the book down for a moment. He lit up another cigarette and drank some more. Really it was too much. To carry out such an act, to deliberately invoke in consciousness the negative aspects of creation abhorred him. But this was precisely what had to be done, and he had to work with that vile creature, that obnoxious god. It was no wonder why it had been rejected; it was repulsive. What Grantham was enforcing was no different from a form of therapy; in psychological terms, embracing the shadow. Each time this god appeared it seemed to threaten Capri, as if it was about to overwhelm him with such colossal force he could only shun it. This he could no longer do. The symbol Angel had given him was the key to exploring the Negative, Grantham's Recremental Space. But he didn't want to have anything to do with it.

But I don't want the Negative; I want God, he wanted to shout out.

Recremental Space, he continued to read, was not, yet paradoxically it was. In other words, it was the Negative. It was still accessible. However, its power had been amassing over the centuries and was now reaching a crisis point. Not only was there a serious imbalance of substantial forces which had once kept the universe in check, it had also been severely disrupted by the selfish, pernicious actions of Atomic Man. Ever since Hiroshima and Nagasaki the fabric of space had been torn irrevocably asunder. Not only did these two events have socio-political repercussions, they also had extra-dimensional ones as well. The thin membranous veil which separates the Negative from the Positive had been torn. Hence the Negative was pouring through. Our world was now seriously under threat. The influx of the Negative was the cause of outbreaks of psychopathological phenomena.

Saddened, Capri threw the book down. He lit up and had another drink as he pondered, looking at Katie sound asleep in his bed, not even aware of such a thing as the Negative and its possible implications. Who would walk with him into its depths? Who would help him to confront it? Who would

go with him to embrace the shadow of life? Nobody. He would have to do it all alone. He wanted to quit, to get out now, run like he always had done.

As soon as this assignment was completed, if and when he handed the drug over to Carlotta, he would start working with it. But could it wait till then?

Begrudgingly, Capri picked up the third and final volume of the trilogy, a far more technical and daunting looking proposition as it appeared to go into more depth regarding Grantham's ultimate theories of the universe and its possible destruction.

The first few pages concentrated on the ideas behind an apocalypse, and how such scenarios had evolved. Grantham claimed all religions had 'borrowed' from an older source, but more importantly, the notion of the end of the world or end of an age was always closely linked with the birth of a new one and an accompanying Messiah or Saviour archetype, a figure who appears 'out of nowhere' and takes the survivors into the new age as a teacher. Grantham's main contention was that this figure was based on the child, an incarnation of the divine principle. In Egypt this was symbolised by the ascension of the pharaoh to his throne, a god-king. The start of his reign marked the end of an old epoch and its history, and the start of a new era or cosmic rule. Documents of the Old Kingdom and thereafter demonstrate that in Egypt history was measured in terms of a pharaoh's reign. This symbolism was later adopted by other cultures, particularly the Chaldeans and Hebrews who presumed the advent of a Saviour-type signified the end of the world. That no such figure had appeared physically for thousands of years, the Christ of Christianity being merely mythic, not historical, validated his theory; the time was still to come, and, according to Grantham's calculations, it was imminent. But as we were well into the new millennium, Grantham's messiah or saviour was obviously overdue.

Interested, Capri decided to read up on this and see how Grantham had concocted this perplexing conclusion. His sources where extensive to say the least, as well as highly suspicious. He analysed the prophetic writings of the religious books of the world believing them to contain archaic traces of this doctrine. They seemed by far to provide the best information on catastrophes as they not only displayed parallels between cultures, but also in most cases overlapped, thus demonstrating a degree of uniformity that could only be explained by them all having one source, or what he called

the original gnosis.

Myth, he was saying, was a historical record handed down from generation to generation orally before the advent of the written word. The purpose of myth was to ensure and preserve the gnosis formulated in magical science; the motions of the stars and planets being a primary example.

Throughout the world there is one prevalent myth, the myth of Eternal Return. That is, the end of the world and a new beginning. This conception is universal and based on the observation of known and identifiable cycles, biocosmic rhythms like the waxing and waning of the moon and its disappearance, the rising and setting of the sun, the motion of the stars and their celestial orbits with their returning to a previous position, the seasons, etc., all enhance the idea of periodic return. Built into this is the notion that the start of a cycle represents a purification, the doing away with the old to pave the way for the new, or a regeneration of the world. All myths agree that there is an act of destruction prior to the inception of a new world. This was the underlying theory also behind the notion of resurrection; the old body died to give birth to the new, a form of rebirth in human terms, but elevated to the cosmic plane, the death of the old world and the birth of a new one.

Further, Grantham was saying that the prophets of old had got it wrong; the end of the world, signalled by a change in the polestar, was incorrect. He was saying we had to look further afield, beyond our solar system. There, he states, we would find the answer, why the world goes into a state of upheaval every so often. The answer was truly occult, he jested, for it was hidden; the outermost planet. As Grantham did not name this planet, Capri assumed he was referring to Pluto, although the descriptions he gave and the dimensions he put forward did not correspond to Pluto at all. Then what was he referring to? Grantham stated it was due to this planet that our world goes through a period of decline and renewal. It has such a large orbit it is almost impossible to calculate. Grantham didn't even hazard a guess as to how long it took for this planet to orbit the sun. It was made more difficult because, like the earth's orbit, it was elliptical, far more so than ours. Not only that, the orbit of the planet's elongation—its eccentricity—was far greater than the earth's. Earth's eccentricity at its greatest measures six percent. Grantham estimated his planet measured

something like fifteen percent or more when it varies to an exaggerated degree. Because of its mass—something else he reckoned couldn't be measured except that it was extremely large—it has a profound affect on all the planets when its elliptical orbit brings it closer towards the sun, a matter of thousands of years. Like the moon's perigee, its proximity to our planet and its perturbations are marked by cataclysmic activity usually associated with end of the world scenarios. He believes that when it does come close to ours it heralds the catastrophes spoken of by all cultures.

As the moon affects the tides of the sea, and possibly the land masses, this planet has the same affect but far greater. Sea levels rise, the earth's crust cracks, there is massive seismic activity; volcanism, earthquakes, etc. As to the other more outlandish phenomena, he explains the darkening of the sky, the blacking out of the sun, the disappearance of the moon from the sky for a prolonged period, the dropping of the stars, are all mythic exaggerations of this planet's affect. What actually happens in some cases when it does come extremely close to earth is to shift its axis out of its obliquity to an alarming degree; either the pole becomes truly vertical or almost horizontal. And, as with all catastrophe scenarios, some periods of destruction are more intense than others. These are dependent on the planet's proximity to ours.

In a word, his planet represents confusion. It acts like a spanner in the works, throwing everything into discord or upheaval. Its disrupting effect has been carefully recorded and preserved in all myths. Grantham also hinted it was the planetary representative of non-being.

Grantham seemed to be reluctant to give any real date in the future when this planet of his would be returning. Or perhaps he couldn't due to the eccentricity of its orbit, leaving it vague indeed, like saying 'round about the turn of the century.'

Capri paused. Did that mean we were still due for the big countdown? He shrugged it off and got stuck in again.

Grantham then went on to quote a text from some ancient Babylonian priest who was writing in the 3rd century BC who described an abortive race consisting of hybrids (half-man, half-fish, or other combinations), and their leader who came out of the sea in the evening and would disappear back

into the sea at dawn. This race was banished to the other side, the dark side, namely Recremental Space. What he meant was; these creatures represented the earliest stages of evolution which had been passed through. As they were mostly abortive, they had been scrapped and superseded by a far more versatile race which eventually became *homo sapiens*. He then went to discuss the fate of the human race, believing that his planet ushers in the reversal which will desecrate the earth. It will bring about a period of confusion. There will be chaos, anarchy, hostility between men, followed by earthquakes, tremendous seismic activity, rising water levels, tidal waves, and all the rest of the apocalyptic scenarios.

As there was no planet beyond Pluto, Capri rejected everything he was saying. It was pure myth, and this forthcoming apocalypse existed purely in Grantham's imagination. Capri wanted to laugh at the absurdity of it all.

If Grantham was a genius, as everybody claimed, then he was a mad genius, for he certainly didn't live on our planet, probably his own, as there was absolutely no scientific validation for any of his theories.

Irritated, Capri jumped to the last chapter dealing with the cult of the Messiah, which at first was mythical, but over millennia various cults had tended to portray him as historical, including the Christians who, according to him, erred greatly for they failed to understand the full import of the original type on which it was based. In other words, he was saying Christianity got it wrong; there was no personal or historical Messiah then, but there will be one in the future.

Once his planet had passed a new saviour would be returning, a Messiah as it had always been predicted, a child of the divine spoken of in all religions, one who is always associated with the end of the world and a new one. The cult of the child is the cult of the beginning. And in the last and final chapter Grantham brought the whole matter to its conclusion by examining all the prophecies which signified a new age, emphasising we were still in the transitionary phase of a new zodiacal sign, having moved out of Pisces, a symbol of the Christian era, and not quite in the next one, Aquarius, appropriately the Water-bearer, an adumbration of another deluge he believed, and not due to commence until the 21st century. Up until that time there would be many drastic events all characterising this transitionary phase. He then went on to cite various prophecies, some of them highly

dubious. Capri skipped through them until he came to the last one. It was transmitted by some American housewife back in the 1960's. Capri was about to dismiss it when he noticed a name she mentioned. She had a vision of Nefertiti and her husband Akhenaten. In this vision she saw Nefertiti holding a baby which was wrapped in soiled and ragged clothes with a small cross glowing above its head. She later saw this cross grow until it covered the whole world. The baby was then enveloped in light like that of a new sun. Akhenaten then walked away and disappeared leaving the mother and child standing alone. Inexplicably, Nefertiti gets stabbed in the back. She dies and the child grows to become an embodiment of the supreme wisdom, combining in himself a fusion of east and west.

Grantham's interpretation of the vision was more interesting. He believed the queen mentioned was not Nefertiti but a symbolic device of a type of woman who had the power to earth the energies of his planet. This sounded intriguingly similar to Crome's description of a Woman of Power. Were these two men talking about the same thing? The parallels were undeniable. Capri read on. She will help to bring the child to birth, not necessarily biologically, but in a maternal role, one that is magical. She will earth his power around the time of the crossing of the planet when it reaches its perigee. That is why in the vision the cross grows and expands to a phenomenal size and becomes as bright as a second sun. The planet indeed is bright, if not brighter than the sun. And when it arrives, it will appear to light up the whole sky. The pharaoh disappears because his function is merely biological. He has passed on his seed for the child to be born. And as in the myth of Osiris and Horus, the father has to die before the child can take his place. The father is the planet; the child is its incarnation on the mundane plane. All divine kingships are based on the same type of model. The pharaoh of Egypt became Horus on his ascension to the throne after the death of his father. The mother too has to die after she has served her purpose in order to allow the child to reach its full powers. Nefertiti is stabbed in the back because she has to give up her role. The child will not necessarily be a fusion of east and west. Grantham believed again that this was purely symbolic, an allusion to the twin concepts of the Positive and Negative, the former being a symbol for the east, as in the rising sun, the latter the west, the sun setting in its primal womb, death. The child will combine both elements in one body. Through him will the imbalance be deactivated and order restored.

This all sounded too far fetched. All these predictions were either way out or make-belief. Nothing had happened of a sufficient degree to suggest any of this was imminent. And as the turn of the century had passed, it looked like it never would.

Grantham's interpretation of this prediction was, well, predictable. Capri yawned as he came to the bottom of the page and read the last few lines, something to do with a certain sign or symbol which will appear spontaneously in man's consciousness other than a cross, a symbol so powerful it will unmistakably be a signal for the catastrophic return. Grantham received it through direct communication whilst working with his planet and claimed he had drawn it in a trance.

Capri casually turned the page…

"No!" he screamed.

He slammed the book shut, his eyes staring into empty space, afraid. A cold wind blew in. He shivered.

"I don't believe it," he muttered.

There was a sound from his bed, a whispering, smooth, mellifluous voice.

"Harmon, aren't you coming to bed?"

He looked up to see Katie stirring. He had forgotten all about her. Now she was smiling at him, her eyes a beautiful crystal sheen. His scream must have woken her up.

"Come on, come to bed," she begged. "Stop reading. Put your book away and keep me warm."

Still confounded he could only let the book fall by his side and, like a somnambulist, he rose from his chair and stood before her inviting eyes.

"That's it. Come to bed. Come to Katie," she purred and pulled back the sheet to reveal her splendid naked body. She opened her legs wide for him.

All sense of doom vanished in the instant of her smile. If the gods want it, so be it, he thought as he let his bathrobe fall to the floor; he, erect and

proud, did what had to be done.

They fucked and fucked, two glorious hours of flesh in flesh, animals, wild and ferocious, he getting it out of his system, she begging for more. For awhile there were no worries or doubts, but fuck after beautiful fuck, exquisitely exchanging their own magnetic fluids. And as the world turned and kept turning they expired again and again, incessantly, recurrently, sighing, dying, being born anew, created and uncreated, ever eternally returning, revolving like the big wheel of heaven, the wheel of time.

After some time Capri was satisfied. He rolled on to his back with a final sigh and closed his eyes. Katie cuddled up next to him and rested her head on his chest. She smiled and fell asleep. Now it was time to make that visit.

He brought up the entrance of the institute, getting it clear and precise, held it steady and projected into it. He found himself hovering by the main entrance. He slipped through into a large foyer. It was white and clean like a hospital. A uniform was sitting behind a desk monitoring some screens. Capri glided by. He found a panel display registering all the personnel and their locations. The sign was fuzzy, too much light. He stabilised his vision and brought the names into focus. He found one he recognised; Mr Anton Landis, room 131. It seemed like a good place to start. He reconnoitred his position, concentrated on the room and was conveyed in its direction.

He ascended up through the ceiling. All the floors were wired, touch sensitive. That didn't bother him. He hovered above the floor and drifted down a long corridor. He found the room and slipped through the door.

Landis' office was how he expected it to be; unoccupied and unremarkable, barely personalised. Plush purple carpet, a false window in the far wall, a computerised desk, row upon row of micro-files along one wall and on the other an in-built aquarium, maybe the only personal touch he was allowed. As he began to examine the room something caught his attention. It was a movement in the aquarium. A rather large rainbow coloured fish swam by, its silvery metallic scales catching the light and throwing it in his path. Then he noticed something peculiar at the bottom of the tank. At first he thought it was another fish of some kind feeding off the bottom. He couldn't see too clear as his vision was partially blurred. He moved in closer. It wasn't a fish. And as he moved closer more came into view, all embedded in the

sand with real fish swimming around them. He strained to see what they really were. Some rare exotic marine specimens? Suddenly he felt sick. There were a dozen of them, all alive and behaving as if they were still attached to their bodies, some of them with pubic hair still intact. The hairs swayed gently like underwater fauna as small currents passed over them. The flesh was perfectly preserved. Some were opening and closing like mouths, emitting bubbles, the lips working in rhythmic movements. Others became big. They rose and fell as if wired up to batteries and on timers. He watched one as it slowly swelled and became erect. It spurted out some white milky substance which floated in the water like a cloud before sinking to the bottom.

Capri recoiled. "This man is sick!" He backed off quick to the other side of the room and hovered. Now he could feel it. He concentrated on it. The whole ambience of the room was filled with it. What at first seemed like an ordinary office was now filled with menace. It was strong, a sadistic pleasure mingled with an intense power bordering on pure anger. It was coupled with an incredible raw edge, biting and cold. But there was also immense intelligence behind it. It conformed accurately to what Mosalla had told him about this man. Now he understood what he meant.

Capri wheeled round the room, not really sure what he was looking for. Anything, he guessed. And he could only look. He did. On the top of the desk he found a small frame with a moving holo inside. It was a 3D photo of some woman, obviously the wife. Not immediately attractive; auburn hair, mid thirties he guessed, and she looked kind of strict and domineering, hardly a gentle appearance at all. Her only pleasant feature was her smile. When she smiled it softened her harsh features. She blew a kiss every few seconds to where Landis would normally be sitting. Capri still didn't know what he looked like. Hadn't even seen a picture of him. There was nothing else here by the looks of it. He decided to exit and scout around the rest of the building.

Outside in the corridor two white coats walked straight through him. He decided to follow. Round the corner they walked towards a door. They scanned their eyes. It dematerialised. They walked through into a tight chamber. It looked like an elevator. Capri came up behind them. The door rematerialised. The coats were talking. He couldn't hear what they were

saying. It was all distorted. Then the room was filled with a pale blue light. It flashed up from the floor to the ceiling and withdrew. A door on the other side opened. He followed the two coats out into another corridor. It was a high risk security area. Big red signs on the walls, warning notices everywhere. He stopped as they passed a door, stainless steel like a bank's vault, security lock and another red sign in big red letters; 'EXTREME TEMPERATURE' and some writing underneath too small to read. He slipped through three inches of solid steel.

Capri found himself in a large freezer chamber like they have in the kitchens of big hotels, grills on the floor and steel walls and ceiling. He drifted to the centre and rotated 360° and stopped. All four walls had rows of vertical tanks with glass doors. The doors were partially covered with a thin layer of frost. That didn't interest him. What did was what lay behind the doors in the tanks that weren't empty; humans. Were they dead? He moved in closer. If they weren't dead they certainly looked it, all naked and suspended in permafrost isolation. Cryogenics?

All the tanks had data readings. Some of them were blipping, others weren't. Presumably the ones that weren't had to be dead. Then the others must be alive. But they were so lifeless he couldn't tell. One other thing really intrigued him when he examined it; the specimen was Chinese. And the one next to it was as well. And a few more. In fact, they were all Chinese and all young.

So Mosalla was right. Landis was shipping in these people from the local community and using them for experiments in cryogenics. But why? Had he succeeded? Had he managed to freeze someone alive for resuscitation at a later date?

He took a closer look. One data display was flashing. It registered -195°C on the cryometer, a degree less than the critical -196°C where all biological activity stops. He checked the contents. The girl seemed to be okay, looked in good condition, but very young. He checked the one next to it. It wasn't blipping and was registering -195°C as well. But the guy inside was very much dead, all emaciated looking as if, as Mosalla had said, his body fluids had been drained off. Then they were obviously having problems at this level of freezing. He could only think of one word as he looked at him—murder!

It jumped into the room so quick he didn't know where it came from. Capri dived straight through into the next room. It followed, hot on his tail. He shot through to another room not even waiting for it this time. He didn't have to. It was right behind him. Capri shot upwards thinking he could evade it.

Whatever it was, it was after him and wouldn't let go. He shot through another roof. Still the fucker was after him. He caught a glimpse of it, black and huge. That was enough for him. He didn't hang around. He hit ground level. No idea where he was. Some kind of boiler room. Capri shot behind a heater and waited, hoping the heat would throw the thing off. It didn't. It reappeared, this time fully formed, some sort of astral sentinel.

He bolted out of hiding and into another room. The sentinel marched straight through the wall towards him. Capri thought quickly. He brought up his astral shield, seeing it as bright blazing white light, concentrated all his energy on it. He stood still and faced it. The sentinel stopped. Now he could see it more closely. It was ghastly, enough to frighten away any intruder, with eyes that swivelled like a chameleon's. They honed in on him. It wasn't going to touch him. He was safe for the time being. But how long could he keep his shield up? The sentinel moved in. It stopped as if surveying him. Capri took a step back. He could dive into the next room. That would be pointless. It would only follow him. Then it raised its arms. Where there should have been hands there were claws, incredibly powerful looking like sharpened steel. This thing was out to do him some damage. He brought round his shield to the front, concentrated it as a ball of light and hurled it straight at the thing. The sentinel recoiled on impact. It disintegrated and finally disappeared.

Relieved, Capri relaxed for a moment. He didn't hang around any longer in case there were more on patrol. He exited and slammed back into his body so hard it jolted and woke Katie up.

"What's the matter?" she asked.

"Nothing," he murmured as he caught his breath.

"You look like you've had a nightmare."

"It was a nightmare."

CELEBRATION

"You're frozen," she said as she stroked his poor head. Capri laughed. "Let me warm you up," she whispered. Her wandering hand found his cock. She caressed it and kissed him full. She climbed on top of him. They fucked once more before falling asleep.

The televid woke him up. He leaned over the side of his bed to answer it.

"Carlotta!" he exclaimed in astonishment. "Do you know what time it is?"

"I know, Harmon, believe me, but I had to wake you up."

"Why? What's happened?"

"You left a message for me, remember?"

"So?" He rubbed his eyes and yawned.

"Well, I've just remembered the name of the road."

"The name of the road?"

"Yes. You wanted to know the name of the road."

"Correct, Carlotta. I did want to know the name of the road. That was over five hours ago. I've got it now, thanks."

"How, Harmon?" she queried looking puzzled.

Capri thought for a moment. "Because I make it my business to know," he paraphrased her.

Carlotta screwed up her eyes. "111 Vermont Drive?"

"Correct. Now do me a favour, Carlotta. I'm tired. I've had one hell of a day. I've been working all night. And now, if you don't mind, I would like to get some sleep."

There was a murmur in the background. Carlotta looked at him for an explanation. "What was that?"

"What?"

"That noise."

"What noise?" he asked, innocently.

Then it came again as Katie stirred to find him sitting up in bed. She reached for his shoulder to pull him down. "Come back to me," she whined.

"That!" Carlotta screamed at him and could see Katie's hand. "You've got somebody with you!"

"No, I haven't." He brushed Katie off him. "Thanks for the info…"

"Harmon, come to me and keep me warm," Katie murmured again.

"You have got somebody with you. And I recognise that voice."

"Goodnight, Carlotta." He went to turn the televid off.

"Wait, Harmon. Wait."

"Bye." He turned it off and drifted back to his warm piece of flesh. She was lying there, her eyes closed, her mouth slightly open. He kissed her, caressed her and, yes, fucked her again.

THE OCCULTIST

'All occultists are schizoidal in that they have an innate tendency to oscillate between varying degrees of reality-consensus frameworks. It is no wonder confusion arises between what is and what is not reality, although they debate to exasperating lengths what constitutes "reality" in the first place. We can only suppose they have an exclusive insight not possessed by normal people which leads one to conclude they may (or may not) be tuned into something far greater than we can ever possibly imagine.'

Professor Henry Malins,
Journal of Psychopathology, vol. 49

—22—
THE LOSS

He halted. He paid his entrance fee. The bouncers on the door gave him a hostile look. He ignored them and ploughed his way in, through the crowd to the bar, gasping for a drink. He ordered. The Chink behind the bar wasn't going to serve him. He hissed and yelled, slamming the bar hard until the fucker was so frightened he was almost pissing his pants. He got served in the end. What was the matter with these people? They knew who he was, so why were they acting strange all of a sudden? He turned round to face the rest of them. They too were giving him hostile looks. He ignored them and drank up, reordered and drank some more. He was late, so he had to make up for it. His head was still sore like it had been split open. And now it was gone midnight. It was better in a way because this place really started livening up around this time. Except it wasn't that alive at all. It should be kicking. There was no beef to it. Everything was dead, stagnant. He could almost smell the shit coming from these corpses around him. What the fuck was the matter with them? He wanted to kick them into life, to kick them hard to get the night started. He was here, so now they had better entertain him and entertain him good.

Even the pussy onstage looked dead. Expecting to be greeted by playful glances, all he got was grimaces, snarls and brush offs. Didn't these people like him anymore? He didn't understand. These people were scum anyway. They knew it instinctively and his distinguishable presence brought out their inferiority—that was it! Well, fuck them. He could be unfriendly too. He

could play them at that game, and play it good. Yet somehow that wasn't the whole problem.

He diverted his eyes to another group of people in the corner. They too were staring him up like he shouldn't be there. They looked away. He went back to his drink, pretended he was some place else. He might as well have been for this sure wasn't like the same club. This club was a morgue.

He didn't worry about it. Chan would he along soon, sort it out for him, tell him what was going on. They'd have a talk, discuss exactly what happened last night and how he was feeling now. Of course he had lost it. Knew he would. It slipped out of him as soon as he hit the Centre and that was it— gone. And all he had now was a memory. It left him feeling hollow, all empty inside, waiting to be filled up again. So it was essential to speak to Chan. He would boost him. They would go out tonight and do it all again, get into that fucking fabulous state of mind and keep it for good this time.

Landis looked up and down the bar for his buddy, scouted round the back and even in the toilets. There was no sign of him and no fucker here he could ask who would understand what the fuck he was saying. Not even his white bit. She wasn't here either, nor the boss man.

Disappointed, he stumbled back to the bar, determined to get back to that state again tonight. It was similar to having a wet dream and just as you're riding with it, getting all excited, reality cuts in and you wake up, shattering the dream. But the next time he wasn't going to wake up. Next time he was going to go with it all the way, make it his, because he had the right to make it his. He deserved it.

He settled for another bottle of this stuff called the God Cure instead, drank it down, surveyed all the ugly slit-eyed faces. He laughed when they shied away. He looked at another pair. They looked away instantly. He placed his eyes elsewhere. The same thing happened. Had the Emperor died or something? Had he stumbled into a nest of vipers? He didn't give a fuck. He'd take out these fuckers any day. He ignored them and carried on with some serious drinking.

Had he touched it? He wasn't sure. He wasn't sure what the hell he had touched last night. All he knew was he was feeling pretty shaky as if he was

poised on some precarious structure and it was going to cave in taking him with it. He'd be crashing down, floundering in the abyss below. But whatever he had hit last night it blew the roof off his head. He had never felt anything like it before. And the aftermath was this immense gap in his memory. He couldn't even remember how he got back to the Centre. Did he walk? More like floated, and the whole world was just so beautiful and different. All the colours were vibrant, streaming with life. And his life was pouring out of him through his eyes, lighting up the city, radiant, glorious. So he must have touched the Tao, right? Or perhaps he had touched God. If so, he reckoned it should be available on prescription like a drug. God is a drug. It's the biggest hit going. Think of the best orgasm you've ever had, some junkie once told him, and multiply it a thousand times. No, even that wasn't anywhere close to what he experienced. Multiply it a thousand times and another thousand; if you could imagine that you'd understand why God was addictive. He should be hooked into your mainline permanently, drip-fed twenty-four hours a day, a divine fix. And you'd never need to jack-up again. But that was the problem; it wasn't permanent: Why? Why was it just a fleeting experience? Why couldn't he keep it? It was so fucking beautiful, it made him come in his pants just thinking about it.

He thought of it in another way. It was like you were this battery driven toy. You performed adequately, functioning mechanically, but then someone comes along and jacks you into ten thousand volts and its like 'Whooosh!' and you're off on a totally different plane, a plane that embraces all the planes, and you know every single goddamned thing in the universe. You know all that needs to be known because you have gone into the unknown. You have become the unknown. And in the unknown you become all. Right out there, man, beyond the edge, beyond the periphery of the universe, and its beautiful, really beautiful. And that was why he wanted it back again. He felt deprived, needy. He wanted another fix of this Tao thing—or whatever it was—because he certainly didn't feel right, not a hundred per cent at all, kind of cheated like he had been ripped off.

Boy, could those girls perform last night. He didn't know how they could keep going for as long as they did, but they had and he wanted them back too. He wanted Chan here now. Where was the fucker?

Then he got to thinking about all the people he had fucked over in the past,

kind of feeling a twinge as his memory skipped over his deeds and what he had done to them and he didn't like it. It made him feel awkward seeing all their bleeding faces, those dead eyes staring at him and even thought of apologising for all the misery he wrought. He definitely wasn't feeling right.

He washed it away with another drink. A conscience? He didn't even realise he had one. But it was somehow making him feel guilty just thinking about his past. What was he? An animal? It sure as hell felt like it, like it was someone else who did all that stuff, not him, his old self, that other self of his. And thinking this way kind of made him feel better. It lightened the burden and he really did feel kind of ashamed like it was guilt getting to him, guilt making him feel like this, guilt tangling up inside making him confused. But the only thing was, he didn't know how to say sorry. He didn't know what to do to make amends. He didn't even know who he was now, just this wreck, inanimate and desolate. By trying to distance himself from his past he was also trying to reach into this other self he touched last night, kind of not quite there but almost.

He didn't like it at all. He was neither his old self nor his new self. This was intolerable. He couldn't stand it. And as he waited for Chan there was only one thing to do; try to get back into his angry self. Because that's who he really was, and then he would be back in gear, fully recharged, out to do business once again. All he needed now was his old buddy.

He turned round to see his white bit. She was approaching him, coming right up to him with a stern look on her face, wearing a cheap dress, the sort only cheap hussies wear, black with white dots, and seeing her now he wondered why he had this fascination for her initially, for she was trash and that confused him. He felt nothing for her, not even getting hard at the thought of her going down on him, taking his steel in whole all the way.

She stopped in front of him, her eyes boring directly into his. "You've got a fucking nerve showing your face here!" she hissed at him.

Landis, taken aback, didn't know how to react. What was her problem? "Look, about the other night, I'm sor...," he blurted, the last word getting stuck in the back of his throat. He couldn't even force it out.

"Fuck the other night!" she spat out. "I don't give a shit about that. I want

to know what you're doing here."

Confused, he tried to gauge her. "What's with the interest all of a sudden?"

"Are you really that much of an asshole you haven't noticed? Take a good look," she said and gestured to the crowd. "Do you notice anything?"

Landis looked at all the faces. They were all still screwing him up and the music had stopped. The place had grown so quiet and intense it unnerved him. He looked at her for an explanation.

"I noticed. They seem to be a bit upset about something."

"They are, believe me. And do you know why?" He shook his head. "These people want to kill you."

"What?" he stammered, uncomprehending. "Wait a minute, whatever their problem is with me I'm sure they're mistaken. They know me. They've seen me around here. And as far as I know, I haven't done shit to upset them. So I don't understand what the problem is."

"There's a big problem here. It's you."

"Look, lady, when my friend shows up, I'm sure we can sort this out."

"Your friend is dead!"

"Dead? Chan?"

"That's right, Chan."

"No, you're wrong. I was with him this morning."

"That's right. You were the last person to see him alive before he was killed by someone dressed just like you. A white American wearing a dinner suit."

Landis finally clicked. "Now wait a minute. It's not what you're thinking. I never killed Chan, I swear."

"Well that's what they think," she retorted, pointing to the crowd.

Landis, now aware of the full implications, noticed they were moving in

closer, crowding around him, and with mean, angry looks. "They think I killed Chan?" She nodded. "That's crazy! I wouldn't do a thing like that! No, they've got me all wrong. I never killed him."

"Don't tell me. Tell them!"

Landis darted his eyes at them again; they were after his blood. "Look, you guys," he shouted. "About Chan. I never killed him, right? I didn't do it. I know how much he meant to you all and how popular he was, but believe me, his death had nothing to do with me. You have to believe me."

He might as well have been talking to himself. His words didn't make a blind bit of difference. He turned to say something to the white bit; she had a gleeful expression on her face like she was loving this.

"You speak their language, you tell them," he pleaded, grabbing her arm and trying to pull her out towards them.

"Fuck you! Why should I help you? I don't give a shit about you."

"But you have to believe me," he argued desperately. "It wasn't me."

"I don't give a shit if it was you or not. You're nothing!" she spat at him.

Landis was raging inside. Who the fuck did this bitch think she was? Under normal circumstances he would have punched her hard. Nobody talks to him like that and lives. "You bitch!" he spat back.

"Nothing. You think you're so fucking cool and smart, so fucking superior to everyone else, that the whole world should he worshipping you. You're wrong. And I hope they rip your balls off. In fact, I think I'll stay and watch. Because there's no way you're leaving this place alive."

For once in his life he was speechless; her words hurt. He didn't know why. She might as well have slapped in the face again.

"You have to help me," he pleaded with her. "You have to tell them I didn't do it." But she wouldn't have it. She gave him a wicked smile of satisfaction, gloating on his fear.

Landis, confused and not too sure how to handle the situation, went right

up to them, each one of them and pleaded with them to believe him. But what was the point? None of them could understand a word he was saying. He felt useless, pathetic, and angry, a whole host of other emotions which were boiling away inside. He ranted and raved, did anything to exonerate himself of all blame. They wouldn't have it. In their eyes he was guilty. The bitch was right. He ran back to her.

"Just tell them!" he shouted at her.

"Why should I?" She howled with laughter.

Landis was on the verge of hitting her. He thought twice about it and made an attempt to leave. A throng had gathered between him and the door. They stood their ground, a wall of bodies, adamant he wasn't going anywhere. His chances of getting out unscathed were slim, but he forced himself towards them. They moved in closer, thicker, at least two hundred against one man. He stopped.

"Where you going?" he heard her shout.

"I'm going to see his old man," he shouted back, not taking his eyes off them. "He would know who really did it. And when I find him I'll kill him."

"Not if they kill you first," she cackled.

He ignored her and thought about running through them, stampeding his way out. He took another step. They stood firm.

He turned round once more to see her casually light up a cigarette by the bar and inhale the smoke, blowing it out slowly like she had been rehearsing it over the years.

She had a wicked smile on her face; he had never hated anybody so much in his whole life. He turned round to face them. This was going to be ugly, but there was only one way out. He ran, ploughing straight through them. They pelted him with blows. He ducked down and shoved them out the way, punching and kicking as he burst through. They retaliated. All he saw was feet kicking into him and felt a rain of fists hammering into his stomach and back. He barged the door and threw himself outside and ran and kept running as a few of them chased after him. He didn't even look back and

was heading God knows where, anywhere but far away from them. He took a turn, down a long alley, panting as the adrenalin flowed in. Soon he managed to stretch the distance between them, his legs working overtime. But he kept running, huffing and puffing, his heart pounding as he made it quickly up another alley and out into the night. He was getting short of breath. Soon he would have to stop, but he kept going, now heading up one long track, the shacks whizzing by, a blur of metal and the sound of running feet trailing off in the distance. They soon stopped. Now he could slow down before he collapsed, thinking they were safely behind him.

He stopped, practically bending in two to catch his breath, sweat dripping from his brow, the silence syncopated by the sound of his heart beating fast and his gasping for breath. He paused momentarily and eventually was able to look up and get his bearings. Where was he? He didn't know. All the shacks looked the same to him and he must have run a good two or three miles. Now he was stuck with four tracks going off in all directions and not even sure which one he had just come down. It was a nightmare, and he was stuck right in the middle of it.

He leant his burnt-out body against the side and rested for awhile. He brushed his hair back and got the sweat out of his eyes. He had never felt so scared. Even his hands were shaking, but at least he had made it in one piece. The damage to his body was minimal. He checked his face. It had received no considerable blows. But he could feel the bruises coming up in his stomach and legs already. What was it with those guys? Why didn't they believe him? Then he remembered he had his gun and knife on him. What a stupid fuck, he thought. How stupid can you get? All he had to do was pull his gun out and then they would have parted like the sea and he wouldn't be in this fucking mess. He definitely wasn't thinking straight.

He pulled his gun out and cocked it in case he needed it. He tried to hold it steady whilst he judged whether this was dangerous territory or not. But then it was all dangerous territory, and there were still probably a few of his pursuers around looking for him. Then he had to be careful if he didn't want his head being served up on a platter. That's what they would do if they caught him. He was certain of it. But why they wouldn't believe him didn't bother him now. Chan was dead. Somebody had killed him. He did warn him. And now it was too late. There was only one thing to do; find

the Sage. But how? Where was his shack from here? If only he knew.

He sighed, red pain in a black night, the moon looming ominously overhead, and not one single cloud. And as he craned his head up all he could see were stars, especially the pole star. But where was the old man's place in relation to that? To the left, right, straight ahead? He hadn't a clue. Neither did any of the tracks have signs or names. How the hell did anybody get their mail around here?

He took a wild guess and headed north up a long alley. It reeked of that familiar, horrible smell of rotting cabbage. It made his stomach turn, but he forced himself on, even thinking about asking some family where the Sage lived. Would they know? Did they speak his language? This was a real shit situation, or what he called a 'shituation.' And now he was truly lost as he came to a dead end. It was a maze, with no way out. He back-tracked, turned off at another corner and headed up another interminable alley, and another one, and another and crossed over when he came to a junction and was wracking his brains out. He seemed to be going round in circles or one huge circle because the pole star was still in the same position and he hadn't even come across any people. It was quiet, not a sound apart from a dog howling in the distance. He couldn't even hear the music from the club. Then it had to be far away. And now he was faced with these endless alleys and tracks which didn't converge anywhere. Now he really hated this town.

He stopped, cursed himself. This wasn't the right way to go about it. He thought about what he learnt last night, what Chan had told him; he was always using logic. All he had to do was drop it, but as he thought about a method of stopping logic he realised he was using logic to do exactly that.

He cursed again. If only he could stop thinking, open his mind up and get into the silence the Sage was always telling him about, the silence he had experienced last night. Or stop thinking altogether, make his mind go blank and open up to intuition. He tried letting go and stood still for awhile. But the harder he tried, the worse it got; the effort made it even more difficult.

"Fuck it," he cursed and gave up.

This was pointless. He snarled and took another alley, kicking and screaming at anything which got in his way, cussing and spitting, getting

back into his good old angry self. He could now feel it coming on like a methadone rush. Now he was feeling better. Now he was feeling really good and anybody who'd attempt to take him out wouldn't stand a chance. He'd be victorious. And he rode the bilious wave of anger. It gave him more strength. Now he wasn't afraid. More energy came flowing in. He was determined to find the Sage and sort out the guy who killed Chan.

He picked up his pace, marched down another alley. He came to the end, turned the corner and wanted to shoot somebody there and then. He had only walked round in a full circle and was now back right where he started.

"Fucking shit!" he screamed and banged his gun against corrugated iron. The sound echoed all around him. Fearing he had given away his position to his pursuers, he scrabbled away quickly and tripped over some sheeting. He clambered to his feet and watched it move.

"What the …?"

He stood back. It was so dark he couldn't make out what it was. Then he saw a face appear from underneath. Some peasant had made his bed for the night right in the middle of the alley. Landis lashed out with his boot, kicking him so hard it sent him flying off the ground.

"Peasant!" he shouted as the itinerant ran.

Landis cursed again and slumped down to the ground. "How did I get into this mess?" He hit the ground with his fist and looked up at the black night sky and sighed. There had to be a way out of here. Perhaps he should wait until it got lighter. Then he'd be able at least to see where he was going. He didn't know. He must have been walking for an hour at least and was still nowhere nearer to finding the old man. He wanted to give up and sink.

He rested his back against the side, splayed out his legs on the ground, not even caring about getting his best dinner suit dirty. It was already ripped in places. He closed his eyes and gave in. He slipped into the blackness, the terrible blackness, his mind reeling as he sank fast. All he wanted was a few moments of peace, get recharged and he'd be on his way. But the stupid bitch's face kept coming back to him in waves. He could see her clearly in that cheap dress of hers. She was laughing at him. Nobody laughs at Landis! And she kept laughing. Her grating voice was echoing down the corridors

of his mind. He grabbed hold of her throat, squeezing hard to shut her up. She still laughed at him. He squeezed harder.

"Fucking shut up, you stupid bitch!"

She continued laughing, cackling, howling. It was driving him mad. He pulled out his knife and slashed her right across the mouth to make her stop. She didn't. She was still laughing, even through her ripped open mouth. She needed to be taught a lesson, he decided.

"Mene, mene tekel upharsin. Thou art weighed in the balance and found wanting," he declared and squeezed her throat tighter and slashed her again, this time a deeper gash with his Pesh-en-Kef and delighted in seeing blood trickling out of her mouth and down her throat. It was such a pretty sight. But she was still sort of laughing, a mute laugh coming from her eyes. They offended him. "If thine eye offends thee, pluck it out." And he was doing just what the good Lord said, following orders, and gouged both right out with his knife, hers not his, you understand, and lobbed them right over to the other side of this shit-hole of a town and laughed back at her. But there was still a voice coming out of her throat. Didn't this fucking bitch ever stop? He'd sort her out. He slashed her throat, cutting his knife in deeper, sawing away until the whole fucking head came loose. Only then did she stop making a noise. He grabbed her decapitated head. It was offensive to his sight. He rammed two rusty nails deep into her eardrums, hooked them up with some twine and whirled the whole trophy high up in the air like a lasso, spinning faster and faster, him yodelling and hollering and laughing as he twirled, then let it go quickly. The head shot off over to the other side of town. He was mighty pleased. And now he was just left with her body, still covered with her shitty dress. It offended him too, so it had to come off as well. And he slashed at the straps, ripped it off and played with her naked body, doing a dance, a dance of death, dancing now like they were in this huge barn and he was swinging her round the dance floor like she was his dame and he was the best man out on a Saturday night showing all the rest of them how to do it, except she kept missing a step or two, so he kicked her, punched her and knocked some sense back into her, but she was useless, couldn't dance to save her life and was making him real mad, real angry, so fucking angry he stabbed her a few times so she could feel his displeasure and threw her down and kicked her hard and kicked her good

all over the dance floor. She was pathetic, a cheap hussy anyway so who cared, but he was going to teach her a lesson because nobody, absolutely nobody, laughs at Landis and gets away with it. They invoked their own death if they did and that's just what he was going to do with her, invoke death in her body, because death is sexy, right? Death is sexy and cool, and it was spilling out of her flesh in luxurious streams of red and there never was such a prettier sight and it was making him all hard in his pants, so fucking hard, man, he had to let his dick out to breathe and was rubbing it good as he skewered the back of her ankles with his knife all the way through until it came out the other side, and he was proud, damned proud of what a fine job he was doing and always thought about doing some body piercing for a living on the side like they all do down at the Strip, and have one of his own little booths, and put a few examples of his work on display, but then the smell would kinda get to him, all those flesh-punctured corpses, so he decided against it and continued with his handiwork, getting some steel meathooks through the fresh piercings in the sinews of her ankles and fixed them securely to a rigid wooden pole, nice clean job, you understand, and strong enough to take her weight, and tied her wrists to the ends of the pole with some rope and then hauled her up with a hullabaloo as he watched her rise in the air ankle-up, all the way up to the rafters in the roof so her headless body was dangling like a deer with her plump titties hanging down, and stood back to admire his work so far and saw that it was good and he was much gratified thereby, seeing her like this, like an inverse holy offering, expiating her sins for the godless creature she was, and now he could get on with some real work and got his knife out again and started whittling away, carving deep into her flesh with love, with a furious frenzy, working his knife at the point which most offended him and grabbed hold of her pubic hair with his big manly fist and did pull thereof as he hacked and the whole mound came away in one glorious piece and he tossed it over his shoulder like a real worker, like he was an excavator, not taking his eyes off the work in hand, and sliced her right down the middle, all the way down from her pubic bone to her chest, a nice clean cut, so clean a butcher would have been proud of him, and cleansed her pubic cavity like he was casting out demons from her sinful body, a body she had no right to be proud of, tempting all the men, making them feel sinful too. Well, it weren't right, so he plunged his hand deep into her wound and excavated the rest of her, pulling out that venomous womb of hers, the filth it had aborted, and

her intestines like filthy rotten ugly detestable serpents and threw them over his shoulder as he got cleaving more, reaching into her abdominal cavity, pulling out more contemptuous vitals, uprooting them, casting them from her abominable body, spitting and cussing and whistling as he worked until she was sore clean inside apart from the most disgusting organ of all which had yet to be removed, the one that was full of shit, the one he loathed the most, her heart, and as he reached in, severing all the arteries with his knife, it was black as cancer, and therefore needed exorcising, so he spat on it, wrung it clean dry with his hands and too threw it over his shoulder until his work was done. And it was done, since now she was all clean inside, truly exorcised and eviscerated, cleaned out, gutted proper, just the way a deer should be, all empty and free from sin, hanging there before him, cleansed and purified of all iniquity, divinely dead!

He was enamoured thereby, and picked up all the entrails which had been housed in that sinful body of hers, playing with them like a kid, examining each one of them in turn, trying to work out how they used to fit together like parts of a dismantled engine, understanding their functions and relationships to one another, and seeing them as the sum of her parts.

As a kid he always enjoyed taking things apart to see how they worked.

He ejaculated into the night then put his knife to the base of his spent cock and dug in deep, pushing it all the way through. He moaned as he ejaculated blood. It was draining out between his legs and he heard the sound of steel cutting into bone and flesh and finally steel and felt the heady rush of a syncope coming on full as his bloody knife fell by his side. Death was coming too as his life ebbed out of him and his mind elevated to the ceiling of heaven. The silence beckoned him on.

THE MENTAL HEALTH BILL

'We can consider the aetiological basis behind any form of mental disorder is really akin to a purgative process in that the mind seeks to exclude from itself all that is inimical or disagreeable, rather like the digestive system of the stomach during an attack of food poisoning. Really there is little difference between the two, except the aperient action of the mind is far more subtle and cumulative. It seeks to regulate itself as its goal is equilibrium. We can thus view all forms of mental disease in a positive, if not a virtuous, way. And I would go so far as to say that really the onset of insanity is the first step towards mental health.'

Professor Henry Malins,
The Myth of Mental Health

—23—
WANDERING IN HOPELESS NIGHT

He staggered into the room clutching himself. The Sage was sitting on the floor, lost in meditation. Landis fell to his knees and gasped. The Sage's eyes flicked open.

"Oh, I'm sorry," Landis gushed. "Did I break your concentration?"

The Sage refrained from replying. Instead his eyes went to the blood-stained trousers of his young disciple and the way in which the blood was seeping into his carpet.

Landis followed his gaze and looked down at his crotch. "That's nothing, old man. It had to be done."

The Sage looked up, without alarm he fixed his eyes on Landis and assumed a blank expression. Landis tried reading him. It was impenetrable, as usual.

"I need your help, old man," he pleaded. "Chan's dead. You know that, don't you?" the Sage nodded gravely. "Someone killed him. I need to find the person who did it. Do you understand? Are you just going to sit there looking at me like that? Or are you going to tell me who did it? You know who did it, don't you? Tell me who did it."

The Sage was slow to respond. His words were perfectly calm, without emotion. "In my country we have a saying: A man full of vengeance is already a dead man."

"Oh, what the fuck does that mean?" Landis whimpered. He sobbed with pain and shot the Sage a spiteful look. "Jesus Christ! Don't speak to me in parables! I need to know who did it."

"What difference would it make?"

"What difference! It would make a hell of a lot of difference, that's what. It could fucking save my ass. All your fellow cronies are out to get me. They think I did it, they think I killed Chan. You have to help me."

"The small has departed, the great approaches."

"Don't give me that shit!" he shrieked. "All I want to know is who did it. That's all I ask. Then I'll leave. D'ya get me?"

"And then you will kill this person?"

"Yes, fucking yes. Of course I will."

"Why?"

"Why! Because he killed your son, that's why!"

"Take a life to replace a life. Is that your philosophy?"

"Yes!" he cried out and buckled with the pain.

"And that will remedy my son's loss?"

"No, but it'll help me. It'll make me feel good and then I can prove to the others that it wasn't me. Please tell me who did it. I know what you're saying and I'm not thinking straight, but I have to find him. Okay, I'll do a deal with you. If I find him I promise I won't kill him."

The Sage sat silent as a statue, unperturbed.

Landis looked up at him, gritted his teeth. "Look, old man, I know we have our differences. I know I'm not the best person in the world, but your son meant a lot to me, he really did, you know that, you have always known it."

"And you feel for his loss?"

"Yes, of course I fucking do. Why? Don't you?" Landis looked at the Sage uncomprehendingly. There wasn't a mark of pain, regret or sorrow anywhere to be seen. His face was completely blank. "You don't, do you? You don't even feel for your son. I can't believe it. You don't even feel anything for losing your son. Just like when you're wife died, isn't it? When your wife fucking died you sat there with exactly the same look of indifference on your face, no emotion whatsoever, and you said something like ... like ... I can't remember your exact words, but it was something like 'That is the Way,' as if she meant nothing to you, as if you were talking about some other woman, as if she wasn't your wife at all and there was no connection between you two, nothing deep or significant, and she died in labour along with her baby, and you still didn't care. You fucking knew she was going to die and you just fucking sat there with that same bland expression, all fucking calm and aloof as if totally unaffected by it. I thought you cared for her because she was your wife. Goddamnit! You knew she was going to die, didn't you?" The Sage didn't respond. "Just like I fucking bet you knew your son was going to die too. You knew he was, didn't you?" The Sage remained silent, impervious. "Yes, you fucking did. You did, old man. You knew your son was going to die and you did fuck all to stop it. You didn't do a goddamned thing except sit there and take it all in like it's all some game out there and it's all the Way, this fucking stupid goddamned Way of yours. You never told him, because of it. That's why, isn't it? Yes, old man. You can read my thoughts. I know you can. Well, fuck you, because I can read yours too. I can see right through your fucking skull, right into that pea-sized brain of yours and I can see you are disturbed inside, deeply disturbed. I can feel it, old man. You are too fucking afraid to show it, aren't you? Because you always have to look calm, you always have to look at peace with the world. Well, isn't that something? One hell of an achievement. The world doesn't affect me, right? The world doesn't influence my judgement. Well, I don't believe that. Too fucking proud to vent your emotions, aren't you? Too scared in case they get the better of you. Well, I'm not scared, see. I'm a man. I show my emotions like everybody else. Like anybody else who is human. Not like you. You're not human. You're dead, dead to yourself. A ghost. You're not real." The Sage was a statue. "You also know what's going to be happening soon, and you didn't tell him."

"Nor did you," the Sage calmly replied.

"No, I didn't," Landis sobbed, shaking his head. "I couldn't, believe me, I kept trying, but the words wouldn't come out. They would get all ... screwed up inside, and I blabbered. I just couldn't articulate it. I couldn't find a right way of saying it. And then I thought, fuck it, why bother, Chan wouldn't have believed me anyway. It wouldn't have made a blind bit of difference."

"Exactly."

Landis looked at him again. The man's face hadn't changed. "I don't believe you. I don't think you're really on this planet sometimes. And soon...."

"The small has departed, the great approaches."

"Fuck it. I don't even know what I'm saying anymore. I feel like I'm going to faint. I feel weak and nauseous." Landis swayed and gripped his crotch tighter. Blood was pouring through his fingers, mingling with the blood already congealed in the Sage's carpet. He looked down to see he was now surrounded by this red pool. He wearily lifted his head to look at the old man. "Aren't you even going to ask me how I got here?" he demanded. There was no response. The Sage was a statue. "No, I guess not."

Landis went quiet as he tried to recollect exactly what happened. He had to force himself on to patch up his memory and get it all into perspective.

"I had this feeling," he soliloquised. "It was a strange feeling. I thought I was going to drift away, just float up and away as I watched all this blood running down between my legs. I lay there, neither in pain nor feeling any pain, kind of somewhere in-between and I couldn't even remember who I was. I forgot who I was, where I was, what time it was, everything. It all became a blur, meaningless, and I didn't care who I was as I couldn't recollect anything. So I gave up, let myself go without a struggle and hoped I would die, there in the mud and caked in all this shit, just die and drift out because it seemed like a good idea at the time. There was no point continuing. I was just this emptiness, this vacant space like a black hole, not even thinking, a void, and something took me over. It picked me up. Put me on my feet and seemed to be compelling me along like I was this blind man being helped across the road, and I didn't even know where I was going. I just went with it as if sleep-walking. Then I woke up and opened my eyes to find myself right outside your door."

The Sage nodded his understanding. "That was the Tao."

"Was it?" The Sage nodded again. "The Tao. Of course, the fucking Tao. I can't escape this fucking Tao thing of yours, can I?"

"It is not mine for it pervades all things and we are all a part of it."

"Right. We are all a part of it," he repeated hollowly.

Landis found he no longer even had the energy to hold his head up. He let it sag and sighed, his eyes flickering close, not even seeing straight. He smiled inanely because the whole situation was funny in a way if you had a sense of irony, and ridiculous at the same time. He still couldn't feel anything, not even pain, just numb all over. It must be due to the significant amount of blood lost, he thought. He didn't know how much, or why he was even here. Something had forced him on and here he was and here he would be perfectly content to die, to just give in and let it consume him. But there was another part of him which wanted to move, to go on, to accomplish all this work he had set himself out to do. His life hadn't been completed yet and he wouldn't be left alone until it had. And that was why he was still alive.

"About last night," he continued. "Why did you bother? Why did you get you son to go through all that trouble and spend all that money on me? I don't understand."

The Sage looked at him thoughtfully. "Yet you experienced the Tao."

"Did I? I don't fucking know. I don't know what I experienced last night. I don't know anything anymore."

"You touched it."

"I did?" he sobbed. He forced his head up and looked at him directly. "I touched it, right?" The Sage nodded. "The Tao. But how do you know? I could have touched anything. I could have touched the Tao, God, Nirvana. I could have even touched death. How do you that I touched it?"

The Sage smiled warmly. "You touched it."

"Oh, great. I touched it. That's it, it has been decided." He lifted his head up and bellowed aloud. "Hey, listen everybody, listen. I touched the Tao.

Okay? I touched it, because the Sage said I did. So I did. Right?" He looked at him again, struggling to keep his head up. "Oh, for fuck's sake," he cursed to himself. "I touched it. So why couldn't I keep it?"

The Sage thought for a moment. "Yet you knew you would not keep it, did you not?" Landis nodded weakly. "You knew you would lose it. That is the way. What you experienced last night was a taste. If a man is addicted to heroin, for example, he will always want more of it because he wants back badly the first hit again. If I was to give him a spoon dipped in it, he would lick it gratefully. And that is what you did last night. You licked that spoon."

"I don't understand."

"You tasted the Tao. It was like a drug to you, and like all drugs, its effect came and went. No drug experience is permanent. And the desire to relive that experience is what makes a man an addict. He wants it back. He feels he has been deprived of a great thing. He suffers from its loss. Analogy ends. The Tao is not a drug. It can be experienced through powerful drugs. Yet a man who relies on powerful drugs to touch the Tao will never make it permanent. He will only get a taster. And what is permanency? Is it something we can keep?

"The boy I mentioned the last time we spoke, he who went chasing after the butterfly, he was an addict. Only addicts chase after fleeting things as he did. He catches them, ruins them, and moves onto another one and does the same thing, always chasing, skipping from one desire to another, restless and disappointed and never gaining what he really wants. The other one, he who held out his hand and waited patiently, he had a treasure there in the palm of his hand greater than the whole world. The butterfly stayed there, and the boy was enriched. He was not an addict. He did not chase after fleeting things. He stayed still. He stopped thinking. He became one with nature. Then the butterfly came to him, landed on his hand and he could see it up close, the beautiful colours of its wings, and he was so still himself, he became the butterfly like the emperor who dreamed of being a butterfly and, when waking up the next morning, he could not remember whether he was an emperor or a butterfly."

"And this butterfly in your story represents the Tao?"

"Maybe. You ask for your mind needs something to grasp. It needs to hold on to something. It maybe the Tao. It may not be the Tao. Yet what you experienced last night was exactly the same. When all desire had left you,

when you wanted nothing, you entered the silence. You were stilled. Then it came to you. You understood. You realised the Tao. It departed. You lost it. That too is the Tao. It is a gradual thing. It comes, it goes. To attain, to make it stay is not always possible. It requires years of patience."

"Then it is hard!" Landis blurted.

"No, I say to you again, it is not hard. It is us who makes it hard. We make it hard for ourselves. We do not trust ourselves. We do not rely on our own intuition. We are at war with ourselves, always fighting for things we want and cannot have. We demand nature should work in a certain way. We have our hypothesis and we are determined to make the facts fit it like hammering a square peg into a round hole. We make it hard, when really it is simple. And like the Tao we have to be simple too. We have to go the other way and relearn for it is us that is out of keeping with nature. It is us that is mistaken. It is us that makes it hard. It is us that is wrong, not nature, not Tao, not anything."

Landis shook his head in disbelief. "And what I am doing, is that wrong?"

The Sage paused. "I understand what you are doing. It is not for me to judge, to commend or condemn. All I say is, you are not prepared. You are helping it, assisting it, but you do not have the full capacity to handle it and it will damage you. Your efforts are praiseworthy and so is your attitude. You are even prepared to die for it, but I say you don't have to. And I have shown you the way."

"But what about your son?" he gasped. "That's what gets me. Why me? Why not him? Explain."

The Sage looked earnestly at his disciple. A sheen came over his eyes. "I remember when my son was born. I had a dream. I dreamt of twenty three horses roaming across the land. They kicked up dust. They thundered through the heavens. They stampeded the earth. They were stallions, wild, untameable. No man could catch them. And they were beautiful creatures, so strong and virile my heart leapt with joy every time they managed to free themselves from their intended captors as they tried to lasso them. I clapped like a child and watched them all escape and I was pleased when they all scattered abroad. They galloped towards the mountains and disappeared. I was so proud."

Landis looked at him. He had never seen it before, but he could swear he saw a tear roll out of the old man's eye as sure as he was the Sage. "And Chan died at the age of twenty-three." The Sage nodded. "Then you knew he was going to die? That he would never survive beyond that age?"

"No. Much greater than that. I knew my son was wild and uncontrollable like those horses. I knew that whatever I said he would always be like them. He was their spirit, and that spirit moved in them and he was them."

"What about me? I'm not your son. I don't deserve this."

"No, you are not my son. When my son first brought you here, I looked at you. You already had it written in you."

"What do you mean? His replacement, is that it?"

"No. You had more than him. You had this look in your eye. It told me you were destined for greater things which would lead you on your path."

"Like I say, old man, your Way is not my way."

"Yet you fight against it."

"No, I'm not fighting against it. I know what I'm doing. Your son and I, we had good times together. We … we were made for each other. But all that is gone now. There is nothing left to be salvaged."

"Exactly. In my country if we lower a pail down a well and it comes up empty, we do not cry in the hope our tears will fill it. We move on and dig another well. You too must move on now."

"And you? What are you going to do? Just sit there and accept it as usual?"

The Sage didn't answer. He reached for his pipe and lit it up as he always did and held it firmly in his mouth. It was Landis' signal to leave.

Landis struggled to his feet. He winced with pain as he hoisted himself up with great difficulty. The room began to spin. Landis wavered all over the place. He looked like he was going to topple over. Even the Sage looked concerned as he watched him.

"Don't worry, old man. I can take care of myself. I know what I'm doing. I'll be on my way now. Crome will sort me out with some of that magical medicine of his and repair this terrible thing I've done to myself. And tomorrow I'll be as right as rain. You'll see, as right as rain. He'll have me howling and laughing like it's New Year's Eve."

He gripped his crotch to staunch the still flowing blood. The pool of blood beneath his feet took him by surprise. It was so large he was astounded he still had some left in him, and enough energy to stand. He took one final look at the Sage. His eyes were unfocused, not resting on him or anything.

"Your son was better than me," he told him and left.

He staggered out of the room, not expecting to hear the Sage bidding farewell, *au revoir, arrivederci, sayonara*, or whatever it was they said in their language. He stumbled out of the tin shack like a brawler from a bar after a fight covered in blood, and groped his way back up the same alley he had come, stopping occasionally when the world spun, once or twice falling down like he had rabies or some debilitating disease, his legs hardly co-ordinating with the rest of him. But when he fell he still had the strength to get up and continue. Everything became blurred, his vision distorted, and he bumped into the side of the shacks and had to grapple to find his way. Slowly he made progress and relied on his own inner momentum to get him all the way out of this godforsaken place. But soon he realised he had lost his way. He must have gone in the wrong direction because none of it was familiar. He didn't recognise any of it. And then he was seized by this mad realisation he was back in exactly the same situation, not knowing where the hell he was or where he was going. He gritted his teeth real hard and fought against the pain coming from his crotch every time he moved. He yelped and clambered against the sides, the world see-sawing like he was on some rocky ride, a ship lost out at sea. It was all chaos and everything was getting swept away. Or so it seemed. Of course, it wasn't moving. Nothing was moving. It was all stable. It was just his mind. It didn't feel right at all.

He stopped to take a breather. Really, he didn't give a fuck where he was going or if he made it or not, but something inside him forced him on as it had done earlier, and he knew if he stopped for too long he would never make it. He would surely die then. And this wasn't the best place to die. There was no hospitals here, no clinics, not even any decent sanitation. This was hell. Eternal damnation. He wanted out of it.

He forced himself on with only one thing on his mind, getting back to the Centre. And if and when he got there he would tell Crome everything. Crome would understand for he knew what he was all about. He knew all about his reckless ways. The man understood him. He was his pal, his old buddy, his teacher, friend, confidant, and he would help him, heal him, put him to rights so he could get on and do what had to be done. His will told him that. So he had better keep moving.

He laughed as he struggled up an alley, a real loud laugh and he was laughing all the way like a madman. He didn't stop because he knew laughter was good for you. He read it somewhere, no doubt in a comic, so he carried on as he could feel all this blood draining out of him as if he was really dying and he had a terrible, foreboding fear of thinking he would never make it back. Only the strong survive, he told himself, and staggered on in a crazy zigzag line looking like he was drunk when all this alcohol must have flowed out of him by now, and he was this wild specimen, this thing the whales had thrown up because they too couldn't see any good in it and had vomited it forth like Jonah from the gut of his whale, and he was regurgitated thereby.

No, he told himself, No, I must stop using that fucking word. It was a stupid habit he picked up from Crome whenever he used to say, 'Thereby hangs a tale,' and it kind of brushed off on him and he wanted to hit the man for he was a cunt and if it wasn't for him he wouldn't be in this fucking mess, stumbling round in the dark like this, not knowing where the fuck he was going, not even sure of anything anymore.

He fell to the ground as he stumbled over another peasant who had decided to make his bed in the middle of the thoroughfare. He staggered to his feet, turned round and gave the fucker a goddamned kicking until the little critter was yelping. Landis watched the wastrel scamper away and laughed like this was his territory, as if he owned it. Well it was his. It was all his now and they'd see tomorrow or this morning or whenever it was and he'd prove them right. He'd prove the Sage right too and laughed again and found it real hard to stop laughing and couldn't control it because it seemed to come out all by itself, just thundering out of his mouth like he was high on some drug and all of this world was fucking crazy, but he couldn't go on like this and he was only halfway in this jungle of tin and iron, and hadn't the fucking faintest where he was going, just going, going wherever this force inside him was taking him, going with the flow, baby, going with the flow, keep going, all the way baby, take me in whole, all the way, baby. Yeah, you can do it, he told her and pressed her hard against the side. Yeah, you know you can, so come on baby, take me into that little delicious cunt-mouth of

yours, open up wide, he implored her, open up wide for me baby, get a feel of my stainless steel, and I'll make you happy—baby!

And he went to shove it deep down into the back of her throat and found it wasn't there anymore. When he looked at her again she wasn't there either. All he could see was bloodstains on the tin wall where he thought she was.

"Shit me!" he exclaimed as he realised he had been rambling to himself good and proper like some old hillbilly who had been on the mountains for too long and wouldn't recognise a good old face if he saw one. And he was still rambling unto himself in a flurry of a fury that he didn't even realise he was salivating all over his mouth and it was dripping down his chin making him look like one of them funny dogs who ain't got no scruples in themselves to swallow and was leaving these trails behind like a snail's and it was oh so untidy he couldn't even imagine how a man of his calibre—one who is upright, upstanding, up anything!—could have fallen into such a state of decrepitude and that it really wasn't him but some other fucker, this animal of a doppelganger who thought he would borrow his personality for awhile. Well, fuck you, buddy, he told him. I'm my own man, see. I got a job to do tomorrow. So don't you stand in my way now. Do you hear?

This is your grandma talking to you, you little shit. Do you hear me? (The words echoed in his mind, and seemed to come from all directions. They made him stand still and look up at the sky.) This is your grandma, and don't you treat me like shit. Why, when I was your age I was as good as gold. I used to be such a clean, fine woman that all the men at the dancing ball would be begging to take my hand. And then you came along and I don't know what the fuck I did wrong. I could have sworn I married the right guy and God blow me to cinders, nay, blow me to ashes, ashes to ashes, dust to dust. Do you hear me boy? Do you hear what I'm saying? This is your grandma speaking to you, so why the fuck won't you reply? I hate you, you little shit. You was always a scumbag. I told your father that. He never believed me. He always used to say, 'My boy is a good boy.' What a fucking load of shit! Your father is blind. Do you hear me? BLIND. I always said his little runt had a chip on his shoulder. 'Nay, mom, nay.' And that was all I got. But I knew you better. I knew you before you was even born. I knew you was always a sinner, ever since you used to strap those boys up to a tree and start shooting at them with that little pellet gun of yours, and then I knew what you was. You was a little piece of shit which crawled out of your mother's arsehole and she thought at the time she was having a baby. Well, I swear at the time you came out the wrong hole, for no way was you a baby. A baby? I ask myself. A baby? Well stuff me a flagpole and impale my guts but since when has a baby ever savaged its pet

dog at the age of three and practically eaten the fucking thing? I knew then something was wrong. I knew you was shit. And you tried to pretend, didn't you? You tried to pretend always that you was the little intellectual one. Daddy's boy, mommy's boy. How cute and how humiliating to be tied to a savage little brat like you. A cunt-person who never did anything wrong, who never was bad, who never made a mistake. Well, listen to me you little prick, you are wrong. That is, W.R.O.N.G. D'ya get me? Wrong, brother. Why, I ought to use you as toilet paper and wipe you against my ass. Yes, but perfect little boy would probably enjoy that, wouldn't perfect little boy? Hey? You listening to me, you little shit, or are you going to pretend? The perfect little boy, mommy, is in pain. 'I am bleeding, mommy.' The perfect little boy will say. Won't he? Because the perfect little boy who likes cutting up mice and rats and insects and little poor cuddly animals is a fucking bastard! Yes, that's right. Did I hurt you? Oh, I am sorry. I didn't mean to hurt you. Here, let me wipe your brow. Let me wipe away your pain. Let me wipe away your brain.

"FUCK OFF!!!"

His scream echoed all around him, coming back to him in thudding waves. He scrabbled to his feet, seriously insane, and came back out into the night. The night was for him. The night is all mine, he wanted to cry aloud. And it would always be. No one could take it away from him. It was his only, and his grandma's voice receded into the thick of it. He wiped it away like the shit paper that she was and was high again as he saw her pinioned body tied to a post, desiccating to desuetude, all finished up and hanging there with a spike going all the way through her, sacredly impaled. He was triumphing, laughing now at her ghost. He had the upper hand.

He remembered stealing into the night, finding her crypt and desecrating her body—for purely religious reasons, you understand—and had his wicked way with her and came up right inside her and was wondering why she wasn't moaning like the rampant bitch she was. He brought away that pubic hair of hers, all dry, matted and grey, rotting away in all of its fetid glory like he was holding proudly in his teenage hands some mascot like the scalp of the Indians at war just as he had seen in the *National Geographic*. The only thing was, he reckoned, they got the wrong end. The soul does not leave the body through the cranial suture or head at all, but through the other end of the body. And this he told himself when he was nothing but a mere whippersnapper and when he had a prime eye for anything that was dead or supposed to be dead like when his father showed him that little dog of his neighbour's which just happened to walk out into the middle of the road, and guess what? Yes, you are right, brother; the fucking thing got run

over and all of its blood was spilling out all over the place and he had never seen such a prettier sight, like it was an oil leak and some local farmer had been drilling for oil, and that turd of a dog just happened to be lying over it at the time and all Hail Mary broke loose and it was hallelujah all over the place, brother, I swear, and you ain't seen fuck all like it, man, because it needs to be seen to be understood, and I'm telling you, bro', that the thing in there, why, it was like strawberry jam all over the place as it spilt its guts, why, I had to just give it a kick to put it out of its misery. Yes sir, kicked it good, to stop the neighbours from hollering, you understand, and make it all quiet in that commotion that was going on and my little brother was none too pleased so I had to kick him too and put him out of his misery. I never meant to kick him that hard, I swear, and how did I know he was going to go into a coma and die on me, but it was a glorious day and a hard day was had by all, I tell ya, a real hard day and so much work to do and so little time to do it in, and grandma was lying there all sullen.

Landis stopped in his tracks. Another voice was coming through …

He talked to her, by gad, he talked to her, till she wouldn't listen, you understand, not realising she was gone from this world. I mean, yes okay, she had always been quiet, she never opening her mouth unless she had to, and he was always asking her things like, 'What happens to the darkness when you turn the light on, grandma?' and she would say it was her power, her will to banish the darkness, and it was a magical act. Well, that kind of got him interested, and he used to sucker up to her like she was some ancient queen riding out high on some bark on some flowing river like the Amazon or something, and he used to imagine there were all these rowers streaming her along and she was the one whom all the crowd were beseeching. Well, I do believe my eye, he was right, for she taught him everything, all he needed to know and he was already practising by the time he was eleven, raking in all this knowledge like so much fodder to the brain, lapping it up, I tell ya, like a cat to milk, all thirsty for knowledge like he could never be satiated and even used to watch his ma and pa in bed when they were getting kinda carried away and he was wondering all the while where he came from. Of course, you understand, his mother was a prim and proper woman, not being from this part of the world, and me being the woman of the house, cleaning, ironing and cooking, and a different colour of skin from his, why, he used to watch me getting undressed and was trying to work out the differences between us like it was some kinda game and there was always that look in his eye which made me feel suspicious. You know what? I caught him once peeking through the door of his sister's bedroom. Yes I did. I swear it on Mary, I saw him, and his was as rigid as a pole as he just stood there watching his sister getting undressed and he

could see every side of her body as she was right there in front of a mirror. Oh, Lord, I didn't know what to say. He was like a different child then, all quiet with no friends. Why, he used to play by himself all day and I swear I could hear him talking to someone who wasn't there, even had a name for him, Bod, or something like that, and he had this deep fascination for unseen things like he used to tell us there was a creature on our shoulder and he would point at it and we would all laugh because that was the only way we could deal with it, you understand, and we is mighty proud people and we ain't gonna let some critter like him down. Okay, he got too emotionally involved, I can understand it. I can understand a curious and evolving mind like his want to understand things, but when he came back that night with what we thought he had in his hand, that poor little cat, we could have all died and he ... he had ... he had ... VIOLATED IT! ... and we, we were lost for words, and his pretty and angelic face was so benign looking, why, I couldn't understand why they'd want to lock up a sweet little child like him. I know he made a mistake and was kinda confused about what all the other kids at school meant when they kept talking about pussy, but I felt real sorry for him. He was always making us laugh, used to come down to our quarters at the end of the garden, we just had to accept him for the way he was. He was always into the dark side of things....

He came out of it from where he had fallen and gripped anything to hand, anything which could get him up and moving. He was stumbling around like some geriatric, blind with it as well, and still didn't know where the fuck he was going. All he knew was, he had to keep going, and he was groaning all the time as he was walking, seeing this stream pouring out from between his legs like some menstruous woman, like it wouldn't stop and the flow was heavy. And he was desperate now, clinging and crawling his way along, hauling his weak body through the night. It was thick and vast and he was wandering insanely in its underbelly, a toad, hopping along, not even sure if he was heading in the right direction.

He fell and spiralled to the ground and lay there like a drunk in the street, all gurgling and making obscene noises like he didn't give a fuck anymore and it was all so unusual as he was getting into this new state of mind and was even prating to himself things he didn't understand.

In the night it comes and we dance like mad children in bright morning sunlight with specks overhead my mind spinning rapidly out of the frame and the ground keeps tossing itself up trying to get a hold of things ... slipping sliding falling away ... fragments whirling ... my vision ... out of focus ... everything seems darker than before ... I ... am not ... sure ... what is happening to me ... could be a dis-ease ... I ... think there is something

terrible about to happen ... I uh ... I ... can't stand it anymore ... won't someone help me? ... a feeling ... pain ... now in my chest ... it is thudding ... I think ... I think ... I ... am ... going ... to ... to .... die.

It hit him right in the centre of his chest like a thunderbolt from heaven, only it didn't come from heaven; it came from deep within him and was making a thudding sound louder than the beating of his heart. And it wasn't his heart either. He knew it wasn't. It was the centre of his being and it was making his mind capsize. And he was still convinced he was going to die because he had never heard it before and especially not loud like this. So he fought against it, grappling with some railing or anything to grip and latch onto as his ship was going down. The road was wavering all over the place, tossing up and down, and he was struggling real hard trying to deal with it, knowing the distortion was coming from deep within him, fucking everything up, throwing everything into waves as his mind was slowly falling apart.

"P L E A S E H E L P M E, P L E A S E!"

He screamed the words out into the dissolving empty night, to all the deaf ears as he lay there watching his mind shift into a new gear that was beyond all he could possibly conceive of, for it was now right there in front of him and he could see it as clear as the sun, a big bright point of light sending out halos of itself in all directions, luminous and radiant, pulling him in as if he was attached to the end of a rope, hauling him in like a beached whale being dragged back into the sea, as it came closer and was getting brighter and brighter, so bright it hurt his eyes. It was like a million suns assembled together forming one sun, its light flooding his mind, and his mind was not fixed in any place, but rather it seemed to be everywhere and it was caving in on itself like it was going down in a funnel, pouring towards this luminous light at the end, a long, dark spiralling tunnel, and he was going down it fast and it was going to swallow him good and proper.

"I DON'T WANT TO FUCKING DIE, PLEASE!"

And his words were just endlessly repeating themselves like he was babbling as his body was hitting the shakes. And he was trembling all over as if he was an epileptic or suffering from the DT's and he could hardly breathe.

"MY GOD, MY GOD, WHY HAST THOU FORSAKEN ME?" he cried out aloud.

And his god came up before him, vast and powerful, and as he rose up his black, shiny body blocked out the point of light. It disappeared and he could see nothing but his god, its eyes penetrating directly into his, and he smiled a glorious smile for he had never seen it so clear, so close as now. And it was a beautiful sight to behold. He cried tears of joy and he was redeemed thereby, filling his heart with love, elevating him, pulling him up, raising him to the regal and standing him back on his feet like he had been renewed, transformed thereby, feeling neither weak nor weary, but with a new vigour in his sails and he was moving again, gliding by, not through his own volition, you understand, but as if his god was blowing the very winds of time into his sails, sending him along. And he could feel his thoughts coming back to him, filling his mind with splendiferous words, singing to himself, ranting away like he was healed, HEALED, man, truly healed, rejuvenated thereby. And he was never, ever going to slip between the worlds again, for, man, that was dangerous, too goddamned dangerous, man, so he had to keep thinking, getting thoughts whizzing round his brain to evade the silence, otherwise he'd be going down that road again.

His god pushed him along, then retreated back into the blackness. He was gone now, leaving him to go merrily on his way. And now he knew what he was doing. He had a job to do, like the good man he was, and he had to do it. A good man has to earn a living now, don't he? He has to earn a living and soon he'd be doing it and it would all be accomplished, very soon. And then he thought of all the work he had done so far and if he didn't attend it would all be wasted and all his efforts would have been in vain. And he had died, been there, out on the edge, right out there on the edge, and had come back into the world, reborn, anew, afresh, a child, a child of the stars, a starchild. And he was noticing those foreboding gaps now coming into his mind, those gaps which let death through, so he struggled harder to think, to get more thoughts filling his brain. Got to keep thinking, come on, keep thinking, don't stop thinking, whatever you do, don't stop thinking.

Son? (His father's voice came through clear and sober.) Do you remember when you were very young and we used to talk to each other without even opening our mouths?—Yes—And you lost it when you grew up, when you got older?—Yes—And I told you there were ways of getting it back?—Yes—And I showed you all the books I used to read when I was your age?—Yes—And I told you there were only two things in life which constitute a man's problems and they both began with W?—Yes—And that they are Women and Work?—Yes—And I told you once you solved one problem the other would sort itself out?—Yes—Then what are you doing, son? Get to! You've got a job to do, son. So bloody well stop arguing with yourself and get on with it!

He looked out of his head and saw lying before him the road which would take him back to the Centre and out of this shit-hole of a town just like it had done yesterday, and, like yesterday, he felt he had been through everything, all compacted in a very short space of time, and somehow he had miraculously survived. He had passed through all the trials, all the ordeals, all the lessons, gloriously, and it was all part of the Tao, man, wasn't it? It was all part of the Tao, and he was now following the Tao, living in harmony with the heavens above and the earth below and feeling like a new man, looking at the world with new eyes, thinking with a new head, and his preoccupation with the state of his dress just slipped into the back seat, for there were better things to think about. There was a new dawn rising and he was on his way—The Way—strolling along, whistling to himself like he was alive, man, ALIVE, and feeling real good inside. And he was intoxicated thereby.

THE MESSIAH

'The original type of the Saviour was based on the mummy (*karast*), for this was the primal transformer in the waters of space that resurrected not in the flesh but in spirit, the *sahu* that was anointed with the oil as symbolic of the living water of fire, or *Sa*, which redeemed spirit from flesh so one then became an *Akh*, a Light One, a being of light purified by its application, the anointed one that gave rise to the doctrine of resurrection or re-erection as the oil was used to stimulate "back to life" the phallus as indicative of the return to body-consciousness. It was this doctrine the Hebrews, and later the Christians, perverted carnally in their ignorance and mistook the notion of the re-arisen one as theological when it was originally physiological.'

Kelly Grantham,
Cults of the Khart

—24—
THE RETURN

I enter a room of impossible symmetry, circular stairs and curving walls. They spiral upwards towards a cupola with an opening looking out on to the night sky beyond. There are no stars. The room is in a tall tower, high up with a black and white floor. Everything is either black or white. I walk towards the centre of the room approaching something which looks like an open window. It is a round hole which appears to be carved out of a wall of ice. It extends from the floor to the ceiling, large enough for a man to walk through. I stop and look out beyond it. I can see nothing but this black expanse of space with a bottomless abyss below. I become aware I am naked. Also, I am neither awake nor sleeping. I stand for eternity alone, lost in the void I survey. I feel the wind of fear. It has made my blood run cold. Two figures appear. They come towards me, both dressed in robes with hoods covering their faces. One of them is wearing a black robe, the other a white one. They do not speak but stand either side of me. The one in black stands to my left, the other to my right. The one in white gesticulates and raises his hand high up in the air. He is pointing. I look up and see a bright star has appeared in the sky. It is directly above us, very far off. The white robe lowers his hand and stands still. He faces me. There is a certain uneasiness coming from my left side. The one in black indicates. He wants me to look where he is now pointing, out of the window towards the void. I am suddenly full of fright, and have the same feeling of someone about to defenestrate themselves. My blood runs colder. He lowers his hand and faces me. It seems I have a choice to make. There is this subtle complicity between all three of us, an unsigned agreement. They back off and

disappear, leaving me. Then there is a flash, a faint memory. I remember seeing a large ornate gold ring on the index finger of one of them. I cannot remember which one. The void before me beckons me on. The one star in sight too beckons me on. There is a vying for my soul. I am being pulled apart, yanked in both directions simultaneously. I vacillate, uncertain of which route to take. They are both equally daunting. Then there is a sudden rush. I am seized with giddiness, a sense of vertigo. I am forced on, impelled by this invisible force towards the window. I try to scream and yell out. My voice does not come, and I am thrown out. I plunge downwards, my arms raised like wings, but I am not flying. I do a backwards somersault as I fall. I am falling very fast into the depths.

* * * * *

He woke up, gasped and clutched the sheets. It took him a second or two to realise he was awake, that he was in bed, that it had been a dream of sorts, too real to be classified as an ordinary dream, and he wasn't falling. But his heart was still pounding. He was sweating profusely as he lay there, the powerful imagery still revolving in his mind. The two robed figures. The window. The fear he felt before he fell. And the falling itself, not even sure for how long he had been falling, only certain he hadn't reached the bottom. For there was no bottom in that dark and formidable space, just this interminable falling.

He tried closing his eyes, praying for a few minutes of quiet to ease his mind, a pleasant reverie or fantasy, anything. But no, nothing would come. Only the dream. Why had he chosen the void? It had chosen him! It had already been decided by some unseen higher power. He therefore had little choice in the matter. He was meant to take the void, to leap into it and embrace it, to become one with it. Then it had to be the Negative, that space he wished to eschew. And it was quite obvious it could be eschewed no longer. Then he would have to pursue it, to take it all the way, to make it his next step. He had already crossed his Rubicon on a higher plane, and now he had to do it physically, consciously. He would do so soon. All he wanted was a few more peaceful moments, to lie next to Katie, to feel her fresh reassuring flesh against his skin.

He rolled over to her side of the bed to cuddle up next to her. He groped empty space. He opened his eyes to see she was no longer there. He sat up to see if any of her clothes were still lying on the floor. No, she had definitely gone. Then he noticed a small note on the side with his name

written in capital letters. He had quite forgotten it was Friday which meant she had not only left him, she had left LA and gone home.

He picked up the handwritten note and read it through bleary eyes.

> Dear Harmon,
>
> Sorry I didn't wake you. I thought it would be better this way, to just leave as I hate to say goodbye.
>
> You have been a little treasure to me, so kind and you were right. I did enjoy myself, but now I have to go. I only hope we'll meet again some time, perhaps in a different place and then we can do it all again. It's a small world, and who knows, it might happen. I think it will, and I hope you have faith in it too. Until then, I will miss you.
>
> Good luck with your mission. I will remember you always.
>
> Yours,
> Katie
> xxx
>
> (Kissy kissy, bang bang!)

Capri laughed at the last words, not even sure whether he was bothered about her being gone or whether he really wanted to see her again.

"Ah, well. The Lord giveth and the Lord taketh away," he recited and threw the note to the floor and snoozed for a bit longer before realising that if she had gone then it must be late. He checked his watch. It was.

"Shit!" he exclaimed and jumped out of bed and rushed to the bathroom for a quick shower.

A few minutes later all vestiges of the dream had gone, washed away, and he was feeling better. He strolled back into the room working out what his plans were for the day. Mosalla's temple was at the top of his agenda. He didn't know why, but he just he had to go there. He'd head there first thing. He started getting dressed when he noticed there was a light on the televid signalling someone had left him a message. He turned it on to find it was from Carlotta:

```
Harmon,

I'm coming over to LA. I am catching the next shuttle.
Something tells me you are in trouble. As I assume you
will be leaving before I arrive, meet me at the temple
around 12. Pack your bags and leave.

Carlotta
P.S. I have already paid your bill.
```

Capri was filled with rage. What the fuck was she doing? Why couldn't she just leave him to it and mind her own business? And why did he have to leave? He wanted to confound her along with all these other women who insisted on telling him what to do, interfering with his life. He kicked the bed hard and switched the televid off. Fuming, he finished getting dressed and grabbed his belongings, including the books, and marched out of his room like a man possessed, slamming the door behind him, bounding towards the elevator.

By the time he was in his car and out on the Strip he had cooled down, and was thinking more clearly now. It seemed he had no control over his life. Everything had been decided in advance. They, whoever they were, were pushing him along, controlling his actions, and manipulating every event in his life. He fucking hated it and pressed the accelerator right down on the floor, flying south down the 101. It was, thankfully, fairly empty. Good. That meant he would get to Long Beach, according to Cindy, at around 11.00, well before Carlotta could turn up and stick her oar in. Why couldn't she just stay back at New York? Didn't she realise he was on a mission, that he had a date with destiny? Wasn't that what it was all about? Something very important was about to happen. The dream told him that. The divination told him that. Everything told him that. It was all slowly connecting up. His inexorable jigsaw puzzle was finally cohering, its jumbled mass purposely slotting into place piece by piece. And soon the picture would be complete, finished at last. Then he would know and understand. It would announce the end of his suffering, an end to indecision, to doubt and uncertainty. His period of darkness would be over. There would be no more mental and physical instability. No more compulsively wandering the streets like an ambulatory ghost as if searching for a key, one which would open the door to peace. Everything would make sense. Then he would be blessed with peace.

But why the temple? Why was he going there? He wasn't sure. All he knew he had to go. He was meant to go there like he was meant to come to LA. Like he was meant to meet Mosalla. Like he was meant to have that

experience in the lab. And everything else in the last couple of days. This was not some stupid fucking mission to find some elusive drug. This was a mission of another nature altogether, his destiny. Or at least that's how it felt. Everything seemed purposeful, loaded with meaning. And it would all make sense when he got to the temple.

He hit the accelerator as he cut a swathe through onto the 5. Cindy was telling him there was an emergency broadcast bulletin. He ignored her. He had more important things on his mind, and was so busy concentrating on the future he didn't even notice all the other cars were going in the opposite direction.

He hit the outskirts of Long Beach early, earlier than expected as there were hardly any cars on the road. In fact, Long Beach looked like it was deserted. There were very few people. What was going on? He passed abandoned cars and people dashing out of their homes, families carrying clothing, belongings, anything of value and bundling into their cars. He slowed down as he entered another street. More of the same; people frantically packing their belongings into cars and driving off in a hurry. Was there a war going on or something?

He pulled up beside a family busily loading up their car. "Hey, what's happening round here?" he shouted at them through his window. They ignored him, too busy to stop. He tooted his horn. The old man ignored him and went back to what he was doing. Capri tried again. "What's going on? Why is everyone leaving?"

Another man stopped packing his trunk. He came over to Capri with a look of irritation in his eyes. "Ain't you heard?"

"Heard what?" Capri replied innocently.

"Jesus!" he bellowed at him. "They've been blaring it out all over town all morning. Don't tell me you ain't heard. The whole coast is being evacuated. They reckon we're gonna be hit by a tidal wave, a big one too, within the next few hours. If I was you, buddy, I wouldn't stick around. You don't want to be here when this thing hits."

The man went back to his car, locked the trunk and piled his family inside. He sped off quick, leaving Capri dumbfounded and confused. A tidal wave? He wanted to laugh out loud. It sounded ridiculous, having just been reading about the bloody things. It had to be a coincidence, and now he

was enraged again. It was not only women interfering with his life it was Nature as well, as if it was determined to prevent him from taking his next step. Well, he was determined more than ever now. Nothing was going to stop him, not even a stupid tidal wave.

He hit the accelerator and sped through the rest of the suburb. It was all the same, practically deserted. The few people left were busy bundling into cars and leaving. He checked the emergency bulletin. The man was right. Due to extraordinary meteorological conditions there was a tidal wave building up in the middle of the Pacific. It was heading this way. And it was moving in fast. Now he couldn't laugh it off. He had a deeper suspicion, one he was afraid to even contemplate. What if Grantham had been right after all?

He didn't bother answering his question. He hit Vermont Drive only to find that not only was it right down by the coast, it was also on a lower level than the rest of the town. How unfortunate could he get? What a fine site Mosalla had chosen for his temple. But then, as he drove down the street, it didn't look right at all. He couldn't imagine a temple being here. Bland old office type buildings either side, about three or four stories, with steps leading up to the main door, all grey and all equally unappealing.

He slowed down at what he hoped was the correct address. The number of the building tallied. It was hardly what he expected. He parked the car and climbed out. He ran up the steps. The building looked empty from outside. He tried the door. It was locked. He got out his skeleton keys, checked no one was watching—there wasn't a soul in sight—and twiddled the lock. It clicked. He was inside, closing the door gently behind him. The dim hallway was equally bland, musty with old flowery wallpaper which went out of style decades ago, peeling off the walls in places. He tried one of the doors. It creaked open, an empty old office, everything coated in dust, the windows all begrimed. He tried another door, the back office, and met the same sight, tables and chairs covered in dust, sun marks on the walls where pictures once hung. He tried turning on the light. No electricity. No life, nothing. He hit the stairs. They creaked like old wood, moaning with age. The first floor was exactly the same, empty offices, disused for years.

He tried the next floor. Same thing again, except the back room was a kitchen. It was filthy. He checked the window looking out on to the back. He wiped it clean to see a backyard overgrown with weeds, a narrow path leading out on to the drive at the back. That got him thinking. Perhaps he was going in the wrong direction. Perhaps he should have gone down instead of up. These old buildings had big basements. There was no more

perfect a site for a temple than down below. But the only problem was, he hadn't seen an entrance to the basement on the ground floor.

He retraced his steps. He was right. Perhaps it could only be accessed from outside. That didn't seem right. Knowing Mosalla he would have some special entrance for it just like his cubby hole in the library. Capri searched the rooms again, and as he was searching, he could now understand why Mosalla had chosen Long Beach for his temple. Although part of the town was being redeveloped, this street was replete with old buildings, very old, probably pre-war and therefore possibly listed. They would never get converted or pulled down. What better location could you choose, especially if you were going to spend megabucks on rocks to furnish it? But where was it? It must be here somewhere. He went back to the hallway, certain there had to be a secret door. Perhaps behind the stairs? No, it was a solid wall. Then he examined closely the wooden panelling by the stairs, the way the balustrades supporting the rails came down and connected with the floor with three sets of panels in-between. One of them had to be a door. And they were all wide enough to let a man pass through with ease.

He looked for a latch or a touch-sensitive stud, anything to open one of them. He tapped the panel on the left. It was solid. He tapped the middle one. It sounded hollow and gave slightly. The one on the right was solid. He whipped out his ID card and ran it up and down the gap between the panels, first on the left side, nothing, then on the right until about halfway down it struck something. He eased the card in deeper and pressed it harder. There was a sound like a latch opening. Next, the panel flipped out. He found what he was looking for. Delighted, he pulled it open all the way.

He was now standing before a dark passageway, a set of narrow steps going all the way to the bottom into the blackness. As in his dream, he was suddenly overcome with the same feeling of foreboding. Only this time he physically felt the wind of fear turn his blood cold. This was it. This was the deciding moment.

He pulled out his flashlight and switched it on. He pointed it down the stairs. Not only were they narrow, they were pretty steep too, and had to descend a good fifty feet all the way to the temple below. He was just about to take his first tentative step when he felt someone tap him on the shoulder. He whizzed round expecting to see Carlotta standing there only to confront empty space. And like the man in the cafeteria, he too felt stupid. He was certain he felt something. Or was it his imagination?

He shrugged it off and continued, taking each step carefully. The wooden stairs let out an eerie squeal as he descended. A few more steps and he could smell it, a pungent, overwhelming fragrance. It wafted past him and out the door. As he descended further the smell became stronger, like freshly burnt incense. He was right. The temple was still being used, and somebody was performing a ritual.

Instinctively, he whipped out his Preston, and took each step diligently trying very hard not to make a sound. Whoever was using the temple were in for a big surprise; he'd walk straight in there and catch them off guard. They were probably Mosalla's killers. They had to be. It made perfect sense.

Now full of a curious mixture of fear and anticipation, Capri descended very slowly. He paused halfway down when he heard a voice emanating from the bowels of the earth. It was making a chanting sound and only confirmed his suspicion. He resumed his descent. The voice became louder, more distinguishable. It was the voice of a female, sonorous, in a language he was unfamiliar with. She was getting louder as if reaching a crescendo. Now Capri had only two or three more steps to take. He flashed his torch at the ground; all damp concrete. There was a low arched ceiling of brickwork leading to a set of curtains at the end. As he stepped towards the closed curtains there was a distinct impression of cloyingness as in the lab. It was exactly the same, and now he was really on edge.

He was about to open the curtain slightly to take a peak when the voice stopped. Had they heard him, or was it just a coincidence? He froze on the spot. He hesitated, even thought about running all the way back up before he could be detected. Relieved, he heard the voice come back with a new chant, a dithyramb of some description, again in a foreign tongue.

He listened to this woman's voice and wondered who it could possibly be. The very words she was using were being forced out, expelled from her throat with such volatile force that it was powerful enough to waken the dead, each word being stretched out, the syllables being emphatically pronounced, then trailing off with a sibilant hiss. And in his now treacherous state of mind he was seized with another uncomfortable notion. It jarred him painfully. Was it her? He couldn't even bring himself to mention her name, but the voice was strikingly similar. Her utterance stopped again as he was about to pull the curtain aside and pry. Again he froze and hung back. He waited.

The voice came back again. He pulled the curtains apart a fraction, his breath on hold, his finger pressed tight against the trigger of his gun. Bright candlelight hit his eyes, a soft glare danced across his face. In the soft glow of the candles he could see a figure standing directly in front of him wearing a black robe and, as in his dream, it was hooded, its voluminous material covering the brow and the rest of the face hidden in shadow. She was doing the spell, coming almost up towards him as she drew some figure in the air with her outstretched finger. He wasn't able to see anything beyond her for she blocked his view, but he reckoned there were more of them, possibly one or two, and waited for her to finish and move on.

She stopped. She stood still with her arms down by her sides as if surveying what she had drawn in the air. She then turned round, her back now towards Capri, and again stood still. Was she now indicating to the rest of them she had finished? Whatever she was doing he was still unable to see much, only a brief hint of black walls and floor, and as he suspected they were shiny, highly polished just like Jack's temple.

He watched her walk to the other side. As she did so more of the temple was revealed. It was massive, spacious, far bigger than he initially assumed. It was so big it was almost impossible to imagine the temple being just under one building; it must be under the whole block of offices. Perhaps Mosalla owned the entire street. The ceiling seemed incredibly high, the columns in the corners were remarkably tall, and the floor was as long as a football pitch. So betaken by its astounding architecture Capri hadn't even noticed the row of figures were now all lined up and facing him.

"Why don't you come in?" a man's voice bellowed.

Capri flinched and slinked back. They couldn't have possibly seen him.

"We know you are there," the voice came back. It was an English accent, almost Etonian in its pronunciation. "We've been expecting you," he said.

At first he didn't believe his ears. What did the man mean? How could they have known he was coming here? What if it was her and he had been set up all along? These questions raced madly through his brain. They only made him more confused and panicky. He gripped his gun tighter.

"Well? Are you going to stand there all day?"

Capri hesitated. He wanted to take them by surprise. Somehow they knew he was coming. But how?

"Why don't you come in, Mr Capri?"

He flinched when he heard his name. There was only person who knew he would be coming here today. She had set him up. He couldn't believe it.

He poked his gun through the curtains and edged his way in. They were standing there like statues, all six of them, and all wearing the same long black robes, their faces obscured by voluminous hoods.

"Ah, there you are." The voice spoke authoritatively. "You're earlier than we expected. Do forgive us for not being properly prepared."

His mind was numb. Who were these people? And prepared for what?

He moved in cautiously, his gun aimed directly at them, wavering across the line of figures, he on edge and poised to shoot at the slightest provocation. "You've been expecting me?" he asked meekly.

"Indeed we have. And may I say what a pleasure it is at last to finally meet you." The voice was patronising and condescending.

"What do you mean?" Capri stopped in his tracks. "I don't know you."

"Oh, but you do, old chap. Or should I say in one way or another." The man stopped and gestured to Capri's gun. "I assure you," he continued, "the gun isn't necessary. We mean you no harm."

Capri wanted to snarl. The man's voice was mocking him. It only made him grip his gun more firmly and point it at the one in the middle who was talking and obviously the leader.

"If you don't mind," Capri gibed, "I'd rather keep hold of it."

"As you wish, if it makes you feel better. But I'd rather you didn't point it at me or any of us, for that matter."

"Who are you?" he demanded impatiently.

"I thought I had already said," he replied indignantly.

"That wasn't an answer. Be more specific. Who the fuck are you?" he shouted. He was slowly losing his temper. He scowled at all of them.

"Well, if it's specifics you want, then I suggest you move closer. I have absolutely no intention of shouting. My voice isn't as good as it used to be. Please come closer. We have been waiting a long time for this moment."

Warily, he took a few steps towards them, his eyes darting from one end of the row to the other and then back to the man in the middle. Behind them was some sort of altar upon which tall tapers were burning. The light made the robed figures look like silhouettes. He stopped and shot a quick overall glance at the rest of the temple. The slabs of rock were expertly hewn. They had been slotted into place with such precision it was hard to distinguish where they joined one another. He doubted he could even slip his ID card in between them. It was a miracle of engineering. He was impressed.

"You can come closer than that, old chap."

He took a few more steps until he was right in the centre of the temple. He stopped and scanned them, then flashed his eyes down quickly at this strange design carved into the floor. It was a weird series of interconnecting lines resembling a giant cobweb and he was standing right in the middle of it. The imagery made him feel uncomfortable, like a trapped fly.

"That's better," the man said. "Now I don't have to shout. You want specifics, do you not? You want to know who we are and a host of other things besides as it is quite obvious our identities elude you. I wonder what is going through your mind? Do you suspect that we are your enemies? Or conversely, that we may in some roundabout way be your friends?"

"I don't know who you are. Just tell me. Let me see you."

"As I said before," he responded calmly. "You do know who we are, or at least know of us. Perhaps not directly or personally, but I can certainly say with some conviction, our identities are not entirely unknown to you."

Were they the remnants of Mosalla's old group? Is that what he was hinting at? Had they reformed or something? Capri was losing his patience. Why couldn't the man just tell him?

"Really?" he remarked unimpressed. "I know you, do I? Let me see. Let me hazard a wild guess. As Mosalla is dead, a fact you're aware of no doubt, you must be connected with his old group. Is that it? Am I getting warm?"

"Excellent, Mr Capri. You show promise. Although I should point out you're only slightly warm and half right about the group. But I wonder; can you get any warmer?"

"Perhaps, but I find games of this sort rather puerile. So why don't you just come out with it and tell me who you are exactly."

"Come, come, Mr Capri. You give up too easily. You should learn to be more pertinacious," he said in a mocking voice. It reminded him of what Carlotta said to him in the Grand Gallery that day. It was unnerving.

"You were doing so well," he continued. "Do you not like challenges, the solving of imponderable riddles? Why don't you have another guess? Let me give you a clue. You have heard all about us and now you are finally meeting us. You should be pleased with yourself, that you have followed so assiduously the clues which have led you to us. And here you are. We knew you would be coming here."

"Oh? How?"

"Because it was inevitable, Mr Capri."

"Was it?" The hooded man nodded. "Really? And you've been expecting me?" He nodded again. "That still doesn't explain anything. Now just tell me who the fuck you are and take off those bloody hoods."

"I am surprised. Did you not feel compelled to come here? Indeed you did. You knew you had to come. But I understand your impatience. I am not a patient man myself. Nor do I like being treated like a fool. So I expect you to oblige me and do the same. Now, who would you like to go first? Me perhaps? Or my colleagues?"

The man gestured to the rest of them. As he did so, Capri noticed a large gold ring on his index finger not unlike the one he had seen in his dream. It was uncanny, and something clicked in his mind. Now he remembered which one of the figures it belonged to. The recollection was disconcerting.

If he was right, then she had planned the whole thing in advance, and had to be here, collaborating with her old flame. He was the one doing all the talking. It could only be him, the one with the distinctive English accent and the joke about age; it could only be one man.

"Why don't we start with you," he suggested, pointing his gun at him.

"Very well. If you insist."

The man slowly raised his hands to his hood and started to pull it back. Capri prepared himself, smarmily expecting not to be surprised, but could only gasp. With the hood pulled back it revealed a face which was old and wrinkled, not what he expected at all. Capri could not hide his look of confusion. Indeed he was old, very old, and the overall impression was of a man who had done many things in his time. For the lips were tight and slim verging on purple, the cheeks incredibly withdrawn, the nose long and thin. From another angle it was almost aristocratic. The hair was receding and slicked back to reveal a large forehead that probably housed a large brain. But it was the eyes which disturbed Capri the most. They were cold and grey and penetrated straight through him. His dead eyes looked like windows inviting people to jump through to their deaths. He had to tear his own eyes away for an instant before gazing at this tall man once more. The skin was bloodless, bordering on white, a deathly pallor. Yet the face did not conceal the once handsomeness of his youth. He now looked extremely ravaged by time being an octogenarian at least, and therefore Capri doubted whether it was him at all.

"You're not Crome!" he gushed.

But the man could only laugh and shake his head. "No, I'm not Crome," he replied and smiled wanly. "You're obsessed with the man."

"Then who the fuck are you?"

"Come, come, Mr Capri. Do I really elude you that easily? I thought you were a man of intelligence," he laughed. His colleagues joined in.

"How the fuck should I know who you are?" he slammed, angrily.

"Because I am in your mind," he snapped. The remark hit Capri straight in the face. "Think, Mr Capri. Where have you seen me before?"

"I don't know," he blurted.

"Oh, I am sure you do. Let me give you another clue. How about a set of stairs in a large house, hmm? Does that not help?"

Capri tried to think, his mind racing round. A set of stairs? Where? Then it came to him. Of course, last night, Mosalla's house, the thing he saw.

"Yes, I remember, but I thought it was a hallucination."

"I wouldn't call it that. Why not call it a premonition."

"So what? I thought I saw someone or something at the top of the stairs. It could have been you or anything. That still doesn't tell me who you are."

"I am disappointed. I am convinced you are not trying hard enough. Another clue; you are reading my books."

Capri gasped as it hit home. It couldn't possibly be, could it? He was so shocked he nearly dropped his gun. The others made a move towards him. Quickly, Capri reasserted himself.

"Stand back. All of you," he ordered, his gun waving madly at them. "Don't any of you move or I'll …"

"You'll what, Mr Capri? Shoot us? What good will that do? Don't you find this situation intriguing?"

"Shut up, Grantham. I thought you were dead."

"Well, I'm sorry to disappoint you, but as you can see for yourself I am very much alive. Unless of course it is another hallucination."

They all started laughing at him. Capri suddenly felt very weak. He asserted himself once more. "Shut up, all of you." He looked at Grantham again with new eyes. "What are you doing here, Grantham? What's all this about?"

"I thought you knew, old chap," he retorted icily. "Am I to take it you don't? That you really haven't the foggiest notion why I am here, why we are all here? Are you really that ignorant?"

Capri ignored the last remark and flashed his eyes at the rest of them. Yes, he knew why he was here. He had been set up. But for what reason he couldn't fathom. That didn't bother him now. All he wanted to do was make certain she was present, hiding under one of those ridiculous hoods, probably laughing at him inwardly, having roped him in, duped him and was now, to complete it all, betraying him. Well, he would prove Grantham wrong. He wasn't the weak, pathetic fool they thought he was. And the woman standing next to him could only be her.

"You!" he blurted out, shaking his gun at her. "Remove your hood now."

She looked to Grantham for his consent. "Oblige the man," he told her.

She pulled back her hood. Capri, on seeing her face, wanted to die. It wasn't her. Rather, it was some old woman, in her sixties or early seventies who, like Grantham, had also been ravaged by time and yet still bore the hallmarks of a beauty she sadly no longer possessed. Her features were marred; the skin was slack and yet she was still attractive in an indescribable way. Haggard, the cheeks sagging and the large bags under the eyes, caused her to have a drooping expression which formed striations about the lips running down to her chin. Her eyes, although possessing a faint allure with their thick mascara, conveyed the impression they were steeped in some heavy narcotic, yet brimming with friendliness. They smiled benignly at him, like a mother to its child. Her grey-silver hair was tied back making her look like a Russian or Polish gypsy. Capri was confounded.

"You're not her," he stammered.

"Who?" Grantham queried.

"Yes, who?" she asked, concerned. "Who did you think I was? Admittedly, you are not to know me as you've had no dealings with me," she remarked.

"Allow me to introduce my wife," Grantham said. "This is Natasha."

"How do you do," she said as if this was some sort of parlour game. "We mean you no harm, as my husband said. Do not be afraid, for you have been drawn here by powers far more miraculous than you could ever possibly imagine. Do not think unkindly of us either. All will be explained in due course. Do not fret. Think how marvellous it is to be here, to be at the very edge of time itself."

He looked at her as if she was mad, then to Grantham for an explanation.

The old man smiled. "My wife has been one of the most successful operators I have ever worked with. Without her help I never would have got this far. You see, age gets the better of us all, and now alas she really is quite useless, having served her purpose, she is content. She has done her will. And now she is ready to depart from this life," he said tearfully.

Capri ignored him, more than ever determined to get to the bottom of this charade. She was here. He knew it. There were at least two more candidates for the role. And like Grantham had implied, this was a game and he had better play it good. He surveyed the other hooded figures standing in the row, ignoring Grantham's wife who seemed to be fixated on him with incestuous desires. There was another person standing to the other side of him with breasts visible under the robe and therefore a woman. He decided to give it another try. Grantham followed his eyes curiously.

"You!" Capri shouted at her. "Take off your hood," he ordered.

Again this one looked to Grantham as if they were all under his spell. Grantham nodded and slowly the woman turned towards Capri and pulled back her hood with aplomb, he bracing himself, ready to pounce on her should his assumption prove correct. Again he was seized by unknowing for it wasn't her either.

"You're not her..." he whined.

Again Grantham butted in. "Who?"

Capri ignored him and looked at this second female sternly. She was younger, perhaps attractive if you could call it that, but not to his liking. She didn't do anything for him and he thought of her as being a cruel, malevolent bitch, one he would not be able to trust, with her domineering brown eyes and auburn hair. She was vaguely familiar.

"Who is she?" Grantham prompted him on to get the game moving. Capri shot him a glance. "Think, man," he said. "You saw her recently. Surely she cannot escape you that easily?"

Capri diverted his eyes back to her. Did he know her then? He didn't think so. In fact, why should he know her at all? Slowly he was getting the drift of what Grantham was saying. Yes she was strangely familiar. Perhaps he had

seen her recently, but where he didn't know. He wanted to tell Grantham where to go. This whole scenario was inane. This wasn't what he wanted.

He looked at her again. She blew him a kiss. Then he remembered. It was last night on Landis' desk, the holo image. He smirked with satisfaction. Now he knew who she was and what Grantham was really implying. He laughed. Grantham picked up on it.

"You see," he said. "You do know."

And he could only agree, although not in the way he originally thought. If this was Landis' wife then he had to be here as well since couples always stick together. If he was correct, this was the nasty little group Mosalla had told him about, the sinister band he mentioned whom Landis had sided with. It could only be the one standing right next to her.

"You. Take off your hood," he demanded and gestured for him to do so. This one, however, did not look to Grantham this time and proceeded straightaway to pull back his hood, revealing a sprightly mop of blond hair and a pair of blue eyes which, like Natasha's, suggested a drug of some sort as they were hardly focused on him at all, glazed over with a sheen. He had marks about his face which gave him a thuggish appearance like a ruffian. He also came across as cool and calculating, but with the sort of look which suggested menace and deviousness as if he couldn't be trusted. And like in his office, Capri felt the same raw edge coming from him, one of power, nigh uncontrollable. A smooth, smarmy type of character, sophisticated but with an expression of rascality about him, a philanderer, one who could so easily charm in one instant and kill in the next. Mosalla was right. And it unnerved Capri when the man simply smiled at him. In that one instant, Capri decided he detested him, instinctively.

"The one and only Anton Landis, I presume," Capri remarked with smug satisfaction. He could nearly hear the applause circulating round the arena as the man nodded his head. Capri stopped and thought. He had never seen him before, yet there was a frisson of recognition he couldn't ascribe to any known source. His thoughts were clamouring for attention, pounding into his brain. He stopped smiling.

"Well?" Grantham asked him. "Where have you seen him before?"

Capri chose to remain unfazed. He couldn't think where, gave up and looked to the last two hooded figures. One was obviously female. The other

gave him bad vibes. He didn't like it at all. It just seemed to stand there dead still like a sentry. He skipped it and faced the hooded woman. This could only be her as she had the same figure and was the right height. With confidence he moved in closer, right up to her face, gloating on his own self-assurance. He ordered her to pull back her hood and smiled.

His smile vanished quickly. She had done away with her hood to reveal her attractive features. The recognition refused to hit home. Capri gulped as it struggled through into his feeble brain. Then it hit home forcibly. The ground fell away from his feet. His mind recoiled. He didn't know whether to laugh, cry, lash out or simply die. It couldn't have been any worse, but it was. His eyes clashed with hers, still refusing to see as if they were disconnected from his brain. He murmured something unintelligible and gawped at her like a simpleton.

But it couldn't be her. It just couldn't. He found his legs retreating back towards the centre as if distance could deny her existence. And in one terrible moment he had to accept it was her, "Katie!" The word came out tremulously from his throat. He squealed with anguish. "No!" he blustered. But it was true and it hurt. He shook his head in defiance. Had he been led up the garden path by her? Had he been too blind to see what she was actually doing? He cursed himself for being such a dotard. Of course. It was she who had set him up, and the smile creeping across her face and the look of satisfaction in her eyes only confirmed it.

She breathed in deeply, her magnificent chest heaved, the loose folds of her robe now revealing her ample cleavage. She placed her hands on her hips in a gesture of domination. She had defeated him; she was proud of it. His eyes, still not registering her fully, skirted round her, avoiding her eyes and settled on the rest of her; the silver-blonde hair now exquisitely bundled up in a spiral fashion and trailing over her shoulders, the heavy lipstick bringing out the voluptuousness of her mouth, and like the others, she too conveyed a sense of being under the influence of some drug as he allowed his eyes to veer perilously close to hers. But it wasn't her really. It wasn't the Katie he had known, trusted, confided in, kissed, caressed, and fucked. This was another Katie, a more mature version, not the silly little girl of yesterday. And like a chrysalis she had transformed overnight into this butterfly, but a deadly one at that, oozing with cunning and menace. Or had she been like that all along? Had it all been an act and this was the real Katie? He knew instinctively there was something not right about her, that she wasn't really as superficial and shallow as she made herself out to be. And like the fool he was he had let his weakness get the better of him and now he was paying for it, having accepted her unquestioningly. He should

have realised, been more discerning. It had been too good to be true; her appearing at his door like that. He felt this bilious rage building up inside him. He was not annoyed with her but with himself. Then she must have been keeping an eye on him. It was too much of a coincidence her staying in the same hotel as his. Was she the one Mosalla was referring to, the one who still looked after the temple, one of his original members? It didn't make sense. None of it did.

"I believe you are intimately acquainted with Mrs Pearson," Grantham casually remarked.

His words cut into Capri. Jack's wife? This was unbelievable.

He didn't know what to think, praying he was still in bed, that this was a continuation of his dream and he was still falling. For it certainly felt like it; the bottom had irrevocably dropped out of his world. He gripped himself and steadied his position. He tore his eyes away from her and noticed Landis smirking inanely at him. Then it clicked. He looked back at Katie, then back to Landis. Yes, he had seen him before. It was confirmed by the sibling resemblance.

"Well?" Grantham demanded, as if reading his thoughts.

Capri gestured to him to wait, to give him time to think, but he wasn't certain. Where had he seen him before? Then it slammed into him. He was sitting admiring a blonde strumpet. He couldn't take his eyes off her. He thought she was ravishing and was quite content just to sit and watch her and continued drinking, wondering all the while who was going to join her; her husband perhaps? As he got up to leave he noticed she had been joined by a handsome young man with blond hair. He tried to get a closer look, but the people between him and her blocked his view. And when he saw her later she was telling the truth, in her own perverted way. She had been having dinner with her brother, Anton Landis.

He looked at her again with new eyes. "I prefer you in black," he sighed.

She didn't take any notice, the bitch. She stood there as if she owned the place. Then he thought about the way the sigil came into his mind that night, seeming to appear out of nowhere, spontaneously. It wasn't Angel who had given it to him; it was her, so he would experience Recremental Space? Why? Why go to all these elaborate lengths? The conspiracy—which this certainly was—didn't amount to anything if it was only to get him here.

What the fuck is going on? he wanted to shout out loud.

In his confusion he dropped his guard. Landis seized the opportunity and lunged towards him. Capri caught him in the corner of his eye and became instantly alert. He quickly drew up his gun and backed off, all the while pointing it at them not sure who to kill first, them or himself.

"Well?" Grantham barked, edging in closer towards him. "Are you going to stand there all day?"

"Stay where you are. As long as I have this gun in my hand, I am in charge. Now do as I say." Grantham stopped. "Good, and that applies to the rest of you." They were inwardly mocking him, delighting in his confusion. Then back to Grantham. "Why have you gone to all this trouble?"

"We had to make sure you would be here. For reasons you are evidently ignorant of. It is quite apparent you don't know why you are really here."

"I know why I am here," he told him with a quiver in his voice.

"Are you sure? Do you?"

"Yes. I know perfectly well why I'm here."

"Then tell me, Mr Capri."

"I'm here because...because..."

"Yes, do go on. I'm still waiting."

"I'm here because..." He tried to get the rest of it out. It wouldn't come. It was tangled up inside somewhere, a confused, chaotic mess. Not to be undermined by this man he blurted out anything. "I knew this temple was still being used. I came here to see if it was true."

"Really? As you can see, your assumption is correct. This temple is still being used. It always has been, although the previous owner wasn't aware of it. But what does that tell you? How is it going to help you?"

Capri thought anxiously, struggling to get more words out. "It is going to..."

"It's going to what? Help you find this drug you are searching for?"

"The drug?" he blurted out.

"Yes, you know, the drug, your mission to find it, the one which brought you to LA in the first place. What connection could it have with here?"

He thought hard. There was another reason why he was here, but it wouldn't come to him. Finally, he just said anything to appease this man. "I thought it may lead me to it."

"Really? If you truly believe that then you are a pathetic excuse of a man, are you not? You know full well there is more to it than that. So why do you insist on deceiving yourself?"

His words bit into him. He hated him. "Okay, then, Grantham, since you seem to know far more than I do, why don't you tell me."

"It looks like I'm going to have to, doesn't it? And hopefully it will put you out of your misery, for I can see you are a man suffering from some great burden. But allow me first to digress for a moment, a necessary digression I assure you. Then you can judge for yourself whether I speak the truth.

"You see, we knew there was a guaranteed way of getting you here. We just had to make sure we fed your inquisitive mind the requisite morsels. That was Katrina's role," he uttered, gesturing towards his old Katie.

She smirked with self-satisfaction and purred like a cat. He always thought Katty suited her better.

"And her brother," he continued, indicating Landis, "relayed everything back to me. You see, your walking into this temple was no mere accident, I fact I hope you have by now concluded."

Capri nodded. "Yes, I know now. It seems you have gone to a lot of trouble to make sure I was here. I certainly felt I had to come."

"But you still don't know why?"

Capri shook his head. "No, I don't."

"Well at least we are making slow but sure progress. When I was told everything was going according to plan I was more than satisfied. I was assured the gods were working marvellously for us on our behalf whereas no doubt you thought they were working for you. But you were mistaken. You took the bait and we reeled you in. That is how we knew you would come. Katrina intimated you were planning on making this visit first thing. We prepared ourselves. You arrived slightly earlier than we anticipated. But that makes no difference. Something else confirmed your proposed visit."

Grantham stopped and turned towards Landis. Landis smiled and was motioned to continue. He started walking towards Capri. "Something happened last night," he began as he encircled Capri, "which only confirmed you were on the right track. It seems some fucker was snooping around my institute, sticking his nose in. Of course, we couldn't detect him as he was doing it astrally, and I was only informed about it early this morning. Whoever it was put one of our servitors out of action," he whispered into Capri's ear and continued perambulating. "When I was told, I could only think of one person. And my sister confirmed it," he whispered again and stroked Capri's hair. Capri flinched.

Landis laughed and proudly walked back to the rest of them. Capri felt sick inside. He looked to Grantham who was fixing his eyes intently on the last hooded figure at the end, so intently as if he was in direct telepathic communication with it. Capri, disconcerted, wondered what was going to happen next. He didn't have to wait long. The hooded figure immediately ripped away the hood and bounded towards him. Capri recoiled. He lurched backwards as it came right up to him, talons outstretched and poised directly above him as his knees buckled. He couldn't believe it. The thing was visible on this plane and looked equally repulsive, reeking of some mephitic odour. His stomach turned somersaults. He wanted to retch.

"Well? Aren't you impressed?" he heard Grantham call out.

Capri couldn't respond, nor could he tear his eyes away from the servitor. It dwarfed him, its chameleon-like eyes revolving, boring into his. Not only was it visible, it also appeared to be partially tangible. It was truly hideous.

"Get it off me!" he shouted.

Grantham laughed in the background. He stopped and the thing retreated a few steps then stood like a sentry once more, his eyes firmly fixed on Capri.

"Do I take it you're not much enamoured of my creation?" he slyly remarked. "Pity. I think it is exquisite. I suppose it requires a bit of getting used to. Familiarity I'm sure will breed admiration. But I can understand your reluctance to embrace it since it's like Recremental Space. But that could be due to the fact that it is made from Recremental Space," he said and laughed. "You see, I can manifest thought-forms on this plane, not only making them visible to physical sight, but virtually tangible as well. Far better than a holo, don't you think? And it causes me considerable expenditure of energy every time I have to recreate one of my own creations. Please try to refrain from destroying this one if you can."

Grantham laughed again. Capri shot him a look. He detested the man. He raised his gun and aimed directly at the thing's mid centre.

"Don't be a fool, man," Grantham mocked him. "How can you shoot at something which does and does not exist?" He laughed, so did the others.

Capri felt stupid. He turned his gun towards Grantham instead. "But you exist. I can shoot you. As you are this disgusting thing's creator which exists through you, if I kill you it will also technically be killed. Is that not so?"

"Excellent," he cheered. "You show admirable knowledge of occult laws. Indeed, you are correct. But I'm sure you don't want to kill me just yet."

"I wouldn't be so sure if I was you, Grantham. Right now I've got half a mind to blow your head off. This game has gone far enough. I could shoot you without compunction. Your death would not worry me the slightest. In fact, I think I would be doing the world a favour and getting my own back for Mosalla's death. You are the ones who killed him, aren't you?"

"Ah, yes, Mosalla. I'm glad you mentioned him. Yes, what a pity the man had to die. It was also another confirmation you would be here. We knew you would be paying another visit to his house last night. That was why I was there, astrally speaking, to see if you would arrive and follow the clues. And that was also why we had to remove some documents before the police arrived. You see, if you saw them, you would have put two and two together rather too quickly and perhaps been dissuaded from coming here."

"Answer me!" he shouted angrily. "Did you or did you not kill him?"

"We do not kill people, Mr Capri. We simply remove them."

"Same thing. But why? Why for God's sake? He was a harmless old man. What could have possibly warranted his death?"

Grantham scrutinised him closely. "You have a lot to learn," he replied, showing little remorse. "Unfortunately, time does not permit a full lecture. Let's just say he was an inconvenience, a threat to our plans."

"Plans? What fucking plans?"

"Your reason for being here, Mr Capri."

"Grantham! You have no morals whatsoever. Only a coward would kill someone in such an underhand fashion."

"A coward? Rubbish! You are not aware of the full picture. When you first went to visit him he gave you sufficient information to act on, but like any man he had a weakness. His was drink, and the more he drank the more voluble he became. If your second visit took place he would almost certainly have said far too much, especially if you mentioned Katrina here. If you described her, he would have made the connection."

"And told me more about his old group?"

"And more. You see, he was a stubborn old man who had in his possession one thing he refused adamantly to let us have. Katrina tried all her charming methods to persuade him to part with it and, as you are aware, she can be extremely persuasive at times. She always gets what she wants in the end. But Mosalla proved a tough nut to crack. He had to be removed before we could get our hands on it."

"What the fuck are you on about, Grantham? Get hold of what?"

"Take a good look, Mr Capri. Take a good look."

He stepped aside to reveal the altar and its centrepiece. Capri felt sick again. He recognised it instantly having seen it so many times. It was horrific.

"I see you recognise it," Grantham gloated. "Why don't you step forwards and take a closer look."

Capri couldn't. His feet were welded to the floor. Looking at it from this distance was bad enough. He could see every feature clearly; the strange bestial head with the long snout, the upright ears, the body of a fish, the coiled tail of a serpent which formed its base, and the huge leathery wings upraised like that of a bat, and all crudely wrought in some unearthly dark metal which curiously shone, possibly hematite. It was a statue of Grantham's obnoxious god which had been on display in Mosalla's alcove.

"You stole it from him," Capri uttered.

"Poppycock. He had no right to possess it in the first place. He didn't understand its true significance. You see, it fell into the wrong hands. I merely reclaimed that which is rightfully mine. Don't you think it's beautiful and so powerful?" he mocked him again.

Capri could only feel resentment at the man's remark.

"Well?" Grantham demanded intrusively. "And does it not also repulse you? Hmm? I see that it does, and that it is more than familiar to you for you have experienced it in its own space, and yet like Mosalla, you too do not really know what it represents or its true value."

"I hate it," he sneered.

"Of course you do, but as you would've read in my books somewhere, you have to embrace that which you despise to become fully enriched thereby."

"I still hate it and I have no intention of embracing it or worshipping it. It is foul. It is odious. It is ev..."

"What was that word?" Grantham snarled at him. "How could you possibly think of using such a word when you know full well there is no such thing? Evil was invented by the Christians to explain phenomena they did not understand. Out of their ignorance they created the Devil. They made him the adversary of their false god to explain the disasters that befall man, disasters which are part of nature. How can nature be evil? How can anything in the world be evil? How dare you mention that word. You are no better than them.

"This statue is the embodiment of Recremental Space. It is primal, archaic, so antiquated we cannot even ascribe a date to it. It is your fear of it which hinders your true understanding."

"I loathe your god."

"Rubbish. You speak out of fear. It is fear which turns you against him. You fear it because it threatens you. If you were a real man, Capri," he said, dropping the 'mister' out of impatience, "you would face up to all you fear. You would no longer be a man but a god. That is the only reason you have a personal disliking for our god, because you cannot face it."

"I don't want to. Why should I? This god of yours, whatever its name is."

"He has no name, for he was before any known speech. And he is returning, assuredly once more, to take his rightful place at the head of creation. And this is why it was of paramount importance we had his statue back in our possession, of which there are only seven in existence. When our god is nearing his return he disgorges images of himself around the world. That is how it came into Mosalla's possession when he visited Iraq fifteen years ago. Nor is it of this earth. It comes from somewhere else. Can you guess where, I wonder?"

"I don't give a shit where it comes from. What's all this leading up to? What do you intend to do now you have it in your possession?"

"Again you would know if you had my books."

"I tried to, Grantham. I read them very quickly; they are absolute drivel. They are worthless. All your conclusions and predictions are way out. And furthermore, you can't even write properly."

"Don't try to mock me. You know nothing. My books deserve careful attention for they are written in such a manner so as to stir the primal layers of subconsciousness into activity. They are not meant to be read but dreamed on, for it is through the dreaming mind where they really speak and come into power, contacting the vast reservoirs of Recremental Space and siphoned into the conscious mind. For have you not experienced strange dreams of late provoked by their reading? You know as well as I the conscious mind particularises and rejects that which it cannot comprehend. More information slips through by writing in an offhand fashion, a twilight language, a linguistic surrealism based on irrational content that goes beyond logic and concrete rationality simply because it preceded it. My books communicate with the primal layers directly, bypassing conscious censorship altogether so my message takes hold, grows and clarifies."

"You mean festers like a wound, an insipid cancerous growth."

"Humbug," he retorted heatedly. "Why do you persist in rejecting all that I tell you when you know it is the truth?"

"The truth! What do you know about the truth? You're full of shit, Grantham, just like your god and you know it."

"And I thought you had such a fine head on your shoulders. Sadly it seems I am mistaken. You are addicted to your ego. That is why you are deaf and blind to what I am really saying. You refuse to give up this preposterous notion of self and cannot accept the truth."

"I still say you are wrong. I mean look at this absurd prediction of yours that the world was going to end at the turn of the century. Here we are, well into new millennium, and it still hasn't happened."

"You do me an injustice. I did not say at the turn of the century. I said around the turn of the century, implying sometime afterwards."

"Even so, you are still wrong. The earth isn't going to be destroyed by a great flood. The inner planes aren't going to implode and they never will, because all your theories are based on the words of charlatans, false prophets and lunatics. It is never going to happen."

"Oh, but it is."

"Oh yeah? When?"

Grantham leaned forward, his eyes firmly fixed on his. "Now!" he hissed.

"Bullshit! I don't believe you."

"It makes no difference whether you believe me or not. But I assure you, it has already started."

"Rubbish. You're dreaming, Grantham."

"Then listen closely," he suggested and raised his hand and ordered everyone to be silent. Everyone went quiet and listened intently. A faint stirring sound could be heard from beyond the confines of the temple. A

tremendous wind was picking up speed and hammering the sides of the old building. It wheezed and groaned with resentment.

"Is that not the sound of its coming?" he asked with a genuine prophet of doom's voice.

"It's the wind, Grantham. So what?"

"Ah, but listen closer."

Everyone remained in silence, listening to the building as it trembled. It sounded disconcertingly as if it was being torn from its foundations.

"That is merely the start, the first intimations of its coming," Grantham howled with glee. "For has it not been predicted calamity will strike soon?"

Capri remembered the broadcast bulletin announcing an impending tidal wave. Did this man really think that was it, the start of his great apocalypse he had predicted all those years ago? "Yes, they said there would be a tidal wave hitting soon. But surely you don't think it marks the advent of the end of the world?"

"Oh, but I most certainly do."

"You're mad, Grantham."

"Am I? Why do you have such little faith in me, I wonder? Is it because your refuse to believe? This is merely the start of it. Soon there will be more. The seas will rise up violently. Whole coasts will be obliterated and washed away. There will be tornadoes, hurricanes, typhoons, earthquakes, volcanic eruptions. The whole world will be thrown into upheaval."

"Yes, but you still can't be serious."

"I am. This is merely the beginning. As it was predicted. As I have clearly expounded in my books which you read with such fascination last night. A phenomenal deluge will sweep over the earth, erasing whole cultures, wiping out cities, erasing them from the land like a veritable palimpsest as my god makes his return. Everything will be thrown into disorder. There will be chaos, panic, millions of people will be killed. Nation shall sink after nation. This is merely the beginning of the end which will last for several years until the whole of earth is wiped clean like a slate and man, as the very

dust he is, will be eroded away. Then only will the world subside and be reborn, a re-genesis."

Capri couldn't believe this man. "You're mad. Fucking mad."

"Silence, imbecile. I speak the truth. Your incredulity is of no consequence. You're taxing my patience," he barked at him, his eyes aflame with blood. "You know nothing. You don't even know why you are really here, so who are you to question my judgement. Verily, what I say is true. The tidal wave is merely the beginning, announcing the return of my planet."

"Of course! Your fucking planet. It doesn't exist, Grantham."

"Ah, but it does, and it is truly occult. Not even the most powerful telescopes can bring it into view."

"And you reckon this time it is going to come closer than ever before?"

"Oh, I'm absolutely positive. Although I'm incapable of predicting exactly how close, all I can say is it will be far more dramatic than previously, perhaps even to the detriment of the entire human race or even to the whole world, announcing the start of a new age. Who knows? But don't dismiss it so lightly, Capri. My research into this has been more than thorough. I could go on to prove my point, but I won't. There are already intimations of its arrival. And that statue is proof that the time is now."

"I don't believe you. I don't believe a word you say."

"Scepticism is an admirable trait, but not when it refuses to the point of denial to accept what is right before one's eyes. That it resurfaced after having been buried under the sands of time for thousands of years can be empirically verified. Here it stands along with six others scattered throughout the world, each one is powerful, as you yourself can confirm."

"Oh, I can confirm it's powerful. But it exists on a separate plane."

Grantham raised his eyes high up to the ceiling and asked, "What is that?"

Capri followed his gaze. Directly above him he could see etched in the ceiling a similar motif to the one he was standing on. It had the same spiralling lines like a giant cobweb except in the centre was something he hoped he would never see again; the sigil.

"Well?" Grantham prompted him.

Capri tore his eyes away from it and looked at him fearfully. "It's the sigil of the Negative," he blurted.

"Correct. And what is it used for?"

"For entering the Negative, or what you call Recremental Space."

"And?" Grantham asked. Capri looked at him blankly. "What can be used for going in to, can also be used for going out of. It is a gateway. And like any gateway it can be used both ways; we can enter it from this side, but we can also bring through what is on the other side."

"You mean you're going to use it to bring the Negative on to this plane?"

"Exactly. Indeed we are."

"You cannot be serious. It could do untold damage. It will affect us all."

"Not all of us. It will only affect those who haven't worked with it. Those who have will be immune from its impact."

Capri was staggered by this man's casual attitude. "But that amounts to nearly the whole population of the earth. They aren't prepared for it."

"Then they should have worked with it. They should have read my books and attuned themselves to it. It is not my fault. I warned them. And now they will have to pay the consequences. In the next few hours they will feel it coming through, not just leaking as it has been doing over the last few decades, but pouring through. And we are going to assist it. Most of the herd will die anyway once the apocalypse really gets under way."

"You're joking."

"I never joke about my work, Capri. Through our assistance the Negative will have full effect. Like the planet, it will sweep its influence across the lands overturning everything. Only then can the cosmic balance be restored as our planet drifts back out again."

"What? Just you lot are going to help bring it through? I don't believe you."

"Not just us. All the rest of us put together. There are six other groups around the world, each with a statue. The Seven Churches, we are called."

"Right out of Revelation, hey? Not only are you mad, you're tyrannical."

"Imagine it, Capri. Imagine bodies floating in the streets, homes being washed away, families running to safety. Bah! There will be no safety, nor refuge, nowhere to run to. And we can do nothing to prevent it. We are here today merely, I repeat, to assist it. The great wheel is turning full circle. We cannot stop it from turning."

Capri was shocked. This man standing before him was speaking no different than a doctor examining a gangrenous limb and deciding upon its amputation as a cure. His attitude was one of absolute cold detachment.

"I don't believe any of this," Capri stammered.

"Nevertheless, it is so. Let's put an end to this confab. Enough's been said."

With that Grantham turned round to face the others and ordered them to start getting ready.

"Grantham!" Capri shouted at him. "I cannot let you go ahead with this."

"Really?" he said snidely. "And what, pray, are you going to do? Kill us? Will that solve anything? Will that stop it from happening? And what about the other groups? Are you going to kill them as well, that is, if you can find them? Don't be a fool. There's nothing you can do. You're powerless. Accept it as we have. It's already been ordained. We have been bidden to aid it. We're merely doing our wills. I suggest you do the same."

"You're just a jumped dictator. You're hyperventilating on all this power bestowed on you. It has gone to your head. You have no mercy."

"I warn you, Capri, I'm losing my temper. I am the Magus, a magician, not a man. And my will is not only closely allied with the will of the universe, it is identical with it. I suggest you too bend your will in the same way. Be a magician, Capri, nay be a god, for once in your life."

The temple shuddered as another blast of wind hit the building square on. Grantham stopped. His eyes were now raised to the ceiling. Everyone became alarmed as if the whole temple was going to collapse any minute.

Perhaps the man is right after all, Capri thought, as another blast came in, this time more powerfully. It was no ordinary wind either. Nothing could knock the building that hard. Capri looked at this dangerous man before him. He noticed a gleeful expression in his eyes. Grantham lowered his eyes and levelled them with his. He smiled with pleasure.

"It is time," he roared. "Let us prepare ourselves. Let us welcome our god with open arms. Prepare yourselves, my children. Raise the Ark!"

What the devil was he referring to? But before Capri could ask, Natasha had gone over to the side of the altar and bent down. She pulled a lever. There was a rumbling deep beneath the floor. Capri could feel it shudder. He looked to Grantham for an explanation.

"Prepare yourself, Capri," Grantham wailed instead.

"How can I? If your prediction is correct, we are all going to die."

"Not all of us."

"What do you mean by that?"

"Stand back, man!" he barked.

Now Capri could feel it. The whole floor was shaking. There was also a strange whirring sound. Where he was standing the floor seemed to be moving. Capri looked down only to see it was. He quickly leapt back. The floor opened from the centre of the design, its sections retracting like the blades of a diaphragm. Capri watched puzzled as the hole became larger and finally stopped as it reached the design's circumference. He shot Grantham another glance. The man could still only smile. Now Capri felt it full. The floor vibrated and something appeared to be rising up from the hole. At first it reminded him of an extremely large silver bullet, snub-nosed and shiny, as it poked its way up above the ground, rising slowly like a phallus of steel. It stopped and stood vertically, pinioned into position above a platform with seven circular steps leading up to it fashioned from basalt rock. Capri could only guess the rest of this rocket, or whatever it was, still remained underground, only the capsule being visible. And as he looked closer, the top part of it was covered with a glass lid through which he could see a padded white interior. It reminded him of a coffin. It was large enough for only one person.

"What's the meaning of this?" he asked Grantham warily.

Choosing not to answer him, Grantham turned to Landis. "Brother Anton, what is the saying in Pyramid Text 267?"

Landis smiled and faced Capri and recited proudly, "A staircase to heaven is laid for him so that he may mount up to heaven thereby," saying the last word with added emphasis.

"Exactly," Grantham rejoined. "As I said, not all of us are going to die." He then gesticulated to his wife. She pulled another lever. The capsule broke away from its shaft and swung slowly on its pinions into a horizontal position. Grantham glared at Capri. "And there you are."

Capri caught on. "Oh, I see. Once you have done your devil of a god's bidding, destroyed the entire human race, he is going to reward you with a tomb to lie in for the rest of eternity like some Egyptian pharaoh, not only spiritually ascending to heaven, but also physically. Is that it?"

"Not exactly. It isn't for me," he said calmly.

"Oh? Then who is it for?"

Grantham leaned forward and announced with glee, "It's for you!"

Capri was stunned. He didn't know whether the man was being serious or joking. "You are off your rocker, Grantham. I thought you were slightly eccentric, a bit weird, but by God, you're as mad as a hatter. I'm out of here, Grantham. This joke has gone too far."

"A joke!" he barked. "Why, you ignoramus. You think this is all a bloody joke, do you? Did I not say earlier I'm absolutely serious about my work?"

"Oh, you did. But you are sadly mistaken if you think you're going to get me in that thing of yours. I'll leave you to it. It's the end of the world, isn't it? So, if you don't mind, I think I'll go and enjoy what time we have left."

Capri turned round and started walking away briskly, only to hear Grantham shout, "Wait!" He stopped in his tracks and without turning said, "There's nothing you can say to me anymore, Grantham."

"Oh, but there is. We have only just started. Besides, don't you want to know who you really are?"

Capri turned round to face them indifferently. "I know who I am."

"Are you sure? So far your life has been nothing but a mockery."

"Shut up, Grantham. I've had enough for one day. I don't give a shit about you and your bloody fantasies."

"But don't you want to know why you are really here?"

"What? So you can put me in that thing of yours, offer me up to your god as some sort of sacrifice? No thanks. I've seen that film before."

"You're not who you think you are."

"Aren't I? And of course you know, is that it?" Grantham nodded. Capri shook his head in disbelief. "You know nothing."

"Do you honestly think we would have expended considerable time and energy in preparation for this momentous occasion, because it is some joke? Forty years we've been preparing, forty years since the day you were born."

Capri went numb. "What?"

"You heard me. Think about it. Use your brain properly for once. Stop pissing about and do what you are meant to be doing with your life. This mockery has got to stop. Nor can you laugh it off any longer. It's so easy, isn't it? To laugh something off, because it is far easier to deal with then, isn't it? Or even perhaps run away. Like you have always done. Like you are doing just now?

"Do you honestly believe you are this psychic detective called Harmon Capri who is searching for a drug which may or may not exist and that you have been drawn into some conspiratorial plot by a group of magicians who are going to sacrifice you to their god? Or are you a man who has been living a lie for the past forty years simply because he does not know who he really is and is thereby suffering from some existential conflict simply because he cannot find his true position in life? Which is more likely?!!"

CELEBRATION

Capri ran back to him, furiously. "Fuck you, Grantham."

"How long is that jigsaw puzzle in your head going to remain fragmented? Isn't it a pain to carry it around in shards when none of the pieces will fit together because they don't appear to belong to the same puzzle? Does the truth hurt that much that you have to keep running away from it? Wouldn't it be nice to have all those pieces fall into place, an end to the confusion at last, and to have the peace you've always been dreaming of? Then don't walk away from here. Be a man, Capri. Nay, be a god. It is time to wake up. Open your eyes."

Capri was raging inside. He bounded towards Grantham, possessed, and raised his gun, aiming it directly at him. "I've had enough. Do you hear me?" He stopped right in front of him, his eyes searing with hatred. He looked at the rest of them, so cold and unemotional; it was as if he was the only human being in the temple. "Let me get this straight, since you seem to know so much about me, more, it appears, than I do myself. You have lured me here today so when all this is over and I am dead you are going to put me in that coffin of yours. Correct?"

"No. And it is not a coffin."

"Then what the fuck is it?"

"You will soon see. Nor are you going to die."

"But everyone else is, yes?"

Grantham refrained from answering. Nor did he look at Capri waving his gun in his face. "I can understand how you feel," he began reflectively, "for I too was placed in a similar position as you. I too struggled with things I could not comprehend and had to face the truth in the end. It is only with that hindsight I am able to tolerate you and empathise with your mixed feelings about all of this.

"You see, when I first got involved with magic I didn't really know what I was doing. Then I hit on something very powerful. It threw me out of the orbit of the common man into the dark terrain of the unknown. I tried piecing it together, to make sense of it all and found there a whole grimoire just waiting to be written and tried my best to bring it through. That was the theme of my first book, admittedly not that good. Later I entered a crepscular stage where things started making sense vaguely, being fed

certain pieces of information at the most apt times when I needed them, as if I was being led by some unseen hand or being guided by some mysterious force. At first I ascribed it to coincidence, but when these things recur repeatedly that label seems the most absurd. I had to sit up and take note. It was too explicit to be ignored. I then felt I was being pushed along by a inner momentum as if, yes, the very forces of the universe were behind me. It was only then I felt I was doing my will and the second book was written in next to no time. It was as if every single element of my nature had been balanced and sorted out accordingly, being divested of any superfluities not essential to the work in hand, so that I could be free from them and get on and do what had to be done. And that culminated in the third book, which practically wrote itself. I was able to bring through my grimoire onto this plane and augment it with the findings of other seekers and pioneers of consciousness. I was able quickly to transfer to canvas and paper as fleeting as they were, exotic and wondrous landscapes, buildings, creatures of a forgotten time, which I incorporated into the book as illustrations, the ones which so horrified you, even placing in my possession the sigil itself. It was like a transmission. It was only on completion I realised my will and hence I was no longer beset by any more obstacles. Nothing impeded my path. Everything thereafter flowed smoothly as if something was happening on planes far higher than this one. In short, I felt I was being made to do things I did not want to do, and did them because I felt they were meant to be done, a factor you yourself have no doubt come across."

"Yes, but it was different for me. You planned all of this. You made me come here, not some higher guiding agency. You said so yourself."

"No, not entirely. We merely made sure you followed the path. We think, pathetically, we are the masters of our own destinies, that we can choose consciously what paths we can take. But the freedom of independent existence is taken from us the deeper we become involved. We try to escape but sooner or later we find ourselves back in it. It may he that we lose something precious, our loved ones, our jobs, our families. We enter into a period of profound suffering and melancholy that can only afflict the most sensitive of souls. We want to die rather than suffer this torment. Everything seems to be against us. We feel we are being mocked and ridiculed, until we accept. Only then does the darkness lift. Everything comes into focus and starts making sense. Everything falls into place. We know. We will. We dare. And we keep silent. We follow the path direct. And we are here to show you your path."

"I want nothing to do with this."

"That is only your ego speaking, not you. Don't be a fool, man."

"I'm not a fool!" he retaliated. "Why, I still feel like blowing your head off."

"Then why don't you?"

Grantham stood still and invitingly opened his arms exposing his chest like a martyr, prepared to die for the cause, willing Capri to fire with eyes of allure and absolute calm. Capri dithered and wavered, his gun shaking in his hand as he raised it to take aim. Even his whole body felt it was going to topple over any minute.

"Shoot me!" Grantham implored.

Capri tried, his finger on the trigger, but couldn't. He tried harder this time and raised the gun resolutely to the man's forehead. But it wouldn't fire. And the harder he tried, the worse it became. His whole strength seemed to abandon him, being sapped out.

"See!" Grantham said triumphantly. "You can't. Why, I wonder? I will tell you why. Because that within you which is greater rules your actions. It knows I speak the truth. That's why."

Capri dropped the gun down to his side and wiped the sweat from his brow. He breathed in deeply to calm his nerves, his face an ashen white, and glared at this man he absolutely detested. "I can't kill you," he finally murmured. "I don't know why. All I know is, you've got the wrong man."

"You will so? Have we really? How pleasant it would be to transfer your will to somebody else, the easier it is to bear the burden. You are the one who is dreaming, not me. It is your ego which is rebelling. Communicate directly with your Holy Guardian Angel. Ask it!"

"My Angel?" he asked him feebly.

"Yes. After all, it knows more about you than anybody else. Ask it!"

Capri thought for a moment. He and Angel had been out of rapport for too long now. He dismissed Grantham's suggestion and instead looked to these other mysterious people who were regarding him as if he was some geriatric in a hospital, yet without the pity or sincerity he would have expected.

Instead, they were merciless, so clinical they were automatons. He couldn't believe anybody could be like them.

He heard something, an alien voice whispering sweet, soft words in his ears, the reassuring chant of Angel. Ah, Angel! where would I be without you? He heard the voice again, neither born of a male nor a female but both simultaneously. 'True, true, true!' was all he could here.

"You see," Grantham said joyfully, "we do speak the truth."

"No!" he shouted in anguish.

Katrina stepped forwards. He fearfully watched her come right up to him through tear-stained eyes. "Yes," she whispered. "You have been chosen. You are the chosen one. It is your destiny, it is you our god has selected to lead the way in the next age."

"No!" he shouted.

"Yes," Grantham retorted. "You know it. You have always known it. Accept it now, once and for all."

"I will not," he sobbed.

All of them apart from the servitor made a move towards him as if ganging up on him. Capri leapt back and nervously raised his gun at all of them.

"If any of you so much as moves, I'll blow your fucking heads off."

They stayed their positions.

"You know we speak the truth," Grantham beseeched. "Why do you persist in this folly of yours and try to deny it from yourself? The greater part of you has accepted, the lesser part has to as well. That is where the confusion lies. Give in. Submit. Become whole. Stop punishing yourself like this."

"No!" he shouted. "It's a trick. You're all against me. I won't let you win."

"Come, Katrina," he gestured towards her. "Let us not waste any more time. I feel another rumble coming on. We must get ready."

"Wait!" he shouted. "Don't you understand? I want no part of this!"

Grantham turned to look at him directly. His face was completely blank. "You are privileged. You will survive, and outlive us all. You'll be reborn as a god, Capri, uniting in yourself the Positive and the Negative, perfectly balanced. You'll repopulate the earth once more."

"What? All by myself?"

"No, of course not. As I said, there will be six others whom you will join. At this very moment they are preparing themselves and you will lead them. They have accepted their destinies; why don't you!" He then pointed to the capsule. "Our Ark will save you. You will go into space and orbit the earth in a profound sleep for many days. Once it is all over you will awaken and return to earth and take the survivors into the new age."

Capri shivered. "Sleep? You mean you're going to put me in suspended animation like those people I saw in the tanks last night? But some were dead, man! The technique hasn't even been perfected. I will surely die."

"No you won't!" Landis butted in. "We may have had a few problems in the past. They've all been sorted out. It has taken us many years of research to get this far. All of our latest experiments have been successful. We won't fail you. Believe me," he assured him, as a man deeply attached to his work.

"You're all mad."

"Mad? Or divinely intoxicated? It is not my choice. It is not my destiny, but it is yours." He then turned to the others. "Come, he is wasting time. He refuses to accept the truth. We will have to resort to the other method. Katrina, if you will be so kind..."

"Wait!" Capri shouted as Katrina stepped forward. She stopped and glared at him as if depriving her of some personal pleasure. "How dare you inveigle me into this shit. You lie!"

"You lie to yourself, Capri," Grantham angrily countermanded. "So stop trying to foil our plans." More sympathetically he said, "Peer deep inside yourself, Capri, there you shall see it in all its glory. Go down deep, sink all the way, past your adult memories, past your teenage years and further backwards, reaching right into the past, to one experience especially which still haunts you to this very day."

I am lying in bed, ill. I toss and turn and still can't get to sleep. There is a pale light coming through the windows. I can only watch it. Then there are shapes moving, forming shadows on the curtains. They come up to my window. They are going to take me away! I scream. Daddy comes rushing into the room. He turns the light on and asks me what the matter is. But I can only point at the window. "There, outside," I yell frantically and he looks at me anxiously. He pulls the curtains aside and peers out, baffled. "There is no one there," he assures me. He checks my temperature. He smiles and tells me to go back to sleep. When he is gone I lie back and try to close my eyes. I turn back to look at the window. The shadows have gone. Then they reappear, this time coming closer. I hide under my sheets hoping they will go away. I sneak a look. They are still there! They are moving about outside. They have strange heads. One of them looks like he is wearing a funny crown. Another has pointy ears and this long protruding snout which makes me scared, and the others I can't distinguish as they keep moving, shuffling around as if walking in a big circle outside. I must take a look and see if they are really there. I reach up and pull the curtains back and peer out. I gasp. There's no one there. They have gone. I am safe once more so I lie down to sleep, and still it does not come. But they do! They are back and I can see their shadows on the curtains. I call out loudly. Daddy rushes back into my room and again looks outside to show me there's nothing there. They are there! Why won't he believe me? He tells me I am dreaming, that it is because I am unwell. But I know they are there; I know they have always been there.

* * * * *

And now he realised that one in particular had been looking after him all the time; Angel! And the others he was uncertain of, yet one was definitely the beast, this devil god of Grantham's.

"Well?" the man demanded. "Now do you believe us?"

The man's words cut through him. Capri wanted to hit him. He couldn't. "You're right," he finally blurted.

"Good. At last. Then let's get on with it. We have much to do."

"But I can't!" Capri shrieked.

Grantham looked at him furiously, his eyes spitting out flames. "Can't!" he bellowed. "What is wrong with you, man? It has been proven. You know it

has. We will initiate you, push you through and put you into the beyond. You will live as countless others die, as we too shall die and go on to that holier place. You shall inherit the earth."

"I can't."

"There is no 'I' only 'thy', and thy will shall be done. If you doubt me, then speak to your Angel. I demand it this time!"

* * * * *

Grantham and the rest slipped sway on an endless void. The temple receded into obsidian night. The candles transformed into stars, a brightly lit canopy above. They were so bright they seemed to cover the entire region of the visible sky and cast down their glare, turning everything to a radiant glow. It paled and soon became dull. He was now able to see where he was standing, this desolate landscape, an expanse of sand and Angel in the distance walking towards him slowly, gracefully, but had changed. Angel was now this woman of rapturous beauty, her hair shining with silver exaggerated by this one bright star directly behind her on the horizon. It shone one ray of light across the land like a path on which Angel trod. To either side was a gulf of darkness. 'Ah, Angel!' he whispered with joy. She smiled. Her whole face lit up. It too shone with a brilliance he had never seen before as if the star imparted to her some spark of life. She was dressed in one long flowing robe of gold which trailed behind her and her hair was covered with a rich headdress abundantly bejewelled; stones of yellow diamonds, topaz and stones of precious water. And as she approached his heart was uplifted. She stopped before him and stood silently upon the golden sands. She was too beautiful to look at. It made his soul swoon. When she smiled it was a smile to shake the world apart, for she was love, an embodiment of love, a love so pure it healed his wounded heart as he went to embrace her, to lay his weary head on her bosom.

'Ah, Angel!' he whispered. 'Are you not the Light of the World?' But she answered him not. She pulled out this prestigiously wrought key of gold in the shape of a Calvary cross. She held it out to him in her right hand as her other hand drew back the folds of her robe like a magnificent curtain revealing this dim outline of a figure, a keyhole. He scrutinised her for the meaning of this. She simply smiled and gestured for him to take the key. That was all he had to do, take the key and insert it in the lock and turn.

Nervously his hand went up to reach for the key. "Yes, go on take it," he could hear Grantham saying in the back of his mind. Capri touched it. He halted. It wasn't a key. It was the weight of the world! He threw it down.

* * * *

Capri collapsed to the ground sobbing.

"Fool!" Grantham shouted at him. "You bloody fool. All you had to do was take the key and turn. Why do you do this to yourself? You could have saved yourself so easily." He looked down at this gibbering wreck; there couldn't have been a more pitiable sight. It only increased his irritation.

"Save yourself, man," he continued. "You have known all along this is true. You have had repeated confirmation throughout the whole of your life. And each time it comes to acceptance you baulk like a coward hoping it will go away. Well this time it won't. That is why it has come to this. I warn you, Capri, you are now balancing precariously. You are on the very edge. You risk insanity and a death a thousand times worse than what we shall go through. Save yourself. Call her back. Do you hear me? I said call her back!"

As he lay on the floor all he could hear was Grantham's irritating voice.

"Quick, apply it," Grantham ordered. "We must prepare for the black time. The darkness is already moving in closer."

They grabbed hold of him, dragged him off the floor and tried to hold him still. His legs were boneless and he kept slipping from their grasp.

"He's really out of it," Landis remarked, holding one of Capri's arms steady.

"So I see," Grantham remarked casually and turned towards Katrina. "Get on with it," he ordered her. "And hold him still," he shouted to Landis.

Capri could see Katrina now moving menacingly towards him. She had a big smile on her face, a cruel sadistic smile which made his heart turn to ice. He looked blearily to Grantham who ignored him, then to Landis holding his right arm, then to the servitor clutching his left, then to Natasha who stood off in the distance, her head turned away as if unwilling to look. What was going to happen next, he simply didn't know. Katrina was now standing in front of him. She was even taller looking now, a giant Amazon standing proudly above him, her hands on her hips gloating on his

suffering. She smiled again, reading his anxiety, feeding off it. She wasn't the same. This wasn't really Katie, he had to tell himself. Then she pulled back the middle seam of her robe, revealing her legs. She was wearing long black leather boots with peculiarly sharp toecaps and high stiletto heels. The boots went all the way up to her thighs. Capri looked on confounded. Then she pulled more of her robe apart to reveal the top of her thighs. He caught a brief flash of crutch. He looked at those legs he had lain between only last night. Every movement she now made was deliberately slow, lovingly slow. She was delighting in the perplexity she was creating in his mind. And very slowly her right hand went to a small black holster just above her boot. She drew out a gun. It was long, silver and shiny like his. At first he thought it was his. Then he recalled their conversation over breakfast that time, how she was afraid of guns. But it wasn't his gun which must have fallen to the floor. He swung his head round to see where it was. Grantham had picked it up and was calmly examining it, indifferent to his plight. Capri looked at the one Katrina had in her hand. She raised it up towards his forehead, poked the muzzle deep into the bridge of his nose and held it steady. He tried to pull away. Landis' wife, who was now standing behind him, gripped his head firmly and held it in position.

Katrina smiled again, intoxicated on his fear. "Goodbye," she breathed.

"Yes, go on. Kill me, you fucking bitch," he fumed at her. Capri closed his eyes. He succumbed and could almost feel the bullet exploding into his brain as she started to squeeze the trigger.

This was it. This was the end.

THE SHADOW

'The ghost-treader moves between the worlds with the greatest of ease, like a shadow.'

Lamal,
Interstellar Magick

—25—
THE RITE TIME

"No, not yet." Katrina released the trigger and pulled the gun away.

Capri flicked open his eyes and sighed. This torment was unbearable. What were they going to do now?

He watched Katrina go up to Grantham, gun in hand, a lascivious, naughty look upon her face. She said to him, "Correct me if I'm wrong, father…"

"Father!?!" Capri blurted.

Katrina flashed her eyes at Capri and smiled. She went back to Grantham and continued, "But did you not say it would be part of my reward having brought him here to savour this our last moment together?"

Grantham reflected deeply and nodded. "Indeed, I did," he answered laconically.

"And that I could do anything within reason I want with him?" she asked.

He nodded again. "Yes. But do get on with it, Katrina. We have wasted enough time as it is."

"Good. I will do father. Let me just have my way with him," she said smarmily as she slithered over to Capri, still riddled with that evil smile of hers. "Now, what game shall we play, my brother?" she asked Landis, her voice nearly singing with delight.

"How about something fitting," he replied. "Why not one of the games we used to play as children where you were the top and I the bottom."

"Oh, what a good idea. 'The Mistress and Her slave' trip. I can see it all now. Let me prepare myself."

Capri had enough. "Landis!" he shouted at him. "What happened to you? I thought you were Crome's protégé, that you were following his path?"

"Oh, shut up, Capri," he replied bemused. "I envy you. Do you realise that? We're all going to be wasted. Yet you shall live on. I don't know why you're making such a fuss over such a trivial matter. As for me, I've found my path. I delight in it."

"Because it brings you pleasure! I've heard all about you. You're sick. People like you should be strung up. How can you commit such atrocities?"

"Very easily, actually," and laughed maniacally.

"You're mad!" Capri shouted at him. "You're just as bad as Grantham. And you," he yelled at Katrina, "I bet you're the same."

Katrina started at him with a look of absolute contempt as if no one should talk to her like that and slapped him in the face, hard. "Silence!" she barked.

"No, I won't. You are mad. I can see it in your eyes. Like the rest of them." He struggled to free himself. His captors held him back. "I have never come across such a degraded bunch of perverts in all my life. I have tracked down some of the most ruthless people you could ever come across like rapists, paedophiles, kidnappers, arsonists, bank robbers, some of the most deranged, fucked-up, psychotic killers in the world..."

Katrina silenced him by pressing the muzzle of her gun under his chin. "How utterly goddamned heroic," she uttered.

"But I have never, ever come across such a sick, insane bunch like you. Especially you, Katrina. I thought you felt something for me?"

"Me? Feel something for an urchin like you? You're nothing but a slave. That is why it was so easy to get you hooked. You were the easiest coup I have ever made. You walked right into it. Do you honestly think I would fall for someone like you? But then, who can blame you? Who can resist my irresistible charms? Aren't I the greatest."

"You arrogant, selfish, juvenile little bitch!"

"Silence, slave. I will have no more of this. You will only speak to me when I order it. Do you hear?" she asked him, pressing the gun hard under his chin, nearly forcing his neck to breaking point. "You are a slave. Like all men. You shall be treated like one. You're no better than a dog..."

"Or a pig," Landis suggested. "Get him to squeal like a pig."

"No. We've done that scenario too many times. I'm bored of it. I want to hear him whimper like a snivelling dog. Do you hear me?" she asked Capri, the muzzle still pressed tightly under his chin. He didn't answer. She brought it right up and ran it over his face, pushing it into every niche. "Whimper! You snivelling dog!"

"No, I won't," he shouted back. "What a nice family you are. Next time you have a party, remind me not to come."

"There will be no next time," Katrina hissed through pursed lips.

Grantham turned to Katrina and said, "Get on with it."

"We have a disobedient dog here, father," she said with dissatisfaction. "I dislike intensely disobedient dogs, especially when they won't do what their mistresses tells them." Her eyes were aflame with anger, as she continued roaming with her gun, exploring each contour of his face until she found his lips and ran the muzzle over them. Capri tried to flick his head back. Landis' wife checked him. Katrina pressed it harder against his lips, nearly hitting his teeth as she tried to force it in. Capri kept his mouth shut tight. She pushed it harder, forcing his lips apart until he could no longer fend it off. The gun went straight to the back of his throat, making him choke.

"Suck it!" she demanded, her eyes vivid with excitement. "I said suck it. Do as you're told. Obey your mistress. Suck it." Capri refused and tried swinging his head round. His captors were stronger. "Do as you're told. Suck it. I want to see you suck it like a man's cock, you cocksucker."

Katrina flashed her eyes at Landis. He smiled in return as if there was a stirring of some memory between them. Capri could only look away in disgust. Finally he managed to wriggle out of their lock enough to get his

mouth free. The gun flew out of his mouth. He gathered up all the saliva he could muster, and in one glorious stream of hate, spat it straight into her face. "Bitch!" he shouted at her. "If you're going to kill me, then kill me. Get it over and done with."

Katrina's eyes boiled. He thought she was going to explode. With contempt, she wiped the spittle and threw it back in his face, took one large step backwards and in one blinding flash brought the toecap of her boot with incredible speed to his groin.

Capri doubled in two as the air went out of his body, his testicles shot into the back of his throat and out of his mouth in a loud guttural cry. His scream resounded in the temple, shaking its walls.

"Don't damage him, Katrina," her father yelled at her. "Now, bloody well get on with it. Finish it."

Capri's body sagged limply to the ground. If it hadn't been for his captors, he would have sunk into it for his body wasn't there at all, just this huge overwhelming pain which made it numb all over. But they pulled him up, struggled to get him back to his feet and brought his head up once more. He could hardly distinguish who it was standing before him with hands on hips, gleefully enjoying the result of her corrective discipline.

"I am not going to kill you. Anyway, I can think of better ways than shooting somebody. I like to see my slaves go down in pain, in exquisite pain, grovelling at my feet for more before they finally leave my beautiful presence. Pain, Capri. Beautiful, glorious, rejuvenating pain. It is the only way to explore your body. And you'd be surprised how much it can take. You see, my slave, I like pain. Don't you?" she asked him and gripped his chin to bring up his head so she could look straight into his eyes. "Answer me! Do you like pain?"

"Only if it doesn't hurt," he whimpered.

"No, I am not going to kill you. I am just going to put you out of your misery with a little pain, a little pain to take away the big pain, then you'll gain. No pain, no gain," she whispered into his ear. She then walked round him in a circle. His eyes tried to follow her, watching her suspiciously, then finally focused on her when she stopped in front of him. She was no less

than an inch or two away, her protruding breasts pressing against his chest. He could feel her nipples. They were hard. Her game had more than aroused her. She smiled at his realisation. She brushed her face against his. "No pain, no gain," she whispered again.

Capri tried to wrench his head back. He wanted to head-butt her as hard as he could. But it was held in check. Her mouth then came down to his, her lips hovering longingly over the surface of his. Again he tried to wrench his head back. They held it in place.

Quickly, she landed a peck on his mouth. Her kiss tasted like poison. He flinched. She laughed and then brought her mouth down again, her tongue extended, poking between his lips. The smell of her breath repulsed him more than anything else. It was laced with some malodorous substance, a drug he wasn't familiar with. She retracted her tongue, her eyes fixed on his, peering deep into the recesses of his skull. She smiled. She then opened her mouth revealing those bright shiny teeth of hers, so perfect they simply couldn't be real. At first he thought she was going to kiss him again as she craned her neck and lowered her mouth to his. She stopped. She then nibbled his top lip gently, suddenly clamping her teeth shut and in one excruciating jerk she pulled her head back, the flesh of his lip still caught between her teeth, and drew it back then released it. Capri could only yell out as it brought more tears to his eyes.

"I said don't damage him!" Grantham barked.

"Let me kiss it better," she breathed and gave him a full, big kiss, trying to wriggle her tongue into his mouth. Capri fought back. She desisted and closed her eyes and breathed all over him, brushing her breasts firmly against his chest, her hand slowly working its way down to his groin. Her eyes flicked open in dismay.

"You're not hard!" she spat at him with resentment. "How dare you not be hard when I let you come so close to my voluptuous body. Slave!"

"You're mad," he said agitatedly as he tried to get free. "Fucking mad."

"Silence, disobedient dog. How dare you not be hard for your adorable mistress. Why, I ought to hang you up by your genitalia. I will make you hard before we're through."

"No you won't, Katrina," her father bellowed. "We don't have time for that. Now get on with it."

"But he's not hard, father. I want him hard."

Capri wrestled with them some more. Katrina turned round to face him. Finally he managed to get some more words out, "You stupid bitch. Of course it's not hard. You just kicked me there. What do you expect?"

"Silence, slave. I rule this space," she said, indicating the whole temple. "This is my space. Nobody talks to me like that here. I rule here. I am the mistress here. And you will do exactly as say." She stopped talking and walked round him once more. "What a failure you are," she continued. "I detest failures. All this trouble I've gone to as well. And you won't even acknowledge my superiority. Well, we'll see about that. It is a pity I do not have my whip with me. That would put you right. Then you would submit. I am a Mistress of Whips. Do you know what that means?" she asked offhandedly. Capri shook his head, too far gone to care. "You really are an ignorant person, aren't you? Just like my father said. So much to learn, so little time in which to learn it. I am a Goddess of Power, the Goddess of Blackleatherspace, this space, my space," she whispered in his ear.

Katrina backed off and stood still. Capri endeavoured to read into her mind. It was as inscrutable as a closed book. So far her behaviour had proved all too erratic to estimate her next move. He simply had no idea what she was going to do next. Fearfully, he waited.

"Kneel slave!" she barked cruelly. His captors forced him down onto his knees, his arms forced rigidly behind his back. He was made to look up to her like some queen.

"I am the goddess of Blackleatherspace," she intoned solemnly. "Therefore you shall worship me as such. Now worship me!" she hissed.

"No. You're no goddess," he countered.

"Worship me."

He shook his head. "No. I won't."

Impatiently, she took three steps forwards and with the toecap of her boot brought it up under his chin, pushing his head up, making him look directly into her eyes. He turned away. She fumed at his disobedience and pushed his head right back. A gurgling cry came from the back of his throat. She laughed hoarsely and rested her boot firmly on his shoulder, deliberately pulling back the folds of her robe so all he could see were her long, never ending legs and a brief hint of crutch. She cast her eyes down to his, smiled wickedly and uttered again, "Worship me." Capri shook his head once more. "Worship me," she demanded, her gun resting on the knee of her boot aimed directly at his temples. Again he refused. He could tell by the look in her eyes he was pushing it. Soon she would have to kill him. That's what he was praying for, to put an end to it all. "Worship me," she repeated. Now was the time; she was on the edge, losing her patience.

"FUCK YOU!" he screamed at her.

With that, in a movement so quick he didn't see it coming, she whirled round, booted him straight in his chest, pirouetted once more like a ballerina on one leg, stopped and settled it again on his shoulder. Capri, taken aback with the force of her kick, could only splutter.

"I said don't damage him!" Grantham yelled. "How many more times?"

Capri spluttered again and coughed. He tasted this foul liquid in the back of his throat. He spat it out. It looked like blood. He winced.

Upon seeing it, Katrina smiled. She ignored her father and came down even heavier upon him this time.

"Worship me!"

"No, never," he cried as loud as he could. "I will not. You're no goddess, nor a mistress. You're no Woman of Power either. You don't even menstruate!" Katrina looked livid. "Now do as your father says. Fucking kill me. Get on with it."

Before she could kick him again, Grantham rushed forward and grabber her arm and pulled her back. "You've had your little game," he told her. "Your time's up. Now go and get ready." Katrina, her eyes filled with bitter hatred, gave Capri one more look and walked back to the altar. Grantham stooped

CELEBRATION

down and said reassuringly into his ear, "We're not going to kill you. You will have to forgive my daughter. She gets a bit carried away, the headstrong girl that she is. I do apologise for any pain she has caused you. Please forgive us, but if you had simply accepted what I had said it would never have come to this."

Capri shook his head in disbelief. "Grantham, I don't give a fuck anymore. Whatever you intend to do with me, just do it and let me die in peace."

"You're not going to die either. Soon you will be prepared and placed in our Ark. You will be long gone from here before the apocalypse gets under way." And with those words, as if on cue, another bruising wind shook the old building. Grantham looked up. "The time is coming, the rite time, the time of his passage. We must get ready. And to you," he said to Capri with a paternal voice, "you will be undergoing the major initiation of your life. The final one, the one you have been putting off for years. It is now time to work with the Dark, to unite the Light and Dark in your being. We will guide you safely into the beyond and you will come back a new man, nay a god. You shall achieve immortality. I swear it."

"I don't believe you. I don't believe any of this. You've got the wrong man, I tell you. And you are wrong about the end of the world, I'm sure of it."

Landis stepped forward, saying, "We speak the truth. The time has come. It has been intimated for many years. A great friend of mine too has known of the coming doom. He has prepared himself just as we all have. We cannot stop it from happening. The small has departed, the great approaches."

"After today," Grantham continued, "there shall be no more Harmon Capri, but a god. I swear this is true. And it is absolutely imperative we have your full cooperation. One slight mishap could jeopardise the whole operation. If we don't get the balance right you could come out of it a hideous monster or a megalomaniacal tyrant like a false Messiah of old. Please allow us do to our wills without hindrance."

Grantham then turned to Katrina and whispered something in her ear. Capri couldn't hear what he said but it certainly helped to shrug off the brooding look on her face. She beamed and proudly marched towards Capri, gun in hand.

"Wait!" Capri shouted. "What about the drug?"

With a look of annoyance clouding his features, Grantham swung round. "What about it?" He eyed him critically and gestured Katrina to stop.

"Does it exist?"

"What's it to you?" she asked. "It doesn't matter whether it does or not."

"It does matter," he countered. "I have to know."

Grantham indicated for his daughter to hang back and stepped forward himself. "My daughter is quite right. I can see no reason why we should satisfy your curiosity, unless of course it is a means of buying more time in the hope you'll be saved because you won't. To answer your question, it does exist, and you were on the right path. But it is far more difficult to obtain than you think. That is why all my efforts have failed. That will suffice for you; that is all you need to know." Then he turned to his daughter. "Get on with it, girl."

Capri, anxious, for it must have gone twelve by now, was desperate to get him to talk. But for how long? Carlotta should have been here by now. Where the hell was she?

A curious silence stole over the temple as if Grantham's words not only terminated his speech, they also terminated the end of the world. Grantham again gestured to Katrina. She took a step towards Capri.

It looked like this was it. Soon it would all be over. Carlotta was not going to show. Had she let him down deliberately? Or was there some other reason for her non-appearance? Maybe the shuttle had been delayed. The panic due to the imminent tidal wave could be the cause. He simply had no idea what was happening up there, but he was determined to hang on for as long as possible.

"Wait!" he shouted.

"Oh, for crying out loud, Capri!" Grantham shouted back. "We've wasted enough time as it is. Stop trying to buy more time. Your time has come."

"But surely, if you were a gentleman," he rejoined, looking at Katrina as she

CELEBRATION

stopped in her tracks, "you would grant a dying man his last wish."

"You may think you are going to die, Capri, but not in the form you hope."

"I don't care what you mean. All I know is I came to LA looking for a drug on behalf of Carlotta, and I was fairly certain she would be here," he let slip.

"Be here?" Grantham snapped.

Realising he had made a mistake by mentioning her, Capri decided he now had to go along with it. "Yes. Be here. I thought she was one of you."

"Oh, I see," he wheezed. "Now I understand. Now I can see why you were so dismayed when not finding her under our hoods. You really thought she was one of us, that she had betrayed you. Is that it?"

"Yes. Don't laugh at me. I was certain of it."

"Well, let me assure you, old chap; she has nothing to do with us. She was long gone before we took over. After she left she thought the group had been dissolved. And so it had, temporarily. Then I stepped in. Took over the reins and resurrected it. Made some modifications to this temple. Not even Mosalla was aware it was being used. Nor did Carlotta. She doesn't even know we are here."

"Oh, but she does!" he exclaimed eagerly. This was his last trump card.

"Rubbish, Capri."

"I can assure you she does. And she's on her way right now, this very minute and bringing the police."

"You're imagining things in your delirium. Carlotta is safely ensconced in New York, thousands of miles away."

"Afraid not, Grantham. She's on her way here with the Calvary."

"Don't be a fool. Stop trying to waste time. You talked to her long distance last night. Katrina heard you and tried to prevent you from telling her what your plans were for today."

"Ah, but this morning, first thing, I told her I knew who Mosalla's killers

were and that I was going to track them down here. She didn't believe me and insisted on catching the shuttle over. She should be walking through that door any minute."

"Will she, indeed. In that case we had better get a move on. The last thing I want is some stupid woman interfering with my plans. Get on with it Katrina," he barked at her.

"No, wait," Capri begged.

"Ignore him. Do it, my girl."

Katrina smiled with delight. Capri struggled. His captors gripped him tighter as he tried to wriggle free with one giant effort. Katrina, her eyes cold as steel, came right up to him, gun outstretched. She stopped two inches away, her head bowed down to his, her breath brushing against his skin like dry ice. He flinched and tried to wrench his head away as she kissed him quickly on the cheek. He winced again. She walked to his side, raised the gun to his neck and said in words devoid of any emotion, "I've been dying to do this for a long time. Goodbye, Harmon. It was nice knowing you. In a way, I meant what I said in my note. I will miss you."

"Well, the feeling isn't mutual," he responded wryly.

She fired. He felt the hit instantly, buckled to the floor as his neck took the whole force. The sound of the shot wasn't as loud as he had expected, more like a quick spurt of escaped gas. And the pain wasn't what he expected either, just a quick, sharp jab in his neck. It sort of flowed through in gradual waves, pulsating down towards his lower trunk, but bringing with it a queer motion of sinking. Then his eyesight blurred momentarily as the full sensation took effect, and the whole temple seemed to be slowly melting. He could see Grantham staring at him anxiously, his brow still knotted, and those dead eyes looking even deader. The temple seemed to spin as he felt himself sink into the ground. He was sinking deep into it and could feel his body melt at the same time. He had to struggle to interpret what was actually happening as Katrina stepped back and watched him. His captors, he now realised, had also let him go and that was why he was sinking, and the ground was swallowing him up. And nor could he stop it. Any strength he had left seemed to dissipate. It seeped away and he was on this endless

CELEBRATION

tide, floating on its surface, his arms by his side as the ceiling of the temple came into view. His head fell back and hit the floor with a deadening thud. It was the only thing he could feel beneath him. Instinctively, his hand limped to his neck to pull away the pain. His numb fingers pulled it out. He brought it before his eyes, seeing it through half-blurred vision, a small steel dart dripping with blood.

"Quick," he heard Grantham say, all muffled. "Make sure he lies straight."

Then he saw Landis and his wife hovering over him doing something to his non-existent body. It simply wasn't there as if he had been decapitated and was only this head pinioned to the floor. He tried turning it to see what they were doing to him now. Only Katrina was visible. He saw her shrug and throw her gun away and turned to look at him. She smiled wickedly at him. He wanted to curse her. But his voice would not come. All he could manage was a croak. He forced his head round and could now see Grantham bending down towards him, his dead eyes looking straight into his. He reminded him of a doctor examining his patient just as he was going under prior to surgery. His voice reinforced the impression as he heard it coming through to him indistinctly.

"I'm sorry, brother. It was the only way. You left us little choice. It is a mild drug, a concoction I prepared myself, sufficient to paralyse you from the neck downwards. Normally, I would have taken precautions and I administered a larger dose to paralyse your entire nervous system. But knowing you, I decided this amount should be adequate. Besides, we don't want you trying to slip away from us astrally, do we? As you will retain full consciousness until you enter the freeze you will not be able to. You will feel a slight discomfort. It is perfectly normal, I assure you. It will make you feel nauseous. You will feel the need to vomit. It is a side-effect which will wear off shortly. Do not be alarmed. Do not panic," he cackled.

Grantham cackled again as he stood up. He looked to his colleagues to see how they were getting on. Capri could only look straight up at the ceiling with little idea of what they were doing to his body. And now Grantham's words were proving true as the drug took full effect.

Then they lifted up his head. Now he could see what they had been doing to him all this time. He wanted to gasp, thinking this was a dream, that it

wasn't really happening. His clothes had been removed and his naked flesh covered with thick layers of bandaging as if he was a mummy, the bandages having been wrapped tight, his arms and legs left separate and not bound together. And now they were doing the same to his head, wrapping bandages round it as they held it in position, And lastly his eyes, using only a thin layer of gauze so at least he could see partially. His nostrils were left free so he could breathe. Then they let his head back down gently and stood above him, each admiring their handiwork. For the first time he saw on Grantham's face a little smile play about his tight, thin lips. Capri now realised how fully he really despised the man.

"Did you know," he said as he bent down towards him, "this is the exact method they used in Egypt. You see, their practise of mummification was practised on not only the dead, but also the living as a means for effecting trance and exploring other realms. And now here you lie like a mummy ready for your great initiation. And you will undergo it, my brother, and you shall pass into a land that the ignorant call death and yet you shall live, rise up like a glorified *sahu*, a risen mummy, resurrected, one that died and yet was reborn and need die no more."

Capri felt his head shake. It was a tremor from deep underneath, but forceful enough to stop Grantham speaking. The man quickly looked up and waited. Another tremor came. It brought a smile to his face.

"Ah, my children," he chanted jubilantly. "At last the time is come, the rite time, the time of his coming. Listen as he approaches. Is that not the sound of his coming? We must prepare our brother for his great awakening."

Capri saw them through distorted vision bending down. They gently lifted him up off the floor. He was being conveyed to the infernal machine, the Ark that was not his tomb but his womb, or so he thought. And they gently lowered him into the padded interior as a baby in a manger. All he could see above him was that dreadful sigil. He could also see the spiralling lines around it that would open up like the floor and allow him entry into the beyond, blasting through the floors above. Then he would be all alone in space for—he knew not how long. Eternity perhaps? Or until everything on earth had subsided and returned to some form of normality. How long would that take? He did not know. He just saw himself as a satellite circling the earth with the other six satellites. Then he would come back down to

earth and join them in their quest to repopulate the earth on a new level of consciousness like a god.

He lay there snug inside, motionless, as the glass lid came inexorably down sealing his fate. Then there was this whirring sound, trembling deep beneath him, as the capsule started to shift into a vertical position. He saw the sigil recede past his head and then he saw the opposite wall, the curtains of the doorway. And still there was no sign of Carlotta, no hope of a reprieve. It was too late as he stood erect in the capsule and was now waiting for the sleep to come, that sleep he had dreamt of, the thousand odd days, and the accompanying peace it would bring and hoped never to awaken from it. And he could see them joining hands before him as the ceremony was about to begin, as they started to invoke their obnoxious devil of a god, how they seemed to be laughing at him. Was this really what his life had amounted to? Was this really the end, the end of his life and the end of the world? What a fool he had been to have embarked on this mission that not even his terrible sense of foreboding could stop him from undertaking. And all because he believed he was helping a woman he thought he loved.

As the liquid nitrogen came seeping through in waves of white clouds, rolling over his body, dancing around his nostrils, making his head feel numb and cold, he could see himself as if from a distance; an upright mummy, now on the verge of resurrection. Having lain flat as in death, he was now upright, a living *sahu*, a risen Horus, a Christ rising from his tomb.

He was out high above earth, floating in the dark and icy coldness of space, bound like Christ to a cross of steel which shone brightly, reflecting the sun's rays as it slipped behind the western hemisphere of earth. And all became dark and he was isolated in this tenebral gloom, a figure no one remembered anymore, forgotten, doomed to eternity and space, awaiting for the light of the east to rekindle his naked spark.

He floated endlessly like a hawk over the earth. He could see the harbour of New York as it came into view, the formidable landscape of concrete fingers pointing up to the sky. In the silence he saw the gallery, its twin pyramids conveying a sense of poignancy as he now understood on a far deeper level what the building meant. Then he saw the cafeteria and the very table where he sat with her, remembering how beautiful she looked

that day. Then he saw the archives section, all those paintings by that genius, and the one where he first met her. He saw the fisherman's boat shored up in the harbour, the blue placid water, the hills in the distance encompassing the water as if it were a lake, the scattered broken clouds above and the dark sky stretching up beyond them, and the hallowed image of the cross suspended in space. He saw the Man, his face hidden, his head drooping down in the ecstasy of death. And then it moved as if being stirred to life, slowly awakening, his head lifting to look directly at him. And he saw the face. It was his own.

He saw the second picture, the Madonna enthroned, her hands joined in the attitude of prayer, her eyes closed in supplication, her countenance exuding peace. Yet strangely it wasn't Gala. And, as if being disturbed from a deep sleep, she too slowly opened her eyes, looked at him. It was Carlotta.

And he saw the child playing about her lap, full of innocence, a gift of love. It forsook its playing, looked up at him. He saw the face. It was his own.

A montage of images flew through his slowly decaying mind. Gala smiling, holding the baby. Mary mourning the death of Christ. Isis mourning the death of Osiris. Nephthys wailing like a kite. Stephanie slowly losing her mind. And a host of other women paraded themselves before him, each one meaningful but too fleeting to glimpse. Lastly he saw Nefertiti seated on the throne with her husband Akhenaten sitting next to her. They turned to face each other, smiled, then turned towards him. He could see her face clearly. It was Carlotta. Then he saw her husband's face. It was his own.

As the freeze bit into him deeper, making his teeth chatter, the only thing he could utter to himself was, "I am cold, Carlotta, I am so cold. So cold. Help me."

His life began to slip away. Slipping away from his fingers. Slipping away.

All slipping away as the jigsaw pieces finally fell into place.

And lastly he saw the stagnant sea, the jagged horizon, the dead sky above and the waters rising up, the head appearing above the waves with its eyes of burning coals staring directly into his, and the upright ears that looked like horns, the hideous scaly body...

THE COMING ONE

'All myths of a "Coming One," a parousia or putative Messiah, are derived from one source and one source only, an origin that was never anthropomorphic—that came later!—but natural and physical, namely the annual inundation of the Nile which announced each year 'Life, Prosperity and Health' in all of its abundance, for it was undoubtedly the saviour of the land that had its reflection in the physiological processes of the phallus, the Coming One being another synonym for the waters, the waters of life in the loins of man. Both were interchangeable, the inner sometimes being signified by the outer. Yet it was with the outer that this natural phenomenon was personalised as the Coming One they called *Messu*, the child as *Repa*, the Prince of Peace, the perennial giver of life to the land as Hapi, the river, Horus, the Child or *Iusu*, the origin of the word *Jesu* or Jesus, who was figured by the Egyptians as *Iu-Em-Hetep*, He Who Brings Peace, the son of *Iusaas*, She Who Is Great With *Iuasa* or *Iusu*, the Ever-Coming Child, the Messiah of the inundation.'

Kelly Grantham,
Cults of the Khart

—26—
THE SAVIOUR

If only he had known; if only he could have delayed them for a bit longer, for Carlotta was on her way.

She was struggling to get the key in the front door as the wind beat at her face. It ripped off her hat and sent it high in the air. She swung round to see it being tossed down the road in the same direction as the taxi, it too fighting against the formidable wind and the rain. The taxi sped away back up the flooded street, sending a spray of water as it disappeared up the hill and was gone. She cursed the gods and fumbled with the lock. Finally she managed to get the door open and threw herself inside and slammed it behind her, panting. She leant against it to catch her breath, her scarlet coloured coat soaked and ruined, her hair bedraggled. She brushed it out of her eyes and the rainwater from her face, too flushed to be bothered about the way she looked. She had made it in one piece, regardless of her make-up and the wet mascara that ran down her cheeks in small black rivulets. There was something far more important to do, to find Harmon and get the hell

out again. At least his car was outside; it had to be his as there were no others in sight. She faced the panelled door; he had to be down there.

She took a deep breath and moved towards it and flung it open all the way. Before stepping inside something immediately struck her as odd. She stopped and listened. From the blackness below there was a curious sound bellowing up the stairs, too inaudible to make out what it was. It sounded like some people were singing. What the fuck is going on? And as she listened closer she realised it wasn't singing at all; it was chanting. But who? Why? Didn't they know what was happening? Her mouth dropped open in shock as another thought struck her. The smell of incense confirmed it. She reached into her handbag and pulled out her gun, a silver Lady's Beretta automatic with ivory inlaid grips, her hands trembling with nerves.

Not perturbed, she descended the innumerable stairs as silently as possible and with trepidation, on edge but determined to find out what was going on. The chanting grew louder and louder the further she descended and at each step her heart seemed to miss a beat. In the inner chamber she warily edged her way up to the curtains. Whatever was on the other side she was prepared to accept it. Harmon was right, and this gave her strength. Time, however, was not in her favour. It was now or never. She raised her gun. "Now!" she told herself and lunged through.

"Carlotta!" Grantham snapped, his consciousness slamming back so hard into his body it made his hood fall off.

Carlotta could not hide the look of surprise from her face as she found herself in the middle of some bizarre ritual. She stopped midway and went numb as she examined the circle of celebrants. They seemed to be worshipping some large metallic object standing upright in the centre of the temple. Fazed, she tried to take it all in simultaneously.

"What the fuck is going on here?" she barked at the man she barely recognised, having only seen him once or twice.

"What does it look like?" he howled back.

She ignored him, her gun aimed at his chest, but her eyes surveying all the other hooded figures. Was one of them him? "Harmon?"

CELEBRATION

"You're too late, Carlotta."

"Where is he?"

"Never mind him. Do you realise what you have just done? You have broken our circle of power by stampeding in here. The whole operation could be jeopardised."

Again she ignored him. There was something else bothering her, an uncanny sense of malevolence. It seemed to be brooding throughout the temple, cloying and clinging to the walls. She thought she was going to be sick. She fought against it and tried to abolish the repulsive smell. It too made her stomach turn. "I don't give a shit about your operation. All I know is, Grantham, whatever it is you are doing, it is evil and I'm glad I'm putting a stop to it. Now, where is he?"

"I've told you, you are too late."

"Grantham, I will not ask you again. We don't have much time. Do you fucking realise what is going on up there?"

"Of course I do. Why do you think we are all assembled here today?"

"I'm not interested why you're here. We have to get out of here. The whole place is going to be devastated any minute."

"We know. We are not leaving. I'm determined to finish my work here."

"Then I am taking him. Where is he? What have you done with him?"

"He is beyond your reach. There's nothing you can do for him. You are too late. Now leave him. Go. You have no business here."

"No, I won't go. I came here to save him. I'm not leaving without him."

"You can't have him. Don't you understand, you stupid woman? You can't take him away. He is inaccessible. Now go," he blared at her as the others stood in resolute silence. "Go, woman. Be gone!"

"You're right, Grantham. I don't understand you, but I did not come all this way, get delayed at some fucking airport for two hours and drenched to

the skin to walk away empty handed. I came here for Harmon and I am not going to leave without him. You understand that, because you fucking better. Whilst I've got this gun in my hand you will do exactly as I say. Now for the last time, where is he?"

"I will not have you ruin a lifetime's work just because of some foolish emotion. You could endanger his life. Now, if you really care for him, I suggest you leave, because if you so much as attempt to take him away from here you will surely kill him."

"I will use this, Grantham," she countered, waving the gun in his face.

"Then use it."

"I mean it."

"So do I. You will have to kill me, Carlotta, because there is no other way you are going to get hands on him."

She paused, looked to the others quickly and counted them, then back to him. Grantham smirked as if reading her mind.

"Yes, exactly," he continued. "You will have to not only kill me, but all of us. We will defy your attempts to remove him. You have no chance."

"Then you leave me little choice. Who shall I take out first? Just tell me where he is before I start shooting."

Grantham shifted his eyes to the capsule. Carlotta followed them, unsure what he was implying. He couldn't possibly mean he was inside that thing, could he? "What's that?"

"What do you think it is?" he replied, smarmily.

"How the fuck should I know. It was never there before. What have you done to this place, Grantham?" she asked, her eyes taking in not only the curious object, but also the even curiouser design in the ceiling which it appeared to be pointing at.

"I see you are intrigued," he remarked calmly. "But unfortunately we do not have time for an intimate discussion, Carlotta. I suggest you leave before it

is too late." Suddenly his voice changed and his words came out in a baritone falsetto, each one slow and reverberating. "You want to leave. You know the situation to be hopeless. You are turning around..."

"Don't use that old mind-trick on me. I can feel your filthy soul trying to burrow into me. Now stop it and just tell me how to get him out of there."

Grantham was brought up short. His voice went back to his normal tone of authority. "I'm afraid we can't. You see, it is time-locked and it's not set to open for another 3 years," he cackled. The others joined in.

"Shut up, the lot of you. I'm warning you. Get him out of there."

Grantham brought his hands together in front of his chest as if in prayer, his fingertips tapping one another, producing an unsettling sound.

Carlotta knew immediately what he was trying to do. It was another of his old tricks. "Stop it."

He desisted and looked her straight in the eye, his voice overfriendly and affected. "You see I would love to help you, I really would. But even if I was able to open it there would be a slight problem of, shall we say, temperature," he cackled again, the others echoing his laugh. "And a sudden, drastic change in temperature could prove fatal. More than that, at present he is in a profound sleep. You will never be able to wake him. So that is two problems you will have to deal with. I'm afraid you simply won't have time. Nor will you be able to get him out of here alone. So you see, you simply have no option but to leave and let us finish our work in peace."

"I don't fucking know what you mean, Grantham, but I came here for him and I'm taking him with me."

"Really? To where? That's another problem. There's nowhere to go."

"Bullshit. There is, and I'm taking him there, miles away from here, miles away from you. Now, for the last time, get him out of there."

"I can't."

"Very well. I will blow him out."

Carlotta redirected her gun straight at the capsule as she moved in closer. Grantham jumped in front of her, shielding it.

"Have you no sense, woman? Don't you have ears? Listen to what I say; it is not only time-locked it is also impregnable. You will never be able to blow it open. Even if you could you will probably damage him. A sudden change in temperature will kill him."

She didn't understand what he meant. Her mind was fixed too feverishly on the strange glass covering that seemed to be housing something inside, something she couldn't make out as the glass was only partially opaque. It seemed to be frosted over. She turned her attention back to him and the others who had moved in a tight circle round her when she wasn't looking. Immediately she sprang back, away from them, her gun darting at all of them in turn frantically, then finally settling on Grantham again.

"I should have known you were behind all of this. I had a sneaking suspicion when Harmon told me he thought this temple was still being used. I never thought it would be you. My own guess was it could only be one person, that bitch of a daughter of yours. Where are you, Katrina? I know you are here. I thought I recognised your voice last night." Her gun pointed at each of the hooded figures in turn. "Come on, you bitch. Show yourself. Take off you hood."

One of them stepped forward and stopped in front of her. Carlotta instinctively aimed as the hood was pulled back in a defiant gesture.

"Ah, there you," she hissed with contempt. "My, you haven't changed much. And still partial to your favourite drug, I see. Well, if you are here, then so must your brother be. Where is that scumbag?"

And another one stepped forward. The hood was pulled back to reveal the face of Anton Landis. He grimaced at her.

"How did I guess? God, how I hate you. I still do after all of these years. I hate the fucking lot of you. Remove your hoods, now!" she ordered.

They all complied except the one standing to the left out of her sight.

"And how nice, the whole debauched family. What a pleasant surprise. I

thought everything here was finished. But obviously I was mistaken. I should've guessed you unctuous creeps had taken over this place. I bet it was you who killed Mosalla. Why? So you could have full control?"

"It is nothing like that," Landis remarked.

"Shut up," she barked at him. "As soon as Alex left the group fragmented. It was all your doing, Anton. Trying to take over something that was never yours. Just like your sister here. I knew we should never have trusted you. There was always something sinister about the pair of you. But how were we to know who your father really was. You were all jealous of us, of what we had achieved. And you destroyed everything. I will never forgive you for that. Especially you, Katrina. You're the worst of the lot. I have never come across such a contemptible person in all my life."

"I thought we had something going, Carlotta," she replied with an affected look in her eyes.

"Don't give me that shit. You bitch. I remember how you wheedled your way into Mosalla's home, pretending to be some poor lost orphan, no parents only a brother, worming your way into Mosalla's heart like some cheap tart, and how the poor man suckered up to it. And you used the same trick on Jack. I wonder; would his death have anything to do with you?"

"No, Carlotta," she replied. "It was nothing to do with me."

"She's right," Grantham interjected. "It had absolutely nothing to do with her. It was purely an accident. He died by his own hands."

"Then what about Mosalla?"

"It was nothing to do with us either."

"Bullshit. You killed him, didn't you?"

"You don't know what you're saying, Carlotta," Landis stammered.

"Shut up. I know perfectly well what I'm saying. You're nothing like Alex, Anton. There is only one Crome. It took over a thousand years to produce a man like him. It must have taken all two minutes of a quirk spurt to produce a little turd like you. You'll never be anything like him. You simply

haven't got it. And the same applies to you, Katrina. Who the fuck did you think you were trying to take my place? Trying to win over my affections just to get into my bed? And then you tried it on with Alex, didn't you? He wasn't impressed. Do you know why? Because you haven't got it. You could never be like me. You could never be a High Priestess. That's what really grated on you, didn't it? You were jealous of me. You're nothing."

"How dare you talk to me like that!"

"I will talk to you any way I want. This used to be my space, remember. Well listen, you silly bitch, I'm back. I'm reclaiming my space. I'm now in control. You do as you're told. Get him out of there, right this minute."

Grantham stepped between Carlotta and Katrina, his eyes fixed firmly on hers. But unlike a normal man's eyes, his appeared to look straight through her. She could feel this horrid stream of energy coming from them, intense and cold. Quickly she tore her face away.

"Stop it. I will kill you," she hissed.

"Then kill me. Go on, shoot me. I dare you."

Her fingers clamped around the grip of her gun. She raised it and held it steady, aiming directly at his chest. "I will," she intoned calmly.

"Then do it. Go on. Because I refuse to allow some stupid woman like you, who doesn't know her place, telling me what to do. This is no longer your space. It is ours. You deserted it. You absconded. And I really don't know why you are so attached to a man you hardly even know."

"It's my fault. I got him into this mess. I'm going to get him out of it."

"Then you will have to shoot me, won't you?"

With that, Grantham stood his ground. He opened his arms wide to invite the bullet and mocked her as if he was invincible. Carlotta held on to her attitude of defiance. Her fingers gripped her gun tighter. Her eyes raged. She summoned her courage, knowing that this was the only way, and began to squeeze the trigger, half-closing her eyes and preparing for the recoil. It didn't come. The muscles in her arms were locked. Confused, she tried

squeezing the trigger again.

"See. You can't do it, woman. You're incapable of destroying me."

"Don't push your luck, Grantham."

She tried harder. Nothing. It was another trick of his, sapping her strength.

"You can't," he mocked her.

"Yes I can," she shouted back. She imagined being flooded with light. Instantly, a tremendous energy seized her and, without knowing how, the gun fired. The recoil sent her arm high in the air. Stunned, she saw Grantham clutch at his chest, his head bowed in disbelief as he saw trickles of blood seep between his fingers. He raised his head. There was a curious expression she didn't understand. The man was simply shocked. It mirrored her look of disbelief. He staggered back a couple of paces, eyes wide, mouth agape, a strange gurgling cry issuing from the back of his throat as he collapsed to the floor on his knees. His wife rushed to his aid, frantically groping him, her heart sobbing, her eyes filling with tears. She became hysterical as Grantham expired in her arms. Carlotta, still disbelieving she had killed him, found her legs retreating as they all grimaced at her.

"I...I..," she blurted, not even sure what she was trying to say.

"You bitch!" Natasha screamed and lashed out at her.

Instinctively, Carlotta fired a second shot at point blank range. Natasha fell backwards as the bullet went home. She crumpled to the floor clutching her chest, then lay still, and expired with her eyes still open.

Carlotta whizzed round to see Landis' wife hurling abuse at her and then threw her whole weight at her. Carlotta ducked out the way, fired and hit her straight in the back. The woman went down with a thud, dead. Then she felt a kick in the back. She staggered to the floor, fell over Grantham and raised her eyes just in time to see Landis dashing for the exit. She let off a shot. It missed him, going wide of the mark and embedded in the wall. Before she could fire again he was through the curtains and gone.

She clambered to her feet, spun round to see four black robes lying on the

floor. It had all happened so quickly she wasn't sure how many she had killed. She stepped over to one robe, kicked it over only to find it was empty. She didn't understand. It was as if the robe had been dropped from the air. Time didn't permit her to work out what was going on. She went to the others to find them all dead and accounted for. It only left one person still alive, Katrina, wherever she was. She stood still and thought. Quickly, her eyes scanned the temple. There was no sign of her, nor did she have time to escape. Only one person escaped and that was Landis. She didn't give a fuck about him. His sister was more important, the one who kicked her in the back. She still had to be here, hiding somewhere. And the most obvious place was on the other side of the steps.

"I know you're there, Katrina," she called out. "Come out from there."

There was no response, no sound, only the wind still beating against the building high up above. She waited a while longer. A tremor shook the temple. It goaded her on. Gingerly she moved towards the steps, ensuring she made no sound, and edged her way round to the other side, bending down low, her gun ready. She had two shots left, and they were both for her, the bitch. A sound from above made her stop in her tracks. It sounded like the roof was caving in. She looked up to the ceiling to see if there any visible cracks. Out of nowhere a punch to her jaw sent her reeling back. She stumbled as Katrina ran straight for her and hit her again then tried to pry away the gun. Carlotta, only just about sensible, fought back, catching sight of her wild, manic eyes. They were positively blazing with hatred.

She dodged another punch as her fingers refused to let go. She kneed Katrina in the stomach and winded her. She went down, but still locked on to the gun. Carlotta kicked her. She went sprawling backwards. She aimed her gun, but not quickly enough as Katrina threw herself at her, lunging for her like a lioness from the ground. They both toppled to the floor, rolling over each other, tearing at hair, fingers ripping into faces, nails going for the eyes, two alley cats scrapping like mad, the gun waving wildly around in Carlotta's hand. She pulled Katrina away and tried directing it at her, only to get punched in the jaw again. She elbowed her in the face and tried to release Katrina's grip on her wrist. Katrina then head-butted her. Her head slunk back and the force of the blow sent the gun flying out of her hand to the other side. It clattered against the wall.

CELEBRATION

Enraged, Carlotta smacked her hard in the face, shoved her off and pulled herself off the ground to fetch it. Katrina wasted no time, leapt off the floor and with a karate kick caught her in the mid centre of her back. Carlotta sprawled to the ground with a choking sound and gasped as Katrina dived on top of her and started beating her head against the floor.

"Bitch. Fucking bitch. Don't you ever talk to me like that again," she screamed and wrapped Carlotta's hair round her fingers and kept pummelling her head with all the energy she could muster.

Carlotta could only cry out in agony as her forehead swelled with pain. She struggled to free herself from her grip. Katrina was seated on her back, all her strength going into each blow she dealt. Carlotta caught her breath and before the next blow could come, with all her strength, she elbowed Katrina in the side. She gasped and fell from her. Quickly, Carlotta jumped to her feet, swung round, booted Katrina straight in the face before she could rise and watched as she went sprawling backwards.

"Bitch!" she spat at her.

Then she looked for her gun. It was closer to Katrina than her. Katrina saw it, sprang for it. Carlotta hurled herself at her and caught her robe and yanked her back only to have the material come away in her hands and reveal her naked shoulders and breasts. Katrina turned to face her, her eyes wild and staring, shocked at the woman's strength.

"Yes, I'm more powerful than you. Don't ever fuck with me."

Katrina ignored her, whizzed round for the gun and was sent sprawling again as she was kicked in the back. It floored her. She lay motionless for awhile. Carlotta dashed for the gun, snatched it up, turned round only to see Katrina coming straight for her. There was still some distance between them. She raised it to fire. Katrina instantly stopped, backed off three paces.

"Please don't kill me," she whimpered. "I meant you no harm."

"Bullshit. Look what you've done to me," she yelled at her, the gun wavering in her hand. "I will kill you if it's the last thing I do."

A tremor came in. It shook the entire building. Both women stopped and

stared at the ceiling as dust filtered through the cracks. They were frightened, Katrina more than Carlotta. Then another tremor, this time closer. More dust filtered through. The gaps widened. They stared at the rifts. Soon the whole place would be collapsing.

"Spare me," Katrina pleaded.

"Never."

And another which rocked the temple. The very floor seemed to move. Both women staggered to retain their positions.

"Let me go," she pleaded again.

"No." Carlotta aimed and prepared to fire.

"Forgive me."

"Forgive you? I'll spit on your grave first." She aimed. Another tremor threw her balance. Katrina seized the moment and turned to escape. Carlotta fired. The woman ploughed forwards, her arms flaying wildly as she went down.

Carlotta ran up to her, kicked her over on to her back, took aim, this time straight between the eyes. A trickle of blood ran from Katrina's mouth. Her hard, empty eyes seemed to change. They softened and dulled as if a light was going out.

"I'm sorry," she spluttered and sank to the ground; her eyes closed in death.

Carlotta, more than shaken by the events so far, breathed a sigh of relief and dropped the gun to her side. Her face felt like it was raw meat, stinging all over. There was blood too trickling from her mouth. She wiped it away with the back of her hand and threw her head back. Another tremor came in. They seemed to be moving in closer. It only made her panic even more. She turned round. The object, whatever it was, housed her Harmon. Why and for what purpose she simply had no idea. But she was going to get him out. And she ran over to it, up the steps and like a mad woman pried at the lid with her fingers. It was useless. The thing was solid and, like Grantham said, it looked as if it had some sort of timing device, a fortified lock that

would be impossible to break. "Shit!" she exclaimed, and ran down the steps, trying to work out what to do. Surely all her efforts so far hadn't been in vain? She clutched her face in her hands, tore at her hair and bewailed vehemently at these stupid, useless corpses lying at her feet. In an act of desperation and without really thinking about it, she aimed her gun at the lock. She fired. The bullet ricocheted, whizzed past her head, narrowly missing her by inches. It didn't even scratch the surface. She screamed and threw her empty gun at it and beat her breasts. Another tremor forced upon her the urgency of the matter.

She ran to the altar. The holders for the tapers looked like they were made out of solid metal. Thinking they would be heavy enough for the job, she grabbed one, threw the candle away and launched herself at the capsule bringing the holder down heavily on the lock. The holder bounced off, flew out of her hands and scudded to the other side of the temple. She gasped in amazement. The lock was still intact. What kind of metal had it been fashioned from to sustain such force? Perhaps Grantham was right. This was useless and she was wasting her time.

She panicked again, ran back up to the altar having seen a knife and was about to reach for it when she caught sight of that abominable statue Mosalla had been so proud to have in his possession. Looking at it now, and the small vial before it, she still detested it. It was evil. She drew away in disgust, not even bothering to work out how it came into Grantham's possession. Then she caught sight of something lying underneath the altar. The cloth had fallen away to reveal Capri's suit, neatly folded underneath. It was the one he had been wearing when they first met. She bent down and picked it up, and as she did so a metallic object fell out of its folds and clattered to the floor. It was a gun made out of some silver alloy. She had never seen one like it before and picked it up too. There was a small dial under the butt, marked with degrees. She turned it to full. If this didn't work nothing would. She ran back to the capsule, stood a good distance back and aimed, shielding her face with his clothes. She fired. She flounced back as a massive explosion ripped through the temple, sending her hurtling to the ground. She fell on her back and lay dazed for awhile before regaining her bearings. It was as if the gun had been a cannon. And all she remembered was this blast of white light and a crackle of sparks bouncing off the whole capsule. She lifted her head to see the lock had been fairly

split in two, the glass lid had fallen to the floor without even breaking and—more disturbingly—a thick sheet of what looked like dry ice rolled out from inside the thing. Again she did not know what it meant but clambered to her feet and warily approached. Nothing could have prepared her for what lay inside.

"My God, what have they done to you?" she gasped.

She thought her eyes were playing tricks on her and forced herself up the seven steps to take a closer look. Inside was this upright thing she could only identify as a mummy, but whereas the ones she had seen in a museum had been old and tatty, this one appeared to be in immaculate condition and coated over with a thin layer of frost.

"Harmon?" Her voice sounded feeble. She had to force the word out. Her hands reached out to touch it and flinched back on contact. It was so cold it hurt the tips of her fingers. Now she understood what Grantham had been trying to tell her. Now she realised how serious he was, and how mad at that. What was she going to do? The whole of Long Beach was going to sink into the sea very soon and she had to somehow get him out of here. But how? What else had the man said about the dangers of the sudden change in temperature? "Bastard!" she shouted back at his corpse. But it was too late now. If anything, the damage had already been done, and now she had to press on.

She thought quickly. The whole body was frozen. It would take too long for him to thaw out completely. She didn't know anything about cryogenics but knew that to thaw him out too quickly could do irreparable damage. How about starting a fire, anything to get some heat in here? She ran back down the steps, looked around for something to burn. This was stupid, she realised. There was no timber in here apart from the altar. And then she saw once again that thing standing on it. It made her shudder. She drew back and turned towards the capsule again. Her mind, not thinking, more like clutching at wild suggestions, was working overtime. Time was of the essence and she had to get Harmon awake, out of his sleep because she couldn't possibly manage him up the stairs by herself.

She went to look at him again, not even sure if he was asleep or dead. There was no way of telling, but at least the thin layer of frost had begun to melt.

Now she could see clearly all the bandages underneath. She ran up the steps once more and tentatively extended her hand towards him. This time, as she touched it, he wasn't so cold. Her fingers didn't hurt. And it would obviously be better to get him out of the capsule onto the floor, away from the source of the cold. She wrapped his clothes around his torso in the form of a belt to give her some grip and was about to tug him free when a quake roared and the whole temple shook. She clung to him desperately with a horrible vision in her head as he nearly fell forward, her morbid imagination filling in the rest of the sequence, seeing him toppling down the steps and shattering on the floor in a thousand pieces like a block of ice. At least he was free, and with a gentle tug she managed to ease him out. Surprised at how heavy he was, she had to balance him precariously against her own body-weight and let his weight ease him down the steps, rigid like a frozen carcass. With one last effort, he was safely on the floor. She lowered him down and let him lie flat.

"Harmon?" she breathed. "Do you hear me?" There was no response as she knelt beside him, dying to tear away at the bandages. They were frozen together and probably frozen to his skin as well. She wanted to cry, feeling the tears ebbing into her red eyes. There was nothing she could do now but wait. And another quake, this time stronger, reminded her again that waiting was not an option.

"Bastards!" she shouted at all the corpses lying a few feet away. Absolutely useless, absolutely dead. What could she do? She tried to think of a solution, anything. The poor man was stiff and solid as a rock. Perhaps she was too late. Perhaps he was dead and she would be too soon if she hung around any longer. She moaned again, wailing like a kite and fought back the tears. Again she thought of making some sort of fire. Heat is what she needed. She got up and stamped her feet in rage. She let all her anger assail her and expelled it with her breath in one loud, mad scream. And as she looked up, again her eyes fell upon that dreadful statue. How she loathed it. And she directed all her anger, all her frustration at it. Then, as if seized by inspiration, the gun in her hand came up and without thinking she aimed it directly at that vile, monstrous piece of work and fired. There was an explosion. It threw her back. She landed squarely on the floor and opened her eyes wide to see a huge ball of flame shooting out from the statue. That and the altar went up in flames like an inferno. She couldn't believe how a

thing like that could emanate such heat. But it did and it was intense and from where she lay, she could feel it blasting against her skin. It was perfect and with delight she jumped to her feet, pushed Capri's body along the floor towards it as close as she dared and then ran back as the flames leapt up, vicious tongues of fire snaking their way up the wall. Within fifteen minutes the temple had become a sauna. Her face was covered in perspiration and she pronounced it a miracle as she watched his frozen body slowly melt. A pool of water now lay all around him. She watched fascinated as it spread across the floor. The flames subsided reducing the altar to a mass of charred embers. She waited for the heat to die down before going anywhere near him. And what had once been standing on the altar was no more, only a molten heap of metal. She thanked the gods and jumped to her feet with joy and ran over to him. The bandages were soaking wet, but at least he lay limply now, the stiffness had gone and the bandages came away in her hands as she frantically pulled them off his face. She cried ecstatically when she saw his eyes were still open.

"Yes! You're alive, Harmon. You're alive."

She kissed his white forehead and clutched his face in her hands. It brought warmth to his cheeks and she watched as the colour returned. The blue lips now turned a pale scarlet. There was hope yet.

"Thank God, you're alive," she sobbed and bent down to kiss him once more. But was he? She listened intently for any signs of breathing. Startled, she quickly ripped away the bandages around his neck and felt his jugular. At first she thought the pulse was absent. Then as she pressed harder she could just about feel it. It was so minimal she was surprised to be able to feel it at all.

"No!" she cried, and tore away at the rest of the bandages around his chest. She beat it with her fists, pummelling his heart back into life. Still the pulse was slight. She gave him the kiss of life. Stopped. Listened for his breath. Still it didn't come. She beat his chest again, climbing on top of him as she methodically pumped him. A strange gurgling sound came from the back of his throat.

"Yes, that's it. Harmon, breathe, goddamn you, breathe."

She gave him another kiss of life, slapping his face hard as if to shake him out of it. She panicked when there was still no positive response and pumped his chest some more.

She crawled round to the back of his head pushed him up and hit his back hard. Another gurgling sound came out of his mouth, this time followed by some liquid. She hit him again to get all the water out of his lungs, pushed him down face forwards as it dribbled out of his mouth. Once or twice he choked and his whole body went into a spasm. She pulled him back down and cradled his head in her lap. There was this terrible blank expression about his face. He looked dead. But he couldn't be. He had to be alive. He just had to. And the fear of God made her beat it back into him.

"Don't fucking die on me, Harmon. Please. Live! Fucking live!"

She kissed him feverishly, her warm hands rubbing his face. It shone with a rosy hue, but it was the eyes. There was nothing in them. Not even a glimmer of a spark.

"Live! Goddamn you. Live!"

She hit his back again. More liquid poured out of his mouth. He vomited and his whole body went into another nervous spasm, writhing with convulsions as if shaking off death itself.

"Live!" she cried, her eyes full of tears, her face flushed, her lips tremulous.

Capri stirred briefly, struggling to get some words out. Like water, they dribbled out unintelligibly.

"Hush," she quietened him. "Can you hear me? I thought I had lost you. I care for you, Harmon. Do you know that? And I'm sorry for getting you involved in this, but the thing is, we haven't much time. Do you understand?" His expression was blank. "Please try to understand. We have to get out of here. We can't stay. And I can't carry you up the stairs all by myself. See if you can move, please. Just try."

It was hopeless. Not only did he make no movement at all, she wasn't even sure if her words were registering. She stifled her sobs. There was a look of wonderment and genuine affection in her eyes. And she realised how much

she really did care for him in a roundabout way. Yes, Grantham was right. She hardly knew him, but to her he was all she had left in the world. Perhaps she shouldn't have been so hard on him, but there were few in her life she really cared for, and none of them matched Crome. None ever would and she had to accept it. Maybe, with time, she could make something of it with Capri. Now, with great passion and tenderness, she was determined to keep him, to get him to safety.

As if to shake her out of her deliberations another shudder sounded. The whole floor seemed to leap up in defiance. And a bigger crack appeared in the ceiling. She craned her head to see a boulder balancing precariously above the remains of the altar. Another shudder would send it crashing to the ground. Then the rest would follow. They had to get out quick.

With all the stamina she had left in her she got to her feet and started dragging him on his back towards the exit. She left him there, retraced her steps, picked up his clothes, his gun and her handbag and went back to him in time to feel another shudder and, as she had anticipated, it did indeed bring a slab of rock down. She turned in fright to see it dislodge and go crashing into the altar sending up sparks everywhere. She screamed. This was a nightmare. It was too frightening to even believe in. She grabbed Capri, struggled to get him to his feet, leant him against the wall and quickly threw his jacket over his partially naked body. As soon as she let go, he flopped forward. There was not a single bone in him.

"No," she cried, caught him and leant him back against the wall. "Harmon. I can't do this all by myself. Do you hear me? Try, please try." She let him go, stood back and watched in horror the way his limbs weren't coordinating as if he was suffering from ataxia. She caught him again. Another shudder produced by a quake from underneath the floor made it heave. Her imagination possessed her once more, imagining some foul demon trying to push its ugly head up to the surface. And, to match her fears, another quake made the floor split. A few inches at first appeared. The split in the floor went from one wall to another. She screamed when another quake stretched the floor even wider apart, revealing an impossible depth of emptiness below. The corpse of Grantham was lying right on its edge. She saw it move as another quake came. The body jolted an inch forward. She could only stand in acute horror, mixed with uncanny

fascination, and observe as the body dangled over the edge. The floor widened and she screamed again as another quake came as if it was determined to reach up and pull him down into its lair. She watched hysterically, her whole body numb as Grantham's body slipped over the edge and disappeared into the abyss below. Hell reclaimed its sovereign.

"Move!" she shouted at Capri and bundled him towards the curtains, throwing her whole weight behind him. He sprawled. She caught him and pushed him like a rag doll up the stairs. She drew on the last of her strength, manipulating his legs for him as they tried clumsily to negotiate the stairs. He fell down. She cursed. She wasn't having any of it, yanked him up and hurled him head long up the last flight of stairs and out into the hallway as a gust of dust billowed up behind them. The last thing she heard was a crashing sound as the masonry fell.

In the hallway she caught her breath, eyeing the pathetic but pitiable figure of the man she cared for. He lay motionless on the floor, an entangled heap. She fought back more tears which threatened to besmirch her face and pulled him up, dragged him towards the front door, opened it, and with one arm over her shoulder marched him through to the outside.

She gasped. How it had changed. What was happening? It was so dark it could well have been night, and the rain she thought would soon vanish only teemed down harder. Even the unfriendly wind seemed to be stronger. The road had disappeared. It was now a torrent of a river and looked as if it was ready to wash the car away.

She pressed on, got him down the stairs, waded through the water and propped him against the side. She dug into his pockets, found his ID card and rushed round to the other side. She got the door open, climbed in and was horrified to see the water was trying to seep in across the floor. She was inserting his card when another thought struck her.

"Shit!" she exclaimed and hit the steering wheel. She dashed out again. Ran round to him and clutched hold of him.

"Harmon, can you hear me? You can't drive so I will have to. But I can't drive without knowing your PIN. I need to know your number. Please tell me," she begged and grabbed his face. It was pointless. She might as well

have been talking to a drunkard on the verge of passing out.

"Please!" she screamed shaking him, her fingers wrapped round his lapels. "Please," she sobbed. And now the tears came and she couldn't hold them back any longer. She didn't care now, letting them flow as she panted. She snivelled and gave up, ran back round to the driver's side and climbed in. She punched in the first four digits which came into her head.

The computer came online. It was a cold metallic voice, a female's; 'ERROR. YOU HAVE ENTERED THE WRONG NUMBER. PLEASE TRY AGAIN.'

"No, wait. Listen to me. I don't know the right number. Please help me." Her plea went unheard. She tried another four.

'ERROR. YOU HAVE ENTERED AN INCORRECT NUMBER AGAIN. PLEASE TRY ONCE MORE. ANOTHER INCORRECT ENTRY WILL BE DEEMED AS POSSIBLE THEFT.'

"Please help." The computer went silent. She thought about asking Capri again, even getting him to write down his PIN. She thought of everything.

'STILL WAITING FOR ENTRY.'

As a last resort she ejected his card, rummaged in her bag for her own, inserted it and punched in her PIN.

'WARNING. YOU HAVE VIOLATED SECTION ONE TWO ZERO NINE THREE OF THE VEHICULAR REGISTRATION CODE. YOUR ACT HAS BEEN TREATED AS THEFT. ALL SYSTEMS SHUTTING DOWN.'

"No!" she screamed. She died in her seat and slumped forward, clutching the steering wheel, sobbing her heart out. To have got this far only to be defeated by a fucking computer. She wished she was dead.

'MISS BIANCI?'

She thought she was hearing voices, raised her head deliriously and waited.

'MISS BIANCI?'

It was the computer. She clapped with joy. "Yes. Yes. Yes," she cried.

'OF CONTACT NUMBER NEW YORK THREE ONE NINE THREE THREE ONE?'

"Yes, that's my number. My name's Carlotta Bianci. You have to help me."

'WHY HAVE YOU INSERTED YOUR CARD? THIS CAR IS REGISTERED TO MR CAPRI. YOU ARE AWARE OF THAT.'

"Yes, I know. I ordered it for him. Look, I haven't got time to explain. Mr Capri can't drive. He's not very well. I don't know his PIN. That's why I inserted my card. He's had an accident. He's leaning against the car on the passenger side. Feel him if you don't believe me." The computer went quiet again. She waited anxiously only to notice the water was now flooding the interior of the car. She screamed. "Help us, for fuck's sake. We have to get out of here. The whole place is going to be flooded."

'I AM PERFECTLY AWARE OF PRESENT METEOROLOGICAL CONDITIONS, MISS BIANCI. I DID WARN MR CAPRI BUT HE CHOSE TO IGNORE ME. THE CURRENT LEVEL OF WATER IS RISING RAPIDLY. IF IT SHOULD PENETRATE MY CIRCUITS IT WILL NOT DO THEM ANY GOOD.'

"Then fucking hurry up and get us out of here! Let me use this car, please, you stupid computer. It's an emergency."

It went silent again; another pause. It lasted for eternity. She couldn't bear it any longer and wanted to cry even more.

'YOU MAY PROCEED.'

She sat up and clapped her hands jubilantly. She hit 'start.' All the lights came on. She could hear the soft hum of the motor. She sighed with relief.

'DO YOU WISH TO SAVE ALL PRESENT OPTIONS?'

The holo wound up on the windscreen. She took them all in quickly. "Yes, save all present options."

'ALL WE REQUIRE IS CONFIRMATION OF PAYMENT. PLEASE

STATE YOUR BANK ACCOUNT NUMBER.'

She gave the computer her number, told it to open the passenger door, ran round to the other side and helped Capri climb in. Back in the driving seat she ordered the doors to close, the car lifted, she swung it round and hit the accelerator. The car tore up the street, sending a spray of water as it disappeared over the hill and was soon out on the empty freeway. Behind her she heard an almighty bang. It sounded like an explosion and so close it made her immediately stop the car and turn to have a look. She caught sight of a brilliant white light like an arc light cascading down to earth, leaving a trail of smoke behind it. It crashed somewhere not far from where they had been parked and exploded. She couldn't explain what it was then noticed Capri's small bag on the back seat. She made a mental note not to forget it.

She hit the accelerator, driving like a woman possessed up the rain soaked freeway. She estimated it would take less than an hour to get to the airport. She patted Capri's knee. He rolled beside her each time the car took a bashing from the wind, his eyes still wide open, but curiously not seeing anything. It must have been a terrible shock for him. All he needed was some warmth, peace, affectionate love, and he'd soon be back to normal.

"We'll be at the airport soon, Harmon. Computer?"

'MR CAPRI SELECTED CINDY AS MY NAME. DO YOU WISH TO CHANGE IT?'

"No, Cindy. That's a fine name. Save it. But what I want you to do for me right now is get me LAX. Make sure they have still got my reservation and ask them to wait for me. If they give you any shit, tell them I'll sue them."

A few moments later Cindy came back. The last shuttle would be leaving in the next half hour. The whole of LA was being evacuated. If she wished to get out, she had to put her foot down. Carlotta didn't understand what the fuck was going on. First it was Long Beach, now it was the whole of LA. It was no wonder the airport was so busy. If only I had gotten there earlier, she thought as she looked at Capri. Perhaps then he wouldn't have been in this state. She put her foot right down. In less than half an hour she was racing down the long strip which led to the airport. She could see from the distance a shuttle taking off, praying it wasn't theirs, and a whole line of cars

abandoned outside as if the drivers were in too much of a hurry to park them properly. What she could see of the rest of the city didn't look too promising either. It was dark, nearly desolate as if everyone had left already.

Then perhaps they were the last ones to be leaving.

An official in a bright yellow jacket waved them through and ran on behind them as she screeched to a halt by the side of the runway. There was only one shuttle left and it had to be theirs. A queue of people were struggling up the ramp; hostesses and stewards were frantically trying to get them all aboard. Carlotta had never seen anything like it. This was mayhem. She ordered the doors to open, bolted out and grabbed their things.

'WE HOPE YOU HAVE A PLEASANT FLIGHT, MISS BIANCI.'

She ignored Cindy, retrieved her card and waved to one of the hostesses to help her with Capri. The woman gave her a peculiar look when she rushed over. Only then did Carlotta realise that her appearance wasn't particularly salubrious or fitting for a woman of her wealth. What would they say if word got out she had been involved in a fight? The bruises to her cheeks and forehead, the cut lip and the state of her dress proved it. Nor did Capri help, half dressed in bandages and a jacket. She explained he was a hospital patient, hadn't had time to get him dressed properly. The hostess gave her a plastic smile and obliged her and helped her carry him up the ramp, clutching his small bag of belongings.

They were dumped in the last two seats at the back, he by the window, still blank and apoplectic. She smiled as she heard the reassuring sound of the engines and the door close and soon they were taxiing down the runway. The orgasmic pull of the take-off made her smile even more and she could see out of the window what was left of LA. The sight disconcerted her; the whole coast was being eaten away by the sea. Soon there would be nothing left. All visibility was lost as they penetrated in to deep, dark, thick clouds.

Now she could relax. They were on their way, safe and sound and could be together forever. She patted his knee again and looked down at his bag on her lap. It was partially open. She noticed lying at the top were some books, something she could read perhaps during the flight. She reached in and pulled them out. Three of them were some thick volumes by Grantham.

She shuddered when she read the titles. They had been part of Mosalla's collection. Perhaps Capri had bought them off him, but why? And underneath was a small book bound in a dark blue cover with a gold seal on the front. It was a curious design. Out of interest she opened it and read the title and the short ink inscription. She smiled. It was some poetry Alex had written. He had always been interested in poetry. Finally he had published something. She lay it on her lap. She would read it later. All she wanted to do now was sleep.

She clasped Capri's hands between hers, patted them and smiled at him, and a tear rolled out of her eye as she realised now more than what she had told him. She didn't just care for him; she felt more deeply for him than that, and what she had been through to get him out of there and safely away only confirmed what her emotions were telling her. She would prove it to herself and to him they were right as soon as he had gotten over this terrible shock and recovered from his ordeal.

"We'll be there soon," she assured him. "I love you," she whispered.

THE COSMIC CATHARSIS

'And with it, after purgation is dealt,
Nought else can possibly remaineth
Utterly, and only then is relief felt
Soon as the world slips through Uranus.'

Ancient Astronomical Text
(circa 1500 BC)

—27—
THE LAST MENSTRUATION OF THE EARTH

The camera is the Eye of God. It is objective in its vision, filming all things uncritically, without prejudice, bias or motive. It simply records, enduringly for all eternity, continuously from a global point of view. It is an aquatic eye, swimming in the waters of space. It does not blink. It does not miss anything. It records everything. For this reason is it divine, and therefore powerful. It knows all the things that have happened, are happening, will happen. Hence, it is omnipotent, omnipresent and omniscient. Within it lies the Alpha and Omega of all events recorded in light, on view for all to see. And he who does can become divine by travelling back through its lens. He is reborn as a Man of Vision, a Shaman.

The camera does not lie. It is the embodiment of truth. It is only its viewers who distort what it records. And for this reason it becomes a weapon in the hands of those who wield it. They can edit, distort, change events and replay them in whatever form they choose. They can delete, create and manipulate the events of celluloid time to demonstrate their point of view. They can make history, rewrite it, or destroy it. They can make/unmake people. They can, through its use, grant eternity to the chosen few, making them immortal.

Man does not possess the camera; the camera possesses him. It rules in twilight vision. The camera absorbs light, moulds it and preserves it in concrete form for all eternity. The light is its medium, the light that moved across the waters at the beginning of creation, giving rise to form, creating creation, creating life. When the camera shuts down all life is absorbed into it source, withheld in a storehouse of images awaiting to be reborn. This is

when death prevails, the darkness. The first cameraman is known to man. His name is God.

The camera runs on synched time, an endless reel of film moving back and forth, recording, playing, rewinding, and replaying incessantly all it has recorded. It does not only record time, it creates it, twenty four frames per second. And those who assume the mantle of God, the Divine Cameramen or Controllers, can not only create order, they can also create disorder by juxtaposing events. Thus the viewer can be exposed to symmetry or entropy, separately, intermittently or simultaneously. The events can be spliced together in successive sequences, or superimposed over one another, or in reverse order, so conditioning belief or deconditioning it, creating sanity or insanity.

To view a film is a form of time travel. The viewer can be subjected to past, present or future. He can move through film-time forwards, backwards or freeze frame in the present.

The camera is the source of vision. In this mode it creates an intersection known to time travellers as the Gate of Death. Through this gate they can sidestep space-time and move out of the realm of recorded, pre-recorded and unrecorded events. They technically die. Hence they are known as Deathtrippers. And, through will, they can jump into different sections of film-time with impunity, tripping in any point willed. Although technically dead, as revenants, they do not have existence outside of film-time. It is only when they travel through the eye of the lens they become liberated completely. This is the art of film making.

The camera is the Eye of God; the camera is God.

Its film is the astral light.

Its films are the akashic records.

The camera hovers above earth like a hawk taking in all in its glare. The earth is sick. She is rotten to the core. She is dying, bleeding in pain, in acute menstrual agony. Her blood is black. It oozes out of her wounds and swamps her surface. Her skin is peeling away; clumps of dead hair, dried tissue, scabs, are shorn by the hostile winds and the malicious rains, as the earth goes into the agony of menstrual withdrawal, its final menstruation, its

menopause—the Black Time. Her dying skin cracks open. Blood, shit, sanies, mucus, cold discharges come to the surface, obliterating her features, destroying her beauty. The earth is no longer attractive. She is corrupt, old, decrepit, vile, an ugly hag whose time has come. Her body decays. The whole of her surface is being erased.

The winds, lightning, thunders have come to take her away, to purify her rottenness and corruption, to ease her passage into death. They turn her outworn skin into dry timber; ignition by lightning. Fanned by the winds. The thunder is the sound of her burning. The earth is consumed by flames.

"This is the conflagration of the earth, O brothers and sisters," The Preacher announced. "This is the end of the world. The death of nature. Nature unveiled. Lament for her, O brothers and sisters. Lament for our dying sister. She has been good to us. She has served us well. We are the ones who feel the guilt for we have killed her. We have raped her, violated her, pillaged her, and destroyed her. We are her killers, brothers and sisters. Let us give her a good burial. Let us bow our heads in mourning. Let us sing the funeral dirge of the death of our sister whose life is leaving her. Brothers and sisters, be not afraid, we are dying too in this unhallowed, unforgivable hour. We mourn her loss, yea! We mourn our own lives, yea! We have buried ourselves, O brothers and sisters. Prepare your graves, for our time is come too. All hail the earth. All hail the Black Time. All hail the last menstruation of the earth! This is the time of her last bleeding. Feel her pain, brothers and sisters. Feel it in your hearts. Let her know you love her still. Let her know we have not deserted her in this solemn hour. This is the purification of the world."

The camera flies across the sky like a vulture catching snippets of all the chaos and carnage below; torrential rains, flash floods, lightning, old volcanoes re-activated erupting, seismic tremors as tectonic plates shift causing buildings, roads, railway lines and runways to buckle, entire cities to collapse, reduced to heaps of rubble.

Quick flashes of global destruction:

Tornadoes, hurricanes, ripping over the face of the earth, some with wind speeds of up to 500 mph, flattening whole areas. Crop fields left decimated. Houses demolished, flat as pancakes. Barns, outhouses and stables reduced

to splinters. Telegraph poles ripped out of the earth, tossed across fields like matchsticks, embedded in houses. Cars picked up and tossed miles away. Office blocks torn apart. The damage paths resemble gullies carved into virgin earth. Sister tornadoes leaving wreckage in a path a mile wide. Storm surges, their walls reaching 40 feet high, smash inland, flooding whole areas.

Tornadoes, funnels of smoke, chewing up the land, spewing it out, leaving decimation, carnage, mayhem in their wakes. Damage paths, criss-crossing across plains, paths of unpredictability. Relentless, indiscriminate. Bodies torn to pieces. Cattle picked up, whirled around, splattered over highways. Vehicles savaged by the ravenous winds, sucked in, spiralling around, vomited out. Cyclones moving in from Gulf of Mexico, the Caribbean and the Atlantic Ocean like resurrected warriors, samurai surfing on tsunamis, intent on destruction. Satellites forecasting more to come. Seedlings near the West Coast of Africa developing into fully grown hurricanes, vortices of power, churning up the waters of the oceans. Walls of water expanding to ten, twenty, thirty, even forty miles wide. The West coast totally destroyed as they sweep in, killing millions.

Whole land masses disappear and are submerged under the oceans as the ice caps break away. Glaciers, like soldiers, marching down the Pacific coast cutting it away. Small, flat islands lying in their path stand no chance.

Closing shot:

New York Harbour. Rain lashing at the water. It tosses and rises up in revolt. The winds goad it on. Statue of Liberty toppling. It dislodges, plunging into the bay. Manhattan. Dark. Desolate. Empty. The Grand Gallery being badgered by torrential winds. The top half comes crashing down into the lower half. Both pyramids merge. They are united; now one.

* * * * *

(Earth, viewed from a great elevation in space. A flash resembling an electric thunderstorm ripples over the surface of the earth, girdling it in a garment of light. A dazzling array of colours streak down to earth as the inner planes implode. Images project on to its surface, juxtaposing past, present, future events. Archaic images interblend with present space-time. Gods, demons, mythic monsters and fictional heroes manifest on earth.

CELEBRATION

Chthonian creatures come out to celebrate insect time; ants, centipedes, millipedes, lice, cockroaches, scurrying back and forth, engaging in mad erotic frenzies, scour over the land gnawing at anything edible. Pazuzzu unfurls his wings and belches forth hot stinking breath. His wings are swarms of locusts loosened upon the earth. They race through the air, thick dense clouds of death, bringing with them fresh fevers and plaques from the skies. Grasshoppers and crickets resonating sounds of buzzsaws. Scarab beetles roll balls of dung; they deposit them in banks of rivers. They bury the sun. Dagon rises out of the ocean, calling forth his children, the crabs, to join him. They scurry back into his relentless seas. Coyote leads wolves, hyenas, feral dogs away from the Great Winds. They rampage the earth, seizing like scavengers the last vestiges of food. They run to the hills. Two wolves on the summit of a hill watch the moon shed her glamour. Hecate has wizened. She is an old crone. The sound of the wolves howling fills the air. Anubis leads jackals from the gap between the mountains. He strides across the desert. They follow behind him. Thousands of jackals jack-off in the night. Thoth administers the last rites. Baboons stand on hind legs hailing the sun as it sinks forever. A Mayan priest in the temples of Chichen Itza is writing the last codex of time. A *sen* priest in Heliopolis dressed in a panther skin stands outside the temple of Ra orating the last liturgy to his god. Another ascends the pyramid of Khufu. He stands on its summit and unrolls a papyrus scroll. He praises Nut and throws away his scroll. He holds up high a *buja*-leaf, catches a drop of the host of heaven, drinks it and decays. He ascends to heaven as a point of light. Iblis leads a horde of demons from out of their hiding places. They crawl out of ravines and cracks between rocks, clefts, holes in the ground. They stampede the earth, roaming in droves like mad, hungry children, frightening the citizens with obscene gestures. Min rises. He stands naked, his phallus erect. Horus springs from the loins of his mother Isis. Set comes out fighting. He pursues him to the wilderness. Like two giants, their feet crush people into the ground. They clash and each shed blood. Set snatches the testicles of Horus and eats them. He is victorious. Osiris dances with Isis and dies once more at the hands of Set. Humwawa breathes corruption. His face is a mass of seething entrails and writhing serpents. Agni emerges from the craters of mountains. His fire is molten lava. His breath billowing clouds of magma. He is angry. His anger is the rumbling of the mountains, the shaking of the world. Lilith visits men in their death-agonies, sucking out their life-essence

with relish. Ahura Mazda and Angra Mainyu are fighting. Their battlefield is the earth. Angra Mainyu wins and reigns supreme. Mot triumphs. His victims are burnt carcasses of beasts of the fields, birds of the air. Mulungu appears. He is wrath with his people. His wrath is the fury of storms, the hostile winds, and the flood of torrential rains. Shamash disappears forever. Windigo eats human flesh. Yama turns the cosmic wheel full circle. The bridge to Chinvat collapses. The souls are hurled into the bottomless abyss. There is the sound of screaming and death cries. Sheol opens its jaws, consuming more souls. Its belly is full. Tlaloc is victorious. His body is the tempestuous rains, his breath the destroying winds. Amaterasu turns black. She disappears into the abyss. There is wailing at her loss. Reshef appears. His wings are plaques, his eyes fevers. Merodach awakens. She opens her legs and lets loose upon the world her poisonous excrementitious matter, killing thousands and blacking out Surya. Reshef is joined by Erra. They consume the world with sickness. Mara reigns, tempting the last survivors. The few that escape are captured by Cizin. He destroys them with fetid breath, biting off their heads. Saturn devours his children. The bridge to Qiyama too collapses. There is no heaven, only hell on earth. And all the souls are tried and found wanting. Thor alights from thunderous clouds. He holds in his hands his mighty Miolnir and does battle with the serpent Midgard. Both are defeated. The Beast arises out of the lake, his blackness is the clouds of smoke of erupting volcanoes. He unfurls his huge menstrual wings. They shadow the earth with primal night. Atum rises out of the primal mound. He fists his phallus giving birth to more gods, more demons. Harpocrates floats down the Nile seated on a lotus. He is silent. Allah captures the Buddha. He buggers him ferociously. The Buddha smiles serenely as he defecates sacred sperm. Kali dances the dance of death. She skips, hops, twirls over all the bones of the dead in all the graveyards of the world. The world is now one big graveyard. She gloats salaciously as she licks blood from her lips. Shiva lies in the corpse posture. Shakti bestrides him. She kills him with frantic copulations. Tiamat gathers her body about her. She is defeated by Marduk. Kingu divests her of her garment of shame. Ea comes out triumphing. He floods the lands with his waters as they pour from the skies. Ravana defeats Rama. Gog and Magog appear destroying the last vestiges of civilisation, first with fire, then with water, sweeping away the world into oceans of chaos. Baal destroys Nergal. Erishkigal opens her limbs, embracing the dead. Hades revisits the earth, opening fissures in

the ground for the dead to pass through. A hawk pecks at the eyes of Jesus as he hangs upon the cross. Mary laments her son's death. Sekhmet roars and burns up the lands with her heat. Everything lies parched in her wake. Shu collapses. Nut and Geb are lost in a last embrace. They merge, become one. Maat throws down her scales. Quetzalcoatl joins Beelzebub. They fly through the air, blackening the lands. Erzulie dances naked. Baron Samedhi sits at crossroads pointing to the Gate of Death. Poseidon rears his head above the stormy seas. His body is the rolling, treacherous waves. He scoops the lands back into his folds and sinks them. Pan comes dancing out of the woods followed by satyrs. They dance across the lands, trampling over the dead. Ishtar laments the death of Tammuz. Zeus strikes rocks with his lightning, splitting them asunder. Vulcan rises. His fury is the sounds of volcanoes erupting, his wrath ravines of molten lava. Nun spreads his body over the world, submerging whole cities.

A sulphurous fog hangs in the air, choking the last of the people. Some die through asphyxiation, others in agony as their skin peels away as if eaten by acid. The seas have turned black. A star falls from heaven into the abyss. The moon has turned red. It resembles a bloodshot eye. Christ reappears. He emerges from his tomb. All is silent. He is enveloped in a halo of light. His light fills the world. There is hope. The angels of the Last Judgement blow their trumpets awakening the dead. Peace. The Four Horsemen ride out of the sky. They descend to earth, the hooves of their steeds churning up dust. Christ is hacked to pieces by the sword of the red horseman. Peace is destroyed. All hell is let loose on earth as it is laid to waste. The Four Horsemen are triumphant and gallop across the lands, raping and killing anyone who gets in their way. A lamb lies bleeding. The angels sound the death knell of the world. The Book of Life lies open, its spine cracked, its pages burning. The beasts arise out of the seas, the lands, the seven hills. A seven headed hydra whirls and shoots lightning bolts from heaven, destroying the last remaining cities. Everything is destroyed. The red dragon covers the world with his body. It turns all things red. The seas become blood. The Whore showers the world with poison from her cup. Plumes of purple smoke rise to the skies. The sun turns black. Shaitan stands triumphant, gloating on the carnage. The cemeteries are overflowing. The dead rise from their graves. Scrawny fingers push up against the earth. Desiccated bodies climb out of holes in the ground. Putrefied corpses are re-animated. They stampede the earth, wild, ravenous zombies. Some are

dressed only in rotting flesh. Others are just bones. They rattle as they feast on the living and are engorged with blood. The Beast is unchained. He crawls out of the bottomless pit. He waxes strong and smites the Word of God. He prevails...)

* * * * *

The camera glides over Los Angeles, scanning the land for signs of movement. Its vision is blurred as the rains lash at its lens. Roads have become rivers. Trees uprooted. Buildings lie in ruins, heaps of rubble. Sound of distant thunders. Lightning flashes across the skies, immense jagged arrows striking the earth. The land lies barren, deserted. Bodies, wrecks of cars, carnage.

It is night. In the darkness the camera picks up movement. It is a man running. His black robe billows in the wind. A Great Wind tears at him. He runs faster trying to escape it. It appears to be chasing him, right on his tail. It catches him. He is lifted bodily off the ground, his legs kicking in the air. He is tossed around, his fists beating at it like a madman. He is hurled to the ground.

He lies in a crumpled heap. He is screaming obscenities at it. He scrabbles to his feet. He is up and running again, running madly down a flooded road, his feet kicking up water.

He runs past torn up fields, massive fissures in the ground, stumps of trees. Down another road, deserted. Abandoned cars, bricks, rubble, debris, collapsed buildings. A tree has been rammed into an old wooden house. Its roof is missing. He runs past it. He clambers over fencing. Trips over. Falls to the ground. Picks himself up. Turns. The Great Wind is behind him. He continues running. Past a tree. Sound of thunder. Lightning. A flash of light. The tree is struck. An explosion. A charred stump.

The man stops running. He looks all about him to get his bearings.

There is fear on his face. His blond hair is drenched. He wipes it out of his eyes. They are wild and frightened. Skin glistens with the light of the full moon. He catches sight of the wind, resumes running. It comes up behind him. It clutches at him again. He is seized, twists round to face it. Struggles. The Great Wind rips at his black robe as he fights against it. His robe is

shorn from him. He runs on naked with nothing but a bandage round his loins. Down a long winding track. Dead, leafless trees either side. Past an iron gate on the left. He stops, looks quickly back. Catches sight of the wind, looks to the gate. He heads for it and reaches it just as the wind comes up behind him. He throws himself over and runs down a cobble-stoned path.

An old stone church at end of path. Deserted. Dilapidated. A twisted steeple devoid of a cross. The stone cross lying broken on the ground. Headstones. Long grass. Graves overgrown with weeds.

An arched doorway, the door half broken. The man reaches it. He forces it open and runs inside.

The church is empty, shrouded in darkness. Pews on either side of aisle are thrown over or broken. Stained glass windows are smashed except the tripartite division high above the dais.

The central portion. A gothic rendition of Christ hanging upon cross. His halo is infused with light of moon behind it.

The naked man runs down aisle towards pulpit. He staggers on to the dais as if struggling for breath. He clings to the pulpit and quickly surveys the interior of the church. The Great Wind can be heard beating against the doors as if trying to get in. He smiles. He is safe. He wipes his brow and flings his head back, still panting. Then looks down at the old bible lying open on the pulpit.

The bible, pages turned yellow with age and covered in dust. Hand wiping dust away revealing title in bold type: PSALM TWENTY-TWO.

The man is laughing as he reads it. Eventually he stops. He simmers down to sobbing.

He jumps down from dais looking all around him. Then he stops as his eyes catch sight of portrait of Christ, the eyes, half-closed.

The man falls to his knees in centre of aisle facing altar. He looks exhausted or in a trance. His eyes fixed on portrait. A tear rolls out of his eye and down his cheek.

He says to himself, "And I am redeemed thereby."

He shakes his head and sighs. He lets it drop as he kneels with hands placed on legs and looks at bandaged crotch.

There is the sound of scurrying and movement in shadows. The man lifts his head up and looks to where it is coming from: the pulpit. A beetle comes into view. It scurries across the dais and onto the floor, large and black. Then it moves across the floor into the light. On its back; a visible mark in the shape of a cross, white on its closed black wings.

The man starts laughing dementedly.

More sounds are audible.

More movement in the shadows. The sound of hissing. Something dark comes into view. A snake, black with gold markings. Its red flashing tongue darts at the man.

He is still laughing, his eyes fixed on the snake.

The snake moves. It uncoils and drifts down the side of the dais towards the empty space in the front of him. It now lies on the bare paving stones. It coils into a figure of eight. The cracks in the paving stones beneath it suggest a sword.

The man laughs even more, tears rolling out of his eyes. He looks insane.

The snake uncoils and drifts to the left side of the church and disappears through a hole in the wall.

The man stops laughing, his head now drooping down. Still sounds of insects and small rodents can be heard in the background. The man falls to the ground and spreads his naked body out on the cold stone paving. He rolls onto his back and stares into the dark recesses of the arched ceiling.

He can see dark shadows. Rotten timber. Patches of light poking through missing slates. Cobwebs.

He smiles. He closes his eyes and rolls over onto his left side in the position of a foetus and falls asleep.

CELEBRATION

The camera focuses on all the windows. Glimpses of intense meteorological activity outside. The sky is still dark. Flashes of lightning. Rain. The portrait of Christ. His face. The moon still shining behind it. Rapid succession of alternating phases of light and dark, face appearing and disappearing, then total darkness. Face blackened. No light at all. No sound. Slowly a soft glow appears behind the portrait. A new dawn. Christ's face lights up. There is the sound of faint humming beyond. The sound builds up in intensity. Suddenly a large piece of glass in the portrait breaks away. It flies towards the camera and falls to the ground. There is the sound of it breaking on the floor in pieces, then silence.

The camera pulls back to see the whole interior of the church lit up. Everything, including the sleeping man, is bathed in the light of a new dawn.

THE VISIONARY

'Think not of the future today but tomorrow!'

Will A. Robertson,
Trans-cerebral Hemispheres

—28—
UNION OF HEAVEN AND EARTH

A light. A beautiful light. It was so beautiful I couldn't take it in all at once and had to close my eyes to allow them to adjust. I tried opening them again, not even sure if I was awake or still dreaming. In fact, I couldn't even remember who I was. Everything seemed to have been removed from my mind as if it had been wiped clean, as if all the events of my past—if I had one—had been erased and I was this being surrounded by this incredible light. My memory too of how I got here was absent. Yet in a strange way I kind of expected it. And this realisation almost confirmed my original notion; I had made the transition. I had crossed safely over to the other side. And now I was here, complete and in a body that felt strangely real, not how I expected it at all. It even hurt in places. I could feel these aches in my left side where I had been lying on the cold stone floor and they got worse when I sat up. I let out a light moan and figured they were probably just trace memories left over from my previous life, corporeal vestiges which I presumed would soon fade.

I tried sitting up, my eyes skipping over the interior of this large building. It didn't look real. The incredible light gave it the appearance of some sort of otherworldly ambience. The light came flooding through stained glass windows, some of which were broken, illuminating the high arched ceiling, the overturned pews and a long aisle leading down towards a door shrouded in darkness at the end. Then was I in a church? It sure looked like one. If so, how did I get here? I really can't recall. Was this place a celestial representation of where I had been last? That felt vaguely familiar. It made sense, somehow. And then I looked at my body. I was completely naked except for a bandage round my loins. What happened to me, what happened to my clothes? But then if this is heaven, you don't need clothes, right? I mean, souls are naked. Everything is naked in the Garden of God, just like the original pair. At least that is what I thought. But I wasn't so

CELEBRATION

sure. I guess it takes a bit of getting used to. You need time to adjust to these new circumstances. All I knew was I was here—wherever here was—and I had made it. This was my reward, I think.

I turned my head towards the door. I could hear footsteps. Someone (or something) was walking towards me. Then I remembered what had made me 'wake up.' It was the sound of a door being opened and closed. I could only see this dimly lit figure. It seemed to be gliding, not walking at all. And it was covered in this long dark cape that fluttered all around its tall frame; it was weird, a genuine vision. And it came right up to me as I sat there looking blankly at it. Now I could see it more clearly. Yes, it was dressed in a cape with this big floppy hat on, its brim shadowing the eyes. The face was obscured as well. I couldn't make it out at all.

I struggled to work out what was going on. Was this some kind of angel who had been sent to collect me and take me on to the next state? Was he going to take me to my maker? Was he my guide? And, as if to answer my doubt, this hand came out from beneath the cape and took mine. It pulled me up and put me on my feet. Then it removed its cape and flung it over my shoulders to cover my naked body. The cape was warm. It had soft silk lining which tingled against my skin; it wasn't what I expected. I looked at this angel in blank dismay hoping it would tell me what was going on, if I was worthy or not, what sins I had committed which would be held against me. Perhaps angels don't speak; they don't need to. They exude this wonderful air of peace and calmness, so warm and gentle it drifts over to you like a summer's breeze. And this one made me feel good. His very presence was reassuring and therefore there was no need to speak.

Then it laughed. Do you angels laugh? I thought it most unusual, and it only laughed again, not at me, you understand, but kind of with me as if this was all a big cosmic joke. And I could see its teeth. They were big and shiny, pure white like the light surrounding us, so white they sparkled. I eyed it curiously. It obviously sensed my incomprehension for it doffed its hat as if to greet me. I was taken aback when I saw the face. It wasn't what I expected either; slit-eyes, ebony pupils, the face so real, so young and fresh looking and the skin that not only looked sallow, it was yellow. And I mean yellow, man. This angel was a Chink. And it was like looking at me inquisitively for a sign of recognition. Did I know him? Was I supposed to?

I stood there dumb for awhile, my mind kind of jarring and not connecting together at all. But the angel smiled at me and that smile filled me with this wonderful joy. I could feel it bursting inside, sending my heart into a swoon. It was pure love. And it was only then I knew who it was, what this angel represented. It was my old friend. And he, having departed recently, had come to greet me. And this realisation brought tears to my eyes for I loved him as if he were my own brother.

"Chan!" I gushed with joy and went to take his hand. But he stood back and shook his head. "You're not Chan?" I asked him and he shook his head again. I didn't understand. Then he smiled at me tenderly. I could have sworn it was Chan. It looked like him, in a way.

"I am not Chan," he replied in this soft voice, very friendly. "Chan is dead."

I was shocked. "Yes, but so am I."

Then he laughed again, his voice echoing around the building. "No, you're not dead."

"I'm not?"

"No," he replied and smiled benignly as if appreciating my perplexity. "You are alive," he continued. "This is not heaven. This is the new world. And I knew I would find you here."

"And you're not dead either?"

He laughed. "No. I am perfectly alive, my friend. Nor is this a dream."

"You mean this is real?"

"Yes. This is real and you are safe now. There is a lot to explore. We will explore it together."

"We? Who are you?"

"Your old friend. Do you not recognise me? Do I look that different?"

"Yes. No. I mean, I don't understand. If you're not Chan, who are you? You do have a name, don't you? I mean, I'm not imagining you, am I?"

CELEBRATION

The man stopped and looked at me as if reading my soul. He thought for a second then calmly said, "The great has departed. The small approaches."

I couldn't believe it. "No!" I shouted.

"Yes," he replied and smiled.

"But you can't be. I mean, you look so young."

"Does not a snake shed its skin when it is old and worn out? I too have shed my skin, for is that not the way of the Tao?"

We both laughed together. This made us draw towards each other. We embraced like old friends. He patted my back.

"Here," he said, giving me a hip flask. "Drink. It will make you feel better."

I took it. There was this vague memory in the back of my mind, something to do with the last time I accepted a drink from a Chink which was black in colour. I couldn't quite remember what it was. He gestured me to drink. I did. It was beautiful, so refreshing, I kept drinking till it was all gone. It made me feel warm. The pulse of life surged inside me. I felt alive.

"Better?" he asked me. I nodded. He placed the flask back in his pocket. "Come. We go now. There is a whole new world out there waiting to be discovered. It's not how you would have remembered it as many things have gone. You have been asleep, my friend, for a very long time. We are now entered upon a new phase, one I wish to share with you. I have many things to teach you. You have much to learn."

He took me by my arm and escorted me down the aisle towards the door. He stopped me in front of it. "Be prepared," he said, and opened the door. I could only gasp as my eyes fell on this incredible landscape. It was all covered with the same white light, so pure, so fresh like dew covering shoots of grass in the early morning. I breathed in. The air was invigorating. If I wasn't dead, if I hadn't died, then it felt like I should have. I was reborn. I could only sigh. It was too much.

He patted me on my back once more and led me through the door with the grace of a father to his son. We walked out into the renascent dawn.

THE SUPPLICATION

'I want to die
Between the legs
Of a brave, young girl
Who would call
On the hearts of America
And the itinerant poor.'

Harmon Capri,
Scatological Snapshots (unpublished)

—29—
CAPRI SMILES

[The following are extracts from the personal journal of Miss Christina Carlotta Bianci during the time she was nursing Mr Harmon Capri. Although her entries are extensive and copious, we saw fit to include only the entries deemed relevant. We have reproduced them as accurately as possible without too many omissions.

As to the nature of the method employed by Miss Bianci in her endeavours to help Mr Capri, we feel we should warn the reader; the method is highly questionable. We have pointed out the errors in her summation on certain points and can only advise the reader not to place too great a reliance on it or attempt to emulate it in any shape or form for whatever reasons.—The Editors.]

Monday, 16th Dec. Still the same as yesterday. I don't know what to do. It seems to be dragging on for too long. I am now becoming extremely anxious. He still hasn't shown any sign of recovery so far. I thought the warm bath I gave him yesterday would have a beneficial effect, but when I checked him first thing this morning upon awakening he still showed no sign of improvement. I can only describe his condition as resembling a species of catatonia rather than a coma. I don't really know the difference between the two, indeed if there is a difference. He sits in a permanent trance with no sign of awareness of outward things. His pulse is stable, but there is not the slightest response or reaction when I touch him. He seems not to hear anything. His eyes are forever open, but blank as if he sees nothing. I have repeatedly tested this by placing the light of a candle directly in front of his pupils. There is no dilation or contraction as one would expect. Although I have to spoon feed him, he can only manage small

quantities at a time, and I'm not even sure if he's digesting it properly. He is rather like a baby with anorexia. His drink intake also is minimal. Needless to say, his weight loss is also causing me some concern. I know he was thin when I first met him, but he has almost been reduced to a skeleton. He looks so emaciated at times it frightens me. Of course, I have to help him to the toilet like an invalid. That is only rarely. He is suffering from acute constipation still and barely passes water, once a day if that. His limbs seem to be fairly flexible, but his muscles are wasting away due to lack of exercise. I noticed this morning how soft and smooth his hands have become, like the hands of a patient who has been confined to bed for a long time. The only thing he can manage to do by himself is sit up straight in that funny cross-legged position of his[1]. It appears to be the only thing he does now, sitting on the floor facing the fire but not even aware if the fire has gone out. He doesn't sleep. At least not what I would call sleep. Nor does he lie down. Sometimes I wonder if he is really there at all; I feel I am just left with this empty husk. He might as well be dead for all I care.

It has now been exactly 49 days. I know the Tibetans mention trances of this length in their book[2]. I cannot believe anybody can survive like this for so long. I have to accept that it is all my fault. This has been bugging me, as recorded, for the last two weeks, and each time I see him, I am filled with guilt and recriminations. Perhaps I should have left him and not interfered, taken Grantham's advice and fled and left them to it. But if I had done that I never could have forgiven myself. In retrospect, I don't consider it was that selfish of me. I honestly thought what I was doing was right, and now I've got to suffer the consequences. I hope I'll be forgiven, especially by Harmon, if and when he finally comes back from the dead. I can only pray he will make a full recovery.

I'm still intrigued after all this time. What were they doing that fateful day? And each time I ponder on it an overwhelming feeling of dread engulfs me. I am perturbed. Yet I know the answer lies in front of me; the three books by Grantham. All I have to do is read them. Each time I so much as glance at them I am repulsed and cannot even bear the thought of doing so. They also remind me of Grantham, the look he gave me. I want to throw them away, to get rid of them as they make me nervous. I cannot think of a good reason why Harmon obtained them from Mosalla in the first place. What does he want with them? To have brought them with him only confirms he

intends keeping them. And for that reason I am confident he would kill me if I was to dispose of them. They are all I have for company, them and Alex's book of poetry which I am sick and tired of reading. I've decided I hate poetry, particularly his style. It's so masculine and typical of Alex. I can't bear to read it any more.

I still don't know what these pieces of paper I found inside refer to. They are notes written in Harmon's handwriting, but it is barely legible. It seems he was drawing inferences on one of the poems he mentioned to me. He believes one of them contains the formula of the drug. At the top of the page he has put a title; *The Kalanitic Equation*. But for the life of me I can't find a poem of that name although I have come across one called 'Invocation of the Scarlet Woman' on page sixteen. He mentions on the first line the words 'Scarlet Woman,' so I presume he is referring to this one. I've read through it at least five times and although I understand it on a symbolic level (Alex used to call me his 'moon' and he was my 'sun'), I still do not see the significance. Obviously Harmon did. I'm trying to read his writing. It's all abbreviated; I don't know what the abbreviations refer to. I wish I could remember what E.R.[3] stands for. I will ask him when he comes out of it.

(I also found another piece of paper. It looks like a drawing of a snake in the shape of an 8 encircling a sword. What the significance of this is I do not know nor how it connects to the poem.)

I wish I had never taken the drug now. But then love makes you do stupid things. You go out of your way to make someone happy only to get kicked in the teeth for it. You suffer and feel betrayed and are forced into accepting that it was you who betrayed yourself and the partner is never really to blame. It was my fault. I honestly thought it would work out between us. The trouble with a man like Alex is he thinks on too far great an orbit to be able to take others into consideration, particularly if he is adamant on achieving his goal, his mind being 'filled with one thought, one conception, one purpose,'[4] and will stop at nothing to fulfil it. Everything else to him is secondary. I knew he was special, a man of great sagacity, one bent on learning with a strong desire for knowledge that powers all of his being, one who 'drinks deep of the fountains of knowledge, and is still insatiate.'[5] I cannot help wondering where he is now, if he has survived.

CELEBRATION

He isn't a man; he is a god. Gods don't die. He is still alive somewhere, one of the few hopefuls who have found shelter from the terrible calamities which have turned our beautiful world upside down. My love for him has left a wound that will never heal. Not even kind words can do that. As Brabantio says, 'Words are words; I never yet did hear that the bruised heart was pierced through the ear.'[6]

I only hope Harmon can heal it for me. We have only each other now and we must salvage what is left of our lives, what remains after this unbelievable tragedy and start again. Looking at him now I am seized with a strong, almost maternal desire for him. I held him close next to me earlier, hugging him, his head resting against my breast and we sat together in the silence rocking back and forth staring into the fire. Poor thing, he is so defenceless and vulnerable I really do feel he needs a mother. Perhaps that is my new role, what is to be expected of me. I feed him and wash him as if he is my own. I do it out of love. And it is my love which will bring him back. I'm positive of that. When he is better, when the world has recovered and everything is back to normal, perhaps then we can get married. Or I am being stupidly optimistic? What if he never recovers and stays like this for the rest of his life? What if he comes out of it not loving me, but hating me, despising me for what I have done? What if he blames me for everything?

Stop being so stupid, Carlotta, I had to tell myself. Thinking like this really won't do you any good. I don't think anybody can possibly imagine what it is like being stuck up here in the middle of nowhere, cooped up in a small cabin for days on end with no electricity, no communication with the outside world, no real company. It is absolutely soul destroying. You don't know what is left of the world. Most of it could be submerged under the sea and this is the only summit remaining above the waves. There maybe nothing left of the world at all except this. We could be the last survivors just waiting to die. I hope not. It is only hope that sees me through the day. Sometimes it is so dark outside I simply have no idea what time it is. Everything seems to be shrouded in darkness, a long interminable night. I know it is not unusual for this time of the year, but it has been like this ever since we got here. We rarely see any genuine hours of sunshine.

I feel so cut off at times. There is no one to talk to, only Harmon and he can't respond. When you are like this, isolated from the rest of the world,

your mind tends towards yourself without cessation. You are always looking at yourself, thinking about yourself, remembering past events long forgotten. There's nothing much to do here except wait. For how long? What are we waiting for? For some mystical sign to appear in the heavens to tell us everything is o.k., that we can come out now as it is all over, normality has been resumed? I don't know. I only know one thing; I am sure to lose my mind if it carries on like this.

I don't sleep much at all now. I kind of just lie there drifting on this insomnia. My mind keeps me awake. I find that I am always worrying about him. In the early hours of this morning I thought I heard something coming from the main room. I opened my eyes and looked to the door adjoining it.

I was stunned to see this peculiar glow seeping through. When I got up to investigate I could have died. It was coming from Harmon. It seemed to be radiating off his body like a halo and it was so bright I had to shut my eyes and turn my face aside. It was only when I had grown accustomed to it I saw he was hovering a good foot above the floor. He was actually levitating in his sitting posture. I sunk down the wall and sat there watching him, half frightened, half fascinated. I have never seen anything like it before. I thought he was dying, that this was the end, and he was now going to leave me. I cried for many hours.

Then when this light eventually dispersed, it was followed by something equally disturbing; a black cloud seemed to envelope him and he came down to the ground gently.

What the fuck is going on?

Tuesday, 17th Dec. I awoke today having had little sleep, my mind still restless after last night. I only hope the strange phenomenon doesn't happen again. Whatever it was, it couldn't possibly be a good thing. I think something is happening inside him, yet I don't know what it is.

Went for a walk earlier on, only a quick one as I don't like to leave Harmon for too long. It is still fairly dark outside. The sun seems to be hidden on the other side of the mountain as if refusing to show his face. It is cold but bearable. There is still a thick blanket of snow on the ground. It is too dark

for me to see far. Visibility is poor. It is the first time I have actually ventured out. The view I get from the top is of a massive lake surrounding the whole mountain. It makes me shudder to think we could truly be the only ones left alive like survivors of a shipwreck. This is reinforced by the boat having left us here. Nobody comes to visit us anymore. Perhaps they are dead; I don't know. We are stuck up here on this island at the top of the world. I pray the water will recede and we will be able to make our way back down soon.

The air was captivating. It seemed so fresh. I felt elated and was overcome with joy. I think it was enhanced by the complete lack of sounds. No noise whatsoever. I presume it is a positive indication. Nature has now restored herself to harmonious order, an elemental rapprochement. There was just this deep serenity, a fantastic calmness which swept me off my feet. It was so peaceful I felt heaven had finally descended upon earth, the two were ecstatically uniting in a carnal embrace and we were right at the juncture of their union. This feeling was also mingled with a curious sense of aloofness. I am hard put to describe it. There were two trains of thought going through my head at the time. One was we were all alone; the other one was we were especially chosen to help propagate the human race, to build the numbers back up and make up for the devastating loss of lives. I revelled in it and saw Harmon and I on our new mission; the repopulation of the world. We were Adam and Eve in the Garden, simple and innocent without care or worry, and we could do whatever we wanted. We would make up for lost time and get on with plenty of fucking. I would have children, hundreds of them, and I saw them running about this island all naked and splendid, pure natural bundles of joy.

As soon as I returned to the cabin this feeling of exaltation left me. In its place I was seized with such misery as if I had been literally thrown down to earth. I think it was the shock of finding the fire had gone out. I try to keep it burning at all times, but there is little wood left and the few trees remaining are far too big for me to cut down. Luckily, Harmon hadn't caught a cold. His temperature was normal. I went outside and promptly prepared some more wood for the fire. Some of the logs were too large. I had to chop them down to size. It was then that I had this peculiar experience. I was chopping a log. All of a sudden Grantham's face appeared on it. It was as if he was mocking me. I saw his face etched on the wood

and all my anger and frustration came to my aid. I was fuelled by this incredible strength and kept chopping the log until I was exhausted, utterly drained of energy. Then his face simply vanished. I got it out of my system. My fear of him left me. It was then I decided to start wading through his dreadful books to see if I could find what they were really doing that day.

And they are dreadful books[7]. I don't know how anybody could read them. I was struggling after the first page. It took me half an hour to read it before I could even understand what the hell he was talking about. I still think he was mad. How anybody could believe him let alone understand him is entirely beyond me.

I remember the first time I met him. It was during a brief trip to London. I heard all about this occult organisation he ran on an international scale. A friend of mine was a member of it in California. Somehow Grantham managed to gain control of it. I was invited to an open evening. I had a sneaking suspicion he knew of my involvement with Alex and that was the only reason he invited me. It was an informal gathering in Ladbroke Grove, an old house where he sequestered himself away from the world and the prying public eye. Few knew of its location and I was sworn to secrecy and led blindfolded into the house so I couldn't see which number it was. After the blindfold was removed I found I was in a reasonable sized room with a small circle of middle-aged well-to-do people of both sexes. Grantham stood out straight away. He had this powerful air which seemed to emanate from him. He was handsome; his dark hair swept back, his face pleasant to look at, his eyes calm and alert, and a real gentleman, almost aristocratic in temperament, yet disturbingly sinister on a deeper level. It was then I realised I didn't like him, and all the stories I heard about him were true. He was involved in some real heavy shit. It clung to him like tobacco smoke clings to your clothes. Of course, he showed me especial interest. He made it quite plain I could be of use to him and required my 'services,' endearing me with quaint words like 'You're a natural,' 'You have the power within you,' etc., and advised me to join his group to act as High Priestess. The underlying motive behind his charm and suave sophistication didn't go unnoticed either. He simply wanted to get me into bed. But being the strong woman I am, I immediately put my foot down. He desisted and we sat through a pleasant evening of social intercourse instead. I got into a rather heated discussion with his sweet Polish wife Natasha over the

symbolism of the besom handle employed by witches. She insisted it had its origins in ancient Egypt and was based on the *sekhem* sceptre[8] and was employed for exactly the same purpose. I disagreed and found her ideas to be preposterous. But then they were all borrowed from her husband, so what do you expect. I left dismayed.

Then I bumped into him 'accidentally' a second time when he came over to the States. I made it very plain to him I was with Alex and therefore wasn't interested in him. Besides, they both loathed each other as they were both working on the same thing but from opposite ends of the spectrum. I should have known of course it was either him or his son who was responsible for the setbacks we all suffered.

A further thought has just struck me; did Grantham have anything to do with Jack's bankruptcy? He was conned by a fraudster and lost everything. I am positive it was him.

Anyway, back to the book I am reading. It is called *Cults of the Khu*—'khu,' I think, means spirit in Egyptian. In it Grantham is talking about an imminent catastrophe around the turn of the century. If he is by any chance referring to what we have just undergone, then his predictions were correct. Perhaps that was what he was trying to warn me about in the temple that day. I always believed he was mad. That is why I didn't take any notice. But having read this first chapter, I am now wondering whether he was trying to make the prediction come true. I mean, look at it this way. The ritual they were performing that day was extremely bizarre. Was Grantham therefore trying to make the catastrophe occur through invoking his devil-god as represented by that disgusting statue? Surely it is possible. A powerful magician like Grantham and his whole retinue could make it happen on a global scale. Then if so, what is Harmon's role in all of this? Why had they locked him up in that freezer and put him in a trance? I don't understand his part in it at all.

Now, this is my next line of thought. Assuming I'm travelling along the right lines as regards the above, Grantham warned me I was interfering with their operation. If I was to take Harmon away I would be jeopardising it. Now this has got me thinking. Since I carried out my plan of action and saved him (before it was too late), did that action put a stop to the total devastation? All the extraordinary phenomena stopped abruptly for no

reason. In fact, it stopped as quickly as it had started. Was its cessation due to my actions? Is it possible? Can a woman like me really have that kind of knock-on effect by breaking the chain of causality? If I hadn't interfered would the devastation have continued? Would Grantham have succeeded in his aim by destroying the world completely?

Grantham's style of writing doesn't help either. Nor does he explain clearly what he is trying to say. Some of the symbolism he employs I am not familiar with. My leanings are towards the Greek and Roman myths. I feel they are part of my ancestry. I have no kinship with the Egyptian iconography he employs throughout the text, except only on a superficial level. I can identify with some of its great queens like Cleopatra (who doesn't count because she wasn't Egyptian[9]). Also Semiramis[10]. Alex used to call them 'Women of Power.'

I gave up and was about to throw the book down through exasperation when I happened to glance briefly at the illustrations. I was gripped with a trembling fear as my eyes skipped over the rugged lines and contours of obnoxious beasts and landscapes and had to fairly slam the book shut, the after-effect of my perceiving them too lingering for a long time in my mind. They absolutely repulsed me like that statue. It was only after my nerves had calmed down somewhat I was able to resume reading and settled for the last book instead. This appeared to be a repetition of the previous two, the only difference was Grantham was concentrating on the future and possible predictions and prophecies which may come true. As I started flicking through I came across an illustration at the back on the last page similar to the one Harmon has drawn. Why did he copy it? At the bottom is a brief note regarding the 'sigil,' as it is called; it is a means for activating the gateway to Recremental Space (whatever that is!) and I now remember where I have seen it before. It formed the centre of the diagram in the ceiling in the temple. Is that what they were using the temple for?

I turned to the first chapter, making my mind up I was going to read it all the way through before going to bed. It is called 'The Messiah,' an examination of the parousia of Christ as hypothesised by the Christians. Grantham was saying they got it wrong and discusses in great detail the symbolism behind the cult of the Child (the meaning of the word 'khart'). The cult of the Child is based on the notion of a being who is far superior

to the rest of humanity, who acts as a teacher or spiritual guru from one age to the next. When I read further, and finally understood what he was actually saying, I realised what he meant. It all started sinking in and I went numb.

My God, what have I done?

Wednesday, 18th Dec. I feel dreadful today. I cannot shake off the burden of what I learnt last night.

I don't believe it is true. Or perhaps it would be more correct to say I cannot accept it is true. My whole world has been shattered with that one iota of knowledge. He can't be one of them, surely?

Yesterday when I was outside this mountain was to me a veritable Forest of Arden[11] and like it too, a refuge from the real world (or what is left of it), somewhere to settle our conflicts, where they could be resolved and then we could 'fleet the time carelessly as they did in the golden world.'[12] But now that idyllic notion has been stripped from me. I am bereft of all hope. I fear greatly for him now. God, please forgive me, for I feel I have done something terribly wrong and I now know I should have listened to Grantham. I only hope the man was wrong. I was screaming to myself all last night in bed he was wrong. He simply has to be. I want my old Harmon back, not somebody else.

I am still stuck in a predicament because I have no real idea who (or should I say what!) I am nursing. If Grantham is correct, then God help me. What if he does come out of it as one of them? What if he doesn't and through my interference he comes out as something else? What am I to do then? The experiment wasn't completed, and my action has probably severely changed the outcome.

First thing this morning I picked up the book and resumed reading. The second chapter is an extension on the mythic child which is not a child in the strict sense but an embodiment of the divine principle in man. In Egypt this was typified by the god Horus. The child thus represents a type of spirituality which Grantham (I think) believes is the closest anyone can get to pure spiritual consciousness. In the following chapter he focuses on the Messianic cults of the world and demonstrates they were all based on the

Egyptian mummy as a type of the transformer. It goes through a death-rebirth experience in order to become a spirit. On another level it is based on a formula involving the physiological tumescence and detumescence of the penis, that it has to die in order to be reborn[13]—or something like that. I really do not understand what he actually means. It all seems a bit far fetched and I'm sure he was perverted like his son. He seems to reduce everything to sex and body functions. As the word 'messiah' simply means 'anointed,' Grantham believed the first part of a man to be anointed prior to resurrection was the penis because it was the first to resurrect, or re-erect, as he puts it. He appends a small illustration beneath this passage to underline his point. It is a vignette taken from the Egyptian *Book of the Dead* showing an upright mummy. A priest is standing behind it wearing a jackal's mask. In front of the mummy a female mourner is on her knees and looks like she is performing an act of fellatio on it[14]. I cannot believe that is actually what she is doing; Grantham is really perverting the picture to suit his own ends. He then goes unto say, 'The Anointed One was then essentially the phallus long before it was symbolised as Christ.' But it has given me an idea and I am going to try it out. As Harmon is in the same sort of trance as the mummy, he will not come out of it until some act is performed on him. Thinking this way, perhaps I am just as perverted as Grantham. I hope not. Nor do I care. For all I know we could be the only two people left in the whole fucking world, so what the fuck does it matter. I'm so desperate; I am going to try it anyway. And if people think I am shameless, then fuck them: I am shameless!

(I have decided to write this up as part of my magical record like I used to when I was monitoring my periods and biorhythms prior to ritual workings, just like Alex taught me. After all, I am doing a magical experiment.)

Time: 8.00 pm
Operation: Resuscitation of H.
Method: *in manu Regina*[15] + oil
Duration: 45 mins.
Result: Failure

Comment: Op. was hard work. Intended result was not achieved due to lack of response from patient. Only slight swelling apparent. No visible facial expression. Hence failure.

The above operation was followed by an investigation into H's erogenous zones. I tried all the ones I could think of. None of them aroused any sort of response. I do believe he is not even aware of his body, as if he is permanently dislocated from it.

Another experiment was followed after this. I placed a long sharp needle at the acu-points[16] of his body. Again no response. I pricked harder with the same result. I then tried pushing the needle all the way through tender parts of his flesh. Not only did this not produce any reaction, it did not even draw blood. Conclusion; he is oblivious from all pain like some sort of fakir. I inserted a needle (after sterilising it) all the way through his earlobe, then his cheek and even his nipples. I am sure he is dead to his body, not even inhabiting it at all. I know fakirs are capable of such techniques and are totally oblivious to pain. I have seen pictures of men hanging from beams by hooks embedded in their chests. I am wondering if the same principle applies to him. I simply don't know what to do. This method seems to be useless.

Time: 10.31 pm
Operation: As above
Method: As above + *per os*[17] + oil
Duration: 55 mins.
Result: Failure

Comment: I was hoping a combination of methods would work this time. Although swelling increased, it was not that much more pronounced than previous op. I did note, however, something which I had never noticed before. There is a small stream of heat running along his spinal column. This area is significantly hotter than the rest of his body, yet it increases around the top of his head. I am worried as I don't know what this heat is or what it means. I can only assume my op. was in some way responsible for producing this side-effect. Is it a good sign or a bad sign?

Back to Grantham's books again. I really can't read them. They're so heavy and wordy, I find myself nodding off halfway through a sentence and 'wake up' to find nearly a good 10 minutes have passed. It was in one of these lapses I found myself recollecting the time I grew very close to his daughter.

We were lying in bed, splendidly naked, her soft, warm body against mine. I

kissed her cheeks, her lips and her breasts. She caressed my waist, my pelvis and her hand eventually found my powerful cunt, touching the lips and my clitoris, as she lay there. She murmured and pressed her large breasts against mine, taking my hand and placing it against a vagina that was, to my surprise, completely hairless, like a child's. I parted her legs a little, kissing her chin and her stomach and, finally, her vagina, my tongue firm and controlled as I licked her clitoris. She gasped and arched her back. I came up, grasped her head, found her mouth and kissed her full on the lips, her tongue firmly in my mouth and her hairless pubis hard against my vagina, moving with a rhythm that was at once gentle and demanding. I shuddered, yielded completely as I felt the first stirrings of a magnificent orgasm. I moaned. She stopped. Then I felt something smooth, cold and hard brush against my leg. At first I was afraid. I didn't know what it was. She brushed it against the lips of my vagina and began slowly, delicately to insert it. I shrieked as she inserted it all the way and started pumping it mechanically. I tossed. I rolled. I was half in pain, half in ecstasy. It seemed so large, but I took it in all the way and lay back as she dominated me, my fingers finding her hot, wet cunt. We orgasmed simultaneously.

Later, I awoke to find her bringing me a cup of tea in bed. I sat up and arranged the pillows for the both of us and patted the bed. She slipped in next to me, resting her head on my chest. My fingers ran through her long hair, brushing it. I rolled her off me and found her pubis. It was bristly, not as smooth as it had been.

"Do you shave down there?" I asked her.

"Hmm. All the time. That's the way he likes it," she breathed.

"Who?" I asked her, not knowing who she was referring to.

"Anton, of course." She giggled. "I like it too."

"Does it hurt?"

"No, not really. It just itches occasionally. Why don't you try it?"

"Oh, I couldn't. Besides, I don't think Alex would approve."

She giggled again. So did I.

I never did understand her. I could never work out what was going on in her head half the time. I guess she was just a fucked up kid, or it was all an act? She was very good at that. She made people believe her sob stories, emotionally manipulating them. It was all down to the malign influence of her father. Of course, we never realised who he was until many years later. The same applies to Anton. Another smart, intelligent, but very fucked up kid. Katrina and Anton had such a tight relationship; they used to go to bed together all the time, ever since childhood. Reckoned they were continuing the Egyptian tradition, keeping it in the family. This was encouraged by Grantham, no doubt, who also had weird ideas, a bit like Gardner[18].

I am reading Grantham again. He believes mummification was used on the living (not just the dead) to effect trance. And that's what I guess he was trying to do with Harmon. But to get him into a trance and do what? Unite with his god? To become a god? I don't know.

I don't believe a word Grantham says. It is all a load of rubbish, this magical interpretation of mummification, etc. The thing I certainly cannot agree with is his statement that the word 'Christ' comes from the Egyptian 'karast'[19]. I refute his claim. It goes against everything I was taught at school. Being raised as a Roman Catholic I thoroughly believed in Christ and that he actually lived and died for ours sins. Grantham claims there was no historical, personal Christ, and that the original type was based on the child, the *khart*, which was always symbolic.

I have just come across a picture of this god he worships, in the illustrations halfway through the book[20]. It seemed to leap out at me and I had to fling the terrible book to the floor. It was only with enforced courage I was able to pick it up again and allow myself a closer inspection. It so clearly resembles the statue. They must be one and the same thing. This is the Devil! Yet he says this beast was the first to ever be worshipped by man in the remotest past. What utter rubbish. I don't care if it embraces all the elements[21]. It lacks the most essential part: spirit! Therefore it is unholy and I will have nothing to do with it.

Thursday, 19th Dec. Eventually roused myself from bed late this morning after a most hideous night. I am sure reading into the early hours of the morning affects my sleep for it was full of the most gruesome and hideous dreams. I seemed to have been plunged into the nightmare landscapes so

vividly conveyed by the illustrations. It was as if I was actually there, pursued by monsters. The atmosphere was horribly claustrophobic and intense. I awoke surprised to find myself safely in bed. It was frightening. I have never been so scared in my whole life. I staggered from the bed, threw on my bathrobe, made my way to the kitchen via the main room and was again horrified to see H surrounded by a halo of white light which was then followed by a dark cloud. Very worried. He's now been like this for 51 days.

Time: 11.33 am
Operation: As previous
Method: *In manu Regina* + *per os* + oil
Duration: 65 mins.
Result: Failure (with a modicum of improvement)

Comments: I put the above in brackets because although the intention was not arrived at there was improvement compared with yesterday. Swelling better. Erectile force apparent for a short length of time. Needed constant maintenance to keep it up, but no ejaculation. I persevered, believe me I did. But it is hard work when you have to do it all by yourself and there is no feedback. I felt a wee twinge of guilt whilst doing it today for it is rather like taking advantage of a child (how apt the analogy!). I felt like a molester. I banished this guilt with the words; 'Apo pantos kakodaimonos,'[22] as Alex taught me, and was able to proceed without hindrance.

How sad and distressing all this is. My thoughts run rampant. I am frustrated. I try to express them when the only avenue for them is this diary, and I find my heart pouring out on pages nobody will every read. At times I wonder why I am writing this at all. Why don't I just pack it all in?

Just had a bath. I needed one. It is so hard to get the water hot in the old tub. I am now reduced to bathing only once a week. The fire takes ages to heat the water; I tend to lose my patience. The hot water soothed me. I lay back and relaxed and let it engulf me. I soon found my hand straying towards my delicate flesh. It is hard to believe nobody has touched me there now for nearly 7 weeks, not since that magnificent fuck with Harmon. I am incredibly frustrated. I cannot go without it for such a long length of time. I don't know how celibates manage. I am an active, physical woman of the flesh. I love the flesh. I love my flesh mingling with others, brushing against strong muscles, being gripped by giant demanding hands, yielding at

the slightest touch. I had to bring myself to complete orgasm in the bath. But I was still left unsatisfied. I think it is one of the side-effects of the drug. It seems to increase libido as well as push the parameters for sexual satisfaction further. It takes a lot to satisfy me now. Not having anyone to talk to up here is bad enough, not being able to have sex is even worse.

I remember well my first visit to Haiti many years ago. Alex took me to a powerful Rada[23] rite dedicated to Legba[24]. He was invited personally by the local *hougan*[25] as word had got round he had an interest in voodoo and could speak Creole. The ceremony was one I will never forget in all my life. The bringing down of this major *loa* into one of his initiates bore all the hallmarks of a divine possession. The man became incredibly strong, violent, aggressive[26] to the point it frightened me and the women laughed at my fear. I was invited to join in, a rare privilege for a white woman. I regrettably declined. I did not like the idea of losing control. It seemed to me as frightening as watching a man being 'possessed' by an epileptic fit. The loss of control wasn't something I could tolerate then. It was only much later I learned to accept it and allow myself to be possessed by my goddess. In fact, I think it was this experience in Haiti which sparked off my initial interest in anything magical or mystical.

Anyway, that is beside the point. What I have got here is a situation I am thoroughly unfamiliar with. I can only tentatively assert Harmon is indeed 'possessed' by something. This is quite evident in his periodic levitations. These strictly nocturnal occurrences confirm something is happening inside him. I don't know what though. When he eventually 'returns' then I better be prepared. If he comes back as the Devil—and I know it sounds stupid—what do I do? Kill him before he kills me? The situation is unbearable.

I have to learn the lesson of Lear; we are all frail being 'human, all too human'[27] and it is a sad reflection on our human condition that it is not readily equipped to deal with what I can only call the 'impossible.' Have I done something wrong? I am being punished for my sins? I am reminded of Voltaire's *Candide*, particularly the episode wherein a natural disaster is interpreted as an act of vengeance by God for punishment of sins. I am left with the same feeling of contempt. '"The end of the world is come!" Candide shouted.'[28]

The satire would be amusing if it weren't so pertinent.

'Expose thyself to feel what the wretches feel/That thou mayst shake the superflux to them/And show the Heavens more just.'[29] And like Lear I castigate myself for my own actions. I know this is all highly illogical and I am not in the right state of mind to make sense of it all, yet it is my emotions which persuade me I am right. Back to work, Carlotta!

Time: 11.19 pm
Operation: Same
Method: Same
Duration: 35 mins. (I was very tired due to lack of sleep)
Result: Only slight improvement

Comment: I was tempted to put down failure as the desired result wasn't forthcoming. But I feel a definite improvement has persuaded me that what I am doing it correct, whereas before I was prone to dismiss it as idiotic and stupid. Now I am convinced it is working. Erection maintained far longer than previously. No gleet or ejaculate appeared, nor were there any visible signs of recognition. Most of it was tongue work. I am inclined to use the other method, but fear erection not strong enough to take it. I will try it when I'm confident. Heat is still there. It runs from either the base of the spine to the crown or vice versa. I am unable to determine which.

I am going through a chapter entitled 'The Dark Work.' It is all very interesting but I can't really understand what he is saying. I feel sure Harmon has been through this chapter—don't ask me how I know, but I know he has. Grantham talks about assimilating those aspects of creative evolution which are no longer available to man and have been cast out. I presume he is referring to the Qliphoth[30] which I have to assume featured heavily in his workings. This he makes quite clear in the following paragraph when talking about excreta. I had to put the book down at that point for what he was suggesting—indirectly I know—brought vividly to mind my recollection of seeing Pasolini's 'Salo'[31]. I felt physically sick, especially by the poor girl who was railed with commands of 'Mange! Mange!' and was forced to eat what the man had deposited on the carpet. It is the only film I have seen which indeed made me physically sick. If this is what Grantham is proposing as a new doctrine, a 'transcending of one's aesthetic culture,' as he puts it, then he can certainly count me out. Goodnight!

CELEBRATION

Friday, 20th Dec. Again, assailed by bad dreams. I should really call them nightmares, but it seems silly for a woman of my age. It is not only brought on by reading his books but by me being peculiarly sensitive. It is because it is so quiet here. There are no distractions whatsoever. That is why I keep finding myself picking up these idiotic books of Grantham's and browsing through them. As they affect me I have decided to discontinue reading them. I simply must sleep. I was restless last night. Entered the same landscape and awoke this morning sure I had been tainted by something foul. I simply refuse to read them any more.

Good. I feel better after that. A quick note on Harmon. Still in that fucking stupid trance. I went over to him this morning and shouted 'wake up' really loud. There was no response. I want to kick him, beat him, to claw and scratch his eyes out. How can he do this to me? How can he leave me here all alone? I risked my life saving him and this is the fucking thanks I get!

Went out for a brief walk. Calmer now. My emotional outburst came upon me suddenly, and I got it out of my system by walking several miles. And how good it was to get out, to feel the air in my lungs. The darkness is more like a twilight, somewhere between dusk and dawn. It is getting lighter outside. And of course tomorrow is the winter solstice. I look forward to that and will celebrate it as I always do. The snow is soft underfoot. It is hard to believe at times that this is the real world. It seems like a landscape in some fantastic dream. Or am I losing touch with reality?

Later I grew bored after my meal and found myself dipping into Grantham's books again, quite forgetting my resolution to never pick them up. I can't help it. There is nothing else to do. I find it hard to understand why I keep getting drawn to them. I cannot refrain from taking a morbid interest in them. My curiosity has been piqued. I will continue.

Just finished third volume. A lot of it I found dreary and totally preposterous, especially towards the end when he discusses all those stupid prophecies. I can't believe any of them, yet I am forced to consider that perhaps he was correct regarding the Child. Looking at Harmon now I know what he means and reading it has forced me to accept certain truths.

In one chapter Grantham talks about the corporeal manifestations of the Child, how he appears physically. As the Child is a symbol of divinity which

has transcended duality, he embraces within himself both genders and becomes a third, a sort of divine androgyne, as he calls him. This androgyne is not specifically hermaphroditic, but does display all the signs of an intersexual being. It (rather than he or she) has both within it, one who is both male and female at the same time, but also neither. In other words, it is capable of manifesting either gender.

I would like to take solace in ignorance. But I can't. Looking at Harmon only proves how true the statement is. He is the true divine androgyne, an eternal youth, one whom 'nature doth not live nor falter'[32] and is perfectly balanced gender-wise as he displays not only the supple limbs, the thin waste, the wide hips and lack of body hair, he also has developed breasts. By the latter I mean the flesh on his chest has exaggerated to a degree whereby it is loose, the fold of flesh resembling breasts. He has also developed something of a pot belly. It reminds me of the pictures I have seen of Akhenaten. In a way, Harmon looks just like him now. Also, Harmon's age seems to have retarded, if not reversed. He looks younger!

His appearance has been replaced by a 'youthful' quality, one that was only there superficially originally as he has never looked his age. I always thought he looked young for 40 when I first met him despite the degrading life he has been through. However, it is now more confirmed. And it is for this reason I am now more definitely inclined to accept what Grantham says. Harmon is the Child of the New Age!

The waters still haven't receded, and I feel like Noah waiting in his ark which was 'lifted up above the earth'[33]. If that myth has any historical basis I still have nearly a hundred days left before the waters are 'abated.' But unlike that myth, the waters have not covered the mountains—well not completely anyway. This is Ararat[34] not the Garden of Eden, a virtual prison. We are stuck here with no dove to send forth. In fact there are no animals in sight at all which is even more worrying as we are running low on provisions; the cupboards are nearly bare and all I have left are a few tins. I have tried to ration them but I can see if the waters do not subside soon we will surely die of hunger. The situation is intolerable.

Time: 11.45 pm
Operation: Same
Method: Same

CELEBRATION

Duration: 1 hour
Result: Improving

Comment: Only one op. today as I am losing my faith. I really don't know why I am bothering. It doesn't appear to be working and I can either blame myself for lousy technique or Grantham for being totally mistaken in his theory. No one has ever complained about my handwork or mouthwork before. I say 'improving' for there is a marked tendency for the erection to be maintained, but as soon as I desist it goes limp requiring constant vigilance. That is why it isn't appropriate for me to use the method I would prefer; full conjunction. Impossible at present, but that is what I am hoping to achieve within the next few days. I am taking Grantham's ideas further; I believe what Harmon needs is a good, full orgasm. It should bring him down to earth. It has to be a full paroxysm of the body which will dismantle his character armour[35]. In fact, I am going to borrow the theory of Reichian therapy and apply it to Harmon. If I can get him to experience a 'convulsion of the total organism'[36] it is sure to produce a response. All he needs is one good orgasm, not 40,000[37]. Easier said than done. I can't even get a decent erection out of him let alone an ejaculation. But I will persist. My fighting spirit keeps fighting on.

Saturday, 21st Dec. Winter solstice. The first thing I did upon awakening late today was to go out and explore. The sky, if I am not mistaken, is becoming lighter. I am sure it is as the whole mountain is now more visible than it has ever been and I am led to the conclusion it is not a case of the sun being absent, but that it cannot penetrate a deep, thick cloud hanging over the hemisphere like a dark veil. The mountain also seems higher. This I can explain. With the amount of water and the colossal downfall of rain, all the lower lying lands have been eroded away creating the impression the mountain has 'risen' from the waters of chaos themselves. The waters are now subsiding; hence it appears to have risen.

There is something miraculous about being up here for this length of time. It is as if you are coming face to face with God. I feel spiritually I am in direct connection with God. Over the last few days I have met my demons; they have been exorcised through these pages. My soul, like the sun, is gradually clearing and becoming brighter. I rejoiced in this by celebrating the winter solstice with a small ritual; breaking and eating some cakes,

drinking some wine, and performing a lustral oblation to Mother Earth herself, seeing her being healed, reborn and coming out of her time of darkness. This filled me with a great joy, a marvellous serenity, and for once during these terrible months I can honestly say I am proud to be alive. My morbidity has finally departed.

I gave some wine to Harmon. I don't know why as he was totally incapable of drinking it. But it was the last of an old bottle I was saving especially for this occasion. It is all gone now and it is back to water again.

Speaking of Harmon, it is time for another assessment of his condition. I am afraid to say there is little change. He still sits there in his posture. His eyes are forever open but blind. He has not said a word since the day in the temple. I am wondering if he ever will. This afternoon I was sitting with him and a whole 2 hours passed without my noticing. It was rather like a drug addict staring at his shoe oblivious to the passage of time, as related by Uncle Bill[38].

Time: 4.35 pm
Operation: Same
Method: Same with partial *conjunctio*
Duration: 90 mins.
Result: Disappointing

Comment: Before the op. I bathed him all over, got him to lie on his back with great difficulty as his legs were rigid. I massaged him with oils, worked on getting a good erection. I felt incredibly sexually charged. I wanted to make full use of it and tried slipping him inside me. It was useless. No sooner had my manual touch finished, he went limp and it slipped out. I might as well have resorted to using a dildo for all the good it would have done me. Not to be deterred I tried again. Lost the erection and gave up. I wish there was some other way. I am afraid there isn't.

Reading Grantham's books again. They exert an elusive fascination. I now believe everything he says is true. I no longer reject his theories. They are perfectly plausible once they are stripped of their tendency to blur the lines between fact and fantasy and his hyperbolic style of writing. For the latter, take the following passage as an example;

'Space as a continuous morphologising spectrum of possibilities, an endless void of potentiality, fixed without limit and in nowise capable of complete reification dependent on known space-time parameters, refracting into polydimensional existence, straining death in oneiric landscapes ever transmuting with protean energy along synthetic lines. With the fructification of the light ever unerring in the ceaseless escarpment of mind in a cosmogenital occultation of experimental astrochemistry whose power of correspondences are slowly coalescing into a tangential whole. DNA as PAN! The life of the void floating out in ophidian networks as nu-ovulations, subtle vibrations, opposite elements copulating, eternally doubling, the spermatoic logoi wrapping round aetheric substances creating bundles of energy self-replicating in highly technologised patterns of infinite variety; a zymotic cannibalism reaching backwards through quantum states into the heart of eternity.'[39]

WHAT THE FUCK DOES THAT MEAN?

I woke up this morning with more hideous memories and ghastly vestiges of a nightmare I thought I would never awaken from. Tonight it will be the same thing. I can only take comfort in this mysterious assumption I have got in my head that we are being looked after, and it is this insane notion that is keeping me sane.

Sunday, 22nd Dec. Yes, it is true. More dreams again this morning. In all I had about four hours sleep. During that time I was assailed by the most monstrous of creatures. I entered the same landscape and was besieged by terror. Woke up screaming and have now vowed to never read them again. I only hope this time I can keep my oath and not break my resolution.

The whole problem I am experiencing here can he classified quite easily. First, no distractions. Secondly, lack of company. Third, loss of interest. When a man or a woman is placed under these difficult conditions it is rather like being in solitary confinement. The walls of one's cell echo back your thoughts. They bombard your consciousness like cannon fire, and each blast leaves you feeling dazed. It is this tyranny of (self-) assault which undermines and unhinges the mind.

Had short siesta.—More dreams. I am sure they are produced by my

unconscious as compensation for the dull and uninteresting conscious life I am forced to endure.

I went out for a walk. My assertion that the sky is getting lighter has been corroborated. It is true. It seems to reflect my own internal position. Visibility of surrounding area is greatly improving. When I was walking around in my mink coat I honestly felt alive. The very mountain seemed to speak to me. The snow responded as well, so fresh and vital as if it was animated with life. God is present here, I am certain. I feel him move all around me. I breathe him in deep into my lungs. I heave my chest and he fills me with warmth, with love. Previously I was dead to him. I could not hear him nor see him. Now I can. Now I am alive to him. Everything was speaking to me; the snow, the water, the sky: they all spoke to me.

Returned to the cabin and my emotions were in disarray. The elevated, exalted state of mind diminished as soon as I saw Harmon. My obligation of responsibility pressed at me from all sides and I am still inured to care for him. No sign of life at all. How can this be? How can it drag on for so long? My mind numbs at the thought and I have run out of ideas.

Time: 4.25 pm
Operation: Usual
Method: Same as before
Duration: 130 mins.
Result: Dismal

Comment: What can I say? Nothing, except I keep trying. I persevere and I am left feeling constantly disappointed. I go through a series of oscillations where I am at one time filled with life, at another filled with death. It is in these latter moments of despair I am left trembling at the edge which lures me into the depths. I'm beginning to understand a pattern though. It is this:

When I am high I a get a better response from Harmon than when I am low. So far, going back through my journal—which is what it is for—confirms this. Today's dismal failure was a result of my miserable state of mind. I have taken a vow: I will wake up fresh and invigorated tomorrow, and when I do I will be throwing my whole self into the act. Now all I want to do is sit and pray things are picking up.

Time: 1.05 pm
Operation: Same
Method: Same as earlier
Duration: Only 30 mins. (too tired)
Result: Still disappointing!

Comment: As stated, I was too tired. I thought I was feeling good and this feeling would be transferred to him. Fatigue hampered the effort. I resorted to doing it in an offhand, perfunctory way. Lethargy and my lackadaisical attitude are to blame. It is no different from trying to fuck a eunuch! It was a complete waste of time. Erection there but only slight. Not strong enough to give good penetration. Went limp. Left me feeling hollow and empty. Ended up satisfying my desires by my own hand which has put me in the mood for bed.

Monday, 23rd Dec. Today feeling better. Sleep most satisfying. I awoke refreshed and determined to get on with life.

After I had attended to Harmon I went for a quick walk. The chill is lessening, sky still dark yet showing signs of becoming lighter. It is so gradual it is barely perceptible. Water level lower, slightly. I caught my reflection in the water. I realised my appearance leaves a lot to be desired. I don't wash myself as often as I should or brush my hair. It is unkempt and knotted in places. I don't know why I have allowed this area of my life to slip. I have run out of make-up and it seems pointless doing myself up when nobody is going to see me anyway. I used to be such a strong believer in personal appearance. Now I simply don't care; it doesn't matter anymore.

As for Harmon; no sign of improvement. It is most discouraging to have to face him day in and day out and be met with the same picture. I really cannot believe this. I am getting desperate now.

Time: 2.34 pm
Operation: Same
Method: Same with only partial *conjunctio*
Duration: 90 mins.
Result: Dismal

Comment: Exhausted. I can hardly write this. My hand has been working

overtime and it does not have the strength to grip the pen. Erection, however, is definitely improving. It took at least 30 secs to get it strong enough to give penetration. As soon as it was inserted it went limp on me. I tried repeatedly. Lost patience. I am now ... [40] although I have an idea. Alex taught me certain exercise techniques of Tantra[41] to give better orgasm. I pride myself on my versatility, and have decided at this late stage to go back to practising Vajroli Mudra[42] at least 3 to 4 times per day. Will start now.

Quite surprised at the amount of grip. There seems no problem in that department. Did a cycle of ten repetitions. I am sure this is the only way. Urination good. Flow stemmed with great ease after drinking three pints of water on fairly empty stomach. Shut-off technique quite superb. My whole system was flushed and left me feeling animated, vital. Will repeat shortly.

Yes, again, two hours later, already showing definite signs of improvement although there was no deficiency in this area originally. Muscles are strong but could do with some extra strengthening. Contraction greatly improved. Inserted two fingers; grip more than adequate and retained for a fairly long time without too much effort. I was quite chuffed at how strong the hold really was. People will think I am depraved. Fuck them. I don't give a shit what they think; if any of them still exist!

Same if not better. I'm now overwhelmed with confidence. I think it's time.

Time: 10.11 pm
Operation: Same
Method: Same with extra vaginal control
Duration: 60 mins. (approx.)
Result: Better

Comment: I say 'better' for the result because this time erection was fully maintained. It was firm and strong enough to allow full penetration. My vagina worked at him like a suction pump and I was able to experience a good, healthy orgasm yet without a corresponding one from him. There was no ejaculation from him at all. In fact, it was rather like making love to a corpse. This has given me an idea. I will try it out tomorrow as I am now too tired to continue. I will transform it into a full scale sexual rite. I wish nothing more now than to curl up with him before drifting to bed.

Tuesday, 24th Dec. I am sure there is a corresponding link between my state of mind and nature. I am feeling lighter as the environment becomes lighter. It is as if a great weight has been lifted from my shoulders, leaving me 'heady' and light of spirit. The 'girders of my soul' have been greatly expanded and oceanic feelings of unity rush in with nature penetrating my whole being. I feel wonderful.

After attending to Harmon—still no improvement—I went for a walk as is my wont. Came back feeling high after an incredible experience. I feel I have to write it down before it eludes me. Those translucent threads of thought will escape if I don't articulate them properly.

Outside the air was still, with only the occasional gentle breeze to break the monotony producing a brief flurry of snow which lies upon the ground like pure crystals of light. I was walking, or I should say drifting, where my body willed. I let go and let the momentum carry me without conscious control, immediately I was seized by a blissful state wherein my consciousness was not confined to my body. I was no longer stuck in my head. My soul had become the world. The whole place was alive and I was connected intimately to every part of it so there was no distinction between inner and outer; I was the mountain, the mountain was me. And down by the water's edge I felt as if I was present at the very dawn of creation. The darkness had departed and 'the Spirit of God moved across the face of the waters'[43]. It embraced me and wrapped me in a shroud of purity. The mountain was transformed. It became sacred, holy, blessed. I felt I had been 'caught up into paradise'[44] and everything was known to me. There was nothing I did not know. The whole of existence had been revealed to me and I understood. I knew what the passage in Isaiah (11.9)[45] meant as if it was here the passage was referring to. God had come out of hiding. I felt he had touched me personally, consecrated me with his hand. For a few seconds I wasn't there; I was the mountains, the sky, and the sun. There was no Carlotta. Even space and time had been abolished and I felt immense, infinite. It was the most wonderful experience of my whole life and left me feeling elated all day. Nor did this emotion leave me as I returned to the cabin. My feet did not walk on the wooden floors; they walked on air. I was guided to Alex's book. It fell open at page sixteen. I knew this time it was going to work.

Time: 5.55 pm
Operation: The giving of life!
Method: As previous, ritualised with invoc. of 16th[46]
Duration: 2 hours
Result: Successful, but see below

Comment: Yes, it was unbelievable, although I hesitate at using the word 'successful,' as will now be explained.

I ran through my mind the imagery of the 16th poem, slightly adapting it so it could be recited by a woman rather than a man. I read it aloud as I prepared his body, getting him to lie flat and gave him a ritual washing. I poured a lustration of water all over him, applied oil to his sensitive areas, my fingers working dexterously around his penis. I got a good strong erection out of him, all the while chanting the poem. I personified the Scarlet Woman, seeing him as the Beast and bestrode him. I was not only the Moon, I was also the sky, the heavens, the inverted cup of creation flushing him with my lustral light. I felt empowered and saw my vagina as cosmic, filled with radiant energies, with light. I infused the divine immortal spark into his being, igniting his body, turning him into the Sun. I was Shakti, he was Shiva, and I was re-animating him. I suddenly became charged with energy. I saw my womb sucking up his whole being and gloriously he exploded inside me. He actually came! There was so much love-juice it created a small pool around us. I have never seen so much of the stuff. It was wonderful, except—and this is why I hesitate in saying it was successful—there was no spasmodic movement of the pelvis, no change in his facial expression, no movement at all from him. There was an ejaculation but not commensurate with orgasm, or what I would call a proper orgasm.

I wonder if the change will come through gradually. I see my performance as exerting a subtle effect on him and that it has to come down from some higher source before penetrating through the subtle sheaths until finally manifesting in this world. I am sure I am right.

Wednesday, 25th Dec. I can't remember exactly what time I fell asleep last night. I am not even sure if I fell asleep at all. I think I had a dream, although I am not happy with that word. For what followed 'I cannot in the least believe that it was all sleep'[47].

CELEBRATION

I was lying on the sands of a golden beach bathing in the brilliance of the radiant sun. My heart went out to it and the sea lapped with small friendly waves at my feet. I was alone, not a soul in sight. I and nature were strengthening our bonds. I 'dozed' for awhile and slipped into a profound lethargy. Something arose out of the sea. It was brilliant and shiny like a metallic serpent dispersing these multifarious hues in all directions. Its eyes were two bright points of light. It seemed to lull me into a deeper sleep as if hypnotising me. I was not afraid of it. In fact, there were few emotions to speak of. I could feel its oleaginous skin brush against my naked flesh as it slithered up between my legs and disappeared inside me. I could feel it move and each movement created a wave of sensations which thrilled me with a 'languorous ecstasy.' Then it left and crawled back into the sea and was gone. Yet a part of it was left behind. It is still inside me.

The 'dream' has produced in me a very peculiar condition. I seem to have no craving for anything. I have no desire to do anything, yet it is wholly different from apathy. My mind is calm. For the first time I am content to just sit and cuddle Harmon by the fire like a mother with her baby. I don't even feel like going for a walk. The need to continue the operations also has left me. My head feels curiously empty.

As I was staring into the fire it suddenly dawned on me and my heart leapt with joy. I now know what the dream means. I am pregnant!

I can't wait to tell Harmon. I know he will be so pleased. I am sure he will be. I want to tell the whole world, and I cried with joy for hours until I was sure I had run out of tears.

Then, this evening ...

Glory, glory! I thank ye gods. I praise ye in all of your wonderful names: Harmon smiled![48]

EDITORIAL NOTES

1. *Padmasana*. Lit. 'lotus posture' of yoga.
2. *The Tibetan Book of the Dead*. Miss Bianci is referring to the limbo or intermediate state between death and rebirth known as *bardo*. An individual's consciousness enters the *bardo* after death which is said to last for up to 49 days prior to rebirth in human or non-human states.
3. Presumably 'Elixir Rubeus'—the red elixir.
4. Mary Shelley's *Frankenstein*. Miss Bianci is equating Crome's fanaticism and dedication to his work to that of the protagonist's of the novel.
5. Percy Byshe Shelley's *Alastor*.
6. Shakespeare's *Othello*, Act I, Scene III.
7. The titles are as follows: *Cults of the Khu* (1977), *Cults of the Khaut* (1978), and *Cults of the Khart* (1979), all published by Kerygma Press, London. They are collectively known as the *Thanatosian Trilogy* and have never been republished. An original set is exceedingly scarce and can fetch around £5000 if in decent condition.
8. One of the royal insignia of the gods and pharaohs of ancient Egypt. It was a symbol of power and for that reason it was intimately associated with the goddess Sekhmet. The crux of the argument is: Grantham believed the *sekhem* was originally a dildo used for inducing trance in temple priestesses prior to it being turned into a cultic symbol, and it was the prototype of the witch's besom handle which was used for the same purpose. The latter-day myth of the witch riding a broomstick comports the same idea.
9. Cleopatra was of course Greek, the last of the great Ptolemies before she was overthrown in 30 BC by Octavius.
10. Babylonian queen circa 1900 BC. Legendary for her 'depraved and polluted mind,' a paragon of 'unbridled lust and licentiousness,' Semiramis was believed to be the basis for the 'Woman' or 'Babylon' of the *Apocalypse*. It is understandable why Miss Bianci should feel an affinity with her.
11. Or Arcadia, the artificial world of Shakespeare's *As You Like It* where the Duke Senior remains exiled for most of the play. Equivalent to the island in *The Tempest*, it was much enamoured of the Romantic poets of the 19th century literary tradition and the source of their inspiration.
12. Shakespeare's *As You Like It*, Act I, Scene I.

13. Miss Bianci has seriously misinterpreted this view. Grantham's use of paronomasia is never more than suggestive.
14. See the *Papyrus of Ani*, an Egyptian scribe, 19th Dynasty, c. 1250 BC, Spell 1.
15. *In the hand of the Queen*. Miss Bianci masturbated Mr Capri.
16. The pressure points of acupuncture.
17. *By the mouth*; i.e. an act of fellatio.
18. Gerald Gardner (1884-1964) was responsible for reviving witchcraft, what later came to be called 'neo-paganism.' He was not adverse to using flagellation in some of his more dubious rites.
19. The derivation is as follows: Egypt. *karast*, for 'to make the mummy.' Alternative spellings: *karas, karis, kares*, etc., especially *krst*, the 'upright mummy,' a type of the resurrected Christ (*Christos* in Greek, *Chrestus* in Latin). The *karast* is literally the person who has been mummified or embalmed and anointed (christified). It symbolises resurrection.
20. See Grantham, *Cults of the Khaut*, pl. 31.
21. The symbolism, as tentative as it is, can be deduced as follows: the wings = Air; the head (mythical, perhaps a salamander) = Fire; the body (of a fish) = Water; the tail (of a snake, hence chthonian) = Earth.
22. Greek; lit. 'Depart from me all evil spirits.'
23. *Rada*. From Ardra or Allada in W. Africa is the gentler side of voodoo rites. The Rada *loas* are said to be more benign in comparison with those of the Petro which are malign and far more hostile. However, the difference is never moral; it is essentially musical. The Rada rites being performed to an on-beat rhythm of the drum, the Petro rites to an off-beat one.
24. The major *loa* of Rada rites. His symbol is the knotted stick, possibly a reference to the phallus. He acts as intermediary between the *loa* and man, opening the doorway so man can speak with the *loa*.
25. The voodoo priest = male; *Mambo* = female.
26. Characteristics typical of possession by Legba.
27. The phrase is from Nietzsche's book of the same name.
28. *Candide* by Voltaire (1759). The sailor represents 'the common man,' Pangloss 'the philsopher,' and Candide 'the innocent.'
29. Shakespeare's *King Lear*, Act III, Scene IV.
30. The evil or averse side of the sephira of the Qabalistic Tree of Life.

31. *SALO or The 120 Days of Sodom* (1970), a film by the Italian director Pier Paolo Pasolini. Set in Mussolini's fascist state, it depicts the director's complete renunciation of hope in a moral wasteland. At the time it was controversial for its explicit scenes of obscenity, including coprophilia, and potential viewers were advised it may 'upset those of a nervous disposition.'
32. Source of quote unknown.
33. *Genesis*, 7.17.
34. The mountain upon which the Ark of Noah rested (*Gen.* 8.4).
35. The term developed by Wilhelm Reich (1897-1957) to denote an individual's defence mechanism against emotional excitement. This is a remarkable observation on the part of the diarist. She sees the problem as being a complete lack of emotional response, a trait of character armour, for it is said to result in the same rigidity of body and 'deadness' exhibited by Mr Capri.
36. Reich's definition of an orgasm. Orgiastic potency is said to be inhibited by character armour (see previous note), hence orgasm is never fully experienced by those afflicted. Miss Bianci is making the connection a genuine orgasm will break the deadlock and produce an emotional response sufficient to restore him to full awareness and normal functioning.
37. A gross exaggeration on the part of Miss Bianci. It reveals something of her psychology. The truer figure is closer to ten times less. Reich believed a normal healthy person should experience at least 4000 orgasms in his or her lifetime to obviate any form of neurosis.
38. Possibly a reference to William Burroughs, author of *The Naked Lunch*. The reader is referred to the book's introduction, 'Deposition: Testimony concerning a sickness,' wherein he describes the harrowing withdrawal from heroin addiction. The addict is rendered 'senseless,' incapable of doing anything and could stare at the end of his shoe for eight hours, totally oblivious of time.
39. Kelly Grantham's *Cults of the Khaut*, p. 111.
40. Handwriting illegible.
41. *Tantra*, lit. 'loom, thread, web,' etc. Known in the occident as the 'Indian Cult of Ecstasy,' its possible translation could be: *Tan = expand, tra = liberate*. It seeks to render man in cosmic terms through the utilisation of sexual energies. The female is always primary in their rites.

42. A Tantric exercise in body-consciousness, the control of the body through mental and physical exercises by way of muscular functions, either sphincteral or urethritic. Practised by Tantrics to enhance sexual performance and prolong orgasm through preventing flow of semen or, in this case, tightening the vaginal muscles for greater satisfaction.
43. *Genesis*, 1.2.
44. *Corinthians* (2), 12.4. The passage in full is as follows: 'How that he was caught up into paradise, and heard unspeakable words, which it is not lawful for men to utter.'
45. 'They shall not hurt nor destroy in all my holy mountain: for the earth shall be full of the knowledge of the Lord, as the waters cover the seas.'
46. Invocation using the 16th poem. Not to be confused with the 16th formulation of the drug.
47. The quote is from Bram Stoker's novel *Dracula* (1897).
48. The journal abruptly ends here.

THE FLOOD

> 'Like the beauty of a lunar glow,
> Is that alluvial, sanguine flow.'
>
> Shri Paramhansa,*
> *Mahakala Tantra*
> (Quoted in Grantham's *Cults of the Khaut*—
> * Crome's pseudonym for this work)

—30—
CONCLUDE

Crome is seated in the dark watching the copulating couple. He hardly moves. Occasionally he slowly raises his right hand to his mouth and inserts his cigar without taking his eyes off the scene. He draws and exhales. The smoke wafts about his face like a visor, partially obscuring his features. He takes a sip of brandy, swallows and gently lowers his glass down by his side.

The couple are building up to a climax in time with the orchestral piece as it picks up tempo, reaching a crescendo; they are perfectly synchronised as they climax. Their bodies melt into one another and lie inert for awhile, blissfully satisfied. The woman disengages her legs from the man's hips allowing him to lift himself off her slightly. He raises his head. His face becomes visible. It is Crome. He looks down at her and smiles as he brushes her long black hair from her face. She is smiling. It is Carlotta.

The picture goes dark and fades out. The music stops.

Crome reaches for the remote, presses a button and turns off the holo-projector. He presses another button to turn off the sound system. He claps his hands and all the lights come on. He takes a final puff of his nearly finished cigar and exhales slowly. The smoke eventually clears. His face becomes visible. He is smiling.

THE THINKER

'I have written well over ten million words and I still can't stop thinking: Methinks I think too much!'

Paul K. Jarrup,
The Confessions

—31—
A CLOSING

The Buddha was right.

The Sigil of Recremental Space
(From Grantham's *Cults of the Khart*)

Made in the USA
Charleston, SC
01 November 2014